ELEPHANTS, THE GRASS, AND A TEACHER

Recollections and Reflections on the Nigeria / Biafra War

(Revised Edition)

Chinyere E Egbe

Printed in the United States of America

ISBN 979-8-89114-077-6 (hc)
ISBN 979-8-89114-076-9 (sc)
ISBN 979-8-89114-078-3 (e)

Library of Congress Control Number: 2024905140

2024.04.26

MainSpring Books
5901 W. Century Blvd
Suite 750
Los Angeles, CA, US, 90045

www.mainspringbooks.com

TABLE OF CONTENTS

DEDICATIONS

This book is dedicated to my parents, Mazi Pliny Igwe Abel Egbe and Anna Nnenna Egbe; to our father Mazi Igwe Egbe, whose good work and personal influence shielded the family through those challenging years and close calls with danger and annihilation and to our mother, Anna Nnenna, whose patience, and endurance shepherded the family through the stresses of the challenges. This book is also written in honor of the trues heroes of the tragedy, the malnourished innocent, and helpless children who perished needlessly because of the conflict. I must also honor and thank the Nigerian Army commander who arrested my mother and the family and was gracious enough to release them without a scratch in recognition of our father who was his teacher. He was truly a patriot who fought the war to achieve its proper purpose – to unite the country. He was truly a professional soldier. Finally, this book is dedicated in remembrance of our big brother, Lt. John Chukwumaeze Egbe who died in action during the war. Finally, I will honor my little sister, Dioma Egbe of blessed memory and my big sister, Nneoma Uchendu (Nee Egbe), also of blessed memory. My two sisters survived the war, but they also suffered with us and endured the hardships as we provided mutual support to each other along the way. May their souls rest in peace.

ACKNOWLEDGMENTS

I must acknowledge first that I am not the sole author of this book. The complete authorship of the book is attributed to me and my brothers and sisters who contributed immensely to the narrative about the ordeals that the family went through.

While they did not join in telling the story, I must acknowledge the support and encouragement of my wife, Brandi, and other members of my family Ogechi Lizzy Egbe, Amechi Egbe and Enyioma Nwagbara. I must also acknowledge Mazi Obiesie Azunna for valuable information on activities during the Nigerian Army occupation of Ovim. Also, credit must go to Chief Uwadiegwu Ogbonnaya who ferried our dad across enemy lines during operation Open Corridor in May 1969 and told me the story.

Finally, I must acknowledge the partial financial support of the Professional Staff Congress of the City University of New York (PSC-CUNY) as well as the guidance of the editors from 2Nimble Publishing.

Cover Design by Christopher Daniels

WARNING: Occasional Strong and Explicit Language Chapter VIII, Page 139 and Page 140, and Chapter IX, Page 149. Reader Discretion is advised.

NOTICE: The names of some individual persons in this manuscript have been distorted. Others are identified only by their first names or nicknames to protect their identities. Any persons that are fully identified gave their permission that they should be fully identified, or they are members of my family. If the distorted names identify any real person or persons, such is coincidental. Please note that I did not interact with such persons in the course of events during the period of the Nigerian civil war. Furthermore, other events herein described do not refer to them.

FOREWORD BY

NAVY COMMANDER (RTD) OCHIABUTO IGBOKWE

When I saw the title of this book, my first thought was the connection between the Elephants, the Grass, and A Teacher. But titles can be deceiving. The content is more of a well-researched chronicle of events of the over 30 months of the Nigerian civil war. In the opening chapters, I said to myself "what may have led to the author's dislike for Ojukwu". But as I read further it became more interesting and I could now see also that it was not the issue of dislike but a fair judgment of the events that followed every action or inaction.

The incursion of the Biafran government into the Midwest and the events that followed up to the period of withdrawal of troops is, as the author put it, a misplaced judgment and adventure. Especially after having been advised by far more knowledgeable diplomats, colleagues, friends, and even emissaries from Britain, the USA, and the Nigerian side. One of the most interesting parts is that when you finally settle down to read, it also becomes difficult to put the book aside. However, some of the chapters are quite long and winding looking as if there were repetitions. Only towards the end of the chapter would you find that these were intended for emphasis. Many reference materials were quoted, but the author pulled out the ingredients of each work thereby not leaving the reader with the pains of looking for the reference materials for further understanding. Of much interest is to know that various authors knew how and why some statements were made and certain decisions are taken, yet they go ahead to quote part of such to the extent as to portray the speech in a bad light.

This book made a great effort to look critically at some of the earlier works as written by the major players and or witnesses and made effort to analyze them. He further came out with opinions as to whether the actions or inactions were right then and even now. This is very interesting as it will leave readers especially those interested in war documentaries to further research. For me most of the outcomes are personal opinions. In any case, the author never implied that his opinions were that of the Elephants or the Grass except they came from the Teacher.

Of great interest was the management of other parties, according to the author, the so-called minority groups of Eastern Nigeria. The mistrust that characterized their behavior and actions against Biafra are still there today. The creation of states with the false understanding that it would amount to self-government, or some kind of autonomy, helped in their actions against Biafra.

This book is more of a collection of various works, personal experiences, and evaluations. It's an example of a very hard and time-consuming piece. A must-read for those intending to understand the intrigues, actions especially from the Nigerian side as well as the personal interest of the key players.

I recommend the book for schools, libraries, individuals, and those intending to further research works.

Commander Ochiabuto Igbokwe
Nigerian Navy Rtd.

FOREWORD BY

VICTOR ANAZONWU

An Audacious Account of the Nigeria Biafra War

About fifty years after the guns fell silent in Biafra, a new generation of writers has emerged to review the events of Africa's most tragic civil war. Some were minor actors in the war. Others were too young to fight. Yet others were born after the hostilities and relied on what they heard or read from other sources. They have one thing in common: They offer more dispassionate and objective perspectives on that war's complex issues and events.

Dr. Chinyere Emmanuel Egbe belongs to this newer generation of writers. Currently a tenured professor at Medgar Evers College of City University of New York (CUNY) and Consortia faculty of the CUNY School of Professional Studies, Egbe was in his teens when the war broke out in May 1967. Although he did not initially enlist in the Biafran war effort, he had an older brother who signed up early. Young Chinyere eventually left the "comfort" of hiding in the bushes with women and children to operate on the fringes of battle when he got older towards the end of the conflict.

These life-transforming experiences are at the heart of his new book, now available in major online bookstores in ebook and paperback. *Elephants, The Grass and a Teacher...* chronicles in fine detail the horrors and heartaches of a brutal war. And the chilling retrospect that it was all in vain and could have been avoided – if the leaders of Biafra and Nigeria were less self-serving and more mature.

Egbe recaptures the tragedy of Biafra with vivid simplicity. He tells stories of suffering, hunger, dislocation, anxiety, and death away from the battlefields. He takes you back in time, into private and family lives, to feel the pain and anguish of everyday living in the shadows of war. The eventual loss of his older brother, the frequent separation of family members and the family's close call with execution in the hands of federal soldiers all left indelible marks in the mind of the author.

He makes the point that wars are not only fought in battlefields but in the hearts and households of every victim. So, it is not just the soldiers and statesmen who bear the brunt of war. The common folks bear an equal burden, he suggests. Not only because they too are killed and maimed by flying bullets and bombs, but also because they have loved ones fighting in the trenches with whom they share inseparable bonds. More still, because they (the common folks) are helpless victims with no hand in either the making of war or in its outcome.

The author goes out of his way to review extant literature on the Nigerian civil war. He fearlessly points out the fables, misjudgments, and deliberate mischief in some of the claims and narratives – especially by major actors who sought to justify their roles or defend their sides in the conflict. He backs his arguments with painstaking research, sometimes delving into ancient military history and other relevant disciplines.

Across over 400 pages, Egbe repeatedly turns in a guilty verdict on the leaders of both sides, perhaps saving his most stinging criticism for the leaders of Biafra. In his view, they failed to make sensible military preparations, paid scant attention to internal and international diplomacy, and relied too much on propaganda.

As an intellectual, Egbe acquits himself quite well in this book. As a professor of Business Mathematics and Economics, he deserves praise for cross-disciplinary accomplishments in a field he embraces purely as a matter of private interest. This book will go down as an audacious contribution to the historiography of the Nigerian civil war. Not to mention a crash program in military history. Here, his detailed rebuttal of Brigadier Alabi's claim that the Second Punic War between Rome and Carthage was the first time elephants were used in battle, comes to mind.

For younger Nigerians, born after the war, and wondering why their fathers and grandfathers seem fixated on the events of 1967 – 1970, this book serves as an immersion in virtual reality. If they come away in anguish and tears, Egbe would have successfully delivered his message in this literary labor of love: That everyone is a loser in war. Perhaps even more so in the Nigeria-Biafra War.

Victor Anazonwu is a Journalist in Lagos, Nigeria

FOREWORD BY

LAWRENCE NWAGBARA

The book, ELEPHANT, THE GRASS AND A TEACHER is a very interesting and fact-filled rendition of the story of the Nigeria Biafra war with the objective of leading the reader through the events that led to the conflict, the hopes and tragedies that followed, and the collapse of the quest for independence by the Biafran people. The book showed that despite the will and determination of a people, a lot more was needed to win a war. As I read the entire story and especially the account of the attack at Abagana in the then East Central State, I literarily saw myself as the story!

I had been at the Abagana sector where our Platoon laid in ambush for the Nigeria soldiers. We were moved from Otuocha Aguleri where we had stayed in our trenches for over six months watching and in readiness to defend the Biafra land. Cynically, we were dug in near a Primary school where the enemy soldiers were stationed, and we could clearly hear the sound of their metal water container when placed on the cement floor of the building, clear evidence of a superior force that cared very little about the capability of its enemy. We did not make any move and they never attacked us.

After the famous Abagana attack where the enemy lost strings of armored cars and other military vehicles and equipment, we made effort to retreat but our Platoon was hit by a mortar bomb which resulted in the death of my precious brother, Sunny-Lee, who had been with me right from our recruitment and training at Umuahia in 1968. To me, that was the beginning of the end of the civil war. I was at that point convinced that the bravest soldier is the one that survives the war. As luck would have it, a few months later, I was invited for an interview to be assigned to the Pay and Record Department popularly known as the "Pay and Roll" Department where I spent the last few months of my military service.

The writer's account of the events of the second half of January 1970 after Biafra surrendered and the following February represents the experience of almost every young college-age young adult on the Biafra side. We had little or no money but our parents still found a few pounds to pay for our high school and college applications. Many of us returned to the nearest secondary school from our home to complete our West African School Certificate examinations.

The brilliant display of historical chronology and the perfect analysis of the economic and social impact of the war on the Igbos in particular and Nigerians, in general, will give any reader and generations to come to a clear picture of the conflict, its effects, and the consequences. The description of the brutality and man's inhumanity to man in the book is completely apt and a central point in the war. Both sides showed little regard for human life. Nothing mattered except individual survival.

The author warned that, paradoxically, little lessons appear to have been learned from the experience of the conflict. In his view, Gowon's closing signature tune of "No victor, no vanquished" does not appear to have any significance as the victor continued its winning streak and the vanquished remained in anguish. Every action of the winner was clearly designed to prepare for another war, a war of suppression, repression, oppression, and neglect. Even the political posture of the post-war civilian regime was no less divisive than the very atmosphere which led to the war. This led the author to clearly and rightly so, declare, with a sign of finality, that there were "no lessons" learned from the gruesome three-year war. What a tragedy, the author concluded.

I believe that this book will serve the need of future generations who would wish to know the truth about the civil war, the Professor who wishes to educate his students from the perspective of historical facts, and a reader seeking knowledge about the great Igbo race of Nigeria and the basis for their continued aspiration for a country they can call theirs. Their struggle for self-determination has continued to this day.

Lawrence Nwagbara
Houston, Texas USA

FOREWORD BY

DR. AUGUSTINE OKEREKE

The causalities of war are not only those who sit in air-conditioned offices to negotiate, are not those who exert and implement policies, are not the rulers who make war policies; rather the causalities of war are the poor, downtrodden, inconsequential masses on both sides of the divide. These are the ones that suffer the pangs of war. Chinyere Egbe's book, *Elephants, The Grass, and a Teacher: Recollections and Reflections of the Nigeria Biafra War* captures this theme. Egbe makes the point that leaders do not seek the opinions of their citizens before making the consequential decision of going to war. But eventually, the ordinary citizens are the ones who suffer the effects of war.

Narrated from a first-hand experience, the book captures vividly the deceit, ugliness, and sordidness of war. The author, who was very young during the Nigeria Biafra war was motivated to write this book after encouragement from his acquaintances to document his experiences during the Nigeria Biafra civil war. He was, additionally, motivated to document these experiences for his younger siblings who could not recollect their collective war experience in detail. But, most importantly, Egbe was motivated to author the book as a "reflection on the issues surrounding the war." According to him, "more importantly, it is about my thesis about war, the motives and behaviors of the ruling establishments that led to the war on both sides, the suffering of the masses of ordinary peoples". This assertion aptly captures the sentiments expressed in John Pepper Clark's poem "The Casualties". Clark's poem illustrates the evil nature of war; that war benefits no one and should be avoided. Egbe's book is emblematic of this moral instruction. Furthermore, Egbe uses his book to correct the assertions made by earlier writers about the war and proffers objective assessment. According to Egbe, both sides of the war offer dishonest representations of their accounts of the war. For instance, Egbe notes that Samuel Unweni in his book *888 days in Biafra* recounts the sufferings and violence he endured at the hands of his Biafra captives but fails to mention the atrocities of the Northerners during the pogrom. Similarly, Yakubu Gowon exhibited "plain dishonest presentation of events" in his victory speech in 1970 where he referred to the pogrom of the Igbos in the North as "much-regretted riots". The Biafra side was no better either.

Some of Ojukwu's advisers failed to give him objective assessments on the prosecution of the war. Egbe also highlights Ojukwu's attempts to make peace and for the Igbos to return to their displaced place of abode in the North in May 1966. Egbe observed that the real cowards of the war were the Nigerian leaders who could not hold their people accountable for the massacre of the Igbos in the North. At the same time, he also faulted the Biafra proponents of secession for selfish reasons. No doubt, the massacre was the main reason that precipitated the war and led to Igbos leaving the federation and declaring their own statehood for survival.

Egbe in *Elephants, The Grass, and a Teacher* describes the dishonest discussions and activities that led to the civil war as "the callous irresponsibility of our political leaders and ruling establishments." Those who suffered in the war are the common people. As he puts it, when the elephants fight, it is the grass that suffers. Egbe posits that the war was avoidable, but the callousness, selfishness, and mindlessness of the players and policymakers forestalled all avenues of reaching a peaceful resolution. The concept of "Monkey De Work, Baboon De Chop" is espoused in the book. The ruling warmongers and demagogues continued to ride in their Mercedes Benz cars and enjoyed the spoils of war while the "ordinary people, the villagers, the farmers, the common laborers, the market traders in the urban areas (the lumpen), the talakawas…." These are the ones that died from the violence of the war. The vividness with which Egbe describes the suffering of the common man is remarkable. This is not surprising because he experienced that suffering as a young man who, at times, served as a war messenger on the Biafra side. He reminisced on this experience in a harrowing account: "I found myself suddenly on the verge of losing my education. I found myself weekly, in a leaky dugout boat rowing ammunition and other military ordinance across a turbulent river, though I did not know how to swim; …. I endured shell fire for days and meandered under a tropical rainfall for 36 hours in a dark and treacherous swampy forest, with no food, towards the end of which I nearly collapsed, and then captured, tortured, and nearly killed."

In the end, Egbe in *Elephants, The Grass, and a Teacher* demonstrates that the war was avoidable. The Aburi accord would have presented itself as a perfect platform for peace to prevail but the actions of the negotiators, particularly on the Nigeria side, thwarted every chance of peace. The prohibitive demands made by Ojukwu advisers did not help matters either. Gowon and his advisers did not make efforts at enforcing, at least, the non-controversial parts of the Aburi accord. The attitude of the Nigerian government did not create an atmosphere for peace. In the end, the casualties were the ordinary people who were bombed mercilessly and not those who were negotiating the peace. Egbe remarks that the fact that the Biafra side was also provoking the war does not justify the bombing of defenseless, ordinary civilians by the Nigerian army. This barbarity is akin to what is happening in the present Russia Ukraine conflict. The Russian army continually bombs hospitals, mosques, fleeing refugees, and defenseless civilians. These unwarranted, brutal actions also happened during the Nigeria Biafra war.

In his objective sense, Egbe devotes time to reflect "on the Folly of the Igboman." He outlines the folly of the Igboman during the civil war in three categories. One is complacency in their misguided sense of superiority, which I believe is tantamount to arrogance. A second is lack of cohesion, which led to ineffective leadership. Finally, is their failure of diplomacy. This objectivity stands Egbe's *Elephants, The Grass, and a Teacher* out from most of the other books written about the Nigeria Biafra war. It is this objectivity that differentiates Egbe's book from most other books written about the war. Egbe's *Elephants, The Grass, and a Teacher* could be classified as historical war writing infused with informed analysis. This informed analysis adds to the authenticity and validity of the narrative. Egbe's account is factual, authentic, and grounded in plainness and vividness. His analysis positions him as a teacher reminding the citizens of the evils and fruitlessness of war. He moralizes on the Nigeria Biafra war where the elephants (herein the ruling class and the privileged) begin a war but the grass (herein the general population) suffers the pangs of war.

Augustine Okereke, Ph.D.
Professor of English at Medgar Evers College & Formerly Provost & Sr. Vice President,
MedgarEvers College of the City University of New York (CUNY)

PREFACE

It has been more than fifty years since the Nigeria-Biafra War ended. Stories and documentations have been written, and debates and discussions, and analyses are still going on. Even more will be written about this celebrated cataclysm two hundred years from today. There are still agitations for break up, and the issues that gave rise to the crisis are still with us—ethnic and sectarian tensions, alienation and frustration, and allegations of real or suspected corruption. It does not appear that things are getting better or that we learned any lessons.

I was motivated to write this book because I have told my story to friends and acquaintances, and they have found my experiences interesting—enough that many of them have suggested that I publish these experiences. At other times, from the end of the war to the time that I commenced this writing, I have been engaged in discussions and debates about different aspects of the war. But the catalyst to my writing this book was that I began to read the writings of ordinary people who documented the experiences of ordinary people—authors like Uriel Ogbechie, Diliora Chukwurah, and Alfred Uzokwe.1 Uzokwe and Chukwurah were highly inspiring because Uzokwe and Chukwurah were younger than 11 years old when the crisis and even the war began. The experiences of the war must have been so catalytic in their young minds that they could recollect events as they unfolded and document them in impressive detail. In adding documentation of my experiences to the literature on Biafra, I am expanding for posterity a collection of stories that will add to more complete documentation of events. Equally important, this book is written for the sake of my younger siblings, who experienced the events but were too young to recollect or document any details. Finally, I am writing this book as a tribute to my father, Mr. Pliny Igwe Abel Egbe, an educational pioneer whose energies and intellect mitigated the hardships arising from the war and whose personal influence shielded the family from annihilation during the war. It is possible that after I publish this book, the people of my village and my hometown in Ovim will be inspired to embellish the story for incorporation into a second edition—or maybe not.

This book is not just about my experiences and the experiences of my family during the Nigerian Civil War (July 1967–January 1970). It is also a reflection on the issues surrounding the war. More importantly, it is about my thesis regarding the war: the motives and behaviors of the ruling establishments on both sides that led to the war and the suffering of the masses of ordinary people. I take issue with the personalities, especially the secessionist leader and the ruling establishment on both sides. I have also expressed opinions about the organizational flaws of the leader on the Biafran side as well as some military analysis of one or more of the commanders. I will also use this opportunity to address some issues that do not fit logically or neatly into the main narrative. For example, Brig. Gen. Godwin Alabi stated that Hannibal captured Spain and introduced elephants into ancient warfare, a tactic for which the Romans had no answer. Such statements are flatly wrong (elephants were introduced about 500 BCE, and the Carthaginians had used them against Rome at the Siege of Akragas in 264 BCE, which was more than forty years before Hannibal's Second Punic War between 220 BCE and 202 BCE). I am addressing and correcting these errors for the benefit of people who do not have extensive knowledge of history and who have not read history books and literature and who would depend on an apparent expert for a reference. For example, while I was growing up, a man whose opinion I respected believed that Scipio Africanus was so named because his father had gone to the First Punic War with his pregnant wife and begat a son whom he named Scipio Africanus. However, this belief is not true because Scipio Africanus was born ten years after the First Punic War and his father was no more than ten years old when the First Punic War ended in 241 BCE.

My Approach to Writing this Book

Many books have been written about the civil war in the form of memoirs and historical documentation. However, a lot of the writings—not all–have been characterized by selective memories. Writers have been one-sided either by design or because of their perspective or limited information. Even on a personal level, if I had written this book twenty-five years ago, it would have been different. I would not have had the wealth of information that I have now, and my perspective might have been different. Accordingly, I will address some of the points that authors and spokespersons (on both sides of the conflict) have made. Examples would be Samuel Umweni's *888 Days in Biafra*, Mohamed Haruna's statement about Ojukwu after Ojukwu died, and Brig. Alabi's comment that no genocide had taken place during the war. Authors like Gen. Olusegun Obasanjo carefully avoided discussing the mass slaughter of Igbos that occurred from September 1966 through December 1966, in that he failed to explicitly recognize that it established the conditions that made secession an attractive and feasible option and then possible.

Selective Memories and Festering Wounds

This double standard of insensitivities pervades much of the writing about the civil war. Samuel Umweni, a senior official of the Midwest government of Nigeria, was captured by the Biafran Army and brought to Enugu in August 1967 and then imprisoned for the duration of the war. He suffered harrowing experiences and wrote a book, *888 Days in Biafra*.[1] In his book, Umweni detailed his experiences and his ordeal and documented the treatment of some Biafrans who were alleged to be saboteurs. As he saw the torture of these alleged saboteurs, Umweni stated, inter alia, that:

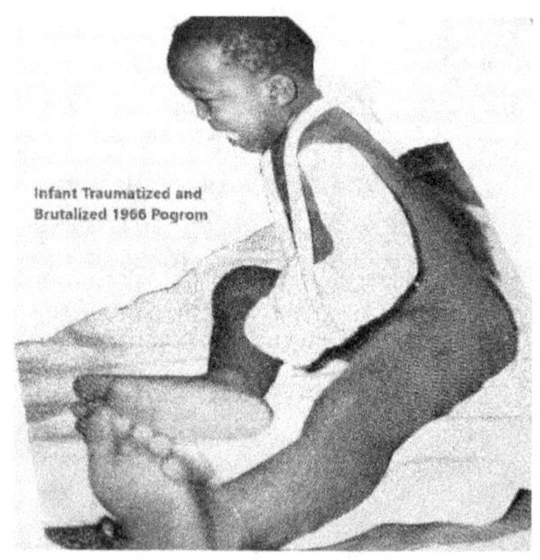

"... Honestly, I never knew that a human being could be as barbaric as that... how they all managed to survive that beating is still a mystery to me. I should regard that as one of the wonders of the world for it shows how much human beings can endure."[2]

I also wonder how Umweni survived the ordeal in Biafran prisons. Perhaps Umweni is being dishonest. He failed to witness the barbarism of the northern pogroms against Igbos, or he chose to be impervious to it. He should see the sampling of the pictures on this page and the next page and then explain why he thought that such endurance did not matter. After all, Umweni was still in the Midwest during the pogroms of 1966 and he should have traveled to Enugu or even Onitsha, a few miles from Benin to witness the victims. Umweni should have wondered how the child or man on this page survived the ordeal of being brutalized in the manner that they appear here.[3] In all likelihood, observers like Umweni were aware of the statement that Lt. Col. David Ejoor (later major general) made, which stated, inter alia,

"...It is true that recent events have taken a heavier toll on lives and properties of persons from a particular region...It is also true that people of that region ... have shown conspicuous restraint in

---

[1] *Samuel Umweni, 888 Days in Biafra (London: iUniverse, Inc., 2007), 159-61.*
[2] *Umweni, Pp. 160 – 61.*
[3] *The pictures are from Nigerian Pogrom: Crisis 1966 by the Government of Eastern Nigeria, 3-20.*

the face of reckless destruction... Speaking for myself and well-meaning Nigerians, they deserve nothing but praise... for the calm demonstrated in the face of fearful odds..."

The denialism of Umweni is exemplified by others such as Ayuba Mshelia,[4] who make it appear that the only reason that Igbos fled from the north and other parts of Nigeria was because Col. Ojukwu called on them to depart. What would Mshelia and Umweni have done if they had been subjected to molestation and murder simply because they spoke a particular language? What would they have done if they were leaders of the afflicted and the victims of such horrendous mayhem? All that Ojukwu did was to advise his people to depart from where they were not wanted, and the East would give them safety. At no point in their rendition of events did these two and similar authors recognize that the molestation of Igbos and other Eastern Nigerians was a major contribution to the discontent of the afflicted and was just as subject to condemnation and disapprobation. Umweni's, and similar others, imperviousness explains the double standards in human behavior. The Igbos have a saying: a coffin that bears the dead remains of a neighbor's grandmother is considered as nothing but a wooden box.

The Eastern Nigerian government published its view of the Crisis of 1966. According to the Eastern Nigerian government, *"...On January 16th [1966] the civilian government of Nigeria transferred power to the Armed Forces ... This transfer followed the revolt by a dissident section of the Army on January 15, a revolt which led to the killing of some army officers and four leading politicians..."*[5]

What a dishonest presentation of events. In the first place, the Eastern Nigerian government carefully avoided the emotions that had been evoked by the one-sided killing of leading politicians and army officers on January 15, 1966. Although the coup included several officers from other parts of the country, the preponderance of the commissioned and noncommissioned officers who carried out the coup of January 15, 1966, were Igbo. It is equally disingenuous to refer to the coup planners as "some dissidents" as if the military governor of Eastern Nigeria and other military leaders could not be traced to the conspiracy.

Well, the latter might be speculation, yet there was no excuse for the military boys and Ironsi, an Igbo man, to take over the civilian government, if, as stated by the Eastern Nigerian government, the coup of January 1966 was stopped by members of the armed forces who were still loyal the elected government. The army's government takeover was, in my view, an indication of complicity or opportunism by the Army boys

Another example of plainly dishonest presentation of events can be taken from Yakubu Gowon's victory speech in January 1970 and his and Mohamed Haruna's March 2012 characterization of the pogrom of 1966. Specifically, Gowon casually dismissed the events occurring between September and December 1966 as "much-regretted riots." If Gowon truly regretted the riots, he should have provided stronger support for the victims. Besides the troops that he sent to Kano from Kaduna in October 1966, Yakubu Gowon should have ordered the dispersal of the soldiers who barricaded the bridge at Makurdi that extracted soldiers and civilians alike to be murdered gratuitously. These soldiers should also have been detained and dismissed after the war. Gowon should also have permitted the international community to use Uli Airport immediately after the war to rush relief aid to the victims of the war. Yakubu Gowon should not have imposed internal and external blockades against the Eastern Region even before hostilities commenced. About the pogrom of 1966,

---

[4] *Ayuba Mshelia, Pp. 250 – 51*

[5] *Ministry of Information, Government of Eastern Nigeria: Eastern Nigerian Viewpoint, Nigerian Crisis 1966, Enugu, Nigeria, Page 3.*

Mohammed Haruna[6] states that "The riots of 1966, said Malam Magaji, became worse when soldiers of the 5th Battalion mutinied, killed one, Captain Audu Auna, and another, RSM Abdulmumini, both of them Northerners, in the process of their attempt to stop the mutiny." In reading this presentation of the events, one could think that the northern Nigerian noncommissioned officers were killed by Igbo soldiers—a careful and crafty distortion of the truth. Furthermore, this retelling could give the impression that some Igbos killed more northern Nigerian officers in the Fifth Battalion of the Nigerian Army, thus triggering a worsening of the riots against Igbos that were already going on. What I surmise happened there was that some well-meaning Northern Nigerian Army officers were opposed to the anti-Igbo riots and their fellow angry Northerners shot them dead in anger and simply joined the civilian riots. When these soldiers, and later policemen, joined the anti-Igbo riots, the Igbos who had laid low and hoped that the situation would blow over lost their nerves and joined the exodus of Igbos, creating a clear break between Igbos and the rest of Nigeria. Worse yet, there was thus a breakdown of protection for Igbos in almost every part of Nigeria, except in Eastern Nigeria and most of the Midwest.

I titled this book *Elephants, the Grass, and a Teacher* for a reason. Elephants represent the ruling, privileged establishments that precipitate war for which we, the ordinary masses (the Grass), suffered. The teacher represents my father (a celebrated teacher) who, both by his presence and even his absence, saved and shielded my family from annihilation. For example, after my siblings and my mother were tied up to be executed by Nigerian soldiers in early May 1969 (they missed me narrowly), one of the soldiers discovered a photograph in which my dad was pictured with the very battalion commander who had sent them to go and arrest the entire family. Moreover, one of the division commanders in the war was also in that same picture. The commander ordered the release of my family when they were presented to him. My father was not present.

Misleading Notions and Blasphemy

Now, I want to take issue with some of what I consider distortions or even misleading notions by others who have written about the civil war. I will begin with Brig. Gen. Godwin Alabi.[7] In giving honor to whom honor, Brig. Gen. Alabi wrote one of the most thorough and well- documented books about the war that should be considered a "must-read" for anyone who desires to experience what we all went through during the war. In particular, I could not agree more with Brig. Alabi when he implies that those who cause war are not the same people who fight in the trenches and suffer. As Alabi would put it,

"I wonder whether the Nzeogwu Ifeajuna coup of January 1966 was worth it, ... What good came of it for the people, except for some opportunists at the expense of the masses of the people... Now I know that we were just fighting for our pockets... What makes a military leader think as if the people sent to fight and die were not other people's children and of course, their own children are kept quietly abroad while others die for their greed...[8]"

In effect, *the children of the warmongers are all overseas in comfortable places while the poor and ordinary people's children are dying in the trenches.* This is exactly one of the theses of my book. However, I disagree with the Brigadier's argument that there was no genocide occurring in Biafra and with his misrepresentation and distortion that Biafra was executing Nigerian prisoners of war while the Nigerian side was feeding Biafran prisoners of war. What would he say of Col. Murtala Mohamed and Maj. Gen. Ibrahim Haruna's cowardly and barbaric slaughter of innocent children at the Asaba Massacre in October 1967?

---

[6] Mohammed Haruna Ojukwu: the man died but his spirit lives on, newsdiaryonline.com March 2012, http://newsdiaryonline.com/ojukwu-the-man-died-but-his-spirit-lives-on-by-mohammed-haruna/#sthash. DgFLRtET.dpuf

[7] *Brig. Gen. Godwin Alabi, The Tragedy of Victory: On the Spot Account of the Nigeria Biafra War in the Atlantic Theater, Ibadan, Nigeria, Spectrum Books, 2013*

[8] Brigadier Alabi, Ibid, Location 3416 in the Kindle Reader (E-Book)

With All Due Respect: A Point of Information and Point of Correction on Misleading Notions – An Essential Digression

Godwin Alabi appears to be puzzled about why the Biafran commanders sent one hundred men to capture Port Harcourt, two hundred men to capture Akwete, and three hundred men to capture Azumini.[9] Indeed, it would have been better if the six hundred men had been deployed to one axis, as Alabi had suggested so that the Nigerian forces would have had to be diverted to redefend Calabar and Ikot Ekpene. What the Brigadier did not understand was that the Biafran leadership and, speaking truth-to-power, Ojukwu were not militarily prepared to fight a real war. Ojukwu depended much on internal and external propaganda and bluff to fight the war. The whole idea was to announce the capture of these little places, gain some minor tactical victories, and make a big announcement to raise hopes that Biafra was about to recapture Calabar and Port Harcourt from the Nigerian invaders. The government of Biafra will sustain illusions and the morale of the population, and the masses of troops engaged against the enemy. This also explains the foray into the Midwest in August 1967 and the silly military action of bombing of Kano and Lagos shipyards in 1967 – Much like a childish fantasy that imitates the German bombing of London in World War II without the numerosity of bombers.

I am not here to argue with the Brigadier's notion of battle tactics. However, the Brigadier's assertion that the military operation of the war from Calabar to Port Harcourt was similar to what the Romans did to Hannibal's Carthage is flatly wrong. Specifically, Alabi makes several misleading or factually incorrect statements. First Alabi claims that

...it was like Hannibal advancing into Italy after capturing Spain in 218 BCE. The Italian generals[10] had no answer for this African (Carthaginian) general who introduced elephants into the battlefield ...He attacked and captured everywhere and anywhere that he wanted until a Roman general called Scipio Africanus thought of attacking Hannibal's supply route. The strategy was to allow Hannibal to continue to advance into Italy but his home base and supply route from Carthage would be captured and his supply route cut off ...That was exactly what happened ... Hannibal's counterattack to Scipio's attack on Carthage should have been to continue his advance to Rome and use Spain as his supply route ... because he turned back creating a vacuum in Spain... he lost his momentum ... and lost the war ...[11]

Every single assertion in Alabi's narrative above is incorrect. First, Hannibal lost his momentum after Cannae (216 BCE) because his troops had been badly depleted and the Southern Italians, in as much as they had declared for Carthage, did not provide the needed manpower and material support that Hannibal needed to attack Rome and weaken Roman political resolve and military capacity.

Hannibal of Carthage did not introduce elephants into battlefields during the Second Punic War (219–202 BCE). As I stated earlier, elephants had been used in battlefields of the ancient world as

---

[9] *Ibid at locations 3427 - 3446*

[10] *Better to refer to Roman generals because the Punic Wars were between Rome and Carthage. Many Italian cities and potentialities were not exactly on the side of Rome but, in many instances, against Rome and only refrained from aligning with Hannibal because they were afraid of possible reprisals from Rome if Hannibal did not win.*

[11] *Godwin Alabi, Tragedy of Victory, Locations 3268 – 69.*

far back as three hundred years earlier.[12] Even to Western European warlords, elephants had been encountered more than one hundred years before Hannibal fought against the Romans in 218 BCE. Specifically, Alexander the Great encountered elephants at the Battle of Hydaspes (327 BC), against the Punjabi (Indian Potentate) Porus of India, and in the Magadha empire east of the Punjab, halting his advance. Even before the Hydaspes (327 BCE), Alexander had encountered elephants at the Battle of Gaugamela (331 BCE) and the Battle of Issus (333 BCE). Alexander's successors employed elephants beginning from about 318 BCE. As for the Romans, Hannibal was not the first to use elephants against them in battle. King Pyrrhus of Epirus used elephants against the Romans at the Battle of Heraclea (280 BCE) and at the Battle of Asculum (279 BCE). The Romans were frightened of the elephants at Heraclea but at Asculum, the Romans devised a way of attacking and capturing them.[13]

In the struggles between the Romans and the Carthaginians, Carthage had used elephants against the Roman army in 263 BCE at the first encounter between the two rivals during the First Punic War and also in 254 BCE at the Battle of Akragas under the Roman commander named Lucius Caecilius.[14] In 251 BCE, Lucius Caecilius defeated the Carthaginian general Hasdrubal at the Battle of Panormus (Modern Palermo) and captured 120 elephants.

Hannibal did not have to capture Spain to invade Rome. For several centuries, the Carthaginians had been influential in Spain and colonized at least one-third of the peninsula. However, at the end of the First Punic War (264–241 BCE), the Carthaginian senate in its foolish greed held back on paying the mercenaries that helped them fight Rome. A war ensued between Carthage and the mercenaries. Taking advantage of the distraction, the Romans opportunistically occupied Carthaginian possessions in southern Italy, especially Sicily. Having lost their possessions and source of resources, Hamilcar Barca, Hannibal's father, immediately occupied what was left of Spain, except for a sliver of territory north of Spain.[15] After Hamilcar died (229 BCE), a treaty was signed by Hasdrubal in 226 BCE that marked the boundary between Rome and Carthage at the Ebro River (see map). The Ebro River is practically at the boundary between Spain and the Pyrenees. Therefore, when Hannibal set out to invade Rome through the Alps beginning in 219 BCE, he did not have to capture Spain because most of the Iberian Peninsula was under Carthaginian hegemony or influence and probably included parts of Lusitania (present-day Portugal).[16]

The reason that Hannibal advanced from northern Italy through to the south had nothing to do with the inability of Roman generals to answer to Hannibal's elephants. Hannibal set out with about thirty-seven elephants, but fewer than five survived the crossing of the Alps or engaged in any battle.[17] Therefore, Hannibal fought the battles without the elephants. That Hannibal advanced through Italy was certainly not because the Roman generals allowed it as a means of stretching his supply lines. On the contrary, the Romans did their best to stop Hannibal and confronted him every

---

[12] *Heraclea (280 BC) Weapons and Warfare, History and Hardware of Warfare* https://weaponsandwarfare.com/2018/03/19/heraclea-280-bc/, March 19, 2018 *for a synopsis of the introduction of elephants in Warfare. See also Richard Glover, The Elephant in Ancient War, The Classical Journal , Feb., 1944, Vol. 39, No. 5 (Feb., 1944), pp. 257-269 and Mark Cartwright, Elephants in Greek & Roman Warfare World History Encyclopedia 16 March 2016,* https://www.worldhistory. org/article/876/elephants-in-greek--roman-warfare/

[13] *Richard Miles, Carthage Must be Destroyed: The Rise and Fall of an Ancient Civilization, London, Penguin Books, 2010, Pp. 162 - 63*

[14] *See also Ibid, Pp. 179 – 89.*

[15] *Daniel A. Fournie Second, Punic War: Hannibal's War in Italy, Military History magazine, March/April 2005. See also Richard Miles, Op. Cit.*

[16] *See Richard Miles, Op. Cit. See also John Prevas, Hannibal's Oath: The Life and Wars of Rome's Greatest Enemy, Boston, DeCapo Press, 2017, Pp. 7 – 28. See also Patrick Hunt, Hannibal, New York, Simon and Schuster, 2017. Also Keith Milton , How Hannibal Hammered the Roman Army:* https://warfarehistorynetwork.com/2015/11/15/how-carthaginian-hannibal-hammered-the-roman-army/ *November 15, 2015*

[17] *Charles, Michael and Peter Rhodan, Magister Elephantorum: A Reappraisal of Hannibal's Use of Elephants, Classical World, Vol. 100, Summer 2007, Pp. 363 – 89.*

inch of the way—at the Battle of Ticinus River (218 BCE), the Battle the Trebia Lake (217 BCE), the Battle of Lake Trasimene (217 BCE), and finally at the Battle of Cannae (216 BCE). Each of these battles ended in defeat for Rome and, at least Cannae was a frightening and disheartening disaster.[18]

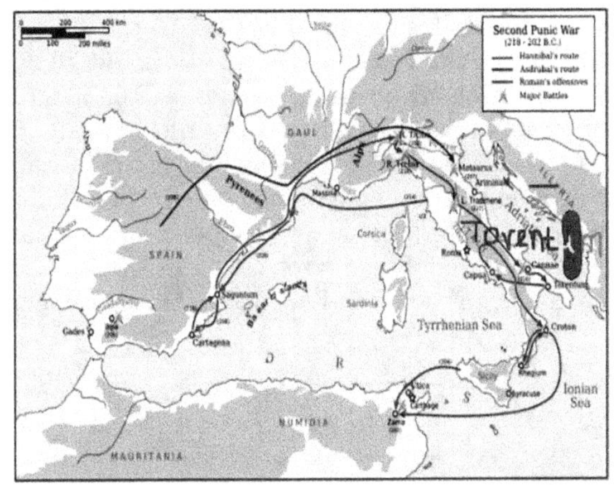

I am not disputing the Brigadier's assertion about who was stretching whose supply lines during the Nigeria-Biafra War or why or whether it was the right thing to do under the circumstances that he was referring to. Stretching supply lines and attacking the enemy back and the front is well known in military science. The Nigerian civil war's Battle of Abagana could arguably be described as such, and Gen. Barclay De Tolly's decision to retreat and draw Napoleon deep into Russia from the beginning of Napoleon's invasion (1812) as continued after the Battle of Smolensk (August 1812) could also be argued as an example.[19] However, with all due respect to the Brigadier, Scipio did not initiate stretching H a nn i ba l ' s s upp l y line, and Hannibal's ultimate defeat from a strategic point of view had nothing to do with stretching his supply lines.

After Cannae, the Romans, on the advice of appointed dictator Quintus Fabius Maximus (nicknamed Cunctator or "delayer"), decided not to confront Hannibal directly any longer. Thereafter, the Roman Army and Navy simply harassed Hannibal and engaged him and the Carthaginian navy in minor confrontations.

In 212 BCE, Hannibal captured the port city of Tarentum, further south and east of Rome. Hannibal failed to besiege Rome because, as some historians have argued, he did not have the siege engines or sufficient forces to attack, invest and capture the city.[20] After Hannibal's capture of Tarentum (Modern Taranto) in 212 BCE, his brother Hasdrubal tried to resupply him through the Alps. By itself, that choice by Hasdrubal, which stretched Hannibal's supply route, was a continuation of Hannibal's original decision to invade Rome from the North. Why they chose to go that way from the beginning of the campaign is a subject of discussion by itself. After all, Tarentum was much closer to Carthage than traveling all the way north of Italy and then traveling southeast. It might have been because the Romans were menacing the Tyrrhenian Sea and a move by Hasdrubal to resupply Hannibal across the Tyrrhenian Sea might have been considered riskier.[21]

---

[18] *James Lacey Ghosts of Cannae, by Robert L. O'Connell, Book Review: Ghosts of Cannae, by Robert L. O'Connell (historynet.com). See also Robert L. O'Connell, Ghosts of Cannae: Hannibal and the Darkest Hour of the Roman Republic, Random House, 2010. See also Greg Yocherer Second Punic War: Battle of Cannae, Military History Magazine, February 2000*

[19] *When the French invasion of Russia began in 1812, Barclay de Tolly was commander-in-chief and initiated a scorched earth policy from the beginning of the campaign. After the Battle of Smolensk (August 16, 1812), the Russian Tsar (Alexander I) removed De Barclay and appointed Mikhail Kutuzov as commander-in-chief. However, Kutuzov continued the same scorched earth retreat up to Moscow and eventually gave Napoleon a battle at Borodino on September 7, 1812. Arguably, the scorched earth policy and retreat of both De Barclay and Kutuzov were designed to stretch Napoleon's supply lines.*

[20] *See Josiah Ober, Hannibal's Dilemma, Military History Quarterly, Summer 1990, Pp. 50 – 60. Other sources include Richard Garbriel, Why Hannibal Lost, Military History Magazine, May 2016, Pp. 58 – 63. Or Hannibal's Big Mistake, Military History Magazine, November 2011. Of course, you may also consult, Patrick Hunt, Op. Cit, John Prevas, Op. Cit. Others are B.D Hoyos, Hannibal, What Kind of Genius, in Greece and Rome, Vol. XXX # 2, 1983,*

[21] *After the naval battle of Ecnomus (255 BCE) of the First Punic War, the Carthaginians effectively lost their place as the preeminent naval power of the region and the Romans were able to effectively challenge Carthage at sea.*

In any event, in 211 BCE, Gnaeus Cornelius Scipio was assigned to stop Hasdrubal in Spain. Later, Gnaeus's brother Publius Cornelius Scipio was assigned to join him. Publius took along his young son of the same name, P. Cornelius Scipio Minor. The objective was to disrupt the supply line that had already been stretched by choice. During that year, the senior Scipios died in battle at the hands of Hasdrubal at the Battle of the Baetis Valley. The Consul Claudius Drusus Nero was assigned to replace them, but Hasdrubal duped him and managed to slip his soldiers out through the Alps.[22] The younger Scipio pursued, defeated, and killed Hasdrubal at the Battle of Metaurus in 208 BCE. None of this was about the younger Scipio's thoughtful or ingenious idea of stretching Hannibal's supply route. The defeat of Hasdrubal had the effect of starving Hannibal of reinforcements in addition to the fact that the Carthaginian Senate had modified their strategic objective in the war. Simply stated, the Carthaginian Senate wanted to recover their lost possessions in southern Italy. Therefore, it is easy to understand why they were reluctant to provide money and manpower to reinforce Hannibal. This modified strategic objective was simply a mirror image of the Roman strategy for the war, which was to consolidate Roman hold on southern Italy and to make stronger their foothold in Spain. Specifically,

Both Carthage and Rome viewed the war in a far broader strategic context than did Hannibal. Rome sought to preserve gains it had obtained during the First Punic War and perhaps seize Iberia, while Carthage aimed to retain Iberia and recover territory in Corsica, Sardinia, and Sicily it had lost in the previous war. Rome clearly perceived Carthage's strategic intent ... What Carthage wanted most from the war was to retain possession of Iberia, with its lucrative silver mines, commercial bases, and monopoly on the inland trade. It also wanted to recoup its bases in Corsica, Sardinia, Sicily, and some of the offshore islands and thus control the sea-lanes in the eastern Mediterranean ... If Carthage had established a significant military presence in its former possessions, it would have been in a strong position to retain them once the war ended and negotiations ensued...[23]

The Romans proved resilient and would not negotiate with Hannibal. Under these circumstances, it would have been futile to attack Rome. Once more, Josiah Ober[24] provides a cogent explanation. Instead of Alabi's proposition that Hannibal should have attacked Rome,[25] Hannibal should have taken the gamble of amassing forces in a joint infantry and naval assault on Sicily and southern Italy to recapture lost Carthaginian possessions and to defend Spain and Carthage. This should have been done immediately after capturing Tarentum or immediately after he unsuccessfully attacked Rome in 211 BCE, the latter of which was done as a means of diverting the Romans from divesting him of Capua immediately to the South of Rome.[26] The failed attempt on Rome in 211 BCE should have taught Hannibal a lesson. Hannibal should also have revised his thinking after his brother Hasdrubal was killed at Metaurus (208 BCE).

Lingering in southern Italy for another three years that enabled Cornelius Scipio, the younger, to mobilize and attack Carthage was a fatal error. If Hannibal had moved to occupy southern Italy and if he had taken Sicily, the Romans would have been forced to withdraw forces from Spain to defend their southern flanks. The Carthaginians would then move to reconsolidate their hold in Spain where the Romans were beginning to attack Carthaginian interests and which they took afterward. Indeed, the moment Hannibal lost his hold on Capua, he should have advised his brother and the Carthaginian Senate to halt all reinforcements through the Alps. Hasdrubal would have consolidated his hold on Spain and Hannibal should have attacked Sicily. The outcomes would have amounted, at least, to a stalemate that would have earned the Carthaginians a more lasting peace. Gabriel agrees with me

---

[22] *Joshua J. Mark,* Hasdrubal Barca, *https://www.worldhistory.org/Hasdrubal_Barca/ 05 April 2018*
[23] *Richard Gabriel, Why Hannibal Lost*
[24] *Josiah Ober, Op. Cit*
[25] *Alabi is not alone in expressing this opinion. Even Gabriel (Op. Cit) suggested that Hannibal should have attacked Rome even as a feint because Rome would have been forced to withdraw their forces from Spain.*
[26] *See Patrick Hunt, Hannibal. Pp. 168 – 71 and Richard Niles, Pp.193 – 98.*

on this.[27] Simply stated, the capture of Tarentum provided Hannibal and Carthage the opportunity to modify the strategic landscape and give Carthage their more long-term objective. Rome might not have been defeated, but Carthage might have avoided or withstood the Third Punic War. Following the defeat of Hasdrubal at Metaurus, the younger Scipio requested that he be permitted to take the war to Carthage. In 205 BCE, the Roman Senate grudgingly assigned Scipio troops from disgraced veterans of Cannae. Scipio landed in Africa about 203 BCE.[28] The Carthaginian Senate recalled Hannibal and the two military giants met at Zama in 202 BCE. Hannibal was defeated and the younger Scipio was invested with the sobriquet "Africanus." Thereafter, P. Cornelius Scipio Minor was called by the name Scipio Africanus. Therefore, the name Scipio Africanus was not in existence before P. Cornelius Scipio Minor invaded Carthage in 202 BCE.

Though the Brigadier suggests that Hannibal should have attacked Rome—as many historians agree—Hannibal did try to attack Rome. Specifically, in 212 BCE (see map) after Hannibal captured Tarentum, the city of Capua defected to Hannibal.[29] The Romans attacked Capua under the leadership of Quintus Fulvius Flaccus and Appius Claudius Pulcher and were defeated by Hannibal. In 211 BCE, the Romans, once more, besieged Capua. Hannibal marched on Rome as a means of diverting Roman attention from the siege of Capua, but the Romans called his bluff and Hannibal retreated to Tarentum, leaving Capua to fall to the Romans. What I wonder is why Hannibal did not head for the City of Rome after the Battle of Lake Trasimene (217 BCE). Instead, he went further away, south and east of Rome, and ended at Cannae where the Romans engaged him and met yet another disaster. In the end, this all goes to prove the point that Hannibal did not have the resources to invade and capture Rome.[30]

In writing this book, I have tried to be objective. To the extent possible, I have put myself, in turn, in three different positions: I tried to put myself on the Nigerian side and ask the question, "what if I was a Northerner and I was subjected to murderous brutality due to the actions of a few Northerners." Alternatively, I ask the Igboman, "what would you do if your leaders were murdered in cold blood and their murderers took their positions in government, which in turn might jeopardize your livelihood and basic comfort?" I would ask other Nigerians, "how would you feel if you were subject to harassment to which there was no end in sight? Would you have remained in the locations where the mayhem was taking place, considering that everyone is not equally lucky in being spared or escaping the assault by enraged assailants?" I have also analyzed the actions of the leaders and tried to take the view of a neutral observer to reflect on why they took certain actions while cognizant of the consequences. For example, after the peace talks in Ghana, why did Yakubu Gowon not at least order the payment of three months of salary to federal civil servants who fled their places of work, because it was agreed to at Aburi. This singular act alienated the Igbo and Eastern Nigerian populations and gave them a reason to support Ojukwu and the secession. On the other hand, I can understand why the civil servants in Lagos, Nigeria, objected to the payment, citing the lame excuse that it would have an adverse economic impact. Simply put, paying such monies would transfer resources to a potential adversary. But my argument is that the decision-makers should have weighed the pros and cons of the alienation of those affected and the goodwill that it might have brought the federal government if they had paid the salaries. At the very least, they would have done their part to bring about peace. My conclusion is that the comfortable top civil servants did not care about the consequences of their inaction because they would not be the

---

[27] *Richard Gabriel, Supra.*

[28] *James Lacey Book Review: Ghosts of Cannae, by Robert L. O'Connell (historynet.com) See also, Robert L. O'Connell, Ghosts of Cannae: Hannibal and the Darkest Hour of the Roman Republic, Random House, 2010*

[29] *Michael P. Fronda , Hegemony and Rivalry: The Revolt of Capua Revisited, Phoenix , Spring - Summer, 2007, Vol. 61, No. 1/2 (Spring - Summer, 2007), pp. 83-108*

[30] *William C. Morey, Second Punic War (218-201 B.C.) in "Outlines of Roman History". New York, American Book Company (1901), published in https://factsanddetails.com/world/cat56/sub407/ entry-6249. html#chapter-9*

ones to go in the trenches and fight a war where they would face bullets and endure the discomforts of battle and exposure to danger.

Many people who read my opinions in this book may find my conclusions and analysis objectionable. Others may find that I have been objective and be understanding. For the former, I will beg their indulgence and plead that they try to do what I have done, which is to place yourself in the position of those affected by the developments of the crisis. Consider the ordinary person who suffers as a refugee in a refugee camp, beset by hunger and discomfort. I urge that people who read this book do so with an open mind. Think about the fact that those who instigate war are not the ones who end up being exposed to the dangers of the dagger, the sword, and the guns. Think about the fact that in every conflict, there are usually alternative avenues for compromise and peacemaking. In the Nigeria-Biafra War, there were numerous such opportunities that the leaders on both sides in the conflict overlooked or rejected.

INTRODUCTION

Nigeria was created in 1914 by the amalgamation of the Northern and Southern Protectorates of the British. At the time of the amalgamation, three regions were created: the Northern Region, the Eastern Region, and the Western Region (see map). Each of the regions included several ethnic groups, with a dominant ethnic or cultural group in each of them. Northern Nigeria was dominated by the Hausa-Fulani Islamic ethnic group. The North also included numerous small groups such as the Igala, Tiv, Nupe, and Idoma, to name a few. There were also the Kanuri, and Gwari, which, though substantial in their

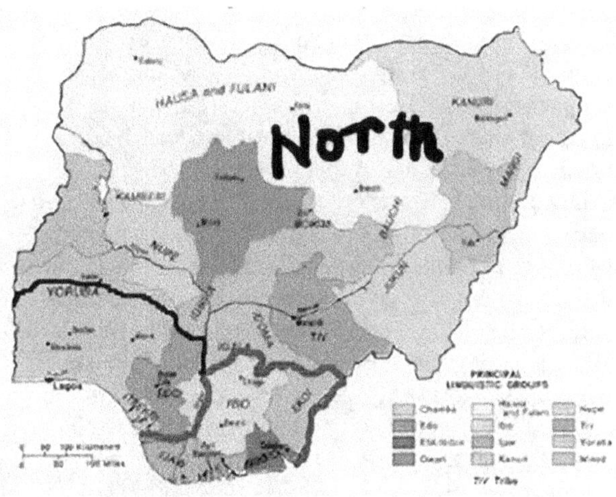

populations were nevertheless potentially subject to domination or paralyzing struggle against the Hausa- Fulani group. In the Western Region, the Yoruba dominated in terms of their population, but it also contained the Edo of the pre-colonial Benin Kingdom that was fairly influential and could engage the political domination of the Yorubas in a mutually paralyzing political struggle. In 1963, the Midwest Region was created, which left the Western Region to become monoethnic Yoruba. However, the resulting Midwest Region was multiethnic, with the Edo ethnic group being the largest single group among the Itsekiri, the Igbos, and the Urhobo. The Igbos of the Midwest Region were a minority and were linguistically related to the dominant Igbo ethnic group located in the Eastern Region. In the Eastern Region, the Igbos were the dominant group; other ethnic groups included the Efik-Ibibio, the Ijaws, the Ogonis, Kalabaris, and the Ekoi-Ogoja group. Although the Efik-Ibibio, Ekoi-Ogoja, and the Ijaws were considered a minority, collectively they constituted a substantial percentage (45 percent) of the Eastern Nigerian regional population. The appearance of domination by the Igbos was not exactly potent but was also a portent of debilitating political struggle and a creator of discontent.

On October 1, 1960, Nigeria gained independence from the British. The new country adopted the Westminster system of parliamentary democracy based on political parties. The ethnically-based political parties were dominated, in each region, by the dominant ethnic group of that region. The dominance of political parties by the dominant ethnic group was a portent for perpetual distrust that made real ideologically based coalitions difficult. Less than four years after independence, the country was beset by a series of crises, beginning with an election crisis in 1962 in Western Nigeria and the imprisonment of Chief Obafemi Awolowo, the first Premier of Western Nigeria. The political instability in Western Nigeria and at the center was followed by the Tiv riots in 1964, which were quelled with military force. During the same period, the country was bedeviled by an election crisis not only in Western Nigeria but across the country in the Federal Parliament (1964–1965). There was cataclysmic violence in Western Nigeria, and one of the leaders of the independence struggle, Chief Obafemi Awolowo, was in jail on allegations of treasonable felony.

On January 15, 1966, less than six years after Nigeria was granted independence, the elected government was overthrown by a military force led by a group of dissident soldiers who had decided to take matters into their own hands. The ringleaders of the coup of January 1966 were Igbos of Eastern Nigeria, though there were officers and rank and file of every region and major ethnic group in Nigeria. The coup was described as an attempt by Igbos to take over and rule Nigeria. This perception gave rise to riots in Northern Nigeria against Igbos and eventually led to a counter-coup in July 1966 by officers and men mostly from Northern Nigeria.

Following the counter-coup of July 1966, sporadic riots and molestation of Igbos and other Eastern Nigerians in Northern Nigeria were followed in September 1966 and beyond by a horrifying ethnic cleansing pogrom against Igbos throughout Northern Nigeria. During the ethnic cleansing pogroms of September to December 1966, military personnel joined the fray. Estimates of the casualties range from 7,000 to 30,000 and a displacement of up to two million Igbos and other Eastern Nigerians. This ethnic purge and pogrom of Igbos were attended by isolated molestations of Igbos in Western Nigeria. The Nigerian government was not able to control the mayhem and, to some extent, withheld support from the victims of the events. These attacks on Igbos also led Igbos in Eastern Nigeria to initiate isolated assaults against Northern Nigerians and the expulsion of all non-Easterners from Eastern Nigeria (November–December 1966).

During the crisis, there were attempts from August 1966 through March 1967 to negotiate peace between and among Nigerians, especially Eastern Nigerians. These attempts failed because there were warmongers on both sides of the conflict. These warmongers came from the leadership clique in Eastern Nigeria who had hidden agendas and ambitions for establishing a sovereign state; they simply played on the pain and suffering of people who were traumatized and genuinely aggrieved and, therefore, susceptible to instigation. In the north, some people had not ever wanted to be part of Nigeria and so seized the crisis as an opportunity to secede. Some wanted to have nothing to do with a united Nigeria that was not controlled by the Northern ruling establishment and privileged classes. This latter group preferred to manipulate the crisis to precipitate a military solution that they were confident would give them victory. There were also elements in Western Nigeria who felt that any outcome that excluded the east through military defeat would enable them to have privileged access to positions that hitherto had been occupied by Eastern Nigerians, especially the Igbos. When the peace talks failed, the east, under the leadership of their military governor, Lt. Col. Chukwuemeka Odumegwu Ojukwu, broke away from Nigeria and declared the independent Republic of Biafra on May 30, 1967. The federal government of Nigeria declined to recognize the breakaway Republic of Biafra and declared war on July 6, 1967.

The war lasted thirty months and visited immense suffering, including mass starvation and the Nigerian Army's slaughter of Eastern Nigerians. Estimates of the casualties against Eastern Nigerians, especially Igbos, range from 100,000[31] to two million. On January 15, 1970, the struggle for secession collapsed when Gen. Ojukwu went into exile and Nigeria was reunited. Many people, including Nigerians, did not expect the war to last for so long, nor did many expect that the Igbos would endure so much suffering to achieve their objective. During the war, efforts were made to achieve a negotiated settlement, but these efforts were also undermined by the intransigence of leaders on both sides and their lack of sincerity. Biafra failed in part because they were handicapped for resources due to the blockade mounted by the Nigerian government. Another reason that Biafra failed was that the international community declined to recognize the breakaway republic. Biafra also failed because of political myopia and naïveté of its leadership clique. The failure to achieve recognition and even to be able to purchase arms reveals a lesson on the realities of international diplomacy and politics and a further note of caution for those who aspire to self-determination through armed struggle.

---

[31] *This low estimate is attributed only to Sir David Hunt, a British Diplomat who disparaged Biafran propaganda. See Sir David Hunt, On the Spot: An Ambassador Speaks, London, Peter Davis, 1975, pp.168 – 200. Other more credible sources place the estimates of Biafran civilian casualties at least 500,000.*

Characterizing the Nigeria – Biafra War: A Brothers' War or Just About Greed?

It has been difficult for me to characterize the Nigeria-Biafra War. In many ways, it brought out the best in human considerations. In other ways, it revealed the primitivity of the human race. The level of brutality was horrendous. Yet, in many instances, natural humanity led us to spare each other. Friends fought against friends and killed them and then buried them with full military honors and wept. Some soldiers may have captured their friends and allowed them to live. The experience of my mother and my brothers and sisters described earlier and detailed in the main body of this narrative is a good example.

The Nigerian's callous mass starvation of the Biafran population in response to their stubborn resistance is cause for the damnation of the leaders on both sides of the conflict. Nigeria cannot explain what divine right they had to compel Biafra to be part of Nigeria. After all, the other Nigerians subjected the Biafrans to inexplicable mass slaughter and molestation that caused the Igbos to flee from all parts of the country. The Nigerian government withheld support from the victims. Gowon's withholding of a mere three months' salary to federal employees who fled for their lives as agreed at Aburi was nothing short of wickedness in the extreme. On the other hand, if the leaders of Biafra had felt that the security of the Igbos was their primary objective, there is sufficient indication that a mass slaughter would not have occurred if Biafra had given up the struggle. For that reason, there was no justification to subject the population to the mass suffering that occurred. Therefore, I hold on to the view that the war ensued to support the greed and selfishness and the desire for control of resources by the ruling establishments on both sides of the conflict.

Preambles & Insights

In the remainder of this introduction, I want to summarize some of my viewpoints by referencing insightful statements that others have made. Specifically, why did we, as Nigerians, go to war with each other? For the Igbos and all Nigerians, what lessons should be learned?

The Origins of War – Letter from Military History, July 2016

*"There is generally no mystery about what motivates nations, ethnic groups, or other masses of people bound by a particular set of beliefs to fight wars. Conflicts erupt because one group covets the territory (**The Anglo Saxons in England 5th Century CE and America Seventeenth th Century CE, or the British and other Europeans in South Africa and Australia 17th and 18th Centuries**) or the natural resources of another (the **King of Morocco demanded to tax the salt mines of Taghaza in 1590 and threats by European powers during the Arab oil boycott of 1973**)[32] People may be compelled to defend themselves or their lands against real or imagined threats of invasion (**Biafran rebels against Nigerian invaders**), ... Those of one faith seek to forcibly convert others of other faiths who worship different gods or the same god in a different way (**Moslem invasions of Europe and Asia in the Seventh Century, the religious wars of Europe in the 16th and 17th Centuries or even the Christian Crusades against Arab lands in the Eleventh, Twelfth and Thirteenth Centuries**)... Of course, baser human instincts – greed, hubris, jealousy, lust, and others have sparked calamitous warfare since the dawn of time (**Prince of Troy kidnapped or eloped with Helen, the queen, and wife of King Menelaus of Sparta and Greeks made the Trojan War – as per legend**) .... History's Sell Swords ...are willing to fight anywhere for any leader and any cause simply because they are addicted to fighting ... (**Col Steiner of Biafra**) ... People may be driven ...an honest desire to check an obvious evil (**some Biafran mercenaries – the 200 at Calabar and***

---

[32] *For example, when the Askia rejected the demand, the Moroccan king made war and destroyed the Songhai Empire in 1591 at the Battle of Tondibi. During the Middle East oil boycott in 1973, Europeans threatened war and the German chancellor, made a thinly veiled threat that "nations in the past have gone to war to get salt, water..."*

Carl Von Rosen, the wealthy Swedish man who brought Biafran Babies aircraft to menace the Nigerian Airforce); .... In the end, history ultimately teaches us that both types of motivation - the sacred and the profane, the noble and the despicable - will remain part of human nature – This is why wars will remain with us.[33,34]

The Nigeria-Biafra War can be explained by the instincts described in the above statements. There is no denying that the process of nation-building can be turbulent and that there will be conflicts. Fundamentally, any nation-building conflict is bound to be somewhat more intense in a country that was created out of widely disparate historical and cultural experiences, such as Nigeria. Worse yet, Nigeria was created for the convenience of a colonial invader. In this context, the Northern People's Congress (NPC) intense and ruthless pursuit of domination and the Igbo nation's wily penetration into all nooks and crannies of Nigeria was bound to bring the latter into conflict with their newfound neighbors. Along the way, the prospect of oil revenues that would have enriched the elites in all parts of Nigeria may have created hidden and unspoken agendas, ambitions, and vicious greed among the elites that came into play during political maneuvers. Therefore, on both sides, the dogs of war that thrive on chaos found fertile ground to ply their trade and made it difficult to negotiate peace when opportunities arose.

Be Prepared – War is no Child's Play

In the context of the civil war, the Igbo became a victim not only of the power play but also of his follies: self-importance, self-delusion, and the realities of internal politics and international diplomacy. As the Nigerian crisis brewed and tensions escalated between 1962 and 1965, a group of army officers led mostly by Igbos overthrew the government in a gruesome murder spree during the early morning hours of January 15, 1966. The coup was mischievously interpreted to be a conspiracy by the Igbos to dominate Nigeria. In all this, the provocateurs pulled the wool over the eyes of the world and maintained a focus that ignored the Tiv riots of 1964, the gruesome bloodletting of the violent election crisis, and Operation Wetie in Western Nigeria. Indeed, Operation Wetie was the most proximate event that precipitated the coup of January 1966, yet many people today and in the future would look at the war and make it appear as if the war was the culmination of the events of January 1966.

For those who make apologies for the Igbos and those who condemn Ojukwu and the Igbos for the secessions, I can only point to the double standards that attend political diplomacy and the convenient politics of selective memory and analysis. There were serious allegations and indications that the NPC, which was already fermenting and orchestrating the violent bloody violence of Operation Wetie, was planning a coup.[35] Imagine, for a moment, that the alleged plan for Operation No Mercy, the expected coup of Brig. Zakaria Maimalari and other NPC sympathizers had taken place on January 17, 1966, as alleged by Col. Nwobosi and others. Consider further that they killed President Nnamdi Azikiwe (Igbo), Premier Michael Okpara (Igbo premier of Eastern Nigeria), Chief Osadebe (Igbo premier of the Midwest Region), and several Igbo army officers, a few pro–Awolowo Yoruba army officers, one Hausa-Fulani officer, and several top Igbo army officers, including Maj. Gen. Aguiyi Ironsi. There would have been a loud and bitter protest and cry that the "Awusa" people had finally used military force to overthrow and take control of the remaining part of government that had not been in their grasp all those years. The bitterness and apprehensions would not have been different.

Therefore, it is difficult to argue that the description of the coup of January 1966 as an Igbo-led conspiracy to control Nigeria was purely ill-motivated propaganda—though it was so described for purely self-serving purposes: as a reaction to galvanize support for understandable vengeance.

---

[33] *[Military History Magazine – July 2016, Page 21* http://dev.historynet.com/letter-military-history-july-2016.htm

[34] *The bold italics are my exemplars for preceding statements.*

[35] *Hilary Njoku, A Tragedy Without Heros and Madiebo, The Biafra War and the Nigerian Revolution*

Consider equally the possibility that the alleged Operation No Mercy, an "Awusa" coup, had led to a violent orgy that caused the murder of a large number of Hausas and other Northerners in Eastern Nigeria and the uncontrolled molestation of "Awusa" people in other parts of Nigeria where Igbos could influence the population. There is no doubt that the Northern Nigerian elite would immediately have found justification to secede from Nigeria as a result. One cannot argue against such an outcome because that was what the Araba riots were about—The Northerners wanted to expel the Igbos from the North because their leaders were murdered in cold blood, and they did not even want to have anything to do with a Nigeria that included Igbos. The Northerners overthrew the Ironsi government following the January coup, and all evidence points to the Northern Nigerian coup leaders moving their families out of Lagos and away from other parts of Nigeria to the North so Northern Nigeria could secede safely. Furthermore, they had gained control of the government by July 1966. Although there were ongoing negotiations in September 1966 to work out a way for Nigeria to remain united and live together, a full two months after the Northern officers had seized the government, the same army officers from the same region that had seized the government joined civilians to orchestrate an uncontrolled and senseless massacre and expulsion of Igbos that showed no signs of abatement for months. The rallying cry was "Araba" ("let us separate"). Consider further that the federal government reneged on its promises of support for the afflicted and that, while discussions were still occurring, the molestation of the Hausa-Fulani population in all parts of the country continued, there is no doubt that secession of the North would have been fully justified. The point here is that no one can blame the Eastern Nigerians and the Igbos for seeking to withdraw from a country in which the protection of their lives and property was subject to violation, even officially. The double standard, callousness, and hypocrisy of the ruling establishments on both sides of the conflict in the events that followed are palpable. But that is the nature of human relationships and the behavior of ruling establishments throughout the history of humankind. Given the eventual outcome, which was a crushing defeat of the Igbos, the war has been blamed on one and only one man—Chukwuemeka Odumegwu Ojukwu— as if he arbitrarily woke up one morning and started a war. During the war, for example, Brig. Adekunle stated that Ojukwu started a war, and he (Adekunle) had a war to finish. That is a flatly false statement. We Nigerians, through our elites and leaders, collectively must take responsibility for starting the war. For many years, Odumegwu Ojukwu was asked to apologize and express remorse for leading the war against Nigeria. Yet the same people that demand apologies, and even many Nigerians, have never expressed remorse or regrets about the wanton and uncontrolled slaughter of innocent civilian Igbos in Northern Nigeria who held out hope that the instability and the harassment of their members would abate and the crisis would end. When these same Igbos fled from the carnage and sought to protect themselves, they were called rebels who were deceived into Ojukwu's rebellion. The truth is that Ojukwu did not start any war and the Igbos and others in the Biafran Army were not deceived into anyone's rebellion. Ojukwu was not a rebel— or at least he was not the only rebel that emerged during the crisis of 1966 to 1970. If anything was wrong, it was that the Igbos were conned into believing that they had the arsenal to fight a war when in fact they did not. If they had known better, they would have either devoted themselves to ensuring that the arsenal was made available or they would have worked for strategic compromises.

To add to the point on double standards, when the coup of January 1966 was finally suppressed and brought under control, it made political common sense, a good conscience, and political equity to permit the surviving NPC parliament to elect another Northerner as an interim prime minister to replace the Northerner who was murdered in the January coup. Once the Northerners made this offer and the Igboman who was interim president rejected it, the ball was set in motion for apprehension and grudge. Following this apparent injustice, in March of 1966, the Unification Decree 34 was passed, which further fueled the interpretation, arguably so, that the Igboman was actually up to some nefarious scheme. The May 1966 riots, the bloody anti-Ironsi coup of July 1966, the sporadic bloody harassment of Igbos that continued and grew into the horrifying pogroms from September 1966 through December 1966—these all should have served as a wake-up call to the Igbos. They should have either acquired arms to begin to prepare for a confrontation or acted with consideration, knowing that as a people they contributed to the events that followed. When the political and military leaders of another part of the country were murdered in a nighttime conspiracy that was led by Igbo army officers and soldiers and an Igboman took over the helm of affairs against an offer to elect another Northerner—what were the Igbos thinking?

The Igbos around Îsuikwuat<u>o</u> have a saying that the arrow shaft shot by a child had to have been fashioned by the adults in the child's life. It is like a minor child that goes on a mischievous rampage to destroy properties belonging to neighbors. Whether or not the parents sent the child is irrelevant. The parents will be held responsible for the damage. Therefore, it would have been difficult to successfully deny that the January coup was inspired by the leadership of the Igbos. I am not suggesting for a moment that the leadership of the Igbos planned the January 1966 coup. The evidence simply does not lend credibly to any such conclusion. Nevertheless, the circumstantial evidence makes such a conclusion plausible. Igbos and their leaders should have considered the events of September through December 1966, as ugly and unjustified as they were, a predictable reaction of a mob or some self-serving demagogues in Northern and Western Nigeria. The Igbo leadership should have accepted Decree 8 of 1967, prepared militarily to ensure enforcement, and negotiated and bargained with their neighbors in the east for the creation of Eastern states. But the leadership of the Igbos had opportunistic personal agendas.

This Don Quixote Did Not Even Have a Sword to Wield

There is a saying among the Igbos, and even among the Yoruba of Nigeria: "A child that has not learned how to wield a sword should be careful asking how his father died, lest he goes in the same manner as his father." This civil war, like I have argued and will argue later, was not about right or wrong. The apprehension and disillusionment of the Igbos were quite understandable. But if the better part of valor is discretion, then we need to refer to the book of Luke 14:31-32 (King James Bible), viz: Or what king, going to make war against another king, sitteth not down first and consulteth whether he be able with ten thousand to meet him that cometh against him with twenty thousand? Or else, while the other is yet a great way off, he sendeth an ambassage and desireth conditions of peace."[36] There was no compelling reason why Nigeria should have declared war on Biafra. If the Igbos were not wanted and if they had to be driven away in such a bloody manner, then the secession was fully justified. Even if there had been no pogrom, the Igbos could have arbitrarily declared secession if they could have sustained it militarily.

When all negotiations failed or were sabotaged, Eastern Nigeria seceded and became the Republic of Biafra in May 1967. War was declared in July 1967. At that point, the Biafran enclave was not militarily prepared for anything that could be called a modern war. The soldiers who were placed on the fronts had inadequate armaments and even poor clothing. Only the inner members of the Biafran leadership around Ojukwu knew what the armamentaria looked like and should have known that these were inadequate for a military confrontation. Real soldiers like Njoku, Anwunah, Effiong, Madiebo, and others knew that Biafra was not militarily prepared and said so. Even Nnamdi Azikiwe, the sagacious ex-president, admonished against secession, making it clear that such a move could not be sustained. The masses were deceived into believing that "no army in black Africa could defeat Biafra militarily," though, either naïvely or deceitfully, the leadership of Biafra knew better. If the masses of the people and their local leaderships had known the truth, either the level of military preparation would have been better, or other strategic and political alternatives would have been pursued.

All The Eggs in One Basket and Whom do You Think You Are?

There is extensive criticism (or critique) of Ojukwu's leadership in this and other books on the war.[37] Although there is substantial indication and documentation to support a good deal of it, one

---

[36] *Apostle Luke, the book of Luke 14:31-32 King James Version (KJV) of the Christian Holy Bible*
[37] *See Madiebo, Akpan, Uwechue, Effiong, Forsyth, among others*

must consider that there could be legitimate reasons for why Ojukwu took the position he did. His colleagues considered Ojukwu a carpetbagger—maybe rightfully so, maybe opportunistically so, or maybe he was just a child of circumstances. Specifically, he became the ultimate beneficiary of a military coup in which he played no operational role. It would appear, under the circumstances, that he seized an opportunity to frustrate the January coup and was rewarded as governor for his part. For this reason, Ojukwu earned the perception of carpetbagger among his colleagues such as Maj. Ifeajuna and even Maj. Victor Banjo, who treated him as such.

After the July 1966 coup, Ojukwu had no business rejecting Lt. Col. Gowon as head of state and insisting that Brig. Ogundipe, a Yoruba man, be head of state based on seniority. I am not convinced that Ojukwu insisted on Ogundipe purely on principle. It might just have been a convenient crutch because Ojukwu's contempt for Gowon has been alleged by people who were close enough to both of them to say so comfortably. Ojukwu should have known better to rightfully express his objection and accept, even if grudgingly, the decision of his military colleagues. Ojukwu was not oblivious to the collegial system by which military organizations are governed. Soldiers get together and choose a leader. That soldier could be a captain among majors and colonels. Once selected, the captain could be promoted to general by collegial agreement or remain a captain but allowed to run the affairs of the warriors. Ojukwu understood that. There was nothing wrong with him raising objections initially. However, once the matter was settled on August 1, 1966, Ojukwu had a collegial obligation to accept, even if grudgingly.

Many people who wrote about this war compared Chukwuemeka Ojukwu to Yakubu Gowon in terms of their backgrounds and their personalities. One theme that often arises is Ojukwu's elitist and privileged foundations. One writer has stated that Ojukwu never took Gowon seriously.

Forsyth wrote that Ojukwu ejaculated that Gowon was "perfectly capable of making a mess of eating a hard-boiled egg." This illustrates how dismissive Ojukwu was of Gowon. It would appear that, to some extent, Ojukwu had the attitude that he would not serve under Gowon because Gowon was not his senior in the army and not as well educated. And if one were to ask me, it was Ojukwu that made a perfect mess of eating a hard-roasted plantain. Oxford and Cambridge may make us elitist, but it does not make us smarter. With all that comparative educational difference, I could easily say that Yakubu Gowon roundly outwitted Ojukwu in political common sense. Nevertheless, Gowon failed miserably because he also played to Ojukwu's gallery and made it appear as if the matter of the Nigerian crisis was an affair between him and Ojukwu personally, just as Ojukwu himself tried to make it. For example, after the meeting of the Supreme Military Council in Benin in March 1967, Gowon wrote a letter to Ojukwu pleading, inter alia, that:

...the constitution can provide all safeguards necessary for state governments. Also, the program envisages the immediate appointment of a revenue allocation commission to find the new formula on basis of the principle of derivation and the need to provide adequate funds for essential government functions. The program will ensure justice and fair play for all the country. Therefore, I earnestly appeal to you to cooperate to arrest further drift into disintegration. On the basis of the foregoing, representatives of all governments can meet without further delay to plan for smooth implementation of the political and administrative program adopted by your colleagues of the Supreme Military Council. Most immediate...[38]

In this missive, it was clear that Gowon was pleading with Ojukwu and referring to revenue sharing and constitutional arrangements for power-sharing. It appears that Gowon was recognizing that Ojukwu and the ruling Eastern Nigerian elite were concerned about the money they would make based on who controlled the anticipated oil boom and the attendant riches that would flow. But at that time, Yakubu Gowon was still withholding the civil servants' salaries that had been agreed

---

[38] *Vincent Oluwatoyin Adepoju, Drums of Reconciliation, Drums of War: Efforts Between 1966 and 1967 to Persuade the South-Eastern Nigerian Leadership Not to Precipitate War, https://www.scribd. com/ document/117715610/Drums-of-Reconciliation-Drums-of-War-Efforts-Against-the-Eruption-of-the-Nigerian-Civil-War-of-1967-1970*

upon at Aburi. It was clear that Gowon was not sensitive to the public opinion of the Igbos and the Eastern Nigerian masses, who would be the ones to persuade Ojukwu to refrain from secession.

The masses did not matter. Yet, the failure to pay these salaries alienated the people so badly that they saw Gowon's actions as callous and insensitive to their plight.

Throughout the crisis, Ojukwu acted like a despot, forsaking critical counsel from other people and possibly taking advantage of the pain and suffering of the people to achieve an apparent ambition. On the other hand, there could have been reasons for him to hold things to his chest as Igbos tend to hunt for rats out of their burning house[39]. It is possible that, under the circumstances, many people were plotting to seize the initiative for their agendas and Ojukwu was aware of this. Therefore, he (Ojukwu) became defensive in his actions. Ultimately, the Igbos stood so strongly behind him that they were willing to allow him to hold the masses of the people to ransom and to give him their destinies. The problem lies in the fact that the Igbos allowed themselves to be held in the grip of a small clique of people and their unspoken agendas, which brings me to refer to a letter from *Military History Magazine.*

Management Style and the Perils of Hierarchy
According to Stephen Harding,

"...Military forces, throughout history, from tribal bands to regional militias, to standing armies, share certain attributes... Most such forces have had some sort of leadership hierarchy, commonly known today as a chain of command... Those with no such hierarchy –have almost universally been self-defeating and understandably succumbed to their better-organized adversaries... .... Effective military organization must have designated leaders at various levels; such forces are not democracies and not everyone gets a vote...overall control of a military force by a single all-powerful person, whose decisions are final and irrevocable - particularly one who believes him or herself to be imbued with godlike powers or infallible judgment – has rarely been a good thing. Czars, dictators, and those who claim to be handpicked earthly representatives of the Almighty With no requirement to heed the advice of inferiors, ... often make decisions that lead to widespread destruction and death, often followed by their untimely demise and the end of their dynasties..."[40]

Such was the situation in Biafra from the beginning to the end. Ojukwu and the inner clique of the Biafran enclave were it—militarily, politically, and even administratively. Ojukwu micromanaged to the extreme: he was minister of finance, minister of defense, minister of foreign affairs, and quartermaster general all rolled into one. With this management system, Ojukwu had had opportunities to make peace yet did not take them. His miscalculation that the world would support him or that he would eventually frustrate Nigeria was as much folly as it was delusional or naïve. In effect, Biafran foreign policy was pedestrian, to say the least. Ojukwu got rid of everyone who stood in his way: Nnamdi Azikiwe (former president of Nigeria who had tremendous personal influence around the world), Michael Okpara (former premier of Eastern Nigeria who had tremendous personal influence with Obafemi Awolowo), and Akanu Ibiam (former governor of Eastern Nigeria and chairman of the World Council of Churches) were virtually under house arrest. Top leaders, even in the military hierarchy, were neutralized. In effect, all the experienced political leaders, including Mathew Mbu in foreign affairs, were either neutralized or served as window dressings or reduced to errand boys. Azikiwe, for example, was tapped on to use his influence to gain recognition for Biafra. This ignominy of wise counsel was lamented pervasively in Biafra and led people to fear and not speak up forcefully enough, all the way to the end of the war. According to Brigadier Njoku,[41] while he was in prison at Achina, the Anglican Bishop of the Niger visited him while he was being escorted to the prison cell and locked him up without a word not even a blessing. This

---

[39] *Madiebo, The Nigerian Revolution and the Biafran War, pp. 377-90.*
[40] *Stephen Harding,* The Perils of Hierarchy, *Letter From Military History – May 2016); https:// www. historynet.com/letter-from-military-history-may-2016.htm*
[41] *Hilary Njoku, Tragedy Without Heroes, Pp. 174 – 175.*

was the same bishop that paid him a courtesy call at his (Njoku) office in Enugu. I guess with the utmost respect and feeling privileged. Now he would not talk to Njoku either because he believed the propaganda against Brig. Njoku or he was afraid that he would be suspected of sympathizing with Njoku. On another occasion Brig. Njoku reports that Monsignor Ezeanya visited him and offered words of comfort and he (Njoku) was allowed to speak to the Arch. Bishop Francis Arinze to clear his (Njoku's) conscience free of all the allegations leveled again him. The Arch. Bishop replied that in Biafra clear conscience is not enough and "… in a country where rulers have no values for the advice of clergy and statesmen, all that is needed is prayer…". And yes, all we did in Biafra was pray because our destiny was now in the hands of a handpicked representative of the Almighty.

All evidence points to the conclusion that Maj. Chukwuma Nzeogwu was set up to be eliminated. Nzeogwu was the most popular soldier among the Igbos and was probably more popular than Ojukwu. He was never given a command. The story of his activities and his eventual death are told by his Aides-de-Camp, Ignatius Chukwuka Onyejekwe, and Charles Abi Enongchong.[42] Several senior army officers, such as Lt. Col. Ivenso, Lt. Col Ogunewe, and Brig. Imo were sidelined and silenced throughout the war probably because they would not support the move to secede from Nigeria and the war that would follow. Brig. Njoku was detained in prison through most of the war. There was this personality cult of Odumegwu Ojukwu, and for that reason, he overruled all decisions— military, diplomatic, and political.

According to Maj. Gen. Alexander Madiebo, Maj. Gen. Philip Effiong, and Lt. Col. Patrick Anwunah, the army was never involved in purchasing weapons or military planning. Even N. U. Akpan (secretary to the Biafran government) reported that Ojukwu, on one occasion, was involved in the offloading of arms that landed at the port. Maj. Gen. Effiong reported that he was able to inspect the soldiers at the front only toward the beginning of the war and saw soldiers wearing slippers, and his list of weapons to be procured well in advance of the war were ignored. According to Lt. Col. Anwunah, only Ojukwu and his civilian advisers knew how and where the weapons were bought. Whatever the circumstances, there had to be a limit to endurance for a single person to act like a god, holding the destiny of a people to ransom until the very end and when all was lost, though there had been opportunities to salvage at least some honor from the disaster.

Look Before You Leap: Desperation and Grabbing at Straws

The strategic outlook of the Biafran enterprise by its leadership was a colossal failure. It appears that there was almost an absence of strategic planning[43]. Militarily, politically, and economically, there was either a lack of strategic foresight or plans were based on untenable assumptions. Procurement of military hardware was haphazard; diplomatic action was pedestrian, especially when experienced diplomats were sidelined. Considering that the major food-producing areas were close to the borders from which the invasion would come, there was little to no provision for protecting the food-producing areas or plan for alternative food sources. To the extent that Biafra was potentially landlocked, diplomatic relations with neighbors were poorly managed and not well thought out.

Military strategy was almost inexistent. As Madiebo would state, no army wins a war by fighting defensive battles. Yet this is what Biafra did—fight almost entirely defensive battles. The strategic assumption was probably to engage in such defensive battles until Nigeria became frustrated and gave up the war. In all of this, let us remember the ultimate strategic objective of the Biafran people and their leadership: to ensure the security of a people who had been rejected and subjected to genocidal extermination. This objective could have been achieved through secession and the creation of an independent sovereign nation and was a fully justifiable option under the circumstances. The

---

[42] *Ignatius Chukwuka Onyejekwe, Nigeria Civil War: The Country Biafra: The Fall of the Iroko Tree (Frederick, Maryland: America Star Books, 2014); and Charles Abi Enongchong, Who Killed Major Nzeogwu? An Investigation into the Greatest Cover-up of the Nigerian-Biafran War (Middletown, Delaware: Century Books, 2019).*

[43] *see Alexander Madiebo, Peter Odu and Elizabeth Bird and Rosina Umelo, among others.*

objective could also have been achieved through modified political and administrative structures as was negotiated at Aburi, albeit modified either treacherously or due to honest differential interpretations.

Within a united Nigeria, the ultimate goal of the resistance was to ensure that the Igbos and other ethnic groups, especially the so-called minorities, played a crucial role based on equality of respect among the constituencies. Given that the secession was failing, there were opportunities for peaceful negotiation and disengagement with honor. But these opportunities were forfeited. When the enterprise showed signs of cracking and failure was almost evident, the Biafran population was made to believe that there were saboteurs. Easy targets like Banjo, Njoku, and Ifeajuna were accused of sabotage and used as scapegoats. The Biafran government began to play crybaby and appealed, partially successfully, to the conscience of the world. These actions did not save the enterprise because war is fought with guns and bullets mixed with valorous determination and attendant discretion. Valorous determination was evident but attendant discretion was absent or inadequate. Once more, this brings me Richard Gabrielle's statement:[44]

"Among the basic distinctions in warfare is the difference between tactics and strategy. The term tactics refer to the operational techniques military units employ to win battles. Strategy, on the other hand, addresses the broader political objectives for which a war is fought and the ends, ways, and means employed to obtain them. For a strategy to succeed, there must be at least a rough connection between tactical objectives and the broader objectives for which the war is waged. Otherwise, battles become ends in themselves, often with grave strategic consequences ... Such was the case with Hannibal Barca, the Carthaginian general widely considered one of history's ablest and most talented field commanders. He invaded Roman Italy in what historians still regard as a classic campaign, won every major engagement he fought, and yet ultimately achieved none of Carthage's strategic objectives... because he never understood his role with the strategic objectives of Carthage."[45]

In the same manner, Ojukwu achieved major diplomatic and political victories but never understood his role in the broader political struggle. This was the basic difference between Ojukwu and the other principal players like Gowon, Hassan Katsina, and Adebayo. These other players worked within a collective leadership and understood their role in a collectively defined strategic objective, whereas Ojukwu usurped the broader strategic objective of the people and replaced it with his agenda.

Even from the standpoint of military operation and planning, the failure of strategic vision in the context of the need for a military operation explains the failure of Ojukwu's invasion of the Midwest Region. This was indeed the case with the entire Biafran struggle, starting from the Northern Crisis and onward. An even larger strategic objective must be considered: political and diplomatic strategies must be considered before a military operation is undertaken. For example, the Midwest should not have been invaded for the simple reason that there was insufficient military hardware and personnel to conquer and garrison the area. More significantly, though, was that it was essential to keep the Nigerian Midwest population neutral, as committed by their governor, and avoid the potential misinterpretation of the objectives and future consequences of such military action. The Yorubas and the Midwesterners had every intention of being neutral as a means of ensuring that their territory did not become a theater of war because they knew they could not estimate the consequences. Besides, there was fairly strong, though divided, sympathy for the affliction of the Igbos. Even if the January coup had been perpetrated by Igbo-led soldiers, many in Nigeria did not believe that it justified the mass slaughter of Igbos, as accomplished by the Nigerian soldiers of the Fourth and Fifth Battalions in Kano and other parts of Northern Nigeria, nor could they commit themselves to the invasion of Igbo territory.

In the final analysis, the Midwest invasion was a suicidal blunder on all counts— military, political, and economic. By most indications, then–Lt. Col. Ejoor (later retired as major general)

---

[44] Richard Gabrielle (Richard A. Gabriel?), Military History, May 2016 (May 2016, Page 59
[45] Ibid

and the Midwest Nigerian population were not enthusiastic about helping Nigeria win the war against Biafra, a position which Samuel Umweni obliquely hinted at[46]. Their posture was either a moral statement or a misinformed belief that Biafra could wage a potentially destructive war if provoked inside Midwest territory. Therefore, anyone planning military strategy would not have invaded the Midwest. And even if the arsenal had been there, one would have needed the political cooperation of the Midwest population to join forces and raise an army to attack Nigeria. However, the Midwesterners were indifferent as to whether they were part of Nigeria or an independent country. Even if they thought about becoming independent, they had sufficient prudence to know that they could not break away and succeed. Therefore, the only way Biafra would have been able to take the Midwest in a strategically efficient move to end the war would have been to raise a major army of at least 45,000 soldiers. Of these 45,000, at least 20,000 would have been deployed to garrison the Midwest while Biafra moved on to capture Lagos. That, again, could only have been feasible if the Yoruba population of the West joined the invasion. Honestly, from ancient warfare to the present, this is the way invading armies conquered territories. Alternatively, the invader would stretch its domestic resources thin.[47] Besides all this, trade flourished between the Midwest population and the Biafran side of the war. The blockade and prohibition to trade with Biafrans were all but openly flouted by the Midwest population. The severe food shortages that gripped Biafra would have been less severe if the Midwest had been open.

Distortions and Crooked Arguments

At the end of the war, Gen. Yakubu Gowon, the Nigerian head of state, declared that there was no victor and no vanquished. Certainly, there was no victor because collectively, as Nigerians, we were all losers. We lost our nation and our vision for a great country. Militarily, there was certainly a victor and a vanquished. If Yakubu Gowon referred to the Igbo victims, then there was a vanquished—the Igbos were considered vanquished not only because they lost several hundreds of thousands of lives through deprivation but because they lost their honor, dignity, and property. Many Igbos lost their properties after the war, some in the North and West and certainly in other Eastern states where Igbo properties were declared as abandoned properties even while their owners were there to point to them and lay claim. Army officers who fought on the Biafran side were detained and later dismissed from the army. Yakubu Gowon also declared a focus on reconciliation, rehabilitation, and reconstruction.

All of these declarations were a sham; there was no reconciliation, there was no reconstriction and there was no rehabilitation. If there had been reconciliation, the Biafran Army officers would not have been dismissed wholesale without benefits. At the very least, they would have been retired at the ranks they had before the war, with full benefits. One could understandably argue that retiring them was for security purposes. And if there had been rehabilitation, the Biafran currency, at the very least, would have been exchanged at some rate with a limit. Instead, it was confiscated, and whatever resources that the people had to rebuild themselves vanished into thin air. The Biafran money that people held during the war was based on some foundation of production and represented a claim to output that had value. Throughout the war, there was even an exchange rate for the Biafran currency to the Nigerian currency. Finally, there was no sign of reconstruction. Roads, bridges, schools, and medical facilities were not rebuilt. It took many years to rebuild the Onitsha Bridge and the industrial facilities were not immediately reconstructed to enable the people to get back on their feet through employment.

---

[46] *Samuel Umweni, 888 Days in Biafra*
[47] *Napoleon left home with almost two million soldiers to invade Russia and returned with less than 30,000; Hannibal – 220 BC to 208 BC had to recruit Gauls along the way; Americans in Vietnam had to stretch their resources at home.*

Blasphemy – Using the Name of the Lord in Vain

The sad irony of war, not least the Nigeria-Biafra War, is that it is all about greed, ego, and the primordial instinct for absolute security. Both and all sides in war believe that they are right and will be vindicated ultimately by victory. When the Nigerian civil war ended, Yakubu Gowon gleefully declared "today we are vindicated." Vindicated by who and for what? Vindicated because you stood by when soldiers under your command engaged in the wanton and senseless slaughter of the citizenry whom you had a constitutional obligation to protect as much as you claimed to have a constitutional obligation to protect the territorial integrity of the country Nigeria? Vindicated by who? By God, to whom both sides prayed during the war? Yes, both sides prayed to the same God of Abraham, Isaac, and Jacob, from whom both sides claimed heritage. Soldiers prayed before they went into battle. Yes, to the same God that the Nigerian priests and clergy prayed, the God of Adam and Eve. It would be different if each side prayed to ancestral deities who could claim propriety based on some self-righteous criteria. Peter Baxter was able to photograph or obtain the picture of a Nigerian veteran of World War II praying before going into battle.[48] Brig. Alabi demanded that he be applauded for doing a good job and so sought vindication by reference to the Christian Holy Bible in the book of John.[49]

In all these references to the same God of Abraham, Isaac, and Jacob, all I see is blasphemy on both sides, whatever their religious avocation. According to the Holy Bible in Exodus 20:7, it says "Thou shalt not take the name of the LORD thy God in vain; for the LORD will not hold him guiltless that taketh his name in vain." Even other parts of the Bible reinforce this commandment. Specifically, Leviticus 18:21 commands, "And thou shalt not let any of thy seed pass through the fire to Molech, neither shalt thou profane the name of thy God: I am the LORD. Also, "And ye shall not swear by my name falsely, neither shalt thou profane the name of thy God" (Leviticus 19:12).

According to Godwin Alabi,[50] [Brig. Adekunle] went back to Lagos ... and granted an interview to the world press ... [promising] that he would capture and give Owerre, Aba, and Umuahia as Independence Day [October 1, 1968] as a gift to Gowon and the people

... The meeting lasted only 15 minutes... I was almost in tears when I turned to Adekunle and said, these officers and men have brought you glory on earth by completing the work you gave us to do and I pray that God in his mercy would reward you and us accordingly." According to Alabi, he was "thinking about the Holy Book, John 17:4," viz: I have glorified thee on the earth: I have finished the work which thou gavest me to do." It appears that Alabi was thinking about John 17:5—which says, "And now, O Father, glorify thou me with thine own self with the glory which I had with thee before the world was"—to mean he was glorified by his commander. But Alabi's commander was Adekunle, not the God of Abraham or Moses.

What a blasphemy to use the word of God in vain and to glorify another murderer with God's word. Whom were they glorifying here? God or Adekunle? The Brigadier should have stopped at saying that Brig. Adekunle should have thanked him for completing the assignments. With all due respect, the Brig. Alabi should not refer to the Gospel of Jesus Christ, because the Lord Jesus Christ said that he who lives by the sword shall die by the sword[51]; He would not glorify the mutual murders

---

[48] *Peter Baxter, Biafra: The Nigerian Civil War, 1967 – 1970, Helion and Co, Publishers Africa @War Series, Vol 16, P. 29*

[49] *Godwin Alabi, The Tragedy of Victory*

[50] *Godwin Alabi, the Tragedy of Victory, Loc. 3568 – 3580*

[51] *King James, Christian Bible, Mathew Chapter 26, Verse 52*

committed by the Biafran rebels and the Nigerian vandals that took place during the war. Why would God and Jesus Christ send the Nigerian Army to murder more Igbos as a reward or continuation of the unjustified mass murders that took place from September 1966 to December 1966?

Crooked Arguments and Cover-Ups

Another sad irony of human experience is comparative pain analysis and selective memory. In analyzing the war and its antecedents, even Biafrans are guilty of discounting and ignoring the arguments from the other side of the conflict. For example, Bridget Edokwe[52] has argued that what took place during the Nigerian crisis, starting from the Northern pogroms onward, was a civil war and not genocide. Edokwe takes the limited and blindsided view that the civil war was caused by Ojukwu's apparent, in Edokwe's view, unilateral, unprovoked, and illegal declaration of the independence of Eastern Nigeria. However, Edokwe completely ignores that it was equally illegal and improper for Nigerian soldiers in uniform to participate with civilian rioters in the wanton and unprovoked slaughter of civilians—including babies—in Northern Nigeria followed by pervasive molestation of Igbos and other Eastern Nigerians across the Federation of Nigeria.

In his book, Brig. Alabi argues that the Nigerian Army was not committing genocide against the Biafrans. I do not know what he would make of events such as the cowardly and criminal massacre of innocent people in Asaba (October 1967) by the Second Division of the Nigerian Army. Similar massacres took place at Item and Onitsha.

The Past, the Present, and the Future

At the beginning of its effort at nation-building, Nigeria failed because of a disarticulated political structure borne out of mutual distrust, a clash of culture, and greedy leadership. Attempts to make peace were not sincere as leaders on both sides had hidden agendas. The greatest difference between the two was that the Nigerian leaders were more cohesive and worked out their spheres of interest and share of the booty. On the contrary, in the Biafran leadership, there was failure or absence of internal and external alliances; Biafran leaders formed a clique with shortsighted strategic thinking and inadequate planning. In the final analysis, the Igbos lost because they lacked collective leadership and were ill-prepared. For example, Biafrans have lamented to this day that, if not for the support of Russia and Britain (strange bedfellows), Nigeria would have been no match for Biafra. What a silly argument! All the historians in Biafra and even elders should have taught the Igbos that war brings together strange bedfellows because war is also an opportunity for people to enrich themselves and make strategic alliances for their future benefits. Sympathy does not win wars. Furthermore, Biafrans should have known that Biafra was not a match for the British and the Russians and so should not have engaged these superpowers in an open attack. This reality is another reason why individuals inside Biafra who could have influenced the British should have been brought in from the beginning. When things began to go bad, the Biafran leadership looked for scapegoats instead of solutions. Saboteurs took the fall for failure, but it was ultimately a big cover-up.

Indeed, Ignatius Ebbe wrote a whole book on sabotage and why the war was lost.[53] In my opinion, the core members of the Biafran leadership were the real saboteurs.

Fifty years after the war, in 2021, nothing much has changed in Nigeria and Igboland. The warning sign for a fatal catastrophe occurred six years after independence, but the victors learned no lessons and have been engaging in wanton looting of the treasury. The widespread violence of kidnapping, banditry and renewed agitation for separation should be a wake-up call for the victors. The Igbos have learned probably a few lessons, at the least one of which is to build houses in the hometowns while they sojourn outside of Igboland. During the pogrom, many Igbos with wealth and money and

---

[52] *Lasse Heerten & A. Dirk Moses, The Nigeria–Biafra war: postcolonial conflict and the question of genocide, 2014, Journal of Genocide research, Pp. 169 – 203.*
[53] Obi N. Ignatius Ebbe, Broken Back Axle: Unspeakable Events in Biafra, X-Libris Corporation, 2010.

houses all over Nigeria had nowhere to sleep when they fled back to their hometowns in a hurry. On the other hand, today, because of corrupt leadership, the Igboman has not created opportunities or established lasting foundations for self-reliance. In the event of another disturbance, the Igbos will starve to death and will likely blame some adversary for using starvation as an instrument of war. Igbos still elect corrupt people into their leadership, each of us, among the voters and ordinary folks hoping to be beneficiaries of the cannibalistic fraud. There are no roads, schools are breaking down, salaries and pensions are not paid, and people are disillusioned. The only exception to this general rule for the Igbos was during the first return to civilian rule in 1979 when Sam Mbakwe, the civilian administrator of Okigwe Province of Biafra, was elected governor of Imo State. He immediately embarked on rebuilding the state and his ward of Igboland. Finally, Igbos must make themselves credible to their neighbors by appreciating alliances. The Igbos must honor their dead and all who stood with them through thick and thin. Brig. Njoku, Okokon Ndem, and Maj. Gen. Phillip Effiong must be honored.

Chapter I

FROM THE END TO THE BEGINNING

January 13, 1970–February 28, 1970 Walk Home, Regroup, and Readjust

As I limped along that road in a lonely trek home, I ruminated in silent soliloquy. I had just dismissed my relatives and no longer had any assured support just in case. I was now on the way to Âfô Umu Ûdâh and then onwards to Amorjî, Nkpa. The road was wide but, as usual, unpaved though motorable. It was a dusty morning during the dry harmattan season on January 13, 1970, to be precise. The forests nearby were quiet and bare, and though the woods of the tropical forest that lined the dusty road were not exactly dry, you could see through the thicket because there was no underlying brush or tropical bush shrub. There were no longer any sounds of gunfire or artillery bombardment. I looked to the crowd of people streaming down toward the Nigerian checkpoint with me, trooping out of that village where I and other Biafran soldiers had congregated for the last time. This village whose name I never found out was at some point between Mbâ Âno and Ônûchâ Ubo'ômâ. Other people were trooping out from other villages where other losing Biafrans had congregated aimlessly and hopelessly for the last time. There was nothing special about the look on their faces—or maybe I expected more. There was simply no sign of the anguish, the fear, and the fact that we had just been running from place to place like animals. Surely, like myself, the people I saw walked in a frenzied silence. How could I see, in people's faces, thoughts about the whereabouts of relatives who may have fled from the mayhem? After all, no one could see in my face my thoughts of my older sister or my dad or my mother and my younger brothers and sisters. Yes, I felt an internal melancholy and my heart was lugubrious, but I am not certain that any of this was evident on my face. If the sorrows of the last 24 months did not show evidently on my face, then why should I expect it to show on the faces of the other people that moved on both sides of this road that I trod? The stolid silence may have reflected the anguish and some inner sorrow and shock over this abrupt ending of a quest that was never realized despite the immense suffering and sacrifice; the bloodshed; loved ones lost or yet unaccounted for and the uncertainty that awaited us all.

At this point, though, what was uppermost in my mind was my mother. I wanted to make sure that she saw me, or someone, as soon as possible. However, the movement of people on both sides of the road was as if they had just come back from a spectator masquerade dance, a soccer match, or the marketplace— people moving about their business. I cannot recollect if anyone said anything to anyone along the way, except as in my case to my relatives. At some point, I said to myself, so this is it? All these people that died, all the destruction, the loud bang of artillery bombs and gunfire. This is it? If anyone should start a war again in my lifetime, that person and his or her family will be the ones to go to the front and the battlefields. And if war must be, I will be the commander-in-chief and stay in the bunker while others go and exchange fire. I just could not imagine that so soon after we went through all of this that people would just head home as though they were returning from an everyday errand or event. Maybe if the war had ended in a tidy way—a negotiated peace, for example—there may have been gatherings of people, even on the wayside, discussing and weighing its merits and demerits. Or maybe even rejoicing that we got something out of it after all. I think, maybe, what I witnessed was sullenness because the war ended abruptly in an unconditional surrender—in chaos and utter helplessness. It was over and we had no idea of our destiny. We had no idea what the future would hold for us. If it meant that we would be massacred, then it would come. If we were going to be spared, I guess, we would begin the task of picking up the pieces. For me, my mind was set on getting home alive to assure my mother.

I continued to limp along on my lonely journey home. A little earlier, the wound under my foot became very painful, so I stopped and asked my two cousins to help me clean and dress it. They did, and the pain eased considerably, so I asked them to move on because I felt that I was delaying them. So, they accepted and moved on. Not long after my cousins moved on, I encountered a man with a small child (a little boy, about five or six years old). I said nothing to him and continued along the road, minding my business. But this man approached me and confronted me angrily, saying that I was one of those Biafran soldiers who treated them badly. I realized then that sending my cousins along may have been an unwise step. "See, you? What you people did to us." I lashed back at him and said to him, "But you do not know me." I kept close to the little boy just in case he decided to do something ill-advised. Eventually, he acknowledged that he knew nothing, nor did he care about who I was. He moved on and left me alone. In hindsight, I think the man may have been one of those opportunistic turncoats. Even under the circumstances, the war had just ended, and we should have all been glad and pulled together this man was interested in generalized recriminations against anyone he thought was a Biafran soldier. I regretted asking my cousins to move on. For all that I knew, they had probably been prepared to keep me company to the end, or at least until we got to Nkpa.

It was about 7 p.m. when I arrived at Nkpa. The community was teeming with people moving in all directions. A lot of people were going north toward Ovim. I stopped very briefly, and I certainly did not stop to eat, as I had no money. Even if I had dry garri, I would not have bothered to ask anyone for water to soak and drink some of it. My mind was focused on getting home. I walked down the slope northward to Ovim, mixing into the crowd that was moving in the same direction. I came down through Obichie, which is now inside Ovim. As I walked through the bush paths and toward the road leading to Akara junction, I found myself in a nightmare, as if the goons of Michael Jackson's "Thriller" caught up with me years in advance of his dance of the dead from a graveyard: a graveyard of the unknown was spread out in front of me. Human remains that were not properly buried. I was horrified by what I saw. For two hundred feet on the edge of the forest and inside the forest and along the wide dirt road these skeletons, some partial and some full-bodied, were scattered all over the place. The luckiest were half-buried—their bones protruding from the soil. The others lay in open fields for all to witness, like the Spartans after the Battle of Thermopylae – Go tell the people, thou who passeth by, that here we lie, obedient to her laws. This time though, where are their kings and peoples to fete them and honor them for their sacrifices? I saw none! These anonymous souls were obedient to the greed of the privileged. They were the anonymous and dispensable sacrificial victims to the gods of war, of greed, and the power struggle. They would never taste what they fought and died for. They would never rejoice in honor for victory or suffer the sorrow and opprobrium of defeat. But there they lay.

All over the field, there were human skulls and bones—limbs, hands, and ribs—all over the place. It was a dense field of skulls and fragments of lifeless human parts, cleaned and bleached from the rain and sun. I could hardly find space for my feet to step on. I simply waded through it, sometimes pushing aside skulls and bones so I could keep moving. This was clear evidence of death and destruction, a reminder of the carnage and mutual slaughter of the people—someone's brother, nephew, cousin, father, uncle, husband, or child dead and not properly buried; given up for missing in action. I was further disheartened and dismayed, and my anguish multiplied. And yet! That was it. It was over like a soccer match or a masquerade dance.

I kept moving down to the road that led from the southern part of Ovim through Ahaba and Akara junction. I veered west toward Umuanya to Ngele Oyîrî and then north again to the village where my aunt, Ugo, was married. I managed to drag myself up the craggy, hilly compound and felt that I was now home and could stop. My aunt and her family were exceedingly happy to see me. It was getting dark, around 8 p.m. Amaeke, my home village and destination, was about one mile from my aunt, so I stopped for rest. My aunt cooked for me—four big lobs of boiled yams and pepper soup. I ate heartily and took a nap for about thirty minutes. When I woke up, it was dark, but I insisted on getting home that night. Uppermost in my mind was to take the speculation from my mother's mind. The war was over, and it made sense for her to see at least one person arrive home. I walked on and arrived in Usaja, but I did not bother to stop and inform my mother's family at Usaja that I was home. I continued my journey until I arrived at the compound of Ndi Egbe. I walked through the door and immediately saw my mother. She and all my brothers and sisters exclaimed with joy; a mixture of joy and apprehension. My mother exclaimed "…you are home, but where is your dad…? Where is your big sister? By this point, my mother was holding me in her arms, excited, but also weeping and asking about my big brother. I assured my mother that my father would be back in time, and I explained

Dad returned with a shotgun like this.

that I had been with my sister in the same army camp but that we scattered in all directions as the war was ending. I was confident, for some strange reason, that they would all be back. My mother was worried that if my brother was not around then the burden of leading the family would be too much for me. I assured her that we would make it. To reassure her, I handed over the foodstuff that I had. Under the circumstances, that food lasted us about a week, supplementing whatever else was available—a ten-pound bag of rice, some beans, one good-sized yam, stockfish, Formula-2, and some cans of corned beef.

For a week, we were all but rudderless. We had this confidence that all would be well. One week later, my father walked in—with confidence, as usual—holding a bag and his briefcase. What was remarkable about my dad's return was that he had a gun—a Glock-like shotgun and a bag of fifty or sixty 0.9-mm bullets. It was amazing, but I was not surprised. My father was a remarkable human being. I knew that when we were at Biafran Organization of Freedom Fighters (BOFF) camp, he was the liaison officer for the regional command of the BOFF and had a standard-issue shotgun in his possession. How he managed to bypass all the checkpoints mounted by the Nigerian soldiers to enter the compound with the gun, however, I cannot fathom.[54]

Mama was happy and wept with joy and sadness. "See my husband—see how lean he has become." I did not see the leanness, but I too was happy that he had finally returned. That was important. My oblivion to the leanness was not deliberate – I just did not see it. It took another four or six weeks for my big sister, Nneoma, to return from the war. Though we waited, for some strange reason, we were confident that she would be back. I was convinced that she departed our last location before the end of the war in the company of Ama Orji, the commandant at the BOFF camp and the commandant would ensure that she was safe. I am probably right because after she returned home, she talked about the frequent confrontations between this man and his girlfriend - a girl from the present-day Rivers State of Nigeria. Therefore, I can conclude that my sister stayed with the commander for a while before returning home. Remarkably, and sadly, we, as a family, never got to sit down to reminisce about what happened—how my sister got to where I retrieved her (a story that I will tell later) or how she journeyed home from the time we all fled Ônûcha Ubôma to wherever she went; how she got there and how she came home. My dad would have had a good story to tell, but it never occurred to me to ask either of them. Where was my dad on the day the

---

[54] *The gun in the picture is only similar to the gun that my father had in his possession when he returned home. I did not record the name of the gun.*

war ended? How did he get back – on foot or did he hitch a ride and from where? How was he able to evade the checkpoints and manage to bring home a gun? Now they are gone.

In any event, Papa returned early enough for us all to talk confidently about the future. By the time Papa returned, announcements about rehabilitation had already been made. The Nigerian government was, in some cases, generous and in other cases cruel and insensitive. Civil servants were instructed to report for work. Being from the East Central State, they all had to return to Enugu. It was announced that school would begin mid-February (this was in 1970).

A few days before or after our father returned, the East Central State government announced that all civil servants must report for work by January 30, 1970. My dad reported to Enugu, along with other civil servants. Based on the story that my high school principal told me and other members of his family, I believe that my dad traveled to Enugu, mostly on foot and, at best hitching a ride from some Good Samaritan.

They had no money, and the Nigerian government made no arrangements to provide free transportation by road or even by the railway line. I recollect, though, that one of my teachers recounted that they traveled by foot and that it took them three days. I failed miserably at documenting the history of what happened because I did not even ask how they slept along the way since it took them three days to walk to Enugu. How did they eat or drink water? The latter is easy, as they might have come across rivers and streams along the way. How they survived it all is probably not hard to find, given that our people were in solidarity and found ways to assist each other in the effort to survive. It is also possible that they found a way to arrange credit for themselves and said nothing. It was not the business of children or wives to ask such questions. Remarkably, when they reported at Enugu, my dad and other civil servants received salary advances up to maybe half a month's pay or more. For my dad, who was a top civil servant, that would have amounted to more than £N75. By the end of the month, they received their full salaries. Shortly after his return, my dad decided to go to the occupying unit of the Nigerian Army quartered at the Mission Hill where the girls' secondary school was located to retrieve his car or at least inquire about it. When our dad fled from Owerre in September 1968, he had returned with his car (a yellow Peugeot 403, Plate EU 413) and parked it partially inside the family compound in the village. Luckily, the Biafran Army did not commandeer it for their service. When the Nigerian Army occupied Ovim in March 1969, six months later, we abandoned the car in the village as we fled into the forested parts of Ovim. Even after the army came and arrested my mother and the family, the car was not towed away and was still there around May 20, 1969, when I escaped to Biafra—about seven weeks after the occupation. Someone in the village informed him that they had seen the commanding officer with the car. But before we get to my father's trip to retrieve the car, there is an interesting story about the car and the Nigerian Army's attempts to move it.

According to the story told by people in the village, notably Nwachukwu, Orji, and Egesi Egbe, the army tried several different approaches, but the car could not be moved. They worked at one angle for a whole day but could not move the car. They returned another day and tried a different approach—and a third or fourth time before they finally managed to move the car. People believed all kinds of things, as my dad was somewhat of a legend. Some even believed that he had mythical powers. This mythical power that my dad was supposed to possess was what made it difficult to move the car. No! Our dad had no such powers. The fact is that having been stuck in one place for about nine months, the engine of the car would not readily start. The car was buried a little bit in the mix of mud and loose sand in the topography of the area around the village. Also, there were huge protruding rocks and depressions and ditches. These could make the towing of any vehicle difficult. In addition, the passage area around the village between our compound and the other family compound is quite narrow which limits maneuverability. So much for legends and beliefs!

My dad had gone earlier to the officer at the Mission Hill. The officer there pointed him to the Annunciation Secondary School a little northwest of the Mission Hill. On the day he went to the Annunciation, he took me and two of my cousins, Nwachukwu Egbe and Orji Egbe, along with him. When we got to the school, we met the commander—a man from Idah, a community little north of Nsukka. The commander was very friendly. The car was still there. As it turned out, only the chassis was there as the commander had changed the engine. The commander spoke Igala or Igbira, both of which my dad could speak a little as he had worked in Idah. After a short conversation, the commander was generous and gave my dad £N50 and returned the car engine to my dad. My dad greeted or thanked him, expressing some pleasantry in the man's language[55]. I did not know the meaning of the words he said, but the commander was elated as we left. My dad gave ten shillings to my cousins as well as the engine of the car. Nwachukwu was a very competent mechanic and knew what to do with the engine. Nwachukwu and Oji used a wheelbarrow to transport the engine back to our village—about four miles away. For about one month or so after the war ended, the Biafra pound was still in use. The exchange rate was about £B44 to £N1. Yet a week before the war ended, I was told that the exchange rate was £B32 to £N1. How was the exchange rate determined? This should be an interesting question for theoretical analysis. The exchange rate for the Biafran currency could have been based on pure speculation for post-war gain. Since the Biafra currency was the legal tender before the Nigerian invasion, the people in the "attack business" had nothing but Biafran currency to trade with. There was nothing that Biafra exported to Nigeria. I would bet that the Biafran currency had less value the farther a location was from the war front. Because the availability of Nigerian currency was limited in Nigerian-occupied Biafran territory, the local people had no other currency to do business with. Accordingly, the value of the Biafran currency would depend on the calculated value of real output in the local area and the proportion of Nigerian currency to Biafran currency.

Back to Nigeria (February–March 1970): Debriefing and Readjustment

When I arrived home the day after the war had ended, I was incredibly happy. It gave me much-needed peace of mind. My mother was happy to see me. I was happy to see her and my other brothers and sisters. The fact that I arrived home only one day after the cessation of hostilities helped me recognize my natural, though sophomoric, complacency, a realization for which I thank God to this day. I was happy for my mother because my arrival relieved her of speculation. At least one of us from the Biafran war front was home. While I was in Biafra, I worried helplessly about how she and the children were coping with the war situation. Even Kanu Edede of Ndi Egede in our village of Umueye, who went on the "Attack Trade," probably informed me only once that my mother and the siblings were fine. In the end, it is only by the grace of God that none of them were harmed beyond being frightened on the day they were gathered for execution. How they ate or took care of their health, I could not tell or control. The best that I did on the day that I was departing for Biafra was to leave for Agu, our two-year-old baby brother, a few bottles of children's vitamins from our mother's evacuated medicine store I also left pain killers and anti-malaria medications. As I was departing for Biafra on that fateful day, I do not recollect ever providing any instructions on how to use any of the medications. I was only confident, rightly, or wrongly, that whatever I left behind would be helpful.

The coincidence of my quick return after the war was that I was less than twenty-five miles from home when the war ended. On the other hand, there were people who, a mere sixty miles from home, took two weeks to complete their journeys. For example, Mr. Uzôkwe's sixteen-year-old brother was cut off at Ôhô'ofia a little over one hundred miles away from his home. It took Uzokwe's brother at least two weeks to get home to Nnewi.[56] It took some people up to two months to get home—my sister arrived between thirty and forty-five days after the war. Our dad arrived home in one week. Sunday from Umudinja in Ovim, whose brother was later to marry my sister took sixty days to get home. The latter joined the war at the beginning of July 1967 and never wrote home to tell anyone where he was or how he was doing.

One afternoon, about the end of January 1970, my dad called me into our living room and told me that he had heard that the Nigerian Army was going to go to people's houses and search for guns.

---

[55] One of the expressions that Papa used was "..munzaama makopchi.."
[56] Alfred Obiora Uzokwe, Surviving in Biafra: The Story of the Nigerian Civil War, Lincoln, Nebraska, Writers Advantage, 2003, Pp. 154 – 58 and 167 – 78.

Late that night, my dad called me in a room at the back of the house and put his gun in a black bag and the bullets in another black bag. He instructed me to go into the bush opposite the Aelia'aegwu compound, at the vegetable garden, among the palm tree groves and cocoa farm, and hide the gun. He intended to retrieve the gun when the apprehension was over. I proceeded as instructed, sneaking out the door from the east. I looked out the dirt road stretching from Abo, across the front of the compound of Aeli'aegwu to ensure that there was no movement. The time was from about 10:00 p.m. – about 1:00 a.m. I walked casually down and walked down the steep slope toward Iyi Nta, the stream of spring water from which we fetched water for our needs. I walked straight toward the stream and made a right along the railway lines and into the bush as if walking back south. All along I had the gun in my hand. I thought, wisely or not, just in case. If I encountered a Nigerian soldier, I would of course run for my life, since I knew the bushes better than such a soldier and the consequences of doing something stupid.

Think about the possibility that a huge snake could tangle itself around me. I probably would not have a chance to fight back. There is also the possibility that such a beast missed me momentarily. In any event, I had a torchlight (Flashlight) which I flashed now and then as I entered the bush. The intensity of the light might have frightened alerted such a huge snake to move. Of course, I would be able to fire back with a gun if I was alerted on time by a potentially dangerous beast. I knew those bushes well enough. Therefore, I knew where to locate a rock that had a cleavage of the earth below it. Once more, that is where a snake could hide. But before I made my approach towards the rock, I flashed my light intensely into the rock to cause any nocturnal animal to move or change location, hopefully.

I found a location that was ten to fifteen paces from the railway line that I could remember easily. Even forty-five years later, I am confident that I would be able to locate the rock if no one has dug around there to remove it. I had brought a farming hoe along, and with it, I began to dig. I dug a pit that I thought was large enough to contain the gun and the bag of bullets. Before I placed the gun in the bag to wrap it up, I fired a shot from the gun. What a foolish thing to do! That shot could have easily called attention to the area, instigating a search, or it could have got my dad worried that something may have happened to me. In any event, I wrapped the gun up twice in the plastic bag and did the same to the bullets. I placed the gun and the bag of the bullets side by side and covered both with a heap of earth. As I was leaving, I counted my paces to be sure that I could locate the place where I hid the gun. With my flashlight, I found my way back safely. Upon my return to the house, I reported to my dad that I had completed the task. I do not recollect that he said a word to me in response. My dad also never asked me to retrieve the gun—maybe because he thought that it would be dangerous, or he did not think it was relevant. He could have also acquired another gun, for the man was remarkable.

It was also announced by the third week of January that schools would reopen around February 15, 1970. By the time that school was to reopen, my dad would have money to support our schooling because they received salary advances before the end of January 1970. During the second week of February, when we were instructed to register for school, my dad gave me £N4 to travel to Owerre to register for school. In 1970, £4 was a lot of money. My dad intended to ensure that I would not encounter any financial difficulties along the way. I set out to Owerre several times between February 7 and April 15, which was when school finally started. Therefore, each time that I traveled, he gave me £N4. The closest public motor transportation available was in Okigwe, seventeen miles away, for at least several months. To get there, I had to put my portmanteau on my head and walk for seventeen miles. During each of the journeys, I had £N4 in my pocket—four ten-shilling notes, for a total of £2, and the remainder in five-shilling notes. As I was leaving for Owerre on my first trip, my father gave me a written note intended for our vice principal, who was from Umudinja, Ovim. This would make it easier for me to find shelter and or protection. I was to stay in his house when I finally registered in school.

Since I had to walk to Okigwe to get public transportation, I found a shortcut through Îsuikwuato. I walked down the path from Ndi Egbe to Abo, near Ama'aba. I veered northwest along the railway lines into the villages in Otamkpa and worked through the villages. I emerged as far as I could toward Okigwe, hugging the wide dirt road and eating fruits along the way—the fruit that our people called uké (oukay) that tastes like ut̲u̲ except that it grows on a shrub-like plant, looks like a vine, and climbs on other trees. The "uké" fruit has a soft and thin pod that can be popped open between the palm or even between an index finger and the next digit. U̲tu̲ has a large yellow thick pod that is more easily cut open with a sharp object and may be usable for other purposes. These fruits were found closer to Umu'nnekwu and I would foray into the nearby forest for this fruit. Finally, I would emerge at the Ugba junction, hugging the valleys where there was a cashew plantation, and then walk to Okigwe. When I arrived in Okigwe, after four and a half hours of walking, the available transportation was minivans. At this early stage after the civil war, Igbos did not have the resources to invest in transportation capital. Most of the vans were owned by Yorubas, and there's one in particular that I recollect boarding on a few of my trips to Owerre. This van driver sang a war song—or at least a song that was cursing Ojukwu during the war. I could not translate his song, but it sounded like:

Olorun Majé, Ojukwu Ifani Nwogbee, Odaahh!

This man sang this song throughout the trip to Owerre. When we arrived in Owerre for the first time in February, we simply registered for school. When we reported for school on February 15, we were informed that the opening of school was moved to March 5, 1970. I had to return to Ovim and travel at least twice more on March 5 and March 15, 1970. By March 5, 1970, my sister had finally returned. (Or it may have been by the end of February. I am no longer certain.) Her school was at Ovim Girls' Secondary School. Therefore, there was no question of traveling to register her for school. I insisted on returning to Owerre because of my elitist attitude toward school and education. I could easily have sought and gained admission to Government College Umuahia or Methodist College Ozuakoli, where my dad was an alumnus. At Umuahia, my brother was extremely popular as an athlete, a cadet, and an activist. When we finally returned to Owerre on March 15, 1970, we were informed that our school was occupied by the Nigerian Army. Therefore, we had to share a campus with Emmanuel College, which meant that we could not live on campus. For me, this was a non-issue. It was more important for me to complete my secondary school education at the same school.

Approximately two weeks after the war ended, my big sister had not returned. It was somewhat disturbing to the family and for me. This was someone that we had lost momentarily for six weeks. I retrieved her from a forest, stayed in the army camp with her for six months, and then she disappears again. It was especially disturbing because I had told my mother and the remainder of the family that I was with her in the camp. We waited helplessly. As narrated earlier, about two to four weeks later, she returned home and the family moved on. The speculation was now on for what may have happened about our big brother.

My sister's return was joyful but uneventful. She fled in the company of Mr. Ama Orji, the regional commandant of the BOFF. When she walked into the house, she had little of significance in her hands. I did not even ask where she was and how she found her way back. We were simply happy to finally see her. My dad did not ask either, so it is possible he concluded that she was under the care of the commandant or that if she died, there was nothing that anyone could do about it. I can only believe that my mother only prayed about it. Like all of us, my big sister settled down and returned to school.

When school finally started, we had a short term that lasted fewer than six weeks. No exams were given. We only had a few of our original teachers and needed to bring in new ones. We had a few new teachers, including one whom we called "Sefuwa" who owned a motorcycle. We thought he was just a businessman taking his salary as a supplement. By the beginning of the second term, we moved from one room in Owerre township into the Vice Principal's house at Shell Camp, a few miles from Emmanuel College. By then it was the end of April 1970. The rainy season had set in, so when I returned to school at the beginning of the second term, it was very rainy. On the stretch between Nkwere and Orie Amara'aka, the rain was quite heavy. At that point, the Igbo people were beginning to procure some vehicles, but they were rickety vehicles. On one occasion, I joined other passengers for a ride originating at Okigwe, but before we arrived in Orie Amara 'Aka, the tires blew. Worse yet, the van barely had a roof, and whatever roof it had flapped back when the rain and high winds blew too hard. We tried to drive slowly with a flat tire, with the hope of changing the tire, so we were all drenched by the time we got to Orie. When we got to Orie the driver changed the tire, but it was not a good tire. The ride toward Owerre was bumpy and we prayed and wished aloud that we would be able to get to Owerre, where the driver hoped to purchase better tires. As we crossed the marketplace, I saw no other than Capt. Nwoko standing by some junction around the marketplace. I pointed frantically at him and screamed "Captain Nwoko!! Captain Nwoko!!! Captain Nwoko!!!" but the van moved out of sight. I got to Owerre and continued school until the next memorable event that I described as a digression— my bout with a severe form of yellow fever.

One of my guides, Fabro, reported that he met Capt. Nwoko at Aba and recognized him. Capt. Nwoko did not recognize Fabro, but Fabro introduced himself and reminded the Captain about the incident, several years earlier. Fabro explained to the Captain that he was the person whom he arrested in 1969 when he (Capt. Nwoko) was commander of the 82nd Battalion of the Biafran Army and flogged us sixty times. The Captain appeared to be remorseful, and Fabro assured the Captain that there were no hard feelings and they shook hands.

After my big sister's return in mid to late February, the speculation about our big brother ended sometime in March or April 1970. The last time we had seen our brother was in March 1968, as he had returned home every two months between July 1967 and March 1968. Sometime before the end of April 1968, his aide-de-camp (ADC) came to the house and said that our brother requested that our mother give him £B10 of the allotment money that our mother received from our brother. After that visit, we did not hear further from our brother or his ADC. Our brother may have already died, and his ADC was just trying to get money from us. Either way, no one in our family heard a whisper about our brother. There was some rumor or gossip that he was at the Ikot Ekpene sector of the war, which was south of Umuahia and more than fifty miles from Ovim. However, while I was at the BOFF in July/August 1969, an army officer who was from Ovim made a statement that led me to a conclusion and early closure regarding my brother. This officer told stories about the activities of the Second Battalion of the S Brigade of the Biafran Army. My brother had been a company commander in the Second Battalion of the S Brigade and may have even become the battalion commander. If this officer mentioned nothing about my brother in this unit, then I surmised he must have been gone. On the other hand, some people had joined the army at the onset of war, who never wrote home and never sent messages, and were "lost to the wind" yet returned after the war.

While we waited and hoped that there would be some miracle or that we would hear some news after the war, my mother did not get into a wild goose chase looking for her son. She did not endure the heartbreaking searches, humiliations, and exploitation that Uzokwe described about his mother in his book, *Surviving Biafra*.[57] I recollect that one day during the war, and probably around that April or May 1968, my mother shuddered, shivering as if some electric shock ran through her muscles. She slapped her chest and said, "Chukwuma'eze Nwa'm," which means "Chukwuma'eze my son." It was like a spiritual reaction, as if the bullet that felled our brother struck at her soul, causing her to feel her son's death.

Finally, one day during the last week of March 1970 or early April, as I was walking into the compound from outside, I heard women wailing. My dad was leaving the compound teary-eyed— the first time I saw my dad with that level of emotion—and he urged me to go into the house and comfort my mother. As I got to the middle of the compound, the wife of one of my uncles told me that my mother had finally received the news of my brother's death. I walked into our house and heard my mother wailing and lamenting that her son must have been felled and rotted in the middle of a forest like a wild animal. It was at that point that another woman from our village commented that the news of my brother's death had been received about a month after the news of the death of Hallerie from Umuanya Ovim, which had been big news. Hallerie D[58] was another popular young man in Ovim – somewhat of a trailblazer. The people who had heard of the death of our brother kept it a secret, in part because of the great empathy that they had for the village and the Ovim community. Indeed, this occurred shortly after the letter that I had written to my brother was returned undeliverable. In

---

[57] Alfred Obiora Uzokwe, Surviving in Biafra: The Story of the Nigerian Civil War, Lincoln, Nebraska, Writers Advantage, 2003, Pp. 154 -78.
[58] Hellerie D is a pseudonym to disguise the real name.

my letter, I asked my brother to communicate with us. The letter's return did not faze me, though it should have given me a hint. On the other hand, he could have been posted elsewhere.

The disclosure of the long-held secret brought some closure regarding the fate of our brother. But I continued to miss our brother and harbor hopes that even if he was dead, I could find a piece of him like a surrogate or hear the story of what happened. Though I missed him greatly, I had to move on. One night while I was at school in Owerre in 1970 or 1971, I dreamed about my brother. In this dream, I saw my brother in a gigantic silhouette and he took long strides toward me. His lanky, tall, and imposing features came silently in my direction, much like Banquo's ghost. He said nothing to me, but shook my hands firmly and moved on, a grand shadow towering over me. All that I can say is that my brother was a towering figure, a gregarious go-getter. He was loved by his friends, and for a long time, he was a reference point for me or any of our other siblings.

Our big brother was the best among us. Besides being gregarious, he was dexterous, vivacious, amiable, and amorous. In many respects, you could have considered him a lady's man. I almost brought a real closure to my brother's end in 1973/74. While I was a student at the Institute of Management and Technology (IMT) Enugu, Nigeria, someone heard my name and asked if I was the brother of John Egbe or Egbe, J. C. I promptly responded in the affirmative. He said, "Yes, you look like John." He told me that he had fought with him in the Enugu sector of the war. There was a day when my brother and a detachment of soldiers laid an ambush against Nigerian forces at the Coal Camp section of Enugu. After the successful ambush, my brother relaxed under a tree with the small radio that he often played, apparently on the Biafran side of the combat zone. However, the routed Nigerian soldiers returned and found him. Before they got to him, he returned fire, but the Nigerian soldiers still overcame him. According to the storyteller, my brother may have had a grenade that he detonated, or the Nigerian soldiers outgunned him and shot him dead. Before he could complete his story, someone called me, for whatever reason. Indeed, the caller was persistent, as initially, I ignored the call. Regrettably, I eventually answered the call and moved away from the storyteller. I now wish to God that I had ignored that caller so that I could learn more details about what happened. I wish I had ignored the call, but it's too late. Another version of the story corroborated the first story in sum and substance. Chuks, as my big brother was fondly called by his friends, and a detachment of Biafran soldiers were assigned to an operation to regain control of a location called the Green House. After the operation, Chuks and his group fell into an ambush set by Nigerian forces. The Nigerian side challenged them and yelled at Chuks and his group of soldiers and demanded that they advance to be recognized. Chuks is said to have yelled back at the Nigerian soldiers and chided them, upon which the Nigerian contingent opened fire. Chuks died in the crossfire, but the others managed to escape. I heard the first story before our mother passed away in 2012, but I did not tell her about it because it would have caused her a lot of grief. Each story brought greater closure to the matter for me. I heard more than the rest of the family, but for me, as a historian at heart, it mattered. The loss of a loved one is a reality that we must all face.

Health Scare After the War

The end of the war gave me some reprieve from my bouts of malaria and yellow fever. However, only six months or so after the war, yellow fever caught up with me. Toward the end of June or early July 1970, I caught a bad case of yellow fever and couldn't help but recollect the death of our camp cook, Ogbo'ogbo, who had caught the fever in mid-December 1969. During the last two or three days of December as we were hurriedly evacuating our camp, the cook died. We gave Ogbo'ogbo a twenty-one-gun salute and buried him at the camp. That was my first experience seeing a dead person. It was frightening. On previous occasions, if I was told that a person had died, I simply kept my distance. About May 1970, our next-door neighbor caught the same strain of yellow fever and suffered for two months. It was said that anyone who caught the fever should stay away from oil and any fried foods. Nevertheless, we were told that this man's wife fed him fried eggs daily. Eventually, the man recovered. However, there were still a lot of people who died shortly after the war from this strain of yellow fever. If the war had lasted a little longer, there would have been mass deaths from the disease in proportions that would have been unspeakable. In any event, as Providence would have it, the war ended due as much to the guns of the Nigerian Army as to the weakening of the physical ability of the Biafran population and concomitantly their spiritual resolve to continue.

For me, it happened one day as I was walking to school at Emmanuel College from Shell Camp Owerre, where we lived with our vice principal. I felt very weak. Unknown to me, this disease had set in and had turned my eyes a bright yellow. On our way back, one of my classmates, whom we teased for the size or shape of his nose ("opara imi ozho," whatever that meant) looked at me and screamed. He said to me, "You better go and take care of yourself. Your eyes are bright yellow. You better go home and get some attention, or you will die soon." I immediately recalled what happened to our camp cook, among other stories of death, and our next-door neighbor who suffered for two months. I managed to get home. By the next morning, I felt very weak. I woke up early and with whatever little money that I had in my pocket, I took a commercial bicycle ride from the Owerre/Orlu road and headed to the motor park. At that point, I could barely walk. However, I garnered as much strength as I could and took a taxi to Enugu where my father lived. When I got to the Enugu motor park, I took a bus, all the while feeling weaker and weaker. When I got home at Abapka Nike Housing Estate and discovered my dad was out of town and nobody else was home. Somehow, I had the key to the house, so I entered and slept to get some rest. I had to have cooked for myself, but it was clear to me that oil should not be part of my diet. I ate food that had no oil.

The following morning, I woke up and headed out to town. When I started toward the Abakpa Nike bus stop area, I could not walk faster than a two-year-old toddler. I took a bus to the railway station at Ogui Road and managed to buy a train ticket to Ovim. By the time I bought my ticket, it was almost too late to catch the train, as I was to discover. In any event, I shuffled through the underground passage toward the platform, where the train was preparing to leave. I heard the last whistle, signaling the preparation for departure, but I was still a good twenty yards to the train. I found some reserve of energy to motivate me to run. I ran and barely made it as the engine belched its initial puff of sound to commence. I was not quite able to get to the passenger coaches, but I did manage to grab onto the door of a goods wagon and climb into it. I was exhausted. I simply rested myself until we got to the next station—a major station where the train was expected to wait up to ten minutes before its next departure. At this station, I managed to climb down and toddle to the next passenger coach and traveled in it for the rest of my journey. I disembarked at Ovim and managed the two or so miles to the village and our compound at Ndi Egbe. Luckily, my mother was home. All my mother knew was that this kind of yellow fever was not cured with "White man's" medication. Only bush medication worked, or so she had heard. I put myself totally in the care of my mother and Almighty God. I knew nothing else. My mother boiled Dogon Yaro and made me drink it, and my older cousin, Papa'm Nwa'ikwu, suggested that there was something better that people used. He explored the bushes and found two herbs that he claimed were better. Indeed, this medicine, which I accepted in good faith, was very effective. Even my fearless uncle, Nweni drank it and swore that it was great. One of the herbs had a sharp bitter taste, but the other herb had the smell of stout to me, tasted a little bland, but it was not bitter. Papa'm Nwa'ikwu said that he almost lost hope and had to wade deep into the river Nne Ochââ to obtain it. For the next three or four weeks, my mother cooked for me. Whatever food she cooked had no oil. My dad, who was usually on the road on business, had no idea that I was ill until he visited Ovim en route to whatever destination and saw me there. Along the way, I craved rice, which our people eat with tomato sauce (or stew). My mother could have made Jollof Rice, but she chose to make tomato "stew" with no oil. This tomato stew had crushed dried fish and some stockfish, and the tomato was stewed down dry and very tasty. I have never tasted stew so good, not since that day in July/August 1970. It took about five weeks for me to make a full recovery. Just before, I was to head back to school, I saw Martin Nwa'ikwu at the Ovim railway stop and he told me that palm wine helped with recovery from this strain of yellow fever. I obliged a bottle of palm wine and drank it slowly. I felt a lot better. I am not certain whether it was this palm wine or just my faith, but I felt a somewhat rapid improvement. In any event, I returned to school after a five-week absence, five days before final exams. I crammed for the final exams and came fourth in the class. I returned to Ovim and Enugu shortly after the final exams to report jubilantly to my dad that I was at the top of the class. My dad was very proud. Throughout my ordeal, my mind often flashed back to the dead cook and the fact that I fell ill very frequently during the last eight weeks of the war. If the war had lasted into July of 1970, I am not sure that I would have made it. Even on the day that I was walking home at the end of the war, on January 13, 1970, I was gravely ill and could barely walk.

The Genesis of Events—Wherefore Could We Not Say Amen!?

When I reflect on how it all began, I can only say that this was a confrontation between viciously selfish elephants for which we all, the grass, suffered. This was an intraclass struggle where we, the ordinary people, were simply hapless and helpless puns in a game in which the powerful figures of society fought to maintain their relative advantages. In the process, we were trampled. I will never cease to lament how the war ended like a soccer match as if nothing happened. Ken Saro Wiwa would say that the war ended in an untidy way, and I don't think he could have said it better. As we trekked home in droves and crowded highways, through the village paths; as people left and emerged from jungles, hitherto unknown to them, they were disoriented to varying degrees, some utterly disoriented; the ruling establishment flew out in airplanes to exile and re-established themselves in lucrative businesses. Those that remained in Nigeria returned to comfortable quarters, some of them still in possession of their automobiles, driving around in search of resettlement. This was not a war of who was right or wrong; it was an intraclass struggle in which the underclass served as cannon fodder, benefiting little from the outcome of the fracas, the imbroglio, the staccato, the pandemonium, the carnage from their wounded breasts, broken bones, and broken hearts.

Most wars do not break out because one side was right or wrong. To even look at this war in that way, one must first ascertain who the war was against. The ruling classes fought against each other. Neither side was right. They were all wrong because the issues at stake for them could have been negotiated. However, each wanted it all and believed unrealistically that they could take and control it all. There was the ruling Northern People's Congress (NPC; the Northern Nigerian establishment), the diffused aristocracy of Yoruba land, the amorphous and disarticulated aristocracy of the Igbos, and the disarticulated aristocracies of the minorities of Eastern Nigeria and the Ijaws of Southwestern Nigeria, depending on where one draws the boundaries.

In the struggle (fracas and conflagration) that ensued, the *talakawas*, the ordinary Igbo and Yoruba men, and, in general, the proletariat suffered. They were, throughout Nigeria, the cannon fodder, and pawns in the game. For me and most people, time froze. As Ogbechie put it rightfully, there was an eclipse on noonday. We stopped school for three years. For me, that was a source of pain in addition to the deprivation, fear, uncertainty, and hardships at various levels. People who fled from Northern Nigeria less than one year earlier, for the most part, had not even had time to readjust and therefore, marked time. For people in Eastern Nigeria, many were disrupted because of the war and so they marked time waiting for the war to be over. Some people were born at the beginning of this war and did not survive it. They never had a life. For their parents, the life of parenthood was suspended until the war was over. For the babies who survived, real-life did not begin until the war was over.

On the one hand, I suffered what I consider to be excruciating pain. On the other hand, my pain caused me to explore the horrors of war and observe that lots of people suffered more than I did at levels or depths that I could not fathom and that I did not even know existed. When I read the accounts rendered, especially that by Diliora, I find a reason to take consolation but also to question the purpose and justification for war. Worse yet are the pictures of the malnourished and those that suffered from the blasts of bombs during air raids. Even worse and extreme are the soldiers who faced the gunfire of the Nigerian Army and suffered hunger and pain in trenches for days and weeks. How about those that endured the horror of the pogrom in 1966? People who were chased out of their homes, their properties looted, and who lost their relatives and breadwinners. Against this background, one must analyze the scheming of the elite ruling class and their machinations to exploit the situation for their personal gains.

While I lament my torture at the hands of the commander of the 82nd Battalion of the Biafran Army, I have read about people who were truly tortured—their eyes gouged out, skin burned with electrical shocks, their bodies whipped and beaten until they swelled and bled for days. I consider my "uncle," who was said to have been beaten and then basted with carbolic fluid until he blistered and roasted to death under the heat of the sun. I have read about the torture chambers and practices of tyrants, even in peaceful countries. While I lament the suspension of my life and school for three years, I have read about people who were born into wars in other lands and who never saw school and grew from the day of their birth until they were old enough to fight in the war, voluntarily or because they had no choice but to join the war. While I refrain from imagining how people endured the level of pain that I have learned about, I feel strongly that neither I nor the masses should endure the pain and agony that results from the intraclass conflicts of the privileged that they incite just so they can maintain their relative comforts and privileges.

Some people, Nigerians among them, have traced the foundations of the war to our colonial heritage—the forced amalgamation of Northern and Southern Nigeria and the attendant cultural conflicts. I disagree with such an analysis. The excuse that the British brought groups together in an artificial entity is at best a lame and poor excuse. In my opinion, the "White man" did us a favor. They created for us a country that has vast rich and varied resources and created a common market that made communication and interaction smoother than it would have been had we been independent as different countries. But we made a mess of it because of ignorance, incompetence, and greed.

I believe that the manifested conflicts were the results of our bad luck in the kinds of individuals who surfaced into the leadership of the country. The top leaders may have been idealistic and probably found a way to limp along. However, several elements in the cauldron of leadership were crude and despicable demagogues. It is equally possible to blame the problem on the founding fathers themselves and the way they sought to resolve conflicts among themselves. There are many practical reasons why Nigeria should be united as one country rather than focused on our differences and mutual deprecations. For example, the United States is home to all the languages of the world; all the races and hues and colors of the human race, yet they can manage a functioning democracy. American democracy has flourished based on its credibility—the belief, among the plurality of its people, that certain behaviors lead to rewards and that the system is fundamentally fair and equitable. The United States is today inhabited by people who arrived in waves from different parts of the world (and their descendants) for different reasons. The pattern of migration into such a vast area of land and confronted by various peoples who claimed prior ownership of the land could easily have given rise to a fractious conflict that could have still been with them today. When America fought its civil war, it was about ideology, and the various cultural groups aligned themselves along the lines of ideology, not of religion or ethnicity or anthropo-cultural differences. However, America was blessed with political and intellectual leaders who rose above those parochial differences and interpreted events much more objectively than the leaders of other countries. Nigeria may well have been blessed with such leaders, but it was not to be. Indeed, Joe Garba (author of *Fractured History*) has chastised us for dwelling so much on our differences and the colonial foundations of our problems. Garba made it clear that our leaders failed to take the high road. Others have blamed Ojukwu, the Igbo people, the Yorubas, and their election crisis, or the Northern ruling establishment for precipitating the war. My attitude is that the Biafran conflict was the result of our collective irresponsibility as a people, especially such as was displayed by our leaders; the selfishness and sophomoric miscalculation of our leaders that caused senseless conflicts for which the rest of us are puns.

Because of my perspective, I have no intention of dwelling on the colonial foundations of our problems or the historical and cultural reasons for why we are incompatible. I believe that we can rise above colonialism. We had time from 1900 to 1960 to overcome the mutual suspicions arising from being introduced as strangers to each other. Therefore, I will focus on the practical, proximate events that precipitated the conflict and some conclusions that have been adduced by various analysts. Specifically, the catalyst for the Northern crisis of 1966 in the context of the civil war and Ojukwu as a factor in the internal conflicts among members of the ruling elite. Within the context of my perspectives, I will narrate and analyze my personal experiences and my involvement. My narrative will be factual, taken from personal recollections and credible research or documentation. I will conclude with an explanation and analysis of my perspective— why do I hold my views of events? Why do I characterize Ojukwu and the other members of the ruling establishment as brutal despots whose mindless greed precipitated the crisis at whose altar millions of us were sacrificed? I could not agree better with Alexander Madiebo and Joseph Garba: the events that led to the civil war were the result of our irresponsibility and our collective inability to govern ourselves once we were handed independence.

Chapter II

A CRUCIBLE FOR WAHALA

The Genesis of a Brothers' War

There is a false impression that the most proximate event that led the country to civil war was the military coup of January 1966. The coup was interpreted as a sectional coup, which led to a counter-coup that was sectional and to widespread riots in Northern Nigeria that were focused on the citizens of one section of the country. There were unsuccessful efforts to find a political solution. These efforts were characterized by a mix of insincerity, insensitivities, obstinacy, hidden agendas, mutual duplicities, and false promises. But, before the coup of January 1966, Nigerian leaders failed woefully because of their greed and their incompetence to forge alliances and conduct simple elections that could have kept the country together.

Nigeria was indeed created for the convenience of a colonial master who brought together peoples from disparate cultures, languages, histories, customs, and perspectives. However, by the time of independence, sixty years after the amalgamation of the Northern and Southern protectorates, Nigerians had begun to get used to each other. We had begun to savor each other's food and even adopted the names of our foods and widely began to speak each other's language and wear each other's clothing. We even began to adopt some clothing across ethnic boundaries as national attires. Intermarriage was beginning to become commonplace. I would guess that a good deal of intermarriage began to happen because we began to sample each other's women and found that if the stuff was good, it did not matter what language it spoke. Before the war, Yakubu Gowon, the Nigerian head of state during the war, had an Igbo girlfriend but had to give up his delicacy because of the conflict and to keep his position without suspicion. Gen. Babangida fulfilled his dream during the war when an Igbo woman from Asaba captured his heart as the Nigerian Army invaded Asaba. Consciously or otherwise, Lt. Col. Bamigboye, the governor of Kwara State in Northern Nigeria was captured by an Igbo woman as a husband. Evidently, he did not regret it. Even, Lt. Col. Olusegun Obasanjo, the hero that led the Nigerian aggressors to defeat the Biafran rebels, grabbed a prize of an Igbo woman as one of his wives. Chances are that he had had a sample as he advanced against the rebels and decided to take one home. When the Nigerians were about to complete their capture of Umuahia in April 1969, they entered one of the villages at Olokoro, Umuahia, and found two Hausa women who had fled from the North in 1966 with their Olokoro husbands (I guess to keep the good Igbo stuff that was just as delicious as Hausa goods). The Nigerians were so impressed that they treated Olokoro people very well, though they were captives.[59] In my hometown of Ovim, there were at least two people who returned with Yoruba women as wives.

Odogwu relates an interesting example[60]. There was a Yoruba man (Western Nigeria) who had resided in Onitsha for about forty years as of 1967. When Ojukwu issued the quit order that all non–Eastern Nigerians should leave the East, this man stayed put. He had been married to three

---

[59] Anne Nnenna Ezeogueri-Oyewole, "The Role of Olokoro Women in The Nigerian Civil War, 1967-1970," *Asian Journal of Social Sciences, Arts and Humanities* 4, no. 2 (2016): 78-87, ISSN 2311-3782.
[60] Bernard Odogwu, No Where to Hide, Page 242.

Igbo women who, between them, had borne him eleven children. In early 1967, vigilantes brought him to Enugu for disobeying the quit order. This Yoruba man spoke Igbo better than most Igbos and had not visited Yoruba land since he arrived in Onitsha with his Yoruba blacksmith father in the 1920s as a boy. According to Odogwu, besides his obvious tribal marks, he was not distinguishable from an Igbo man. This Yoruba man argued, apparently successfully, that he would not return to Yorubaland because he would become a stranger in his region of the country.

When Nigeria gained independence in 1960, its leaders had worked on and pressured the colonial mother country, Britain, for more than twelve years to achieve independence. Several constitutional conferences and caucuses and meetings were held to prepare for the outcome. During this period, true national leaders would have been able to forge alliances across ethnic groups based more on ideology than on ethnic and tribal demagoguery. The main political parties that sought to lead the nation, were made up of people from numerous ethnic groups; and though some were large, the major parties ended up becoming ethnically based. Each of the ethnically-based parties dominated their regions of origin and could not form a majority in parliament that cut across ethnic boundaries at the Federal House of Parliament.

On the eve of independence, there were three main political parties: The National Council of Nigerian Citizens (NCNC), the Northern People's Congress (NPC), and the Action Group (AG)—though it bears noting that the Nigerian National Democratic Party (NNDP) formed after a split with AG. Minor parties that had a significant following include Northern Elements Progressive Union (NEPU), the United Middle Belt Congress (UMBC), and the Dynamic Party (DP). There were minor movements, such as the Kano People's Party, Igbira Tribal Union (ITU), the Niger Delta Congress (NDC), and the Borno Youth Movement (BYM), to name a few.

What is clear is that all these parties were ethnically based. Had any of them hoped to command a national majority to win an election to govern the country of numerous ethnic groups? The answer is simply no! The leaders knew it but did not make any sincere or serious effort to create coalitions or integrations that would present a national character. With the constellation of parties, the major leaders had an opportunity to forge alliances and coalitions that would erase the ethnic connotations of the parties and win elections that could have cut across the country to truly govern. Sometimes, there were halfhearted attempts to form alliances across ethnic boundaries, but they were either crushed [61] or could not get off the ground probably because of greed or hardened parochial thinking, and a lack of political skill. For example, the alliance between the NCNC, an Igbo-or Eastern Nigerian–based party with substantial power in parliament, formed an alliance with the NPC in the Northern Nigerian parliament but never took such an alliance to the extent of forming a national movement that presented a national front all over Nigeria or even to conduct an election in Northern and Eastern Nigerian with a common name. The NPC and the DP, an Eastern Nigerian party led by the Igbo-born Chike Obi, the famous mathematician, could have formed an alliance that would have erased their ethnic outlooks and presented a common front in elections in their respective regions or even across the country.

The NCNC and the AG had, by their names, at least a façade of intention to be national parties. The NPC did not pretend for a moment to seek to represent Nigerians broadly. Even by their very name, the ethnic populations of the East (Igbos and their neighbors) and the West (Yoruba) would not have been motivated to vote for them in a national election or agree to represent them in their regions. On the other hand, the generic names of NCNC and AG could have been presented in a façade of national agenda to seek support in all parts of Nigeria. In this regard, the NCNC had significant support in Northern Nigeria, though it never gained traction. The NCNC also attempted to build coalitions with the UMBC of Joseph Tarka of the Tiv ethnic group and with the NEPU, though without much success. Similarly, the AG attempted a coalition with the NEPU and the BYM. The latter appeared to have gained some traction, however, the NPC suppressed it with ruthless force (see also Ajiroba).[62]

---

[61] *Jiroba Yemi Kotun, A Stab in the Back, The Nigerian Voice, June 2013 https://www.thenigerianvoice. com/news/117069/a-stab-in-the-back.html*
[62] Ibid.

The BYM was founded around 1954 by young radicals of Borno origin in Northeastern Nigeria. One of their early leaders was a man called Ibrahim. Ibrahim Imam had earlier resigned his position as secretary-general of NPC and had joined NEPU. He merged NEPU activities in Borno with that of the youth movement. However, the alliance with NEPU did not last long, so BYM forged a new alliance with the AG. The BYM also had strong ties with the UMBC, which had also allied with the AG. If these three had formed a strong union, they would have made a strong showing in Northern Nigeria and the power of the NPC would have been attenuated. However, Mr. Imam was accused of embezzlement and almost went to jail[63]. Though he was released in 1959, through the efforts of the supporters of the NPC, Ibrahim Imam's house was attacked and burned, causing Imam to flee from Borno land. About 1961, Ibrahim Imam, it was alleged, was offered, and awarded a non-negotiable, mouth-watering, multi-million-pound contract only after Imam had promised to turn against Awolowo,[64] the leader of the AG, who was later jailed in 1962 on charges of treason. This, in a nutshell, describes the ruthless suppression of any political opposition against the NPC in Northern Nigeria.

It was against this background of disarticulated political structures, with barely a pretense of ideological agendas, that Nigeria conducted elections in 1959 in preparation for independence in October 1960. The NPC won a majority of the seats in the Northern Nigerian Legislature. The AG won a majority of the seats in Western Nigeria, and NCNC won a majority of the seats in Eastern Nigeria. At the federal level, the NPC won a majority of the seats, followed by the NCNC and the AG, being the third-largest party. The NPC and NCNC (Dr. Nnamdi Azikwe's party) formed a coalition to create the first government of the newly independent Nigerian government, with Alhaji Abubakar Tafawa Balewa (the deputy leader of the NCP) as the Nigerian prime minister. Awolowo left his position as premier of Western Nigeria to form the opposition in the Federal Parliament. Chief Akintola, his deputy in the AG party became premier of Western Nigeria. Nnamdi Azikiwe left his position as premier of Eastern Nigeria to become the first indigenous governor-general of Nigeria. Dr. Michael Okpara became premier of Eastern Nigeria.

Shortly after independence in October 1960, Chief Akintola, Deputy to Chief Awolowo in the AG Party, fell out, and there was turmoil in the AG. Sometime in 1962, the Western House of Assembly passed a vote of no confidence on Premier Akintola and expelled him from the party. The then-governor of the Western Region, the Ooni of Ife, Sir Adesoji Aderemi, demanded Chief Akintola's resignation as premier and named Alhaji Dauda Adegbenro as his successor. Akintola's expulsion from the party and his replacement as premier precipitated a bloody crisis in Western Nigeria. The Federal Prime Minister Sir Abubakar Tafawa Balewa–led federal government intervened by imposing a state of emergency and appointed an interim premier of the Western Region in June 1962. However, Akintola formed the NNDP—essentially adopting the name of a party that had its origins in 1922—allied with the NPC to form the NNA (Nigerian National Alliance) and returned Akintola to become premier in December 1962. In 1963, Chief Ladoke Akintola, Alhaji Tafawa Balewa, and Alhaji Ahmadu Bello plotted to have Chief Obafemi Awolowo arrested for treason. Awolowo was tried and jailed for ten years.

A good deal of what happened could be explained as part of the strategic machinations of the NPC to dominate the federal government of Nigeria, using the NNDP and working better with the Western Nigerians than with the Eastern Nigerians. Some have opined that Awolowo was meddling too closely with the government of Western Nigeria because of personal interest in the privileges of office. Several theories explain the split within the AG. According to Francis Famoroti[65] October 2012, "Various historical accounts abound on the circumstances that led to the rift between the two political leaders. While some historians claimed that the genesis of the political crisis in Western Nigeria began with the sacking of Chief J.F Odunjo as the Chairman of the Western Region Marketing Board by Akintola over interfamily squabbles. Others attributed the offshoot of the crisis

---

[63] Kotun, *op. cit.*

[64] Ibid

[65] Francis Famoroti, Western Region crisis: How Awolowo, Akintola Parted ways, October 2012, https://kwekudee-tripdownmemorylane.blogspot.com/2013/11/chief-samuel-ladoke-akintola-celebrated.html

to the hardline stance of the AG leaders over differences that could have been amicably resolved within the party." Some have even opined that there was a rivalry between Akintola's wife and Awolowo's wife.[66]

However, there were also strong ideological differences between Awolowo and Akintola. Akintola is said to have preferred a more conservative approach to government and society. Awolowo was more of a social democrat, favoring public support for ordinary citizens, such as free education. One way or another, the NPC through the Sardauna of Sokoto (Ahmadu Bello) could easily have taken advantage of the rift between Awolowo and Akintola to consolidate their grip on power and control that the NPC and the Northern (Hausa-Fulani) power superstructure had sought all along.

The proximate events that precipitated the civil war began with the Western Nigerian elections in 1962. These elections were the crucible within which the cataclysm was hatched. All the principal players—Azikiwe, Awolowo, Ahmadou Bello, and Abubaker—were invested in the outcomes of the elections because whatever happened in those elections had implications for the federal elections that were to be held in 1964. As a ten-year-old child, the turbulence in Western Nigeria came across to us as a confrontation between the NCNC and the NPC. The events were so rancorous and the drumbeats so loud as to raise the consciousness of even the children. As a precocious child, I followed the events closely and analyzed them, along with my elders—and of course, they influenced me. Therefore, as an Igbo, and considering that our leaders were parochial and not ideological, we were influenced to side with the NCNC as an Igbo-based party. During this period, the United Progressive Grand Alliance (UPGA) was formed. The older youth understood the meaning of UPGA. As a young child, I did not understand what it meant but I supported them because the older ones did. Indeed, one of the older youths in our village, who was called Chigbu Ocha (light-skinned Chigbu), adopted the name "UPGA" as his new nickname.

My ten-year-old mind during that time only remembered that there was tremendous trouble in Western Nigeria. Being an educator, my dad made me read newspapers so I could follow the events too. I recollect on one day, at Umudike in Umuahia, my dad ordered me to go to the library of the Rural Education Center—where he taught—and read the news of the day and to report back to him what I read. Along the way, I veered off and went to play soccer (football). When I was done playing football, I began to walk towards the library, only to encounter my dad walking down the slope of the hill from our house. He asked what I was doing on the road. I responded that I was on the way to the library, as he had instructed me. He was livid and reminded me that it was at least two hours earlier that he told me that. My dad had a signature walking stick that he made by himself and proceeded to whack my bottom with his walking stick. I ran off and then did what I was asked to do. I understood little of the analytics, or at least, I did not read the news with a critical mind. Much of what I read, in hindsight, was more like propaganda from each of the parties. In Eastern Nigeria, we read the *Nigerian Outlook* and the *Daily Times*. My recollection of events was that we thought that the conflict in the West was a struggle between Awolowo and Akintola, especially since Akintola had sided with the Sultan of Sokoto. In all honesty, it was whether we would support "Awusa" people or not.

Though the crisis continued, I do not recollect any personal experiences at the village level until 1964 or 1965. Of course, the federal elections were held at the end of 1964 and all hell broke loose again. The political alliances formed during this period included Chike Obi's DP and the NPC. One remarkable feature of political rhetoric in my childhood was the politics of bombast. Our people, especially the Igbos, were impressed with bombastic English words that ended with 'isms' and the like. These were the days of Zikisms, in honor of Dr. Nnamdi Azikiwe, the first President of an independent Nigeria. He also set the tone for these bombastic usages and produced the likes of Ogali A Ogali, a journalist that wrote the popular marketplace or street drama book, "Veronica My Daughter". In Veronica My Daughter, the character of "Bomber Billy" was riding his bicycle "and was descending the declivity … at…such an excessive velocity … and precipitated on the

---

[66] (See also The Awolowo – Akintola Leadership Tussle: A Reinterpretation by *Emmanuel Oladipo Ojo, the Journal of Arts and Humanities, Vol 1 (5) 2016 (https://theartsjournal.org/index.php/site/ article/view/896)*

Macadamized thoroughfare…". Bomber Billy also admonished another character to "… beware of ponderosity, … pomposity, proticity, verbosity, and rapacity and to learn to respect my integrity…[67]"

True to form, one of the newspapers had accused Chike Obi of irresponsibility and hooliganism. Many of us tried to mimic the role models. I can recall playing soccer with my agemates at one of the soccer fields of the Government College Umuahia in 1963/1964 and during a soccer game, an agemate (Gabriel) tackled me hard. In return, I chastised him for irresponsibility and hooliganism. He took great offense at the appellation and protested. I promptly dismissed him for excessive loquacity and then called him a stupendous ignoramus. He then complained to another person that the tackle that he made did not rise to the level of cursing him out with such big words. When I reflect on it, I don't even believe that I knew the exact meaning of the words that I used. But I knew them very well. One might wonder how I came about these big words. First, it was just the vogue, as I explained earlier. Knowing the big words was a sign of great facility with the white man's language and those who had such facility were considered the best qualified to represent us when dealing with our colonial masters. I was in elementary school Standard Six (American 7th Grade) in 1963/64. From the 5th Grade, those of us whose parents could afford it bought and walked around with a book – red in color or similar color – called the "Student's Companion". It had in it as many big English words as one could imagine. We used to, more or less, learn and memorize as many big English words as we could. I certainly owned one.

In preparation for the 1964 federal elections, Chief Akintola (with the NNDP) and the NPC allied as the NNA. As a counterweight, the NCNC joined with the AG, the Northern Progressive Front, the Kano People's Party, the NEPU, the UMBC, and the Zamfara Commoners Party to form the UPGA. Despite their best efforts and partial boycott of the federal elections, the UPGA lost the election at the federal level in 1964 and at the Western regional elections in November 1965. There were allegations of widespread vote-rigging as some alleged that the NNA bragged that it would not matter whether the people voted for the NNA or not—they posited that the NNA would win the election anyway. Several months after the federal elections, an estimated 2,000 people died in violence that erupted in the Western Region.

By January 1965, I was at the government secondary school (Government College) in Owerre. The elections had led to political mayhem. In general, we had heard about the conflicts in Western Nigeria and at the federal level, with accusations and counter- accusations of corruption and election malpractice tossed back and forth. My classmates were mostly precocious twelve- to fourteen-year-old brats—very noisy but mostly bright. We followed the political developments very closely and discussed them practically daily like we had any real clues or solutions. Essentially, we recited what our parents and elders said. One big real difference, though, was that we were more actively involved and knew a lot more details than most people our age. One remarkable thing that we did regularly was read the newspapers that most people our age would not do or had no access to. We also pursued information on subjects that were of interest to us and for each person on our free (Wednesday) nights to come in front of the class and brag about some new knowledge that they had gained. My special area of curiosity was history, wars, and mythology. On Wednesday nights or over the weekend, I would go to the library and explore my interest in these subjects. Every two weeks, I read this pamphlet titled, "Legendary Beasts." In this pamphlet, the legendary beasts of different cultures over time were portrayed. It was here that I learned about the griffin, gnomes, tokoloshe (South African), and a lazy Russian man-like beast that is greenish or dark with grass on its head instead of hair.

I do not recollect any public presentation of my explorations. However, there was one particularly boisterous member of the class, Eugene, who was exuberant about his stories. Eugene specialized in updating us about the latest political news. It is conceivable that the ongoing political crisis motivated Eugene to become so boisterous about broadcasting the news. Because he was so enthusiastic about

---

[67] Ogali A. Ogali, Veronica My Daughter, in Veronica my Daughter and Other Onitsha Market Plays and Stories, Reinhard Sander and Peter K. Ayers, Eds., Washington, DC, Three Continents Press, 1980, Page 148 & Pp. 158 - 60 Veronica My Daughter was originally published in 1958 as popular literature.

sharing his explorations, we nicknamed him the Journalist—a nickname that he carried throughout our school days. He loved it and probably hoped to be a journalist someday. Eugene did eventually study political science and earned a master's degree in the United States[68]. At the end of that year, 1965, my dad was transferred from Umuahia, where he was principal of the teacher's college, to an administrative position as senior inspector of education in Owerre. I was not aware of it until the close of school. Federal elections were held in October 1965 and the results led to more mayhem. It did not appear that there was any hope for a calm settlement. Still, my classmates and I followed the events with keen interest.

It was amid the irresponsibility of our leaders, their mutual intransigence, personal interests, and the attendant violence following the federal elections that a group of army officers struck and overthrew the federal and regional governments in a military coup. The military coup took place on the morning of January 15, 1966. This military coup gave rise to a counter-coup, and the events that followed spiraled out of control and precipitated the civil war.

The Original Coup and Aftermath

During the early morning hours of January 15, 1966, a group of Nigerian Army officers overthrew the elected government of the Federal Republic of Nigeria. The officers were mostly majors in rank. Although the coup was carried out with the collaboration of officers from all regions and ethnic groups, the true ring leaders (Maj. Nzeogwu, Maj. Ifeajuna, Maj. Obienu, Maj. Don Okafor, Capt. Humphrey Chukwuka, Capt. Ben Gbulie, and Maj. Tim Onwuatuegwu) were mostly of Eastern Nigerian origin (Igbos) and four others (Maj. Wale Ademoyega, Lt. Olafemiyan, Second. Lt. Oyewole, and Capt. Adeleke) were Yoruba people from Western Nigeria. Lt. Bob Egbikor was a non-Igbo from Midwestern Nigeria. It has been quoted that several officers from Northern Nigeria also participated in the coup of January 1966, though it is not clear whether such officers may have played minor roles, simply looked the other way while the plan was hatched, or just sat on the sidelines waiting to cooperate with the coup ring leaders. According to Max Siollun, "Among the prominent northern soldiers that helped Nzeogwu to overthrow the Northern Region's government was John Atom Kpera… Atom Kpera later became the military governor of Benue State."[69] Siollun also asserts that "many of the soldiers that accompanied Major Ifeajuna when he abducted the Prime Minister, Tafewa Balewa, were also northerners…"

During the military coup, the plotters murdered several Nigerian political leaders and the leadership of the Nigerian Army. Almost all the eliminated leaders, military or civilian, were from Northern and Western Nigeria, namely, the Prime Minister Abubaker Tafawa Balewa (Northern), Ahmadu Bello (Northern), Samuel Akintola (Western), and Okotie-Ebo (Midwest, non-Igbo). Among the military leaders that were executed were Brig. Abogo Largema (North), Col. Kur Mohamed (North), Lt. Col. James Pam (North), Brig. Zakariya Maimalari (North), Col. Ralph Shodeinde (West, Yoruba), Brig. Samuel Ademulegun (West, Yoruba), and Lt. Col. Arthur Unegbe (East, Igbo). Considering that most of the coup leaders were of Igbo ethnic origin and the preponderance of the fatal casualties of the coup was non-Igbo, the impression that was propagated was that the coup was intended to perpetuate Igbo control of Nigeria. This perspective led to the counter-coup that occurred in July 1966.

On January 15, 1966, the Nigerian government of Azikiwe and Tafawa Balewa was overthrown by military officers in a coup. The officers were led by an Igbo man, Maj. Chukwuma Kaduna Nzeogwu. Maj. Gen. Aguiyi-Ironsi, an Igbo man, also emerged as the new head of state. There was general euphoria around Nigeria, celebrating that the corrupt political rulers had finally been

---

[68] True to his ambitions, our Journalist eventually studied at the Claremont Colleges in California and at the Johns Hopkins University School of Advanced International Studies in Washington DC and obtained a Master's Degree in 1980, before returning to Nigeria. He occupied critical positions in the Federal and state governments.

[69] (Barrel of a Gun and also The Inside Story of Nigeria's First Military Coup, http://www.gamji. com/ article6000/news6574.htm,

militarily overthrown. It did not come as a shock to many people, though it was somewhat of a surprise. The surprise was more from a new lesson learned: until the coup, the politicians appeared as invincible to our people. To our surprise, a group of young boys, with guns, could shoot them out of office. Our experience with modern, European-style government and processes did not prepare us over the last less than one hundred years of the European era to address the erudite politicians who controlled the process. Therefore, it came as a shock that this could happen. For the ordinary person in the village, it was neither here nor there. The leader that emerged was an Igbo man—what else? If there was anyone who could replace the White man from such a lofty position as major general, it probably would be an Igbo man. Though my Oxford Dictionary of Modern English helped me familiarize myself with military ranks, I did not know who was where in the Nigerian Army. I had no idea that there was even a Nigerian Army. Indeed, I recollect when I was about six or seven years old my Aunt Ugo singing from a book about attitudes toward a person being a soldier. The song went something like this:

Alughu'M di Soja! Alughu'M di Soja!
Alughu'M di Soja, mgbe chi boro, ye'etiwe'M Ogboni
Hey, hey, hey ya, mgbe chi boro, ye'etiwe'M Ogboni

In English, the song translated to:

I'll marry no soldier, I'll marry no soldier
I'll marry no soldier, day by day, he beats me (Punches me out)!!

With the perspectives in society and my indoctrination from people around me, I never even bothered to know any soldier and never asked if anyone knew of any soldiers. I grew up around Government College Umuahia, adjacent to the teacher's college where my dad taught and held a position as senior staff and, later, principal. Government College Umuahia had a military cadet training program that we called the Cadet Unit. Many students joined this Cadet Program, including my older brother. I saw the Cadet Unit as no different from a glorified Boys Scouts program. The Boys Scouts program was glamorous but never really interested me. My dad was a Scout Master in his schoolteacher days. He was Col. Adekule's Scout Master at Okene or Idah, based on pictures that were in our house. About these kinds of activities, my elder brother mimicked him a lot. Given my attitude, I never took the scouting thing seriously. I joined the Boys' Scouts program in high school but dropped out—though what we had for the Boys' Scouts program at my school was, in hindsight, a joke. In any event, nothing surprised me when I realized that the sergeant who was the training officer for the Cadets at Government College Umuahia was a Northerner. We referred to him as a Hausa man. His son, Aiki, played soccer with us sometimes during the years 1963 to 1964. After all, it was "Awusa" people that would join the army and would know military things along with the Munchi people (the Tivs) of Nigeria. Given these attitudes, it is equally ironic that the military boys who overthrew the government were mostly Igbos, and the military head of government was Igbo—but I was not surprised. How did they get there and how did it happen? This is the stuff of ill-informed prejudice.

As expected, when we returned to school on January 23, 1966, Eugene was quick to stand up on the desk in front of the class to give a gist like no journalist could have given to us. Eugene updated us on the latest developments, the politics of the coup and the events that led to it, and the events that followed. Of course, we had all read about the coup in the newspapers. There was a general euphoria about the coup; happiness that the corrupt government and their politicians had been overthrown. Our euphoria reflected the euphoria in the general public, among our parents and elders. No one thought about the potential fallout from the coup. Among my classmates, it was remarkable that Michael Okpara, the premier of Eastern Nigeria, and Nnamdi Azikiwe, the president of the country, were spared. For Azikiwe, it was easy to understand. Over the years, especially as young children, we believed that Azikiwe possessed the magical ability to disappear from captivity or potential harm. We all thought that Igbos were astute. After all, Osadebe, the Premier of Midwestern Nigeria was also unharmed.

Our Journalist serenaded us with the action at the residence of the Sultan of Sokoto. Pictures of Nzeogwu, the presumed leader of the coup, were all over the newspapers. His hands were bandaged, indicating that he sustained a wound while carrying out the coup. According to the Journalist, Major Nzeogwu sustained the injury because he needed to smash the glass windows to the Sultan's house to get in. Honestly speaking, many of us saw the Igbo-led coup as what would ultimately lead to the realization of an Igbo-led Nigeria. Of course, we were naïve kids. We saw the outcome of the events as naturally reinforcing our naïve understanding of political and social events. But also, no one mentioned to us that Major Ademoyega, a Yoruba army officer, was part of the coup or that some Northern Nigerian officers participated in the action.

We all hailed the new government and were full of admiration for the new leaders. To me, there was nothing particularly remarkable about the new leaders, except that they wore military uniforms. In March 1966, Lt. Col. Ojukwu, the military governor of Eastern Nigeria, was scheduled to visit Owerre, and the Government Secondary School Owerre was a place that he was expected to visit. This was my first opportunity to see Ojukwu or any military leader in person and as close as I could get. On the day of Ojukwu's visit to the school, we were all required to be at the parade ground to welcome him. An honor guard was mounted for him in one of the soccer fields in front of the main assembly hall, opposite the principal's office. Based on the elitist attitude that I had developed over the years as a child, what I observed of Ojukwu on that day reinforced my impression of what a soldier—or, better yet, an officer—should look and act like. My understanding of military tradition was based on my reading of European history. Even before there was a military disturbance in Nigeria, I used the Oxford Dictionary of Modern English to master the ranks of the military: the Infantry, the Navy, and the Air Force. I learned that Ojukwu's father was a millionaire. Therefore, I was not surprised that he was an army officer of that rank and now the military governor of the Region. Indeed, my ideas were even more reinforced when I learned that Lt. Col. Hassan Katsina, the governor of Northern Nigeria, was the son of the Emir of Katsina. However, I never inquired about Gen. Aguiyi-Ironsi, the commander-in-chief, or about the other governors. I may have presumed that they too must be scions of some powerful parentage or aristocracy, based on my limited history of military leaders in old Europe. Besides his pedigree, Ojukwu had this stern and serious look of discipline on his face. He was not smiling. On the parade ground, there was a soldier who had a glitch on his uniform. Ojukwu pulled on the uniform to fix it. With his stern look and his fastidious attitude toward the soldier's uniform, I was further impressed that this is what a military officer should be like.

The next opportunity that I had to see Ojukwu in person was in May or June 1966, when I visited with my Aunt Ugo in Enugu. The governor was hosted in the main athletic stadium. I made it my business to get into the stadium to get a glimpse of him more like Zacchaeus climber the sycamore tree to see Jesus Christ. The first northern riots over Decree 34 (that we'll discuss later) had occurred. The counter-coup had not yet taken place, and Lt. Col. Hasan Katsina, the governor of Northern Nigeria, was still in enough good grace, for Igba 77, the Igbo folk musician, to fete him. Igba 77 was playing at the stadium and his music went something like:

Ojukwu Chiri Anyi Gawa (Let Ojukwu be our leader), Unu anugwo (Hear ye!! Hear Ye!!) Hassan Chiri Anyi Gawa (Let Hassan be our leader), Unu anugwo (Hear Ye!! Hear Ye!!)

Once more, Col. Ojukwu had this stern and unsmiling look on his face. When Igba 77 pronounced Ojukwu "Chiri Anyi gawa," Ojukwu gave this curt applause that comes only from the elite. To say that I was impressed by Ojukwu's curt and stern look is an understatement—after all, I expected as much from a highly regimented and elitist institution like the army or police.

Because I was living in the boarding house at school, I did not have an opportunity to discuss the contemporary events of the coup or politics with my father. For one, like other Igbos of his time, he welcomed the coup, though not probably as a means of perpetrating Igbo domination, for my dad was a cosmopolitan Nigerian. He spoke several languages and had friends across Nigeria. I recollect visiting his office in Owerre during that year when he was the senior inspector of education. We had a conversation about my future, even though I was only fourteen years old. My father told me he could already see my future, opining that he saw me majoring in history and earning a bachelor of arts degree and then going on to complete a PhD in international relations and diplomacy. I said nothing to my dad, as we were conditioned not to challenge our elders, not least our fathers. My dad was not aware that I had utmost scorn and contempt for political diplomacy as an aspect of human behavior. As a child, I had a sharp sense of truth and fairness. My experiences, based on observations of village politics and historical knowledge, made me disdain political diplomacy. I saw political diplomacy as lacking consistency and integrity. The truth was commodified and was purchased or sold, buried, dismissed, or ignored based on the convenience and interests of the arbiters of human affairs. My attitude was later to be reinforced by the diplomatic outcome of the civil war that followed the coup.

While one might argue that the coup of January 1966 was not an Igbo-led coup designed to subject Nigerians to Igbo domination, events that both preceded and followed the coup could arguably lead to such a conclusion and its consequences. Other perspectives on the January coup include one that claims that the coup of January 1966 was a preemptive coup to forestall a planned jihad by the ruling Northern establishment and, therefore, was justified. Another claim was that the coup was engineered by Western Nigerian Yoruba army officers to release Chief Obafemi Awolowo from prison and install him as president of Nigeria. Though of purely speculative academic interest at this time, these alternative postfactum conspiracy theories may be arguable considering the events surrounding the coup and the turbulence that characterized Nigerian politics ex-ante. Furthermore, they provide grounds for me to hold on to my thesis that our leaders lacked the discipline to sustain a functioning democracy and for that reason plunged us all into a catastrophic crisis. Even the military takeover did not solve any of the problems that they claimed they set out to solve.

In my opinion, the military had no business plunging into the political fray, as the events that followed their entry into politics would show. Even they, the military men, lacked the discipline to bring matters under control and were indeed clearly tied to and aligned with the elite ruling class in such a manner that they too were part of the problem[70]. Their takeover of the government under the pretext of correcting its corruption, tribalism, or incompetence can only be described as opportunism, as I will argue later. The military intervention served no useful purpose. If the military had not intervened, even the Western Nigerian crisis would have resolved itself over time. Awolowo would have been out of prison within six years of the coup in 1972 or two years after the civil war that followed the coup. Awolowo might have even been released before he completed his sentence as part of a political bargain, after which he would have reasserted his political influence among his people. There would have been no violent crisis in the East, and though in the North there were strong undercurrents of potential violence, such as the Tiv crisis of 1964 that led to military intervention, those too might have been resolved through political negotiations by the creation of a Middle Belt state that would have granted substantial autonomy to the aggrieved Northerners. These events may have taken place by 1972 without the cataclysm of war and acrimony, mutual suspicions, and the wanton destruction of property and lives.

Igbo Military Coup – Seriously?

The general knowledge of events following the coup was that there was widespread support for the coup. There was euphoria and jubilation that the corruptly established government had been overthrown. For all intents and purposes, Western Nigerians were happy that the unpopular government of Samuel Akintola had been overthrown. Subliminally, there might have been hope that Chief Awolowo (or Awo as he is popularly known) would have been released from prison to become the leader of the Yorubas. Besides the hypocritical complaints about corruption, tribalism, and nepotism, a sore point for Nigerians was the bloody violence and turbulence in Western Nigeria and Northern Nigeria in addition to the allegations of rigged elections. For example, in Northern Nigeria, the NPC had used the Army in 1964 to forcefully suppress the demand of the Middle Belt people of Nigeria for a Middle Belt Region. Northeastern Nigerians were equally not happy about

---

[70] See Madiebo, The Nigerian Revolution and the Biafran War

the dominance of the NPC in the Borno area of Nigeria. Shortly after the military government was established, pledges of support, allegiance, and loyalty poured in from all corners of the country. Nevertheless, there were reservations in the subliminal recesses of certain segments of the country.

Another evident issue was that the objective of the January 1966 coup was to remove the heads of government, but the premier of Eastern Nigeria, Dr. Michael Okpara (Igbo), and the Premier of the Midwest Region, Chief Dennis Osadebe (Igbo), were spared. The explanation was that the soldiers who had been set to execute the coup in Eastern Nigeria mismanaged their task and made it possible for the premier to escape. In the Midwest, there were no military installations. Therefore, any pre-coup movements of troops to prepare for a coup would have been suspicious or so obvious to the point of appearing arrogant. One may buy this argument, but for those Northern Nigerians who were aggrieved and who found offense in the enterprise, these details were irrelevant. Even more than that, there was an unexplained gap in the deployment of personnel to execute the coup in Eastern Nigeria, where the First Battalion of the Nigerian Army was located. Finally and critically, if the objective of the coup planners was the overthrow of the civilian government, why did they eliminate the military leadership of the Army and, once more, in a lopsided manner.

In any event, the January coup was not successful. It was effectively suppressed, and the leaders were arrested and detained. That the coup was squashed was meaningless to the aggrieved Northerners and Western Nigerians, whose civilian and military leaders were killed. Even more, the leader that emerged from it all was another Igbo man, Maj. Gen. J. T. U. Aguiyi-Ironsi as the supreme commander and head of state. Furthermore, in the months that followed, the new Igbo head of state failed to bring the coup planners to trial. Worse yet, the behavior of the Igbos and the policies of the new government could have easily been interpreted to reinforce the conclusion that the January coup was an Igbo scheme to dominate Nigeria.

Before we discuss the events that set into motion the tragic civil war and the counter-coup that preceded these events, it would be appropriate to discuss some of the counter-arguments against the perception of an Igbo-inspired coup to dominate Nigeria. Some of the arguments are weak and lame and others are apologetic. The aggrieved might consider some of them an insult to their intelligence. The same would go for the apologetic and intellectually crippled arguments that accompanied the coup of July 1966 and the subsequent Northern Nigerian pogrom against the Igbos. Although the counter-arguments against an Igbo-inspired coup of January 1966 can be weak and uninspiring, their weakness does not necessarily lead to a definitive conclusion that the January coup was an Igbo effort to dominate Nigeria. There is simply no proof of any organized Igbo leadership conspiracy to impose a government on Nigeria through military force. Even without the civil war and its conclusion to prove the contrary, the Igbos did not have the military force to achieve such a goal. And if the Igbos had ever conceived of such an idea, it would only go to demonstrate their naïvety and self-delusion. Although there may have been no organized Igbo leadership conspiracy to overthrow the government by military force and impose Igbo rule on Nigeria, some of the coup operators may have had such an agenda, which can explain why the coup went the way it did. One thing is for sure, as will be argued later: all the major political leaders (Ironsi, Ojukwu, Azikiwe, Awolowo's followers, Ahmadu Bello, Tafawa Balewa, and probably Michael Okpara) across the country were complicit in precipitating an imbroglio, the consequences of which they could not have predicted. The coup turned against the Igbos because they were not cohesive, and the superstructure of Igbo social organization was complacent or disoriented. For all the available evidence, the leaders on all sides of the political landscape knew that the coup was coming. They were all scheming to muscle the system to their respective advantages, but they were all caught off guard.

Other Ethnic Groups Joined the Coup Foiled by Igbos – Really?

The major ringleaders of the January coup were mostly Igbos, with one Yoruba man (Western Nigerian). While one might argue that the officers implicated in the coup were from all parts of the country and represented all major ethnic groups, there was a preponderance of Igbos, for whatever reason. Omoigui (based on a police report) cites a long list of non-Igbos who participated in the coup. This list includes officers of other ethnic groups and lower ranks, such as private soldiers. Involved sergeants, corporals, and lance corporals were mostly Igbo but included other ethnic groups. It would also appear that the members of other ethnic groups played minor roles or simply went along.

Madiebo's account of the composition of the troops that accompanied him to the premier's lodge casts a cloud on Omoigui[71]. According to Madiebo, "...It was very striking that Nzeogwu conducted the coup almost entirely with soldiers of Northern origin..." Madiebo also observed that "top civil servants of Northern Nigeria were called for a briefing at Nzeogwu's headquarters, and their faces portrayed nothing but joy and excitement. The only exception was Alhaji Ali Akilu, the Secretary to the Northern Nigerian Government..." Furthermore, Madiebo states that after the coup at the premier's lodge that killed Ahmadu Bello, he saw Lt. Bob Egbikor (Midwestern non-Igbo) and Lt. Olafemiyan (Western Yoruba) who stated that "they were participating in an authorized exercise only to suddenly realize that it was a coup, and they were forced to take part against their will." Madiebo "could not possibly believe them because of the amount of equipment ammunition that they (Egbikor and Olafemiyan) took away without my permission... I... advised them to return the guns to barracks as they were not necessary for the exercise that they were doing.... They did not carry out the instruction...[72]"

Yes, these two officers were non-Igbo. But they may have been complicit and would have been Igbo-oriented collaborators had the coup succeeded. The fact that they were non-Igbo does not necessarily mean that the affair was not an Igbo-inspired conspiracy. Generally, in conquest or colonization, there are always collaborators from among the conquered. These two non-Igbo officers may also have been coerced into cooperation while the coup was going on. From the available evidence and documentation, Maj. Nzeogwu conducted a practice run and night exercise the night before or a few days earlier around the residence of the Northern premier. During the actual exercise on the night, the premier was murdered, Major Nzeogwu informed the soldiers with him, including the Northerners and Westerners, that this time they were going to kill someone. Therefore, one could not conclude that these non-Igbos voluntarily participated in the coup. On the other hand, as Nzeogwu was to state later when these Northern and Western Nigerians realized that they were there about to kill their spiritual leader, they should have turned around and killed Nzeogwu himself. Furthermore, as Nzeogwu would testify, they were armed, but Nzeogwu was not armed. That would have ended the whole affair. As for the non-Igbo officers Egbikor and Olafemiyan, why would they take away so much equipment and ammunition without informing their commander, Lt. Col Alexander Madiebo? It leaves them open to suspicion that they knew what they were doing.

In the final analysis, there was a lot of dissatisfaction with the government at the federal and regional levels. Meanwhile, the Yoruba collaborator could have been anti-Akintola and the Midwestern (Egbikor) could have been an UPGA collaborator. Therefore, there is no reason to dismiss their willingness to seize an opportunity to remove the government by force if they calculated that such a scheme would succeed. Brig. Njoku[73] who was a lieutenant colonel at the time of the January coup and actively involved in the reorganization efforts with Maj. Gen. Ironsi, states that Akintola was shot by a Tiv (non-Igbo and Northern Nigerian) soldier. It's difficult to discount the veracity of this statement, considering that the NPC/NNDA government had used the military to violently suppress the Tiv riots.

Following the coup, Njoku (Page 21) reports that

"...jubilation gradually turned into dejection ... Lagos was in a joyous mood ... Abeokuta and Ibadan were no less affected ... Jubilation was mixed with reprisals, vendetta ... Opponents of Chief Akintola ... took time off to set houses of their political opponents ablaze ... Many leaders fled the town [and] hidden iniquities perpetrated by the Government ... began to surface ..."

There were undercurrents of grievances among members of all ethnic groups that would have motivated many non-Igbos to participate in the coup. Therefore, the fact that most of the officers who led the coup were Igbo could have been because it would have been risky to co-opt more non-Igbos

---

[71] Madiebo, The Nigerian Revolution and the Biafran War, Pp. 17 – 25.
[72] Ibid, Page 18
[73] Njoku, Op. Cit, (Page 21)

in a violent conspiracy. The chances of a leak would have been much higher, with unpredictable consequences for the plotters.

In the aftermath of the January coup, it was claimed that there was no plan to execute the coup in Eastern Nigeria. Therefore, the premier of Eastern Nigeria was spared. In addition, Igbo and Eastern Nigerian Army officers were spared. This account, aside from its value for propaganda and provocation, is probably untrue though it could be a smoking gun. In the first place, besides Maj. Gen. Aguiyi Ironsi, all other officers of Eastern Nigerian origin, and Igbos were at the rank of lieutenant colonel and below. Of the three colonels (Adebayo, Shodeinde, and Kur Mohamed), one was Northern (Moslem) and two were Western Nigerian (Yoruba). There were four brigadiers (Ogundikpe, Largema, Ademelegu, and Maimalari). Two were Northern (Moslem) and two Western Nigerian (Yoruba).

From all accounts, all but one of the brigadiers were eliminated (Ogundikpe was not in town). Of the colonels, two were killed as Adebayo was in London. According to extant accounts "...the General was marked down for elimination by Ifeajuna and .. one man that could have exonerated Aguiyi-Ironsi was the Inspector-General of Police, the late Alhaji Kam Salem who [Enahoro] says telephoned the military commander to inform him that the police were reporting usual troop movements in Lagos..." Furthermore, Max Siollun[74] stated, "...Nzeogwu's reasoning is chilling in its simplicity ...We wanted to get rid of rotten and corrupt ministers, political parties, trades unions, and the whole clumsy apparatus of the federal system. We wanted to gun down all the bigwigs on our way. This was the only way. We could not afford to let them live if this was to work. We got some but not all. Gen. Ironsi was to have been shot, but we were not ruthless enough. As a result, he and the other compromisers were able to supplant us..." Other detailed accounts, for example, Forsyth, indicate that Ironsi was to have been eliminated along with the other top officers of the army. According to[75] Forsyth "Ironsi's phone rang ... It was Lt. Col. Pam (who died shortly after) ... Ironsi dropped the phone ... jumped into his car ... He was stopped at the roadblock by Ifeajuna's soldiers who pointed their gun at him. Ironsi climbed out ... and roared 'GET OUT OF MY WAY[76]'"

Brig. Njoku would corroborate a similar story of Ironsi being a target to be eliminated along with other senior officers. According to Njoku[77] "After the party at ... Ikoyi, the group met at Major Ifeajuna's house ... [and] Obienu was given the task of returning to Abeokuta for three ferret cars ... one ... to be used for the arrest of General Ironsi

... [who] encountered Captain Orji ... whom he ordered to take these children back to the barracks ... I never told you that I wanted to be President." According to Njoku (Page 29), the coup plotters planned to use Ironsi to give legitimacy to their actions and dispose of him. These two accounts are not the only ones that allude to the possibility that Ironsi was also a target. Ironsi may have gotten away because the roadblock where the coup plotters confronted Ironsi was manned by Captain Orji, who was from Ironsi's hometown. According to Henry Onyema who quotes Obasanjo, "...Oji had a change of heart after exchanging words with the General in their local dialect..."[78]

Why did the coup fail or not take place in the East? During the crisis leading up to the war, there was an apocryphal gossip, or popular story, that said that Maj. David Ejoor was supposed to carry out the coup in the East and eliminate Premier Dr. Michael Okpara. Maj. Ejoor cleverly avoided his task because he (Ejoor) had a wedding in December 1965 and Dr. Okpara had given him extremely generous wedding gifts. This account seems to be "fake news" because though I have searched high and low, I have found no evidence that Lt. Col. Ejoor ever had a wedding ceremony. In an

---

[74] *Max Siollun, Oil, Politics and Violence: Nigeria's Military Coup Culture (1966 - 1976), New York, USA, Algora Publishing, 2009*

[75] Frederick Forsyth, The Biafra Story: The Making of an African Legend, Page 30,

[76] *Frederick Forsyth, Op. Cit.*

[77] *Hillary Njoku, Tragedy Without Heros, Page 22.*

[78] *Henry Chukwuemeka Onyema, July 29 1966 on my Mind: Did General Aguyi-Ironsi Deserve to Die? Part Two: Ironsi's Role in The January 15 1966 Coup (Nigeria), https://www.author-me.com/nonfiction/julyonmymind2.htm*

interview with Max Sioullun, David Ejoor made references to his wife and children during the Biafran invasion of the Midwest in August 1967. The failure of the coup in the East was due more to fortuitous circumstances, poor planning, or plain treachery by Nzeogwu's co-conspirators. Based on what can be gleaned from all the narratives (Luckham, Forsyth, and Njoku), it is not clear that anyone was assigned to arrest and eliminate the premier of Eastern Nigeria. The assignment in Enugu can only be inferred. For starters, the battalion commander of the Nigerian Army in Enugu was Lt. Col. Fajuyi, who had just been sent on a course and thus was not in Enugu at the time of the coup. Lt. Col. David Ejoor was to take over for him but was in Lagos at the time of the coup. Therefore, Ifeajuna, Okafor, and probably Ademoyega and Anuforo ordered the second in command, Lt. Col. Okonweze, to arrest and eliminate the premier. However, the premier was just concluding a visit from Archbishop Makarios of Cyprus. According to all available narratives, the assigned assassins permitted Okpara (premier) to see Makarios off at the airport. Okpara was arrested after Makarios departed the airport[79].

In the East, Njoku (Page 22) offers another explanation as to why the coup in the East failed. Specifically, the boys that were supposed to carry out the coup in the East and eliminate the premier did not start on time. Upon hearing a broadcast that there were army dissidents who had rebelled against the federal government, these soldiers dumped their weapons in the Ogun River near Shagamu and were later caught and taken to the Second Battalion headquarters of the Nigerian Army. But Njoku's story does not fully explain or provide details of whether there was any action in the East that would have come close to eliminating the political leaders in Eastern Nigeria. What can be inferred from Njoku's narrative is that Maj. Ademoyega (Yoruba) and Anuforo (Igbo) may have been assigned to carry out the coup in Enugu. The question that arises is why were they in Lagos or Western Nigeria when they were supposed to be in Enugu for an assignment? On this point, Forsythe and Robin Luckham have some thoughts.

Based on Luckham's narrative (Page 22), Ifeajuna was responsible for ensuring the arrest of the premier of Eastern Nigeria. It appears that Nzeogwu blamed Ifeajuna for the failure[80]. According to Forsyth[81].

"...Troops of the First Battalion moved against the Premier's house around 2:00 AM on January 15, 1966 ... They surrounded it but awaited orders before attacking the house and its inhabitants ... The troops ... largely of Middle-Belt infantrymen from Northern Region crouched around the house as dawn rose and awaited orders ..."

These orders had to have come from Maj. Okonweze, who was not part of the coup conspiracy. Okonweze received orders from Lagos, apparently from the coup planners in Lagos, and became suspicious and only threw a cordon around the Premier's house. Coming to understand that the coup in Enugu had not been carried out, Ifeajuna and Anuforo decided to speed off to Enugu in their car. Before they got to Enugu, Lt. Col.David Ejoor had arrived Enugu by air under command of Maj. Gen. Ironsi, who had taken over the coup from the operators in Lagos.

These narratives do not make it clear whether the conspirators intended to eliminate the Igbo premier—not that I am suggesting that he should have been eliminated for the sake of peace. The elimination of the Eastern premier would have diminished the suspicion of an Igbo conspiracy, or at least that part of the argument would not have had the benefit of questioning why the Igbo premier was spared. The big question that casts a cloud on the argument of the conspirators would be that they did not reveal who exactly was assigned to Enugu – who was on the ground - at the time (the H-Hour) of the coup. Since David Ejoor was not there and they knew that he was in Lagos and Major Okonweze was not part of their conspiracy, who then did they expect to execute the coup at Enugu? Furthermore, Njoku (Page 19) indicates that after a wedding party for Brig. Maimalari (January 13, 1966), Ifeajuna was supposed to have been posted to Enugu the following day to be part of the

---

[79] *Robin Luckham, The Nigerian Military: A Sociological Analysis of Authority and Revolt 1960 – 67, Cambridge, University Press 1971 Page 22.*
[80] Luckham, Op. Cit, Pp. 22 – 27
[81] Forsyth, The Biafra Story, Page 30

First Battalion. One would then think that he (Ifeajuna) would have executed the coup in Enugu. Why then did he stay back in Ibadan to participate in the action in Lagos and Ibadan? Either he was playing games or he needed to explain why they did not recruit someone in Enugu who would not be in any doubt about what needs to be done and who would not, like Capt. Okonweze, become suspicious and only throw a cordon around the Premier's house awaiting orders. The last unverified allegation is that Maj. Chude Sokei (Midwest Igbo) was assigned to execute the coup in Enugu (Effiong, Page 41), but Sokei was sent to India for a course before the coup was to be executed. He was to be replaced by Lt. Ogechi. Effiong claims that Ogechi had an unexplained problem of resources and space that was complicated by the visit of Archbishop Makarios of Cyprus to Dr. Michael Okpara, the Premier of Eastern Nigeria. Furthermore, events soon caught up with Ogechi and his mission was partially successful. However, Effiong did not explain what these events were and what problems of time, space, and resources bedeviled or constrained Ogechi. Is it possible that Ogechi (Igbo) became a mole or fifth columnist in the scheme? After all, he was not part of the original plan. He may have accepted to be part of the coup to save his skin so as not to be a target of the coup plotters when the action began. Simply put, Ogechi was only a lieutenant in a scheme that majors developed. What could have led the majors to select a lieutenant for their plan when higher-ranking officers may have been available?

Following the elections of 1964 and the violence and allegations that attended them, Nnamdi Azikiwe (Igbo), who was president of Nigeria at the time, suggested that the army should intervene to restore order. According to Adeeko (Vanguard Online Community, February 2015 - http://community.vanguardngr.com/profile/ OtunbaJuliusOlusegunAdeeko), "following the crisis [in 1964], Dr. Nnamdi Azikiwe requested the military general office commanding (GOC; Ironsi, an Igbo) to intervene and reorganize the elections in the Western region to avoid catastrophe, but the military high command refused and Dr. Azikiwe was briefly held in house arrest for making such a request..." However, following the elections in 1965, again with attendant violence and allegations of rigging, "Azikiwe and the prime minister (Balewa) were scarcely on speaking terms, and there were suggestions that Nigeria's armed forces should restore order." Who was making these suggestions? In any event, in late November 1965, Dr. Azikiwe departed the country on medical leave. While he was on leave, the Commonwealth Conference was held in Nigeria in January 1966, which did not motivate Azikiwe to return. It was shortly after the conference that, on January 15, 1966, Maj. Nzeogwu and other army officers struck and overthrew the government.

Azikiwe's disappearance and absence from major events during the days leading up to the coup of January 1966 is at least a smoking gun. What is important in Zik's story is that he was expected to have returned to Nigeria at the end of December. He declined to return, and his physician abandoned him overseas and returned to Nigeria. The smoking gun could indicate that Zik was aware that a coup was about to take place because he was tipped off by Maj. Ifeajuna, his kinsman who was the leader of the coup. One cannot ignore the allegation that Zik had requested military intervention in 1964. It might also be that he was so frustrated about the events that he simply could not care about what was going on in the country and felt powerless as president. As alleged earlier, Zik was barely on speaking terms with Tafawa Balewa; the prime minister whose inconsistency he must have disapproved of called Commonwealth Conference to consider Rhodesia instead of talking about Nigeria.

Azikiwe's apparent foreknowledge of an impending coup does not implicate him in an Igbo plot or even a personal plot to overthrow the government as a means of restoring normalcy. Extant research and reports provide a circumstantial or direct indication that the ruling establishment of Northern Nigeria was also plotting to overthrow the government. The coup that took place on January 15, 1966, was plausibly a preemptive action against another coup. At this point, this is more than of academic interest, but the information supports the thesis that the crisis and the civil war that followed were the culmination of the callously selfish and greedy schemes of the ruling establishment. According to Njoku (Pp. 12-13 and Pp. 19-27), "...Zak (Brig. Zakaria Maimalari, who died in the January 1966 coup), while in a drunken state, talked of a military coup to come and often ran his hand across his neck as a sign of killing ..." Further on Page 13, Njoku asserts,

"...At Ikeja Airport that morning of January 14th [1966, the day before the January 15th coup], was Major Hassan Katsina [Northern Fulani and son of the Emir of Katsina] bore it that he had flown to Lagos to report to the GOC [General Ironsi, the Igbo man that eventually took over the government after the coup] ... about a plot to overthrow the Federal Government by Brigadier Ademulegun... Zak had revealed a lot in his drunken state on January 12th ... and here was Hassan..."

One implication of the allegation is that Maj. Katsina was in Lagos to disclose a coup plot to Maj. Gen. Ironsi and that Katsina was not in favor of the coup. The question that arises, though, is why Ironsi did not immediately move openly to investigate the allegations? It is entirely plausible that Ademulegun and the ruling NPC establishment were plotting a coup. The ruthlessness of the NPC in destroying the AG and holding political and military sway has already been described. Meanwhile, Madiebo (Pp. 10-14) provides an extensive description of Ademulegun's alliance with the NPC and the ruling Northern Nigerian establishment. Ademulegun was so aligned with the NPC establishment that he openly campaigned to be the GOC following the departure of the British. Ademulegun was instrumental in supporting the ruthless rigging of elections in Western Nigeria and in supporting the alliance between Akintola and the ruling NPC. According to Madiebo (Page 14), the commander of the Fourth Battalion of the Nigerian Army arranged for ballot stuffing during the elections and also for the training of Akintola and his ministers on the use of automatic weapons. It also alleged that Chief Akintola, the premier of the Western Region of Nigeria, shot at his assailants with a semi-automatic rifle during the coup of January 1966 and was killed only after he ran out of bullets. Moreover, Ademulegun also supported the ruthless suppression of the Tiv rioters. Besides these, according to Forsyth, the ruling NPC had made certain moves that would have facilitated the military or other forceful control of the government of Nigeria.

"...On January 13, 1966, there... was a secret meeting between Samuel Akintola [Pro NPC and Sardauna of Sokoto] and the Sardauna with Brig. Ademulegun, a pro-Akintola military officer ... Previously [I guess shortly before this alleged secret meeting], the Federal Defense Minister [Alhaji Ribadu] had ordered Maj. Gen. Ironsi [Igbo commander of the Army] to take his accumulated leave ... The Inspector General (IG) of the Police, Louis Edet (Easterner – Efik or Ibibio) was ordered on leave and Deputy IG, a Westerner was sent on premature retirement to be replaced by Alhaji Kam Salem (A Northerner) ... who would have been in control by January 17th, 1966...[82]"

According to Njoku (Page 21), Major Emmanuel Ifeajuna contacted Gen. J. T. U. Aguiyi-Ironsi about the coup. "...Ironsi said that he would not be a party to a coup. He [Ironsi] warned the Prime Minister [Balewa] through the Chief Secretary to the Federal Government. " Why did Tafawa Balewa not take up the matter to immediately arrest the plotters, and why did Ironsi not move immediately to order the plotters to a location where they could be arrested and dislodged (such as surrounding their houses and sounding sufficient alarm to disorient the scheme)? There is innuendo that on the night before the coup, Tafawa Balewa (Prime Minister, a Northerner of Hausa-Fulani establishment) was invited by the British high commissioner to spend the night at the commissioner's residence, but Balewa declined. It is possible and plausible to infer that the British diplomat had intelligence on the coup and thought that Balewa must receive the information. The latter decided that he would not hide, either because he was confident that it would fail or because his NPC scheme would eventually prevail. It's equally plausible that the prime minister had become sufficiently sick of the prevailing political environment that he would support a military takeover, in all likelihood by his allies in the Army.

Gen. Ironsi is implicated in the plot in more than one way. First, Njoku twice quotes Ironsi's utterances "...that they promised that there would be no bloodshed..." immediately after the coup was supposedly foiled. Ironsi's government takeover after the foiled coup is grounds for suspicion, complicity, or opportunism or both, and his subsequent policies could also implicate him even more so with an Igbo plot to control the government—through the implementation of policies were

---

[82] *Forsyth, Op. Cit. Pp. 26 – 27*

muddled with internal inconsistencies. One could argue either that Ironsi thought that the other constituencies were stupid, or one could say that he (Ironsi) was disingenuous.

On the day of the coup in January 1966, an alarm was raised after the Maj. Gen. Ironsi effectively took over the coup. Lt. Col. Njoku (Page 19) was with Ironsi and Yakubu Gowon (who became the head of state after the July coup), and Ironsi said, "…But they said that they would not kill anyone. " During a conversation, the GOC (Ironsi) repeated his earlier statement "but they said there would be no bloodshed." These two statements implicate Ironsi with foreknowledge of the coup. Furthermore, he was forewarned that the action would be violent and that he [Ironsi] asked and received assurance that there would be no bloodshed. This corroborates the earlier reference that Ironsi had declined to be a party to any military coup. Why then did he not act, as it appears that he received ample forewarning—and by ample, I mean several days or weeks in advance? A coup this elaborate could not be planned and executed in fewer than sixty to ninety days, especially considering the turbulence and bloodshed that had been occurring in Western Nigeria. Any forewarning to Ironsi and all those that were planning different coups had to have had at least one to two weeks advance knowledge of the event. Even with two days of forewarning, the machinery of government would have been able to act and arrest the plotters.

The Majors' January coup was effectively foiled through the efforts of Maj. Gen. Ironsi (Igbo) and his officers, including Lt. Col. Njoku (Igbo), Lt. Col. David Ejoor (Midwest, a non-Igbo), Lt. Col. Yakubu Gowon (Northern Nigerian, not Hausa-Fulani), and some non-commissioned officers, sergeants, and lower ranks. By the following day, January 16, 1966, negotiations began with Maj. Nzeogwu and the coup leaders in Northern Nigeria. Lt. Col. Ojukwu, who was commander of the Fifth Battalion in Kano (Northern Nigeria), had declared support and loyalty to the new supreme commander. Maj. Ifeajuna and Maj. Anuforo, who were in Enugu in Eastern Nigeria, had been neutralized, and Ifeajuna, having failed in Enugu, fled to Ghana from where he was later extradited.

Other evidence that has been brought to bear on the nature of the January coup includes the testimony of an Igbo army officer (Second Lt. Godwin Onyefuru) who was a witness to the plans for the coup. It is also claimed that the coup was foiled in large part due to the efforts of senior Igbo army officers, including Maj. Gen. Ironsi, Lt. Col. Njoku, Lt. Col. Ojukwu and Lt. Col. Madiebo. Second Lt. Onyefuru was to testify that the planners had intended to install Obafemi Awolowo as president after the coup (Njoku, Page 180). Onyefuru testified, during a post-coup investigation and interrogation, that he participated in the coup against his will and witnessed the murder of some of the officers. Onyefuru also witnessed a meeting at the house of Maj. Ifeajuna. According to Second Lt. Onyefuru (Njoku, Pp. 180 – 81 Appendix I), "At the briefing in Maj. Ifeajuna's house… Capt. Udeaja was detailed to go to Calabar to release Awolowo; Awolowo would be made president as soon as the OP was over." If it was stated that Awolowo would be installed as president after the coup, who is to say that Awolowo or his supporters did not mastermind the coup but used Igbo army officers who were sympathetic to his cause or the cause of UPGA, Awolowo's party, in alliance with the NCNC? It is equally plausible that Onyefuru was covering or fronting disinformation, post-factum, for his compatriots or was sympathetic to Awolowo and his supporters in the fracas that took place in Western Nigeria. After all, this investigation was conducted on January 18, 1966, three days after the coup.

Besides the post-factum claim that the [Igbo] coup plotters arrogated to themselves the responsibility of correcting the federal and regional elections by handing over government control to Awolowo, it is also claimed that the coup was foiled by Igbo army officers (Ironsi, Ojukwu, Madiebo, Njoku) along with other non-Igbos. The question is, to what purpose? It would appear from subsequent events that they were all opportunistic, including the non-Igbo officers who participated in foiling the coup. Maj. Gen. Ironsi escaped assassination (apparently; see Njoku) and moved immediately to confront the disorder in the wake of the ongoing coup. That he foiled the coup, even with advanced knowledge and reassurances that there would be no bloodshed, does not necessarily mean that he meant to restore order to the legitimate government. Yet that is what the commanding officer of an army should do. However, he may have foiled the coup to save his neck. If the coup planners had succeeded, he may not have survived it or he may have ended up in detention for a long time. Ojukwu also played a pivotal role in foiling the coup. In a televised YouTube interview,

Odumegwu Ojukwu objected to the theory of an Igbo-inspired coup, saying, "...who foiled the coup..." like he could fool anyone with his answer.

On the day of the coup, available literature gives the impression that Lt. Col. Ojukwu was in Kano at the house of the Emir of Kano, Alhaji Ado Bayero. The Fifth Battalion of the Nigerian Army was in Kano in Northern Nigeria. According to Alexander Madiebo (The Nigerian Revolution and the Biafran War, Page 19), he called Lt. Col. Ojukwu in Kano to apprise him of what was happening in Kaduna. Ojukwu's response was only a series of ".. Good... good... good..." Ojukwu must already have been aware of what was going on. Lt. Col. Ojukwu foiled the coup by his actions, but to what purpose? And what was his motive? It would appear from Nzeogwu's statements that Ojukwu was complicit in the coup plan and hedged his bets if the coup failed.

On January 16th, 1966, the day after the coup, Maj. Nzeogwu promised to deal ruthlessly with those who had shown signs of sitting on the fence (Madiebo, Pp. 22 – 25). Nzeogwu announced that Ojukwu and Katsina were enemies of the revolution, and he accused Ojukwu of being a let-down (Page 23). Maj. Nzeogwu later sent Capt. Udeaja to Kano to collect £N500,000 to pay his soldiers, but Ojukwu, who was commander of the Fifth Battalion in Kano, arrested Capt. Udeaja. The same day, after the coup had failed in Lagos, an announcement was made, indicating that some soldiers had mutinied against the government: "...The commander of the 5th battalion in Kano, Lt. Col C.

O. Ojukwu, seized Kano airport and intercepted an aircraft sent by Nzeogwu to collect money from the Central bank in Kano...[83]" Omoigui further documents how Major Hassan Katsina, along with Maj. Alexander Madiebo of artillery in Kaduna and Lt. Col. Chukwuemeka Ojukwu in Kano, "...began playing a very cunning game of isolating Nzeogwu, while appearing to cooperate by assisting in sending out some signals and making troops available for odds and ends. Indeed, it was the undercover role played by Ojukwu and Hassan in support of Ironsi during this stand-off that got them both the military governorships of the East and North respectively...[84]" Ojukwu's actions took place after the coup was already foiled in Lagos. Any attempts to launch an attack in the East and West of Nigeria, including Lagos, had already been discouraged by Lt. Col. Alexander Madiebo (see Madiebo Pp. 23-25). If Nzeogwu accused Ojukwu of being a let-down, then Ojukwu must have been part of the plot—or at least fully aware of it—and worked to foil it after it failed in Lagos, as a means of profiting from whichever side won the battle. Therefore, Ojukwu's intervention to foil the coup bore fruit for his ambitions either way. If Maj. Nzeogwu had succeeded, Ojukwu would have been happy, for it is alleged by many authors, including Col. Ben Gbulie, that Ojukwu had been harboring a coup plot as far back as Independence Day in 1960 and as recently as 1964. In effect, Ojukwu became a carpetbagger.

---

[83] *Nowa Omoigui, "January 15, 1966: The Role of Major Hassan Usman Katsina" January 15, 1966: https://dawodu.com/katsina1.htm.*
[84] Ibid

Chapter III

FROM THE MINEFIELD TO THE PRECIPICE

Handing Over the government—Seriously? Not Really True!

Once the January 15 coup was suppressed, the general officer commanding of the Nigerian Army, Maj. Gen. Aguiyi Ironsi (Igbo), became the new head of state.

The claim was that the civilian government—ministers and the parliament of senators and representatives—handed over the government to Ironsi, and although the political parties and social organizations of various communities and ethnic groups pledged their loyalty to the new government, there is controversy as to whether the remaining members of the civilian government voluntarily handed over the government to Ironsi and the army. Furthermore, the subsequent actions and policies of the new government were not accepted by segments of the community, especially Northern Nigerians whose leaders had been murdered by the January activists. Notwithstanding the controversy over the events that led to the handover of government to the military, the policies of the Ironsi regime immediately set the Northern ruling establishment and their collaborators into a conspiracy mode that eventually led to the overthrow of the Ironsi regime barely six months after it took office.

After Maj. Gen Ironsi had good control of the rebellion, he met with the remaining ministers of the government of Tafawa Balewa. According to Chief Richard Akinjide (a minister of education in the Balewa government before the coup), "when Balewa got missing, we knew Okotie-Eboh had been held, we knew Akintola had been killed. We, the members of the Balewa cabinet started meeting ... unanimously, we nominated an acting Prime Minister amongst us... Having nominated Zana Dipcharima as our acting Prime Minister in the absence of the Prime Minister, whose whereabouts we didn't know, we approached the acting President, Nwafor Orizu to swear him in because he cannot legitimately act as the Prime Minister except, he is sworn-in. Nwafor Orizu refused... He said he needed to contact Zik who was then in the West Indies." What the ministers did was correct under the circumstances. Constitutionally, Nwazor Orizu, as president of the senate and acting president, had all the powers of the president and could have legitimately sworn in Zana Dipcharima as acting prime minister. Dr. Orizu requested to see the National Council of Nigerian Citizens (NCNC) colleagues of the Northern People's Congress (NPC) and find out if they would support the nomination of Zana Dipcharima as acting prime minister. The testimony appears to be that the NCNC colleagues responded that they would prefer Mr. K. O. Mbadiwe (NCNC) as their choice of acting prime minister. Once more, According to Akinjide, Maj. Gen. Ironsi requested to meet with all the cabinet ministers and made the case that he would not able to control the army plotters unless the cabinet handed over the government to the army.

Whatever the circumstances, Ironsi's government takeover was a clear violation of the constitution. No provision in the constitution allows the Cabinet to hand over the government to a military unit or organization. More importantly, Maj. Gen. Ironsi was not a mastermind of the coup and, therefore, had no interest in taking over the government from coup plotters. If Ironsi testified that he would not able to control the coup plotters, he was not being honest. By the time he met with the Cabinet, on or shortly after January 16, 1966, Ironsi had effectively neutralized the coup; Nzeogwu would not have been able to match him in the southeast let alone in the southwest in Lagos, where Ironsi was firmly in control. It is equally telling that before Ironsi came to plead his case before the cabinet, he met privately with Dr. Nwafor Orizu, the senate president. No one knows the subject or content of their conversation.

Sheer political fairness should have justified the NPC ministers' decision to select Mr. Dipcharima as interim prime minister. It was political insensitivity for the NCNC, junior partners, to reject Dipcharima in favor of K. O. Mbadiwe, an Igbo man, to take over from Tafawa Balewa (Northerner) who had just been kidnapped by Igbo army officers. The fact that Dr. Orizu (Igbo and president of the senate) rejected the NPC nominee after he met privately with Ironsi was reason enough for the NPC leaders to be suspicious and indignant. The rejection of the NPC nominee was political insensitivity for the simple reason that Tafawa Balewa was a Northerner and for him to be killed in a bloody coup and replaced by another Igbo would have given the Igbos the prime minister, the president, and the head of the army all at once. There was ample reason for the Northerners, correctly or incorrectly or for cynical reasons or an excuse, to see the coup as an Igbo plot to take over the country.

The Fall of the Government of Aguiyi Ironsi and the *Counter Military Coup – July 1966*

Once Aguiyi Ironsi received the mantle of office from the civilian government, the plotters of the January 15 coup were confined in prisons around the country. Ironsi then settled into governance and formed the Supreme Military Council (SMC), which he populated entirely with officers from the military and the police. The members of the council were comprised of the head of state, the military governors of the four regions, and the chiefs of staff of the Navy, Army, and Air Force. The members of the SMC were Maj. Gen. Johnson Aguiyi Ironsi (supreme commander), Brig. Ogundipe (chief of general staff), Lt. Col. Yakubu Gowon, (army chief of staff), Adekunle Fajuyi (governor, Western Region), Hassan Katsina (governor, Northern Region), David Ejoor (governor, Midwest Region), Odumegwu Ojukwu (governor, Eastern Region), George Kurubo (chief of air staff), and Akinwale Wey (chief of naval staff).

While Ironsi was settling into governance, a combination of events occurred in such a sequence that brought about his downfall and the downfall of his regime. At the foundation of these events and their dynamics was the seething anger of the Northern Nigerians—or at least their understandable consternation over the elimination of their political and military leaders. The catalyst for the eventual strike against Ironsi can be found in a series of policies within a crucible of paradoxical internal contradiction in his operational style. Another major matter that caused trouble was the behavior of Igbos around Nigeria, especially in Northern Nigeria. As mentioned earlier, it appeared that the Igbos were bragging about and celebrating what they considered an Igbo victory against the other ethnic groups; thus, the impression was created.

Many things set the scene for bringing down Ironsi's regime: first, of course, there was an outcry that called the January coup an Igbo conspiracy. It was, therefore, incumbent on Ironsi to try to dispel this perception. He tried to do this in a few ways, such as rapid promotion of certain Northern Nigerian army officers. He also tried to appear transparent in some of his policies, a decision that led to accusations of making compromises with Northerners that emboldened them to plot harder for his overthrow.

Ironsi began his role by setting up the machinery of government, including plans for the future of Nigeria and establishing committees for development and the appointment of commanders and administrators as part of the reorganization of the army. In February 1966, Ironsi appointed Francis Nwokedi (Igbo man), a permanent secretary in the Ministry of Foreign Affairs, as the sole commissioner to establish an administrative machinery for a unified Nigeria, though he already appointed a separate constitutional review panel under Rotimi Williams. At the time of the appointment of Nwokedi, the Constitutional Review Committee had not submitted a report.

From about the middle of March 1966, the atmosphere began to get tense. In the middle of it all, bad news came that our cousin, a pilot in the Nigerian Air Force (commissioned in 1963 or 1964) had died in a helicopter crash. I cannot recollect exactly when, but I believe that he was set up. His body was later to be returned to the compound. It caused me a lot of pain because he was a shining star in the family, the grandson of my grandfather's sister.

Another source of suspicion in the army was the promotion exercise carried out in May. There were three complaints about it: First, it should not have happened at all because there was a moratorium on promotions at the time. Second, it "favored" Igbo officers and consolidated their control of the military. Third, Northerners were also "favored" along with Igbos while Yoruba officers were "marginalized." The sources of each of these lines of thinking are easy to guess. Eleven majors were promoted to permanent lieutenant colonels, whereas fourteen majors were made temporary lieutenant colonels. Of these twenty-five new lieutenant colonels, nineteen were Igbo or Igbo-speaking easterners and Midwesterners, five were northerners (Katsina, Akahan, Shuwa, Muhammed, and Haruna), and one was Yoruban (Olutoye). On the surface, it looked like a crude attempt to favor Igbo or Igbo-speaking officers. But in reality, no Igbo or Igbo-speaking officer was promoted who was not due for promotion, considering that between 1955 and 1961 the vast majority of officer recruits were of Igbo or Igbo-speaking origin. Faulty or not, the appearance of a lopsided promotion of Igbo army officers reinforced prevailing conspiracy theories, notwithstanding that three Igbo majors (Obienu, Aniebo, and Chude-Sokei) were also bypassed. This promotion exercise was followed soon after by the Unification Decree exercise, which practically erased all doubts about prevailing conspiracy theories.

Another factor that turned the coup of January 1966 against the Igbos was the behavior of the Igbos themselves. When I was a young teenager, I can vividly recollect a picture of Maj. Chukwuma Nzeogwu, the acknowledged leader of the January coup, standing astride the dead body of the murdered Sardauna Sokoto and another picture of the Sardauna saying something from within or under a death shroud. Another picture in the newspapers depicted a picture of Nzeogwu and the Igbos saying that he (Nzeogwu) was the only person who could knock sense into the heads of the Northerners. What a false sense of indignation and complacency! In his biography titled *Power with Civility* by Oleka and Ofondu[85] Rear Admiral Godwin Ndubuisi Kanu, an Igbo easterner who later fought in the Biafran Navy states: "...That Igbos, including soldiers in the barracks, teased their Northern counterparts about what they regarded as swapping of fortune, served to fray tempers..." It was not long before Northerners vented their spleen on their Igbo guests. An orgy of Igbo killings throughout the nooks and crannies of the Northern Region kicked off. In his book, *Revolution in Nigeria: Another View*, late Gen. Garba describes how his soldiers in the federal guard broke down in tears in the Jankara market in Lagos when they heard the album "Machine Gun." Gen. Danjuma (Retired) says even the wives of Igbo soldiers were taunting the wives of Northern soldiers.

In early May 1966, Maj. Gen. Ironsi passed Decree 34 (the "Unification Decree") that unified the administrative structure of Nigeria. At least in words, the Decree abolished the regions and proposed a unified administrative structure for the country under a central government. Given the historical apprehensions in various parts of Nigeria, and especially in Northern Nigeria, such a proposition was ill-advised, to say the least. It did not make theoretical or operational sense besides the fact that Northern Nigerians, whose leaders had just been murdered, would not entertain it and their leaders. Traditional rulers, leaders of thought, and civil servants of Northern Nigeria immediately expressed their opposition to the Unification Decree.

Extant literature on the civil war written by those who have done extensive research indicates that the idea of unifying Nigeria was strongly opposed and that the SMC was still discussing the decree when Ironsi suddenly passed it. According to Okey Anueyiagu (*Biafra: The Horrors of War, The Story of a Child Soldier*), his father led a delegation to advise Ironsi against passing such a decree. In April 1967 during his last interview (with Ejindu), Maj. Nzeogwu was quoted as saying that the Unification Decree was "unnecessary, even silly..."

---

[85] *Ogbonna Oleka and Ndubuisi Ofondu, Power with Civility. A Biography of Rear Admiral Godwin Ndubuisi Kanu. Nekson Publishers, 1998*

According to Brig. Ogbemudia (rtd), who was then Brig. Maj. at the First Brigade, during a visit to Kaduna, First Brigade Commander Lt. Col. Bassey tried to advise Gen. Ironsi to back off from the controversial decree, but a civilian adviser (probably Francis Nwokedi) who came along with the general retorted saying: "...Colonel, the General understands Nigerians more than you here. You will find that the people will soon see him as the much-sought redeemer of our dreams. Do not worry. Everything is under control...[86]" It was claimed that national surveys had been done and showed that the decree was welcome all over the country. With that said, the Eastern Region Governor Lt. Col. Ojukwu did not help matters for the general when, the day after the promulgation on May 24, he announced publicly in Enugu that Igbo civil servants would be transferred to other regions and Lagos, based on seniority. Such a statement sent shivers through the northern civil service because that region was not only educationally disadvantaged but traditionally paid the lowest salaries in the federation and thus automatically relegated northerners to the bottom of any unified civil service. Furthermore, the Unification Decree proposed that governors should be prepared to serve outside their regions—in any part of the country.

Whoever advised and pressured Ironsi to pass the decree while it was under discussion and opposed by an influential segment of the country, and against the advice of even some intellectuals in Eastern Nigeria, was either oblivious of Nigerian history or callously and recklessly insensitive to the attitudes of Northern Nigerians. Alternatively, such a person was utterly incompetent. Even if, arguendo, unification was the most appropriate structure for Nigeria, such could only be achieved through an evolutionary process that would have taken numerous decades. Indeed, the Ironsi government was alarmed and warned on several occasions that there was a plot afoot to overthrow the government again. Ironsi took several measures to forestall the schemes, but his attempts to protect himself and his government failed. His adversaries were determined. Meanwhile, the contradictions in his policies and operational modes were antithetical to success.

Between the January coup and the Unification Decree, the seething anger of Northern Nigerian officers, provocative disinformation by maliciously motivated instigators in the Northern ruling establishment, Ironsi's contradictions, and the behavior of Igbos all combined into a lethal recipe for the downfall of the Ironsi regime. Immediately following the Unification Decree in May, riots broke out in various Northern Nigerian cities. During these riots, the targets of the attacks were Igbos; estimates range from one thousand to three thousand dead. But even before and after the Decree and the riots that came in its wake, there was an undercurrent of a scheme to overthrow the Ironsi government by aggrieved Northern Nigerians, who did little to hide or camouflage their intentions or their feelings.

Aguiyi Ironsi was warned and alerted about these schemes to overthrow his regime, and so to mollify the Northern Nigerians, Ironsi granted "skipping" promotions to selected Northern Nigerian Army officers to make up for the senior officers that they lost during the January coup. Secondly, he made paradoxically curious efforts to impress other Nigerians that he was not plotting with Igbos to dominate Nigeria. Finally, he undertook a peace-seeking tour of Northern and Western Nigeria, excluding Eastern Nigeria to assure other Nigerians that neither the Decree nor the actions of his regime were intended to establish the Igbo domination. None of Ironsi's efforts helped because (1) in a misguided sense of complacency, Ironsi did not take adequate steps to protect himself, (2) there were flaws in his policy actions that easily created doubts in his credibility—somewhat half-witted and above all, and (3) his adversaries were determined and implacable.

Madiebo[87] opined that Gen. Ironsi surrounded himself with more Northerners than Tafawa Balewa did at the height of his (Balewa's) political power. Madiebo did not provide much evidence to support this assertion besides noting that Yakubu Gowon, a Northerner, was appointed chief of army staff. In addition, Alhaji Kam Salem, also a Northerner, replaced Mr. Edet (non-Igbo Easterner) as chief of police. This was somewhat inevitable. After all, in a diverse country, offices at the pinnacle of power should be distributed in a diffused manner. Other offices, like the chief of navy, were held by

---

[86] *Nowa Omoigui, OPERATION 'AURE': Northern Nigerian Military Counter-Rebellion, July, 1966, Uhrhobo Historical Society, 17 Aug 2002*
[87] *Madiebo, The Nigerian Revolution and the Biafra War, Page 31*

Yorubans (Akinwale Wey, whose Ibibio mother was from the East). The chief of air staff was from the East (George Kurubo, a non-Igbo–speaking person from the Rivers State). Any other distribution would have lent credence to the charge that the January coup was Igbo-inspired to establish Igbo domination. One thing to note is that the replacement of Edet was already in the works before the coup of January 1966.

Reports also have it that Ironsi went out of his way to demonstrate that he was not in conspiracy with the Igbos. In doing so, Ironsi may have exposed himself recklessly.[88] For example, one of Ironsi's aides-de-camp (ADC) was Sani Bello (a Northerner). Someone that close should have been watched closely through a highly skilled informant or spy. According to Max Siollun, "To prove that he was not heading an 'Igbo regime,' Ironsi had, with great courage, entrusted his security to northern soldiers (including Major Yakubu Danjuma, Lieutenants William Walbe, Titus Numan, and Sani Bello). One of his ADCs was the younger brother of Lt-Col James Pam (who had been murdered during the January coup). By surrounding himself with northern soldiers, Ironsi sealed his fate…[89]" Very often, Ironsi discounted reports of the plot to overthrow his government. For example, in June 1966, a report from a certain Mr. Anueyigu (father of Anueyiagu cited in this book) stated that a certain Alhaji Suya (this is a pseudonym) had disclosed a plot to kill Igbos in the Northern part of the country but was dismissed by Ironsi, with a reprimand of Madiebo.[90] Specifically, Madiebo, Mr. Anueyiagu (chairman of a peace committee in Kaduna), and Col. Okoro met with Alhaji Suya to receive a report that outlined a plan to create fake mayhem in Kaduna and give the impression that Igbos were at it again, killing Northern soldiers. This would then justify the killing of all Igbos in Northern Nigeria (June 1966). At the end of the meeting, Madiebo flew to Lagos to relay the reported story to Ironsi. At the meeting, Ironsi made a point of requesting that Madiebo repeat his story in the presence of Maj. Mobolaji Johnson (Yoruba administrator of Lagos Capital Territory). Following this narration,[91] "Aguiyi Ironsi summoned Lt. Col. Yakubu Gowon (Army Chief of Staff), Kam Salem (Chief of Police) and Yesufu (Head of Special Branch) and asked that Madiebo repeat his story… The three men promptly denied the story and requested that Ironsi treat the story as a maliciously motivated rumor designed to tarnish their image." Ironsi reprimanded Madiebo for rumor-mongering and assigned the three men to investigate the matter and report to him (Ironsi). Ironsi also "summoned Lt. Col. Njoku and ordered him to dispatch a company of soldiers to Lokoja to locate and destroy the … alleged training camp and destroy it." According to Madiebo, Ironsi lost a major opportunity to survive by ordering the leaders of a private army that was plotting to overthrow him to investigate their scheme and report back to him. Furthermore, assigning Njoku to locate the training camp for the rogue insurrectionists in the presence of their commanders was senseless. The plotters would simply relocate the camp.

In a similar narrative, (Anueyiagu Pp. 48 – 49 Son of the same Anueyiagu who met with Madiebo on Pp. 45 – 49), "… My father led a group of [*Igbo*] intelligentsia to meet General Aguiyi Ironsi … to deliver intelligence [regarding] plans to kill Igbo and other Easterners in the North before it was too late … and noticed that Ironsi's ADC was a Hausa man … and started to speak in the Igbo language … He was promptly interrupted and directed that the meeting be held in English … My father knew that the meeting would be fruitless … Any sensitive information about the plans by Northerners divulged to Ironsi in the presence of his ADC would be carried back." This account appears to corroborate the story that Madiebo relates concerning the report to Ironsi. At this time, the cat has already left the bag, depending on who was there first. In any event, Madiebo and Anueyiagu should not have gone independently to Ironsi to report the same matter. As Igbo leaders, they should have coordinated their plan to meet with Ironsi and begin to plan for their defense or the protection of the Igbo community in the North or plan for an ultimate showdown, if it would come to that.

---

[88] *Anueyiagu Okey Anueyiagu, Biafra: The Horrors of War – The Story of a Child Soldier, Atlanta, Georgia USA, Brown Brommel Publishers, 2020, Pp. 48 – 49 and Madiebo, Op. Cit. Pp. 46 – 47*

[89] *(NigerianNews, July 28, 2016, The Northern Countercoup of 1966: The Full Story - By Max Siollun)*

[90] *Anueyiagu, Op. Cit.*

[91] Madiebo, Op. Cit. P. 49

Besides his misguided sense of complacency, Ironsi, as already narrated, had appointed an Igbo man as sole commissioner to recommend an administrative structure for Nigeria—the Unification Decree. After the riots that attended the Unification Decree and Col. Ojukwu's frightening ejaculation that Eastern Nigerian civil servants would be posted around the country, Ironsi proposed a tour of the country to assure the concerned constituencies that the Decree had been misunderstood. The leaders of Northern Nigerian met in June 1966 and made three demands of the Ironsi government. The first was that Decree 34 must be repealed. They then demanded that the coup plotters of January 15 be tried, and finally that there should be no investigation into the riots that attended the Unification Decree[92]. By all indications, any plan to put the January coup plotters on trial was not made known to the public or any of the concerned constituencies. The right thing to do was to put the January coup plotters on trial. As such any hesitation on the matter could justifiably cast doubt on Ironsi's credibility and sincerity. It is equally plausible to speculate that Ironsi's adversaries were aware that the SMC had made the decision[93]. to try the January coup plotters but made haste to overthrow him before the decision could be implemented. If the decision were made public and the trial commenced, the situation could no longer be used as justification for resenting Ironsi's government. Indeed, one of the military governors acknowledged at the Aburi meeting that the trial of the January boys was set for August and then moved to October 1966[94].

Nothing could have saved Ironsi's regime from its downfall. If Ironsi had taken appropriate precautions and if he had made security arrangements, he would have, at best, escaped with his life. The coup would have taken place, with the exception that Ironsi would have been driven from Lagos. Such an expulsion might, at worst, have led to an earlier civil war or tensions for a while and the tension would have died down. Given that Ironsi may have been influential with the British or other foreign regimes, he may have been able to live peacefully in exile and negotiate a peaceful transition to a new government.

Although the Unification Decree was the last straw that justified the takedown of Ironsi's government, it is clear from events that the motive for a northern counter-coup was established immediately after the January coup. The army officers from Northern Nigeria and their political allies and instigators only wanted an opportunity and further justification. Whenever they had the opportunity, Northern Nigerian officers got together to plot and scheme on how to carry out a counter-coup. It is reported that during a platoon commander's course in Kaduna, young northern subalterns came together to share ideas and vent frustration. These officers even wrote a letter of protest to the Army Chief of Staff Lt. Col. Gowon, openly stating that if senior Northern officers did not act within a certain time frame, then they would and that senior Northern officers would have themselves to blame for the catastrophe[95] Aggrieved Northerners were implacable. To inflame the Northern population, malicious disinformation was spread about an Igbo plot to carry out another coup and murder more Northerners. According to Ibrahim Babangida, who testified during the Oputa Commission (military president of Nigeria, 1985–1993), civilians also instigated against the Igbos. Specifically, Northern civilian propagandists used the tools of psychological warfare and worked tirelessly to incite the Northern military.

Gen. Babangida put it this way: "...There was a very calculated and subtle but very efficient and effective indoctrination of the Northern officers by civilians. They kept hammering on it that our leaders had been killed and we were doing nothing; that we were cowards...." Gen. Shuwa (Retired) described documents passed around Kaduna purporting to show plans for senior Igbo officers to meet at Hamdala Hotel to plan the liquidation of the remaining Northern officers. Indeed, the rumors were so detailed that operational code names using animals were even ascribed to parts of the alleged grand Igbo plot to continue: Operation Damisa (leopard), which had already taken

---

[92] *Madiebo, The Nigerian Revolution, Page 44.*
[93] *Max Siollun, Oil, Politics and Violence, Pp. 95 – 96*
[94] *Government of the Federal republic of Nigeria, Meeting of the Nigerian Military Leaders held at Peduase Lodge, Aburi Ghana, January 4 – January 5, 1967, Federal Republic of Nigeria, Aburi Meeting Minutes, Page 39.*
[95] *See Nora Omoigui, Operation Aure, Op. Cit.*

place on January 15th; Operation Kura (hyena), to eliminate certain chiefs; Operation Zaki (lion), to eliminate the remaining chiefs; and finally, Operation Giwa (elephant), to carve the country up into individual districts administered by Igbos[96].

Babangida also testified that there was ...

...a whispering campaign of highly provocative but unproven stories about the grotesque way some of the northern politicians and soldiers had been killed in January. There are northern officers I have spoken to who still say Prime Minister Balewa had his phallus cut off and placed in his mouth by Majors Ifeajuna and Okafor. Another story had it that a kola nut was placed in his mouth after being shot to taunt the northern custom of eating kola nuts - a curious story considering that all Nigerian tribes, especially the Igbo, value kola nuts in their custom...

Additionally, *This kind of uncorroborated preposterous disinformation is what informed the nervousness with which certain traditional rulers approached the conference of traditional rulers in Ibadan on July 28.*

I will digress and comment about Babangida's perspective that the insertion of kola nuts in Balewa's mouth is curious and preposterous. First, I do not believe that the coup plotters who murdered Tafawa Balewa, though they were grotesquely violent, would have inserted a kola nut in his mouth to mock him. Having said that, the allegation that Abubakar's murderers inserted a kola nut in his mouth is not preposterous or curious. Indeed, it is an informed, calculated instigation based on the known behavior of Igbos. Though all tribes in Nigeria value the kola nut in their culture, the Igbo kola nut that is used in ceremonies is different from the gworo that the Hausa-Fulani and even the Yoruba eat. Although many Igbos, including me, prefer to eat gworo for pleasure, the Hausa-Fulani culture, I believe, eats the gworo as a stimulant. I have seen some of them chew it continuously and then spit it out.

The Igbo kola nut is different from the gworo that Northerners eat. Compared to the Igbo kola nut, the gworo, is more crispy, more pleasant, and tastier. The Igbo kola nut is dry and more bitter in taste. Continuous chewing and spitting of the gworo over time leaves a yellow mark on the teeth and the lips. I suspect that some people may have seen the yellow mark on Abubakar Tafawa Balewa's lips and teeth. For that reason, the Igbos called him "Eze gworo" or the man with Gworo teeth or you may say yellow teeth. Therefore, the allegation that Abubakar's murderers had extended their villainy to sticking a gworo in his mouth as a form of mockery is plausible and such an allegation could not be preposterous.

What is probably preposterous is the allegation in Eastern Nigerian propaganda that Northerners would bring leprous men to rape Igbo women during the pogrom before killing them. There were no reports of women fleeing from the ethnic cleansing in 1966 who eventually caught leprosy or who spread it. If the Northerners truly desired to hurt Igbos by having leprous men rape the women, the best thing would have been to have the leprous men rape the women and ensure that they are put on a train with instructions that they must be transported safely to the East. This would have ensured that leprosy would spread to the East.

Amidst the rumors, mockeries, threats, and tensions following the riots of May 31 to June 4, 1966, the Ironsi regime took the initiative to bring about peace. In early June 1966, the General issued orders to arrest anyone displaying offensive behavior in pictures, songs, or statements. Gen. Ironsi also sought to enlist the support of the Emirs to appeal to the Northerners to calm down. At least for a while, there was a sign of goodwill and probably confidence and trust among the leaders of the North. In mid-June 1966, the Sultan of Sokoto broadcast an appeal to his people and asked those [Easterners] that fled from the North to return. Even Lt. Col. Odumegwu, the governor of Eastern Nigeria, encouraged those that had fled the North to return after the leaders of Northern Nigeria made promises of safety. In June of 1966, the Emir of Kano, Alhaji Ado Bayero, was appointed as the new chancellor of the University of Nigeria. During the emir's visit to Nsukka, Ojukwu used the opportunity to express his concern for the safety of Eastern Nigerians in the North, against which

---

[96] (see Nowa Omoigui, Operation Aure by the Urhobo Historical Society.

the emir promised to guarantee safety. During a June 1966 conference between Northern emirs and chiefs and Lt. Col. Hassan Katsina, the [Ironsi] regime stated that the May decrees did not affect the territorial divisions of the country.

While the key leaders of the nation were trying to bring about peace and calm the crisis, the issue of how to address the January boys remained a sore point between the regime and an undercurrent of unrest among military personnel and political leaders. The dogs of war, as already depicted (see Babangida's testimony) remained active and would not let go. Meanwhile, Ironsi blundered again. The regime announced that military prefects would be deployed at the local level and then further proposed the rotation of military governors. The latter proposition immediately reawakened the suspicion that Ojukwu could be posted to Northern Nigeria. By this point, nothing could placate the dogs of war.

To further reach out to Nigerians, Ironsi embarked on a tour of Nigeria—Eastern Nigeria excluded—in July 1966. The purpose of his tour was to explain the merits of the Unification Decree, despite the people's vociferous rejection and opposition to it. Ironsi started his tour in the North, continued through the Midwest Region, and finally arrived in Ibadan, the capital of Western Nigeria. There, he invited the emirs of the North and the chiefs, among other traditional rulers from both Western and Eastern Nigeria. This visit to Ibadan took place on July 28, 1966.

In July 1966, smack in the middle of the second term of the school year, we were jarred in our classrooms by news of a counter-coup by the Nigerian Army. Specifically, Northern Nigerian soldiers led a counter-coup. Soldiers led by Maj. T. Y. Danjuma kidnapped Maj. Gen. Aguiyi Ironsi, and shortly thereafter, we heard a broadcast that the new head of state would be Lt. Col. Yakubu Gowon, a Northerner. In hindsight, I cannot recollect whether we, the kids or I, had any negative opinion of Gowon. I took note that he was a Northerner. After all, Abubakar was a Northerner. When I saw my father next, I heard him and his friends make special note of the fact that Gowon had made a speech that spoke of how power had returned, once more, to a Northerner. That speech had a less-than-reassuring effect on people's minds, especially among the older folks. With this new takeover, tension heightened. There was speculation about what would happen next, as the May anti-Igbo riots were not far from people's minds.

Three things happened: First, there was speculation that Ironsi could still be alive somewhere. However, more experienced people had no illusions that Ironsi was still alive. There was a boy my age in the village who was an apprentice mechanic. His name was Chukwuma Ocha. He told me that his boss said to another man, "Onye ndi army jî, ô nâ â di ndû?" That is to say, "How do you expect that a person that was kidnapped by soldiers would be left to live?" The air was pregnant with speculation, and with Ironsi's whereabouts unknown, the Igbos had received a wake-up call. Secondly, the euphoria over Nzeogwu and his coup-making comrades was greatly tempered, if not altogether chilled. But this countercoup was not the end of it. Finally, by the end of August 1966, the sporadic killing of Igbos, now led in part by Northern soldiers, turned into mayhem. All hell broke loose.

While visiting the North, rebel officers of Northern Nigeria probably plotted to kill Ironsi. According to Hillary Njoku, gunshots were heard in the vicinity of Ironsi's location. However, it is also reported that dissenting leaders of the community dissuaded the would-be assassins because they did not want Ironsi's blood to be shed on Northern Nigerian soil.[97] During his visit to Ibadan, Ironsi and his host, Lt. Col. Francis Fajuyi (governor of Western Nigeria) were abducted by army officers of Northern Nigerian origin and murdered. This counter-coup of July 1966 was a revenge coup by a constituency of army officers who, understandably, felt aggrieved by the apparent betrayal and treachery of their colleagues in January 1966. The details of the plot are documented very well by other writers including Omoigui, Akpan, Effiong, Garba, and Madiebo, among others[98]. On the day of the coup, Brig. Ogundipe (Western Nigeria Yoruba), the chief of general staff and next in authority to Gen. Ironsi, attempted, without success, to foil the coup. The soldiers who were

---

[97] I do not know why that should matter to anyone.

[98] *Omoigui, OPERATION 'AURE', 17 Aug 2002, Akpan, The Struggle for Secession, Effiong, Nigeria and Biafra: My Story, Garba, Fractured History, and Madiebo, The Nigerian Revolution and the Biafra War*

involved, including the ordinary rank and file, would not take orders from him and made clear they would take orders from no other officers except their Northern Nigerian superiors. Ojukwu was in constant touch with Ogundipe, urging him to fight the rebel officers and argued fervently that if Ironsi was absent, then Ogundipe was the next in rank to be in control of the government. At some point, Brig. Ogundikpe had to go into hiding for his safety but eventually resurfaced in London, where he was appointed high commissioner for Nigeria. Among the Igbos, the circulating story was that Brig. Ogundipe had gone into hiding, but it failed to mention that the Brigadier had put up a heroic effort to bring the crisis under control before he gave up. Specifically,

"...About this time, first Major Johnson and then Brigadier Ogundipe himself gave an order to a northern NCO deployed to the Federal Guards Company. The soldier blatantly said he would not take orders from the Brigadier unless approved by Captain J.N. Garba. So, Captain Garba was sent for and came to the Police HQ. He was initially interrogated by Lt. Col. Anwunah, searching for information about what was happening in the country. Garba then aggressively confronted Anwunah with the grievances of northern soldiers and why they had struck. When Anwunah reported Garba's intransigence to Ogundipe, Ogundipe told Garba ... I wish you boys had waited. I have just received the report about the January coup this morning and it is on my table right now. Try to talk to your friends in Ikeja, and I am sure we can settle this matter, even at this stage."[99]

There is no denying that the July 1966 coup was a revenge coup. However, it was equally an attempt to balance the ethnic distribution of commissioned and senior officers in the army. Following the abduction and murder of Ironsi, the Northern Nigerian Officer Corp acted with an utmost vengeance. According to Maj. Gen. Theophilus Y. Danjuma (though he was Maj. Danjuma at the time of the coup), there was no intent to kill Ironsi and his host, Fajuyi. Maj. T. Y. Danjuma testified that the intention was only to arrest Ironsi and remove him from office as supreme commander. In a documented telephone conversation, Lt. Col. Yakubu Gowon called to talk to Fajuyi, but Danjuma answered the call. During their conversation, Danjuma told Yakubu Gowon (chief of army staff) that he was in the building to arrest the supreme commander (Ironsi). Gowon asked if he (Danjuma) was able to achieve that. Danjuma's testimony is that Ironsi was arrested and handed over to soldiers who promised not to bring harm to the supreme commander. Unknown to Danjuma and other ring leaders, however, the soldiers assigned to the care of the supreme commander took him to an unknown location and shot him dead, along with his host, Fajuyi.

There is also the allegation that Lt. Col. Yakubu Gowon (army chief of staff and Northerner) was part of the conspiracy to abduct and kill the supreme commander. However, Maj. Gen. Joseph Garba (a captain at the time of the July coup) in his book, *Fractured History*, states that Yakubu Gowon, who emerged as head of state after the July coup, knew nothing about the planned attack. On the contrary, Maj. Gen. Phillip Effiong (then Lt. Col. Effiong and chief of ordinance staff for a while under Ironsi) has argued otherwise[100]. While Yakubu may have not been part of the original conspiracy to overthrow the Ironsi government, he probably knew the details and withheld the information from Ironsi.

It is hard to argue that Yakubu Gowon did not know about the July coup. Earlier reports by Madiebo[101] provided sufficient reason for Gowon to investigate and gather intelligence. On the other hand, I find it difficult to accuse Gowon, post-factum, of being an accessory to a crime because he failed to inform his immediate superior who had taken him into confidence. There was obvious tension in the country. The planners of the July coup may have approached him to be part of it. Secondly, "In Kaduna, the Platoon Commanders Course at the NMTC provided an opportunity for young northern subalterns to come together to share ideas and vent frustration. These officers included Lt. Shelleng, Lt. Hannaniya, Lt. Muhammadu Jega, Lt. Sani Abacha, Lt. Sali, Lt. Dambo, and others. These were the junior Northern officers that wrote the threatening letter to Lt. Col.

---

[99] Nowa Omoigui, MD, *OPERATION 'AURE': Northern Nigerian Military Counter-Rebellion, July 1966, Uhrhobo Historical Society, 17 Aug 2002*

[100] Phillip Effiong, Nigeria and Biafra: My Story. See also The Caged Bird Sang No More by Effiong.

[101] Madiebo, The Nigerian Revolution and the Biafran War

Yakubu Gowon and demanded action.[102] The better part of valor is discretion. Therefore, Yakubu Gowon could have had information about the plan to assassinate his supreme commander and was careful not to leak the scheme in such a manner that the leaks could be traced to him. Alternatively, he could have taken the attitude that Madiebo had provided Ironsi sufficient warning about the nascent plot. Therefore, the Supremo should have protected himself. On the matter of Gowon's role and attitudes, Effiong has an extensive discussion.[103]

For a while, the wrath and the rampage of Northern Nigerian officers extended to all officers from all Southern parts of Nigeria. Available literature reveals that then-Maj. Samuel Ogbemidia, Benjamin Adekunle, and Olusegun Obasanjo were in danger and went into hiding or were chased by the rampaging officers. With some wise counsel, the Northern officers realized that it was better to leave Western Nigerians off their rampage. They then focused on Eastern Nigerians, especially Igbos. Madiebo, Regina Maduabum, and Effiong all provide extensive firsthand accounts of the events in Northern Nigeria and how each of them escaped. Madiebo's account is particularly dramatic.[104] Max Siollun corroborates Maduabum's eyewitness account.[105] In the end, more than 150 Igbo and other Eastern Nigerian officers and men were murdered in Northern Nigeria. Several others were executed in Western Nigeria, bringing the total to about 168.[106]

Efforts to stem the rampage were fruitless. Among the demands of the Northern Nigerian officers was that they would not stop the killing until the North was allowed to secede from Nigeria[107]. Chief among the proponents of Northern secession was Lt. Col. Murtala Mohamed, the leader of the coup.

The massacre and mass slaughter of Igbos intensified through September and October 1966. At the end of September 1966, Lt. Col. Gowon made a speech, in effect condemning the riots and the killing of Igbo people. Instead of abating the riots, the anger of the people boiled over. On October 4, 1966 (*Time Magazine*), soldiers of the Fourth and Fifth Battalions sacked the Kano Airport and began to massacre Igbo people—passengers and staff alike. This act of vandalism and barbarism spread like wildfire and even the police joined the violence.

The carnage that transpired was horrendous. Descriptions of the event could not impress on my young mind until I witnessed it myself. As N. U. Akpan did not spare details as he described the situation in his book:

"...There was no human being with a soul, blood, and life who saw it and was not revulsed at what happened... and this was true of even Northerners resident in Enugu." I have never been able to

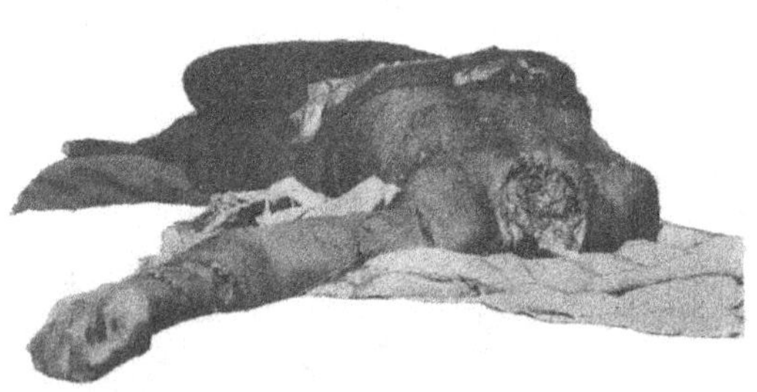

HORROR OF SAVAGERY

Head chopped off with an axe. Stomach ripped open and intestines flowing out. Six-foot Onwuanaibe Anyaegbu was travelling by train from Pankshin, near Jos and met his tragic end at the Oturkpo Railway Station in Northern Nigeria where he was beheaded by Northern savages and his body put back in the train travelling to Enugu in the East. Many more men, women and children were beheaded in other Northern towns. The picture summarizes the grief of Eastern Nigeria.

forget the shock... one early evening— ... what came out of the train was beyond description... Some came off the train with severed limbs, broken heads ...But the most chilling sight was a woman who came out completely naked, clutching the head of her child. ..Unfortunately not many in the rest of Nigeria knew of the horrible situation... This could be seen from the obvious horror which struck the ... chiefs of Western Nigeria ... who visited later and were taken to the General Hospital ... They were all so shocked that they could not enjoy the

---

[102] *See Nora Omoigui, Operation Aure, Op. Cit.*

[103] see Effiong, Nigeria and Biafra: My Story, Pp. 120 – 35.

[104] *Maduabum, A soldier's Spouse, Pp. 81 – 94* and *Madiebo, Op. Cit, Pp. 72 – 80.*

[105] Max Siollun, Pp. 135 – 36

[106] Njoku, A Tragedy Without Heros, Pp. 184 – 86

[107] See Akpan, The Struggle for Secession, Madiebo, The Nigerian Revolution and the Biafran War and Njoku, A Tragedy Without Heroes.

hospitality offered them ... and before they left, they surrendered everything they had collectively and individually..."[108]

Akpan's description is graphic. Such graphic descriptions and newspaper articles circulated in Eastern Nigeria during my childhood—specifically my teenage years. I saw a lot of them. But they did not mean much to me until I visited home in late September 1966 for the second term break, in preparation for the last school term from October to December. I witnessed for myself the horror of the events that were so vividly described in the newspapers and Akpan's book. I was frightened but also got a vivid picture of the gravity of the events that were taking place in Northern Nigeria. Even at this point in late or mid-September 1966, the mayhem was not yet as bad as it eventually became.

My hometown, Ovim, a hilly geographical area, was crisscrossed by the rail lines of the Nigerian railway system. There was also a train station in Ovim. My village and our family compound were so close to the rail lines that you could see and hear the trains from our house and several other compounds. Furthermore, the rivulet or stream of water that served our village was adjacent to the rail line. Therefore, either while I was fetching water or just visiting the neighbors in our village or the adjacent village, I could see the trains, even across the forest behind our house. In the middle of the day, the rumbling noise of the trains could be heard.

It was from these vantage points that I was able to witness daily the gravity of what happened. The trains were packed full of returning refugees. Some people even sat on the roofs

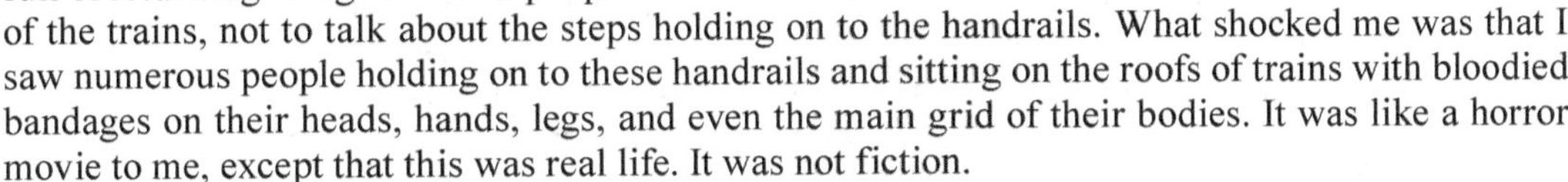

of the trains, not to talk about the steps holding on to the handrails. What shocked me was that I saw numerous people holding on to these handrails and sitting on the roofs of trains with bloodied bandages on their heads, hands, legs, and even the main grid of their bodies. It was like a horror movie to me, except that this was real life. It was not fiction.

It is quite remarkable that pictures or videos of the events and mayhem in the North in 1966 are not readily available. The Nigerian government did its utmost to keep the horrific events off the record. Foreign journalists were barred from publishing the events. On the contrary, there are extensive pictures of the Biafra conflagration, the starvation, battlefield action, and speeches even though modern technology was more available in 1966 Nigeria than in 1968 to 1970 Biafran enclave. The Nigerian government's denial in 1966 prompted one journalist to lament that the truth would never be known, and no proper lessons are learned[109]. Without a doubt, the developments in contemporary Nigeria and the behavior of our leaders indicate clearly that no proper lessons were learned from the events of 1966.

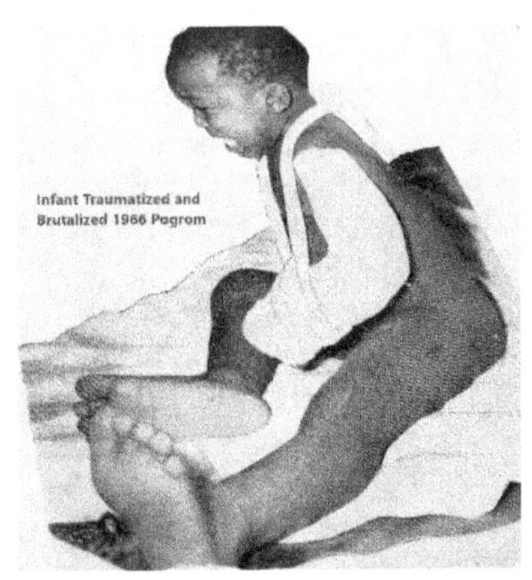

As our people returned from Northern Nigeria, I also met, for the first time, relatives that I had never known existed—immediate first and second cousins of the same last name: Egesi Egbe and Oji

---

[108] Ntieyong .U. Akpan, The Struggle for Secession, 1966 – 1970: A personal Account of the Nigerian Civil War, London, Frank Cass, 1976, 1971, Pp. xii - xiii

[109] Times Magazine, October 4, 1966

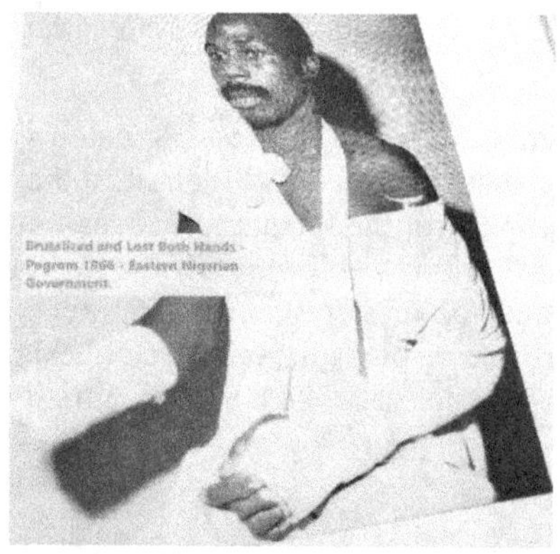

Egbe, the sons of Nyeye or Egbe ncha (little Egbe—I always knew of them). However, I never knew about Ukennaya Egbe and his wife and children, nor did I know about Nwachukwu Egbe, the immediate younger brother of Egesi. Ukennaya Egbe was the older brother of Egesi and son of Nyeye (Egbe ncha) by an earlier wife. Nyeye was an animist to the very end and died in 1958. The man adamantly refused to go to church and worshipped our traditional gods to the end. I could never forget his diligent calendar of sacrificing to the gods, his incantations, and liturgies by the gates of the compound. He placed tender leaves of *ichikara* between his thumb and the adjacent finger and popped it loudly as a means of chasing away evil forces. He sacrificed chickens and made a tasty pepper soup that tasted very much like Jamaican jerk chicken. Nyeye's older son, Ukennaya, was a barber in Northern Nigeria. The crisis displaced him, and he hardly recovered from it. Before the end of 1966, around November 1966, the last of our people returned to Eastern Nigeria. My newfound relatives, once we saw them all in the compound, felt that it was all good for us. Coincidentally, I was amid some older relatives and other women from the village who came to celebrate that Ukennaya was back and safe with all his children, and the women said, *"Ndi Awusa wusarou nga ha."* This was a poetic statement in rhyme that meant, in sum and substance, "Let the Awusa people be dumped in their land." The word *wusa* in my local dialect of the Igbo language means literally, to be dumped loosely in some heap.

Part of the tragedy of the Nigerian civil war is that it was fought to supposedly unite Nigeria and was the culmination of military coups that lamented and decried all forms of corruption and tribalism. From my point of view, Nigeria had been more united before the crisis and even the level and type of corruption and decadence were much less than what we have today. As I often say to people, I grew up in Nigeria when Nigeria was Nigeria. What do I mean by this?

In Nigeria before the coup, we had corruption and tribalism. Both simmered underneath and were somewhat of a nuisance, but they were nothing like what we have today: putrefaction that set in from the 1990s. As Madiebo noted, by the time of the coup in January 1966, ordinary Nigerians were getting used to each other. The ordinary people intermarried and lived and worked freely in all parts of Nigeria. I attended grade school with Nigerians from all over Eastern Nigeria and even Western and Midwestern Nigeria. I remember that my father had friends from all over Nigeria working at Umuahia. I still recollect very fondly one of those friends, a man called Mr. Okpeku. He was not an Igbo man, but he and my father did business together and probably even owned property together. My schoolmates included other Eastern Nigerians, Kalagbari, Ibibio, Efik, Yoruba, and all who spoke Igbo fluently. I also recollect Igbo schoolmates who spoke the neighboring languages very fluently, including Yoruba.

I attended the Government Secondary School Owerre with a mix of Nigerians from all over Nigeria. Their ethnic origins did not matter. Amenities were distributed equitably, based entirely and transparently on merit and equity. In those days, we had to pay to attend secondary school and even part of elementary school (the last four years). The private schools (community-funded schools, religious schools, and privately owned schools) were more expensive than the publicly funded secondary schools (Government College Umuahia, Owerre, Afikpo, Comprehensive Port Harcourt, and Queens College, Enugu for Girls). The private schools, if approved, received government grants ranging from £N3,000 to £N9,000.

In the government-funded schools at admission, five out of the sixty that were admitted receive a scholarship. At the end of the first year, five additional scholarships are awarded based on performance for the top five students. In January 1966, at the beginning of my second year, five scholarships were awarded to the incoming students. Two of the five scholarships were awarded to two students who were from Western Nigeria, both Yorubas and were cousins. This is a school that was located in the heart of Igboland. Better yet, it was after the January 1966 military coup. As the post-coup crisis wore on, even after the July 1966 coup, there was no difference in the campus atmosphere. We just carried on as students. Needless to say, things began to change after November 1966, following the mass slaughter of Igbos in Northern Nigeria and the molestation or harassment of others in parts of Western Nigeria. As a reaction to these events, Ojukwu expelled all non-Eastern Nigerians, and some Igbos extended their anger to other Nigerians who did not leave immediately or who were perceived not to be truly Igbos. I recollect that Williams, a self-described Sierra Leonian, was called *Kpanla* ("cord fish") by another student on the soccer field, but I think this was in 1967. Though Williams spoke the Yoruba language fluently, he also spoke the Igbo language well and grew up in Aba, a mere 40 miles east of Owerre where our school was located.

During this crisis, an event occurred that shocked my conscience. It illustrates how, although corruption was a known fact of life in Nigeria, it was condemned and resisted and often dealt with. Corruption was on the same level as armed robberies—like a rare occurrence. Ordinarily, there was, to a substantial extent, a good deal of merit and meritocracy. The ordinary Nigerian still expected to achieve mobility or gain access to public resources or amenities based on merit. This event that occurred only reinforced my disdain for political diplomacy—a cankerworm eating into the fabric of our society and which, over the years and especially after the civil war, took over in an odious way. In late 1965, we had a new principal called Chief Jumbo. At the beginning of each term, the school used to supply each of us with a can of yeast. We sprinkled this yeast powder into our soup and other foods, such as rice, to enhance their taste. We did our best to use the yeast parsimoniously to last throughout the term. Some of us who were a little more financially endowed arrived each term with an extra can that enabled them to lambaste their food more generously with extra yeast.

During one of the terms of 1966, the new principal decided that we would not receive our usual supply of yeast. We waited for two weeks and then in the third week, we inquired and were informed that the principal thought that the yeast supply was a needless luxury—and yet his sons came to the dining hall with privately purchased cans of yeast and openly used them. Did he mean that it was not a luxury for his sons but for the rest of us it was?

On the morning of the third week, while we were assembled after the morning parade and inspection, the principal was about to commence announcements and instructions when one of the school prefects (a senior boy) sneezed in a manner that sounded like, "YEAST." Then another school prefect and then another. The principal responded by saying, "Stop that!" With that, the same perfect or another prefect sneezed again, "YEAST! YEAST! YEAST!" The principal responded next by dismissing the teaching staff. After dismissing the staff, the principal warned us about the consequences of disobedience. If the principal had expected us to cower, he was sorely disappointed. In response to his warning, there was now a loud and concerted chant of "YEAST! YEAST! YEAST! YEAST!" It was an endless, scintillating chorus and the principal realized that he could not stop us.

For me this was shocking. I had this naïve feeling that there was corruption, but it was not this bad. For example, during my first year in the boardinghouse, we heard that the Eastern Nigerian government was distributing scholarships. The scholarship was supposedly merit-based—merit of some kind. We also heard openly that people received the awards if their parents paid a bribe of £N50. How could someone hold public resources and blatantly deny us a supply of yeast that was already fully funded? Later that evening, one of the teachers, Obieke, C (One of my classmates) and I saw Mr. Osakwe, one of the teachers, pull up or step down from a pickup van with cartons of yeast by the principal's office. Obieke and I approached him, and he asked us if we had seen the principal. We said no. I do not recollect if Mr. Osakwe asked us to go and fetch the Principal in his house or said something to someone that the other person did not understand, and Mr. Osakwe called him "Ewu!" or goat. Mr. Osakwe was often nicknamed Sach by some of the senior boys. Sach was a sobriquet for people that were considered to be a little crazy in their ways and Mr. Osakwe behaved a little crazy sometimes.

The new year, 1967, began with two remarkable events: all our schoolmates from Western and Midwestern Nigeria did not return. Once again, my naïve assumptions were shocked. All through the crisis in 1966, the principal remained calm and professional in his activities in the school. There were strange intrigues inside the school. Some senior boys—upper and lower sixth boys—were accused of conspiring with the kitchen supplies staff to misappropriate and sell our food supplies. They were expelled from the school in the middle of the night and the school prefects among them were demoted. I was shocked at the inconsistency; this was the same principal that had just attempted to deny us yeast, and yet he expelled people for trying to steal our food. I am not suggesting that the culprits should not have been disciplined, but I was shocked by the inconsistency of those who are with sin and they are casting all the stones against other sinners and doing so with a straight face.

Not long after this incident, in the middle of some night in early 1967, some boys at the school went to the principal's house and poured melted bitumen into the exhaust pipe of the principal's car—a Mercury Zephyr. After this incident, there were demonstrations against the principal, and we ran amuck in the school chanting "Thief Jumbo" in place of Chief Jumbo. I think, in hindsight, that this disorder was just an extension of the tension that had gripped the country during the previous year. The police were called in to disperse us. I was continually active during the demonstrations, and I threw stones at the police. In about two or three days, the principal had replaced his Mercury Zephyr with a brand new car. Oh my God—already? That is it! He must be truly corrupt and eating our money. Cars are not cheap; how could the principal already buy a new car? I now realize that insurance still worked in Nigeria at that time and his insurance company may have replaced the car under vandalism coverage. Alternatively, the principal was an influential man, and he could have persuaded the government, legitimately, that students at the school destroyed his car for no good reason and that the government should replace his car. In any lawsuit, he could easily have won.

I was later questioned by Mr. Joseph Ukwot (Bob Joe), our mathematics teacher. He questioned me and I vehemently denied any active involvement in the riots. Bob Joe tried to play on my mind by telling me that he would bring witnesses that could testify that I was throwing stones at police. I still vehemently denied that I did anything like that. The next morning after the demonstrations, we were in the assembly hall and the principal addressed us, renouncing the demonstrations, and said that this was the typical behavior of Igbos who go around the country making trouble. This was the source of my shock about political diplomacy. Did this principal not see what was wrong with the mass slaughter of our people in Northern Nigeria? How could a living human being with a soul, a life, and blood fail to see what was wrong with the wanton mass slaughter of men women, and children, instead attributing it all to the trouble-making tendencies of the Igboman?

When we returned to school at the end of January 1967, several boys joined us from government secondary schools around the country. Okoli, A joined from Government College Ugheli. Okoli prided himself in being able to sing like Elvis Presley and imitated Elvis very well. Others who joined included Okoro, D, and Uzoegbu, C from Kings College, Lagos. I cannot remember others in higher classes. I could remember those in Class 3B and Okoli, A in Class 3A because, for some reason, I interacted with him a lot. Okoro D was a star soccer player and Bob Joe made a joke of calling him, Dandioro Okoro. Ukaegbu was humorous, or you may say in our parlance, a mischievous chap. He was a good artist—remarkable from my perspective, because I had never been a good artist myself, and at that age, I was impressed with his ability to draw so accurately. He was fond of drawing cartoons of Bob Joe on the board and mimicking Bob Joe's grunt. One day, as he was about to complete his little mischief and before he could wipe it off the blackboard, Bob Joe walked into the class and caught him red-handed. "Ukaegbu, I am gonna fiiiiix you." Needless to say, Bob Joe punished Ukaegbu with a few runs for his misbehavior. Besides poking fun at a teacher, which was rude, Ukaegbu was supposed to be seated and working quietly. Two offenses.

Another remarkable thing that happened was that despite the crisis and potential violent breakdown of the polity, the bloody counter-coup of July 1966, and the pogrom against Igbos through November 1966, new American Peace Corp teachers arrived to replace the ones whose term ended in December 1966. At the end of 1966, our American Peace Corp teachers and other foreign aid teachers whose terms had ended left the country. Mr. B. Bally (geography) and Mr. H. Briner (French) were Canadians. Both were excellent and impressive teachers who made an impression on me and motivated me to learn. Mr. and Mrs. Utroshkah (United States Peace Corp) taught me biology and English language and English literature, respectively. The Americans were replaced by Mr. John. Kitchner. Mr. Kitchner taught me chemistry, and I remember him very well. While in a chemistry lab one day, I played around with chemicals by writing chemical equations and causing explosions in the classroom. After two unheeded warnings, Mr. Kitcher sent me out of the class. On the parade ground the following Saturday, I was punished by the vice-principal of the school and placed on full detention. Mr. Ball and Mr. Brin were not replaced by foreigners. The French teacher was replaced by Mr. Anyanwu, an Igbo man.

As refugees streamed from all parts of Nigeria into Eastern Nigeria, health facilities and other social facilities started to burst at the seams. School facilities were overcrowded. In the communities, relatives accommodated others. Despite this, our people heaved a sigh of relief—we were now finally on our own and had our destiny in our hands. When my relatives returned from Northern Nigeria, the common experience that they narrated was that the battle cry of the rioters was "Araba," meaning "we should separate." As will be analyzed later, there was a clear indication that the Northerners wanted to have nothing to do with us any longer. Even for the less educated, the outlook was that we no longer belonged to Nigeria. From August 1966 through March and April 1967, efforts for peaceful or negotiated settlement were mixed with truculent rhetoric on both sides. In August, for example, Chief Obafemi Awolowo, the leader of the Western Nigerians and the Yoruba ethnic group, was released from Calabar prison. This may have given hope to our people that the Yoruba people would side with the Igbos in the event of a crisis or military conflict. I am not aware that we discussed it among ourselves on campus, however. To the extent that this was the sentiment of our parents and elders, we all probably went along with that simplistic notion of political diplomacy. Many have attributed a statement to Awolowo that he gave assurance that if the East was forced out of Nigeria, the West would follow suit. I recollect, very well, my dad making a big issue of the statement. The Igbo community was also emboldened by their interpretation of the statement and felt that they now have allies among the Yoruba ethnic community.

This naïve interpretation of political statements has for a long time been a source of resentment for Igbos against the Yorubas of Nigeria. In due course, this loaded statement will be explained. The Igbos naïvely interpreted Awolowo's loaded statement and his subsequent role and the role of the Yorubas and, in my viewpoint, such a statement did not mean what Igbos thought it meant. Therefore, Awolowo's role and the role of the Yoruba ethnic group do not amount to betrayal.

All over Eastern Nigeria, especially in Igboland, there were demonstrations against Gowon in response to the pogroms against the Igbo population in Northern Nigeria. Lt. Col. Ojukwu was relentless in rendering galvanizing speeches about the events and boasting about our ability to withstand any aggression. Demonstrators demanded *"Ojukwu nye anyi Egbe, Ojukwu nye anyi nma ka anyi gbuo Gowon,"* or that Ojukwu should give us guns and knives to kill Gowon. Gowon was the scapegoat for the pain and suffering and misfortunes of our people.

We returned to school at the end of January and, as usual, the brainy brats discussed the Aburi meeting as if we had a clue to its implications. We were happy that the crisis may well be settled peacefully. We waited expectantly for the Aburi accord to be implemented and matters to be resolved peacefully. About the end of March 1967, Ojukwu made a galvanizing speech, which revealed to us all that Gowon had reneged on the Aburi accord. Specifically, Yakubu Gowon and the federal government of Nigeria enacted a decree that implemented the Aburi accord but left out critical aspects of it, one of which was the payment of three months of salaries to federal civil servants who fled from other parts of Nigeria. The effect of this omission from the decree was devasting and critical to the eventual breakdown of trust between Eastern Nigerians and the federal government— it was taken as a clear indication of betrayal and lack of faith and caring on the part of the federal Nigerian government.

At the end of his speech, Ojukwu stated, "On Aburi we stand... No Compromise[110]." When I returned home for the first term break, my big sister and dad were big on that statement: "On Aburi we stand." I felt that the agreement, whatever it was, must have favored Eastern Nigeria and may have been a just compensation for the injustices that we suffered. My understanding was that Lt. Col. Yakubu Gowon must have flouted the agreement. It must also have been, as some of my elders interpreted it, that Ojukwu invoked and took advantage of his superior Oxford University education to outwit Col. Yakubu Gowon. Upon return from the meeting at Aburi, Gowon must have felt bamboozled and, therefore, decided to renege on the accord.

---

[110] A speech given by Lt. Col. Ojukwu, Governor of Eastern Nigeria, in March 1967. I listened to this speech myself and recollect it vividly.

With the apparent breakdown of the Aburi agreement, I observed that the Eastern Nigerian government began to recruit soldiers for a possible military conflict. Trenches in a zigzag formation were being dug around our school. The explanation given was that these would be shelters in the event of air raids. I was frightened. Could it be that this conflict could rise to the level that we would be fighting in our school premises, even if only to dodge aerial bombardment by the Nigerian Airforce? In any event, school life went on despite the tense atmosphere.

During this period, from January to March 1967, I had the opportunity to interact with my older brother, Chuks who was an athlete for his school, Government College Umuahia. On one occasion he came to play tennis in our school in a match between his school (Umuahia) and my school at Owerre. Chuks was a star tennis player. On another occasion, he came with the team from their school to play in a cricket match against our school. I was excited and immensely proud of him. I made sure that he had yeast for his food in the dining hall. I cheered him on so much that Obieke, C criticized me for supporting Umuahia instead of my school Owerre (OGSSIAN). Well, I was in a difficult position. I cheered him on because I wanted him to play well. If that meant that he would play well enough for his team to win, so be it. After all, the Umuahia team could still win, even if my brother were not on the team. I cannot recollect how the match ended. The atmosphere was tense with the war of words between Gowon and Ojukwu.

Ojukwu's initial issue was that Gowon was not the rightful person to succeed Ironsi. In Ojukwu's view, it should have been Brig. Ogundipe. At the time of the event, this very issue was not clear to me and all but irrelevant. For me, the issue was the pogrom against Eastern Nigerians. The demonstrations continued as the Eastern Nigerian government and Radio Television Kaduna in Northern Nigeria bombarded their populations with provocative propaganda. After Ojukwu's March 31 broadcast regarding the Aburi accords, Ojukwu enacted the Revenue Edict that transferred all revenues due to the federal government to the Eastern Nigerian government. Sometime in April, Ojukwu reorganized the political structure of the government of Eastern Nigeria. There used to be twelve provinces, but Ojukwu announced the creation of eight more provinces to bring the total number of provinces to twenty. I could not make sense of it, but in hindsight, as I will explain later, I think it was a halfhearted and half-witted attempt to appease certain minority groups in Eastern Nigeria, dividing and conquering.

As the war of words continued, there were undercurrents of peace initiatives. For all I knew, Igbos in particular wanted nothing but secession from Nigeria. There was anticipation and hope and dreams of an independent nation. Igbos were confident that our ethnic neighbors were on our side. After all, the injuries against our people were obvious and anyone with a conscience would see it. After a meeting of the Eastern Nigerian Consultative Assembly on May 27, 1967, the federal government enacted a decree and created twelve states in Nigeria, altering the political structure of Nigeria's administration. The tension grew and the anticipation of Ojukwu's next move grew. Would Ojukwu agree to it? If so, how are we, the people of Eastern Nigeria, to respond? If the Igbo ethnic group was sequestered into a state all our own, would we accept Gowon's creation and still allow Ojukwu to keep his power and speak for us? Following suit on Gowon's edict, on May 30, 1967, Ojukwu made a speech and declared that Eastern Nigeria would now secede from Nigeria and become the sovereign Republic of Biafra. There was jubilation that, finally, we were free from Nigeria, if even as an act of defiance and just settlement for the pogroms and Nigeria's insensitivity toward the people.

Following Ojukwu's declaration of the Republic of Biafra, the propaganda war began. Yakubu Gowon and the Nigerian government began to advise that secession should be renounced and that we should retrace our steps back to join the rest of our fellow Nigerians. For me, the secession and the sovereignty of Biafra were a fait accompli. What was the benefit of returning to Nigeria after we had finally freed ourselves from their clutches?

For me, this was a major shift in my life. I was now a Biafran, and I could refer to former Nigerians as people from a different country.

Chapter IV

NO SCHOOL WILL HAVE JOB

Secession and the Shooting War Begins

On May 30, 1967, Lt. Col. Chukwuemeka Odumegwu Ojukwu declared that the Eastern Region of Nigeria would secede from Nigeria to become the Independent Republic of Biafra. We were all jubilant. There was euphoria. We had finally responded to the mass slaughter of our people and shown our rebellion when Gowon would not give us Aburi. I can easily recollect how we glued our ears to the radio, listening for the news of the declaration.

Not long after Ojukwu declared Biafran independence, on July 6, 1967, Gowon declared what he called a limited police action. For us, Yakubu Gowon's declaration of so-called Police Action meant nothing but war. Nigerian forces attacked simultaneously at Gakem, north of Ogoja, and at Obolo Afôr, north of Nsukka. In response to Gowon's police action, Ojukwu made a speech and declared that Biafra would engage in a total war with Nigeria. Truth be told, recruitment of soldiers and officers was already taking place, at least at Owerre. I remember there being a recruitment exercise in my school, not of the secondary school students but from the general public. The war had begun. I believed that the Nigerian invasions were nonsense. How could the Nigerians hope to defeat Biafra? Biafran propaganda was strong. Radio Biafra broadcast repeatedly that gallant Biafran forces had driven the Nigerian forces back into Nigeria. The first news that I recollect was that Biafran forces had captured Oturukpo and Idah, clearly in Nigerian territory, north of Nsukka. Good for them!! I was not surprised. How could Nigerians be better than Biafrans and how could we let them unravel what we had gained?

On July 10, 1967, as we assembled in the hall in preparation for classes, we were informed that schools would be closed due to the war. We were to go home dismissed? These were the very paintings of my juvenile fears – that a war could be disruptive of my dreams. I was not surprised. I believed that when war comes, things like this might happen. For me, missing school, even for a considerable length of time, was a small sacrifice to make for the ominous possibility that we could be massacred in our beds as had happened in Northern Nigeria. Secession and the attendant sacrifice of missing school for a brief time could also just send a message that behavior such as what happened in 1966 was simply unacceptable. Maybe, this is what happens in wartime. In any event, with the Biafran forces drubbing the Nigerians, I felt that the closure of schools would be temporary and that we would return to school as soon as Biafran forces drive the Nigerian forces back into their own country.

My dad was stationed at Owerre, close to the school and just behind the police station. I packed up and put my belongings, including my books, on my head and walked home. Upon dismissal from school, I stayed at Owerre for a few days, and I left Owerre to stay with my mother at Ovim. I did nothing else except go to the farm with my mother, read my books, and glue my ears to the radio to listen to the news. I could only hope that Biafra would defeat Nigeria soon so that I could return to school. My big sister stayed with our father in Owerre. I had no particular need to stay close to my dad.

Unknown to me and the rest of the family, except our mother who was briefed, our older brother, Chukwumaeze (Chuks) had joined the Biafran Army as an officer and was commissioned as a second lieutenant. Our big brother was astute and quite boisterous, ebullient, vivacious, and any other adjectives that have similar extensions of such descriptions and connotations. He always wanted to be a military man, though he was quite a versatile person—a ladies' boy, gregarious, outgoing. Even before he left high school, he had a string of girlfriends and was bold enough to bring them home freely. As a soldier, I got the hint from one of his friends, Okpechi, that he was dating a woman from the Enugu area—a beautiful young lady. This story was later corroborated by a man from Ovim that my brother had tremendous respect for. According to Mazi Obiesie Azunna, whose father was a celebrated pioneer educator in Ovim, Chuks brought this lady to the officer's mess at the army barracks in Enugu and intimated that he would marry this lady. The lady was said to be tall and extremely pretty and later was featured to appear regularly on Ukonu's Club.[111] Chuks also intimated to Mazi Obiesie that he would never submit himself to being a prisoner of war. As a student at Government College Umuahia, where he attended high school, he joined the Cadet Officer's program where they received military training. He looked impressive in military attire, as he had this tall gait and was proud to take a picture holding his gun in a military-style uniform. Therefore, we were not surprised that he joined the Biafran Army so early during the war and became a commissioned officer.

As a young child, my brother serenaded me with war stories and cited, with confidence, how many warships fought in different battles of World War II. As a child, he was heady and had a very uneasy peace with our father. But our father respected him for his versatility. At the age of eleven, our father sent him to a boarding primary school for the last two years of primary school (the Seventh Day Adventist School at Ihie Mbosi). This school had a primary school, a secondary school, and a teacher's college. The experience transformed him completely—our father sent him to primary boarding school as a way to control his restlessness. At about age 11, he would travel on inspection tours with our dad, who was an education officer and an inspector of education. By age 14, he was able to drive the car and even make minor repairs. Even when he was probably less than fourteen years old, he was tall and lanky. I remember one day in 1961, when he was almost fifteen years old, my brother took me on a ride in our father's car. He made a mistake and we fell inside a ditch and had to be pushed out with the help of people passing by.

As a student at Government College Umuahia, Chuks showed his versatility in more ways than one. He studied technical drawing, technology, and the sciences. He constructed his electrical guitar and played music with his friends, Okpechi and Fabro. He was so fond of music that he would buy gramophone records and play them slowly to their ruination but was able to extract the lyrics from the music. He was fond of East African music—I can still remember one of them: "Siiiku tuuuwa, siiiku tuuuwa, nia ninga ange ringe, tohhh yuma gwusu, gwuuu gwuwaaa, ehhhh." Besides his electric guitar, he also built a battery transistor radio that I played throughout the war before I departed for Biafra in May 1969. The battery for the transistor radio lasted a long time, but I can recall times when it got to the point where the sound from the radio was so faint that I had to lie flat on my stomach and glued my ear to the radio to follow the news of the war.

Chuks was also a star athlete. He played lawn tennis and cricket. His best performance was in lawn tennis, a prowess he acquired from our dad who also played tennis in his own time and as a youth. In 1965 or 1966, Chuks was a runner-up in the Eastern Nigerian Tennis Championships for secondary schools. He was also a good photographer— yet another skill he inherited from our dad, who was also an avid photographer. In 1965, Chuks won first place in photography at the Eastern Nigerian Festival of the Arts. In the end, I

---

[111] *Ukonu's Club was a very popular radio and later also a television show in Eastern Nigeria before the war, during the war, and after the war.*

was not surprised at all when, in July 1967, our brother visited home from the war front. His visit from the front gave me a lot of confidence that he would simply fight the war and return. Before the war started, he had graduated high school from Government College Umuahia and sought admission to study engineering at the College of Technology in Enugu.

One day in late July 1967, our brother breezed into the house at the village wearing an impressive army uniform and the insignia of an army officer at the rank of second lieutenant. He essentially

commandeered our daddy's yellow Peugeot 403 (Plate Number EU 413) and drove around town. During the early stages of the war, Biafran soldiers were paid regularly. The salary of an army officer was that of a university graduate, about £N60 per month. That was big money. Our mother received regular allotments of £N20 per month from our brother's salary. This was a lot of money at that time when the Biafran pound was still backed by the Nigerian pound. In July, when Chuks entered the compound, he gave £1 each to all the grown women in the Egbe family compound. There was dancing and rejoicing, and the women sang and asked, "E nyêrê'M kâ'M nye onye," meaning "Was this money given to me to give to who?" Of course, the money, £1, was a lot of money for the women because they had never earned that kind of money in one day.

Chuks visited home again in September 1967, November 1967, January 1968, and March 1968, regularly every two months. For us, this had become regular anticipation. Therefore, we waited for him in May 1968 and July 1968. By his visit in November 1967, he had become a full lieutenant and carted an AK-47 semi-automatic assault rifle. When we did not see Chuks in May 1968 or July 1968, we only prayed and hoped that all was well. In or about June 1968, I wrote a letter to him with the expectation that he would respond. He was commander of the "C" Company of the Third Battalion of the S Brigade of the Biafran Army. During his last three visits—in November 1967, January 1968, and March 1968—he was in the company of his "batman" (aide-de-camp; ADC). We never knew his name, however, sometime during the last week of April or early May 1968, his ADC visited us and gave us a message that our brother asked our mother to give him (our brother) £10 from the allotment money. This gave us confidence that our brother was still alive. I am not certain whether he showed us a letter. My mother believed him and happily handed over the requested money. We never saw the ADC again. Sometime in June, as I was visiting the family compound from my residence at the marketplace, the wife of one of my uncles walked frantically and expectantly away from the square, toward me, and told me that there was a letter for me and that I should go and read it. I went into our house and obtained the letter. It turned out to be the letter that I wrote to my brother, returned to me as undeliverable. I was unphased by the return of the letter, though in hindsight it should have been the first hint to me that our brother must have fallen in action. If our mother reached a conclusion, she did not show it. But I dismissed the return of the letter as inconsequential. I simply thought of the possibility that our brother was deployed to another sector of the war.

The war wore on. I remained at Ovim and simply woke up each morning and read the newspapers and listened to the news. In late July 1967, the Nigerian Army attacked and invaded Bonny on the Western Coast of Biafra and the oil export terminal. The Biafran Army recaptured Bonny shortly after and kept the Nigerian Army from capturing Port Harcourt. The menace of the Nigerian Army around Bonny made it difficult for Biafra to import goods from the outside world, a fact that soon began to bite.

And so it happened that, about September 6, 1967, there was an announcement over the radio that we would return to school. Meanwhile, Nigerian forces had occupied Bonny Island, they had almost recaptured the Midwest that Biafran forces had occupied on August 9, 1967, and they were making good progress toward Enugu. I packed up my belongings, books, and all, and prepared to return to school. I could not have expected better. How could the Nigerian vandals keep us from school? With the announcement, my father came to Ovim to take me back to school. We were still in my dad's car, in and around Emekuku, when the announcement came over the radio that the order to return to school had been rescinded. I was disappointed and my father took me to our house in Owerre. After a few days, he took me back to Ovim.

1967 – September to October – I am a Chemist

Shortly after we arrived back in Ovim, my father approached me, saying that I had sufficient knowledge of science and chemistry to take over the drug store that he had opened for my mother at the marketplace. Honestly, his confidence in me was not for a moment misplaced. I was a Class Three student at Government College Owerre by the time the war started. Within two days, I went to the Oriendu Market and informed the curious young man who manned the store that he was fired. Indeed, before March/April 1967, I had never approached that drug store. Once or twice that I went there at the marketplace, the young man would be sitting outside the store. I felt that he was somewhat derelict. I never inquired about his credentials to manage a drug store. But I asked no questions. On the day that I went to the place to fire him, once more, he was sitting outside the store in his wrapper cloth and was drinking some palm wine by the tinker's shed. I called him and informed him that he no longer had a job. It was early in the morning. I did not give him a day to prepare. I took inventory just as my older brother had kept meticulous inventories and an inventory book that I took over. By late afternoon, the young man left the store and raised no objections. I did not give him a reason, nor did I think that I owed him one.

The Oriendu had been modernized from early 1960, in part as part of an OCL (Ovim Community League) initiative. My dad was instrumental in the leadership of the OCL that put the initiative together. One of the things that he did was set up this medicine store for my mother. The store had all kinds of modern medicine. There were antibiotics (Terramycin and tetracycline), pain killers, first aid materials like bandages (plaster in Nigeria), iodine, hydrogen peroxide, morning-after contraceptives, and even abortion pills (Dr. Bonjean's pills: sugar-coated green oval, and Apiol and Steel pills: sugar-coated white hexagonal), pain killers, anti-malaria prophylactics and therapeutics, condoms, and the cure-all May Baker (M & B) pills, among others. The store was a semi-detached unit, with two chambers. The front chamber was the store with shelves and a little space for customers to discuss their business with the store clerk. The inner chamber was a sleeping room for the store clerk. There was also a fenced (thatch) backyard with a little kitchen shed for the store clerk and also a pit toilet (outhouse). Whoever manned the store took care of themselves in every other respect the way most Nigerians did at that level of development.

Life at the marketplace was routine, lived one day at a time. My closest friend was my cousin Okechukwu, the son of my great uncle. He ran his father's general store across from my medicine store. We did little else than sell what was in the store and collect revenues for our parents. On one or two occasions, we closed the doors of the stores and went fishing. I caught little fish only a few times on those trips. Sometimes we bought and set fish traps, other times we used hooks. During the early stages of the war, we noticed that prices were rising, and inventory was declining. For me, the signal to restock the store and raise prices was when a customer came into my store and asked for the price of one bottle of Aspro (the aspirin-based pain killer). I gave him a price based on what my big brother had set before he joined the army. Promptly following him, Okoronkwo Mgbo from my village, who had been sitting by the door of my store, asked that I set aside one bottle for him. I promptly raised the price for the next customers and kept away the remainder of the inventory. A few days later, Okechukwu and I went to Umuahia, twenty miles away to purchase more supplies for our store. I traveled with a big carton and loaded it up with supplies. I made the trip a second time in the company of Oso Nde from Ama Akwu in the Obayi section of Ovim later in 1967 or early 1968. The remarkable thing about that particular trip was the difficulties that were beginning to set in. I traveled with a carton, as in the first trip, but returned with limited stock to replenish the inventory. It ended up being good, though, because we could not find transportation back to Ovim and had to walk the twenty miles on foot, carrying my few purchases in the carton. On another occasion, we traveled to Isiagu to buy goods of all kinds, including dried Nchi or bush rabbit (which was a giant rodent) and fish. I bought a few things, but I was not that kind of trader to buy goods and retail them in the local marketplaces. Therefore, I probably ended up eating quite a bit of what I bought over time.

I interacted with practically everyone who lived around my store. The semi-detached unit that contained my store was part of a long building that had four stores in it: my drug store, the tailor (Anyalewechi of Ndi Ekwu'ukwu), Sondi the photographer from Ohonja, and Jeniya who kept what may have been a bar. Opposite the building was my great uncle's general store and my uncle Kanu's bar and restaurant. The tinker shed of a man from Ohoroho and Mazi Ukeje of Usaja, father of Aja, was a little to the left on the opposite side. In a small building to the west of our store was, initially, a grinding mill for corn operated by Igwe, a man from Umuahia. Igwe was called "Idea," and when we asked him why, he explained that he had been a mechanic sometime in the past. It happened that a problem arose with a vehicle for which no one had a solution for a considerable amount of time until he came up with a great idea. His idea resolved the problem, earning him the nickname "Idea" among his fellow mechanics and apprentices. Igwe eventually left the marketplace to be replaced in the building by Ogbonna Ndi'isi of Ndi Ugbo, near Ndi Ekwu'ukwu. Ogbonna worked and lived with Ada, a young lady that he would eventually marry. The tinker made pots and pans in his shed. He was a diminutive man who worked with a young apprentice from Amune, Ovim, whom we called Agent 007, and another young apprentice called Nweke, a refugee from Ugbo'oka, near Enugu. They joined him in the marketplace after the fall of Enugu in October 1967. Finally, there was Azik, the photographer, and his brother, both from Umudinja. These people moved into the marketplace after the fall of Enugu, not long after I moved in there myself. Enugu fell into Nigerian hands on October 4, but the evacuation of Enugu began to occur late in September of 1967. Finally, there was a trader called Ogbuagu. He was probably from Ezere but married to a rather attractive young woman. He owned a store on the promontory on the rising section of the hill leading to Elugwunta at the intersection of the road leading to Umudinja. He also has a store assistant called Chileme. At some point, there was gossip that he had taken his assistant on trips and had an affair with her. On one occasion the young girl came to my shop and lingered for a while as other girls did, and I figured that she was probably waiting for the other customers to depart. I was right. When the customers departed, I let her into the inner chamber of the store and sold Apiol and Steele or Dr. Bonjean's pill to her; A morning-after birth control or, you may say, an abortion pill.

There was a friendly atmosphere and we lived together as a community at Oriendu. Sunny the photographer was a congenial man and did his business very simply. The elderly man among us was Mazi Ukeje of Usaja. Everyone accepted his leadership and guidance. One day, Mazi Ukeje assembled us and proposed that we all swear an oath of mutual respect and protection, so to speak. When we assembled the following day, kola nuts were cut into small pieces and placed in a bowl. Mazi Ukeje made incantations, poured libations to God and our ancestors, invoked the rites, and finally poured some of the palm wine on the kola nuts. He asked, in part, that we should all pick one piece of the kola nut and pledge that no one should bring harm to another person in the neighborhood among us, scheme to bring harm, conceal any schemes of conspiracies that any person should witness against another member of the community, and anything else he thought was necessary. We all did as we were asked. However, Azik, another photographer from Umudinja, declined to participate. Later, he volunteered to me that he did not want to participate because it would not be right for people to hurt other people or do something bad to another person and then propose the swearing of oaths. I said nothing to Azik, as I had no idea the basis of what he was saying. I did not ask for elaboration. At that age, I did not think it was wise to ask for details. In any event, I found it interesting.

In all of this and at this stage of the war, my mind was focused entirely on going back to school at a moment's notice. I was confident that we would win the war very soon. After all, we had captured the Midwest so swiftly. Somehow, we would recapture it soon. Biafran propaganda was not making my illusions any better, although we were steadily losing territory. The tailor also was very congenial. He had two half-brothers from a polygamous family. In 1968, he married a light-skinned girl named Comfort, and they had a baby sometime in 1968. There was a lot of excitement those days, especially with some of those surprises that come with new fatherhood—the behavior of babies and God's miracles. I recollect one day, the tailor observed that babies feed on breast milk that is whitish or cream-colored, yet their poop takes the "orange or red color" of their mother's food. I was also astonished at that biological process.

I did my business very simply. I interacted respectfully, according to our traditions, with everyone. Of course, I had name recognition to some extent with everyone since families at Ovim were easily identifiable. Customers had confidence in me and approached me with their medical concerns or asked for interpretations of dosages for medication. I was able to read the medical indications and provide advice on dosages for all medications. On contraceptives, the boys came and purchased prophylactic condoms, and the girls approached me to purchase the "morning after" abortion pills. They would come and linger around as if they did not know what they wanted, especially if there was another customer around. I would figure out what they wanted and either asked them to wait or eventually brought them across the counter to provide confidentially for their needs. Occasionally, a customer would ask for a fresh wound to be dressed using the "first aid" kit that I stocked. I would wash the wound with hydrogen peroxide, which bubbled and cleansed most fresh wounds, and then drop some iodine on it and then gauze and "plaster." Indeed, more than forty years later, a person from Ndi Ugbo, who was somewhat younger than my fifteen years in 1967, told me that he remembered me: he had had a scrape on his leg and I treated him successfully.

Besides the soldiers that invited me to write a settlement, Biafran soldiers confronted my "uncle" Kanu. As the war progressed, imported goods became scarce as a result of the economic blockade imposed by the Nigerian government. However, smugglers were still able to import goods through the Cameroons. My uncle Kanu was one of those enterprising and fearless persons. I do not believe that he engaged in smuggling, but whoever smuggled goods into Biafra, my uncle was among those who knew where to obtain the goods. He was also brash and outspoken. His straight and fearless talk earned him a lot of respect but may equally have made enemies. This probably accounts for what happened to him later in the war. Specifically, around April or May 1969 after the Nigerian Army captured Ovim and we returned from our hideouts to our villages, my bold "uncle" left his house, enterprising as he was, to reach out to the Nigerian Army. He had his pot of palm wine on his head—a man full of confidence and diplomatic skills. But he never came back. For a long time and even after the war, there was endless speculation as to what happened to him and why. We waited all day and for several days. We hoped that he may have been detained for questioning and probably would be released at some point. After a few days, news came that he had been killed by Nigerian soldiers. What was their reason? What did he do? Up until today, I believe that someone betrayed him. He was short of neither friends nor enemies. Alternatively, he was killed out of frustration by Nigerian soldiers who probably had a bad day on the battlefield with Biafrans. Whatever happened, may his soul rest in peace.

For now, it happened that someday Biafran soldiers came to his restaurant and found goods that were now scarce and generally no longer found anywhere. This was in October 1967. There was Fanta, Pepsi-Cola, Heineken beer, and other assorted restaurant goods. "Where did you come by these kinds of goods under these conditions of scarcity and deprivation?" asked the soldiers. Mgbo Kanu responded that he bought them. "From who?" the soldiers pressed. Mgbo Kanu responded that it should not matter. The soldier, still in shining military uniform at that early stage of the war, proceeded to count the cartons of soft drinks, stacked almost to the ceiling, "One, two, three..." Mgbo Kanu immediately quacked the soldier, bouncing him off, gun and all! "...What grubs my stomach is for this man to come in my shop to count... one, two, and three... Who are you...?" My uncle slammed the door behind the soldier. I cannot recollect exactly what may have followed except that none of the goodies left Kanu's business premises on that day. In my opinion, at that time, I could not understand why it was the soldier's business to question how my uncle acquired normal business stocks. This event is characteristic of the governance style in Nigeria and much of underdeveloped post-colonial Africa. This governance style of displaying power was equally, the harbinger and precursor to events that characterized the relationship between the Biafran military and civilian population throughout the war. As much as our people endured, it was also indicative and instructive of our people's resilience and determination to face hardships, deprivation, and degradation just to make the point that if we are rejected, we were willing to suffer.

Mgbo Kanu was equally a bold, gregarious, jovial, fearless, and humorous man. On another day, I was over by his restaurant listening to Biafrans tell stories of the progress of the war. This was in 1967, so things were still going fairly well. But a man came by and changed the topic. "What happened?", my uncle asked. There were these two women at the railway station, well known to Mgbo Kanu and the storyteller, and one or two other persons in the crowd, listening to the story. The two women fought, cursed each other out, and battered themselves. So, what next? They beat up on each other and stripped each other naked and fell all over the place and even spread their legs. My uncle asked, "…so you mean you saw everything in and out and all the hair?…" Of course, it was entertaining. "… Entertaining? … Now, get the hell out of here… You mean you were there and feasted your eyes and you come here to tease me and everyone else with your juicy story…".

I can recollect several remarkable and interesting incidents and events that occurred between September 1967 and March 1969, when the Nigerian Army occupied Ovim. I remember a man who bought old money and elephant tusk, and another man that came to the marketplace to sell what he called Biafran Omo (a detergent). There was also the time a crazy man came into the marketplace at the tinker's shed. The crazy man claimed that he was building a hovercraft that could be used to attack enemies behind the lines—a story that ironically sounded like Bernard Odogwu's story[112] about Col. Steiner, except that Steiner was an experienced and educated soldier and this man at Oriendu, at best, completed two years of elementary school. However, Odogwu's description of Steiner's proposed craft for "Operation Capture Gowon", described a little later in this chapter, was not different from what this madman was putting together. I can only conclude that Steiner had lost his sanity, or he believed that he could fool a bunch of illiterate Africans. The hardships that the war would bring began to set in discernibly by November 1967.

However, our people, who had not lived much better than our ancestors from the late nineteenth century, resiliently bore it and simply hoped that things would improve. My uncle Kanu was a baker at the railway station before the war started, and I remember that he had a "modern" bakery that had impressed me. In late 1966, my mother sent me to purchase ten loaves of bread from him at the bakery. We could afford to buy that many loaves at a time. We were equally numerous in the household—my mother had nine children. When I arrived at the bakery, I saw that the dough was rolled mechanically, and the oven was huge (based on what I knew about ovens). The usual wholesale deal for bakers then was that they tossed in two extra loaves if you bought ten loaves—to provide a profit for street vendors—but Kanu gave us three extra loaves. That was good. Being a good boy, I did not eat the one extra that I received. However, as resources dried up, Mr. Kanu quickly invested in setting up a bar and restaurant at the Oriendu market adjacent to where my great uncle (my mother's uncle and guardian) had his general store. Such enterprising behavior characterized our people's response to the hardships of the war.

Some of the hardships were difficult to conceal. For example, newspapers were no longer available. The last time I read a newspaper, about August or September 1967, it was published on sheets of paper taken from a classroom exercise book. In the same vein, sometimes about November 1967 or early 1968, a man appeared at the marketplace, purporting to sell what he represented as Biafran Omo. Omo was the brand name of the usual granular laundry detergent we used, whereas the other brand was Surf. Omo was blue in color. To prove himself, the man took a small sample and dissolved it in water, and showed that it lathered like a normal detergent. It was also blue in color like the Omo that people knew. I was impressed. In hindsight, I suspect that the industrial producers of the laundry detergent at Aba ran out of resources to import the materials for making their product

---

[112] *Benard Odogwu, No Where to Hide: Crisis and Conflict Inside Biafra, Pp. 115 – 17*

and so some managers sold the liquid stage of the product to this dealer, whereas Omo was usually granular. The man did not come again during the next market day—eight days later. A few market days later, this man came back and Azik the photographer came out and told me that this man did not have anything that could be called Omo. As he put it, what the man was selling was nothing but potassium ferricyanide and that he probably bought the liquid materials from Aba or Onucha." Azik was a photographer and simply tested the chemical in his film processing unit. Ordinarily, potassium ferricyanide is used in photography. A related compound, potassium ferrocyanide also has a blue color. I could not say what exact compound this vendor had, but, to me, the event was remarkable in that it was indicative of the beginning of a long and difficult road.

The Oriendu market usually congregated every eight days on Oriê Ntâ (Little Orie). I took interest in a man who came regularly on the big market day to buy old money. He bought copper bars for sixpence and elephant tusks. He impressed me with his antics and sales pitch, and he was different from the usual marketplace tricksters—the ones that offered to double your money or quasi-lotteries. The money doublers would usually come with some small cylinder-shaped wraps that they claimed contained money. If you bet sixpence, you could get money depending on your luck. On one occasion, I saw them play the trick of demonstrating how much money a person could potentially make, and a man bet three pence and was asked to select one of the wraps. When the bettor opened the wrap, he saw two shillings inside. What a lucky man! Of course, they warned you that there was no guarantee of how much you could win. Another man bet one penny and opened his wrap and found one shilling and sixpence. Wow!! This was looking good.

Then came a woman who bet sixpence and opened her wrap and found only two pennies. She burst out crying because she now could not buy the crayfish that she needed for her cooking. These people came regularly for several market days but then stopped. I suspect the story went around that the people who won money were simply part of their gang, for they stationed themselves at different locations in the marketplace on the same day. But back to the buyer of old money. Usually, his sales pitch sounded much like that of the tricksters. He offered to buy your elephant tusk for so much. However, he said this thing that tickled or amused me. He essentially provided a statement of full disclosure, to ensure that there was no doubt about his business dealings. As he put it in sum and substance, "I like to make things clear in my dealings… for that reason, I do not try to copulate with a woman that is asleep, lest she is a dead person. When the time comes, I will nudge my partner and if she were to ask me, what the matter is, I would alert her that the friendly monster is ready to befriend her…" In effect, he was saying, "If you present what you say is an elephant tusk, we will agree on the price, and I will set the money aside. I will then slice the tusk at the tip. If the color is right, I will pay the agreed price. If not, I will return your product to you. The damage to whatever you presented to me is yours." In the end, it will be like cooking an egg in water. When all is said and done, the water will go its way and the egg will go its way. No quarrels and no complaints.

We usually congregated around the tinker's shed to tell stories and discuss the war. All kinds of stories were told. A major problem of the Biafra war for us Biafrans was the lack of weapons for the war. Our people were resilient, enduring and hopeful to the very end. They were equally naïve and ill-informed about the requirements for modern warfare—I am referring now to the ordinary man in the village with limited or no education. By early 1968, it was becoming clear that the war would not be a quick victory against the incompetent "Awusa" people. It was equally common knowledge that the setbacks we were suffering were due to a lack of weapons. However, hope stayed alive. Suggestions were made during conversations that Ojukwu should pledge the oil wells to get help. Others, even people in the village with limited knowledge, spread the story that weapons were on the way and so there should be continued hope. One day, there was a man around the tinker's shed assuring everyone that he had news that weapons were on the way from China. Everyone turned and asked how soon the weapons were expected. The man certainly had no concept of geography. He promptly assured everyone that the huge ship was currently docked in Lagos and would be proceeding to Port Harcourt in a few days. Both Port Harcourt and Calabar were still in Biafran hands. I promptly responded that a shipload of armaments destined for Biafra could not be docked in Lagos—in enemy territory. It would not make sense. I also pointed out that a ship from China would not need to be traveling through Lagos, because it would not make sense. A ship from China would simply travel directly from South Africa and straight into Calabar. The storyteller promptly told me to shut up. "You are a small child, what do you know?" I kept quiet and left the place.

On another occasion at the tinker's shed, a man was bending and joining wires and probably asking for the tinker to allow him to weld the wires together at the joints. What was he building, we all inquired? The man claimed that he was constructing a craft that was able to fly quietly and would be deployed behind enemy lines and would enable Biafran soldiers to attack and defeat Nigeria. Remarkably, he claimed that his first experiment was successful. The last he flew it, the craft landed in a cocoyam patch behind their family house. However, the craft that he was constructing was no wider than a dining room chair and had no props, no engine, and no roof. I wondered how the craft would fly, given my knowledge of technology and science. Equally remarkable was the fact that some people around believed him. He then left, saying he was going to collect additional materials. The following day, I went to the tinker and asked if the man came back. The tinker promptly responded to me, saying that the man was crazy. I told the tinker that I thought as much. The moral of this story goes to the level of desperation that our people experienced. As said earlier, Bernard Odogwu told a similar story. Remarkably, Odogwu's description was like this madman's story, with the exception, as said earlier, that Steiner was well-versed in warfare, famous to boot, and also exposed to Western technology and education.

November to December 1967: Life in the Marketplace

Growing up as a child, I had heard some horrible and degrading stories about prostitutes. Around October or November 1967, while I manned the store at Oriendu, I had one of the most curious experiences I could imagine, at that age, regarding a prostitute. The story that I am about to tell confirmed my worst imagination about prostitution and prostitutes. The war was still in the romantic stage. Biafran soldiers still returned home in shiny uniforms. I was the chemist manning the medicine store that my mother had at the Oriendu marketplace.

One afternoon, I was called out by a soldier—a sergeant of the Biafran Army. The soldier asked me if I could read and write. I replied that I could read and write very well, as I had been in Class 3 (tenth grade according to American standards) before the war started, and a precocious young man for my age. The matter was about a physical confrontation between a young man, probably in his early to mid-twenties, and a pregnant woman. A young pregnant woman, about seven months pregnant with a visibly protruding and heavy-looking stomach. The sergeant intervened to settle the matter, for the simple reason that the young man would not let the pregnant woman go. Meanwhile, no one seemed to care. I was asked to be a witness and to draft a settlement between the man and the pregnant woman, which I did. I later told my friends Nnabuchi and Dibango the story and they told me that, if they were in my position, they would not have agreed to write the settlement agreement. What was the matter?

The young man claimed that the pregnant woman owed him ten shillings change from prior sexual service in Enugu, where he had given the now-pregnant woman one pound. Where did this happen? The man stated that the woman was a prostitute at the hotel where Celestine Ukwu, the musician, performed. The woman agreed that she provided sexual services to the man, promising to return the change to the man because she did not have change at the time of the transaction. But neither the soldiers nor the man could read or write fluently or well enough to draft a settlement in English. I was invited to write the settlement and I agreed. Of course, I had pen, paper, ink, and carbon paper to make a duplicate copy for each of the parties. I asked for the names of the parties and where they came from. I proceeded to draft an agreement that both parties agreed to, which included the pregnant woman's admission that she owed the balance and a promise to pay the man. Whether she eventually paid or not, I never found out. In the end, I was shocked that the man would be so bold as to confront a woman in the marketplace, admitting that he had received sexual services from a prostitute or that he would sink so low as to demand the money in the marketplace. I was equally shocked that the woman admitted that she was in such a trade. With my conservative attitude at that age, I that age, I also wondered how a man would agree to marry such a woman, as she also said that she was now married.

In as much as I had a derogatory attitude toward prostitutes, I equally despised men who visited them. Indeed, I was so conservative growing up that I also despised people who ate food in restaurants, which we called "hotels" at that time. When I was about nine or ten years old, we lived at Umudike in Umuahia. Frequently, I would find myself on the paved road leading from Umuahia township to Ikot Ekpene, thirty-two miles away. One day, I happened to be on that road, adjacent to where our primary school was located. Men were working on the road—a road gang of common laborers. Some of the men had roasted yams, cocoa yams, and salted palm for their lunch. There was of course a woman who walked around with the cooked food that she was selling by the wayside for the men, whoever was interested. This was common practice at that time. Two of the working men approached the woman and asked for garri (foo foo made from grated cassava that is called farina in the West Indies) for two pence and meat for one penny, for a total of three pence. One of the men then asked her to take the meat out and give him more garri for an additional penny. It saw this happen and my conclusion was that these were decadent men. I stood there and made sure that I could bear witness that they did it—I mean to eat food that was not cooked at home and waste that much money on "hotel" food. They must be bad and wayward fathers. However, it never crossed my mind that my dad was usually out of town on business (an inspector of education who went on tour a lot of times and may have had to eat food that was not cooked in the house). On all the occasions that I traveled with him, we lived in rest houses and cooked food in the rest house. But what about those times that he traveled alone? How did he eat? In any event, as I was there, I calculated that each man might have spent their three pence on crayfish that would have made enough soup for all their children. I had no idea if they had children or if they were married—in my mind, they were just decadent. My attitude was such that I adamantly refused to eat in any restaurant until I was caught up in the war myself at age 17 and found myself in difficult situations. So long for my life in the marketplace. I will narrate more of it as the war wore on.

Chapter V

JULY TO SEPTEMBER 1967
THE TRUE SHAPE OF THINGS

Are You Seeing What I am Hearing?

The war officially began on July 6, 1967. The Nigerian Army attacked in Gakem Ogoja, northeast of Biafra, and at Obolo Âfôr near Nsukka, in the north of Biafra. According to Gowon, the operation was in the form of police action—a form of highly limited military action intended to send a message that the Nigerian government was serious about forcing the Eastern Nigerians to return to Nigeria. However, the operation was carried out by a brigade of soldiers armed with artillery and armored cars. Though the Biafrans were determined, its government under Ojukwu was inadequately prepared and probably underestimated the determination of the Nigerian Government as well as their level of military preparedness and force. Though the Nigerians were far better prepared than the Biafrans, the level of force that they had was not adequate to overcome the level of determination of the Biafrans. Similarly, the Biafran military arsenal could not keep the Nigerians away.[113]

Biafran propaganda made it difficult for us to know the exact situation and effectively hid the truth of what was happening on the war fronts. Of course, this happens in every war. However, in the case of Biafra, our people were so determined to defend themselves and felt so aggrieved that they believed that providence was on our side and even the spirits of justice and world opinion would help us win the war. There was also misguided confidence that we were better than Nigerians. Therefore, we easily and quickly believed much of what we were told. Whenever the propaganda was confounded, we convinced ourselves, thanks to our belief perseverance, that the situation would eventually be reversed.

According to Alexander Madiebo,[114] "the enemy attack began at Gakem on July 6, 1967, with two battalions (approximately 750 strong per battalion or 1,500-armed infantry, excluding administrative staff) of soldiers preceded by three ferret cars, a Saladin and a Land Rover on which was mounted a 106 RR anti-tank gun that rained bullets in all directions and knocked down the mud huts of the village... The Biafran forces faced the two battalions of Nigerian forces with four platoons (21 soldiers per platoon) of soldiers. In effect 42 Biafran soldiers against 600 Nigerian soldiers – well armed with heavy artillery." Based on Madiebo's account, the Nigerian soldiers were routed because the Biafrans bypassed the armored cars and the anti-tank gun on a Land Rover. Furthermore, the Biafrans captured a prisoner whom Madiebo described as a boor that muttered to himself that the Biafran's were armed and that no one could stop them.[115] In a counterattack, the Nigerians engaged the Biafrans in a heavy bombardment, and "For some reason, enemy guns opened a heavy bombardment of their troops and also on Biafran troops ... The troops got mixed and scattered in all

---

[113] *See Major General Alexander Madiebo, The Nigerian Revolution and the Biafra War, Enugu, Fourth Dimensions Publishers, 1980, PP 123-143 & PP 145, 148 & 154.*

[114] Ibid *PP. 123 – 143*

[115] *Ibid, P. 126.*

95

directions ... the Biafrans running south and the Nigerians running north ... As the enemy resumed heavy shelling of Gakem ... There was no question of counter bombardment for there were no guns or mortars available to us (the Biafrans)."[116]

At Obudu, in Ogoja, and near Gakem, "The enemy attacked with a ... battalion ... The shelling was heavy... and the (Nigerian) infantry was beaten back ... From then on, all the enemy did was shell our (Biafran) position ... We could not shell them back neither could we go into the offensive because of our inadequacy in equipment, communication and ... support." In the Nsukka sector, "the enemy (Nigerians) had pounded their way through Okutu town and ... the enemy had bypassed all the obstacles with armored vehicles ... and Brigadier Njoku was very unhappy ... because he had failed to convince Ojukwu to disclose to him where all the weapons were hidden ... He (Njoku) could not plan and issue any reasonable orders... On the 4th day of battle (July 10, 1967), Nsukka had fallen, and the enemy was at Eke, 12 miles from the capital of Biafra."[117]

Once more, according to Madiebo[118] "...The support for the First Battalion (Biafran Army) was impressive by our (Biafran) standards ... There were two 81mm guns and three 3-inch guns with 68 and 100 rounds of ammunition, respectively ... At exactly 05:30 AM, the (Biafran) mortars opened ... and made a terrifying impact on the enemy ... In less than ten minutes, the mortars were exhausted, and soon the enemy counter bombardment began with two artillery guns and about eight 81 mm mortars..." (Page 135). "... On July 30, 1967 (Madiebo, Pp. 139 -141), Eke came under heavy artillery ... for 30 minutes and then stopped ... When the commanding officer (Biafran, Major Amadi) recovered from his daze, he ordered the Tampella mortars to ... fire the remaining ten rounds of Biafran shells... When this happened, the enemy shells also stopped completely, and it seemed that the enemy infantry assault would (follow) immediately ... When this did not happen, our force of two companies advanced to ... contact ... the enemy ... What we saw ... The whole enemy force, numbering several hundred, was seen scampering away in all directions in absolute confusion ..." Madiebo[119] further explains that the Biafran forces captured several Nigerian soldiers, including the commander, who explained that the Nigerian contingent had fired off five hundred rounds of ammunition in less than thirty minutes and stopped. It was at that point that the Biafran troops began firing their leftover ten rounds of shell bombs. Little did the Nigerian officer know that the few shells that the Biafran contingent fired were all they had.

The pathetic lack of Biafra's preparation and, to a degree, even Nigeria, is rendered by P. J. Odu.[120] Odu was an operational officer of the Biafran Navy who had been in the Nigerian Navy and managed to hijack a Nigerian Navy ship during the runup to the war. According to Odu,[121] "Unfortunately, if there had been an overall strategy for the Defense of Biafra, we in the Navy were not aware of it ... Perhaps, it had not occurred to the leaders of Biafra that ... Nigerian forces could squeeze Biafra from the north as well as from the south ... Not only that but the matter of naval intelligence was also overlooked completely." The invasion of Bonny, an island near Port Harcourt to the south of Biafra, began around July 25, 1967. Odu[122] describes the event very well. "On July 25, [1967]... I could see that an assault was being made on Bonny by three Nigeran Navy ships accompanied by a troopship ... The largest of the Nigerian ships was the NNS Ogoja ... a naval vessel with a 3-inch gun ... under the command of Akin Aduwo ... As we came into view the ship detached and fired a few volleys at me ... I opened fire with my comparatively puny Bofors anti-aircraft gun ... The gun jammed and ... I devised a maneuver... By the time I did this maneuver three times I had drifted ... into shallow waters ... Having thus been beached, my ship became a fixed target for the enemy ... We were only a few yards from the riverbank, and I ordered the crew to abandon ship[123]." With

---

[116] *Madiebo, Op. Cit.*

[117] *Ibid, P. 131*

[118] *Madiebo, The Nigerian Revolution and the Biafran War, P. 133*

[119] Madiebo, The Nigerian Revolution, Pp. 140 – 41

[120] Peter J. Odu, The Future that Vanished: A Biafra Story, Thorough Fare, NJ, Xlibris Publishing, 2009

[121] Ibid, Pp. 124 – 25.

[122] Peter Odu, Op. Cit. Pp. 114 – 118

[123] Peter Odu, Op. Cit, Page 115

this event, the Nigerian Army occupied Bonny on July 27, 1967. However, Odu continues, "Typical of the planning on both sides ... the Nigerian Navy did not think to press their advantage ... If they had steamed up the Bonny River that day, they would have occupied Port Harcourt without firing a shot ... As it was, the Nigerian Army settled in Bonny and while they sought to consolidate their hold, we found time to prepare our defenses."

All in all, by the end of July 1967, less than thirty days after the war began, the Nigerian Army had captured much of Biafran territory across the Northern boundaries and had also attacked by the sea at Bonny, south of Biafra. Indeed, a good deal of the job of capturing Biafran territory was achieved during the first week of the war. Madiebo's rendition makes clear that Biafra did not have the materials to hold Nigerians back, and P. J. Odu, the operations officer of the Biafran Navy, agrees.

Odu gives further insight into the woeful and damnable preparation of the Biafran leader and his cronies. Odu describes the blockade of Biafra and later the invasion of Calabar, west of Port Harcourt. According to Odu "All this propaganda about the blockading of Port Harcourt was meant for the consumption of our foreign friends ... The fact is that I have not sighted any naval vessels within 20 miles of Bonny ... But we do continue to receive ships ... Those vessels that dare to will continue to deliver supplies ... To maintain a steady patrol outside the Bonny estuary would require a plan ... that the Nigerian Navy is quite prepared for." In an apparent reference to a conversation with a senior officer, Odu continues, "Perhaps we should think in terms of a ruse to attract the [Patrol] ship close enough ... to rake the upper deck and capture the ship ... Our operation was supposed to last for 12 hours ... but after patrolling about five miles outside of the entrance of the Bonny estuary for almost 36 hours, no Nigerian navy ship showed up.[124]" Even the so-called blockade was not well equipped by Nigeria. Nevertheless, it was effective, though things did not begin to get unbearable until Nigeria's final capture of Port Harcourt in May 1968. But this does not tell the whole story of the recklessness of the Biafran adventure.

On October 13, 1967 (Odu Pp. 124 - 27), "Helicopter reconnaissance revealed two enemy warships at anchor in Bonny along with unspecified smaller vehicles ... either reinforcing or evacuating troops ... As it turned out, they were withdrawing troops for an assault on Calabar, which took place the following day ... We had reported as much to DHQ and requested any type of air assault on the numerous ships that were milling around Bonny so brazenly... We were told that nothing was available ... Unfortunately, there was nothing they could do ...Colonel Adekunle ...utilized naval bombardment to dislodge any ground resistance ... and landed one battalion and ... the landing craft steamed back and forth down the river to the passenger ships anchored there and reinforced the forces on the ground ... By the end of the day, it was over..."

The remarkable thing about this story is that "The Nigerian Navy routinely used merchant ships as troopships during the war" and that the Biafran Army or Air Force could do nothing about it. If the Biafran side had been adequately armed, even if Nigeria had superior armament or even assuming the level of preparation and the skill of warfare that the Nigerians demonstrated, the Biafran forces would have been able to keep the Nigerians at bay for a considerable length of time. Biafra might even have been able to take the battle to Nigeria very early in the war. Having essentially fought the Nigerians to a standstill at Nsukka, at least temporarily, Alexander Madiebo began planning an operation to take the war to Northern Nigeria at the end of July 1967, but it was not to happen.

The gist of all this is that the Biafran side was not prepared for war and also that the Nigerian side had underrated the Biafran determination to resist and was also inadequately prepared. If the Nigerian side had estimated that the Biafrans were determined to fight, and with a little more push from Gakem and Nsukka, they would have captured Enugu from two fronts in less than two weeks. Similarly, as Odu recounts, both the capture of Bonny and the capture of, Calabar each was achieved in one day, the moment the Nigerians arrived at each location. Biafra could not even manage to attack merchant ships that Nigeria used to transport troops.

The setbacks at Nsukka, Bonny, and Ogoja sectors were greatly demoralizing to the people around me. Based on initial Biafran propaganda, we believed that the Nigerian forces were being defeated. Indeed, during the first week of the war, while Nigerian forces had captured Gakem, Obudu, and

---

[124] Ibid, Pp. 104 – 27

Nsukka, Biafra radio gave us the impression that Biafran forces had captured Oturukpo and Idah, north of Nsukka in Nigerian territory. Shortly after these broadcasts, and in the weeks that followed, we heard the disheartening broadcasts about accomplishments of gallant Biafran forces in the Nsukka sector, the Obolo Âf̱ọr sector, and the Ogoja sectors of the war, deep inside Biafran territory. If we had captured territory north of the border of Biafra, why were we fighting at Nsukka and Ogoja, well inside Biafra? The low morale of Biafrans was to be assuaged shortly after the end of July. On August 9, 1967, quite early in the war and with the demoralizing reversals in the Northern sector of the war, we woke up to the announcement that the Biafran Army had captured the entirety of the Midwestern Region in one stroke of genius—or so we were made to understand. For me, what made the news better was that the operation was led by Lt. Col. Victor Banjo, a Yoruba man of Western Nigerian from the other side of the conflict. Wow! That must imply that the Yoruba ethnic group was on our side or at least the Yoruba man would be able to convince his people to join the Biafran side of the war. I had no idea how Victor Banjo ended up on the Biafran side of the conflict.

In any event, two weeks or so after the announcement that Biafran forces had invaded and captured the Midwest, we were informed by radio news that Biafran forces had captured Okitipupa and Ore on their way to Lagos. However, this happened around August 23, 1967. We were also informed that Biafran forces had also captured Agenebode, a border town on the banks of the Niger River. From Agenebode, it would have been easy to attack Idah, east of the Niger and north of Nsukka in Biafra. Such a move would have put pressure on the Nigerian units inside Biafran territory. I was hoping that the Yoruba people would use this opportunity to rise against Nigeria and finalize the disintegration of Nigeria and secure the independence of Biafra. But none of this happened.

The invasion of the Midwest held fast for a while and morale was high in Biafra. This singular, though eventually momentary, feat reinforced my feeling and the feelings of many ordinary people that we Biafrans were superior to Nigerians. Verily, verily, the Biafran Army had captured Okitipupa and Ore, for soon, we were hearing about battles in the Ore sector of the war. For all that I knew, the Nigerians would not stand still and see Biafra take Lagos and Ibadan without a fight—though if they did let Biafra capture Ibadan and Lagos without a fight as they did in the Midwest, that was all fine and good. Though the battles raged, I was confident that Biafra would win and eventually capture Lagos. However, the propaganda machines on both sides spewed out their rants that made the civilian population on both sides believe that all was going their way. On the Biafran side was the inimitable Oko Okon Ndem. In hindsight, Biafra should credit Oko Okon Ndem with keeping the morale of the people high throughout the war. His eloquence and journalistic editorial skills could only be surpassed by a few. Indeed, Gen. Obasanjo wrote that when he eventually conquered the Biafran rebels, he made it his business to get Oko Okon Ndem to do a little gig of his eloquent journalism for his enjoyment. During this same period, a cartoon appeared in the *Biafran Outlook* newspaper showing Ojukwu and Awolowo in a sword fight across the Niger Bridge and Awolowo backing off and running away from Ojukwu. But that was also when I noticed that the quality of the newspapers was beginning to diminish and the size of the newspapers was getting smaller. I attributed these changes to war-induced rationing.

By September 1, 1967, battles were being fought at Auchi inside Midwestern Nigeria. I looked at the map and found the location of Auchi and wondered when all of this happened. I thought we had gone beyond that. We are supposed to be inside Northern Nigeria. How come then are we still fighting at Auchi and Agbor? About the same time, I was in the village at Ovim and overheard a woman, who was not educated, telling another woman about what Nigerian soldiers had done to Igbos in Sapele and Warri in the Midwest of Nigeria. So, whatever happened to the capture of Midwestern Nigeria? It was about this time that the announcement of school reopening was made and then rescinded.

Soon it dawned on me that Biafra was losing ground. How did we lose the Midwest after capturing it in a blitzkrieg? A few weeks later, about the third week of September 1967, a certain Maj. Albert Okonkwo broadcasted that the territory previously known as Midwestern Nigeria would henceforth be known as the Republic of Benin. To what purpose, I asked, if we are losing ground? I was now hearing about the Agbor sector of the war. My big sister, who was nearby, responded that Yakubu Gowon would have a heart attack on hearing the news that the Midwest was also seceding. Once more, I assured myself that this was just the nature of war. The Nigerian advance would be halted before they could take the entirety of Midwest Nigeria—I was confident. However, in hindsight, the announced secession of Midwest Nigeria from the remainder of Nigeria is one of those incidents that we were just grabbing at straws.

Not long after hearing about the fall of Agbor in the Midwest, we heard about the massacre of Igbos in Asaba, and the news about how the Nigerian Army tried to enter Onitsha (Onucha) and were driven back by Biafran forces was another reality check. By the end of September, the entire Midwest was lost. Morale was waning. Nevertheless, Biafrans were determined. I was still hopeful and confident. As the Midwest was falling, so also Enugu, the capital of Biafra, was falling into Nigerian hands. Madiebo (Pp. 171-72) and Akpan (Pp. 104-5) both extensively describe the delusion and the pathetic, wishful thinking that prevailed during the fall of Enugu. Though the Nigerian Army was within twelve miles of Enugu, and Ojukwu could see the Nigerian soldiers from a hilltop, he still believed that these were Biafran troops or just the sound of thunder (Akpan Pp. 104 – 5). Some civilians reported that the shelling and machine gunfire came from saboteurs who were in collaboration with the enemy. As the enemy advanced toward Enugu, C. C. Mojekwu, Ojukwu's uncle or cousin who is alleged to have eaten a good part of Biafran money, was convinced that the Biafran Army could still push back the enemy. According to Madiebo (Pp. 174 – 75), Mr. Mojekwu did not see the point in evacuating Enugu. Mojekwu opined that "During the Second World War the Germans were within three miles of Stalingrad and the Russians still pushed them back." But what the privileged Mojekwu failed to learn from his military history was that in Stalingrad, during the World War II, the Russians matched force with force. According to Madiebo (Pp. 175 – 76), there was no point explaining to the military historian that "while the Russians in Stalingrad matched force with force, the Biafran forces had little or no weapons to check the enemy." Though Biafrans were determined to stay put, Ojukwu and much of the civilian population, after stubborn resistance, eventually evacuated Enugu around September 28 or 29, 1967.

The table below provides comparative responses of the Russians at Stalingrad in light of Mojekwu's alleged flippant and mindless ejaculation. Although Biafrans were outmanned, if they had 50 percent of the artillery and battle tanks like the Russians had against the Germans, Nigeria would never have entered Enugu, at least not for the following next nine months.

Comparative Force - German vs Russia at Stalingrad (1942)	Germans	Russia	% of Russia to Germany
Initial (July - Nov 1942)			
Personnel	270,000	187,000	69.26%
Artillery Pieces	3,000	2,200	73.33%
Battle Tanks	500	400	80.00%
Aircraft	600	300	50.00%
Soviet Counter-Offensive (Nov 1942)			
Personnel	1,040,000	1,142,000	109.81%
Artillery Pieces	10,250	13,451	131.23%
Battle Tanks	500	894	178.80%
Aircraft	402	1,115	277.36%
Casualties	800,000	1,129,000	141.13%

The enemy entered parts of Enugu around September 29 or September 30, 1967. Indeed, my fear that Enugu had been captured despite our delusion that we could hold the town struck me in the middle of a Radio Biafra broadcast. As I glued my ears to the radio, lying on the floor, I overheard a broadcaster or a staff person saying hurriedly to another "Kâ anyi pûba ... kâ anyi pûba," which means "Let's leave, let's leave," and suddenly the airwaves went silent, and the broadcast was shut down. I did not hear a broadcast for another few days. I wondered if that was it. Was Biafra over in less than four months of battle?

Not so soon! The available firsthand accounts confounded me and, as events unfolded, my hopes were restored. Amid the lost euphoria of Biafra's military success, the misleading propaganda, and the desperation, all I had was speculation about what would follow next. The Biafran Army Commander, Alexander Madiebo "went around town to see what troops were still available and ... was astonished that they were still there in good number but lacked ammunition ... and the Head of State who held all the ammunition was gone." Madiebo "... still met Colonel Amadi at the foot of the Miliken Hill still fighting ... to check the enemy thrust[125]." Biafra still had a fight. For me, though, that was the end. We lost all the Midwest; Onitsha would be under attack, naturally, and Enugu had fallen. What else was there to fight about? From where? Once more, the people's sheer determination was the only thing that buoyed up the lack of preparation and kept the struggle going.

As Biafra was losing ground in the Midwest and the enemy was putting pressure on Enugu from the middle of September through the last week of September 1967, the big news that shocked listeners were a broadcast to the Biafran population: Treacherous saboteurs were undermining our victories and the efforts and gallantry of our soldiers and the people. It may well have been true to some extent. Suffice it to say, it will be helpful here to identify the extent to which sabotage made a difficult situation worse. On the other hand, sabotage is the stuff of war. There are always turncoats and double agents in any war or conflict.

By the third week of September, shortly before the enemy entered Enugu, the "sabos" (as they were stylishly called in Biafra, i.e., Maj. Alale, Mr. Agbam, Maj. Ifeajuna, one of the coup plotters of January 1966, and Lt. Col. Victor Banjo) were tried and executed publicly in Enugu. The other saboteur, Maj. Nzeogwu was killed in action in July 1967. Another discredited soldier, Brig. Hillary Njoku was incarcerated through the remainder of the war. It was not clear that Njoku was a real sabo, and I do not believe that Brig. Njoku was a saboteur. I think he was a victim of a power tussle with Ojukwu.

Finally, at the risk of shocking the sensibilities of Biafrans and sending shivers down their spines and raising disquieting eyebrows, I will mention that Nzeogwu, for his reason, was a real saboteur. However, Ojukwu would not accuse him openly. If Ojukwu was ever prudent, it showed in how he dealt with Nzeogwu. Maj. Chukwuma Nzeogwu was next in popularity to Ojukwu, if not more popular. If Biafrans had the slightest notion that Nzeogwu was not in favor of the war, it would have dealt a blow to Ojukwu's scheme to keep Biafra out of Nigeria. For this reason, it was easier, as will be argued later, that Ojukwu set him up to be killed as if he died in action fighting for Biafra. The argument for Nzeogwu's sabo status will be presented below.

There were rifts inside Biafra, much as in any other society. However, Biafran secession and the subsequent war were fraught with treacherous behaviors, the explanations of which go beyond the normally expected betrayals that are often motivated by petty greed or unscrupulous individuals who engaged in sabotage for money, namely turncoats who were bribed. From the beginning of the crisis in January 1966 through internal debates about whether or not to secede, some people had personal reasons for why they felt that they should undermine the war effort.

As I will argue here, Victor Banjo had his personal and political/ideological reasons for undermining Biafra, but Ojukwu thought he could trust Banjo—or both were trying to exploit the other, only to be mutually destroyed in the process. It is worth noting that it is quite possible that Victor Banjo, as I will state briefly here, must have held Ojukwu in contempt for being a carpetbagger. Banjo also had a hidden personal agenda, part of which may have included the fact that his wife and children were still in Nigeria and the other being that he did not believe in Biafra, or perhaps that he was hoping to achieve a personal political ambition that he had no chance of achieving in a successful Biafra. Based on the extant evidence it appears that Victor Banjo had an agenda that was different from Ojukwu's agenda. Either Ojukwu was trying to play Banjo and use him, or Banjo was trying to play Ojukwu and use him. However, each side believed in their pipe dream. For starters, evidence

---

[125] Madiebo, The Nigerian Revolution, Page 175.

would indicate that Banjo made clear his belief to Ojukwu that Nigeria should remain one.[126] See also Deji Yesufu, Ikenga Chronicles, June 6, 2017. Ojukwu equally made clear his intention that Biafran sovereignty would not be compromised. Somehow, Ojukwu convinced Banjo to continue to stay in Biafra and assist in the scheme for Biafran secession, with the hope that Banjo would have something to gain by achieving his agenda in Western Nigeria.

Consider Olayinka Omigbodun's *(Banjo's daughter) statement published in The Nation (2017),* "He said he would not change the principles he lived for ... He said he cannot fail to condemn what he described as the vindictive and vengeful killings of Easterners. He warned that unless the killing stops, the bloodshed will be prolonged for a longer time. He warned the Yoruba of the West not to keep quiet on the killings saying they must not think that they are temporarily safe." In response to the question about differences in opinion about secession, Olayinka continued, "*And you don't think his not agreeing in the secession was a reason he got into trouble with Ojukwu?* Well, they were friends and friends do disagree. They probably must have disagreed on that (secession) before then because my father never hid his patriotism ... He knew my father was up for one Nigeria. Even before drafting him into the war on his side, he knew my father was a patriot who wanted one united Nigeria."[127]

Banjo sympathized with the Biafrans and their cause. But also consider the following statement, quoted verbatim from Bernard Odogwu's book: The text of Banjo's self-defense during his trial by Ojukwu's military tribunal in September 1967. A full text of depositions and cross-examinations can be found in Odogwu's book [(*Nowhere to Hide)* The statements below have been numbered to facilitate reference and were transcribed from *I Am Not Dead Yet*[128]:

1. *"My stay in Biafra, after having been released from prison, has been due to my friendship with Col. Ojukwu. I clearly remember once telling him that I would return to the West. He told me that he needed me here because he felt he needed someone who could talk to him without ceremony; someone in a position to give blame for his mistakes. Most of the political maneuvers that Col. Ojukwu planned early this year in connection with achieving Southern solidarity against the North, were planned with me..."*[129]

2. *"When he decided to declare an independent Republic of Biafra, I pleaded with him to postpone it as both the people of the West and Mid-West were not ready or at that stage, sufficiently strong militarily to take the same stand, even though they would wish it..."*

3. *"I pointed out to him his declaration of Biafra at the time was not consistent with our plans and agreements. I told him that the people of the West who were acting on the basis of the fact that I would bring assistance to them from here would consider the decision to declare Biafra at that time a betrayal of our arrangements. I told the military Governor that I would leave Biafra for the West or for the outside world after his declaration of Independence..."*

4. *"However, when I discovered the emerging trend that followed the declaration of Independence of Biafra, it became clear to me that a war with the North was imminent. I decided to stay behind and assist in the prosecution of the war, both for the sake of my friendship with Colonel Ojukwu and in the hope that having assisted to fight back the Northern threat to Biafra, he would assist me with troops to rid the Mid-West and Lagos of the same menace..."*

5. *"I came into the war at a moment of temporary collapse of the Biafran fighting effort, when it became quite clear to me that the fighting effort of the Biafran Army was not only being incompetently handled, but also being sabotaged. Since then, it has been my fortune to command the Biafran troops on their successful exploits..."*

---

[126] The Nation – Olayinka Omigbodun, <u>Sunday Interview Archives - Latest Nigeria News, Nigerian Newspapers, Politics (thenationonlineng.net)</u>

[127] Olayinka Omigbodun, Banjo's Daughter, Loc. Cit.

[128] Deji Yesufu, "I am Not Dead Yet: The Sad Story of Banjo's Death, "I'm Not Dead Yet!": The story of Victor Banjo | aljazirahnews, June 2017

[129] *Odogwu, Op. Cit, Page 88.*

Banjo's statements here clearly indicate a defensive posture, one that admonishes Ojukwu that he had mis stepped and was bound to fail. It also gives away the possibility that his subsequent actions when he invaded the Midwest of Nigeria may have been designed to, not necessarily sabotage Ojukwu, but to go out on his own to hedge his bets, realizing that the Biafran objective of taking the war to Nigerian territory would not be feasible. In paragraph 3, above, it might also appear that he was giving away a potentially sinister scheme that got the Nigerians thinking, hence the allegation that Biafra's invasion of the Midwest was an indication that Ojukwu desired to rule Nigeria and not to liberate Biafra. The latter argument could not stand the strain of logical scrutiny. Specifically, the mere invasion of the Midwest, in and of itself, could not necessarily lead to the conclusion that Ojukwu desired to rule Nigeria. Ojukwu's subsequent actions might implicate him and betray his ambitions. In that regard, Ojukwu had to have been out of his mind because he did not have the military capability to achieve the capture and overlordship of Nigeria.

To reach the ultimate conclusion about Banjo's behaviors, one would then have to begin from his (Banjo's) interactions with Madiebo at the Nsukka sector during the early weeks of the war and how he manipulated himself into the position of essentially becoming the commander of the Biafran Army. Banjo then halts an operation that Madiebo was planning, takes the arms to go to the Midwest. From then, after Banjo's invasion of the Midwest, his (Banjo's) broadcasts in Benin, his letter to Ojukwu is instructive in the analysis. The manner of the withdrawal of the Biafran Army from the Midwest and correspondences between Ojukwu and Banjo reveal their motives and differences thereof[130].

The Nsukka Sector and Banjo

At the Nsukka sector in mid-July 1967, Madiebo provides details of his interactions with Victor Banjo that lend support for the argument that Banjo was the real sabo[131].,

"...The ill fortunes of the 53 Brigade were so frequent ... that they no longer appeared to be coincidental... For a long time, each time they planned an operation against the enemy, they were attacked exactly 30 minutes before the H-Hour on that ... front, thereby neutralizing their proposed offensive ... My fears of foul play were heightened by the fact that Col. Banjo and Major Alale were already going around spreading a rumor that saboteurs existed in the 53 Brigade and Army headquarters ..." Madiebo continues (Op. Cit.), "... It was difficult for the Army to understand how a Yoruba man who found himself in Enugu by chance and a civilian ... could be the first Biafrans to detect sabotage in the front lines ... from their offices in Enugu ... yet everyone believed them ... It was much later that I learned from [Colonel] Eze that Banjo insisted and did attend all his briefings preparatory to his futile offensives and near disasters ...".

Banjo went on a rampage to campaign against Brig. Njoku, the army commander and convinced Ojukwu to permit him to form the 101st Division of the Biafran Army. Now, as commander of the 101st Division, Banjo proposed a plan for Madiebo's next offensive at the Nsukka sector, a plan of action that Madiebo (Page 148) considered to be absolute nonsense that showed a remarkable ignorance of basic military tactics. Under pressure, Madiebo was forced to attempt Banjo's planned offensives, all of which eventually turned out to be disastrous, as with other operations that Banjo planned at the Nsukka sector of the war[132].

Nigerian forces entered Obolo Âfôr on August 6, 1967. The struggle continued. But Biafra needed a morale booster. And so it happened, on August 9, 1967, that Biafra invaded the Midwest Region of Nigeria under the command of Victor Banjo. So, what happened and how did Nigeria recover the Midwest? The developments are interesting. According to Madiebo (Page 156), the first he heard of

---

[130] Njoku, Tragedy Without Heroes Page 217, Par. 6 and Page 218 Par. 14). Also Akpan, The Struggle for Secession Page 101 – 102, Oyewole, and Njoku, Tragedy Withiut Heroes, (Appendix 18 in Page 224
[131] Madiebo, The Nigerian Revolution, Pp. 145 – 47
[132] Ibid, Pp. 146 – 156.

the operation to invade the Midwest was on August 7, 1967 (two days before the invasion) during an early morning visit with Banjo, who revealed a detailed plan to take the Midwest in a lightening operation, move to Ibadan, Lagos, and the southern territories of the Midwest of Nigeria.

As expected, the Nigerian Army was taken by surprise on August 9. I recollect hearing a broadcast on Radio Biafra, a few days prior that the Nigerian Army was no good and the only credible troops it had were stationed in the Midwest. Even at that, their capability and effectiveness were doubtful. Therefore, when the Biafran Army announced its capture of the Midwest in a lightning operation, I was elated and convinced about the invincibility of Biafra. I reflected on the broadcast that I heard that the effectiveness of the Nigerian Army in the Midwest was suspect and explained it to myself.

After crossing the Onitsha Bridge in the early morning hours of August 9, 1967, Banjo and his troops immediately captured Benin before noon on the same day, without firing a single shot or losing a single life[133]. The speed of the operation was such, as will be obvious later, that the Nigerian military governor of the Midwest (Lt. Col. David Ejoor) was captured in the process. Only God knows who else had been part of the conspiracy, only to back off when they saw that the operation would get nowhere. In a similar lightning speed, the remaining territory of the Midwest to the south was captured. The inhabitants of these areas, such as Ughelli and Warri, were caught by surprise at the appearance of Biafran forces[134]. The events that followed were interesting.

According to Madiebo (Page 157), for reasons best known to him, Banjo conveniently ignored the principle of speed as a principle of war and "chose to remain in Benin to reorganize troops that had not yet fired a shot... Much time was lost while the argument raged between Benin and Enugu on who was going to be governor of the Midwest. From his statement, it appears that Madiebo was not aware of the tremendous details of the plans that took place. Njoku reveals that the plan was made in utter secrecy. "...The plan was to carry out the operation on August 4, 1967... On the 7th of August 1967, I went to Onitsha to prepare the 54th Brigade for the impending operation into the Midwest...[135]" Madiebo, the General Officer Commanding in the Biafran Army, was out of the loop in all this secrecy. For that reason, he would not know why Banjo wasted three days in Benin arguing with Ojukwu. From what follows next, it is clear that Banjo had his agenda, or he was convinced to be a turncoat—better yet, these events, described next, make a clear argument that Banjo knew exactly what he was doing from the beginning: to sabotage Biafra and profit from it. As soon as Banjo got to Benin, he got in touch with Yoruba leaders and other influential people. As a matter of background, the people of the Midwest had in many respects wanted to remain neutral.[136] Furthermore, it appears that Ojukwu had maintained communication with Ejoor, governor of Midwest Nigeria, before and during the war.[137] According to *Deji Yesufu, in the Ikenga Chronicles of June 6, 2017,* "...The Mid-West, now Delta and Edo State, at first took a middle position as far as the crisis was concerned...[138]" Just before the war was about to begin, Lt. Col. David Lt. Col. Ejoor made a broadcast that renounced the impending war as a war of revenge and domination. Also, Col. Adeyinka Adebayo, the governor of Western Nigeria, on May 4th, 1967, condemned the potential use of violence to settle the political crisis in Nigeria.

Deji Yesufu also stated,

"On the side of the West, there was mixed reaction in the minds of Yoruba people when news of the Biafran takeover of the mid-West reached them. On one hand, they saw the Biafran brigade led by a Yoruba, as a liberation army and they looked forward to their coming... But as news of the atrocities being wrought on the non-Igbo of the mid-West by the Biafran army reached the West, the

---

[133] Madiebo, The Nigerian Revolution and the Biafran War, Pp. 157 – 60,

[134] Oyewole, The Reluctant Rebel, Pp. 44-54.

[135] Hillary Njoku, A Tragedy Without Heroes, Pp. 152 - 53

[136] *Samuel Umweni, 888 Days in Biafra, New York, iUniverse, inc, 2007, Pp.14 – 16.*

[137] *John de St. Jorre, A Brother's War*

[138] *Deji Yesufu, I am Not Dead Yet, https://www.thegazellenews.com/news/ im-not-dead-yet-story-victor-banjo-yoruba-man-assisted-biafra-executed-ojukwu-deji-yesufu/*

Yoruba's became less convinced that the Igbo were ... coming to liberate them from the shackles of their colonizers[139] – the Hausas."[140]

Before Banjo left for the Midwest,

"he, (Banjo) had also reached an agreement with Ojukwu to take over the government of Gowon and allow the Easterners to go their way, with a possible secession of the North too ... The mid-West was meant to be a passage through and not a destination. The two of them argued over this matter for days on the phone in Benin, giving the Nigerian government sufficient time to recover from the take-over of the mid-West...[141]"

Yesufu further wrote that

"... Soyinka wrote of how he drove around Ibadan, trying to convince Obasanjo to permit Banjo a smooth sail through Ibadan into Lagos. Obasanjo, the head of the military in Ibadan, would have none of it. Banjo could have rolled into Ibadan successfully, but he would not invade Ibadan without the cooperation of his people. His sister reminded him of (Kakanfo) Afonja and the Ilorin emirate and he said he remembered. He would eventually be felled as another Afonja of the 20th century...[142]"

These events are corroborated by a broadcast that Banjo made in Benin and by the text of a letter that Ojukwu wrote to Banjo[143]. Specifically, Banjo spent time in Benin trying to negotiate with the Nigerians. Indeed, Njoku reproduced a broadcast that was intended to be broadcast by Lt. Col. David Ejoor, the sitting governor of the Midwest. In Benin, Banjo made a broadcast which stated inter alia (paragraph 6, 7, and 14) that "...I am a Nigerian, I believe in the Nigerian nation, and I am fighting for Nigeria ... When I offered my services to my friend ... Lt. Col. Ojukwu ... I requested him ... on his part to assist me by providing me with forces ... to save Nigeria." Banjo goes further to state in paragraph 14,

"... I understand that anxiety is being expressed in some quarters about the safety of Brigadier David Ejoor ... I wish to inform you that I have personally had discussions with David Ejoor and to assure you that he is in good health and is not under detention. Efforts are being made to ensure his continued service in the Midwest ... but until matters are settled, it is necessary that an interim government be set up ... I have, therefore, today, promulgated a decree to set up an interim administration ..."

Banjo went on to state that he had set up a Midwestern Army, a police force that would all be independent of the Nigerian Army and the Biafran Army (paragraph 15, Njoku – Tragedy Without Heroes). On page 219, Njoku discloses a prepared speech that David Ejoor was supposed to broadcast, stating, inter alia

"...Throughout this period, the Government of the Midwest has tried to maintain absolute neutrality and resisted the use of the Midwest territory for the purposes of aggression against the Government of the people of Biafra... I have found it necessary to invite the armed forces of Biafra to join forces with Midwestern troops ... I have today voluntarily resigned my office as Military Governor ... I have handed over the affairs of the Midwestern Government to ... Lt. Col. C.D. Nwawo ..."

However, Lt. Col. David Ejoor refused to cooperate with Banjo, and Ojukwu had a priest to act as an intermediary between Ejoor and Banjo. Lt. Col. Ejoor still declined to make the speech and to go to Enugu (the capital of Biafra) and eventually slipped out to the Nigerian side and reported to Lagos

---

[139] *Ibid*

[140] *See also Oyewole, The Reluctant Rebel and Ademoyega, Why We Struck*

[141] *Yesufu, Op. Cit*

[142] Deji Yesufu, Op. Cit.

[143] Hillary Njoku, A Tragedy Without Heroes, Pp. 217 – 20 and Pp. 224 – 25 – Appendix 18

as the fighting progressed Forsyth[144] told a slightly more detailed but corroborating story. While Forsyth added details that I could not corroborate elsewhere, there could be quite a bit of credibility to it, as he was very close to Ojukwu and may have obtained details that others such as Oyewole, Madiebo (who was not even in the loop), and Effiong (who was oblivious) could tell. Besides being very close to Ojukwu, Forsyth was a highly connected British journalist and could have obtained information from sources that would not have been accessible to many others. Forsyth[145] reports that Yoruba leaders were teetering on swinging to the Biafran side during the Biafran invasion of the Midwest and Gowon had his private jet with engines warming on the tarmac ready to flee Lagos, only to be persuaded and assured of British assistance. Furthermore, upon arriving at Ore, an inspection of dead Nigerian troops indicated that they were principally Tiv soldiers who were part of Yakubu Gowon's guard troops, indicating that if Gowon had to resort to his special guard troops, Yoruba troops had not been available or enthusiastic enough to join the fight.

More credibly, in [146]corroboration of Madiebo and Akpan, Forsyth states that Banjo decided soon after August 9, 1967, that he wished to enter talks with Yoruba leaders in the West, notably, Chief Awolowo "... He (Banjo) discovered the hideaway of Lt. Col. David Ejoor (Governor of the Midwest) though Banjo did not report this to Ojukwu who wished to talk with Ejoor. But Ejoor declined to be an intermediary between Awolowo and Banjo.

"Banjo... relayed the message using the side ban Radio of the British High Commissioner in Benin ... The message was passed on to Chief Awolowo ... The plot, Banjo later revealed ... was to cause the ruin of Biafra by withdrawing the [Biafran] troops from the Midwest on a variety of pretexts, arrest and assassinate Ojukwu ... he [Banjo] would then enter his home Western Region with all his past forgiven ... the second part of the plot ... was that he [Banjo] and Awolowo ... would then depose Gowon ... It seems unlikely that Gowon government was informed of this later postscript."

Banjo's actions in the Midwest appear to be contrary to his plans with Ojukwu. For example, Akpan states that from letters written that night to Col. Banjo, the immediate aim of the adventure was to relieve the pressure from the Federal troops approaching Enugu. For this purpose, our troops were to cross at some point in the North and fight towards Nsukka[147]. From Appendix 18 of Njoku (Tragedy Without Heroes, Pp. 224 – 25), Ojukwu blasted a letter to Banjo, stating, inter alia,

"...After clearing the whole question with my Executive Council, I... have decided to place at your disposal Biafran forces for the liberation of Yorubaland on the following clear conditions... You will have nothing to do with the administration of the Midwest territory ... prior to your move to the West ... On the liberation of Yorubaland, you will be appointed Military Governor of that territory ..... During the period of Biafra's presence in your territory, all political measures, statements, or decrees shall be subject to approval by myself... Should our troops arrive and liberate Lagos, the Government of the Republic of Biafra reserves the right to appoint a military governor for that territory."

This was quite ambitious. Who is to say that the Yoruba leaders did not lay their hands on this letter, dated August 22, 1967? After all, after Ojukwu initially arrested Banjo, he was later to plead his way back to the command of the Midwest operation, the aftermath of which was to cede the Midwest back to Nigeria.

During the confusion between Ojukwu and Banjo, the fighting went on. Biafran forces occupied Okitipupa, Ore to the West, and Okene to the northward and made moves toward Lokoja and Kabba. As a result of their disagreements, Ojukwu ordered Banjo back to Enugu. According to Akpan (Page 101), Ojukwu's agents reported that Banjo had ordered Biafran soldiers to remove their Biafran army emblems and also that Banjo had been saying unflattering things about Ojukwu. In any event, Banjo was brought to Enugu and put under house arrest. Over the period from the end of August 1967 to the first week of September 1967, Nigerian forces reorganized and began to push back the Biafran

---

[144] *Frederick Forsyth, The Biafra Story, Pp. 116 – 19*
[145] *Forsyth, The Biafra Story, Page 116*
[146] *Ibid Pp. 117 – 19*
[147] *Akpan, The Struggle for Secession, Page 100*

forces from Okitipupa and Ore. At lightning speed, the Nigerians under Col. Murtala Mohamed raced toward Benin. Lt. Col. Adekunle under the marine commandos cleared the southern part of the Midwest. According to Akpan, while Banjo was in detention, arms arrived for Biafra by ships through Calabar and by air (Akpan Page 101). A few days after the arms arrived, Banjo went and apologized to Ojukwu and promised never to do anything again to offend the latter and pledged his loyalty to Ojukwu. Thereafter Ojukwu decided to return command of the Midwest Operation to Banjo and sent him and Emmanuel Ifeajuna back to the Midwest According to Njoku, Ojukwu released Banjo and returned him to command of the 54th Bigrade on September 6, 1967, and also made him commander of the newly created 104th Division[148] (Njoku, Page 163). Shortly after, Biafran troops were on the run. By September 17, the troops in the north who would have begun to pressure Nigerian forces at Nsukka pulled back into the Midwest and lost Auchi.

Before Banjo left for the Midwest, he requested the bulk of the arms that had just arrived—the weapons, the ammunition, and the armored cars. Banjo did not request them to fight in the Midwest, of course, but to ensure that the Biafrans did not receive them. According to reports brought by Biafran soldiers returning from the Midwest, the bulk of the arms subsequently fell into Nigerian hands[149]. The rest of the story is where it becomes really interesting: Banjo left for the Midwest on September 6, 1967, with Ifeajuna and Alale. Between September 6 and September 15, the enemy advanced toward Benin. When the Nigerian Army was more than fifteen miles from Benin, Banjo ordered Biafran troopsto withdraw from Benin[150]. Meanwhile, he had arrested or detained several Biafran Army officers, and his companion, Alale, began to spread propaganda that there were saboteurs among the senior army officers of Biafra. According to Madiebo, Banjo also ordered that no stores or equipment should be taken, as there would soon be a counterattack to reclaim any territory that would be captured by the Nigerian forces. Odogwu's report[151] would lend support to the conclusion that Banjo had planned sabotage of the Biafran Army. According to Odogwu Major Alale had told Madiebo and Ezenwugo as far back as the 15th of September 1967 that Benin would fall any minute. Even more, evidence is found in Oyewole[152] that as he was returning to Agbor to take up his new command, Banjo and some senior military officers were driving out of Benin at full speed." When some Biafran soldiers and officers saw this, they joined the race. Oyewole reports further that Banjo and Alale planned the retreat to sow chaos among Biafran troops. Oyewole also reported that he met Ademoyega, whom they had released from prison during the Midwest incursion, and Banjo had been relieved of his command and taken to Enugu . Oyewole also met Lt. Col. Isichei who stated to him (Oyewole) that the withdrawal of Biafran forces (about September 15, 1967) was a blunder and that the Nigerian forces were still more than eight miles away. Less than four days later, Nigerian troops entered Benin on September 18, 1967, without firing a shot. Finally, Banjo, during his trial, stated that the conditions for the successful conclusion of the war no longer existed and that holding the Midwest provided a bargaining power for Biafra within the context of Nigeria[153]. That was a treasonable offense in Biafra to say that Biafra and Ojukwu would negotiate anything in the context of Nigeria. That last statement sealed his fate. And so, Banjo was executed on September 22, 1967.

Major Chukwuma Kaduna Nzeogwu Was Set Up for Elimination

Major Nzeogwu was vehemently opposed to Biafra and was never given a command in the Biafran Army. Ojukwu ordered a halt to military exercise by Nzeogwu in preparation to defend Biafra. He wrote a letter to Obasanjo (See Obasanjo's Nzeogwu an Intimate Portrait, Page 137) and stated that he would form a Nigerian Army inside Biafra. He formed a unit called Nzeogwu's guerillas

---

[148] *Akpan, Op. Cit. Page 101 and Njoku, Op. Cit. Pp. 157 – 163t.*

[149] *Akpan, Op. Cit, Page 103*

[150] *Madiebo, The Nigerian Revolution and the Biafran War, Pp. 158 – 60*

[151] *Bernard Odogwu, No Where to Hide, Pp. 90 – 92*

[152] *Fola Oyewole, The Reluctant Rebel, Pp. 60-61*

[153] *154 Odogwu, Op. Cit, Page 92.*

which even the Nigerian commander at Nsukka directed his troops never to engage and Ojukwu, who never approved of the unit assigned his half-brother to join (See Enonchong, Pp. 137 – 38). Nzeogwu may have had plans to defect. If he did, Biafra would have been devastated. Therefore, it was best to kill him. Nzeogwu died at Nsukka where was doing reconnaissance in an area that he had been disinformed as having been captured by Biafra (See also Onyejekwe on accounts attempted assassination of Nzeogwu).

Chapter VI

SEPTEMBER 1967 – SEPTEMBER 1968
BIAFRA IS NOT DEAD YET

The Struggle Continues

On September 28, 1967, as previously noted, Nigerian forces entered Enugu. By October 8, Calabar fell and Nigerian forces entered Asaba and began to massacre civilians. Biafran forces used the opportunity to reorganize to defend Onitsha and blew up the Niger bridge as Nigerian forces under Murtala Mohamed approached Onitsha.

With the impending fall of Enugu, I saw many of our relatives and hometown men returning and telling the horror stories of their escape from Enugu. Enugu had truly fallen. How could it be? The Biafran people needed an explanation for the reverses and failures: the apparent push back in the Midwest by Nigerian forces, the failure to get to Lagos or at least to remain in Western Nigeria, and now the apparent fall of Enugu although Brig. Njoku, whose command had been momentarily withdrawn, had received new weapons.

The explanation that we got for the failures was what had just happened—the hunt for scapegoats. These failures were the fault of saboteurs and agents of the enemy. Of course, I've highlighted allegations of sabotage already in prior paragraphs, but I bring up their explanation here to bring closure to events that I have described up to this point. The sabotage of Banjo, which I believe was real, and the attempt to overthrow Ojukwu in September 1967 were convenient alibis for the despotic leadership of Ojukwu, the Biafran dictator. For Nigerians, the fall of Enugu was the end of Biafra. But not so fast— Biafra was not dead. Not yet! With the Nigerian Army's brutal massacre of the population at Asaba and the story of sabotage caused by unpatriotic and greedy people, Biafrans became even more determined than ever to continue the struggle.

It must be made clear here that Ojukwu was the boss, the government, the foreign minister, and the quartermaster general all rolled into one—in every sense, in Biafra, *l'État c'est lui* or "the state is him." Ojukwu was the state of Biafra. The Biafran incursion into the Midwest, under appropriate conditions, was a brilliant strategic and tactical move. However, in practical terms, under the circumstances, it was misguided and could be used to justify the allegations that Ojukwu had grandiose illusions of the control of Nigeria. The fall of Enugu makes vivid the lack of preparation, as Madiebo can show[154] and callous disregard for the safety of the people by the inner leadership of Biafra. It equally demonstrated the determination of our people to defend themselves and the sacrifices they were willing to make to achieve that. The attempt to overthrow Ojukwu was a desperate attempt by frustrated comrades (Nzeogwu, Ifeajuna, and Alale) and by dubious friends (Banjo) who had their agendas.

At the end of it, Njoku was branded a saboteur and relieved of his position as commander of the army. Ojukwu set him up for failure and branded him a saboteur or victimized him out of his frustration to cover up his inadequacies. Before the struggle between Biafra and Nigeria, Ojukwu

---

[154] Alexander Madiebo, The Nigerian Revolution and the Biafran War, Pp. 157-62 and Pp. 171 – 74).

was the Quartermaster General of the Nigerian Army for a while. During this period, he became aware of the weaponry available to the Nigerian Army. On the eve of the coup in January 1966, Ojukwu was the commander of the Fourth Battalion of the Nigerian Army. As a high-ranking officer of the Nigerian Army, he was aware that the main arsenal of the Nigerian Army rested in Northern Nigeria— the air force headquarters, the armored squadron, artillery, and several of the battalions that were fully armed. There were two battalions in Western Nigeria and one battalion in Enugu (Eastern Nigeria). Therefore, there had to be six or seven infantry battalions in Northern Nigeria, along with the Nigerian Military Academy or Training Facility. As the Midwest was crumbling and armed with all this information, Ojukwu assigned Njoku to Operation Torch with outmoded weapons against an enemy with armored cars, artillery, and well-equipped modern automatic weapons. According to Madiebo[155] about September 6 or so, when Banjo was sent back to the Midwest, Njoku was handed back the command of the Biafran Army with the admonition that, if he did not achieve spectacular successes, he would lose his command of the army permanently. For this purpose, Njoku was given three 105-mm Howitzer guns According to Madiebo, "As an artillery officer, I ... went to see these guns and found them to be very old guns ... of Second, if not First World War vintage ... The guns came naked ... with no survey or plotting instruments or pamphlets... The barrels were badly worn." Also, "the armored cars were light ... small vehicles ... absolutely bare, with no weapons or equipment inside them ...Those of them that moved at all overheated very easily... With limited supplies, though now slightly better equipped, Operation Torch went off very well and led to the capture of Igumale inside Northern Nigeria but then we had to withdraw because they had exhausted all their bullets and artillery shells...[156]". Apparently or maybe evidently, Brig. Njoku was fired and jailed for the remainder of the war and Brig. Madiebo was appointed commander of the army.

Njoku was not formally accused of sabotage. However, he was thoroughly discredited as a soldier. Njoku's discredit was one of the most despicable injustices of the Biafra war. How would a military leader, who had all the knowledge of the weaponry needs of modern war, send his troops to fight a numerically superior enemy and issue them with limited weapons and expect them to win? Njoku was another scapegoat, so much so that his name was sullied in song, thus said:

"...Ey-woah ebe mu nâ nwanne'm jere'ôgû Akpiri ego!! Ifeajuna rere anyi *Ey-woah ebe mu nâ nwanne'm jere'ôgû Njoku â pûta nu'uzô ree nwanne yaaa! "*	*"... Whereupon I went to battle with my kinsman For the love of money, Ifeajuna betrayed us Whereupon I went to battle with my kinsman Along the way, Njoku betrayed his brethren!!.."*

Njoku did not betray Ojukwu or the Biafran adventure. Like a good soldier, he knew what it takes to go to war. For him, the better part of valor is discretion and if you want peace then prepare for war. Njoku advised Ojukwu about this and Ojukwu was offended. Before the war was to begin and as the storm gathered, Njoku wrote in his book, as will be analyzed later, that God gave Biafra eleven months to prepare for peace or war and Biafra prepared for neither.

For all practical purposes, toward the end of September 1967, Madiebo writes about the desperation that followed[157]. The propaganda continued to blast the message that the impending fall of Enugu was due to saboteurs. Our people, including me, believed it. How could Enugu fall? In desperation, like Caesar and the consuls of ancient Rome, "Ojukwu ordered all provinces to send up their able-bodied men... They came in their throngs and at final count, they were 10,000 ... A few of them brought along their own machetes and den guns ... and those who did not have machetes had to be issued with machetes." Furthermore, according to Madiebo, the order was to have the 10,000 men: "...swarmed the enemy singing war songs and macheting all enemy within sight ... It was futile trying to match determination and machetes against an enemy using artillery and machine guns ...

---

[155] Ibid

[156] Madiebo, The Nigerian Revolution, Pp.157 - 174.

[157] The Nigerian Revolution, Pp. 170 – 74

it was still more dangerous for anyone to suggest an abandonment of the offensive ... their war songs were heard from far places and ... the enemy released a tremendous volley of shells in all directions ... the war songs ceased, and the warriors dispersed in fright in all directions."

What else? I am not certain how this happened, but I heard a similar story from a cousin of mine in the village, Ôshiama Ndukwo of Amuukwukwa, who joined the Biafran Army on the first day of the war. This kind of scenario, once more, was indicative of the desperation and determination of the people, the deceit of Biafran propaganda, and the willingness of the leaders of Biafra to recklessly endanger their people's lives. This is the kind of story that made me say to myself, "betimes me thinks that Ojukwu wert possessed – In effect, Ojukwu, at some point, all but lost his sanity.

The Biafran Incursion into the Midwest

The Biafran invasion of the Midwest of Nigeria in August was erroneous. It was borne out of a desperate attempt to terminate the war in short order by a general commander who did not disclose his limitations to an adoring populace. When the Biafran Army invaded the Midwest in August, it was a morale booster for the Biafran population and a propaganda ploy by the Biafran government and Ojukwu, in particular. In effect, it was meant to neutralize the desperation that was setting in after the Nigerian invasion from Nsukka, to the north of Biafra. For the Biafran population, it was inconceivable that these "Awusa" people could invade Biafra so successfully when previously we had been told that no army in Black Africa could defeat Biafra.

At the time of the Midwest invasion, even my juvenile mind thought that Biafra should have gone north into Agenebode and Idah and then push south to recapture Nsukka. Of course, I did not have any logistical information beyond my knowledge of the map of Nigeria. In hindsight, I can see it was all a losing proposition. On the one hand, pushing back from Nsukka would have put pressure on the Nigerian advance toward Enugu, at least temporarily. On the other hand, capturing Lagos would have destabilized the Nigerian government. Yes, it sounds good in the imagination—after all, an invasion of Lagos might have rallied the Western Nigerians the way the attempted invasion of the Midwest mobilized them. In his naïvety or daydream, Ojukwu called on the Yorubas to rise. However, he ignored the fact that the Yorubas were divided about their support for Biafra. Even if Biafra had successfully invaded Lagos and Ibadan, events in retrospect would lead me to conclude that the Yorubas might have revolted at whom Ojukwu would put in charge.

At best, the invasion decision by Ojukwu was intended to force Nigeria into a negotiation or to just leave Biafra alone. That said, the successful invasion of the Midwest and Lagos and the concomitant destabilization of the Nigerian government would have been a miracle. Given the mutual determination of each side in the conflict, and under the circumstances in Biafra, such a miracle would have been a herculean task. It would have required a garrison of at least 20,000 men to hold the Midwest with a friendly local population and a lot more with a hostile, at least noncooperative, population. Biafra would then have needed a good force of another 30,000 well-armed men to capture Lagos and Ibadan. But the invasion of the Midwest was done with less than one division of soldiers, with a little less than a brigade of 3,000 men holding all of the Midwest and making incursions into Northern Nigeria and another less than 2,000 men thrusting for Lagos. Assuming that Banjo was not treacherous and wasted time in Benin, he might have been able to get close to Lagos in a few days, but the Nigerian Army would not have stood by and watched Biafra's 2,000 men walk into Lagos. There was this dreadfully naïve illusion and pipedream that the Yoruba's would rise and join Biafra and overthrow the Lagos regime. If Biafra had defended Bonny successfully and forced the Nigerians westward on the Bight of Benin, maybe the Midwest population would have been more cooperative. Alternatively, Biafra would need to hold enough resources to equip a Midwestern Army to join with Biafran forces to attack Lagos. Because Benin was taken so swiftly, it would have been prudent to loot the Central Bank in Benin and use the resources to fund a Midwest people's army. This did not happen. But, as Oyewole narrates, the Biafran forces in Ughelli engaged in an orgy of looting and arson that immediately alienated the Midwestern population. News of these atrocities also alienated the Yorubas, who immediately turned against the Biafrans, not least for turning their territory into a war zone.

Before deciding to invade the Midwest, Ojukwu should have considered the danger of opening a wide new front. As a military man and historian, he should have thought about Hitler's invasion of Russia in 1941. During the Second World War, Hitler, leading the Germans, entered a nonaggression pact with the Russians in 1938. The Russians, as it might appear, kept their side of the deal. To their utter surprise, Hitler attacked them one year (1941) after Dunkirk (1940). There is almost a parallel between the German attack of Russia after Dunkirk. I could also argue, in the absence of other evidence, that Hitler was convinced that Britain would be motivated to seek peace once the Germans triumphed in the Soviet Union. If the British did not seek peace, then at least the resources from the Soviet Union would have been available to support continued war with England. In the same manner, Ojukwu must have been convinced that if Nigeria did not seek peace following the successful invasion of the Midwest, the manpower and oil resources of the Midwest would be available to Biafra to bolster the war-making capacity of Biafra. Ojukwu was frustrated at the Biafran Army's inability to check the Nigerian march from Nsukka to Enugu. Instead of concentrating the resources of the Biafran Army at Nsukka to frustrate Nigeria, the treacherous invasion of the Midwest was a way to boost morale because Ojukwu had kept good offices with Lt. Col. Ejoor (governor of Midwest Nigeria), who stubbornly refused to permit the Nigerian Army to attack Biafra from the Midwest. Ojukwu should have kept that faith. The Midwest population also did not care whether Nigeria won or lost the war against Biafra (see Umweni). The commanders of the Nigerian soldiers that were in the Midwest were predominantly of Midwest Igbo extraction and would not have agreed to allow the Nigerian Army to attack from the Midwest, at least on moral grounds and for a considerable length of time. I would argue that they unwisely joined in the conspiracy to allow Biafra to invade the Midwest. If I have anything to say, it's that they should have stayed away and used their contacts to provide the Biafran Army with intelligence, kept up the barrier, and even smuggled food and at least nonlethal supplies to Biafra[158].

The folly of the Biafran invasion of the Midwest is made even more vivid by the extensive excerpt from Maj. Adewale Ademoyega[159] that I have reproduced below. In summary, besides the thin layer of military manpower, which Ademoyega was to recognize toward the end of the Midwest invasion, Ademoyega would agree with me that Biafra lacked sufficient equipment to prosecute such an invasion. Specifically, according toAdemoyega[160]

"...Chukwuka had come to set me free (Page 202)[161] ... but he was yet to gather arms and ammunition ... ... We drove to the police station and took possession of all their old Mark IV bolt action rifles, single round rifles, and all the available ammunition. It all amounted to very little ... Ifeajuna took me to the Edokpolo Army Barracks (Page 204) ... I was to command a newly assembled battalion ... billed to forge its way to Ibadan ... He introduced me to the men of the Battalion ... Everyone was a new soldier ... The best had only been trained for five days ... only a handful of them had any weapons at all ... came in civilian clothing ... in civilian vehicles ... They were about seven hundred in number and would make a good battalion if they were well-armed

---

[158] *Egodi Uchendu, Women and Conflict in the Nigerian Civil War, Trenton, New Jersey, Africa World Press, 2007, Chapter 5, Pp. 137 – 45 and Pp. 237 – 42).*

[159] *Adewale Ademoyega, Why We Struck, the Story of the First Nigerian Coup, Nigeria, Evans Brothers Publishers, 1982*

[160] *Ibid, Pp. 202 – 15*

[161] *Adewale Ademoyega (Yoruba man) was one of the masterminds of the January 15 coup. He was imprisoned in Enugu and later moved to Warri in the Midwest of Nigeria. It was there that Biafran forces released him in August 1967.*

... We had managed to seize a few more weapons from the armory of the Midwest Command ... However, only 100 or 14% of my men were armed ... The Federal authorities in Lagos had ... marshaled a force of company strength, supported by ferrets and mortars to delay the Liberation Army (Page 208)... The 12th Battalion was ... the leading unit in the advance to Ibadan. It had a few Landrovers and lorries ... The remainder were cars and purely civilian vehicles ... ... Actually, the whole division had no support weapons at all, not even 2-inch mortars... Besides a few machine guns, the Division had no high caliber weapons of any description ... The Division Commander went further forward to assess the situation ... After a detailed appreciation of the situation, he ordered the rear unit to return to Benin, followed by a gradual withdrawal of the forward troops... It was the first setback of the Liberation Army in the Midwest.[162]"

Ademoyega continues,

"...As a matter of fact, the Division (101 Division) was very thin on the ground. The only operational battalion was the 12th ... Even that unit had no support weapons ... The 18th Battalion based in Warri ... had only two machine guns ... and there were no support weapons Within a week, we received a single 3-inch mortar Barrel and a few mortar bombs ... I sent the mortar barrel to the 12th Battalion ... and the lone mortar was fixed towards the enemy location, even without sight-setting instruments ... the first mortar fell into the "pot of soup" of the enemy ... The enemy abandoned their weapons ... and fled at full speed ... However, many civilian supporters soon came to us to warn us that Federal troops had occupied Ondo ... A young officer ... reported that the enemy was a division of two brigades ... On hearing this report, Lt. Col. Akahga refused to go and face them with a single battalion ... From then on, any plan to move further West from Ore along the Ijebu-Ode-Ibadan axis was strongly resisted by Lt. Col. Akagha ... who argued that ... we would immediately be cut off from Biafra through any of the several Northern approaches ... and he was neither prepared nor willing to be cut off from Biafra and be finished in the West."[163]

Based on Ademoyega's narrative, it is easy to see how the allegations of sabotage against Banjo and other officers that abandoned Benin about three weeks before Nigerian forces arrived at Benin were partially true. In effect, based on Akpan's narrative, Banjo and Ifeajuna were saboteurs for other reasons, not for money. However, the loss of the Midwest could not be attributed entirely to sabotage. The Biafran leadership used the politics of sabotage to deflect responsibility from themselves. In a way, it motivated officers and men to try their best in the field. However, determination alone could not have won the war. The Biafran population was dedicated to their struggle in response to their pain and anguish, but unknown to our people, the elephants on this side of the struggle had individual agendas so strong and so mutually hidden that there was a failure of coordination among them. They could not even order their priorities to provide us, the grass, enough blades to fight the war and pick up sufficient crumbs in the end.

Onitsha to Abagana to Kampala: October 1967 to March 1968

After the fall of the Midwest and Enugu, nothing very spectacular took place until the Battle of Abagana in March 1968—though Biafra did make a big deal about the battle of Ugwuoba. For sure, the war went on and the Nigerian Army without much effort linked the Southeastern part of Biafra from Calabar through Ogoja via Obubra and Ikom. I do not recollect hearing even one newscast about a battle in Obubra or Ikom. Ifeajuna requested some troops and materials to defend Obubra and Ikom but left them fallow and hiding in a bush, apparently planning to overthrow Ojukwu with these troops, only to be arrested and subsequently executed for treason. Effiong[164] also narrates how some foreign mercenaries that led our troops around the Calabar sector withdrew with speed and

---

[162] *Ademoyega, Op. Cit, Page 210.*
[163] *Ademoyega, Pp.211 - 15*
[164] Effiong, Nigeria and Biafra: My Story Pp. 158 - 160) and Madiebo, The Nigerian Revolution and the Biafran War, Pp. 197 & 236

opened up the link to Obubra and Ogoja, to the north, after they waited in vain for promised artillery and armored cars, thereafter, departing from Biafra. Once the Nigerian forces linked up in Calabar and Ogoja at the Northern border of Nigeria, Biafra was effectively blockaded on its eastern border. As P. J. Odu[165] would say, there was no overall strategic plan to defend Biafra. If there had been such a plan, it would have inevitably included the defense of the eastern boundaries of the country that bordered on the Cameroons. The inhabitants of the area—if not for quasi-ethnic sympathy, as some of them had Igbo names and cultural ties—would have assisted in the smuggling of arms and food for personal profit, but they had no sentimental reason to support Nigeria. I recollect vividly that mid-October in Biafra, while I was manning my mother's drug store in the marketplace at the Oriendu marketplace in Ovim, late at one night, my great uncle Okezie Ihedioha called me in a hush to come over to his store, across from my drug store. Lo and behold, he had huge quantities of canned tomato sauce, tomato paste, and other imports smuggled from the Cameroons, even though Nigerian forces had captured the seaport of Calabar. Instead of recognizing the difficulties that our troops faced in the area, Ojukwu engaged in the propaganda that the fall of these vital links and food-producing areas had been the fault of saboteurs. This was toward November and December [166].

November 1967 to January 1968: The battles for Onitsha – Abagana.

The expectation and desperation in Biafra and the hope in Nigeria were that Biafra had come to an end with the fall of Enugu and the loss of the Midwest. But that was not so. After a brief lull in the fighting, early October 1967 saw Nigerian forces begin to attack Onitsha (Onitsha), a major commercial city in the Western boundary of Biafra, bordering on the Midwest region. About the first week of October, Nigerian forces began their first assault of Onitsha with heavy artillery shelling and also began to invade Calabar. The fall of Calabar and the linkage with Ogoja have already been described, so I will focus on the struggle for Onitsha in this section.

At this stage of the war, more evidence of the determination of our people to resist can be seen when Biafra began to deploy her new weapons that had been manufactured in Biafra, including the new and famous "Mass Destroyer" (*Ogbu Ni'igwe in Igbo*). The Nigerian forces (Madiebo, Pp. 200 – 202) advanced with armor-plated boats across the Niger River and a heavy barrage of artillery. Eventually, Nigerian forces occupied Onitsha when our troops had exhausted their ammunition, as usual. The town of Onitsha was set ablaze and looted by the Nigerian soldiers. A counter-attack ensued and Biafran forces reclaimed the city.

Second Invasion of Onitsha and the Kampala Peace Talks

Nigerian forces attempted a second invasion of Onitsha about two weeks after the first abortive attempt. This time, Col. Murtala Mohamed's Second Division attempted another river crossing from Asaba. According to Madiebo[167] "Nigerian warplanes strafed ... Onitsha .... our troops were in high morale ... and kept vigil... for an invasion, if it did come, would be from somewhere other than Asaba ... There were officers who thought that Colonel Mohamed would not be daft enough as to attack Onitsha again.[168]" Even Olusegun Obasanjo described this attempt and, a third attempt to attack Onitsha across the Niger River, as nothing but bravado. Obasanjo described how these attempts led to near mutiny and disobedience by the troops and an open confrontation between Lt.

---

[165] *Peter Odu, The Future that Vanished, The Future that Vanished, Thorough Fare, NJ, Xlibris Publishing, 2009*

[166] Madiebo, The Nigerian Revolution and the Biafra War, Pp. 236 – 37

[167] Alexander Madiebo, *The Nigerian Revolution, and the Biafra War*, Pp. 202 – 203

[168] *Alexander Madiebo, The Nigerian Revolution, and the Biafra War, Pp. 207 - 10*

Col. Akirinade and the division commander, with the eventual departure of the former. All three attempts ended in a fiasco.[169]

On the morning of October 20 1967 the Nigerian armada of approximately 6 boats were sighted sailing down the Niger from Asaba ... As soon as the boats were in midstream, we opened up again ... hitting one boat after another and sinking them ... The most exciting moment was the sinking of a boat with a Biafran-made rocket ... After six hours of battle, six boats had been sunk ... and the rest were sailing back to Asaba." With this battle, Onitsha was once more saved from Nigerian invasion. The propaganda machine was agog with the news of the victory. Of greater importance to Biafrans was the news or knowledge that Biafran-made rockets and shore batteries (at Calabar) were at work. What an achievement! Inside Biafra, our ingenuity was magnified. Even if the "White man" did not sell us weapons, it appeared that we could carry on with our native weapons.

A third invasion was attempted before December 1967. This time, Col. Mohamed marched from Idah, north of Onitsha, and engaged Biafran forces for weeks, beginning from Amadim Olo[170]. For the defenses of Onitsha, Ojukwu assigned three hundred rounds of shells (Op. Cit, Page 207) against more than 10,000 rounds of shells held by the enemy. Although Biafran forces did their best to check and slow the enemy, the politics of sabotage was brought against them yet again. The enemy pushed on until about mid-January 1968 when the town of Awka fell to the enemy after they had captured Ugwuọbâ. The news on Radio Biafra was that Nigeria had lost about 10,000 soldiers at the Battle of Ugwuoba. To get to Onitsha, Nigerian forces had to pass through Abagana. The battle for Abagana was memorable and provided ammunition for Biafran propaganda. Also, soldiers' accounts of the battle (Madiebo Pp. 224 – 28 and Onyejekwe, Pp. 120 - 23) bring into further relief Biafra's lack of preparation for a war of such magnitude.

The Battle of Abagana (see also Forsyth, Pp. 124 – 26) was the culmination of Nigeria's (two-pronged) third and finally successful attempt to capture Onitsha. After March 15, 1968, the Nigerian Army had to link up Enugu and Onitsha. With almost 20,000 men, 102 troop carrier convoy, 20,000 rounds of shell ammunition, and moving in a massed tight double phalanx, Nigerian forces proceeded to bulldoze their way into Onitsha. In response, the Biafran forces laid an enormous ambush. Once the Nigerian forces had walked into the trap, the Biafrans fired off a lone mortar bomb that landed on a 6,000-gallon fuel tank that was sandwiched between troops and ammunition[171]. The mortar landed on the fuel tank and caused an enormous explosion and set fires and more explosions that lasted three days and practically destroyed the entire force. According to Madiebo (Page 223), the Nigerian Army entered Onitsha on March 25, 1968, "their scandalous losses notwithstanding." Forsyth[172] reports that Nigerian forces entered Onitsha with a little less than 2,000 soldiers out of the 20,000 they had started with. The scandalous part on the Biafran side is that this battle was fought with one mortar round compared to the thousands—or at least hundreds—that the Nigerians had, in addition to 350 tons of other war materials[173]. In any event, the success of the ambush was a clear indication of the determination of the Biafrans and the high skill of their commanders. On the Nigerian side, the story of that battle of Abagana has been distorted. Obasanjo (Page 43) would have us believe that it was pure luck that a mortar bomb hit the rear guard of the ill-advised tight phalanx of the Nigerian offensive formation on the road from Abagana to Onitsha. Pure luck, maybe. But there was also a clear case of planning, as Madiebo and Forsyth would describe in the trend of battles beginning from December 1967 and lasting through March 1968, which culminated in this disaster for the Nigerian Army.

---

[169] *Olusegun Obasanjo, My Command: An Account of the Nigerian Civil War (1967 - 1970), Ibadan, Nigeria, Heinemann, 1980, Pp. 42 - 43*

[170] *Madiebo, The Nigerian Revolution and the Biafra War, Pp. 209 – 10 and Frederick Forsyth, The Biafra Story, Pp. 120 - 24*

[171] Forsyth, Op. Cit, Pp. 124-26 and Ignatius Onyejekwe, *Nigeria Civil War: The Country Biafra and the Fall of an Iroko Tree, Frederick Maryland, USA, America Star Books, 2014* Pp. 120 – 23:

[172] *Forsyth, Op. Cit., Pp. 126 – 27.*

[173] *Onyejekwe, Op. Cit, Pp. 120 – 23 and Madiebo Op. Cit, Pp. 224 – 28,*

What ought to be known is that the officers who effected the ambush had donned the uniform just like Obasanjo and were as skillful and as experienced as Obasanjo, or potentially so. They probably saw their opportunity and knew what to do. Meanwhile, from the Battle of Kadesh (1347 BCE) to Isandlwhana (1879), the blunder of the type that took place at Abagana has usually led to disastrous consequences. Hence after its Pyrrhic victory, the Nigerian Army straggled into Onitsha, much like Napoleon into Moscow after the Battle of Borodino (1812).

The Battle of Abagana was a threshold in the struggle. Before Abagana, the morale in Biafra was very low. In January 1968, the Nigerian government had changed the Nigerian currency, which hitherto had been used in Biafra. Though the struggle for Onitsha yielded a reluctant Pyrrhic victory for Nigeria, the disaster gave Biafra enormous propaganda ammunition. In the marketplace gossip, there was a rumor that Murtala Mohamed was lifted out by helicopter to Onitsha. I do not know how true that could have been. However, what is common knowledge is that according to Odogwu "Col. Murtala Mohamed was so thoroughly exhausted after the debacle ... that once he crossed the River Niger and arrived in Lagos, he took a French Leave and left the country[174]." Truly, Murtala Mohamed was not to be seen or heard of in Nigeria until sometime in late 1970 or early 1971. The next remarkable event after Abagana was the peace talks between Nigeria and Biafra in May 1968, just in the vicinity of the Nigerian capture of Port Harcourt. However, these peace talks, to be discussed later, fell apart and the war continued.

After the failure of the peace talks in May 1968, the Nigerian Army began preparations for what they believed would end the war. Just as the peace talks were about to begin, Tanzania and Zambia recognized Biafra. Nevertheless, Col. Adekunle, the commander of the Third Marine Commandos Division of the Nigerian Army promised Gowon that he would capture Owerre, Aba, and Umuahia by the end of September. In May 1968, shortly after the collapse of the Kampala peace talks, Port Harcourt fell to the Nigerians. Port Harcourt was Biafra's last access to the outside world—it had an airport that enabled Biafra to import armament, and even other needed goods. One might assume that if Port Harcourt fell then all hope was lost. And yet it was not, as Oyewole writes, "Biafran ingenuity kicked in." In light of Port Harcourt's fall, whomever Ojukwu was working with was ingenious—but it makes me wonder why this ingenuity did not extend to other aspects of organizing the war. When Port Harcourt fell, Biafra quickly constructed two airports, one at Uturu, about sixty miles south of Enugu, and another at Uli, a little north of Owerre and south of Ihiala. Despite these airport constructions, the capture of the port had another immediate effect: things began to get much more difficult in Biafra in terms of food and essential items.

Just before the fall of Port Harcourt, Col. Adekunle had captured Ikot Ekpene in the middle of April 1968. This would bring Nigerian forces less than forty miles to Umuahia, the new capital of Biafra. Following the fall of Port Harcourt, Col. Adekunle's next target was Owerre. There was a fierce battle for Owerre, which fell in September. Aba fell in August 1968, and Umuahia was next to close the deal. If Umuahia fell in September 1968, that would have been it, or so I thought. Umuahia is only twenty-one miles south of Ovim, where I lived. After all, Aba was gone, Owerre was gone, so of course, Umuahia would be it.

Diplomacy and Economics

From December 1967 through October 1968, besides military dynamics, there were also diplomatic and economic changes and transformations. Nigeria changed currency in an economic move that was intended to strangle Biafra in the international financial markets and make transactions practically impossible. Economically, by October to November 1967, as described earlier, the eastern boundary of Biafra through the Cameroons was closed off. There were also peace talks, which I will discuss later in context but will also briefly elaborate on within the general context of developments and my attitudes as a fifteen-year-old.

---

[174] *Benard Odogwu, No Place to Hide, Pp. 125 – 26.*

January 1968 began almost uneventfully. There were minor military actions, but most of all, the economic effects were widespread. When Nigeria suddenly announced the change of currency, there was general euphoria in a populace that did not understand the larger implications. Biafran propaganda glorified it. For me, like most people, it felt odd that we had declared ourselves Biafra but had continued to use Nigerian money. It made sense, as Biafran propaganda made it appear, and we were proud to have our own money. I was excited and looked forward to the change. When the Biafran money was eventually issued, the artwork of the currency was impressive and indicative of the greater ingenuity of the Biafran mind.

Then there were the peace talks. In May 1968 and August 1968, there were two peace talks between Nigeria and Biafra. Yet between April and August 1968, four African countries recognized Biafra's independence. These recognitions gave us hope and were celebrated by the ordinary person. To me, it was all but victory and I thought that Nigeria would give up the fight and or that there would be a cascade of recognitions across the African countries. However, Nigeria immediately countered with fervent diplomatic activities that probably stalled further recognitions, as will be discussed later.

Regarding the peace talks, I wondered what the peace talks would achieve. My initial impression was that Nigeria went to the peace talks as an indication that they were now recognizing Biafra or at least recognizing Biafran military credibility. Biafran propaganda gave us the impression that Awolowo had stated that Biafra must surrender and our leaders would be put on trial for treason and, if found guilty, would be punished. That was not acceptable to me. My young sense of justice was revolted by such a notion. Such terms would mean that Nigerians did not accept their share of responsibility for Biafran action. Even if we were to go back to Nigeria, on what terms would we return? One way or another, I was hoping, though, that some kind of settlement could be reached. There was the possibility that we could return to Nigeria. How would that be accepted by ordinary people? I had no idea, but all I wanted was to go back to school or return to some normal life, for obvious reasons—things were getting more difficult, and it was showing in interesting ways.

The observations that I will relate indicate the extent of the resilience of the Igbo people and how much they were willing to sacrifice for the sake of winning the war. First, the concept of Win-the-War cuisine—soup or any food—became commonplace. Win-the-War cooking was a cuisine that did not have the full complement of condiments for the best flavor. The soup was cooked without all the dried fish and often without sufficient meat to provide people a full helping of meat. If anything, dried meat was added to the food, or a small quantity of dried fish was crushed into the soup just for the flavor, which meant the soup would not be as thick (as consistent) as usual. One behavior that I found particularly peculiar was the soup or pepper soup was flavored with dried meat that I considered lightly fermented. Our people love dried meat as it was a method of preserving meat before the era of refrigeration (which continues today as a tradition, for the refrigerator is not yet ubiquitous in our society). Regardless, dried meat is still cherished, fridge or no fridge. What I observed was that the process of drying or smoking meat was modified such that the thigh or forearm of the goat or bushmeat (nchi) was done in such a way that the blood of the meat was left at the onset of mild fermentation that left a slightly strong flavor. The smoking was then accelerated to dry the meat normally. In the end, the mild smell was still discernible in the finished soup or pepper soup product. In as much as I found this repugnant, in later years I read about how fermented meat or fish sauce, and other fermented vegetable have been used as part of human food flavoring throughout the other history of mankind. In Ancient Rome, for example, they produced a fish source called liquamen or garum. Liquamen was produced by what I would consider rotten fish. Specifically, the very best garum, according to the *Geoponica*, is called *haimatum*. It was made with solely the innards of the tuna, including blood and gills. These are put in a pot with salt and placed on the roof of the house and after two months the liquid is garum. According to Muusers, Small fish are covered with salt, spread out in the sun, and turned from time to time. When they have been completely fermented, they are scooped into a fine-meshed basket that is hanging in a vase. The liquid that seeps into the vase is liquamen. In another type of fish source called the *Method Wunderlich*, fish (anchovy, mackerel, tuna) is mixed with salt in a ratio of 9:1, then left in a pot in the sun for several months and stirred occasionally."[175] During my days at Oriendu market, I also heard about okpehe, a kind of food flavoring that was made in the middle belt of Nigeria. According to food experts, "Several species of bacteria especially *Bacillus subtilis, Bacillus licheniformis,* and *Micrococcus* spp were found to be the most actively involved organisms in the production of okpehe."[176] Come to think about it, pungent food flavors abound in Nigeria. Other examples included are *Dawa Dawa* (I loved Dawa Dawa) and ôgîrî (I do not like this one).

Our people also began to eat a kind of cocoa yam that I heard was meant for pigs. In as much as our people were not fond of pigs, I know a few people here and there who kept a pig. The level of pork consumption did not justify reserving or attributing a particular kind of food as being for pigs. This cocoa yam, with yellow egg yolk–like interior was rather flavorful and I wondered why it was not adopted as regular food by our people. After the war, this type of cocoa yam was abandoned again.

Another manifestation of the difficulties was that people began to engage in petty thievery of the kind that our societies despised. Young men and women began to raid farms and backyards to steal chicken and harvest crops that did not belong to them. I was living in the marketplace where I manned the drug store and witnessed how thieves that were caught were stripped naked and paraded in the marketplace. I witnessed several such parades—even one of the occasions was that of a young adult woman in her mid-twenties who had stolen a chicken to make soup. Of course, this response failed to address the underlying cause of the problem – the economic hardship brought on by the war. Punishments such as those I witnessed appear to have been practiced in other places in Igboland. Egodi Uchendu reports that in

"...Umuahia, Ovim (my hometown) and Nkpa (the neighboring kindred town to Ovim), ... youth caught stealing were stripped naked, adorned with a necklace of small shells and dragged around their towns and accompanied by a throng singing defamatory songs ...The excursion ended with the thief being dumped in a public toilet ... an open space designed for defecation... girls were [paraded naked but] not dumped in a public toilet."[177]

I witnessed the dragging around of culprits, but I am not aware of anyone in Ovim being dumped in a public toilet.

Operation OAU – Desperation, Resignation, and Hope

Around the end of July 1968, Col. Adekunle's Third Marine Commandos made a move from Ikot Ekpene to capture Umuahia as part of his famous Operation OAU (Owerre, Aba, and Umuahia). Owerre and Aba fell in August and September 1968, and Umuahia, now the headquarters of the Biafran government, was the final target. With the capture of Umuahia, the final collapse of Biafra was a given. But once more, the operation ended in calamity for Nigerian forces. The attempt to capture Umuahia began around the middle of September 1968. About this time, Biafran forces achieved spectacular successes at Oguta and Ikot Ekpene. Following these successes, Biafran forces intercepted Nigerian forces outside the city of Umuahia. I held my breath and hoped, with confidence that they would not succeed, for Nigerian forces were inching their way to Okigwe, seventeen miles west of Ovim. If they captured Umuahia, that would be it. On September 17, the Nigerian Third Marine Division, previously Third Marine Commando Brigade, began making their way toward Umuahia, but a division of Biafran soldiers intercepted them outside the city and a bloody battle ensued. The terrain around Umuahia consisted of areas of vast jungles and rivers that were littered with mines and Biafran soldiers. For fourteen days, the two sides exchanged

---

[175] *Tannahill, Food in History, New York, Three Rivers Press, 1973 & 1985, Page 83 Also Christianne Muusers, Roman Fish Sauce: Liquamen or Garum, https://coquinaria.nl/en/roman-fish-sauce/,*
[176] *Balogun, M.A. and G.P. Oyeyiola, Changes in the Nutrient Composition of Okpehe During Fermentation, Pakistan Journal of Nutrition 2012 Vol. 11(3) Pp. 270-275 also Fowoyo, Patience Temitope, Microbiological and Proximate Analysis of Okpehe, a Locally Fermented Condiment, Food and Nutrition Journal, October 2017, Pp. 1 – 11 https://www.researchgate.net/publication/331901184*
[177] *Egodi Uchendu, Recollections of the Nigerian Civil War, Pp. 409 – 410.*

gunfire and artillery, resulting in mass casualties on both sides. Adekunle radioed that he needed reinforcements if his entire division were to survive, but the reinforcements never arrived. Nearly 15,000 Nigerian soldiers had either been killed or wounded in the Umuahia sector and on October 1, the Third Marine Division retreated to Port Harcourt while the 16th Division was left isolated in Owerre. Instead of pursuing the retreating Nigerians to Port Harcourt, the Biafrans slowly made their way up the Aba-Umuahia Road and managed to capture Aba on October 15.

The calamity was such that about two-thirds of the 35,000 soldiers involved in that invasion were killed. Following that victory, Radio Biafran spewed out its propaganda and magnified the annihilation of the Nigerian forces. Furthermore, by the end of September, not long after the repulsion of Adekunle's invasion of Umuahia, Radio Biafra's propaganda machine broadcasted that Nigerian forces had been surrounded at Owerre, with over 3,000 men of the Nigerian 16th Division inside the city. This encirclement was to spell the doom of the soldiers in the Nigerian brigade and eventually forced the Nigerian Army to withdraw from Owerre in April 1969. These two victories emboldened Biafra and provided further ammunition for Biafran propaganda. While Nigerian forces were encircled at Owerre, other units of the Nigerian army captured Okigwe in October 1968 by bulldozing their way fifty-six miles south from Enugu. At this point, if they had moved further, they might have captured Umuahia, which was only forty miles away. It was from Okigwe that they eventually captured Umuahia, storming through Ovim, which was seventeen miles east and fighting through Uzuakoli. For the next six months, from my hometown, I woke up every morning to the sounds of shellfire and exchange of gunfire from Okigwe to the west and Afikpo to the northeast. The partial recapture of Aba and the encirclement of the Nigerian forces at Owerre gave us hope. But this capture of Okigwe, seventeen miles from Ovim, brought the war even closer to home. It was like a zero-sum game. It was bad enough to hear the distant crackles of gunfire at Afikpo, forty-five miles northwest of Ovim, and hoping that eventually the Nigerian forces would be driven back or peace would be negotiated. Now that the war was closer and only seventeen miles away, what was our destiny? Would the war finally get to us? Will the Nigerian forces be beaten back as they were beaten back at Umuahia and Aba or will they be encircled as in Owerre and be driven back to Enugu on their way back to their own country? In the end, there was a feeling of foreboding, hopelessness, and fatalistic resignation mixed with a sense of confidence that eventually victory would be ours because our cause was just.

May to September 1968: Living in Oriendu – The Popular Side

Much has been said about Biafran propaganda and its effectiveness during the war. Indeed, Biafran propaganda was effective in taking the facts and graphically shaping them to influence world opinion. Propaganda directed at the world was designed to seek support by referencing the events that led to the war, both proximate and remote. Internally, though, the events that led to the war—the remote genesis of events and the proximate stalemates that precipitated the war—did not need to be dressed up. The communities of peoples that were involved in the war on both sides were still at that level of cultural and intellectual development that it was easy to instigate them into the kinds of actions that would not only precipitate the war but also support it continuously. The other element of Biafran propaganda was creating the impression among the people that Biafra was winning the war—or at least would eventually win the war. These beliefs were made to be strong, even in the face of glaring setbacks on the battlefield, loss of territory, and a constant stream of refugees that flooded Biafran-held areas.

The fear, apprehension, and indignation fueled by the Northern massacres of Igbo people sustained the continuing fear that the Nigerian government and its army intended to exterminate the Igbo race. The atrocities of the Nigerian Army as they advanced into the Biafran territory and the exodus of refugees from other parts of Biafra had the effect of providing manpower for the Biafran army. On the other hand, they also accelerated the shortage of food that led to the mass starvation of the Biafran population.

Biafran propaganda was also effective because the population was not truly educated. At the minimum, sophisticated and intellectual education was not pervasive and did not permeate the general population. Even those who had higher education were not truly educated. Many still believed in magic, were parochial and provincial, or lacked intellectual or ideological depth. Much of what was considered being educated was high school education, to which only a limited proportion of the population had access. Even college-educated people kept one foot in the ancient world of their forebears and the other foot in the modern world—that is, if you consider the modern world to be represented by technology. The so-called educated (those who went to schools and read books, understood the sciences, could pronounce foreign words, read newspapers, etc.) took advantage of their better understanding of the modern world to impress the less schooled into believing what they wanted them to believe. The story of the madman who claimed he was building a helicopter that would fly behind enemy lines is a good example. This is equally true of the man who was spreading the story that a shipload of armaments was docked in Lagos, Nigeria (enemy territory), on its way to Biafra via Port Harcourt. But this man's story was told shortly after the Nigerian Army had captured Port Harcourt in May 1968. The story was intended to assure the audience that the capture of Port Harcourt would be temporary. Strangely enough, the man said that the shipload of arms supplied by the Chinese would soon be docking in Port Harcourt, which had just been captured by Nigeria. Meanwhile, as I explained to the man who delivered this "news," a ship from China (east of Biafra) traveling to Port Harcourt could not travel via Lagos because Port Harcourt is east of Lagos. The fact that much of the audience believed the man was a clear indication of the credulity of the population, the treachery of the "educated" elite, and the desperation of the Biafran population. We were ready to believe anything. Such storytelling, though, was part of Biafran propaganda. It reveals, equally, that by May 1968, the Biafran population had become aware that the Biafran Army was not adequately armed. The barely educated, or better yet, the generally uneducated and ill-informed Biafran public was bamboozled easily by magical stories. The people relied on their educated representatives, as they had done since the arrival of the Europeans, to inform them. What happened was that the beneficiaries of education and those who had access to information simply told the public what they wanted and for their own reasons. Therefore, as the reality of Nigerian encroachment and the attendant fear of a Nigerian massacre of our people in the manner of the Northern pogrom gripped our people, it became necessary to assure them that all would be well. Our people's fears were fully justified. As it is clear during the Northern crisis, the Nigerian government made little effort to protect our people from the frenzy of murder even when soldiers and police, whose duty it was to protect, joined the violence. Our people were equally aware that certain people of goodwill who tried to protect the Eastern Nigerians were also victims of the riots.

As of May 1968, setbacks such as the fall of Port Harcourt were still considered to be temporary. Early successes, such as the invasion of the Midwest and reported repulsions of Nigerian attacks at Nsukka as well as claims about the capture of Oturkpo, gave our people hope that the apparent lengthy setbacks would be reversed as soon as these armaments, docked in Lagos were offloaded in Biafra. Another source of hope for the people was an extant, successive string of recognitions of Biafra by several African governments. With these recognitions, there was hope that armaments would flow, and other countries would recognize us.

For no apparent reason, around late July, or early August 1968. I decided to visit my dad at Owerre where he was stationed at the time. My mother and the children were still in Ovim while I manned the chemist shop at the Oriendu marketplace. Things were still quite normal in Biafra. The difficulties in Biafra, though obvious, were still bearable and people went about their business... Port Harcourt had fallen to federal troops, quite all right, but there was still hope and indeed ebullient confidence that we were still going to win the war. At that point, I was still taking things for granted—the war would end soon, and I would return to school. One morning, I packed a few clothes, closed my chemist store, and headed towards Umuahia. After arriving in Umuahia, I took another public transportation and arrived at Owerre. The Nigerian Army was still far away in Enugu, more than one hundred miles, and had not gone beyond Ugbo'oka on the road to Okigwe. I stayed in Owerre for about five days and left during the third week of August. While I was at Owerre, my dad went to work normally at the Ministry of Education. I wondered what they would be doing at work as schools were closed for almost one year. In the few days that I spent in Owerre, I had quite an experience. The first was my decision to visit town for some unknown purpose. Schools were closed and I had no business in town. I did not have any friends in the main town, but I went there anyway. I did not have any money to take public transportation, so I walked. On my way back home, about half a mile from our house, which was visible from my location near the courthouse, it began to rain. I could see the rain ahead near our house—about fifty yards from the house. However, it was not raining and dry near the courthouse. For about two minutes, I prevaricated whether to proceed home or shelter myself on the corridors of the courthouse. I walked slowly, hoping that the rain might stop before I reached where it was coming down. My thought was that it was not serious rain, since it was coming down at that distance and was not making any progress toward the courthouse. I planned that if it did not stop by the time I got into it, I would run from the starting point of the rain to our house, and I would not get soaked. But I was sorely wrong. I kept walking until I got into the starting point of the rain, at which point I trotted as fast as I could for the remaining fifty yards toward our house. However, before I entered the house, I was drenched!

My second experience was with an air raid. I had heard so much about them but had not yet experienced one. Nigerian Airforce air raids were intended to terrorize the civilian population of Biafra and sap their spiritual energy to continue supporting the war. This tactic had the opposite of the intended effect. It reinforced the Biafran population's belief that the Nigerian government had the intention of exterminating the population or at least to continue the pogrom of 1966. Besides prolonging the war by hardening the determination of the population, Nigerians wasted valuable resources by not targeting the battlefields and discouraging troop morale. If indeed, the Nigerian Airforce had targeted the battlefronts, they may have been able to effectively win more battles decisively and may have shielded Nigerian troops better from Biafran resistance, even from the deployment of Ogbuni'igwe. Biafran propaganda even gave an ironic twist to the air raids. After each Nigerian air raid, several or even numerous civilians were killed. Radio Biafra would announce to the world that thousands were killed. I recollect figures like 10,000 people. If one were to add up the number of the thousands of people killed by air raids at Aba, the entire population of Aba should have been annihilated by the air raids. Another possible interpretation of the air raid policy of the Nigerian Airforce was simply that they were opportunities to continue the massacre of Igbos, destroy more Igbo properties, and humiliate the people even more as an extension of their punishment for the events of January 1966.

It was in Owerre that I witnessed an air raid for the first time. One afternoon, during the first few days of my visit to Owerre, the siren sounded, and I ran out from the house to take cover behind a tree that was close to the servants' (boys') quarters of my dad's house. The air raid's focus was near the center of town around the marketplace and population concentration. Usually, the Nigerian Airforce planes attacked population concentrations such as the center of town or marketplaces. Our house was in a suburb of the main town. It appeared that the raid was over, so I stood in the grass by the tree where I was hiding near the boys' quarters. The fighter jets that raided Biafran towns flew very low, as they encountered no real interference from anti-aircraft fire. Biafra had practically no air defenses aside from some Bofor guns, though there was a limited ordinance to use them. Usually, one Bofor gun would be chasing two or more aircraft with a few shots. There may have been close calls, but I do not recollect any planes downed. In any event, as I thought that the raid was over, I stood at akimbo and saw the fighter plane flying low toward our house. My fists were placed defiantly on my hips as I looked up at the plane, somehow sophomorically brave as if I was taunting the pilot. I could see the pilot. The pilot banked to one side and sprayed the bullets perilously close to me. I quickly ducked and lay flat on my stomach. Now, that was scary and equally stupid! As soon as the pilot flew past my location, I crawled swiftly and changed my location. In hindsight, I believe that the pilot was only trying to scare me or to tell me how stupid I was, standing at akimbo and appearing to taunt him. If he meant to get me, he had every opportunity to spray those bullets more accurately. Three or so days after the raid, I decided that I did not see any purpose for continuing to stay at Owerre. This was about the third week of August 1968. I left unceremoniously and returned to my chemist shop. I can only thank God that I made it through that event. However, the next event is another reason that caused me to wonder how we made it through that war, for at that point in 1968, things were still quasi-normal in Biafra.

In March 1968, Biafra had finally lost Onitsha though the Nigerian Army never held it comfortably for the duration of the war. However, Biafran propaganda made it appear that the Battle of Abagana, which was a widely publicized disaster for Nigeria, prevented the Nigerian Army from entering Onitsha. The Biafran Army victory at Aba'agana in March 1968 was still fresh in our minds. Such major victories gave us hope that we could dislodge the Nigerians from wherever they captured. My attitude was that if Biafra were to lose Owerre, Biafra's doom would be certain. For that reason, Biafra would put up a spirited fight to ensure that the Nigerians would not be allowed to go beyond Port Harcourt. Indeed, I believed that it would not take long before the Nigerian Army would be routed from Port Harcourt. However, shortly after I left Owerre, about September 2, 1968, there was news that the Nigerian Army was assaulting Owerre and Aba simultaneously, under the command of Col. Adekunle. On September 14, 1968, the Nigerian Army captured Aba and began attacking Umuahia. On September 13, the Biafran 14th Division came under heavy artillery fire from the Nigerian 16th Brigade under the command of Col. E. A. Etuk. On September 18, after a fierce five-day stand, the Biafran 14th Division abandoned the fight in <u>Ohoba</u> and <u>Obinze</u> and retreated from the city, leaving Owerre open to Nigeria's Col. Etuk and his 16th Division. Owerre fell to federal forces on September 18, 1968. My dad, evacuating well in advance of the Nigerian Army's invasion, arrived back in Ovim, bringing along his vehicle, a Peugeot 403. Though my dad was home at Ovim with us, and while I remained at the marketplace, he certainly was not idle. Mr. Egbe was a restless man. He was actively involved in the politics of the war. He did not disclose exactly what his role was, but one thing is for certain: the Ministry of Education was no longer active in educational activities—and certainly not in teacher training. Officers of the ministries and government functionaries were now deployed wherever the government of Biafra could use them. I continued with my work at the drug store, did farm work, and engaged in other activities in the village like others. Whenever I could, I would help my mother and other siblings at the farm, fetch wood, harvest cassava, and process it to assist my mother. My youngest brothers, Agu (two years), Okezie (four years), and Iroegbu (six years) were too young to contribute much.

My dad interacted actively with the political and military leaders of the war effort. He was enthusiastic and very active in disseminating the intense propaganda and was quite effective at it given that he was a highly respected man for his education and his pioneering prominence in that area. He also influenced my thoughts about the war. One of the commanders that he interacted regularly with was a major who was in charge of the unit stationed at Otamkpa, along the railway line leading around Ovim and north to Enugu. On one occasion, my dad gave me a bottle of Golden Guinea, probably his last visible bottle, to give to the commander. Indeed, the major came to our house and informed me that my dad had promised him this beer. I handed the beer to him as instructed.

Nigeria's capture of Owerre and Aba was a tremendous shock. The consolation for me and most Biafrans was the events at the Battle of Aba'agana. During this famous battle in March 1968, a large convoy of Nigerian soldiers and their ammunition were destroyed. Biafran propaganda, however, made it appear that the Nigerian soldiers who were encountered at Aba'agana on their third attempt to capture Onitsha never made it there. This third "annihilation" of the Nigerian Army invaders was a morale booster for Biafrans. The first two attempts, one across the Niger Bridge in October 1967 and another in the latter part of the same month and the Battle of Ugwuoba ended in disaster for the Nigerian Army. Biafran propaganda announced that 10,000 Nigerian soldiers were slaughtered at Ugwuoba. However, Madiebo's account does not agree, and though the Nigerian push at Ugwuoba did not yield them a clear victory, 10,000 Nigerian soldiers did not die there. Though the Nigerian Army did not stay comfortably at Onitsha, they entered and held it after Abaagana. The Biafran propaganda, however, kept hope alive. For me, the capture of Owerre and Aba was yet another example of the seesaw of war.

Eventually, we would prevail, but this feeling did not last long. Shortly after the fall of Owerre and Aba in mid-September 1968, the Nigerian Army advanced a scary fifty to sixty miles from Enugu, north of Ovim, and captured Okigwe, which was less than twenty miles from Ovim. What was to stop them from assaulting Ovim the next week? Even more so, from the northeast flank, the Nigerian Army made another lightning putsch and entered Afikpo and Afikpo-Road. Afikpo-Road was not more than twenty-five miles northeast of Ovim as the crow flies. For some reason, the Nigerian Army stalled at these two locations. Every morning, we woke up to the sound of gunfire, but only a few weeks later, we became comfortable with it. Indeed, my dad had a palm oil plantation at Ezu'ukwu Alayi (a stone's throw from Afikpo-Road) that he had been developing since 1956. Besides the palm oil trees that had begun to yield palm fruits, the cassava and yams from the farm were big. We even went to harvest the cassava and the palm oil from that farm during the occupation of Afikpo-Road. It was about ten miles away from home and northeast of Ovim in the direction of Afikpo and Afikpo-Road—and very close to the Nigerian Army formations and perimeter. The fact that we went to this comfortably was a source of comfort for me. In my sophomoric sense of complacency, I thought that because the Nigerians had stalled again, sooner or later, they would be driven back. After all, I was only sixteen years old and not involved in the fighting.

Despite our illusions, things were beginning to get more difficult in Biafra. In January 1968, the Nigerian government changed its currency to deprive Biafra of access to foreign markets, since Biafran currency would not be recognized overseas. Indeed, the Biafran stamps that were issued shortly after were not recognized. The government of Canada is on the record for officially announcing its nonrecognition of Biafran stamps. As a people, we were now resigned to the difficulties of the war. When Europeans arrived in our hinterland, fewer than seventy-five years earlier, our people were still forest farmers that lived off the land. We did not live much better nor did our methods change drastically. People who acquired White man's education and participated in salaried and so-called formal sectors were, in many cases, still tethered to the land. Families were sometimes evenly divided into those whose subsistence methods had not changed appreciably from what it was on the eve of the European era and those who had become transformed into the modern European era in high-paying occupations based on a high level of education or modern industrial skills. Even those of us whose parents were strongly rooted in high-level jobs and top salaries had not exactly separated from the land. My mother had not long severed herself from the traditional modes of living. Her feet were still firmly planted in the traditional, though she had enjoyed the comforts of living the lifestyle of the upper-middle class. My parents were still familiar with old methods—almost as though they were still dependent on them. A lot of people may have felt complacent to have extricated themselves from it. However, it did not take much for them to readapt to it when war conditions compelled them to revert out of desperation. Many people who had lived in the North or other parts of Nigeria as laborers, barbers, traders, carpenters, mechanics, and other vocations in the recently introduced modern sector had only not too long earlier had been farmers and children of parents that raised them in the traditional modes of production and sustenance. Even my dad, the London-educated biologist, had been raised in the traditional modes and was quite familiar with them. However, he effectively applied the best of his training in the modern methods of agricultural science in the development of his agricultural plantation. At Umudike, where my dad was senior staff, vice principal, and later principal of the teacher's college (Rural Education Center), we always had a sizable yam farm. My mother had a poultry and goat farm with at least fifty chickens in it, excluding the chicklets and young chickens that were not ready for the market. We helped to make the mounds and with the assistance of, say, our gardener we weeded the farm, under the direction of our mother. Our mother had a substantial vegetable garden. We hardly bought vegetables from the market, though I recollect that my mother attended the marketplace regularly. During the planting season, we were in the village with others and cultivated the land just like other people, except that our dad may have, occasionally, taken us to the farm or close to the location of the farm in a car—a privilege that more than 90 percent of the population did not have. We learned, like others, how to fetch wood and carry it on our heads. Therefore, unlike Uzokwe (author of *Surviving in Biafra*), much of this lifestyle was not new to us, except that it was more difficult. Much of the population hunkered down, ready for a long haul. What our people did not realize, however, was that we were heavily dependent on other parts of Nigeria for the variety and supplementals in our diets. The beef was almost entirely from the North. The cattle ranches in Eastern Nigeria were not sufficiently developed to supply the additional beef that was needed in Biafra. Though poultry might have made up for the lack of beef, the Eastern Nigeria livestock development system was not prepared for large-scale expansion of meat production. Modern systems of agriculture were extensively developed in the Eastern Region by 1966, but like many things that happened in post-independence Nigeria, our elite took over the white man's positions for the privilege of it, with nary a scheme or plan to apply them to the transformation of society. Even now, more than fifty years after the war, not much has changed in attitude. The discovery of oil, which some claim was the object of the conflict, made things worse. The elite quickly turned their attention to exploiting and spending the oil money. Contributory to the rapid deterioration of matters was the fact Ogoja and Abakeleke, the food-producing areas, were quickly overrun by the Federal Nigerian Army—north and south. The riverine areas that could have produced fish were taken in July and September. There appeared to be no overall strategic plan for the defense of Biafra. If one had existed, arrangements would have been made to expand alternative food production, including the foods that grow and prosper in our area of the country, especially in the hinterland. For example, the fact that Biafra developed high-level technologies—refinery, weaponry, and telecommunication during the war—was in part because of the level of desperation. This level of invention mothered by necessity also points to the possibilities that were never developed and used. Ojukwu went around demonstrating to people that they could eat snails to survive. However, in anticipation of such potential hardships, Biafran leadership should have planned for snail farms that would have greatly expanded the production of snails and other foods that are native to our land. Instead, the Biafran leadership cabal counted on the ability of our people to endure the hardship. At the end of the conflict, they would appropriate all the benefits. In any event, the conditions were beginning to get to the level of becoming intolerable.

However, my family had it a little easier. With the plantation and at Oko'Ofia, the yam and cassava were planted in large mounds that were extraordinary. From September 1968, the cassava planted in early September 1967 was already mature. It was projected that cassava planted in early 1968 would begin to mature by mid-1969. At that rate, much of the cassava crop would go to waste. Therefore, my big sister Nneoma was tasked with going to the farm, harvesting the cassava, processing it, and going to Umuahia to sell the processed food. She shared the proceeds with our mother. My sister went with her friend, Rose, from Amaba. Our mother sold the raw cassava to Rose and Rose would process the cassava in our house. Rose and our big sister would get together three days later and process the garri in our backyard and take it to Umuahia for sale. Usually, in between the fermentation period of three to four days for the grated cassava, my sister and her friend probably returned to the farm to harvest more cassava that they would process later. Once a month or so, maybe six weeks, my mother permitted Ngozi, the wife of her nephew, to accompany my sister to the farm. Even if the war had lasted three years from 1968, we would never have lacked garri or yams or palm oil to support the family. Our only concern might have been meat or proteins, but even that was not yet lacking by March 1969, when the Nigerian Army captured Ovim. However, because of the mass starvation that was beginning to set in inside Biafra, international food and medical relief was being flown into Biafra. There were relief centers in Ovim, but I knew little about it, nor did I care. I never went there, nor was I aware of any member of my family who went to the relief center to collect food relief items.

Amid all this, everything else seemed routine, with the exception that we were now reminded of the war on a daily basis and much more audibly than a few months earlier. The enemy was now seventeen miles from home to the west and a few more miles to the northeast at Afikpo-Road, Uturu (where the airport was located), and Isiagu. We witnessed daily the nighttime flights of the relief planes (or maybe they imported arms into Biafra). We woke up in the middle of the night, greeted early in the morning, and accompanied all day with the sound of gunfire—small arms exchanges and artillery gunfire. Occasionally, we would witness a fighter jet whizzing overhead toward Umuahia. It was not for us, and we expected nothing of it.

Chapter VII

JANUARY TO MAY 1969
REFUGEES AND CAPTIVES

My Daddy Escapes

Yes, for the next five months (and a few days short of the sixth month), the sound and fury of shells and the crackles of gunfire greeted our waking hours and jarred us awake from sleep and slumber during the night. The Nigerian Army captured Okigwe, seventeen miles west of Ovim, in early October 1968. Despite the ominous sounds of battle close to our homes and the daily reminders of imminent danger, we went about our daily chores and visited our farms as if oblivious to the portents of death and destruction around us. The illusion of driving the Nigerians back was beginning to wear thin. But we kept hope alive because our cause was just. One way or another, we would emerge from the struggle with some semblance of justice and peace. We all hoped that the peace talks that began in August 1968, following the failure of the Kampala talks in May 1968, would lead to success and cessation of hostilities and we would all return to normal life. Unfortunately, that would not happen for us at Ovim.

At Ovim, we typically would see an airplane high up in the sky looking like a big bird, but a bird all the same. We heard that airplanes are much bigger than trucks and trailers. Ninety-five percent of the population had never seen an airplane up close enough to realize its true size. I was privileged enough to have traveled to Enugu, where I visited the airport to see the F-27 passenger airplane, but I had never seen a fighter or a bomber aircraft. As a child, I had these nightmares where an airplane would hover so close to my head and above the roof of our house that I was frightened into waking up or the plane would eventually crash into our yard and I would be glad.

Early one morning, it hit home. Sometime in mid-to-late February, or maybe even early March 1969, we witnessed a fly-by during the morning hours. We saw a heavy airplane lumbering overhead. It was pretty much like what I had dreamed about in my childhood nightmares. The plane moved slowly; Biafra had no air defenses. Therefore, the pilot of this plane could taunt us all he wanted. My father and I, along with some others, were in the backyard. My dad and I watched from the window of our bathroom, near our mother's bedroom. We described it for what it was – an Ilyushin Il-28 bomber. It was heavy indeed. Arrogantly, and in labored ponderosity, it hovered in the air like in a fiendish dance by an executioner. The plane flew north or northwest and, unlike the nightmare that I often had during my early childhood, this one was real. We concluded that it was flying to the war fronts that were close by. But, no! The plane banked and then turned around slowly, taking its jolly time to choose its target. This time I was really frightened. The plane descended slowly as if it was coming down right overhead, directly in front of the window where my dad and I were watching from. The plane was huge. You could easily discern its size—it would dwarf the trailer, just as we had been told. It looked like the F-27 passenger plane that I had seen at the airport. For me and my siblings, it looked like a monster. We had never seen such a thing. The next thing we heard was an explosion that shook the foundations of our house. It was frightening. What happened? It must have bombed somewhere in Ovim. The plane turned around like it was leaving. But no! The plane turned around again, descended slowly again, and once more, the ground shook from the explosion. Another bomb had been dropped. It was a major market day at Oriendu. Therefore, the Oriendu marketplace was full. We waited tensely to hear what happened. Luckily, none of us was in the marketplace on that day. But what about other members of the extended family from within the village or in our mother's family? One or two bombs hit the center of the market and killed several people, maybe, four, five, or six people, from what I recollect. Luckily, I was not in the store when this event took place. I call it an act of God. One way or another, I was not in the store at the Oriendu market. Ordinarily, I would have been in the store on a market day, taking care of business. Conceivably, when I saw the plane initially circling the vicinity, I may have left and hurried home. The building where my medicine store was located was not hit. In any event, by the time of the bombing in March 1969, the store was no longer fully stocked. The force of the bomb was so strong that several mud houses in nearby villages crumbled. I believe that a house around Amune Village adjacent to our house, about one mile away from the marketplace, also crumbled. When it was all over, it was discovered that the railway line connecting from Umuahia to the north of Biafra was hit and the rail lines were twisted. That communication link was lost and was never repaired until the end of the war. The houses that crumbled were made of the traditional mud walls and thatched roofs from years back before the era of the Europeans.

After the raid at Ovim, life seemed to return to normal. But again, this was not to last long. A few weeks following the bombing at the marketplace, another flyby occurred. A heavy plane, quite similar to the first one. Once again, the plane descended closely. Some people, in exaggeration, might have sworn that they could see the pilot. No! That was not the case. Nevertheless, the plane descended too low for comfort and danced around arrogantly in the absence of air defenses in Biafra. There was panic. Women and children ran helter-skelter in fright and utter confusion, screaming and crying and looking for someplace to hide. But lo and behold—a cascade of white leaflets fell to the ground in the compounds of the village and the surrounding bushes. The leaflets urged us to end the resistance because the Nigerian forces were our friends and they were not out to kill us. After we picked up the leaflets, we were reassured that this would not be another bombing and we went about our business. "If you are our friends, then go back to your country," I thought. Much of it did not mean much to the people, and I made nothing out of it.

In hindsight, maybe that was a warning about the impending move. It was probably a hint that if they, the Nigerian forces, eventually arrived in Ovim then we should not flee to the refugee camps. At that point, though, we did not see it that way. And so it was and again, one early morning on March 28 or so in 1969, at about 7:30 a.m., we began to hear loud shell fire. The heavy shelling sounded ominous enough to me, so I closed shop quickly so I could get to the village to be close to the family. Also, early that morning, my sister and her friend, Rose, had left for Umuahia to sell their garri. Indeed, the fact that they had left as usual at about 5:00 a.m. signifies that the menacing and ominous shelling did not begin a few days earlier to give warning that danger was imminent or that any serious encounter was anywhere near. Usually, my sister and her friend returned the next day or the same day.

We huddled with our father by the same bathroom window where we had been during the air raid at Oriendu. While there, the shells sounded louder and closer. For the last two or three months before March 1969, there was a small contingent of Biafran soldiers, say two or so platoons, at the girls' secondary school around the railway station along the road from Okigwe to Ovim/Akara. This small contingent was certainly not sufficient to defend the perimeter. Why did the Nigerian Army not try their invasion over the last six months to putsch through this axis? Only God knows. Indeed, one observer, Acho, whose father was a leader of the Obayi Methodist Church, said that by the time the Nigerian contingent arrived near Elugwunta, they were singing and dancing and shooting their guns into the air. Mr. Acho was distributing international relief supplies at Elugwunta, Obayi Ovim, and was able to go and watch the movement of the Nigerian convoy who simply drove by in jubilation and chants. The movement was without opposition or an exchange of fire between Biafran and Nigerian forces. From Akara junction, joining with the road from Abiriba and Afikpo, it was twenty-one miles to Umuahia. It was seventeen miles from Okigwe to Ovim and an additional three miles to Akara. Altogether, from Okigwe to Umuahia along this road, there was a total of forty-one miles, about the same distance directly from Okigwe to Umuahia along the Okpara road. Both were equally unpaved, except for the stretch from Akara to Umuahia.

The shells boomed from the west (Okigwe) and the northeast (Afikpo and Alai). In any putsch, the Nigerian Army or contingents would link up at the Akara junction and then make a final push southward for Umuahia via Ozuakoli. Initially, we felt comfortable that the shelling might stop after a while. It was probably one of those instances where the Nigerians were once more trying to affect a breakthrough. How would the Biafran Army allow Nigerians to make this putsch when their success would effectively end the war? Such a thought was insufferable. However, by 11:30 a.m., it was obvious that the Nigerians were quite close and probably advancing. Our dad, being among the elders, left quickly and met to decide what the next steps should be. By the time he returned, it was decided that all Ovim should move northwest toward the villages of Ohoroho, Obilo'ohia, Ugwu Nta, and Umu'ukwu. We were all advised to take a few belongings. By this time during the war (March 1969), it was becoming evident that the Nigerian Army would not engage in wanton slaughter of the civilian population. Many people from north of Ovim, including such places as Enugu, Ishiagu, and others, were leaving Ovim and returning to their homes behind enemy lines. Even if the thinking was different, the speed of change that early morning in March 1969 was not such that gave us time to flee toward Umuahia. Moreover, fleeing in that direction would have given a lot of people cause for pause. It would mean going to live at a refugee camp. This was an option that people would take only if there was no alternative.

The movement was swift. By 1:00 p.m., all of Ovim south of Amaeke and Ohonja had moved into a few villages further north. Even the people of Ezere and Otamkpa moved out. The people of Ezere probably moved into Ozara, for I visited Ozara while we were at Umuukwu before we came out from our hiding places. By nightfall, we were all huddled at Umuukwu, a village in Amune that was a little less than one mile north of Amaeke Elu. Even my aunt Ugo was there with us. However, I did not see her children, Ngozi, and her brother and sisters, nor did I see her husband. I did not know where they were. Ugo, our dad's youngest sister, kept very close—she had her family, but never really lost the connection. Enyioma, her oldest son, later told me that they were there or close by. I cannot recollect what happened on the first night, but, remarkably, we all survived it. The village of Umuukwu was crowded. If the Nigerian Army had desired to engage in mass slaughter, all they had to do was send a reconnaissance party to locate the concentrations and then send volleys of shells into the villages. They probably did not do this because they were preoccupied with their defenses and the Federal Government had prevailed on them to behave better, for as soon as they joined with their contingent from the Afikpo/Abiriba road, northeast of Ovim, the Nigerian contingent moved toward Ozuakoli by the end of the day and were engaged by the Biafran Army for three weeks. I cannot recollect, day by day, the routine events. However, I can vividly recollect critical and remarkable events, with few frivolities that I prefer not to narrate.

When we moved, we brought some of our goats and chickens with us. We systematically killed and dried them. For thirty days and more, we did not lack meat, and though there was no salt, there was an adequate supply of palm oil, if only from the wild canopy that surrounds Ovim. One of the remarkable events that I recollect is that we slept in the open for the next two or three weeks. There were more than one hundred people huddled in the one-family compound where we were. My mother was granted special privilege and assigned one room, where all six of my other siblings slept with her. The owners of the compound slept in the mud houses that they inhabited, but generously accommodated as many of the refugees as they could squeeze in. Under the circumstances, there were surprisingly no reports of misconduct. Our communities still had standards of behavior that are absent today among the youth and even so-called elders. Remarkably, bands of youth did not visit the villages to loot and pillage. Young women of sexually active or viable age did not visit the vacated villages, as there were young men available, able and willing to brave the odds and risks to go and see or survey the abandoned villages. Even the young boys and men that visited the vacated villages did not engage in looting, or at least none was reported in gossip or open lamentation.

Somehow, people could cook whatever food they retrieved from their homes as they evacuated. There was pepper, as we were close to our vacated villages, and the gardens were within reach of our farms at Ogbakuru and nearby places. We did not go to the farmland en masse, as this could expose us to dangers. There were no reports of Nigerian soldiers, for which reason there was confidence among the people. We went to Ozârâ and Umuâkwuâ (between Ezerê and Ozârâ). There were no reports of people raiding farms to harvest others' crops. At the least, it was not widespread nor did such behavior, if it occurred, give cause for anger or damnation.

Ablution was in the nearby rivers that flowed through Amune. For the young boys and girls, we built a thatched bathroom near the compound. I recollect Ogbonna Ikwu, whose mother hailed from the compound where we stayed, was a close friend of mine. On several occasions were went to that bathroom together and took a bath, using water that was fetched from the nearby stream. We joked that we did not wish to expose ourselves to be discovered by any young girls. On one occasion, we saw one of the young girls from a nearby village that we knew. She was grown up enough to be sexually active, so we joked that maybe we could ask her to give us a little favor—but we did not ask.

At night, under cover of darkness, I was able to return to our compound at Ndi Egbe to survey. On some of those visits, I was with Ogbonna Nweni, my first cousin and son of my father's younger brother. Ogbonna was a little older, maybe six months to at most one year older. It was usual to hear planes fly by overhead, but I could not say whose aircraft they could have been. There could not have been relief planes flying north of Biafra, as the Nigerian Army occupied all territory north of Ovim. Uli Airport was way west. Plausibly, the planes that flew from Gabon would be flying through Ovim and then west, but that would have been strange, as Uli Airport was more northwest of Port Harcourt and closer to Owerre, southwest of Ovim. Usually, the Nigerian soldiers stationed at Ovim railway station, south of our hiding places, would "shoot" at them, presumably with their automatic weapons. These weapons would usually not get to airplanes that high, even at 3,000 feet. My cousin and I would witness the firecrackers and, like the planes flying above, we went about our business. The gunshots were far away and did not appear to be threatening. I could never understand why the Nigerian soldiers shot at the planes or did so with their simple rifles when they could have shot them down with anti-aircraft guns. But one time, it was different. As my cousin and I approached the compound (or maybe we were already inside), a plane flew by. How close it was to the Nigerian soldiers at Mission Hill or the Central School, I couldn't make out. However, the gunshots from the Nigerian soldiers were more intense and more persistent. My cousin and I were still inside the house or just behind on our way out when some of the bullets from the gunshots landed in front of the family compound and behind us. I was wearing only a shirt and a wrapper around my waist. I am not even confident that I was wearing any shorts. My cousin and I fled immediately. The bullets fell harder and closer behind the house. Many of them. We paused for less than five seconds near the udara tree along the path from Ndi Egbe, Amaeke Elu through the first village in Amune abutting Ame'eke. This one was named Otu Ukwu or "large pod." (All udara trees had a unique name). The bullets fell harder, and the firecrackers were more intense. With my wrapper flying around me, my cousin and I fled quickly to Umu Ohkpiâ across the railway line that crisscrossed Ovim in between the valleys. This event, though one of the last, did not stop me from returning to the village. At that age, for some reason, I was remarkably adventurous. Shortly after this adventurous foray and close call, we were to leave our hiding places and return to the compound. This was the last time we needed to go for a reconnaissance inside the compound.

The other remarkable thing that happened was my systematic evacuation of the drug store at Oriendu. I did this during the first few days of the Nigerian Army's occupation of Ovim. Right or wrong, I believed that the Nigerian army was occupied with their fight along the perimeter and would not foray that far into Oriendu market was less than a mile on a motorable road directly from their crossing point on their way to Akara. Indeed, there was a seesaw battle not far from Ngele Oyiri, for the Biafran Army was at Nkpa, just a few miles off. If the Biafran Army had been well-armed, it would have been easy to cut the Nigerian Army off and isolate the unit that was pushing toward Ozuakoli. Even if the Biafran Army had tried to cut through the thin line at the Ovim-Akara road, they would have decimated the population at Ovim, either because the Nigerian Army would have had to form a defense perimeter inside Ovim or the units at Alayi/Ezu'ukwu would have come to their relief, subjecting the entire population of Ovim to deadly crossfire. Pockmarks of bullets from the fighting still adorn the walls of the medicine store at Oriendu where I sold medication from September 1967 through March 1969. Nevertheless, under cover of darkness and while gunfire was exchanged, I packed wares into standard cartons and moved them two cartons at a time into the nearby bushes and onward to Ndi Egbe via Amachiebe. Once again, naïvely, I believed that the Nigerian soldiers would not foray into the villages. Therefore, I believed, right or wrong, that I was not in danger. It's all in the past now, regardless of whether I was right or wrong.

About fifteen to twenty days after we fled to the village at Umu'ukwu, it began to rain. Therefore, we could no longer sleep out in the open. We were now forced to sleep in the corridors of the mud houses on the mud slabs (nkpukpu) that people sat on during a visit to a house. My feet were jutting out in the open, but I was not bothered by it, though that did not last long. The rains became a little heavier in the next few days, a welcome relief as people were getting uncomfortable with what threatened to be a drought. Indeed, it was said that the rain doctors at Amune were holding back the rain unless they were paid. I doubted it openly and a young man, a few years older than I questioned whether these people holding the rain planted their yams in a riverbed.

Stepping aside for a moment, we foraged for vegetables and food in the nearby bushes. There is a species of cocoa yam that had a yellow center that we harvested and ate. I heard that this species of cocoa yam was for pigs. I am not aware that our people had pig farms before the European era, to have a species of food that pigs ate. This species of cocoa yam was not part of the diet and people did not formally cultivate them. Personally, though, I found them to be delicious or so I thought, for I felt that this yellow center tasted a little like the yolk of eggs that this cocoa yam resembled. More importantly, though, I foraged for the Green vegetable. The vegetable, which we called Greens, was a vegetable that was grown for food. It had broad leaves and was tasty, had a great flavor, and grew wild as much as it was also cultivated formally. Somehow, it grew prolifically at Ovim. I foraged as far as Obilo'ohia, Umu Okpia, and even Ndi Egbe for these vegetables—indeed all around Amune. The other vegetable that our people harvested wild and which was a routine part of our diet was *ahiahara*. This vegetable had the slimy properties of okra and was very delicious. It was a compliment to yam or cocoa yam. It might also have been used to make soup. I am still wondering why we did not formally cultivate and nurture the mass development of this vegetable. *Uto nini ji*, *uziza*, and *utaziri* were also abundant. Therefore, these vegetables were harvested freely and sufficiently for all to feed. The only problem was that there was no salt to cook the food. For the thirty days or so that we stayed at Umu'ukwu, we learned to cook without salt and even to savor such food.

Of course, *kwashiorkor* (protein malnutrition) was beginning to set in. It was not as ubiquitous as was presented in many pictures about Biafra. At that point, one might say that there was a correlation between the incidence of kwashiorkor and prior level of wellbeing in children. This is explained in part by the prior accumulation of nutritional reserves and the fact that those who had a nutritional reserve, among children, also had parents that had access to the available limited resources in Biafra at that time. People who lived in refugee camps also suffered more frequently; they did not have access to the farmland or the available livestock.

During the time we took refuge at Umu'ukwu, my father was itinerant and actively involved with the local leadership at Ovim while at the same time working closely with the Biafran Army contingent that was holed up north of Ovim at Acha or near Acha. I saw him only about three times, as he slipped in quietly to visit with the family. Like other community leaders, he was probably exploring ways to contact the field commanders of the Nigerian Army. Under the circumstances, my dad being a visible and prominent civil servant was advised to keep his distance. The situation was fluid and, at the minimum, unpredictable and treacherous. There was uncertainty and faith. From experience, the Nigerian Army would gather young men at whim, at places they captured, and execute them. No one was sure of what they would do. We were at their mercy.

I was not sure of what the elders and leaders were doing. They never told us, and I had no personal contact with any of them. However, during the second or third week, shortly before or after April 21, 1967, the day the Nigerian Army captured Umuahia, my dad sent me on a reconnaissance errand. I went beyond Obilo'ohia, around Ezere and the semi-marshland of Ali'ike. There was a dry red earth access dirt road leading from Ovim through Ezere to Ozara. I forayed into the semi-marshland and surveyed the railway line leading to or from Otamkpa. I saw no sign of Nigerian Army presence or movement. What happened next led to the first and only time that I disagreed openly with my dad. My dad wanted to send me to conduct a second reconnaissance survey. to affirm my earlier findings. This time I requested that I be accompanied by a second person, just in case. My dad declined and I flatly said that I was going nowhere. He became very upset and threw my suitcase outside. My aunt Ugo chastised me openly but also had a conversation with my dad that granted me the dispensation that I requested. After my aunt intervened, Ogbonna, my first cousin, was assigned to go with me. The two of us departed and essentially went to the same locations. We went south from the railway line and crossing leading to Ozara into Ngwara Ezere. We ventured stealthily into the villages of Ezere but declined from going further into the railway crossing leading into Ndi Egbe/Amune from Ezere. That might have been risky, as a stray Nigerian soldier may have noticed us and raised an alert or traced us to the hideouts in Obilo'ohia and Ôzârâ. The inhabitants of the villages in Ezere were absent. They had deserted and fled north. We stepped back and walked back toward the railway line and then hugged the railway lines from the forests going from Umuækwua toward Otamkpa, ensuring that we did not lose our bearings. We returned with the report that no signs of Nigerian soldiers were visible and we noticed none of their movements. Once again, my dad went away with the report.

Following my second report, on or about April 26, my dad appeared in the compound again and asked me to come along with him. Behind one of the houses in the compound plaza on a crossroad leading southward to Ugwuntâ, Agbo Ôhôrôhô and Ndie'Ntu in Ôhôrôhô and Ama Ngelu'ukwu, there was a canopy of trees that provided a shade and cover, especially in darkness. Under this canopy, I noticed an assemblage of soldiers, about a platoon strong, in double file. In a whisper, the leader of the contingent, perhaps a sergeant or staff sergeant (or even a second lieutenant) gave the command, "Attention!" The soldiers stood at attention. Then came the next command, "Present Arms!" At that point, my dad shook my hands and walked in between the soldiers and I walked on one side of the formation until we arrived at the end of the double-file. My dad turned on the side and took a last glance at me and never looked back as the soldiers flanked him and marched into the darkness. That was the last time I saw my dad for a while. As usual, I took it as though my dad was out there just keeping out until the elders and leaders resolved matters. It appears as if the elders had contacted the Nigerian Army, as we began to receive relief supplies. We had onions and some dried fish. The absence of onions in our diet for a while transformed its presence into some magical flavor. Its mere presence in food was sufficient to make the food taste good.

About April 30, 1969, or barely three days after the honor guard at Umu'ukwu, we were ordered to return to our villages and compounds. The news came that Egbe had escaped to Biafra. This news was greeted with great joy and euphoria. I cannot recollect who made that euphoric announcement. It probably came from multiple people at the same time while I was standing with other people in some open place. We all returned. People went back to their villages as far back as Elugwunta and beyond. They even crossed the Ovim-Akara road that was essentially a military zone into Amo'orji Nkpa in Biafran territory. Elugwu Nta abutted the military transit point along which the Nigerian Army would transport their troops and hardware. Any military confrontation between the two armies would have caught the inhabitants of Ovim and neighboring communities in a crossfire.

Papa's escape was eventful. All the time that we were hidden in the northern villages of Ovim, our dad was working closely with a contingent of the Biafran Army that was cut off by Nigerian forces during their putsch. It was while he was working with these soldiers that he sent me on reconnaissance missions. The units were the 71B Battalion under Captain C. C. Njêzê and a detachment of the 64th Brigade under Lt. Col. Ginger. During the Nigerian putsch of late March 1969, these two units were at a location directly and further north of Ovim from where we were hiding. These units resisted the putsch, and, in the process, they were encircled and the Nigerian forces broke through the east of their location and west of their location at a community called Acha and moved southwest into the Abiriba-Umuahia road and southeast and then west on the Okigwe-Ovim road to Akara and then Uzuakoli.

According to Uwadiegwu Ogbonnaya (now a retired journalist and traditional ruler), "the invaders succeeded in breaking through ... except at Ndiokoroukwu. Here, the combined soldiers of Captain Njeze's 70B battalion, the 5th Rangers squadron (guerilla fighters) of Lt. Egwu, a.k.a, "Animal in Jungle", beat back the Nigerian 'Vandals'... With the artillery, mortar, and aerial bombardment going on between Nigerian soldiers and Biafran defenders at Uzuakoli, Radio Biafra was the only link we had with the rest of Biafra ....” After waiting hopelessly to be rescued by Biafran forces, “ ...The order for Biafran pull-out of Acha came on April 28, 1969, after a month's heroic resistance. The pull-out, was perhaps, to avoid a repeat of the Akpanwudele Abakaliki tragedy of 1968 where a whole community was bombarded from every direction by Federal troops to avenge the missing of a Nigerian soldier that strayed into the area. ” The order to pull out was called Operation Open Corridor by their commander. On the appointed day, “... From every track and route to Acha, Njeze and his men pulled out and converged at the Agunta/OgborUdele forest farms, Uturu. At dawn on 30th April 1969, Njeze gave the command for “operation open corridor” from behind the enemy lines With soldiers moving in a single file mixed with civilians, the crossing was tragic for many, especially nursing mothers, many other civilians, and soldiers. Many women threw away the babies on their backs just to save their heads first during the crossing Yours sincerely could not make it that night. While wandering in the bush, I came across other soldiers and civilians marooned. They include Dr. Pleen Egbe,[178] a famous educationist from Ovim, and WO II Josephat Osunkwo from Acha and his newly married beautiful young wife... On May 1, 1969, from the farm settlement, a Biafran sergeant directed us to move to Umuobiala Isuikwuato where the rest of 70B battalion and 5th Squadron Rangers were directed by Major Goddy Onyefuru to assemble.”[179]

It was later at Umuobiala that I joined my father, on or about May 23, 1969. Another casualty of the crossing was a good friend of my father, Mr. Owanta, a former hotel proprietor in Jos from Ozara who was supplying food to the Biafran Supply and Transportation Department in Umuahia. “Unfortunately, Mr. Owanta could not make it as he got missing in action during the ‘operation open corridor’ in the early hours of April 30, 1969.”

All that time, from March 27 to April 22, 1969, while we took refuge in the northern villages, we were hopeful that the Biafran Army would beat back the Nigerian Army, drive them back to Okigwe and liberate us. Such a move would have been dangerous and disastrous for us. Certainly, the Biafran Army was not sufficiently equipped to confront the Nigerian Army frontally at Ozuakoli. The only feasible or viable approach would have been for Biafra to attack the Nigerian contingent from what amounts to their rear, a thinly defended perimeter on the seventeen-mile perimeter to Okigwe. However, we were surrounded from the north inside Ovim. The Nigerian Army could easily have countered such a move. All they had to do was open up the gap between Ovim and the northern formations around Ozara/Afikpo Road formations and suck the Biafran Army into a slaughter while at the same time making mincemeat out of the civilian population. All that hope was lost on or about April 22, 1969, when the news came that Nigeria had captured Umuahia. What next? We had no choice! About five days later on April 27, 1969, the elders and leaders made the crucial contact to order us to return to our villages, with promises of safety from the Nigerian Army.

All this while, I ran another errand for my dad. My dad owned a briefcase or what our people called a portmanteau. My dad had a close relationship with his relatives at Ozara, from where his mother was married at Umuagu, Ozara. My dad made me move the briefcase from location to location. During the last week in March, I had moved it to Ozara in the home of his relatives. The closest relative was called Michael, a police officer, and younger brother, I believe of Nathaniel. I knew Nathaniel more closely and remember him more fondly. I can recollect from early childhood that Nathaniel was known for the jumbo size of his fufu ball that he swallowed. It was legendary to us. It was said that during meals, Nathaniel would swallow four or five of those jumbo balls of akpu and would be done.

---

[178] *Dr. Pleen Egbe refers to our father (Mr. Pliny Igwe Abel Egbe). He was never a doctor in the academic or medical sense of it. However, as referred to by the author, Ogbonnaya, he was a famous educationist but also erudite such that a few people may have thought that he was Dr. in the academic sense, though he never presented himself as such. Our dad was a biologist and agricultural scientist and a well-known educator.*

[179] (Uwadiegwu Ogbonnaya, May 16, 2019 -https://www.nationallightngr.com/byline/by-uwadiegwu-c-ogbonnaya/)

The first time, I left the briefcase at Amune. Then went back to Ozara about the second day of May 1969 to retrieve it. This was about three days after my dad escaped in the company of a contingent of the Biafran Army that was holed up at Acha—a contingent of the 63rd Brigade and another contingent of the 71B Battalion under Captain C. C. Nje'Eze. On the second day of May 1969, I returned to Ozara to relocate the briefcase. I do not recollect exactly when I arrived there, but it had to be early enough in the morning, say 9:30 a.m. The distance was about five miles away. I usually walked through Ezere, but on my return from Ozara, I avoided Ezere and walked by way of Obilo'ohia and Ukopia and Ngwara Amune and up from Umu Okpia. As I approached Ezere from Ozara, after the railway crossing, there was a path that led east from near Ngwara Ezere to Obilo'ohia. There are farmlands there amid the red soil. Around this path, or just near it, I decided to vary my return path. I made this decision just in case someone saw me going toward Ozara during the morning hours. As I was about to veer into the path leading to Obilo'ohia, I saw a lone ripe mango at the very top of a mango tree. I decided to go for the mango. This mango was so high up the tree. I pulled a rope from the forest, made a nap sack from the rope, tied the briefcase to my back, and climbed up the tree. I took with me a small branch. When I got close to the top of the tree and could go no more without risking a broken branch and falling off the tree, I pushed the mango. The mango fell toward me, but it fell to the ground. There was no one around to fight over the mango with me, so I came down and took time to eat the mango.

There is another reason why this mango location is so significant to me. During the early planting season, probably after the Nigerian Army had entered Ovim, Ogbonna and I had been sent to clear the farmland for planting after burning the shrubs and dried vegetation that had dried from the initial clearing. As we set and controlled the fire, a squirrel ran out of the burning vegetation. I gave chase and with my *akparaja* (some sharp Flexi machete) slashed at the head of the squirrel. However, my cousin was in the way. A few more inches close to the squirrel, I might have taken my cousin with the squirrel. I slashed the head of the squirrel but missed my cousin. I can never forget that day— whenever I think of it, I get shivers down my spine and say thanks to the Almighty God for preventing this near-tragedy in my life. This event had to have occurred after we returned to our villages following the Nigerian capture of Umuahia because Egesi knew about how we had captured and roasted a squirrel. We brought our dead squirrel home and roasted it, quartered it, dried it for food, and split it equally.

But back to my trek home! After I crossed from Obilo'ohia, I walked up through the steep hill that led to Umu Okpia and crossed the railway line at that point in Ovim. I intended to enter our house from behind. Ola and the other children were playing in the compound yard when she saw Nigerian soldiers approaching the house. Ola quickly ran through the hallway and behind the house to inform our mother that Nigerian soldiers were on the way to the house, but before our mother could ask a complete question about the whereabouts of the soldiers, the soldiers walked through the hallway and were in the backyard. Ola attempted to flee by jumping through the window only to see more soldiers behind the house with mounted tripod machine guns and others heavily armed. Ola jumped right back and asked for permission to go get our uncle. The soldiers were one platoon strong (thirty soldiers) with a battery of four machine guns.

After the Nigerian platoon entered the house and took all members of my family   our mother and Agu 2 years, Okezie 5, Iroegbu 7, Ulobank 9 and Ola 13, along with Enyioma 9, our first cousin and our uncle, Nweni. Enyioma is the son of our Aunt Ugo. Dioma (15 years old, was in hiding at Eze'Ukwu, in our uncle's place near the palm oil plantation. They also took a boy, Maduabuchi, who happened to be visiting the family. The wife of our older cousin, Ukennaya Egbe and her children, on the way back from the farm, saw the action and diverted to the neighboring family. So, they escaped capture.

The soldiers, according to my siblings, were instructed that they should not kill anyone—not even a lizard, cockroach, or anything that moved or did not move. Ugo and her family returned to Ndi Egbe compound with us and we cooked and ate together. After a day or two, they left, but Enyioma decided to stay because he had Iroegbu and Okezie (two- and four-year-old boys) that he could play with. According to Enyioma, Egbu had admonished Enyioma and was about to give Enyioma a knock on the head when suddenly a swarm of soldiers entered the house, looking for our father. The soldiers believed that our father was still around. It was a mischief-maker who probably desired to destroy the family that told the Nigerian soldiers that our dad was still around. Other family members in the compound were not taken away—our aunt Meme and her children and our other cousins from the family of Egbe Egesi. All this happened before noon. It appears that people settled scores by talking to the Nigerian Army. It was during this period after the raid on our house that my Uncle Kanu disappeared.

As I walked the last stretch at the boundary between Amune and Ndi Egbe, someone walked up to me and told me to stop because Nigerian soldiers were in my house. I cannot recollect the name of this person, but he was one of my good friends, that I knew very well and interacted with regularly within our age group. At that point, I stepped back and went to the house of A. C. (Æchara Nta or Little Achara, as he was called). I hid there for about thirty minutes. This person returned later and informed me that the Nigerian soldiers had left and I could return. Even with that, I stayed away and went to Usaja, my mother's family, and stayed there. Whoever sent the Nigerian soldiers did not tell them about the possible places where stray family members could be hiding, or the soldiers simply did not know that not everyone had been apprehended.

I stayed away. However, by 5:00 or 6:00 p.m.—there was still daylight—all of the family members returned unharmed, except for our uncle Nweni, who was battered and bruised. Mgbo Nweni's head and nose were bleeding. I did not see Enyioma Nwagbara. He returned to his parents after the incident. I could not tell everything that happened along the way. A lot is lost with my departed elders and sister Dioma.

I never asked my mother for details, nor did I ask my uncles, but my brothers told me quite a bit. Based on the mythical belief that my dad was all but invincible and capable of "disappearance" (making himself invisible), the soldiers battered my uncle, believing that he was my dad. According to my brothers, sometimes the soldiers were jovial. Agu was only two years old. They lifted him and called him brigadier and Okezie (five years old) they called captain—but for the most part, they were serious about their business. My uncle, Nweni, was battered with the butts of guns and threatened. "We hear say you dey disappear… make you disappear now; make we see." My mother and our uncle Nweni were tied up with their hands behind their backs, latched to the tall soup vegetable tree (Oha) in the middle of the compound. Some of the soldiers cocked their rifles and meant to execute my mother and the kids as they were lined up against the tree. Ola, the bigger girl covered the eyes of Ulobank and 'Egbu, who were closest to her, with her hands.

At that point, one of the soldiers came out from the house and got into an argument with the other soldiers and suggested that they should go and talk to the commanders before any action was taken. Of course, one of the issues was that my uncle denied that he was my dad. Secondly, among the items taken from the house were pictures of my dad, including a group picture (8 x 10 inches) that my dad took when he was a teacher and scoutmaster at Okene or Idah in Northern Nigeria. In this group picture, Col. Adekunle was among the students (scout cubs). The soldiers recognized their commander, the very one that sent them to arrest the family, in the picture.

My dad was very fond of this picture, as he considered himself a schoolteacher of one of the key division commanders during the war. Indeed, after the war, our big sister told us that Col. Adekule confirmed to her that our dad had been his teacher at Okene. Along the way to their headquarters at the Mission Hill (Girls' Secondary School), the soldiers continued to beat and batter my uncle, until blood began to ooze out of his nose. They even sat the family down and threatened to shoot them, once more.

At the Mission Hill, one of the commanders saw the picture of my dad and exclaimed that my dad was his teacher up north and probably saw a picture of a younger Adekunle and concluded that my uncle was not my dad. The commander also recognized my mother and asked, "…Where is your husband…?" My mother fibbed to the commander, claiming that she had not seen her husband since the Northern Nigerian crisis, three years earlier. Well, I recollect that our mother had advised us never to tell lies, except that it is perfectly ok to lie to the devil. This one time, my mother told a straight face lie. The Nigerian commander, either out of credulity or for convenience accepted our mother's fib. Our mother was then asked to identify her children. Once more, our mother lied and identified her children and our cousin Enyioma as her children. She then claimed that whoever else from the village that was taken was related to her children. Our mother was lucky that no one else from Ovim, or even the informant that snitched on our dad, was around to betray her fib. Our mother told a second fib. Ola, our sister (13) reported that one of the soldiers asked if he could marry her. Our mother responded that in our culture, girls of her age cannot be given in marriage.

The Nigerian commander provided food for the family—okra soup with dawadawa. Enyioma tried to stick his hand in the soup before he was authorized to eat. Apparently, one of the soldiers considered his behavior impolite and struck him hard with a baton. Our mother fell in between him and the angry soldier and offered rather that they hit her instead of Enyioma. The Nigerian Army personnel were quite generous with the food that they served the family. Okezie who was five years old at the time testified that the pieces of meat in the soup were quite big and after he ate heartily at the army barracks, he took another large piece of the meat that he could hardly handle within his fist for the road and ate it along the way. In any event, the commanders ordered the return of the family and provided them with large quantities of foodstuffs and thread for braiding hair and maybe a few other goodies, a guide to take them home, and an order that advised that anyone who ever bothered them again will be severely punished. On their way back home, via Ngele Oyirî or along the railway, it appears that Enyioma was sent to his family, which was along the way toward Ndi Egbe. A man from Ovim that the family can no longer recall who was assigned to lead them safely back to the village, confiscated all the goodies that the commander gave to the family.

When they all arrived back home, I gave my uncle a bottle of Panadol taken from the drug store, about twenty-four tablets, to mitigate his pain from the battery. I also gave him a small amount of iodine, hydrogen peroxide, M&B tablets (panacea among our people), and some bandages and plaster for his fresh and open wounds. The M&B tablets were usually crushed and placed on a fresh wound and covered with band-aid cotton gauze and plaster and bandages. I left the remainder of the medications that I had for the family. Besides pain medication, we had antibiotics that still had an expiration into the end of the third quarter of 1969 or even 1970. We also had children's multivitamins that I kept for our baby brother, Agu.

Three things saved the family, during this event: (1) providence by the Almighty God, (2) the mango, and (3) my father's picture with Adekunle and the scouts at Okene or Idah. If I had not diverted for those ten or so minutes to fetch a mango, I might have been squarely inside the house when the soldiers arrived. The way they surrounded the house, there was no way I could have escaped, even by hiding in some corner of the house, because they combed the house thoroughly before they departed. My sister had escaped to Umuahia before the invasion and my dad was safely on the Biafran side, following his escape.

CHAPTER VIII

NOWHERE TO HIDE MY TURN TO ESCAPE

Hiding in Plain View at Usaja

Once we got over the shock of the events, thanking God for the near-miss, we decided to leave the house and hide away at Usaja. However, somehow, one or more of the soldiers ordered that my uncle and my mother must return to the compound every day until 4:00 p.m. otherwise they would come back and arrest them. The two complied with the order until someone advised them to stop reporting to the compound. Two or three of the soldiers returned and looted the house later. Iroegbu and our mother watched them from the nearby bush as they carted away our mother's clothing trunk box. These soldiers warned that if anyone disclosed that they returned, they would come and set the house on fire. Of course, no one reported them.

While at Usaja, life returned to near normal. With the invasion of the Nigerian Army, ingredients that were lacking in Biafra became more available. For many people, it appeared that the war was all but over, except that schools had not opened. The Nigerian Army began to distribute food items that hitherto had been scarce in Biafra. This brought quite a bit of relief to the pressure from lack of food. They distributed cooking salt, rice, beans, dried fish, some dried milk, West Indian saltfish (our people called this salted stockfish—*okporoko nnu*), and some European grain that could have been barley. Our people referred to the latter as *alikama*.

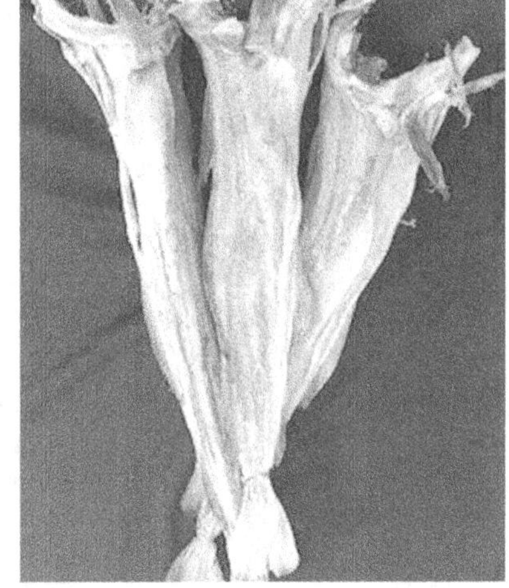

Foodwise, we had access to normal ingredients, such as stockfish, and salted codfish that we had never seen before. This latter stuff mitigated the shortage of salt. We also had onions, milk, rice, and beans, though in limited and rationed quantities. I recollect vividly that frying onions in oil and using it to make okra soup made a world of difference in flavor and taste, even before you added a pinch of dried fish or diced bits of stockfish (Norwegian dried codfish). Before the Nigerian invasion, we had access to locally mined salt from Ubûrû, near Afikpo, and black soap that we produced using the husk of palm oil fruit. Usually, this soap was therapeutic against rashes, probably because of its content of raw potash from ashes. People were excited about the salty stockfish. Some went on a binge eating this stockfish, and of course, after a long period of deprivation, the saltfish was exciting. A story went around that some people had eaten so much of the saltfish that their feet had swollen from it. I was there, on one occasion, when some person came around and admitted that he had been one of those who ate too much of the saltfish. The empty bags of alikama were used to make clothing.

Our people were still loyal to Biafra. However, there arose the issue of "I ga Awusa" or "going to Awusa people." Typically, our people regarded all Nigerian soldiers as "Awusa," though there were Yorubas and people from other Northern ethnic groups among them— even Eastern and Midwestern ethnics. To our people, the war was about the aggression by "Awusa" people—though, of course, it was more than that. Our people essentially ganged up to keep women from entertaining Nigerian soldiers, denying them access to sexual gratification. Of course, this did not have a lot of impact for two reasons. Like in any other war, soldiers forcibly took women of any age that they fancied. At Ovim, the soldiers on parade sang about their exploration of Nyamiri Nduri (Igbo vagina). Their song goes like this, "Nyamiri Nduri baa trigger, yahyah oh, baa trigger..." apparently referred to the absence of the clitoris due to circumcision of Igbo women. Secondly, some women voluntarily went to provide sexual services to the soldiers for their own reasons, especially economic comfort, and security. The saddest part of it all were the instances where the soldiers came and openly took people's wives and returned them at their discretion. Our elders protested to no avail. Those women who went voluntarily were stigmatized, even after the war. Some of them had difficulty finding a husband or even intimate, respectful friendships with men, which exemplifies the contradictions and tragedy of the human experience. Even while we complained about discrimination and prejudice, we perpetrated it against our people—from the mass slaughter of our people to the Igbo man's own self-acclaimed, or arrogation of, superiority over other ethnic groups.

In returning to Usaja and settling down after the raid, life was ordinarily normal. I avoided Nigerian soldiers as much as possible, managing to limit my encounters with them to one time. On this afternoon, I was walking from the compound with Ọdụmuko and one other person in our age group when we sensed the possibility of Nigerian soldiers on patrol around the villages. As soon as we diverted from the path leading from Ndi Egbe through Ndi Agwo and rather went the direction of Ndi Aenye'eru, the soldiers. descended from the path that we avoided. We quickly dove into the bush, and they went by without seeing us. We continued on our business. Aside from that one incident, I lived a normal life. The remainder of the family lived a normal life. Once more, we only hoped and prayed daily that our dad and our sister were well. No one had or heard any news either of them. How were they doing? We did not speculate or ask any person. We went to the farm like others. I did not go and join the relief lines. I am not certain if we ever went further than Amaeke to obtain relief. I know for sure that we had some stockfish, saltfish, onions, and other foodstuffs. In every sense, I was the head of the household. No one bothered us. As de facto head of household, I had no idea what to do to protect or provide for the house. I learned how to farm, and I was ready to gird my loins and work hard. We no longer had access or the courage to go to the plantation at Oko'ofia Ezuukwu. For some reason, I did not want to venture that far, about ten miles north into a thick jungle, with no guarantee of safety. I could raise seventy-five to eighty yam mounds per day, though my age mates among young men could raise 120 to 150 in a day. Somehow, I thought that this would do it.

It helped that the aura of my father's influence led people to respect us. It was also potentially dangerous in a community where people had hidden grudges and mischievous thoughts or could be instigated by sheer greed and mindless treachery. After all, someone went and told the Nigerian commanders that our dad was still around or suggested to them that he was the one who facilitated the escape of the Biafran contingent that was holed up at Acha, whereas all he probably did was join them to be able to escape.

While I tried to stay away from the Nigerian soldiers, I took time on one or more occasions to visit my first cousin, Mr. G. C. Okez, the virologist (his mother was the older sister of my mother) at Amu'uzu. I was very fond of him as a child. After he graduated from the University of Ibadan in 1960, he lived with us for a while. It was at his house that I learned how to play the Monopoly board game and Scrabble. At the Oriendu marketplace, I played with a set of the game that my older brother, Chuks, who also played Monopoly, left at home. I played these games so much that I memorized the entire game board. The most memorable game of Monopoly took place at the Oriendu market. I played with Lawrence Nwagbara, my Aunt Ugo's brother-in-law. Lawrence came often to the marketplace to play with me or just to hang out. On one occasion, we played a Monopoly game that lasted three days. At the end of the first day, no one won, and we kept all the cards in place. He returned the second day and still no one won. On the third day, the day was practically over before he finally won the game.

I remember during one visit to Mr. Okez, we had a conversation with him and one of his sisters-in-law, discussing security-related questions about the war. I declared that some person whom we had mentioned already in the conversation would be considered a security risk. Our in-law retorted that I could say that all I wanted. The next time that I visited, I was with my first cousin all alone. We had a long conversation with him. My cousin was a virologist and had been head of the School of Hygiene at Aba before the war began. He was highly educated and able to discuss or ponder the war at a high level of sophistication.

Just before I left, as it was about to get dark, he disclosed to me that he was planning to write a letter to Ukpabi Asika. I asked how Mr. Asika would know and trust him. My cousin told me that he not only went to school with Asika at Ibadan but also overseas. I then asked if he was not afraid of mistreatment by the Nigerian Army. I did not even bother to ask him how he would get the letter to Mr. Asika, the renegade administrator of the East Central State during the war. It was already getting dark. At that time I had strong loyalties to Biafra and I did not believe that anyone would abandon the cause and go and work for Mr. Asika. I did not think about his proposition in terms of treachery against the cause of Biafra; I just thought it inconceivable that any person would be brave enough to do what he was proposing or would not think first of what people would think of him. Given his level of understanding of matters, I could not fathom what went into his decision. I said nothing to him, nor did I have time to ask any further questions. In hindsight, I might have asked him, if it would be safe for me to go with him. But because of my convictions, I did not and the rest is history. It is possible that he had gauged the situation and considered it safe. During the two weeks or so after we returned to our villages, there were no incidents of the Nigerian Army randomly killing people or other insufferable misbehaviors. On one or two occasions, when the Nigerian Army had a bad day in a confrontation with Biafra, they would gather to randomly arrest a few young men for the slightest pretext and execute them. Such behavior gave rise to strong protests by the leaders of the community.

If our people should learn a lesson from all this, it is that we should nurture our local foods while taking advantage of trading privileges to supplement and enrich our diet. Before the war, all our beans came from the North. Other northern foodstuffs included beef, rice, and even, strangely enough, dried fish. It was therefore easy for the Nigerians to starve us to submission when the northern foodstuffs were cut off. For vegetable protein, we should have developed and expanded cultivation of Odudu and other beans. I was not surprised that even under those difficult circumstances, people who made clothing from empty alikama bags were taunted for it. This is one of the behaviors that keep us backward. On the other hand, the fact that people found ways of making exhaustive use of the alikama bags was testimony to our people's resilience and creativity.

May 20 to June 30, 1969: My Escape from Nigeria

In general, life was aimless because we had no idea when the war would end and what could become our fate at any moment. At night, we sat around in front of my great uncle's house (Mazi Okezie Ihedioha) at Usaja. It was the beginning of the farming season, and we went to the farm as usual. My best recollection of that time was that I went to Ogbakuru in the company of Okechukwu and Nnanna and made about eighty yam mounds in one day. Probably my proudest accomplishment. Okechukwu and I made jokes that were half concealed as messing with girls, which is something we did not do. Nnanna caught the joke and admonished us by telling us we could get a girl pregnant and should be careful. We stayed at Usaja to stay away from the Nigerian army as if it were some great hiding place—but the whole of Ovim knew where we were.

In any event, on the night of May 20, 1969, three men appeared without warning: Fabro— a good friend of Chuks and the son of Mr. Ugoji, who was a good friend of our papa—and Ugwa and his brother, two sons of my father's best friend in town, who was a comparatively older man whom my father relied on for wisdom. They wasted no time in telling me and my mother what their mission was: I had no choice. They were under instructions to get me out of enemy territory. It was a secret mission, and no one was even supposed to hear the conversation. I can recollect very vividly their appearance from a distance. There was no electricity. I saw them in the dim light provided by the moon or some oil lamp, but I recognized them because I was quite familiar with them. Initially, I had pretended to resist the pending adventure. I feigned walking away when in fact, I was glad.

I had heard about people crossing enemy lines and going to the Biafran side and coming back. I had no idea how it worked, but I looked forward to it. To this day, I did not ask my mother or my brothers what happened after I left that night. I later asked Okezie, who was five years at the time, but he had no idea what happened. Apparently, he was not even aware, and neither was Iroegbu or Ulobank. I am not even certain that they were around, or if they just forgot that I was with them. Okezie could only recollect that we were at UmuUkwu and began to return one after the other when the war ended. At age seventeen, I did not contemplate danger. I had this strange and misplaced feeling of confidence that I would always be able to overcome any exposure to danger or challenging situation. My mother intervened in my bluff, urging me to go and telling me that it was the best thing for me. It probably appeared to her that it would be safer for me to be in Biafra than to be in Nigeria, considering that our house had been raided on account of our father. There was always the possibility that people would go and tattle to the Nigerian army that our dad had a son who could be *Ajukwu soja (Ojukwu's soldier)*. On the other hand, she did not consider the potential danger of crossing enemy lines or even joining the Biafran Army on the other side. Whatever her thoughts, I never found out.

After my feigned bluff, I packed up a few belongings—some clothes, my sandals, and probably a tennis shoe that still fit me. At this point, I had begun to wear some of my older brother's clothes as he was six years older and bigger in size. My mother spared me a yam, some rice, about five pounds, and one or two packs of beans, about one pound each. I then packed in some onions, dried fish, and stockfish that I knew were no longer available in Biafra. To pack onions, beans, and stockfish was one of the most foolish decisions I made in my youth. Given that we were traveling at night and crossing enemy lines—trenches and battle locations—the smell of these items could easily give us away. After packing, I walked away with my guides, sandwiched between the—two ahead of me and one behind. It was dark, at about 9:30 p.m. We walked through the side route from the Usaja compound, a little north, and then veered east again into the bush paths between the compounds, toward Nkwo Ovum into Amachiebe. That was the last I recollected. I recollect ending up in the middle of some thick forest, most likely Ogbakuru, somewhere behind Amune and maybe Umudinja.

We stayed in a hideout, a hut in the middle of a dense forest. It was dreary and dark. We dared not go with any kind of illumination. All we had was the knowledge of the jungles and our neighborhoods. But because my mind was frozen, I was not even aware of where I was. Crickets chirped and nocturnal animals rustled around. Hopefully, there were no snakes; we were truly at the mercy of providence. All that ran through my mind was, "what if, what if, what if?" What if some Nigerian soldier or unit was on reconnaissance and found us? What if some wild animal suddenly attacked us or even became agitated due to our presence and howled in a manner that would attract attention to us? What if the right conditions did not exist and we had to stay in that unnatural forest hideout for another day or two? My mother, brothers, and sisters were on my mind. My poor mother! She was a woman that relied on nothing but prayer—all her life. Orphaned at a young age and married off not long after, her whole life had depended on the grace of providence. I ruminated on what might've been going through her mind. Whatever led to this fracas had already probably taken one of her sons. She had no way of knowing the fate of her oldest daughter, who had been caught up in the putsch of the Nigerian Army on the way to Umuahia. She had just survived near annihilation of her entire brood and narrowly escaped execution. Now, she holds her breath for her other son out in uncertain darkness, destination and destiny unknown. I was in danger, but I pitied my mother more and could only ruminate.

My guides roasted a yam, the size of a Star Beer bottle, without the neck. The yam was probably roasted in some underground fire and the heat of the soil cooked it, for I saw no smoke. I kept silent and simply did as I was told. I was more concerned about the ultimate success of the trip than anything else. I was thankful that I had anything to eat, as they sliced the yam into four and gave me a piece. My spoiled and comfortable side could have said, "so that's it for dinner?" However, my discipline and thoughtful side prevailed, for that was not the time and place to ask for comforts. The grass hut had some rafts for a bed. I probably took a nap as my guides took turns to watch the night as we waited for the right time to move, though I was ready to go at any moment. We stayed there until the next day and all day. Luck was on my side.

Early the next evening, May 21, 1969, my guides gave the order to move. It was getting dark, say about 8:00 p.m. We began walking slowly in a single file, down a long gradient as a drizzle was about to commence. Which part of Ovim were we in? I did not know and never will know. We continued walking and came near a thick forest area, crossed by a narrow bush path. This was our embarkation point. The drizzle then turned into a heavy downpour or at least went beyond a drizzle. I stared hard into the dark forest and saw nothing but thick foliage in the darkness. Visibility was zero inside that thicket. This was no seaport or bus terminal. The aura was dreadful and foreboding. At this point, I considered asking to abort the journey. But that was not an option. I could not even see my feet, let alone what was a few feet away. Hopefully, no dangerous critters or crawlers were hanging around for a meal or flesh to latch on to for sucking blood. I was sandwiched between two of my guides and I followed obediently. I did not flinch for a moment; we moved like a linked chain gang.

As we stepped into the forest, within thirty yards, we waded slowly and carefully into a body of water; certainly a shallow stream of the kind that is ubiquitous in and around Ovim. My guides knew the way, so I was confident that I did not have to swim. From that moment on, my mind went numb, and I cannot recollect what happened, except that it rained all night. I stilled my nerves and prepared my mind for the discomfort because it did not take three minutes for us to become fully drenched and dripping with water. Water flowed down my forehead, and I had to wipe my eyes and my face frequently. I had no choice but to be agile and to maintain my consciousness. Any deviation and I would be lost. All that mattered was that we get to the other side safely. We meandered through the forest all night. The forest smelled of rotten everything that could be in a forest. We heard occasional gunfire. What happened during that night, I could not recollect in detail. My mind was focused as my guides, following obediently. All I can recollect was that they would occasionally stop to check for Nigerian or Biafran sentry. On one occasion they thought that they encountered some Nigerian sentries and we had to change direction. Otherwise, generally, we just kept going. We did this meandering under that rainfall all night into the wee hours of the morning.

There is a limit to human endurance, though it may be revived with a little respite. At this point, after ten hours of pounding rain, with no covering, I was beginning to get exhausted. My body was awake and moving, but my brain was asleep and numb. I remembered nothing of what happened along the way, except the monotony of motion and following whatever directives my guides provided. Once more, my guides beckoned me to stop so they could get some reconnaissance. Feeling exhausted, this was welcome. I tried to sit on this piece of rock to get some rest, only to be stung by an ant—a painful sting. Who knows if it was an ant or a larva? Whatever it was, I jerked up only to see a gun pointed toward my head. The soldiers who waylaid us in the sentry ordered us to "advance to be recognized!!", Which means we should come forward and identify ourselves as friends or foes. We had no choice. I consider myself lucky. Whatever stung me could have been a snake or a scorpion on that rock. Lucky it was an ant, for a sting from a snake or scorpion would have been more dangerous. Just as I was beginning to conclude that the agony was over, we were captured – These were the very paintings of my fears – to be captured. My mind went back to my mother for a moment. In hindsight, I can see that we were lucky. Our captors were Biafran sentry from the battalion at Nkpa, the 82nd Battalion of the Biafran Army. They had moved their sentry ahead of where my guides and others who regularly crossed the battle lines would have been anticipated.

We were marched off to meet with the battalion commander at headquarters. It was close to light by the time the soldiers ended their questioning. Conceivably, my guides informed the sentries who captured us that their commander had full knowledge of our coming. They probably were aware of my well-known dad and his presence in the neighborhood. I looked at the palms of my hands and saw they were paper white—bright and glowing as if painted with a shiny high-gloss paint or as if I had been washing endless basins of clothes in cold water. But no! It was the relentless pounding rain that bleached my hands paperwhite.

The battalion was under the command of Capt. Nwoko, a light-skinned man, probably in his late twenties. There were several soldiers in his retinue, about six of them. They questioned us and accused us of being spies for the Nigerian Army. We denied the allegations. My guides reminded the commander that my father, a well-known educator in the region and around our neighborhoods has discussed the matter with the Commander—that I would be crossing from the Nigerian side to Biafra. The commander denied vehemently that he had ever had such a conversation; he had no such recollection. But several other people from the village, mostly women, were around and they reminded the commander that my dad had come and they witnessed the two of them holding a conversation. The commander denied it again and said that he had never met my dad. The women, especially, pleaded profusely with him to spare me any harm because my dad had talked with him. At this point, the staff sergeant asked a simple question, in sum and substance, "This man that everyone is talking so much about, is he a spirit or is he born of a woman?" The people of the village surrounding responded that Mr. Egbe is born of a woman. If this man is not a spirit, I can then torture his son. My big mouth did not help the situation any—of course, I did not say anything nasty, but my incessant plea and reminders to the commander and his staff sergeant that I am the son of Mr. Egbe, the well-known agricultural scientist and educator annoyed or irritated the commander and his sergeant. They then proceeded to begin to torture us. I am glad that I was not female. Rape might have been part of the repertoire because these people were without any compunction. They simply wielded power and abused it to the fullest extent, as in any war situation that I have read about since then.

They pointed their guns at us, and we were to receive sixty lashes of the whip on our bodies. We were ordered to lie face down, our stomachs on the ground. The boys were merciless. They lashed the whip with all their strength; it did not matter that we were human. It was unbearable. At the fortieth landing of the whip on my back, I could not bear it any longer. I scrambled up and ran—I tried to flee, but in what direction? I had no idea of the neighborhood. The soldiers came after me with their guns pointing at me. I ran in a direction that I knew nothing about. I came to a forked bush pathway, and I stopped. I was now in a dilemma: I could continue running and then run into Nigerian Army soldiers who would have shot me to pieces, especially if they saw someone chasing me with guns pointing in their direction. Or would it matter if I ran into Biafrans, who would see the same scene and likely come to the same conclusion?

The soldiers captured me again, and for attempting to flee, I was to get an additional twenty lashes, for a total of eighty lashes on my body. Because they stopped at forty, I had forty more to go. My poor guides—if anything else had happened to me, how would they explain to my dad? Meanwhile, my dad was nowhere near to speak for himself or to protect me. I believe he knew the risk inherent in the move that he had asked me to make. Presumably, he did not want to take a chance at heartbreak if I did not make it. At least he should have asked someone to give him a message at Umuobiala if I crossed over successfully so that he could come and get me. Or perhaps he believed that Captain Nwoko would keep his word and his side of the bargain. After the torture session, around 7:00 a.m., we were sent away to an undergraduate dungeon. It was a dugout hole with a bench or two. We all sat down with no food or water. All the foodstuff that I brought over from Nigeria was confiscated by the captain (battalion commander) and his staff. I had no money in my pockets. I cannot recollect what happened in that cell. All I know is that we just sat there and waited to see what our destiny would be. We were helpless. At about 4:30 p.m., we were led out. We were brought before the captain again. Suddenly and mysteriously, he remembered that my dad had spoken with him. He would now release us. For talking too much, we got an additional twenty lashes before we were released. This time, I was wiser and accepted my punishment. Even as I rose from the ground to continue my journey, one of the soldiers lashed at my bottom about five more times with a palm wine tree bamboo branch.

My guides may have told me where we were heading, but it was irrelevant. We moved on. After about four hours on foot, around 8:30 or 9:00 p.m., we arrived at Umuobiala, the headquarters of the 71B Battalion of the Biafran Army, which was under Captain C. C. Njeze.

The headquarters of the 71B Battalion was in the house of a young man who had a young wife. This man appeared to have been successful before the war. He had an elaborate house in the village, with a boy's quarter that housed the retinue of the captain— cooks and camp boys that took care of household chores. Under the circumstances, the personnel of the Battalion Headquarters occupied a major part of the man's house and compound. He was, likely, allotted at most two rooms in his own house and some section where he did his cooking. I saw his wife only a few times while I was there. They had no children yet. I recollect seeing the woman again in 1970 after the war was over and she was pregnant. There was one other man—a slightly light-skinned man with a little body—and my dad. I never did see where my father slept in those quarters. I had no idea of the other man's status or why he had the privilege of staying at the house. I had no reason to believe that he did anything specific about the work of the battalion. Every morning, he would dress up and just roam around the neighborhood. On one occasion, one member of the kitchen staff made an innuendo that "whenever everyone was away, he would take and fuck another man's wife." The person who made the statement looked at me and said, "if I hear it from you, I will deny that I said anything like that." I have no idea why he would think for a moment that I would tell anyone else. I was wise enough to avoid the potential trouble that such an action could cause, especially where there are guns around. If anyone was foolish, it was him for making such a statement in the presence of so many people. There were about twenty of us in that retinue, maybe twenty-five. While I did not know where my dad slept, I made sure that he had food to eat every evening whenever he was around. As usual, though, my dad was itinerant. He was not usually there—maybe one or two days during the week. I simply took care of myself on my wits and wisdom.

Another remarkable person in the camp was a young man, a teenager about seventeen or eighteen years old. About two weeks into my stay, this young man arrived. He was a relative of the commander, or so it was said. He looked lean like the rest of us. He had privileges, as he did not sleep with us. Two weeks later, one or more of the other boys in the camp was jealous or resentful. "Look at him … when he arrived here two weeks ago, he looked like bones. But see him now, he eats, and his stomach is bulging like a well-fed puppy." I moved out during the last week of June 1969 and returned to visit the camp later around late October on an errand. I saw the young man with a pumped-up chest like he had been pumping iron. The privileged access to better food was now showing. During that war, I did not see anyone else looking that good.

We simply took care of chores around the camp. We foraged, cooked, and fetched water to ensure that the captain and his guests had water to take a bath. One day, while we were out to fetch water at the spring, we found a cascading waterfall of clean-looking water, many of us were suffering flu-like symptoms. Our heads were stuffy and heavy. One of them stopped and waved everyone along, but we were not allowed to stop or slow down. As soon as the last of us walked past him, he scrambled into the bush. As we were on our way back, he came out from the bush and we returned to the camp with him. Shortly after, maybe about forty-five minutes, he assembled us and had a wet piece of warm cloth in his hands and asked us to sniff the cloth. He had harvested a root from the forest and ground it into the cloth. The fumes from the wet cloth were extraordinarily strong and cleared our heads. To this day, I cannot say what root he harvested. I asked my dad, the botanist if he had any idea what it could be, but he had no answer for me.

We ate once or twice a day—mostly garri and soup. I recollect that all twenty of us had this medium-sized basin of garri. As soon as the food was ready, everyone was informed, and we would announce "Gwo Gwo." Everyone would try to grab as much as possible. I grabbed about five big balls of the garri (fufu) to swallow and I would be almost full. If I ate anything else, only God knows how I came about it. I could also remember one day, the cook did not prepare food for my dad. After waiting for a while, I approached him and asked if there would be no food for my dad. He feigned a mistake and prepared food for him.

In general, life was uneventful. While I was at the 71B Battalion, in June 1969, Biafra made a foray into the Midwest and captured some foreign oil company workers. Following their capture, the Biafran government made such a big issue of their capture and attempted to capitalize on their presence. Radio Biafra announced that the oilmen were mercenaries of the Nigerian government and purportedly tried them. According to Radio Biafra, the oilmen were represented by lawyers and found guilty of being Nigerian government spies or mercenaries. The Biafra government proposed that the oilmen be executed, but there was tremendous pressure on the Biafran government to release the oilmen unharmed. I was impressed and hopeful. If Biafra could enter the Midwest again, there was a possibility that Biafra could recapture the Midwest again and menace Lagos successfully. In hindsight, once more, I think it was all a gimmick by the Biafran government to fool the Biafran public into believing that the war was winnable. After all, it had not been long since Owerre was recaptured from Nigeria.

Occasionally, I forayed into the village. I had to be careful because the conscriptors could get a hold of me and send me into the combat units. There was one day while I was in the village when I ended up near a young lady that was a well-known prostitute. She happened to be around and talking with another person and a soldier approached her and presumably solicited her for business. She replied in the affirmative and said, "na money," meaning, it's all about money; if you pay for it, you have it. I felt awful. Was this woman really so decadent? I wrote earlier about a confrontation between a young man and a prostitute at Oriendu. But now, I actually witnessed a decadent man, a truly rotten man, soliciting sexual services that were sold to him like a piece of fish or some other commodity in the marketplace. For goodness sake, this occurrence was real!

I can recollect a few other interesting curiosities at the camp of Captain C. C. Nje'Eze. At the camp, we had a cook. A light-skinned plump-looking young man. He was quiet and went about his business dutifully. One early morning, we woke up and it was announced that the cook has been relieved of his responsibilities. Whether he was deployed to the battlefronts, I do not know, but I do know that he was no longer among us. The story was that he was pilfering special food items, such as stockfish and Royco, a soup-flavoring ingredient, and giving them to his mistress. A lot of us were shocked, including me. First, I was appalled at the corruption, but also, like most of us, because many of us could have sworn that this young man, as quiet and unassuming as he looked and carried himself, would not have recognized a pussy if he saw one. What is more, he had a mistress that he slept with and even knew to pay a bribe for sex. Never judge a book by its cover.

Finally, it appears that the commander had a mistress or relieved himself from time to time by investing in some of the call girls around. One early morning, a young lady left his side of the house in the company of the commander himself. The lady had a whole stockfish in her hands. Fantastic! Her remuneration or wage for the night was quite generous. How could someone have a whole stockfish to herself, when we were glad to get only the flavor of it in our soup. So much for the privilege. In any event, one early morning at the end of June 1969, my dad asked me to pack my belongings and follow him. I had few belongings, to begin with, so packing was quick. With his walking stick, walking slowly ahead of me, I ported my dad's briefcase or portmanteau on my head and whatever I had in a bag and followed. Five miles later, probably southward, we arrived at the headquarters of the Biafran Organization of Freedom Fighters (BOFF), a guerilla army that was initiated by Col. Aghanya, the military engineer behind Biafra's science developments during the war. The BOFF headquarters would be my location until the end of the war.

While I and our dad and our big sister were away on the Biafran side, my mother and my other siblings were left to their own devices. They went to farms like other families and collected relief goods such as saltfish, Formula 2, and other foods. Though the palm oil plantation and farmland of Oko'Ofia that our dad developed at Ezû'ukwu Alai was still there, they no longer were able to access the cassava and palm oil that had matured. Our uncle, Egbula, had been living with his family at the plantation until the capture of Ovim but had to move out from Oko'Ofia into the main villages of Ezû'ukwu. Our uncle moved out of the plantation during the Nigerian putsch because the Biafran Army dug trenches in the plantation as part of their last line of defense, but they were outflanked by the Nigerian Army. After the putsch, our uncle continued farming in sections of Oko'Ofia ("thick jungle") but was not able to use the area where the plantation was located. After the raid on our house and my departure, my mother and siblings returned to the compound only in the mornings to cook their food and eat it but returned to Usaja, where our mother was married from, at night. After several weeks, they were advised that they could return to the compound at Ndi Egbe because it was now safe for them. Meanwhile, our sister Dioma (of blessed memory) was sent away to Eze'Ukwu, which was remotely located about ten miles north of Ovim, to stay with our uncle Egbula as a way of keeping safe from Nigerian soldiers who usually roamed the villages to forcibly take girls for their sexual enjoyment and returned them whenever it suited them. Dioma was already fifteen years old and was considered fair game for the Nigerian soldiers. Though Ola was about thirteen (old enough to be assaulted), our mother never let her attend the relief lines to collect food for the family. It appears also that our share of relief foods was brought to the house for our mother out of deference to our dad as a way to protect her from possible kidnapping by Nigerian soldiers. According to our uncle's wife, Dioma and other young girls of puberty age were sent into hiding in the thick jungle until evening time, when they would return to their homes in the villages. This, in summary, is how the family survived at Ovim after my departure until the end of the war when I met them at our house in the village.

Chapter IX

JULY 1969 TO NOVEMBER 1969
FROM CHEMIST TO SOLDIER

At the BOFF and Military Training

The regional headquarters of the Biafran Organization of Freedom Fighters (BOFF) was at Ama Ôgwûgwû in the Ohuhu area of Umuahia. The regional headquarters facility of the BOFF was what used to be the Adamma Okpara High School, a secondary school named after the premiere of the civilian government that the military overthrew on January 15, 1966. When we arrived, we met with the regional commandant and the Administrative Officer (AO). I was familiar with at least two other people at the camp: a teacher in Ovim (Mr. Ogbonna Azunna), the son of a revered pioneer teacher that preceded my dad in the teaching profession. The other person was Uche, the son of one of my father's colleagues at the Rural Education Center in Umudike, Umuahia. Uche's father and my dad had such a level of trust and mutual support that my dad could ask him the favor of coaching me to pass the entrance exam to the selective government secondary schools back in 1963-64. The regional commander, Mr. Ama Orji, was my father's schoolboy – my dad taught him in elementary school. Both Uche and Ogbonna were "officers" in the unit. My dad introduced me to the Commander as soon as we arrived at the camp.

Before the day was over, the officers assigned me and my dad living quarters in the camp. My dad was assigned a small semi-detached unit with two bedrooms and a kitchen – a kitchen that was separated from the main house by about ten feet, typical of the way dwellings were constructed at that time and what was usually constructed for teachers during that era.

As soon as we settled in, I approached Uche and Ogbonna and asked them if they had heard about or seen my sister. I explained to them that my big sister had been lost during the Nigerian Army's push toward Umuahia in April 1969. They both told me they had heard that someone called Chuks living in a nearby village, would know. They gave me directions on how to get to the village. I proceeded immediately, somewhere south or a little southwest to the named village. I no longer remember the name of the village. There I asked about Chuks. Some person pointed me in some direction within the village, though the vicinity was heavily forested, just like any village in the rural community. I proceeded as I was told. In the middle of this forested village, with nary another construction of any kind, in what was no more than a grass-walled shed, I saw my sister and her friend Rose lying on their stomachs on a bare mat and a dirt floor. The grass-walled shed in which I found them barely differentiated between the wall and what appeared to be a wide entrance area to the shed. My sister saw me and jumped for joy. "Where did you come from?" they exclaimed. I told them that I had crossed the lines from Nigeria, and although I did not go into the details of what had happened and how it happened, I assured them that everyone at home was very well at the time that I departed. Immediately, I let them know that I was at the BOFF camp and that they had to go with me. Whatever, few belongings they had, they packed up and followed me. I do not believe that I ever met this Chuks person. If I did, the meeting between us must have been uneventful.

The retrieval of my sister was simply an act of providence. In hindsight, there was no logical reason for my sister to end up in that location, a few miles away from Umuahia. There was equally no logical reason for me to inquire about her at that point. It did not even cross my mind at Umuobiala while I was with the 71B Battalion. After all, Umuobiala, a kindred community of Ovim, is closer to Ovim than Ama Ôgwûgwû. For some reason, I had not bothered to ask the same question at Umuobiala, where my dad was equally well known and well regarded. It did not even occur to me to ask my dad if he had made any inquiries during the five weeks that we stayed at Umuobiala. I consider it an act of God that I asked at the right place. She could have been elsewhere in the neighboring communities. As the Nigerians were advancing, the dynamics of the situation could have driven her to flee toward Owerre, Obo Owu, or Mbaise. She could have tried to flee beyond where she was in the direction of Umuobiala from which my dad and I had just departed. My sister could have been forced by circumstances to end up near Mbââno. The possibilities are endless. And if I had not found my sister, she could have ended up in a more hostile environment, where she could have been killed or harmed in other ways. In any event, we returned to the camp together. She and I of course were to share one room. The room had a *Vono* (spring) bed in it, but it had no mattress. Our father's room had a similar bed with a straw mattress. We also had a living room with a worktable, a smooth working or office table.

My papa was assigned as liaison officer of the regional office (headquarters) of the BOFF. He hardly stayed in the assigned quarters. As usual, he was itinerant. Once again, his itinerant behavior was probably, in addition to being active and being relevant, a way to avoid interaction and potential disrespect from the young officers in the army camp. Practically all the officers in the camp were young enough to be his children. What's, even more, is that his own son who was their age had not been seen or heard from for about fifteen months.

I hardly saw my dad. He came around only once every two weeks, on average, to check on me and my sister. He ensured that I was on good behavior. Though he hardly slept in the room assigned to him, I did not use the room either. Behind the kitchen, there was a forest and a bush path through which we crossed into the motorable dirt road that joined the main Okpara road to Okigwe, through Ezinnachi and whatever else in between and in the opposite direction. The road ended at the Imo River and one mile to the west. The bush served as a toilet also. Of course, there was no running water. Probably there was a pit toilet, but no bucket toilet as there were no night soil-men to empty the buckets.

The straw mattress in my dad's room was infested with bedbugs. About one week after we moved in, my dad returned to camp, as he was not even there to spend even a night after he showed me the place. He tried to sleep on the bed, only to be harassed by bedbugs. He scrambled up and we placed a mat on the bed for him to sleep on. Later, I took the mattress out and left it in the rain for about three weeks, after pouring a whole pot of boiled water on it. I was confident that the bugs would be gone after being beaten by the hot sun. Three weeks later, I brought the mattress in, just in time for my dad's return. No sooner did my dad lay down on the bed than the bedbugs swarmed all over him. With that, the mattress was taken out and set on fire. Indeed, on that same day, I brought in my mattress in the spare bedroom, which had been exposed to the sun for even longer than three weeks. I had the same experience, though I never used it in the bedroom. I put it down on the floor of the living room, leaving the bedroom for my sister and her friend. Given that the mattress had bedbugs, I had two mats in the living room. I placed the mat on the office table that was in the living room and converted it into a wooden bed. I used the other mat to cover myself like a blanket.

About ten days after we arrived at the camp and settled down, I began military training. My dad was assigned rations like an officer, which I made use of since he was hardly in the place. I began military training in part to prepare myself, just in case, but also to provide myself with a military cover so I could be entitled to my own ration along with the other boys in the camp. I did not sleep in the barracks with the other soldiers of private rank, however.

A few weeks after our arrival at the camp, some of my relatives and people from my village showed up. Kanu Edede of Ndi Egede showed up along with Peter, son of Madiike Onyooma, of Ndi Uzu compound. Also, among them was Ndukwo from Amaukwukwa, nicknamed Oshiama. Following behind them a few days later was Okorie, the son of my father's younger sister, along with Nwachukwu Egbe, a third cousin from the same line of Egbe. Nwachukwu was the son of Egbe Egesi, my grandfather's nephew. I recollect Mazi Egbe Egesi very vividly and was very fond of him before he died. Mazi Egbe Egesi (died 1958) adamantly refused to convert to Christianity or go to church[180].

Oshiama joined the Biafran army as soon as the war started in July 1967. I had a conversation with him a few days after he and the rest of the boys from our village arrived at our camp in early July 1969. Oshiama described the beginning of the war to me. His narrative corroborated what I later heard about Biafra's lack of preparedness. I recollect how he looked when he returned from the fronts in July 1967—a shiny uniform, admired by all. He also told me that he had fought at the Battle of Ôzuâkôli in March/ April of 1969. As he narrated his story, he claimed that there was a lot of desperation at the time that Nigerians were closing in at Ôzuâkôli. Ôzuâkôli is only nine miles from Ovim and twelve miles short of Umuahia. After contingents of the Nigerian Army converged from the northeast and west of Ôzuâkôli at Akara, three miles from Ovim, Umuahia appeared to be a sure bet. But it was not to be. The Biafran Army confronted the Nigerians at Ôzuâkôli, and a battle ensued that lasted for three weeks before they could take Umuahia. Oshiama (Ndukwo) said he was asked the lead the attack. I guess, if that happened, he probably was at the head of a file of soldiers, say a battalion. He told me that he took off his two stripes as a corporal and proceeded to lead the attack. I do not recollect the details of the story, but eventually, they lost the confrontations and the Nigerian Army captured Umuahia.

Oshi'ama was residing at a company that was part of the 70A Battalion of the Biafran Army that had its headquarters a little northwest of our headquarters, closer to the Imo River at what used to be an elementary school. The commander, a major, as he said, had been a businessman in the northern part of Nigeria before the war. Since he was close by, I saw him frequently. I do not know where Okorie, Nwachukwu, and Kanu resided, but they visited the camp frequently. Okorie had sustained a bullet wound in the thigh somewhere, that he never explained to me. Kanu and Peter had never been soldiers. They regularly crossed between Biafra and Nigeria, buying and selling goods across the borders. Kanu may have participated in clandestine guerilla operations, as he was to narrate to me later in this story. I did not witness any of his participation. Therefore, I could not say for certain that he did engage. Nwachukwu had also sustained a bullet wound on his ankle that festered and was healing slowly. He had been a sniper during military operations, which fascinated me. Therefore, I lost no time in asking him some questions about the role of a sniper, and he gladly described it. However, because of his bullet wound, he never went back into active duty. He did, however, carry around a bolt-action rifle that was probably his standard issue.

Our military training lasted about four weeks, longer than regular combat soldiers. We were taught how to shoot, engage in a battle, assault, and how to dismantle and to reassemble guns. Of course, we learned about different types of guns—the Madison (AK-47, with the 7.62 NATO), SLR (Self Loading Rifle – the M16 and the 7.62), the Mark 4 (Bolt-Action Rifle – 7.92), and the "Shebaretta" that loaded .9 mm. We also trained on the light machine gun that packed a 7.92 mm) and the heavy machine gun. We were also taught how to throw Molotov cocktails (essentially a beer bottle that packed some incendiaries) and the bazooka or some weapon more like a rocket-propelled grenade launcher. Finally, we trained on guerilla tactics, which I feel was something of a joke when I look back at it. The obstacle course was also part of our training. We did that regularly for the entire four-week training. It was more of a daily routine, at least one or two days a week with

---

[180] *For a digression, my "uncle" Egbe Egesi, that we called Nyeye believed in everything animist. One thing that I remember about him was that he never missed the routine sacrifices as they were due. One thing he did was pop the tender leaves of a plant called Ichikara (Osinkaro in Yoruba) as a means of chasing off evil spirits. He never failed, as the need arose and probably based on the requirements of the relevant sacrifice, to kill a chicken and make some tasty pepper soup from the roasted chicken. He would then fold the leaves into a spoon to enable us to scoop the soup. Since he roasted the chicken, it tasted smoky, much like the authentic Jamaican jerk chicken that I tasted on the roadside in Jamaica in 1997. He, also unfailingly, sacrificed a little chicklet that was left to suffer in the middle of the shrine at the entrance to the compound.*

some hand-to-hand combat that was more like Judo training. I would not have been able to apply the techniques to outmaneuver any good soldier based on skill advantage. I learned no more from those exercises than an ordinary smart kid would know. Five minutes into our first training using guns and real bullets, Kanu entered the camp from Okpara Road and asked what was going on. I explained it to him (or our trainer explained, for I forget whether the conversation was private after the exercise or while we assembled). He, however, admonished us that the bullets were flying east a few shaves about the heads of anyone walking along the Okpara Road to Okigwe.

Military training was over at the end of the first week of August. I recollect that one day, early in the process, my dad came into the camp and our staff sergeant was looking for me, suspecting that I had failed to appear for the training one that day. My dad was furious and came lashing out at me. Luckily, I still had a gun in my hand; I promptly retorted that I had been out there with everyone else. He then relented and backed off. At the end of the training program, I was issued a Biafran Army number and entitled to my ration like other soldiers. My private ration, along with my dad's ration that I appropriated, enabled me to eat better than the other soldiers. I was also entitled to a monthly stipend, which, till today, I never received a penny of—not even an almost-worthless Biafran penny. I was also entitled to a uniform, which was issued to me in the second week of December of 1969, about two weeks before we commenced our disorderly retreat that ended the war. I promptly discarded it on the last day of the war as we prepared for our final trek home. I also remained in my dad's assigned quarters, unlike the other private soldiers who slept in the dormitory-style barracks.

After my military training, I participated in duties like other private-level soldiers. One of such duties was sentry duty. On my first day at the sentry, I had a partner named David. David was one of those boys who did not have the opportunity to go to secondary school and was resentful because of it. On several occasions before we had been on sentry together, he would confront me as we went to chores or assignments to tell me that college was over, and we were all equal now. In those days, attending secondary school was something that was reserved for a privileged few. Those who did not have the opportunity sometimes envied the ones who did. Many enterprising parents would go into debt to send their children to school or exerted themselves to the limits to send at least a male child to school. David was not so fortunate. On the day of the sentry, David had his opportunity. He not only did not fail to remind me of our equality, but his opportunity came handily. He was older and senior to me at the camp. I never responded to David, in part because I had no idea how to respond and in part because I understood the foundation of his resentment.

At the sentry, I practiced what was taught. Of course, we took turns keeping awake and taking a nap. It was my turn to keep awake. I held my gun between my thighs and, though I had no intention of falling asleep, I dozed off. David snuck up on me and quietly took my gun away. As soon as he did, he came back and asked "Nwa college [college kid] where is your gun?" I realized he had taken my gun, but that was beside the point; you were not supposed to fall asleep on your gun. I knew what I did and so did not bother pleading with David. He promptly reported me to the pope (the regimental sergeant major) and I was charged with dereliction. Pope himself had no education at all and barely spoke Pidgin English. When the sentry was over in the morning, I was arrested and locked up in the detention cell. The narrow cell was seven feet by nine feet and contained a mat and nothing more. I was locked up for two days. I was also whipped between twelve and twenty-four lashes to boot. My dad was not around to intervene, and I had little, if any, food at least on the first day.

The sentry post that I was posted to was behind a building that was either a classroom or dormitory. I think more of a dormitory. Several of the semi-professional staff slept there, and the camp nurses and medical office, and officers were there. I recollect going there for medication and a check-up on a few occasions. While I was posted there, I heard quite a bit of the gossip in the camp. I tried not to pay any attention, but it is virtually impossible to purge one's mind of everything that one encounters. Some things will stick. It was there one night when I heard a lot of gossip about the "Pope" and some woman with whom he had had an affair. One of the boys asked, "But where did he find room or space to be having sex with this woman?" The storyteller replied that he had no idea, but insisted it was happening. On another night while I was on the sentry, the female nurse, who had treated me on one occasion, was protesting the advances of one of the officers or maybe one of the other boys in camp. As she put it audibly, "I don tell you to make you no dey romance me like that." The man was caressing her against her will. On another occasion, while I was on watch, I heard rustling somewhere in the bush adjacent to the building that I was watching. I backed off and stepped into the door that was behind me. "Who goes there?" I shouted—the usual call designed to get a possible intruder to respond or a friend to respond. I shouted again but got no response, so I pumped a few shots into the dark. I may have thought that it was a nocturnal rodent, which, for me, was enough of a presented opportunity to fire off a few shots. Of course, this got me into trouble. I was lucky that the bullets did not fly off and hit someone across the bush. In any event, I shot into the ground. My issue gun was a short noisy gun that looked like the "Shee" that was manufactured in Biafra, except that it had a rectangular breach block, instead of a cylindrical breech block. Both guns carried the .9-mm bullet. When the officers heard the gunshots, they immediately scrambled and came to inquire as to what happened. They questioned me and locked me up again in a narrow room, similar to the one I'd been locked up in before, but this time with one window at the end and a board on the floor for sleeping. There was probably a provision for toilet and urination. I am no longer certain. I was fed one or twice a day during my confinement. I was released after two days. I never discussed the matter with my sister or my dad. I do not think that they even knew about it. It's possible, though, that Ogbonna Azunna or Uche may have influenced my early release. The other remarkable incident during my sentry experience happened when I was assigned to guard the commander's residence. The guard post was in a small guardhouse south of the commander's residence on the way to his outhouse. I was assigned there over consecutive days, maybe four or five days. On the last day, I dozed off, though I was conscious of the fact that more was expected of me. In any event, I was dozing as the commander was on his way to the outhouse. He was probably a few feet from me but had crossed the entrance. I woke up from my slumber and I shouted out, two times "Who goes there?" The commander did not respond. I shouted, for a third time, "Who goes there?" at which point the commander responds. "After the enemy has already passed, you are screaming, 'who goes there.' If I hear that again, I will come there and give you a dirty slap." I said nothing and the commander went and did his business. I was sure to keep awake and make myself visible by the entrance as the commander returned to his residence.

It should be evident, by now, that I cooked my food. The ration that we received was supplemented with whatever we could forage from the nearby forests. For example, we had papaya (pawpaw) and wild Greens (vegetables). Now and then, we also received Quaker Oats and dried milk. Palm oil fruit was abundant around the forests. Indeed, very often my soup consisted of palm oil, which was essentially prepared by boiling and pounding the raw palm oil, without processing and mixing the Greens into it. If I received a little ration of corned beef or some canned meat that looked like Spam (because I cannot remember the name now—lunch meat, I believe), I would mix it in. In hindsight, I can attribute the regular sickness that I felt towards the end of the war to this staple of mine—the palm oil soup (ofe nkpuru nkwu). The other staple of my diet was to boil mature but unripe pawpaw into a small amount of Quaker Oats and some dried milk. I recollect the first time that I had Quaker Oats with the dried milk (thanks to my privileges due to my dad), I had diarrhea—or at least it purged my stomach. By Jove, since this milk was available and not in abundance or adequate if I could not consume it comfortably, then what was the alternative? None! I promptly went to the nurse and asked for antibiotics. My experience at the chemist before I crossed over taught me that antibiotics stopped my running stomach. In any event, all I needed was to take one of those tetracycline tablets and the running stomach would stop. The nurse gave me about five or six tablets. Following this routine about three times, the running stomach induced by the dry milk ceased. Thank God, I did not need the antibiotics any longer. It could have been that the level of deprivation during this period of the war caused my body to absorb anything that was food and use it.

Throughout my service in the BOFF, I never engaged in combat duties. However, I performed combat support duties in addition to running other errands and keeping sentry at night. One of the duties I performed consisted of crossing the Imo River two or so times a week in a leaky boat to cart ordinance across from the other side of Biafra. The Imo River at that point did not have a bridge at all, not even a bridge that was broken. A bridge never existed at that point of the river. There were about four of us. Boxes of ammunition would be loaded into the boat until the water came close to the rim of the boat. There was so much water that it would almost sink the boat. We did maybe two or three rounds before all the ammunition was brought across. Because the boat was leaky, my task was to repeatedly scoop the water out of the boat to ensure that the boat was not flooded with water where it could sink. Without saying it, it was in my best interest to scoop the water quickly enough because I never learned how to swim, even though I had had an opportunity. I can only thank God that I never had to swim across that river. Usually, the river was shallow, but sometimes when it rained the river would overflow its banks rise above a tall Iroko tree that was probably twenty to thirty feet tall. When it overflowed like that, the river would be turbulent. Thankfully, the boat was rowed by this "boy" who was of Rivers State origin. He was quite skillful at it. I could not even accurately describe what he did. During one of those occasions when the river overflowed its banks, the turbulence of the river was such that the boat could not be rowed across in a straight line. The young man would row the boat straight into the turbulence, the water swirling violently. Miraculously, the boat twisted toward the intended direction, downstream. It was very turbulent at the usual point midway across the river. I was amazed at what this young man did. As soon as the boat was pushed forcefully flow-wise, he would place the paddle skillfully such that the boat would turn in the direction of the bank and away from the torrent and we would then row slowly across to the bank. Interestingly, our superiors never for once thought about issuing us life jackets or any kind of support. Every week, when we had to do this chore, I went along with this misplaced confidence that we were going to be successful. At the end of the day, only God saved me from possible drowning in that river.

Once we got to the opposite bank of the river, we offloaded the ordinance and loaded them into a lorry that we called "Okoso in honor of a conical spinner made of metal for rascally boys." Even the drive was called Okoso. Since I joined the unit late in the game, I do not know who gave the lorry the name Okoso. Was the lorry called Okoso and the name extended to the driver or the other way around? I never asked, as once more, I tried as much as possible to be reticent in the camp. At some point, maybe in mid-August 1969, Okoso the lorry broke down. We had to load the ordinance on wheelbarrows and sometimes we carted them on our heads. I can recollect, on a few occasions, we also carted the ordinance to the firing line at the trenches—the operational headquarters of a company. The trenches were visible from the thatched shed, where the soldiers received the ordinance from us.

More on Life in the BOFF

Besides ferrying ordinance across the Imo River, my other chores at the BOFF camp included running errands for the officers. We did not have running water, so we bathed in the nearby streams. Imo River was down the hill to the west, but I never went that far for water. We had little soap, except for the black soap that was made locally using traditional methods. My sister and the other girls in the camp had access to the Lux brand of soap that they used judicially. One good use they made of modern toilet soap was to combine it with some strong species of lime or lemon and mix it vigorously to convert it to body lotion. We had a "doctor" that was a second-year medical student at the University of Ibadan. This doctor diagnosed and prescribed medication. I had no reason to question his competence. However, he did not do surgery. I visited the medical facility several times and saw this doctor when I was ill. Indeed, I believe that the end of the war, six months after I entered military service, saved me. During the last three months of the war, from the first of October to the end of November, I was falling ill with malaria or yellow fever at least once every two weeks. Each bout of sickness lasted about two or three days. When I stepped on a broken bottle and the cut developed an infection, the camp doctor gave me a shot of penicillin that healed the infection very quickly. I had easy access to anti-malaria medication and a small supply of pain medication and such first aid medication as gauze and hydrogen peroxide and iodine. In addition to the medical doctor, we had a nurse, qualified, I believe, or at least one that was in training before the war. This nurse along with another male nurse or orderly constituted the complement of the medical staff at the camp. The female nurse, like other female staff in the camp, was sexually harassed by the soldiers, especially the officers who believed that they had a certain privilege. Talking about the other female staff or even more so the girls who resided in the camp, there was a lot of sexual exploitation. On another occasion, we were at the parade ground collecting our ration of food. Some female cooks did the cooking. In response to a comment, one of the female cooks made, a member of the regimental Sargent's staff said, "<u>O</u> wû mâkâ ihie nwa nsi gi nye'm ma'asoo" or "Is it because of the thing that I asked you to give me to stick my thing in it?" The female cook was embarrassed. In my youthful and innocent temperament, I was equally embarrassed and appalled. I said nothing since I was just an ordinary enlisted person with no say in what people did. I witnessed a lot of that I do not want to mention here. It was indecent, horrible, and despicable.

Besides these experiences, what I did at the camp was routine and I tried my best to stay out of trouble. Another memorable routine from my time in the BOFF was the early morning parades and exercises. Three or four days a week, we ran in the direction of Ezinnachi/Okigwe on the motorable road for about three miles and back, making a total of five to six miles on the double. We sang our patriotic and other parade songs along the way.

"... Hanye nye nye, hanye nye nye, hanye nye nye, anyi ge'egbu ndi Awusa, ...Ya buru ni'iwe, ya buru na'agha, hanye nye nye, anyi ge'egbu Ndi Awusa..." Hope high-da, Hope High-da, Left-right-da left-right-da. Onye obula wayo! A.O Wayo! Pope Wayo!, (Gong Ho, Gong ho, Gong ho, We will kill the Hausa people, Be it in anger or be it at war, we will kill the Hausa People.. Hope high da, Hope high da, Left Right da, Left Right da, Everyone dubious, the A.O. is Dubious, the Pope is Dubious...)

Ka mgbe abali ato, eribele'm ihie, eribele'm ihie, eribele'm ihie, ka mgbe abali ato arabele'm otu, Gowon Mmere gini yeah!!! ..." Ihuru'M na'anya ka'M mara ihie, ...Ihuru'M na'anya ka'M mara ihie, ... Ihuru'M na'anya ka'M mara ihie, onu ahapughi'iko!!!. (It has been three days and I could not eat food... I have had no food ... I have had no food, It has been three days, I have not fucked a pussy, Hey, Gowon what is my offense? ... If you love me, please make it know, If you love me, please make it know... If you love me, please make it know, the word will get out promptly ...

Ojukwu bu eze Biafra!!! E kwuru ya na'Aburi!!! Awolowo, Yakubu Gowon! Ha'enweghi ike i meri Biafra!!! Armored Car, Shelling Machine, Heavy artillery, Ehe'eheh!!! ha'enweike i meri Biafra!!! Okporoko Move ahead!!! Armored Car, Shelling Machine, Heavy artillery, Ehe'eheh!!! ha'enweike i meri Biafra!!! (Ojukwu is the leader of Biafra, ... It was made known at Aburi!!! Awolowoh, Yakubu Gowon, They cannot defeat Biafra... Armored cars, Shelling Machine and Heavy Artillery Aye Aye. They cannot defeat Biafra, Hey – Mr. Dried codfish, Move Ahead!!! ... Armored cars, Shelling Machine and Heavy Artillery Aye Aye .. They cannot defeat Biafra.

On one occasion, I probably did something out of order, the "Pope" reprimanded me, and I talked back. The "Pope" proceeded to smash his baton on my head, but I stopped him with my right hand. The baton smashed into my hand. The "Pope" moved on, but a few minutes later, when I was no longer paying attention, he hit my head again with the baton. It was painful. I am grateful to God to this day that he did not hit me a second and third time. He may have succeeded in breaking my head with that baton.

Though we in the BOFF were technically military personnel, there was a constant threat of conscription into the infantry. Starting around the middle of 1968, the war began to take an ominous turn. The psychological toll had begun to take effect on the populace. Many people began to feel that the war should be over. At the beginning of the war, our people believed that the war would be short. Surely the Nigerian Army would be clobbered and discouraged from approaching our borders. By this time in July 1969, it was becoming clear that the chances of victory were quite slim or even non-existent. As the war progressed, the Nigerian Army advanced their occupation of Biafran territory steadily. For young men, joining the Biafran Army was no longer romantic. At the age of seventeen years, I was old enough to be conscripted.

On one occasion, while we ran errands along the highway from Umuahia to Okigwe, we were arrested by the Biafran Army conscriptors. We were marched to the headquarters of the 70th Battalion along the main highway and packed into a cage. From there, we were to be sent to a processing center and then to training for about one week and then deployed to battle. However, news of our conscription reached our headquarters, about one mile from our processing center. We were released the next day, after spending the night in the cage. On another occasion, late in October 1969, we were once again apprehended and conscripted. This time, we were running an errand in the company of one of the new infantry officers who was assigned to the BOFF. This particular officer, a captain, was a showman. The deployment of this set of infantry officers was a curious story, at least from my point of view.

Sometime in early or mid-October 1969, three infantry officers were assigned to our BOFF headquarters. All three were from our home area in Îsuikwuato. One of them was burly and looked like he was spoiling for a fight and could not wait to engage the enemy. Indeed, this showed later in the year during the final months of the war. He engaged the enemy regularly and gave Situation Reports or sit-reps. The other officer was short and a little stocky. It was clear that the latter officer was in it for the show and the pomp. He knew his way around and knew how to avoid combat. The third person was a youthful-looking guy who probably did not know what he had got himself into. He was visibly shaken and apprehensive. On the day we were conscripted for the second time, we were with the showman. He declared himself to be an army officer and the conscriptors derided him. He was probably not wearing his shiny new uniform. Once more, the news of our conscription reached our camp's headquarters, and we were released.

During our first conscription, Agu criticized me for appearing too enthusiastic and compliant. As we were marched along the road, some showed their grudge by the way they complied with orders and the way they marched or performed the marching orders. I marched enthusiastically as a means of deflecting attention from myself. I had no idea of the possible consequences of showing any reluctance or grudge. Agu did not see that or felt that it was not necessary. In any event, I was hoping that by deflecting attention from myself, I might be able to escape from any encampment where we would be locked up. In hindsight, such a thought was sophomoric.

As of July 1969, the possibility of an outright Biafran victory was a long shot. At that point, we were fighting for a draw or even a negotiated settlement where we might be able to have our leaders share power. Though the Nigerian Army was getting weary of the war, they were more confident of victory. They had occupied most of Biafra by military conquest. On the other hand, world public opinion had forced the government to promise not to massacre the people. Hunger and deprivation had taken their toll, and Biafrans living on the Nigerian-occupied territory of Biafra were living better and more normal lives. For medication and food, Biafra depended more on international relief. Schools were not open and there was no work. Even within Nigerian-controlled Biafran territory that was far from the battlefields, schools were not open, though schools were open all over Nigeria. The sympathy for Biafra was widespread around the world, in large part because the ordinary citizens of the world were fully aware of the cause of the war and felt that punishing Biafra was unjust. The behavior of governments was quite another, as will be explained in the final chapter.

Although the probability of outright victory was a long shot, for me there was still a naïve feeling that somehow we could still win the war. How that would come about, I had not the foggiest notion. In general, though, I was rudderless. I had no idea what to do next. It was clear to me though that the war was not going well, but I had no plans or any idea how to get myself into an advantageous position. I recollect one day, I had a conversation with Agu about the matter. He, in sum and substance, told me that I had an asset that I was wasting. First, my dad was an influential person. Secondly, I could speak a smattering of French. He said, "If I had your leverage, I would go through my dad and find myself where I could show off my ability to speak some French … fritifiti noooooooor." Our leaders were doing it. Whoever found opportunities used them simply to stay safe.

I survived the war by a series of lucky events—or I could say that when I was in situations that worried me or were risky, they were resolved by sheer good luck. Like rowing across the Imo River, another potentially strenuous task was to come into play: the trip to the Supply and Transport (S&T) depot at Ezinnachi, near Okigwe. Sometime before the first of September 1969, our transportation truck broke down. This truck (that we called "Okoso") was used to haul ammunition and food supplies from Ezinnachi into the camp. After Okoso broke down, the boys had to walk to Ezinnachi, about ten to twelve miles away, hauling food and supplies on their heads. Two times a week, a team of eight or ten boys would walk the distance to Ezinnachi for our supplies. Always, it was two big bags of garri, each bag containing 450 cups. Other supplies came in other ways, like across the river—specialties such as stockfish, Royco, dried milk, medication, and whatever else. After about two or three weeks of hauling food on their heads, the boys began to complain that the task was stressful. There was also some grumbling that I (Chinyere Egbe), Mr. Egbe's son, a private soldier like the rest of them, would not participate. "Well, everyone must participate, and privilege should not exclude anyone." But hold on for a minute—one of the other officers had two younger brothers in the camp who lived with him. One was too young. Another was about fourteen years old and did not go to Ezinnachi nor did he participate in other dangerous chores, such as rowing across the Imo River to haul ordinance. Charles (Agu) was also older than I and did not participate, though he was the batman or Aide-de-Camp of one of the officers. Our new admin officer also had a younger brother, about thirteen years old, living with him. Under the circumstances in Biafra, if these boys did not have special privileges, they would have participated in the chores like the rest of us.

As we were out for our chores one afternoon, the boys grumbled about the possibility of walking to Ezinnachi the next week if called on, loud enough so I could hear. I had the impression that the murmuring was made loudly for my benefit, probably expecting me to say something. I said nothing to them, though I was bothered by the whole idea of walking ten or twelve miles while hauling a heavy load of garri on my head. Not long after the grumbling, maybe the next morning, the "Pope" informed me that I would join the team to Ezinnachi. I complied and said nothing.

On the appointed day, the tattoo sounded at 3:30 a.m., the first call for the boys who were on duty to go to the Supply and Transportation depot to show up at the parade ground and get their marching orders. Usually, the leader of the duty troop rose on the first tattoo at 2:00 a.m. so he would have enough time to get to the S&T and complete the paperwork before the others arrived. At 3:30 a.m., I responded to the tattoo and reported to the parade grounds in front of the administrative offices of the unit. I stood there under the trees and waited until about 4:00 a.m. when the final tattoo sounded for the rest of the other boys to report for general duties and the morning exercises. As soon as the remaining soldiers in the regional headquarters were assembled, the Pope asked, in Igbo, "Egbe, what are you doing here?" I responded that I had been standing and waiting since 3:30 a.m. but had not seen anyone. I was certain that I was in the right place, as I had seen them assemble at the parade ground while I was on sentry at the commander's residence. Besides, though their tattoo is sounded about 3:30 a.m., they are usually at the parade ground by the time that the rest of us arrive at 4:30 a.m. or 5:00 a.m. before they leave. The Pope did not believe his ears. He promptly ordered someone to check the barracks to find out what happened. Lo and behold, all the boys were still sleeping in their corners at the barracks; they had failed to report for the parade. I could not say for sure what had transpired, but it is conceivable that the boys had made known their objections to the officers and leadership without my knowledge, as I had not been part of the group. It's equally possible that the grumbling, audibly made in my presence, was an attempt to make me respond and join them in a delegation to the leadership. All the other boys were ordered to report to the parade ground. Upon their arrival, they were whipped for punishment and then ordered to proceed to Ezinnachi or face more consequences. Thereupon, I was issued with an official pass and a gun—a "She-Beretta"[181]—with a fully loaded magazine of ten bullets (.9 mm). The admin officer and the Pope decreed that from then until the end of the war, I would be the leader of the group that goes to Ezinnachi to cart food for the camp. This singular event, I would say, saved me, for I never had to carry the heavy load of food on my head. I attribute it all to an act of providence where the conspiracy spared me from

---

[181] *The real Beretta is a short gun that looks like a Glock. However, Biafra manufactured a semi-automatic assault weapon that we called a "She-Beretta." It operated on a .9 mm caliber and looked totally different from the Beretta Cx4 Storm assault rifle, though they were about the same size. I do not know the origin of the name "She-Beretta." The Biafran version of the gun had a cylindrical breach block and would heat up in about thirty minutes during battle, which may have diminished its range.*

stressful work. Conceivably, this could have been a clever plot by someone to save me by inciting the boys to conspire so recklessly. I am stretching my imagination here. If I joined the conspiracy, then I would be punished along with others, and being the most junior, I would have had to carry the load. Someone had to stretch their imagination to assume that I would not join and when the others disobeyed, I will then be vindicated and made a leader. Therefore, I attribute it all to the scheme of the Lord Almighty. If the conspirators were hoping that I would join their conspiracy, they were also stretching the limits of their assumptions. Considering that my father was so close to the commander and that my disobedience would have had much more significance, there was no way that I could have joined such a conspiracy. The alternative approach for me to avoid the trek to the S&T would have been for me to flex my muscle and either approach the commander or the two senior officers that were close to my dad and appeal to them to spare me the trek. Once I was issued my gun and marching orders, I walked north through the bush path, toward Ezinnachi. I walked with the boys and socialized with them along the way. In this way, we all felt comfortable with each other. On this first day of my leadership, we arrived at the S&T later than others. Nevertheless, we signed for our two big bags of garri and measured them to ensure that there were at least 450 cups of garri in each bag. I signed off and called my boys together. Everyone loaded his big basin of garri on his head and we headed back to camp at Amaôgwûgwû, Along the way, we stopped two times for rest. During one of the rest stops, we mixed some garri in a smaller-sized basin with water. The boys "drank" the garri to fill their stomachs and we moved on. In addition, to that, I realized, on the first day, that each had a small "mudu" measure to take some garri for personal use. A small mudu measure would contain about four cups of garri. At that rate (about forty cups), 4.5% of the garri would be missing and would be attributed to spillage. In any event, the actual number of cups of garri in a big bag was between 455 and 465. Therefore, it was easy to still be within range of the expected nine hundred cups of garri that we were expected to bring to camp. I collaborated with the boys to hold a small bag where they could hide the garri before they went and delivered their loads to the local storage. As we approached the camp, I stopped and hid the garri for everyone near the bush and watched it until they delivered the remainder to our storage. I stood behind the bush and watched them so that no one diverted more food than was allotted as motivation along the way.

My trips to Ezinnachi, in that darkness of 2:00 AM, were without incident. On one and only one occasion, I was confronted by two or three boys as I walked along the Okigwe/Umuahia road. "Who are you and why do you have a gun?" they asked. It was about two hours into the trip, about 4:00 a.m., in the twilight. I did not say much as I slung my gun on my shoulder, except to show them my pass and explain that I was from the BOFF on my way to S&T to cart food for the unit. They inspected my pass with a flashlight and let me go about my business. At the age of seventeen, I never thought that I would encounter a problem that would not go away. It never crossed my mind that I could have encountered ill-behaved people or that my journey in that darkness could have ended in personal tragedy.

My poor mother! She was back home behind enemy lines. There was no communication. I do not recollect anyone returning from behind the lines to tell me that they saw my mother and my siblings. Somehow, I was confident that they were there. What if they had been killed, the way my brother died in action, and no one said a word to the family? I did not think about how they ate or if they ate. While I was behind the lines with them, somehow, we always had something to eat. In any event, I wanted to go and see them. This would require two risky crossings: one to get into Nigeria and the other to return to Biafra. So it happened that one day I tried but failed.

During the war, some people crossed the lines regularly into Nigeria to buy food and other commodities that were scarce in Biafra.[182] Two people from my village, Kanu Edede, and Peter O'Madiike Oyooma crossed regularly. They usually travel to Nkpa, our neighboring community to Ovim, and then cross from Nkpa to Ovim. On one of their trips, I decided to join them. At the time, there was some exchange rate between the Biafran pound and the Nigerian pound. At that stage of the war, it was about £B32 to £N1. At the end of the war, for a few weeks, the rate was £B44 to £N1.

When I proposed that I join Kanu and Peter on the trip, they said nothing. They did not want me to participate as it was quite dangerous. They tried to trick me so I would not join the trip. They came up with a story and diverted my attention and I lost contact with them for a moment. They fooled me, but I thought that I was simply missing something. I did lose track of their movement, so I quickly cut through the forest behind the quarters assigned to my dad and emerged on the main road leading to Okigwe, where I joined with them again. They did not object, and we continued the trip, arriving at Nkpa together. Nkpa was the community adjoining Ovim from the north. At Nkpa, they bought food and fed me, and waited until it was dark. The food consisted of garri (fufu), with no meat in the soup. The meatless soup was the least of my concerns. During the Biafra war, meat was conspicuous in the soup more by its absence than by its presence.

My guides (Peter and Kanu) told me that we would sleep over and undertake the trip to Ovim, across the battle lines the following day.

The following morning, Peter and Kanu told me a story that I did not think was credible. I did not object and the trip across enemy lines was aborted. It was clear to me that they did not want me to cross the lines with them on a risky journey, so we headed back to the camp. Shortly after we returned to the camp, at the end of the next day, I must have been sent on some other errand by the superior officers or I fell asleep.

It did not take much for Peter and Kanu to return to their plan. One or two days later they returned to Nkpa and they went on the operation without me. On their return about a week or a few days later, Kanu reported on an aborted guerilla operation behind the lines. They had tried to fire some Biafran-made rockets from makeshift or improvised launchers at the Annunciation Secondary School headquarters of the Nigerian Army. The rockets misfired and the failed operation gave rise to several arrests and execution of young men suspected of masterminding the failed attack.

Over time, the trips behind enemy lines began to get quite dangerous. The routes for crossing the lines were varied, based on information about the location and sentry points of the Nigerian military or even the Biafran military. When the Nigerian military discovered a route, they would place mines or booby traps to kill violators and discourage them. At Ovim, several young men were adept at helping people cross the lines. For example, people like Mazi Obiesie Azunna, the son of a pioneer teacher and educator, were able to work with a group of operators to assist some units of stranded Biafran soldiers at Afikpo in crossing over into Biafra. Another person who assisted in the crossings was a man called Onuôhâ, from Obichie. Mr. Onuôhâ had been a teacher at Ibadan, and some of the Nigerian Army soldiers at Ovim trusted him and took him into confidence. They went so far as to permit him to visit his farmland behind their battle lines and formations. The leaders of the BOFF got wind of Onuôhâ's relationship with the Nigerian Army and recruited him to provide them information about the locations and formations of the Nigerian units. At some point, the Nigerian Army leaders suspected Mr. Onuôhâ and arrested him. They searched Mr. Onuôhâ and allegedly found some incriminating information and executed him. On another occasion, the Nigerian Army

---

[182] *There is an extensive literature on these crossings called the "Attack Trade" of "Ahia Attack" or Affia Attack. For documentations, see Victor Ukaogo, Ahia Attaakie' and 'Yakambaya' : Interrogating the Moral Dilemma and the Role of Women in the War Economy of Biafra, 1967-1970, JOURNAL OF HISTORY AND INTERNATIONAL AFFAIRS, Vol 5 January 2012. See also Christie Achebe, Isbo Women in the Nigerian-Biafran War 1967-1970: An Interplay of Control, Journal of Black Studies, MAY 2010, Vol. 40, No. 5 (MAY 2010), pp. 785-811 and Egodi Uchendu, Women and Conflict in the Nigerian Civil War, Trenton, New Jersey, Africa World Press, 2007, and Gloria Ifeoma Chuku , From Petty Traders to International Merchants: A Historical Account of Three IGBO Women of Nigeria in Trade and Commerce, 1886 to 1970, African Economic History , 1999, No. 27 (1999), pp. 1-22*

discovered that some stranded Biafran soldiers from Afikpo had stopped over at Ovim. The Nigerian Army decided to arrest Mr. Okoronkwo of Obayi Ovim along with several other elders, torturing them so severely that the elders admonished that young men should no longer assist anyone to cross the battle lines. In addition, the routes for crossing were disclosed to the Nigerian Army. The Nigerian Army made a policy then that any young man of Ovim they saw inside the town would be shot. Two young men, Ndubuisi of Amuuzu and Onwuka were shot and killed because they may have strayed into town when this policy was in force.

When the Nigerian Army blocked all the crossing routes, the young men who acted as BOFF spies received information from Ovim women who were consorts or otherwise had close and intimate relationships with the Nigerian soldiers. Notwithstanding the alternative information sources, the BOFF was handicapped concerning extracting information for their operations. There was a heightened fear of betrayal, and the elders became fearful for their lives and well-being after their torture. Despite the dangers, Mazi Obîesîe promised Col. Ohanehi and Capt. Okafor of the BOFF that he would find an alternative route for crossing and transmitting information to the BOFF. Mazi Obiesie Azunna was warned not to try it. Nevertheless, Obiesie devised a method of circumventing the Nigerian Army. Specifically, Mazi Obiesie got together with men involved in hunting and picked two "boys" and decided to develop a new track through Obayi Mmiri (a rivulet or stream) near Ævum farmlands. These rivulets and streams are ubiquitous around Ovim. Obîesîe and the boys explored a track through Obayi Mmiri, wading through waters to emerge at Ngêle Oyirî near Chief Orjî's fishpond. Although the Nigerian units kept track of the land routes, they did not think of potential water routes.

When Obiesie succeeded in finding an alternative route and arrived at Ugwu Mmam Eso (Spirit Millipede Hill), there was an uproar that Obîesîe had violated the admonition to desist in assisting those that wanted to cross from Biafra into Nigeria and back. The elders decided to recruited other young men to track Mazi Obîesîe and to trap him. However, Mazi Âcho Ukwu, whose name I mentioned earlier, was an informant for Mazi Obîesîe. Mazi Obîesîe worked with Âcho to go and mingle with the vigilantes and identify loopholes in their movements and operational methods to continue with the journeys. Mr. Âcho mingled with the sentries and vigilantes until they fell asleep or dispersed, believing that Mazi Obîesîe would no longer be crossing, but the latter then went through the water routes again and emerged once more in Biafra.[183] There was jubilation. It is even possible that this was the same route that I crossed through.

However, other people from Ovim began to use the water routes and the Nigerian Army got wind of it and planted booby traps inside the waters to alert their sentries. A certain Ekêûgwû of Ohonja may have attempted that route because he was killed around Ngêle Oyirî. After the death of Ekêûgwû, Kanu'Edede decided to end the trips, which was around early November 1969. Peter continued the trips, however, and was captured shortly by Nigerian soldiers around Ngêle Oyirî. I asked Kanu about it and he replied that Peter had been advised, but Peter found people whom he thought were "wiser and have more money than me."

The day that Peter was killed, he was crossing with several other young people. The story goes that the Nigerian Army personnel planted noisy booby lines so that anyone attempting to cross would trip them. Peter and his group tripped on the lines and alerted Nigerian Army sentries. The soldiers opened fire and shot the intruders to pieces. The army personnel then pressured local town criers to sound a gong and advise the relatives of the dead to come to retrieve the dead bodies. However, there was a whisper that went around, warning that no one should go because it appeared that the Nigerian Army intended to use that as a means of identifying individuals or families that they considered conspirators to then execute. Instead, the elders inspected the dead bodies and advised the Nigerian Army that the infiltrators were not from Ovim.[184]

---

[183] *The narrative about the crossing routes is based on am interview with Mazi Obiesie Azunna of Agbo Obayi Ovim.*
[184] *This story about how Peter died is based on interview with my sister Uloaku (Ulobank) Iroegbu (Nee Egbe).*

More on Life at the BOFF Camp

As I already mentioned, life at the BOFF camp was relatively routine. I had no clue or control over the direction of the war, but I did have some strange and naïve confidence that someday soon the war would end, and I would return to school.

Yes, there was David who did not like me, but I also had a good friendly companion called Charles Agu. Agu was in high school before the war. We did camp duties together, but later he became the aide-de-camp of one of the officers. He told me that he had been in some technical school in the Midwest of Nigeria before the war in Class 4. Charles was the only one, among the recruits, with an education level and age close to me that I could interact with on a higher level. We played my monopoly board game together and we talked about school. I guess he was impressed by the bombastic sound.

of densities. He was fond of this English man who taught them physics—this teacher was competent, effective, and impressive. Charles told me about a day in class when the teacher introduced the topics of flux and flux densities. He also claimed he had a sister who was a good businesswoman. As he put it, his sister had been a glamorous woman and met people like Tass Benson, a well-connected businessman, and politician who set his sister up in business. He also told me about his exploits with girls when he was in school. On two or three occasions, some girls came to visit him at the camp, and he told me that one of the girls had been his girlfriend in the past and that it would take many years for my prick to enjoy what his prick had already enjoyed.

Without gainsaying, Charles was savvy in many ways, aside from the fact that he was privileged enough to have access to a high school education before the war. He also had a lot of common sense at a level that I did not have. One day, he discovered that I could speak a little French from high school; yes, I did speak some fluent, conversational French, and indeed, in my free time, while I was running the drug store, I completed all the assignments in my textbook that would have taken another two years of schooling to do. In the process, I increased my vocabulary and grammar. Charles opined that if he was in my position and with covering fire from my dad, he would have gone a long way to achieving more privileges either in the broadcasting service of Biafra or in the foreign service or food relief centers. All he would do was show off his *prowess in the language.* Charles and I did a few other things together in the camp. He often lamented over the good life he lived before the war. He should have left Biafra with his big sister who he said treated him well. One day, Charles's father visited him at the camp from a nearby village.

Another person with whom I interacted very often was I. K. Nwazor. This guy was not a high school student before the war—he was just another kid in the camp that ran errands. Besides exchanging jokes with him, I called him, I. K. Small Road. I had only one remarkable experience with him. One day in early November 1969, we were sent to run an errand together, the details of which I no longer remember. It was along Opkara Road, leading to Okigwe. We were given each a tip of £B1. I. K. did something that I considered awful, at that age, with his money. I spent ten shillings (50 percent) of my money on food with a small piece of meat, probably—something that I did not have regular access to. I preserved the other half of my money for another treat on some other day. But I. K. told me, with a straight face, that he was going to spend half of his money to get sexual release. I asked him how, so he told me to follow him. We walked south, sticking close to our camp, and then west along a narrow road leading into what had to have been a village or some barrio-like business settlement when the high school and elementary schools were active before the war. This narrow road led toward the 70A Battalion headquarters. Along the road lay a tenement with narrow verandas and what appeared to me to be single rooms. In the steps of the houses, there sat some half-naked young girls, legs wide open and fully exposed from a distance. One could see their ware advertised. As we approached the building, I. K. stepped into the corridor and one of the girls stood and turned and followed him swiftly. I could only guess that he had patronized these locations in the past, hence he knew where to go and how to signal his intent. At that point, I stopped and waited for I. K. to emerge from his foray.

Approximately ten minutes later, I. K. emerged and told me that he had a good time. He even described the anticipation of ejaculation to me. "Really?!! It felt that good?" I thought to myself that he had just spent half of his money on what? He reminded me of my attitude toward what I thought at that time were wayward men—fathers, guardians, and young men. My attitude, when I was young, was extremely conservative. I had heard stories of decadence, but I never thought that I would see a boy around my age—maybe a little older—actually pay for sex. What a bad boy! After my errand with I. K., we returned to camp and life went on as usual for the next three weeks. I continued with the errands, including the chores at the S&T and moving ordinance across the Imo River, until hell broke loose at the end of November 1969.

Chapter X

THE BEGINNING OF THE END

November 1969 to December 1969

From the fall of Umuahia and the Biafran recapture of Owerre (April/May 1969) to the hopeful push toward Port Harcourt, there was an apparent stalemate in the war. All was quiet on the Umuahia front. There were occasional skirmishes and morale-boosting speeches. Though military action was at a low ebb, there were diplomatic initiatives in April 1969 in Monrovia, Liberia.[185] Other initiatives occurred in August and December 1969. The biggest concern among the youth during this lull in major battles was the fear of conscription into the Biafran army. You would not usually see young men along the roads or anywhere. But about mid-August 1969, Dr. Nnamdi Azikiwe (known popularly as "Zik"), the first president of Nigeria and one who had been instrumental in obtaining recognition for Biafra, defected to the Nigerian side.

The news of Azikiwe's defection hit me and a lot of people in the camp like a ton of bricks. It sent shock waves to our consciences—It was as if Zik had joined the callous international community that lacked moral values and human conscience. After all, Dr. Azikiwe was instrumental in traveling around the world to gain support and seek recognition for Biafra—and he had been quite successful at it. For me, Zik's defection, though a shock, did not diminish my support for the cause of Biafra. However, I felt strongly that Zik's defection would not augur well for Biafra. Zik had an international influence and the aura of a god in my mind and the minds of many others. His defection was like Zeus throwing his weight into one side of a battle during the Trojan War. I cannot say with confidence that Zik's defection caused us to lose the war because the war was not going well in the first place. Also, I did not witness any diminution of international support for Biafra among her sympathizers. However, Zik's defection certainly hastened the course of events and must have influenced the morale of the troops.

In hindsight, Zik decided like a wise man. While he was in Biafra, the Biafran leadership treated him shabbily and made him look like an errand boy. Dr. Azikiwe was a father and maybe even a grandfather at that time. Azikiwe had witnessed the suffering, in Biafra, of the children the young people, and poor mothers in agony. The level of suffering was at a breaking point. If the war had lasted a few months longer, there easily could have been a plague of disease arising from mass deaths in refugee camps that would have overwhelmed any level of human effort. Besides, as was discussed earlier, Azikiwe had argued against secession and anticipated the war. For Zik to join the war effort, he must have agonized over it and joined reluctantly. Zik was a seasoned, experienced, and smart politician. He was fully aware of the causes of the war and the trend of events that precipitated the secession. On the other hand, Zik did not have to be educated on national and international political dynamics because he understood the internal dynamics of Eastern Nigeria and the relationships between Biafran ethnic constituencies. He could easily foresee the possible trajectories of the war should secession happen. After working with Biafra and Ojukwu for so long and witnessing the

---

[185] *Stremlau, Pp. 318 - 21*

extent and depth of the people's suffering, Zik must have felt that the war needed to come to an end. He also sensed correctly that he could influence the course of events.

Some Details on Zik's Defection

Dr. Nnamdi Azikiwe (Zik), the first president of Nigeria, was instrumental in the survival of Biafra. First, by remaining in Eastern Nigeria during the entirety of the crisis in 1966 up until Eastern Nigeria's final declaration of secession to become Biafra, the world may have had the impression that there was a just cause for Biafra. For a man of Zik's caliber, his presence alone was of significance. It is not clear that Dr. Azikiwe remained in Eastern Nigerian by choice. However, it is plausible that he agonized over the development of events and, like Ralph Uwechue,[186] was not enthusiastic about the secession. However, in consideration of the events of 1966 and the federal government's reluctance or even refusal to guarantee the safety of Biafrans, and the lack of assistance for the victims of the events of October to December 1966, Zik remained with Biafra and provided support. However, as events developed and the mass starvation and brutal battlefield losses took their toll on Biafrans, Azikiwe assessed the situation and still sought to bring the best of his political skills and wisdom to bear on the situation. In as much as he saw that the military and the diplomatic situation did not favor Biafra, Zik figured a way that he could still salvage the situation in favor of Biafra and Eastern Nigerians and bring about honorable peace and end the trauma on both sides. Zik's intentions were not designed to help Biafra to secede, as this was not militarily possible.

Meanwhile, one needs to remember that Zik had advised against secession in May 1967 during a meeting of the Consultative Assembly in Eastern Nigeria.

Dr. Azikiwe was able to influence African heads of state to accord recognition to Biafra. Zik's maneuvers were probably intended to provide Biafra some leverage to extract concessions from Nigeria that would give guarantees to the Eastern Nigerians and Biafrans. Zik then used his influence to bring the Organization for African Unity (OAU) to mediate in the war and make the Biafra war an item in the OAU agenda during the OAU meeting and peace talks in September 1968. According to the Center for Nigerian Progress,[187] quoting Azikiwe, "So, I told Ojukwu, I said now you have an upper hand … I said, look your line of approach is to express appreciation for what the OAU was doing to maintain peace in Africa, but you were prepared to co-operate." Ojukwu was advised, and he assured Emperor Haile Selassie that he would not engage in propaganda in presenting Biafra's case. But Ojukwu violated his commitment and Emperor Haile Selassie was furious.[188] According to Zik, "He [Ojukwu] went back on everything we discussed. He attacked the United Kingdom, the United States, the Soviet Union … and said that … the sovereignty of Biafra' was not negotiable."[189] Zik was still hoping to persuade Ojukwu to compromise, and Ojukwu tried to persuade Zik to bring the matter of Biafra to the United Nations. But Zik, being more experienced about the United Nations, advised Ojukwu wisely that the United Nations would frown at the argument that Biafran sovereignty would be non-negotiable.

After the Algiers, Algeria, conference of the OAU, Zik and a high-powered delegation held a meeting with the French government in Paris, France. At the meeting, it was obvious that the French government was not prepared to increase their support for Biafra, and Ojukwu insisted that the matter of the conflict with Nigeria would be settled on the battlefield. Following this meeting with the French government, the Biafran high-powered delegation held a meeting. At the meeting, attended by Michael Okpra (former premier of Eastern Nigeria), Dr. Kenneth Dike (former vice-chancellor of the University of Ibadan), Dr. Azikiwe (former president), Ralph Uwechue (Biafran envoy in France), and Francis Nwokedi (formerly adviser to Aguiyi Ironsi, the first military head

---

[186] Ralph Uwechue, Reflections on the Nigerian Civil War, Op. Cit., Pp. xxii – xxiii

[187] Center for Nigerian Progress – July 2020, Zik's version of what transpired between him and Ojukwu during the Biafra war https://lawakhigbe.com/2020/07/11/ziks-version-of-what-transpired-between-him-and-ojukwu-during-the-biafra-war/

[188] *John de St. Jorre, The Brother's War: Biafra and Nigeria, Op. Cit., Pp. 228 * 29*

[189] *Center for Nigerian Progress, July 2020*

of state from January to July 1966). All members of the delegation agreed that it was time to come to terms with Nigeria. However, Francis Nwokedi, the man who misled Ironsi, objected to the resolution of the group. Nevertheless, the group drafted a memorandum, making recommendations to Ojukwu to seek peace. Ojukwu fired back a telegraph ordering them to return immediately to Biafra and accused them of treason.[190] Following this order, Ralph Uwechue resigned[191] and Dr. Azikiwe wrote Ojukwu a letter and said:

"...Since you refuse to go to the conference table to negotiate for peace ... since you prefer that the civil war should end on the battlefield and not on the conference table; since you said that the sovereignty of Biafra is not negotiable, I am afraid I cannot continue as a peace envoy because you have destroyed all the vestiges of any optimism for peace. Therefore, I am relieving myself of my services as a peace envoy. I cannot continue as a peace envoy. I cannot continue as a peace envoy because you have let me down. You left me under the impression that if I succeeded in getting the recognition you will go to the conference table. You got four recognitions; you did not go to the conference table. I am therefore going to London on exile..."[192]

Dr. Azikiwe went to London in September 1968 in voluntary exile from Biafra. In February 1969, Dr. Azikiwe proposed a fourteen-point plan to end the war. Zik's plan was flatly rejected by both the Nigerian and the Biafran sides of the conflict. According to sources, Zik made an unscheduled stop in Lagos in mid-August 1969 and met with Yakubu Gowon.[193] Gowon assured Zik of his safety should he decide to return. After the short visit, Azikiwe held a conference in Londotragglingn where he renounced Ojukwu and expressed his belief in one Nigeria. In effect, Dr. Azikwe defected.

While I sensed that Azikiwe's defection could create international diplomatic problems for us and could dent the morale of our troops, I continued to hope for a miracle. For if such a miracle were to occur, short of a sthunder of damnation from God, it would have taken from August 1969 through at least July of 1970 for Biafra to regain all the lost territory to bring diplomatic and military pressure on Nigeria to negotiate to leave Biafra alone. Beating Nigeria back would have involved numerous bloody battles and ingenious maneuvers on the part of Biafran military commanders. For example, even if Biafra recaptured Port Harcourt fully, it would also require the recapture of Umuahia, Aba, Calabar, and Ikot Ekpene. Furthermore, the Nigerian forces would have to be driven back to Enugu and close to Abakiliki, with an open corridor into the Cameroons, and held for a good six months, at which point Biafra could import arms and ammunition that would enable Biafra to establish more military credibility. Such successes might have caused the international diplomatic community to put pressure on Nigeria to negotiate for a settlement. Realistically, even with that, the war would not have come to an end until maybe 1971.

This kind of heroic daydreaming reminds me of my initial analysis of the Biafran invasion of the Midwest in August 1967, which I now think was wrong. When Biafra invaded the Midwest region of Nigeria in August 1967, I was euphoric along with much of Biafra. At that time, I was not aware of Biafra's limited military capability to hold such a vast territory with minimal armament, personnel, and even political goodwill.

At that time, I thought that the drive toward Lagos was an end game for Nigeria. After Nigerian forces recaptured the Midwest, I opined that the best approach would have been to get into Idah from Agenebode and swing back toward Nsukka and put pressure on Nigerian forces to withdraw from Biafran territory, or at least slow the Nigeria forces' advance toward Enugu.

With the Nigerian recapture of the Midwest, any hope of alternative outcomes was lost or shaken considerably. Thinking back to it, though, even if Biafra had captured Lagos and Ibadan as Biafran propaganda would have had us believe, there was no telling whether the Yoruba people would have risen against Nigeria. The Yorubas may have resented whomever Biafra would have put in charge of their affairs. Many people in Nigeria and outside Nigeria argued that the Biafran invasion of the

---

190 John de St. Jorre, Op. Cit, Pp. 229 – 30
191 Ralph Uwechue, Reflections on the Nigerian Civil War, Op. Cit., Pp. xxiii – xxv,
192 *Ibid*
193 John de St. Jorre, Op. Cit, Pp. 363 – 64.

Midwest was proof that Ojukwu's ambition was to rule Nigeria and not to defend Biafra. This was a distortion of truth and disinformation propaganda. Understandably, such distortionary propaganda is a normal instrument of warfare. For Ojukwu, the invasion of the Midwest was a strategic, though poorly thought out, plan to truncate the war.

That said, the miracle that I was hoping for in late 1969, could have occurred in the Midwest in 1967. Maj. Gen. Alexander Madiebo, commander of the Biafran Army, already explained it in his book[194]. Our people were fighting a war, not knowing that the elephants that were leading it had individual agendas so strong that they could not find common ground, or they each calculated that only one of them would get all the spoils. Therefore, they could not even coordinate among themselves or order their priorities rationally enough to provide the people (the grass) armaments to use for the fight.

The final move of the Nigerian forces began about the second week of November 1969. Shortly before this, Ojukwu made one of his morale-boosting speeches. My dad happened to be around camp then, probably for the wedding of one of the officers (the son of the man from Ovim who was one of the pioneer teachers in Ovim). The wedding was witnessed by a small crowd, and the limousine that chauffeured the bride and groom was a Volkswagen car rented from one of the local businessmen in town (a lecherous braggart who visited the camp frequently).

In any event, after Ojukwu's speech, Mr. Ogbagu, the second in command, exclaimed that Ojukwu's speech was a morale booster. He could afford to say that because he and the other officers enjoyed privileges and were never engaged in any military action against the Nigerians. He and the other young officers in the camp simply milled around and engaged in sexual gratification with the young girls in the camp. I do not believe that any of them had a modicum of military skills. At best, they were administrators.

In response, I quickly retorted that these speeches were not helpful and that it was time to end the war. The officers around me were not excited by my comment, so my dad quickly poured cold water on my comment. That probably saved me from untold reprimand or punishment. But I could hold it no longer—I did not see the point in fighting a war without weapons—and we were losing territory. It was not long before that speech that Ojukwu announced promotions of officers. Some of the promotions occurred earlier in the war. Ojukwu was referred to as general, Madiebo was major general, and Effiong was a major general. I had thought that Effiong was a lieutenant general! Upon announcing the promotions. I was somewhat impressed that Ojukwu had for a long time, despite the leadership that he provided and the services that he provided to his people, retained the title of lieutenant colonel all along. I recollect that Effiong had been brigadier for a while and commanders like Onwuatuegwu were already brigadiers. On the other hand, I thought that the promotions were preemptive in anticipation of losing the war. The elephants were trying to protect their positions, win or lose. Therefore, late in the game, they were dishing out high-level promotions. I had become cynical; if the war ended against us, these people would negotiate a surrender that keeps them in their high-level ranks. If the war ended in our favor, that would be enough reason to justify their ranks.

Paradoxically, I considered the promotions ominous and hopeful at the same time. Some hope of peaceful negotiations and a bubble bursting forfeiture of the much-hoped-for independence for Biafra. In response to my opinion, my friend Charles retorted that the promotions were meaningless. "After all, if you are in control of a pot of rice… and you put a large portion of rice in your plate … it did not imply that you deserved that much rice…It only signifies that you are the one holding the store and in charge of its distribution." Overlooking my cynical attitude, the top ranks of the Biafran Army could justifiably argue that they had been in the trenches and exchanged fire with the other side. In any event, a few days after the morale-boosting speech, we began to hear gunfire more frequently and more loudly. We were informed that the Nigerian Army was planning a major offensive. It used to be that we would hear shell fire and operational gunfire for one hour or at most a few hours and that would be it for several days or even weeks. I visited the firing line (company headquarters) a few times to deliver the ordinance that we brought across the Imo River. For me, that was about it for direct combat duty. Starting November 15, 1969, the shell fire was daily and lasted

---

[194] *Alexander Madiebo, The Nigerian Revolution and the Biafran War, Pp. 146 – 61.*

for several hours (six to twelve hours) each day. The gun battles lasted much longer. It appeared that it was the order of the day. Our new army officer, Major Okafor, was out in the front daily. He gave situation reports daily. I recollect that one of those reports happened in my dad's living quarters. I listened intently and was impressed by his ebullience. The other two officers were nowhere to be found. My dad was not present, neither was my sister. Why the situation report was held in my dad's living quarters, I do not know. The commanding officer, the second in command, and the admin officer were present in at least two reports that I witnessed. In any event, the fighting became more intense from late November through December 23, 1969. By December 20, 1969, it became clear to our officers that we had to move. About December 24, 1969, we began to evacuate when the shell fire became so loud that we felt that it was falling inside our premises and was coming from two directions: the Umuahia (Ohuhu) sector and from Okigwe to the northwest. We saw soldiers from Nkpa in the Isu-Ikwuator (Isukwuato) sector to the northeast straggling towards our locations by December 26, 1969. On or about December 28, 1969, our chief cook, Ogbo'ogbo, died. We began to move ordinance, equipment, office facilities such as tables, and household facilities such as beds across the Imo River, about one and a half miles to the west. On one of our last two rounds of evacuation, I was informed that Ogbo'ogbo was buried. I did not witness his burial. On my last round, on December 30, 1969, I was slinging a Biafran-made She-Beretta rifle, but I was not able to take anything from the camp. I recollect that I was empty-handed, except for the gun. The shell fire was so close that I believed that the Nigerian Army was inside the camp. I decided not to proceed. As I was leaving the camp, just as I emerged from the bushes surrounding our camp, guess whom I ran into? Captain Nwoko, the commanding officer of the 82nd Battalion that captured and tortured me and my escorts in May 1969. Somehow, that late in December (30th), there was a little drizzle of rain the previous night or early in the wee hours of the morning. The unpaved motorable road was muddy, which must have slowed the Nigerian advance along the Okpara road toward Okigwe. Captain Nwoko was pushing his heavy motorcycle through the muddy road. His unit had to have been evacuating from their location east of us but more than ten miles away from us and southeast of the Okigwe township formation and perimeter of the Nigerian Army. Captain Nwoko was slinging a Madison rifle (AK-47 look-alike) over his shoulder. The road that abutted our camp was less than three hundred yards from where we met each other, and shellfire was audible.

I was in the company of two or three other BOFF soldiers when Capt. Nwoko appealed to me to help him push his motorcycle but I bluntly responded to Capt. Nwoko that I would not assist him. I moved on past him, probably hugging the forest. I hurried down the road and took the next boat across the river into our next encampment. How the unit would ferry all those facilities across the river, I do not know. However, I did not witness any movement nor did I see any of the facilities in the new camp. Conceivably, none of the heavy facilities were moved. I recollect ordinance and maybe beds and bicycles. We were holed up right across the river in the valley, about 1.5 miles from where we moved or maybe two miles. Batchers[195] had been constructed. These batchers may have been constructed earlier by another unit in anticipation. I did not witness any of that construction. There were a few special batchers for the officers.

Once we settled across the Imo River, we waited and hoped that the Nigerian advance would be halted. We endured shell fire throughout the day. We were not equipped to return fire. The frontline units did all the fighting. Shellfire would last about thirty minutes and stop only to begin again maybe about six hours later for another fifteen or thirty minutes. Usually, a few rounds of shells were thrown around us. Strangely, most of the shells fell short of the Imo River, but close enough to us. When the shelling from the west of the river became intense, we crouched at the base of heavy trees that bordered the river. We endured this shell fire for about four days.

On the night of January 4, 1970, two shells fell across the river, hit our camp, and set the batcher of our army officers on fire. I am not aware that anyone was killed. At that point, we were ordered to evacuate immediately. We began to move that same night toward Ikperejere. All I had was my tennis shoes on me, a pair of sandals, and a pair of bathroom slippers that were half torn at the heels. I had one or two pairs of shorts and maybe a shirt and another T-shirt and of course, medical supplies

---

[195] Grass huts with grass walls and roofs.

that I had preserved. I was assigned to carry, on my head, a full or half box (two hundred units) of .9 mm bullets. We walked for about five miles to Ikperejere. We camped at a schoolyard—most likely a primary school, as I do not recollect any dormitories. Strangely enough, we had food supplies, for I do not recollect any hunger. We had our medical staff, for I recollect that while I was fleeing from our camp at Amaôgwûgwû, I stepped on barbed wire and suffered a severe slash under my foot that I carried for the next eight days, until the day after the war. I visited the male nurse who gave me a shot of penicillin and provided me with a small bottle of hydrogen peroxide, some iodine, gauze, and "plaster." I did not see my sister or her friend at this camp, though I was confident that she was okay. We did nothing except wait for instructions, which we expected at some point would include engagement with the Nigerian Army to stop their progress. I did very little except mill around the camp. I can only remember one frivolous incident. A young girl was doing her rounds with the boys, apparently openly. I. K. Small Road, my friend who patronized the prostitute, was making passes at her. I joined the pass-making for a minute until she called me a small boy and I moved on.

After three days at Ikperejere, the shells began to fall very heavily around us and we received information that the Nigerian Army was close by. We were ordered to move again immediately. This time, we went to Ônûchâ Ubômâ. I cannot recollect the details of the movement, but when we got to Ônûchâ Ubômâ, once more, we were camped in what appeared to be an abandoned schoolyard. The place we camped was much smaller than where we moved from. How I slept, I cannot tell. In any event, Charles and I were sent back to Ikperejere to retrieve something for an officer. I do not recollect what may be a bed or a bicycle. A bed would have required two persons to lift it and bring it back to the camp. If it was a bicycle, then I was assigned to bring something else back. Either way, we returned empty-handed, either because we could not find what we were sent to retrieve or because we had heard severe gunfire and decided that it was too risky. Most importantly, I remember that we began to walk toward our new camp at Ônûchâ Ubômâ. We had to cross a major motorable road, though not paved. Along the way, two remarkable things happened. My feet became so heavy that I could not wear my tennis shoes. I changed into my sandals, but they also became too heavy. I then put on my bathroom slippers, but they also became too heavy. I decided then to walk barefoot for the rest of the way. The second incident was encountering a woman who was selling bananas. I was very hungry, as we probably had not had any food for a whole day. We had no real cooking facilities at the new camp, or if we did, I was not aware of them. I had in my possession £B1, and I asked the woman how much she was asking for the bananas. She asked for £B5. I explained that I had only £B1 and snatched the ten bananas and gave her only £B1. This action has weighed on my conscience for years because I should have at least tried to price the bananas down and then prorated the bananas for the money that I had. I have since prayed that God should forgive me for my behavior. In less than one hundred yards, I had eaten all but one of the ten bananas. I offered it to Charles, but he quietly declined. I felt bad because I realized that I should have offered to share the bananas equally when I bought them. Many years later, as the incident gnawed on my conscience, I thought that Charles may have rejected my offer because of how I treated the woman who sold the bananas. I can only beg God for forgiveness.

January 10, 1970: Walking back from Ikpêrê Jere with Charles Agu

The next morning, January 11, 1970, we held up the staff and raided an international relief center. I can't recollect how we found out about it, but there had been some chaos and disorder that permitted us to enter the center unlawfully. I hauled away quite a bit of foodstuff—rice, beans, cans of corned beef, stockfish, and maybe even yams. When I returned to the camp where we were all crowded together, one way or another, the officers found out about the foodstuff that we carted away. We were summoned to surrender the foodstuff. All the food that I brought in was taken away, save for one ten-pound bag of rice, a few one-pound bags of black-eyed peas (commonly called beans in Nigeria), one can of corned beef, and probably a small yam and some of my salt and one small stockfish. I walked around the camp sulking and carrying a long face. One way or another, my big sister, whom I had not seen for a while during these recent movements found out that I was grumbling and asked me why. I explained to her that most of the foodstuff that I had carted away from the relief center was taken away by the officers, and she asked me if that was the reason I was grumbling and carrying a long face—I confirmed. It was clear to me that she did not approve of my disposition. I left it there and found a way to sleep.

The next morning (January 12, 1970), we had no instructions as to what to do. There was heavy uncertainty and a lack of real leadership. The officers were monitoring the situation as they had all the information. In my mind, I was tired of the whole affair. Nevertheless, I was equally concerned about keeping myself out of harm's way. Suddenly, sometime toward late morning, there was massive and rapid shell fire from all directions. We did not have to be told that it was going to hit our camp very soon. In any event, there was sufficient order from our officers to instruct us to head toward Mbâ'âno. I collected my belongings and left in the same direction as Charles. Charles brought along the bicycle—I placed my belongings on the front frame of the bicycle, and he placed his belongings on the back rack of the cycle. We pushed the cycle along the road to, only God knew, and I guessed to Mbâ'âno. In less than fifteen minutes, we heard a rumbling like a wild animal was ruffling the leaves and branches in the forest adjacent to the sandy road. Suddenly, out from the forest came Charles's little brother. The child was only about ten or twelve years old. We were not expecting him. I knew him, though, because he had visited us once or twice at the BOFF camp, with his father. He must have lost touch with the father and was happy to see us in that chaos. Charles was equally happy. At that point, I had to take my belongings from the bicycle and carry them on my head. Agu's little brother sat on the frame of the bicycle and Charles pushed along his brother and his belongings on the back rack of the cycle.

Where was my sister and the other members of our camp—more than fifty of us? We had no idea. It was chaos. The only member of our contingent that I could see was Charles. In effect, our unit was in total disarray. Hopefully, we would meet up with some or all of them at Mba'ano. In hindsight, it was a hopeless situation. After about two hours of walking, and no later than 12:30 p.m., we came upon a large contingent of Biafran soldiers from around Isu-Ikwu-Ato (three Kindred Barbarians or Invaders)—about 100 to 150 of them. Among them, I recognized two of my immediate cousins. Nwachukwu Egbe (the son of Egbe Egesi who died in 1958)[196]. I saw also Okorie, the son of my father's younger sister (Meme or May-May). Both of them had lived with us in the same compound of Ndi Egbe. I also saw Oshiama (Ndukwo) from Ama Ukwukwa, adjacent to our village (Umueye), and a good friend of the family. Ama Ukwukwa is part of Amaeke-Elu, just like Umueye.

At that point, I stopped and bade Charles and his brother goodbye. I explained to him that these were my relatives and I felt safer and more secure with them. Among the soldiers from my home area were one captain, two lieutenants, one second lieutenant, and several noncommissioned officers. We had leadership. Honestly, I did not have a gun in my hands, let alone bullets. The other soldiers, most of them had guns, real guns— AK-47's, SLR (M-16 rifles), and substantial bullets. It did not appear that they had any artillery guns nor was I aware of any other supporting ordinance. As we gathered there, the officers told us that at midnight they would shoot open a corridor in the Nigerian defense perimeter, we would all drop our guns and go home to Îsuikwuat̲o. Whoever still wanted to continue fighting the war, that would be their choice. We were tired of the war. We were also informed that Maj. Gen. Effiong would make a speech at 3:00 p.m. on that day. The time was not much past noon, but I fell asleep. As a matter, of attitude, I could not care for a moment what the speech was going to be about. At that point, I had made up my mind that I would work with the leadership of the group of soldiers that assembled at the village where we were. Plain and simple, we would not continue the fighting. Nevertheless, I was interested in hearing what Gen. Effiong had to say. After I woke up, I asked about the speech but was informed that the war was over. I did not listen to the speech, but the rendition given by the people present was starkly different from the available official and published speech. It sounded as if Effiong had thanked the Armed Forces of Biafra, explained why we justifiably went to war, and then said, "We are now loyal Nigerian citizens." The actual official text of Gen. Effiong's speech is published below:

---

[196] *Egbe Egesi was the son of Egesi Egbe the half-brother of my great grandfather Okezie Egbe. My grandfather was Egbe Okezie who was in turn the son of Okezie Egbe, hence he was called Egbe Okezie. Hence Egbe Egesi was the nephew of my grandfather.*

Broadcast by (Biafran) Major-General Phillip Effiong on Monday, January 12, 1970

Fellow Countrymen, as you know, I was asked to be the officer administering the government of this Republic on the 10th of January 1970. Since then, I know that some of you have been waiting to hear a statement from me. I have had extensive consultations with the leaders of the community, both military and civil, and I am now encouraged and hasten to make this statement to you by the mandate of the armed forces and the people of this country. I have assumed the leadership of the government.

Throughout history, injured people have had to resort to arms in their self-defense where peaceful negotiations fail. We are no exception. We took up arms because of the sense of insecurity generated in our people by the events of 1966. We have fought in defense of that cause. I take this opportunity to congratulate officers and men of our armed forces for their gallantry and bravery which had for them the admiration of the whole world. I thank the civil population for their steadfastness and courage in the face of overwhelming odds and starvation. I am convinced now that a stop must be put to the bloodshed which is going on as a result of war. I am also convinced that the suffering of our people must be brought to an immediate end. Our people are now disillusioned and those elements of the old government regime who have made negotiations and reconciliation impossible have voluntarily removed themselves from our midst.

I have therefore instructed an orderly disengagement of troops. I am dispatching emissaries to make contact with Nigeria's field commanders in places like Onitsha, Owerri, Awka, Enugu, and Calabar to arrange an armistice. I urge General Gowon, in the name of humanity, to order his troops to pause while an armistice is negotiated to avoid the mass suffering caused by the movement of population. We have always believed that our differences with Nigeria should be settled by peaceful negotiations. A delegation of our people is therefore ready to meet representatives of the Nigeria federal government anywhere to negotiate a peaceful settlement on the basis of OAU resolutions.

The delegation will consist of the Chief Justice, Sir Louis Mbanefo as the leader, Professor Eni Njoku, Mr. J. I. Emembolu, Chief A. E. Bassey, and Mr. E. Aguma. The delegation will have full authority to negotiate on our behalf. I have appointed a council to advise me on the government of the country. It consists of the Chief Justice, Sir Louis Mbanefo, Brigadier P. C. Amadi (Army), Brigadier C. A. Nwawo (Army), Captain W. A. Anuku (Navy), Wing Commander J. I. Ezeilo (Air Force), Inspector-General of Police, Chief P. I. Okeke, Mr. J. I Emembolu (Attorney-General), Professor Eni Njoku, Dr. I. Eke, Chief A. E. Udofia, Chief Frank Opigo and Chief J. M. Echeruo. Any question of government in exile is repudiated by our people.

In any event, the war was over. I was relieved, but not sure what to do next. I am not sure that I ate any food. There was nothing to eat, after all, and if there had been something to eat, where would I cook? The most important thing for me was to stay close to my relatives. If I ate any food that night, my relatives who made sure that I was protected, made such food available.

Walking Home and Debriefing

We all woke up the next morning on January 13, 1970, and I cannot recollect whether or not we had any food. There was probably no food, but Nwachukwu and Okorie are no longer alive to recollect anything that happened. We were informed that there were Nigerian checkpoints and all we had to do was to wave One Nigeria white flags. We began our walk home, with one or more persons leading the way with either "One Nigeria" written on a white piece of cloth or just waving a white piece of cloth and saying, "One Nigeria." We also had to ensure we were not carrying any guns or weapons. The officers and all the soldiers who had guns or weapons buried them or hid them somewhere, or they may have arranged with the local village leaders to surrender them to Nigerian soldiers as a sign of surrender. We walked down the road and about fifty yards in the distance along the way toward Âfô Umu Ûdâh, I saw a Nigerian sentry or soldiers manning a checkpoint. From that distance, all I saw was a casual check of our people's belongings. I double-checked to make sure that the soldiers were not paying attention and ripped all the notes that I had been keeping during the war, at least since I was at the BOFF camp. I was not certain what the Nigerian soldiers would do or think if they saw a fat notebook with copious writing. When we arrived at the checkpoint, I was prudent and politely allowed the Nigerian soldiers to search my luggage, which had probably one item of clothing (I was wearing a shirt and there was maybe a T-shirt and a pair of shorts in my luggage) and no shoes or just my flip flops, but certainly no sandals or tennis shoes. The soldiers barely took a casual look and simply waved us to move on. There was no incident, as far as I could see or hear, which was about fifty feet away after I crossed the checkpoint.

When I woke up that morning and began the walk home in the company of my two relatives, Nwachukwu and Okorie, I had come down with a bout of malaria, a sickness that had set in on me frequently during the last two months of 1969. I also had a gash that ran almost the whole length of my foot on the bottom of my foot. I had gashed my foot on some barbed wire as we retreated hastily from our camp at Ama'Ôgwûgwû toward the end of December, and I thought that it had healed since I was treated by the camp nurse and received a dose of penicillin injection at our camp across the Imo River. I had in my possession a bottle of hydrogen peroxide and a small bottle of iodine, some cotton lint, gauze, and a little roll of plaster (Blank Band-aid). For sure, I had no knife to cut the roll of band-aid, but a small razor blade worked out. In any event, before we got to Âfô Umu Ûdâh, the pain under my foot was becoming unbearable and slowing everyone down. At that point, I asked Okorie and Nwachukwu to help me treat the swollen wound under my foot. Puss has begun to set in again. Using the razor blade, they made a small incision in the swollen section of the gash and cut it open—a small channel—and the puss flowed out nicely. I also had a few antibiotic tablets; I believe tetracycline that the nurse gave me at the Imo River along with some pain medication that I could not recollect, though it was probably some aspirin compound. My privileges at the camp provided me access to these things. I used the cotton lint to put some hydrogen peroxide on the wound and also rubbed some iodine on it. I was confident, but at least the throbbing pain ceased altogether. I was now able to walk without feeling the pain. In all of this, I had lost track of my sister. I had no idea where she was, but I was confident that she may have kept close to Ama Orji or any of those people who were close to my dad. I was focused on getting home that night, about twenty-five miles away. The journey would take the whole day, as I anticipated. After my wound was treated, I told my relatives to keep on moving. I would be able to take care of myself. That was a foolish decision. As I mentioned in Chapter 1, it was a lonely journey home. I did not have any support. Once I dismissed my relatives, I was alone. There was no one along that road back to Ovim that I knew.

Chapter XI

ELEPHANTS FIGHT AND THE GRASS SUFFERS

Monkey De Work Baboon de Chop!

Now, it is all over. The events of the past eight years from 1962 through January 1970 were turbulent. The sudden hold on my education; suddenly living like the
peasant and having to experience going to farm to cultivate my food and having to depend on the yield to feed myself. The constant fear of being killed and the sound of gunfire and sickness and sleeping in the forest without a bed or even in a house. Now it is time to reflect and lament and ask, what was the cause of this suffering?

The background to the bloody civil war is the callous irresponsibility of our political leaders and ruling establishments. Collectively, we, the ordinary people, suffered while the members of the ruling classes, using us as their pawns, fought for their advantages and privileges. Any documentary of the proximate events that precipitated the civil war will make clear that this national tragedy was fully avoidable but for the mindless and desperate greed and callousness of the key players in the social and political superstructure. On the other hand, we cheered them on to free us from colonial bondage and selected them as our post-independence leaders. So, what happened? Did they betray us? Or should we have given them a little more time to do the right thing?

The ancient Roman historian Lucius Mesterius Plutarchus attributes to the Roman reformer, Tiberius Gracchus, a statement that aptly describes social struggles, wars, and human conflicts—not the least of which is the bloody civil war in Nigeria and the crisis that preceded it. Specifically, Tiberius Gracchus is said to have addressed the commons in a Roman forum, saying,

"...the savage beasts in Italy have their particular dens ... They have their places of repose and refuge; but the men who bear arms and expose their lives for the safety of their country, enjoy in the meantime nothing more in it but air and the light; and having no houses or settlements of their own, are constrained to wander from place to place with their wives and children ... The commanders [are] guilty of a ridiculous error, when, at the head of their armies, they exhorted the common soldiers to fight for their sepulchers and altars; when not any amongst so many Romans is possessed of either altar or monument, neither have they any houses of their own or hearths of their ancestors to defend. They fought indeed, and were slain, but it was to maintain the wealth and the luxury of other men. They were styled the rulers of the world, but in the meantime had not one foot of ground which they could call their own..." [197]

Based on this quote, the "savage beasts" describe the warmongers and the demagogues among the ruling cliques in Nigeria and Biafra and much of the ruling classes throughout the history of mankind. Members of ruling establishments start wars, but they are not the ones that end up in the trenches to be exposed to danger. The experience of Fola Oyewole, a Yoruba man that served in the

---

[197] *See Erik Hildinger, Swords Against the Senate: The Rise of the Roman Army and the Fall of the Republic, 2002, DaCapo Press, Pp. 37 – 38.*

Biafran Army, revealed this. According to Lt. Oyewole[198], when he arrived in Lagos after the civil war, people who saw so many prominent Igbos and their top civil servants arriving back in Lagos asked him "... who died...?" For those people who were on the Nigerian side of the war and reading the news about the mass starvation and death in Biafra, it came as a surprise that many Igbos who were working in Lagos were returning in droves. . Of course, the people who died were the ordinary people from the villages, the farmers, the common laborers, the market traders in the urban areas (the lumpen), the talakawas, and the illegitimate or maybe legitimate children of *almajiris*. The sons and daughters of the ordinary people. The list can go on ad nauseam. On the Biafran side, those who died of starvation were the poor malnourished children of low-income villagers who fled at the sound of Nigerian artillery and gunfire for fear that the pogroms that started in the North were going to continue as the Nigerian Army and Biafran propaganda impressed on their minds. They ended up in cramped and improvised refugee camps and became victims of malnutrition, squalor, and disease.

When the relief supplies arrived in Biafra, the well-placed received the choice portions of the food and nutrition. At the end of the war, all these well-placed people at the top still had some mobility and received salary advances that made them comfortable, and they returned to their mansions. The *talakawas* returned to their usual low lives of poverty. I would like to see any talakawas that built a mansion from their salaries as private soldiers, lance corporals, corporals, or sergeants. I would like to see how many of them purchased Mercedes Benz cars—or any cars at all. Quoting Oyewole further,

"... Most of the elite groups on each side who made the clarion call .... The rebellion must be crushed or ... we will fight to the last man ... would not have been so patriotic if they were likely to have faced the same risks as the men in the trenches ... Far more patriotic was the statement made by Colonel Adeyinka Adebayo in May 1967 when he (Adebayo) stated that when we use force to resolve our issues, at the end of the carnage and the bloodshed, we will discover that all of it was futile..."[199]

A good number of the people who died were women and children. The military casualties were refugees or returnees who saw the war as a means of avenging what had happened to them in the North or the unemployed who saw this as a means of making a living. This type of firsthand observation, on my part, informed my rumination in a rueful soliloquy, as I walked twenty-five miles back home along a lonely road the day after the war ended. I found myself suddenly on the verge of losing my education. I found myself, weekly, in a leaky dugout boat, rowing ammunition

---

198 *Fola Oyewole, The Reluctant Rebel, Pp. ii - iii*
199 *Fola Oyewole, The Reluctant Rebel, Pp. ii - iii*

and other military ordinance across a turbulent river, even though I did not know how to swim. What if the boat had sunk? I would have drowned like a rock. I also carted a box of potentially explosive ammunition on my head for miles. The box of ammunition might equally have broken my neck. If the ammunition had sparked and exploded, my head and the remainder of my body would have been pulverized. I endured shell fire for days and meandered under a tropical rainfall for thirty-six hours in a dark and treacherous swampy forest, with no food, toward the end of which I nearly collapsed, and then I was captured, tortured, and nearly killed.

After the war, some key players, such as Maj. Gen. Joe Garba (*Elite Shifts*), N. U. Akpan (*The Struggle for Session*), Maj. Gen. Alexander Madiebo (*The Nigerian Civil War and the Biafran Revolution*), Phillip Effiong (*The Caged Bird Sang No More and Nigeria and Biafra: My Story*), wrote about how the war was avoidable and concluded that the events that precipitated the war could have been managed better.

During the war, soldiers on both sides expressed frustration at the war. There were reports that Nigerian soldiers sometimes offered cigarettes to Biafran soldiers and even played soccer games with them and then returned to their trenches.[200] Nzeogwu is quoted as saying that even if the secession succeeded, he would pack his things and leave and that it would not mean anything to the ordinary Nigerians. Many on the Biafran side, including those who fought the war to maintain secession once declared, argued against secession. Some of those that opposed secession did so on the principled ground that we were better off as Nigerians in a united country. Others argued against secession because of the potential bloodshed, justified or not. Still, many more discouraged secession because secession could not be sustained militarily, even if they favored it or thought that the grievances of the Igbos and Biafrans justified secession.[201] On the Nigerian side, many, including Awolowo, also argued forcefully against the use of force to bring Biafra back because they felt that a war to force Biafra back would be an unjust war.[202] Lt. Col. David Ejoor, governor of Midwest Nigeria, equally condemned the war that he considered a war of vengeance and domination. For that reason, Col. Ejoor forbade the Nigerian Army from using the Midwest as a staging ground to attack Biafra and equally warned Ojukwu not to invade the Midwest.[203]

Nzeogwu, the icon of the coup of January 1966, is quoted to have averred that it would take less than fifteen years for Nigerians and Biafrans to just get back to business as if nothing happened—in effect as if it all were just one country. Specifically, Maj. Kaduna Nzeogwu stated,

"In the first place, secession will be ill-advised, indeed impossible. Even if the East fights a war of secession and wins, it still cannot secede. Personally, I don't like secession and if this country disintegrates, I shall pack up my things and go. In the present circumstances, confederation is the best answer as a temporary measure. In time, we shall have complete unity. Give this country a confederation and, believe me, in ten or fifteen years the young men will find it intolerable and will get together to change it. And it is obvious we shall get a confederation or something near it. Nothing will stop that." [204]

On their part, many Igbos had a desire to return to Northern Nigeria way before the secession was declared, provided that they would be safe. At the end of the war, it did not take long for Igbos to rush back to the North. Even Lt. Col. Hassan Katsina, governor of Northern Nigeria, acknowledged as much at Aburi when responding to Igbo inquiries about returning to the North. According to Col. Katsina, he advised them that it was not yet safe. Conceivably, even under the circumstances, many

---

[200] *See Mike Uriel Ogbechie, Eclipse at Noonday, Biafra, Diaries of Unwritten Stories, London, Xlibris, 2012, Pp. 248 – 50. See also Godwin Alabi, tragedy of Victory – Kindle Reader Location 3339 – 3357.*

[201] *Wole Soyinka and Azikiwe are notable examples.*

[202] *Chief Obafemi Awolowo, in a speech made to the Western Leaders of Thought in Ibadan, May 1, 1967 and published in Daily Times May 2, 1967. Also reprinted in Kirk-Greene, Crisis and Conflict in Nigeria, Volume I, Oxford University Press, 1971, Pp. 415 – 18.*

[203] *A.H.M. Kirk-Greene, Crisis and Conflict in Nigeria, Volume II, Oxford University Press, 1971, Page 5*

[204] *Interview with Major Nzeogwu, by Dennis Ejindu, April 1967. See Phillip Emeagwali (https:// emeagwali.com/biafra/nigeria-biafra-civil-war-major-chukwuma-kaduna-nzeogwu.html). See also Africa and the World, May 1967.*

Igbos found communication channels to get to the governor of Northern Nigeria to ask to return to the North. From that dialogue, it is equally telling that there were warmongers on both sides that did not want peace. After all, if by January 1967, Lt. Col. Hassan Katsina was advising Igbos that it was not yet safe to return to the North, it is safe to presume that there were warmongers among Northern Nigerians who did not want peace and who did not want Igbos to return to Nigeria. The latter, in turn, provides clear justification for the secession that followed.

Although Gowon may have been prepared to discuss settlement, Ojukwu demanded excessive amounts of money that made settlement prohibitive.[205] There is no doubt that Ojukwu's advisers may have purposely made a prohibitive demand to discourage a settlement.[206] Only God knows, if a settlement had been made, whether Ojukwu and his advisers would have quickly pocketed the money or used the money to strengthen their war chest. So, why would Gowon agree to even offer a financial settlement to a potential adversary? On the other hand, why did Gowon not order the payment of a miserly three months' pay to displaced civil servants and the settlement of property that had been scuttled by the civil servants following the meeting of military leaders at Aburi? In as much as he was probably the sincerest among the key players about seeking peace and true unity, history should hold him squarely responsible for failing to enforce the non-controversial parts of the Aburi Accord. For example, in March 1967, the federal government failed to transfer to Eastern Nigeria its allocation of national revenues. Meanwhile, the federal government was on arrears of paying the salaries of displaced civil servants as agreed during the Aburi meeting in January 1967. In response to these acts of bad faith on the part of the federal government, Ojukwu enacted the Revenue Edict. When the secession was announced, the federal government turned around and made the rescission of the Revenue Edict as a condition to avoid war, but it was the federal government that instigated the Revenue Edict to begin with.

There are other incidents in the modern history of the world worse than the Northern pogrom against Igbo people that did not lead to secession. For example, the more vicious and brutal genocidal killings of the Tutsis in Rwanda in 1994 did not lead to the breakup of the country. However, considering that the Tutsi and Hutu dichotomy in Rwanda is somewhat artificial and relates more to caste than to regional and racial locations and identities, it might have been difficult to break the country apart. Yet there are also less grievous afflictions and oppressions that gave rise to secession. When India gained independence from Britain in 1947, by mutual consent, Pakistan broke away and became a separate country. In the separation, there was Eastern Pakistan and Western Pakistan. The East Pakistanis felt oppressed and disenfranchised in many ways, including the fact that their Bengali language was not recognized as an official language for business. There

were protests in Eastern Pakistan that led to the Pakistani Army killing protesters. However, this was nothing near the senseless brutalization and mass murder of Eastern Nigerians the mobs in Northern

---

[205] *K. Whiteman, The Psychology of Secession, 29 July 1966 to 30 May 1967, in Nigerian Politics and Military Rule: The Prelude to Civil War, University of London, the Athlone Press, 1970, S. Keith Panther-Brick, Ed. Pp. 111 – 27. According to Whiteman (Pp. 123 – 24), there were discussions of financial horse trading between November 1966 and the end of March 1967, but what the East was demanding was far beyond what Lagos was willing to consider. Though, Whiteman cited no sources, I doubt if he was referring to the miserly three months' pay to displaced Federal civil servants. Whiteman specifically was referring to properties lost by Eastern Nigerians in the North. See Nowah Omoigui and Aremu, below*

[206] *See Nowah Omoigui at https://www.dawodu.com/omoigui12.htm On March 23 a Ghanaian delegation flew to Enugu for talks. Three days later Ojukwu went to Ghana to meet with General Ankrah over the question of federal debts to the eastern region among other issues. See also Johnson Olaosebikan Aremu, Ghana's Role in the Nigerian War: Mediator or Collaborator, International Journal of Humanities and Cultural Studies, Vol 1 (3), December 2014.*

Nigerian in 1966. Nevertheless, in March 1971, the Eastern Pakistanis declared independence and went to war, aided by India, and won and became Bangladesh.

There were many justifications for the Biafran secession. First, there was no compelling reason for the Nigerian Army to join in the killing of civilians. Secondly, after the Nigerian Army agreed to repatriate soldiers to their regions of origin on August 9, 1966, the killings continued sporadically. Eastern Nigerian soldiers who were locked up in a guard room in Lagos were marched out by Lt. Nuhu and executed, contrary to the terms of the agreement made on August 9, 1966. A full two months after they had removed the Igbo leader of the government (last week of September 1966), army and police personnel joined civilians to engage in a brutal, depraved, and barbaric massacre of the Igbo civilian population living in Northern Nigeria. Soldiers stood guard on the bridge in Makurdi, the link between the East and the North, to extract civilians and suspected soldiers alike to be killed.[207] This is significant for the simple reason that the Northerners had been in control of the government for a full two months. Therefore, what could be their problem? What could be their motive for this systematic and calculated massacre of Igbos? Properties were looted and unspeakable injuries and atrocities were inflicted on the civilian population. The Igbo surmised that if that was to be the lot of the Igboman henceforth, then it would be safer to depart and seek safety in their region of origin. What was going on in Nigeria during that crisis of 1966 was nothing short of genocide. As Odogwu reported, following the massacres of Igbos, Nigerian soldiers also mounted checkpoints all over Lagos to molest Igbos.[208] Wole Soyinka, the Nobel Prize laureate and a Yoruba man who also advised against secession, was not alone in condemning the lackadaisical attitude of the Gowon administration in condoning the genocide and urging Yoruba people to dissociate themselves from those awful events. Furthermore, Wole Soyinka documented that:

"...a progressive pogrom of the Igbo erupted in October 1966... a hunt for easterners of all ages who were unfortunate enough to heed the call of the new regime to return to ... the North ... Even in Lagos, the hunt for the Igbo continued unabated ... Images of death and mutilation ... and television coverage of savage humanity erased the final sense of belonging ... and catalysed their resolve to secede...but it would be a distortion of history and to trivialize the trauma that the Igbo had undergone to suggest ...that it was the allure of oil that drove them to seek a separate existence ... When a people have been subjected to a degree of inhuman violation for which there is no other word but genocide, they have the right to seek an identity apart from their aggressor."[209]

In general, the attitude of the Nigerian government did not, in any real sense, work for peace. Even before war broke out, the Nigerian government mounted a blockade to forbid the Igbos living in the Midwest Region from trading with their kindred in Eastern Nigeria.[210] If the Nigerian government was sincere and truly neutral, the blockade should not have been mounted before the war was declared. The federal government forbade the trading of food between Anioma Igbos and the Igbos of Eastern Nigeria, directing that lorries loaded with foodstuffs from Anioma bound for the East should be seized. In effect, the blockade to starve the Igbos and Eastern Nigerians into submission began even before secession was declared. Indeed, after Awolowo's visit in May 1967, one of the conditions that Ojukwu gave to avert secession was the removal of the blockade against the East. Gowon lifted the blockade like he was demonstrating a genuine desire for peace or like he was making a concession. Why should a blockade be placed in the first place? If the Igbos and other Eastern Nigerians are to be treated peacefully and if the warmongers on the federal side did not prevail, then at least there should not have been a blockade until the war was declared.

---

[207] *See Rose Maduabum, A Soldier's Spouse.*

[208] *Benard Odogwu, Op. Cit.*

[209] *Wole Soyinka, You Must Set Forth at Dawn, Pp. 100 - 102*

[210] Kenneth C. Ryeland, The Up-Country Man, A personal Account of the First One Hundred Days Inside Secessionist *Biafra, Pp. 116 – 18. See also Egodi Uchendu, Women and Conflict in the Nigerian Civil War, Pp. 139 – 42. "... The Federal Government's blockade on the Eastern region necessitated a boycott of the trading links ... The Eastern Region utilized the months before the outbreak of hostilities to stock up on supplies .... Food items were moved in incredible quantities ..."*

Much has been made about how the war was precipitated because Ojukwu was ambitious. It is all fine and good to say so by a victorious army that is in denial about the other events that led to the war, but this allegation against Ojukwu is pure propaganda. But what else is new in political conflict? As is often said, the first casualty of war is the truth. In war, all is fair; the end always justifies the means. We can look at different slices of the events that justified going to war and see that it was all complicated. It is not as simple as any one person's ambition or agenda. Nevertheless, the war had nothing to do with Ojukwu's ambition. Igbos indicated that much when Ojukwu returned from an unjustly imposed exile in 1983. Ojukwu was welcomed with jubilation that should have sent a complex message to all Nigerians. In the same vein that the Igbos rejoiced when he returned, they made it clear to Ojukwu and all Nigerians that the Igbos do not follow Ojukwu blindly. When Ojukwu contested the election under the banner of the Nigerian People's Party (NPN) that was not popular in Igboland, he lost woefully. Nevertheless, in the years that followed that election in 1983, the Igbos continued to fete Ojukwu as a hero, in a manner that communicated to him that he should stay in his lane. "We have applauded you where and when you were right, but now we the people are right." Ojukwu may have opportunistically exploited the situation of the 1966 to 1967 crises, but the war was not his doing. The Igbos and other Eastern Nigerian's who joined them were truly aggrieved and frightened.

According to Odogwu

"...During one of the discussions—Enugu, in December 1966[211]—one of the discussants asked the question ... when will Ojukwu make up his mind to declare our republic – the Republic of Biafra? ... Ojukwu should make up his mind either to lead the people and satisfy their yearnings ... or step aside for someone else who will deliver the goods...Another speaker commenting on the rumor of the possible meeting of the Supreme Military Council in Ghana thought that Ojukwu was chickening out...[212]"

Odogwu's observation was as accurate as any other observation. It reflected the general mood. This is not to say that people who knew better about the possible consequences of secession or the ability to sustain it did not have contrary views or failed to advise against secession, but Akpan summed it up well.

"...The most fervent protagonists of secession were a few individuals with personal ambitions and others who had come home from the massacres of 1966, embittered by the glaring atrocities committed against them, their kith and their kin ... [they] genuinely believed that that secession was the only way of ensuring for themselves and their children security of life and property ... They considered themselves rejected and unwanted by the rest of Nigeria.[213]"

One cannot dismiss these feelings lightly if one considers the sometimes-dismissive attitude of the Nigerian government to the experiences of the Igbos and the false promises or the not-so-credible promises of safety after the May riots in 1966. Under those circumstances, one could describe the mood of Eastern Nigerians and among the Igbos in context, as Njoku aptly quoted, viz:

"Now he'll outstare the lightning (Our people were worked into a frenzy out of anger) ..." "... To be furious Is to be frighted out of fear (Anger diminished fear among the Igbos and other sympathetic Eastern Nigerians) ..." and in that mood, the dove will peck the ostrich (Under the circumstances, false promises of safety and all that, the Igbos were frightened into a desperate defense of their home, their hearth, and their heads and their wives. For it was considered, by the Igbos, that it was better to fight and be conquered than to surrender to certain slaughter); "... and I see still a

---

[211] *Italics are mine. However, the discussion about a meeting in Aburi Ghana was initiated about late November and early December 1966. See also Akpan.*
[212] *Benard Odogwu, No Where to Hide, Pp. 252 – 54.*
[213] *N.U. Akpan, The Struggle for Secession, Pp. iv – v*

diminution in our captain's brain restores his heart. When valor preys on reason, it eats the sword it fights with…"[214]

Against this background, Akpan[215] quotes Nelson Ottah,[216] a journalist,

"…Almost everyone was crying for a showdown … big money men, housewives, motor touts, spivs and pimps … He [Ojukwu] did not do it because he was cleverer than his victims … he did it because his victims … primed with a craze for revenge, escapism, greed, and foolishness … were so ready for destruction and only needed a command … Ojukwu's greatest crime today is that he gave that command…"

Good enough. Akpan had strong reservations about Nelson Ottah's assessment. Even Akpan made clear that not everyone was motivated by greed or even the desire for revenge and, least of all for Igbos, there was no desire for destruction. If it were clear to the Igbos that the weapons were not available for war, they would have been wiser for it as a people. But, yes, Ojukwu's crime was that he gave the command to a people who were wounded but who did not have the wherewithal to defend themselves further. He had the resources to do it but failed miserably at galvanizing and deploying the resources strategically to prepare for a credible showdown. Ojukwu also withheld information from those he was leading. I would thus ask Nelson Ottah what this revenge was about. It is alleged that Nelson Ottah was the journalist who published the provocative article and picture that depicted Maj. Nzeogwu of the January 1966 coup standing triumphantly over the dead body of the murdered Sardauna of Sokoto. If such an allegation is true, he had no business making such statements. Even Ojukwu had his misgivings about secession, and most Igbos would have desired to return to Nigeria at the earliest possible time if it had been safe to do so. But as of January 1967, even the governor of Northern Nigeria stated at Aburi that it was not yet safe to return to Northern Nigeria. Even the army officers who fled from the wrath of their colleagues in other parts of Nigeria were not given any credible assurances of safety if they returned to Nigeria. How would anyone who criticized the secession feel if they had to be in hiding just because they belonged to a specific ethnic group? When it is all said and done, the Nigerian government under Gowon and the supreme military council did a poor job of controlling the Northern officers who continued in their wanton acts of mayhem, savagery, and slaughter.

Regarding Nelson Ottah and his statement, I can only surmise that he was a paid hack who, having endured the war and later escaped from Biafra and defected to Nigeria, was simply writing whatever he had to say to fill his stomach.[217] I would agree, though, with one of Ottah's statements, but only in context. Specifically, "And Emeka Ojukwu exploited the situation to suit his private ambitions." To some extent, I will agree that Ojukwu, as I said earlier, was an opportunist who was in the right place at the right time and simply sought to place himself in a position to expropriate the benefits of the struggle emanating from the people's pain and suffering. For the Igbos, there was no real desire for secession. They simply desired a redress and a genuine acknowledgment of their distress. Truth be told, many Nigerians hated the Igbos and were all too happy to witness and rejoice at what happened, hence the slaughter of Igbos in 1948 and 1953 when there was no pretext of a one-sided military coup. Somehow, many other Nigerians, even today, more than fifty years after the war, justified the mass slaughter of Igbos after the July 1966 coup. Others have dismissed or trivialized the Northern massacres as mere disturbances.[218] For example, Ukpabi Asika, the renegade who was appointed administrator of the East Central State in 1968, trivialized the mass slaughter of Igbos in Northern Nigeria as an "anomy." Nigeria should thank Ojukwu for leading the war. If a less selfish person had led the war, the outcomes would not have been the same. Truth be told, either there would be no secession and thus no war because the other side would not have broken even the most basic

---

[214] *215 Enobarbus, in Shakespeare's Anthony and Cleopatra, Act 3 Scene 13. The italic inscriptions in brackets are my modern English interpretations of Shakespearian English language.*

[215] *N. U. Akpan, Op. Cit. Pp. xv - xvi)*

[216] *Neslon Ottah, Drum Magazine (of Nigeria, June 1970).*

[217] *For details of Nelson Ottah's defection to Nigeria, See Fola Oyewole, The Reluctant Rebel*

[218] *See also Brigadier Godwin Alabi in the Tragedy of Victory.*

promises that would have assuaged the people's fears; or, if there was war, both sides would have come to their senses early enough and would have negotiated peace in good faith.

Nigeria had no moral locus standi to criticize Ojukwu for the civil war. Ojukwu was not the sole cause of the war. Those disobedient officers who continued to execute their comrades even after the agreement of August 9, 1966, and those who participated in the riots of September and October 1966 that killed and stampeded civilians to flee the North were equally responsible. The soldiers and police who manned and barricaded the bridge at Makurdi to extract and kill soldiers and civilians alike were equally responsible. Those soldiers who stormed the Kano Airport on October 5, 1966, should have been court marshalled and dismissed from the army after the war.

In Gowon's victory speech on January 15, 1970, he stated that "Despite my efforts and the cooperation of all other members of the Supreme Military Council, the former Lt. Col. Ojukwu pushed us from one crisis to another. This intransigent defiance of Federal Government authority heightened tension and led to the [regrettable] riots in September/October 1966." However, first, even Gowon knew that the riots of September/October 1966 had nothing to do with Ojukwu's defiance of any federal authority. Indeed, the riots were triggered in part because of a false broadcast from Cotonou, Dahomey (later renamed the Republic of Benin) that told of Northern Moslems being massacred in Eastern Nigeria. Yakubu Gowon responded to the massacres and stated, inter alia that:

"I receive complaints daily that up till now (October 1966) Easterners living in the North are being killed and molested and their property looted ... We should not believe all the talk that other countries and their radio stations make ... ... We should be the people to tell them about our country..."[219]

It is this same Yakubu Gowon, who condemned the riots and denounced the mischief-makers who set up the false broadcast to instigate the riots for their reasons, that said something different with such a straight face. I am confident that Yakubu Gowon knew or understood very well that the mischief-makers instigated the riots because there were still Northern Nigerians in the Hausa-Fulani establishment who desired secession or who did not want to have anything to do with a Nigeria where the Northern ruling establishment was not supreme or at least had ultimate control of the machinery of the federal government. At that point in September 1966, the Northern ruling establishment may also have surmised that they would win in any military showdown. Therefore, they decided to precipitate a showdown so that the matter would eventually lead to a military confrontation.

Ojukwu could have protested all he wanted, but if the depraved orgy of the slaughter of civilians that occurred in September/October 1966 had not begun, the Igbos would not have departed en masse. The ad hoc conference of September 1966 was still going on when the Northern Nigerian and other delegates recessed for consultation with their regions. That is after the Northern delegation made an about-face in their proposition to have a confederation with separate armies and police.

The other statement that is a travesty in Gowon's victory speech is his reference to amnesty. Specifically, "I solemnly repeat our guarantees of a general amnesty for those misled into rebellion." With all due respect to Gen. Gowon, no one was misled into anything like a rebellion. As Madiebo would ask, who was rebelling against who? The Igbos were not misled. There were rebellions in Nigeria during the year 1966. Only one, in my view, was justified: the countercoup of July 1966. The January coup could be explained, though I maintain that it was misguided. The January boys had no business overthrowing the government. The July boys were simply comrades who felt betrayed by their colleagues. For clarity, consider the possibility that the July boys had formed a faction of the army on January 15, 1966, to resist Nzeogwu's coup and succeeded, could they be blamed any more or less than for their rebellion that took place six months later? I think not. The soldiers who massacred civilians at Kano Airport and subsequently joined with police and other civilians to commit the endless orgy of the depraved slaughter of civilians should have been arrested and

---

[219] *Nicholas Ibeawuchi Omenka, Blaming the Gods: Christian Religious Propaganda in The Nigeria—Biafra War, The Journal of African History, 2010, Vol. 51, No. 3 (2010), pp. 367-389. Omenka was quoting West Africa, October 8, 1966.*

tried. Therefore, the question of amnesty for anyone who had been mischaracterized as having been deceived into rebellion is a travesty of truth and justice. Gowon was being boldly dishonest here. However, understandably, Gowon's story is the story of a victorious commander who was at liberty to twist the truth any way that he chose. I do not blame him for opening his mouth to say what he said, but Gowon did not have the moral locus standi to be using the word amnesty. The situation reminds me of a German general during the Nuremberg trials following World War II who was chastised for not being cooperative. Specifically, the German general said, "...If we had won the war, I would have been the one putting you on trial..." Thank God that the German Reich did not win World War II. But, yes, they would have been the ones trying their adversaries, but it would not mean that their heinous ideologies of racial superiority or their depraved genocide against Jews would have suddenly turned from crime to noble conduct. It only reinforces the grotesque point that, in politics, might is right!

Sometime shortly after the end of the war, Yakubu Gowon granted an interview to *Time Magazine,* and an attitude is attributed to him that "His forgiveness, however, was withheld from one Biafran," referring to Ojukwu during an interview with Britain's Independent Television News. Gowon fairly gloated: "How are the mighty fallen and in such a cowardly way." Gen Gowon added, "I hope his conscience will allow him to rest. God knows! Will those who have supported Ojukwu allow him to get away with what he's done—to his people, to Nigeria, to Africa?"[220] I also heard once Gen. Gowon say, in a television interview, that Ojukwu should have taken poison and killed himself knowing what he did wrong. Ojukwu was even called a coward for fleeing from Nigeria. What did Ojukwu do that other people did not do? It was good that Ojukwu left the Biafran enclave to deny Nigeria the unjust victory of arresting and putting him on trial. It is the Igbo man that should flagellate Ojukwu for bungling their affair. If a more reasoned approach had been taken, like preparing adequately for possible armed and violent conflagration or negotiating peace with common sense when the herald was still beckoning, the war would not have been fought or it would not have been lost, even if it were not won. If Ojukwu had been more transparent to co-opt critical personnel and constituencies, the Igbos and other Eastern Nigerians would have come out with a better deal; The long-run strategic objectives of the Igbos and other Eastern Nigerians would have been achieved even if no compensation were paid for loss of life and property in the North.

Referring back to the travesty of forgiveness and amnesty, the questions would be, who is forgiving who here? What did Ojukwu do to Africa that the mass slaughter of Igbo civilians by official military personnel of the Nigerian Army had not done? Some quarters in Nigeria denied that the massacres were taking place and claimed that broadcasting the exodus of Igbos from the North was wicked and false. What happened in Northern Nigeria set an example for what was to follow in Rwanda in 1994. The Pogrom of 1966 to which the Nigerian government turned a blind eye was to indicate to others that barbaric ethnic cleansing and savage slaughter of fellow citizens is acceptable. The real coward here was not Ojukwu. It was good that Ojukwu left the country because killing him would have provided Nigeria with a misguided and false vindication. The real cowards were the Nigerian government leaders who could not see what was wrong with failing to hold accountable the soldiers who, at Kano Airport, engaged in mass slaughter and broke the last straw of endurance and resistance of the Igbos to flee from the carnage that had been going for two months since the July 1966 coup. These bandit soldiers should have been dismissed and detained after the war just like the January boys. The real cowards are the Nigerian military leaders who would not own up to their share of responsibility for the events that followed the July 1966 coup—those soldiers who flouted orders and barricaded the Makurdi Bridge to kill civilians, who flouted orders and marched out and shot surviving Igbo Army officers who were locked up in guard rooms in Lagos, who accompanied Benjamin Adekunle to transport Eastern Nigerian soldiers to Lagos under Adekunle's supervision but who flouted the agreement of August 9, 1966, and pushed Adekunle aside and slaughtered those in their care. They even went after Adekunle to kill him also. One way to take responsibility for their share of the fracas that followed would have been not to dismiss their colleagues who fled as they were being chased by their Nigerian colleagues. The real

---

[220] *Time Magazine, the Secession that Failed January 26, 1970*

cowards are the Nigerian leaders who took thirty years to grant pensions to their colleagues in the army and then took another five or more years to pay the pensions. These Biafran Army officers should not have been dismissed at all. The real cowards were members of the Supreme Military Council who permitted civil servants (permanent secretaries) to hijack their agreement at Aburi to pay displaced civil servants for three months through March 31, 1967. The Supreme Military Council was cowardly in that they would not address the soldiers who stormed the Kano Airport because insubordinate Permanent Secretaries were worried about the possible reaction of the rank and file of the Nigerian Army to the trial of those soldiers.

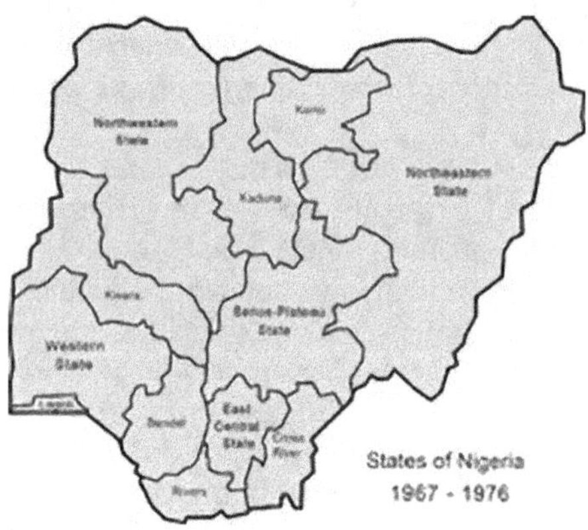

In the end, war breaks out because one or both sides in the conflict believe they can win. The genesis of war is always some dispute that could be genuine or contrived; sometimes war is motivated by greed or a feeling of insecurity that may or may not be legitimate. When Gowon declared war on the eve of July 6, 1967, he referred to or justified his declaration of war on his supposed constitutional duty to preserve the territorial integrity of Nigeria. Who granted this territorial integrity that must be defended or preserved? When did the constituent ethnic groups in Nigeria come together to agree to be Nigeria and to hold all to an oath of being in the same indivisible country? There was no such thing.

In the first place, there is no divine right of any group of people to impose on others to be part of any country. Nigeria was a convenient creation of the British. At the time of the British creation of the Northern and Southern protectorates of Nigeria, Nigerians were not even aware of each other. Certainly, the Jihad of Dan Fodio had tried to force some Yoruba groups to become integrated into the Sokoto Sultanate, but the Yorubas did not feel any kinship ties that indicated a desire to be one entity with the Sokoto Caliphate. Dan Fodio invaded Northern Nigeria and forced the Hausa to be under the Sokoto Caliphate because he calculated that he was able to succeed. If Dan Fodio's military assessment was that he would not win, he would have found a way to integrate his Fulani followers into the Islamic practices of Northern Nigerians the way it was. All he would have to do would have been to preach his version and try to win adherents who might represent a school of thought. The fact that Yoruba communities like Ilorin are Islamic or are part of the Northern and Sokoto Caliphate is the result of conquest. At the time of the amalgamation of the Northern and Southern Nigerian protectorates, the Hausa, likely, were not aware of Igbos. There is no record of their dealings with Igbos as a group either as separate communities or through their potentates. Even the potentates of Igboland were hardly aware of each other beyond those in proximity. When the amalgamation of the Northern and Southern protectorates was completed by Lord Lugard in 1914, the indigenes of the country and their potentates were not consulted. Some historians have referred to some document that was signed by potentates in Northern Nigeria and Calabar (Eastern Nigeria) and another in Western Nigeria. If such a document exists, it could only have been an instrument of cession or at best a glorified surrender to an apparently or evidently superior force. When the Nigerians gained independence from Britain in 1960, all indications point to an uneasy peace. There were several threats of secession from all involved. In the end, there was only one unifying factor: to get the British to leave us alone. The different regions gained independence as one unit because the British forced it. The hope was that we would find a modus vivendi and live peacefully and safely all over the country and build a nation together. In the nearly fifty years from amalgamation to independence, we've had enough time to work out a modus vivendi. However, it turned out that we could not even conduct a simple election, and in less than six years, the artificial entity broke at the seams. The Igbos and other Eastern Nigerians could not live safely in other parts of the country. Aside from the pretext of a one-sided coup, which was totally corrected in July of 1966, Igbos had been previously harassed and wantonly killed in 1948 and 1953.

While the pogrom in Northern Nigeria, was happening, Charles Keil, an American, visited the area around Makurdi and reported that "The pogroms that I witnessed in Makurdi ... [late September 1966] were foreshadowed by months of anti-Igbo and anti-Easterners conversations among the Tiv, Hausa and ... residents in Makurdi ... and fitting a pattern replicated in city after city ... the massacres were led by the Nigerian Army ... After counting the disemboweled bodies ... I was escorted back to the city by soldiers who apologized for the stench and explained politely that they were doing me and the world a favor by eliminating the Ibos ... They are born with greed in their hearts .... They are the ones spoiling Nigeria ... One Nigeria without Ibo ... We make sure they will never worry us again ... The Ibo and their ilk ... vermin and snakes to be trod under foot."[221]

These are the words of a soldier—at once an individual whose opinion should not matter and at the same time a vicarious representative of the Nigerian government who officially armed him and let him and his comrades get away with their bloody deeds. Through all eternity the hands of the Nigerian government will be stained with the bloods of their own citizens for perpetrating the pogroms of 1966. Whether or not the opinion of this soldier represented the official line of the government, the fleeing victims of the pogroms and the implied genocide were seeing something different and were justified in fleeing and feeling insecure within Nigeria after these horrible events

---

[221] *Charles Keil, The Price of Nigerian Victory, Africa Today, Jan. – Feb 1970, Vol. 17, No. 1, Pp. 1 – 3 (https://www.jstor.org/stable/4185054)*

Chapter XII

QUEST FOR PEACE ANTE BELLUM

Si Vis Pacem Para Bellum- If You Want Peace, Prepare for War

If you want peace, prepare for war[222]. This statement by the Roman Commander Vegetius aptly describes the comparative preparation levels of Nigerian and Biafra leading up to the next precipice – the edge of bellicose catastrophe. Both sides engaged in bellicose and pugnacious banter. The Nigerian side was carefully building up and adding to their capacity to make war and manipulating the situation to lead to up to war because they would be prepared. The Eastern Nigerian and later the Biafran side lamented, whined, bluffed, and issued truculent pugnacious threats. In the end, while one can admire or, maybe deride their pugnacious audacity in the war that ensued, the Biafran side never truly prepared for anything like a modern war.

For three days after the countercoup of July 1966, Nigeria was in limbo and on the verge of collapse. There were reports, which may have been interpreted differently, that Northern Nigerian officers commandeered a VC10 aircraft to transport their families back to the North via Kano airport. This event may have taken place as a precaution to protect Northern Nigerian families from the potential danger of a rumored second Igbo coup. It could also have been an attempt to safeguard their families from reprisals following a Northern Nigerian secession [223]. On August 1, 1966, Lt. Col. Yakubu Gowon (at that time he was a lieutenant colonel) emerged as the head of state and made his first broadcast to a nation that was on the brink of collapse. In his speech, Gowon began by acknowledging that events following the coup of January 1966 were unfortunately fueled by "certain parties… [who] caused suspicion and grave doubts about the Government's [*Ironsi's government*[224]] sincerity… certain parts of the country decided to agitate against the military regime which had hitherto enjoyed country-wide support."[225] Yakubu Gowon then made his now-famous broadcast[226] that has been interpreted in different ways. Some interpret it to mean that Gowon meant that Nigeria could not be united or be one nation, whereas others, including Phillip Effiong[227], consider it a masterpiece of compromise and double talk – a statement with a double meaning that played to the sentiments of those who preferred breaking up Nigeria and at the same time appeased those who wanted Nigeria united. Walter Schwarz implies in innuendo that Yakubu Gowon intended initially to announce a secession by stating that "the tone and wording of the broadcast strongly suggest

---

[222] *Publius Flavius Vegetius Renatus's tract De Re Militari (4th or 5thcentury AD). If You Want Peace Prepare for War. The actual original phrasing is Igitur qui desiderat pacem, praeparet bellum ("Therefore let him who desires peace prepare for war.")*

[223] *Phillip Effiong, Nigeria and Biafra: My Story, Pp. 140 – 41*

[224] *Words in bracket italics are mine for clarification*

[225] *A.H.M Kirk-Greene, Crisis and Conflict in Nigeria (Vol I), London, Oxford University Presss, 1971, Pp. 196 – 198*

[226] *Effiong, Op. Cit.Page 138*

[227] *Ibid, Page 139*

that its vital passages had been rewritten at the last moment…he had been intending to announce a secession."[228] I can only say that Schwarz was speculating and reaching his own conclusions.

Specifically, Lt. Col Yakubu Gowon stated, inter alia, *"I have now come to the most difficult but [also] the most important part of this statement … As a result of recent events and other similar previous ones, I have come to strongly believe that we cannot honestly and sincerely continue in this way, as the basis for trust and confidence in our unitary system of government has not been able to stand the test of time … Suffice it to say that putting all considerations to test, political, economic as well as social, the basis of unity is not there, or is badly rocked not only once but several times.[229]"*

I do not see this statement as double-speak or compromise. During the Aburi meeting (January 4–5, 1967), Yakubu Gowon said he was referring to the unitary government that was imposed by the Unification Decree (Decree No. 34 of May 1966). My interpretation was that Gowon was simply saying that killing each other back and forth in coups and counter-coups and mutual slaughter would make economic and social progress and interaction difficult. By extension, political unity as a country would be equally difficult. In the final analysis, Gowon's statement or speech was a call for calm and peaceful conduct among us. What is more telling is that those who quote this speech seem to stop short at a convenient point. Specifically, they fail to cite, or they skip the continuation of Gowon's statement, viz:

'… I, therefore, feel that we should review the issue of our national standing and see if we can [stop] the country from drifting away into utter destruction … a decree will soon be issued to lay a firm foundation for this objective…I sincerely hope that we shall resolve most of the problems that have disunited us in the past and really come to respect and trust one another…[230]"

These latter statements that follow the statement about the basis for unity clearly affirm Gowon's belief that we should have been working toward unity. In my view, the speech leaves no ambiguity as to Gowon's intentions or desire for a united Nigeria. What puzzles me, however, is that most, if not all, who have alleged that Gowon was a secessionist have also chosen to quote only the first part of the speech that justifies their conclusion. Why would they all choose to ignore the remainder of the statement?

The rampage of Northern Nigerian army officers continued unabated through the first and second week of August 1966. While Northern Nigerian army officers in the West and East remained safe, Eastern Nigerian army officers in the West and North were in danger. They were being hunted down and killed. Finally, on August 8 and 9, 1966, a meeting of representatives of the regional governors met in Lagos to search for peace. Besides Ironsi's peace tours that ended in his abduction and assassination, this was another move: Move Number 2. At the end of the meeting on August 9, 1966, it was agreed, inter alia, that all military personnel should be redeployed in their regions of origin[231]. In addition, the military governors agreed to convene a meeting of an expanded committee to discuss the future of Nigeria and the nature of the association among the regions (Akpan, Pp. 41 – 42).

The peace agreement was fraught with treachery on both sides, but none of it was motivated by intelligence of the other side's treachery. I aver that the acts of betrayal were driven by personal agendas. While Northern troops garrisoned in Enugu were escorted with collegial fanfare—toasted with drinks and posing for farewell photographs[232]—the Northern officers in Northern and Western Nigeria engaged in systematic hunting and execution of Eastern officers. Forsyth provides detailed accounts of how between August 11 and 14, 1966, in Makurdi, (after the agreement of August 9, 1966), fifteen soldiers and officers of Eastern origin were marched out and executed. Similarly, (Forsyth, Page 50) details the account of how twenty-two officers and men of Eastern origin were

---

[228] *Walter Schwarz, Nigeria, New York, Frederick Prager Publishers, 1968, Pp. 210 – 11*
[229] *Effiong, Nigeria and Biafra: My Story, Pp. 138 – 39*
[230] *A.M.H Kirk-Greene, Crisis and Conflict in Nigeria, Page 197.*
[231] Akpan, The Struggle for Secession, Pp. 39 – 41 and Effiong, Nigeria and Biafra: My Story, Page 48.
[232] Max Siollun, Oil, Politics and Violence, Pp. 137 – 38.

marched out of the garrison in Lagos and executed on orders of Lt. Nuhu[233]. All this happened in addition to several Igbo and other Eastern army officers being assassinated (understandably) during the heat of the July 29 coup, which happened between July 29 and August 3, 1966. Eastern Nigerian Army officers who escaped after the August 9 agreement achieved it through their own schemes. According to Madiebo, who details his escape, Northern Nigerian troops barricaded the Makurdi Bridge and systematically extracted Eastern Nigerian army officers from trains and even secret crossing points on the Benue River and killed them. This all occurred after the August 9 agreement[234].

At the meeting of August 9, 1966, it was also agreed that a larger committee of the governor's representatives should be set up to discuss and make recommendations about the structure of governance for Nigeria means of coexisting peacefully. The committee was to meet one week later. According to Akpan,[235] the committee ended up being a high-powered ad hoc constitutional conference. In preparation for the ad hoc constitutional conference, Lt. Col. Ojukwu (governor of Eastern Nigeria) appointed a committee headed by Dr. Graham Douglas, the attorney general. The committee met once or twice and then ceased. Meanwhile, Ojukwu had formed a secret committee that was working to achieve his personal agenda. Inter alia, Ojukwu proposed to the ad hoc constitutional delegation to consider what he had said earlier. Specifically, they should consider that a unified military command for Nigeria was no longer feasible. Furthermore,

You have to consider what economic ties will bind the component parts of Nigeria... You [must] consider where the responsibility for foreign relations will lie bearing in mind the necessity for exercising full control over our economic and defense agreements and to establish friendly relations with countries of our choice ... You will have to consider the political arrangement for supervision of common services ... and what type of constitution will be best suited for Eastern Nigeria."

The Northern Nigerian delegation began by recognizing the beneficial value and convenience of belonging to one country, but they also proposed, inter alia, the following in its opening memorandum to the conference on September 1966:

We are different peoples brought together by recent accidents of history ... The powers shall be delegated to the Central Executive Council ... except that the powers connected to external or foreign affairs, immigration can be unilaterally withdrawn by the State Government ... A member state should reserve the right to secede ... and unilaterally from the Union...Each State must have its own Airforce, Army, Police, and Civil Service.[236]

The brief given to the Eastern Nigerian delegation at the ad hoc conference on September 12, 1966, included a proposition that each region would have its independent army [237].Evidently, Ojukwu was already thinking about an independent Eastern Nigeria in one form or another. It is evident from the above that Ojukwu had a hidden agenda, though he set up deceptive committees and consultative groups to make it appear that he was operating democratically. For certain, he was manoeuvring to create a semi-sovereign Eastern Nigeria—independent armies, an Eastern Nigeria constitution, and the establishment of friendly relations with countries of our choice. Ojukwu believed that no one else could read between the lines. Indeed, it does not require the ability to read between the lines to understand Ojukwu's intentions. Even more telling is that Ojukwu was ignoring the wishes of the so-called ethnic minorities in Eastern Nigeria. It is equally evident that the Northern Nigerian delegation desired to retain the right for the North to break away from a united Nigeria.

---

[233] Forsyth, The Biafra Story, Pp. 48 – 50
[234] *Regina Maduabum, A Soldier's Spouse, Pp. 90 - 92 and Alexander Madiebo, The Nigerian Revolution and the Biafran War, Pp. 65 – 77*
[235] *N. U. Akpan, The Struggle for Secession, Page 43,*
[236] *Government of Eastern Nigeria, The North and Constitutional Developments in Nigeria, Nigerian Crisis (1966), Vol 5, Pp. 23 – 27.*
[237] *N. U. Akpan, Op. Cit, Pp. 43 – 45.*

The ad hoc constitutional conference began on September 12, 1966. At the conference, it appeared that the Northern delegation agreed with the sum and substance of Ojukwu's ideas, including separate armies, separate police, and the right to break away from the country. The Conference was adjourned on September 17, 1966, after five days, to let the regional delegations consult their governments. When the conference later reconvened on September 20, 1966, the Northern delegation made an about-face and repudiated all their previous propositions regarding the autonomy of regions—independent armies and secession—and demanded a unified federation with a strong central government. They also proposed the creation of more states with limited autonomy. While the deliberations were taking place, on or around September 26, 1966, the riots and mass slaughter against the Igbos and other eastern Nigerians resumed, this time at unprecedented levels, while the rioters screamed a battle cry: "Araba" (meaning "let us separate"). At this point, the conference was adjourned to October 13, 1966. The Eastern Nigeria delegation left the conference and vowed never to return.

The second wave of massacres against the Igbos and Eastern Nigerians made the case for the secession of Eastern Nigeria in more than one way. One would wonder why the Northern Nigerian delegation decided to consult with their leaders and government. Was there a need to consult with their leaders on the issues at the conference or an excuse and camouflage to stall because some people in Northern Nigeria were about to commence the second wave of killings and were not in favor of continuing the conference? At the time of this conference, all soldiers and officers of Eastern origin had returned to the East or were dead, except for a few non-Igbos who were successful at hiding out in Western Nigeria—such individuals included Maj. Esuene (Ibibio), Lt. Com. Diette-Spiff (Kalagbari). Lt. Col. Etuk (Efik or Ibibio), and Lt. Col. Ekpo (Ibibio), just to name a few. If there was the hope of peace, why start a new round of killings that would spread like an uncontrollable wildfire?

Many Igbos took the risk of being killed in the sporadic riots and waited until the end of September 1966. On September 29, 1966, Yakubu Gowon made a speech in which he condemned the riots and killing of Igbo people. Specifically, Yakubu Gowon said, in sum and substance, that those people who continued to engage in riots were acting beyond reason. After the riots in May 1966, one could not consider any riots within reason—and I would not consider any riots to be within reason. However, it is always possible to explain violent behavior when people are instigated or oppressed to the limit of their endurance. One could explain the May riots by reference to the fact that Northern Nigerians had taken a wait-and-see attitude in response to the January 1966 coup in which their political, social, military and spiritual leadership was all but annihilated—or at least decimated to the extent that theirs had been reduced to a sideline role in Nigerian affairs. While they waited, Igbos engaged them in callous and insensitive mockery in the newspapers and even in personal direct communication . On the other hand, after Northern army officers removed Maj. Gen. Aguiyi Ironsi, the North had full control of the government from August 1, 1966. The riots in the North continued through August with the killing and expulsion of Igbo civilians and army officers from Eastern Nigeria. By October/November 1966, one could not find any justification for the continued riots and the mass slaughter of Igbos. Indeed, the situation became even more damnable when the head of government and the supreme commander of the army condemned the killings and the rioters and their leaders would not heed.

The experience of the Diliora family is a clear example that many Igbos did their best not to flee the North, with the hope that the riots would calm down so that they could settle back to normal life. Besides the family of Diliora, indeed, many Igbos remained in Northern Nigeria with the hope that once the military settled their scores, the crisis would blow over. Many men sent their wives and children back to the east while they waited for tensions to cool down. But their hopes were dashed by the next wave of mayhem. The story of Diliora Chukwurah is instructive[238]. Mr. Chukwura had sent his children and wife home earlier in the crisis and remained in Jos, a non-Hausa community in Northern Nigeria[239]. It took the persuasion of Diliora's uncle to send his wife and children back

---

[238] Diliora Chukwura, The Last Train to Biafra, Pp. 17 – 33
[239] Chukwurah, Last Train to Biafra, Pp. 15 – 16.

to the East. With the support of local leaders of goodwill, such as the traditional ruler of Jos, Mr. Chukwurah remained in Jos with the hope that the chaos would blow over. But no such thing happened. Following rumors of Mr. Chukwura's murder in Jos, his wife decided to go in search of him[240]. Luckily, man and wife returned safely to the East, but the details of the ordeals that they suffered make for an instructive case of the determination that many Igbos had made to remain in Northern Nigeria. Of course, the crisis got worse; the killings went on and became even more brutal and depraved. When the soldiers of the Fourth Battalion of the Nigerian Army fanned out in battle formation and massacred Igbos, it was clear that the Army had officially joined the action.[241] What is worse is that the police joined in the killing action, as evidenced in October 1966 at the airport in Kano. Just before the escalation of the riots at the beginning of October, Gowon issued an order that all federal civil servants from the East who did not return to their posts by October 15, 1966, would be summarily dismissed.

How callous and insensitive could someone be? If you were in the position of Igbo civil servants, would you return to Lagos? The fact was that the Igbos who did not get killed in the North were harassed in Western Nigeria. According to Odogwu[242] "Roadblocks sprang up in many places in Lagos... to deal with hated easterners." Some of these roadblocks were illegal. At these roadblocks, many Igbos were ordered out of buses and killed, yet many survived by claiming to be Yoruba or from another ethnic group. Most Easterners and Igbos, in particular, did not leave Western Nigeria until after October 1966, at which point they felt that the Nigerian government was either unwilling or unable to protect them. Equally, and contrary to Samuel Umweni's vitriolic expression, when Ojukwu ordered that Igbos and Eastern Nigerians depart Western Nigeria and non-Easterners should depart the East, he did so because he could no longer protect Nigerians of Western and Northern origin who resided in the east[243]. It was not to deprive Northern Nigeria or Western Nigerians of educated or competent manpower. After all, Western Nigerians had educated manpower. Furthermore, the Western Nigerians who departed to the east were equally competent, and their positions in the east were occupied by Eastern Nigerians who returned from other parts of Nigeria. In many respects, it was a swap that eased the unemployment situation in the east. Here are a few excerpts from the October 14, 1966, issue of *Time Magazine* outlining the stories of selected survivors of the events of September to October 1966. According to Mr. Colin Legum of the *Observer*, London, October 16, 1966,

"...Men, women, and children arrived with arms and legs broken, hands hacked off, mouths split open. Pregnant women were cut open and the unborn children killed. The total casualties are unknown... In Jos, charter pilots who have been airlifting Ibos to Eastern safety talked of at least 800 dead .... In Zaria, forty-five miles from Kaduna, I talked with a saffron-robed Hausa who told me: 'We killed about 250 here. Perhaps Allah willed it ... One European saw a woman and her daughter slaughtered in his front garden after he had been forced to turn them away...". The times continued *"... The massacre began at the airport near the Fifth Battalion's home city of Kano. A Lagos-bound jet had just arrived from London, and as the Kano passengers were escorted into the customs shed a wild-eyed soldier stormed in, brandishing a rifle, and demanding 'Ina Nyamiri' – the Hausa for 'Where are the damned Ibos?' There were Ibos among the customs officers, and they dropped their chalk and fled, only to be shot down in the main terminal by other soldiers. Screaming the blood curses of a Moslem Holy War, the Hausa troops turned the airport into a shamble, bayoneting Ibo workers in the bar, gunning them down in the corridors, and hauling Ibo passengers off the plane to be lined up and shot.*

From the airport the troops fanned out through downtown Kano, hunting down Ibos in bars, hotels, and on the streets. One contingent drove their Landrovers to the railroad station where more than 100 Ibos were waiting for a train and cut them down with automatic weapon fire.... The soldiers did

---

240 Chukwurah, Last Train to Biafra, Pp. 23 – 25.
241 Times Magazine, October 14, 1966
242 Benard Odogwu, No Where to Hide, Pp. 238 – 42.
243 Max Siollun, Oil, Politics and Violence, Pp. 137 – 38

not have to do all the killing. They were soon joined by thousands of Hausa civilians, who rampaged through the city armed with stones, cutlasses, machetes, and homemade weapons of metal and broken glass. Crying 'Heathen' and 'Allah' the mobs and troops invaded the Sabon Gari (strangers' quarter) ransacking, looting, and burning Ibo homes and stores and murdering their owners.

All night long and into the morning the massacre went on. Then, tired but fulfilled, the Hausas drifted back to their homes and barracks to get some breakfast and sleep. Municipal garbage trucks were sent out to collect the dead and dump them into mass graves outside the city. The death toll will never be known, but it was at least a thousand. Somehow several thousand Ibos survived the orgy, and all had the same thought: to get out of the North.... One officer of the 5th dismissed the whole thing as a prank, but there was no assurance that it would not happen again. When a government representative promised a tense meeting of the Kano Chamber of Commerce that all was under control, he was hooted down ... Assurances are no longer any good...retorted, one local business leader..." As the mayhem went on, Lt. Col. Ojukwu made a broadcast stating, inter alia, "... I have lost confidence in my ability to continue restraining the violently injured feelings of the people of this region ... I have said before that the East would not secede unless she is forced out ... Fellow countrymen, the push has started ...."

Other excerpts: MR. J. P. ONANI[244], *a native of Obubra, who had worked in Kano as a clerk for three and half years, says "...On the 1st of October, at about 6.30 p.m., I was in my house, I heard shooting and so many people shouting in some parts of the streets. As I came out, I learned from a friend that the Nigerian Army and Police were shooting ... but soon after the shooting spread all over the town. I took my family, and we ran from our house into a gutter.... We managed to escape again from the gutter into the bush where we slept for three days because they now entered the gutter and started killing those who escaped from their houses. We saw so many dead bodies lying in the streets as we were running. At the Railway station over 200 people who ran from the town to hide and wait for the Eastern train were killed including Railway workers of Eastern origin...."*

MRS. CHARITY NWOSU, of Ibeku, Bende Division, wife of a trader at Jos, narrates *"... About 1 a.m. on Wednesday, 28th September 1966, I was awakened by a violent stampede and shrill cries that rent the night. On an impulse, I opened a window that over-looks my husband's store. Just across the street, I saw a lorry and a crowd of people in front of the store... Within seconds the store was forced open and looted and Victor (her husband) was hacked to death..."*

These events can be understood in the context of Madiebo's point that there was preparation for a final showdown which could be true sarcastically or paradoxically. During the Northern riots, the clarion call was "Araba," which means "Let us separate." It is no secret that the Northerners wanted to separate from Nigeria unless they were allowed to dominate the politics and resources. As events developed, from the coup of January 1966 to the peace talks of August and September 1966, they could see that either Nigeria would break apart or the structure for unity would not give them the desired dominant position. Therefore, they wanted to kill the Igbos who resided among them as a final blow to their undesirable neighbors. An alternative interpretation could be that there were elements in the ruling establishment of Northern Nigeria who truly did not want a united Nigeria and would not be happy with any negotiation that would ultimately unite Nigeria. Therefore, these riots were part of the Northerners' attempt to force the North to secede as they did not want to have anything to do with a united Nigeria. Indeed, when Yakubu Gowon made a statement in August or September 1966, vowing that he was determined to keep Nigeria united, he was more likely referring to the Northern Nigerians who were determined to scuttle any possibility that Nigeria could resolve the issues and be united.

---

[244] See, http://www.ipob.org/2014/09/european-eyewitness-accounts-of.html). See also Nigerian Pogrom, Crisis 1966, Vol. 3, Publicity Division of the Ministry of Information, Eastern Nigeria, December 1966, Pp. 4 – 20. These events were so disturbing that even the governor of Northern Nigeria, Lt. Col. Hassan Katsina condemned them and was even quoted by the government of Eastern Nigeria.

Finally, the rioting and pogrom were a scheme to provoke actions on the part of the Eastern Nigerian government that would precipitate a military confrontation for a final showdown. Ultimately, the latter happened. The push that Ojukwu is said to have started is true within these paradoxical touches of sarcasm. In a carefully calculated way, the Igbos were pushed into secession and then attacked since the North had the armaments and men to achieve their aims.

Donald Patterson of the political section and Tom Smith of the economic section traveled from the U.S. Embassy in Lagos to the North after the pogrom "The Sabon-Garis were ghost towns, deserted, with the detritus of people who had fled rapidly... Most Northerners ... had no apologies for what had happened to the Ibos, though there were exceptions, in general, there was no remorse, and the feeling was one of good riddance."[245]

After the events of October 1966, Igbos continued to stream back into the East as the killings and disturbances continued into November. For certain, pressure from the outside world led the Nigerian government to provide limited assistance to fleeing easterners to leave the North. Even soldiers and police, from among whom came the rioters and bandits, joined in belated mopping-up operations to repatriate Igbos and other Eastern Nigerians. The peace conference of September 1966 that had been adjourned was reconvened in October 1966, but the Eastern delegation declined to participate unless the Northern Nigerian troops still stationed in Western Nigeria were removed. The fear and concern of the eastern delegation were, in part, justified but also provided a convenient alibi for recalcitrance, intransigence, and pouting. After failing to persuade the eastern delegation to participate, the conference was adjourned to November 1966. Before the conference convened on its November date, Chief Awolowo resigned as the Chairperson of the Western Nigerian delegation and Yakubu Gowon adjourned the conference indefinitely, as it would serve no useful purpose.

From November 1966 to the end of the year, not much happened except the war of words between the broadcasting station in Eastern Nigeria and Radio Television Kaduna, relaying news about the demonstrations in Eastern Nigeria and tension and uncertainty about the future of Nigeria. On his part, Yakubu Gowon vowed to keep Nigeria united. The suspicion was strong that the East was working toward secession. With this in mind, the British high commissioner and the American ambassador to Lagos visited the east to advise Ojukwu, the governor of Eastern Nigeria, against secession. According to Akpan, they warned Ojukwu in diplomatic ways against the dangers of secession.[246] Other delegations from other countries visited to seek assurances, and even a delegation of Obas and chiefs from Western Nigeria visited the east and expressed sympathy and regret for the Easterners that were killed in Northern Nigeria[247]. In response to the delegations, Ojukwu promised strongly that the east had no intention of seceding unless forced to do so.

The Aburi Meeting and After

Following these visits and continued diplomatic efforts, the military governors agreed to meet one more time to work toward the unity of Nigeria. With support from the British government and the military leader of Ghana, the military governors agreed to meet in Aburi, Ghana, from January 4 to January 5, 1967. To ensure his safety, the government of Gen. Ankra in Ghana offered and provided a Ghana Airforce plane to take Ojukwu and his staff to Ghana and back.

The minutes of the meeting and a full record of the meeting was published by the federal government.[248] In general, the level of collegiality, as seen in the minute-by-minute records, is impressive. There was a candid discussion of all issues. It is equally impressive and remarkable that the military governors were able to accomplish so much in two days. Critical issues discussed include reorganization of the army, devolving powers to the regions, recruitment of soldiers into the

---

[245] *Waidi Adebayo, BIAFRA: The Untold Story of Nigeria's Civil War, BIAFRA: The Untold Story of Nigeria's civil war – Nigerian History (wordpress.com), March 2013*

[246] *Ntieyong Akpan, The Struggle for Secession, Pp. 49 – 50*

[247] Akpan, Ibid..

[248] *Federal Republic of Nigeria, Meeting of the Nigerian Military Leaders held at Peduase Lodge, Aburi Ghana, January 4–January 5, 1967*

army, purchase, and distribution of arms and armaments, and addressing the problem of refugees and their rehabilitation. The leaders even discussed the possibility of exchanging assistace among the regions.[249] There was candid discussion of compensating employees who were displaced and recognition of the possibility of double-dipping by individuals. One critical agreement that was made was that civil servants who were displaced from the other regions be paid until March 31, subject to them not having been employed elsewhere. The leaders also agreed to create four regional commands in the army after making clear that such an arrangement should not lead to creating private armies in the regions. Indeed, Ojukwu was clear in making a strong suggestion in this matter.[250] Much earlier, the military governors agreed that there should be no further recruitment of soldiers in the army. At the beginning of the meeting, Ojukwu suggested, and it was accepted, that all should renounce the use of force as a means of resolving future conflicts.[251] They even discussed, at Ojukwu's behest, that either no further arms should be purchased by all sides or that any arms purchased should be distributed to all regions to balance power.[252] There was even a candid discussion of traveling around the regions to ensure that all would abide by the agreement and audit the accumulation and storage of arms. At this point, Yakubu Gowon interjected humorously, saying, in sum and substance, that auditing and verifying arms stockpiles at each region could be done, except for the smuggled arms[253]. This was an apparent reference to the Biafran arms smuggler whose plane crash-landed in the Cameroons.

As soon as the governors and head of state returned from Aburi, their agreement was immediately beset with insidious treachery on both sides[254]. For sure, certain objections to the agreements reached at Aburi by either side were legitimate, but others were intended to set in motion a process for conflict by two sides that were confident of winning in a conflict[255]. The difference was that the antagonists in the east were suffering from a sophomoric self-delusion. The attitude of some of Ojukwu's advisers in the east was that Ojukwu should not have attended the meeting at Aburi in the first place[256].

Their expectation was probably that by pouting and finding excuses, the matter would get to the point that the only alternative would be the secession of the East. They were sophomoric in that if Ojukwu did not attend, then his absence would be used against him. Ojukwu's advisers were making believe that no one would see their tricks. The self-delusion arises from the fact that they did not have the armament to fight a war, yet they did not know it. As soon as Ojukwu returned from Aburi, Ojukwu's advisers were first happy that he had returned alive but retorted to Akpan that the conference had not brought them full sovereignty and independence[257]. But Ojukwu did not go to Aburi to negotiate full sovereignty and independence for Eastern Nigeria. This attitude of self-delusion pervaded all negotiations during the conflict, including peace talks during the hopeless civil war. Ojukwu and his advisers deluded themselves that they were going to win the war by negotiating Biafran sovereignty against an enemy that was steadily gaining an upper hand on the battlefield.

In truth, in my own opinion, Ojukwu and Eastern Nigerians extracted favorable concessions from the conference. I would also say that the remainder of Nigerians should equally have been satisfied with the outcome. The agreements provided for breathing room while tensions cooled down. If the issue were resource control, there was no discussion about economic control of resources

---

[249] *Ibid (Pp. 45 – 52)*
[250] *Federal Republic of Nigeria, Meeting of the Nigerian Military Leaders held at Peduase Lodge, Aburi Ghana, January 4–January 5, 1967 (Pp. 62 – 63)*
[251] Ibid (Pp. 5 – 8)
[252] Ibid.
[253] Ibid, Pp. 6 – 8.
[254] *See Akpan, The Struggle for Secession. Pp. 48 – 55, Effiong, Nigeria and Biafra, My-Story, Pp. 158 – 167, Njoku, A Tragedy Without Heroes, Pp. 118 – 120 & Pp.198 – 201 and Odogwu, No Where to Hide, Pp. 260 – 64).*
[255] Effiong, Op. Cit, Pp. 165 – 66.
[256] Akpan, Op. Cit, Pp. 50 – 52
[257] *Akpan, The Struggle for Secession, Page 53.*

that would have changed existing arrangements. Sufficient powers devolved at the center that the federal side should not have been concerned about. Nevertheless, federal civil servants seemed to have been aghast at the provisions for regional commands without a central command. But the agreement provided for a commander-in-chief of the armed forces and a chairman of the Supreme Military Council (SMC). The fear was (probably) that this commander-in-chief was not granted final decision-making authority. Besides the military issues, which will be elaborated on next, there was the issue of rehabilitating or assisting refugees who were in the employ of the federal government and compensating displaced peoples who had abandoned their properties. It is evident, at least from my point of view, that civil servants on the federal side were out to derail the Aburi accord to precipitate an armed conflict.

After Aburi, two meetings were held in Benin to flesh out and implement the agreements made at Aburi. One of the meetings was for military officers. The east was represented by Lt. Col. Phillip Effiong, Lt. Col. Patrick Anwunah, and Lt. Col. Christian Ude. The Western Delegation was let by Lt. Col. Olufemi Olutoye. The meeting was filibustered by the Western delegation on flimsy or lame pretexts. Again, another indication of bad faith on the part of the Nigerian delegation Specifically, "During the second day of the meeting, the definition of Military Headquarters was brought up[258]." The western and Lagos delegations and the eastern delegations had different views. The western delegation insisted that military headquarters referred only to the army and did not include the navy and the air force. The eastern delegation argued that the air force and navy were part of the military. Lt. Col. David Ejoor (governor of Midwest in whose regional capital the meeting was being held) held separate meetings with each of the western and eastern delegations. Lt. Col. Ejoor and Lt. Col. Eyo Ekpo (Eastern Nigerian who escaped the murderous counter treachery and slaughter of July 1966) rendered contradictory and pusillanimous verdicts of what the leaders at Aburi meant by the military. When the conference was later reconvened[259], the western delegation failed to appear because they were attending the funeral of Lt. Col. Fajuyi, who was murdered during the counter-coup of July 1966. The Northern delegation failed to appear because they claimed that the conditions for flying were not conducive. Nothing further was heard of the meeting of military officers. This was an evident indication that there was no good faith on the part of the federal government and the delegations from the west and the north. Though the supreme military council met in Benin in March 1967, without Ojukwu, Gowon had begun to increase recruitment into the Nigerian Army, apparently in preparation for war and the use of force. Lt. Col. Yakubu Gowon's military build-up in March 1967 was an act of bad faith and treacherous and also shows that all along, the Federal side may have been putting up a façade.

The federal permanent secretaries drafted a decree around the middle of February 1967, which Ojukwu rejected outright. Upon persuasion to honor and keep faith with an agreement that was made freely, the military governors met in Benin in March 1967, and Yakubu Gowon published Decree No. 8 on March 10, 1967. This decree contained practically all the provisions of the Aburi Accord with a few exceptions. One of the deviations from the Aburi Accord was that the commander-in-chief of the armed forces could declare a state of emergency in any region with the concurrence of at least three of the regional governors. While Decree No. 8 reverted all the powers to the regions that they had before January 16, 1966, the decree also restored the provision that no region could exercise its powers in a manner that makes it difficult for the federal government. Much has been made of the impression that only Ojukwu came to Aburi with an agenda and appears to have been well or better prepared. For this reason, many have concluded that Ojukwu used the opportunity to fool and bamboozle his colleagues. However, I see things differently. Njoku[260] speculates that it was not easy to discern Lagos' intention at the Aburi meeting. Njoku surmises that the failure of the federal government to publish a decree on January 21, 1967, as agreed based on the Aburi Accord was due to Col. Gowon being a prisoner of the British, Nigerian establishment politicians, and Gowon's advisers.

---

[258] Effiong, Nigeria and Biafra: My Story, Pp. 166 – 67.
[259] Njoku, Tragedy Without Heroes, Pp. 116 – 17
[260] Hillary Njoku, Tragedy Without Heroes, Page 117

While the discussions at Aburi were entirely between the decision-makers, each one came with intellectually competent secretaries to their government and certainly other capable staff. What I see was that Ojukwu's colleagues were there with a clear intention to motivate him to bring the East back to the fold with significant concessions. Along the way, the other military leaders could discern that Ojukwu would not have the capability to sustain a military confrontation. In effect, they allowed him to play his hands because they saw that his deck was weak, or they, at least, could immediately analyze his vulnerability. Once they saw Ojukwu's weaknesses, they played along just to end the meeting and made concessions, with a clear intention to set Ojukwu up and provoke him to a position where they would strike him down. The only error that the Nigerian side made was their underestimation of the human and material cost and the amount of time that it would take. Even the British, who advised the Nigerian side, believed that it would take two weeks[261]. But they were all sorely wrong.

The Aburi agreement, even as slightly modified by Decree No. 8, gave Ojukwu and the east practically all they demanded at the Constitutional Conference of September to October 1966.[262] Other notable differences between Decree No. 8 and the Aburi Accord were that Federal civil servants who were displaced would not be paid their salaries up to March 31, 1967 (for 3 months, NOT 3 years). The reasoning was as lame as it was callous. One of the reasons given for withholding assistance that would alleviate the suffering of their forcibly displaced fellow citizens was the potential adverse economic impact of such support. For example, it was adduced that the Nigerian Railways Corporation was not functioning fully and would not generate sufficient revenues to pay the salaries of displaced workers for three MONTHS—not three YEARS. Under the circumstances, such support from the federal government should be in the form of emergency or disaster relief and would come from general revenue funds. Besides, for the Nigerian Railways Corporation, workers were displaced from other agencies whose payments did not depend on revenues generated from operations. I feel though that the main reason for withholding the needed support for the displaced civil servants was an attempt to punish the Igbos and establish a provocation given that many on the federal side believed that only a military solution would resolve the impasse. Those on the federal side were prepared and could easily see that during the Aburi meeting. But more on this shortly. After all, there were dogs of war on both sides of the conflict. If not, why would they, with a straight face proffer such a lame excuse that anyone could easily see through it? The intent was a scheme for provocation and alienation that would drive the other side into a confrontation that the schemers were ready for.

The federal civil servants also argued against compensation or relief for Eastern Nigerians who abandoned their properties in Northern Nigeria because the governor of Northern Nigeria was excluded from the meeting to discuss such compensation. Their intellectually lame excuse was that Northern Nigerians who fled the east also abandoned properties. Once more, however, their decision was indefensible and is quickly explained by a desire for provocation and an ultimate showdown. The issues that the civil servants raised could easily be resolved by including the governor of Northern Nigeria in such proposed discussions and meetings so that they could set up the necessary apparatus and processes to resolve the matter.

First, the secretaries that came to take notes at Aburi with the military governors and their head of state were intelligent people who were capable of digesting, on the go, what was being discussed and agreed. They were bound by protocol not to contribute to or interject into the discussions. Nevertheless, they were analyzing what they were hearing. As soon as the military leaders returned from Aburi, it is quite conceivable that the chief scribes of the other governments immediately alerted their colleagues at the office that the agreements reached during the Aburi meeting did not bode well for the future of Nigeria and certainly amounts to the repudiated proposals at the aborted and ill-fated constitutional conferences of September to November 1966. Ojukwu did not help matters by hurriedly holding a press conference immediately after arriving in Enugu on January

---

²⁶¹ Gould, The Biafran War: The Struggle for Modern Nigeria, Page 52 and Forsyth, The Biafra Story, 1969, Page 116
²⁶² See N.U. Akpan, The Struggle for Secession, Pp. 74 – 77

6 or 7, 1967. Ojukwu's announcement was out of order and contrary to the agreement that Gowon would make the first announcement of the outcome of the proceedings in Lagos. His statement that it was agreed that the regions should pull apart for a while may have heightened the alarm among the other civil servants and they immediately set to dissect, dismantle, distort, and mutilate the entire agreement.

In every sense, Ojukwu got his way. The regional commands that were created amounted to regional armies by another name. In effect, it gave him near carte blanche to recruit and build an army under his control. The failure to include the payment of civil servants and discuss the compensation of dispossessed refugees could still have been negotiated after the decree was accepted. Indeed, the failure to pay the civil servants by the end of January should have been a propaganda item from that moment on. He also could have been hammering on the compensation of the dispossessed; on the inadequacy of resources to expand schools and provide medical assistance to the injured. But Ojukwu was not thinking for his people. He was more focused on his hidden agenda to secede anyway. Therefore, Ojukwu rejected Decree No. 8 because it fell short of the entire Aburi agreement. As Njoku said[263], if Ojukwu was a strategic thinker, he would have used the disengagement of hostilities at Aburi to build an army and build up arms. What Ojukwu should have done from at least August 1966 would have been to work closely with more experienced politicians who also knew better the nooks and crannies of the cloaks and daggers of international diplomatic chess games. At least there were lots of highly experienced players in this game who knew corners of the hills and valleys, the moors and ferns and crags that he had either not encountered or experienced, but he chose to go it alone. He would have built up arms sufficient to either make the Nigerians wise enough not to violate the agreements and if they did, he would have been able to defend himself and his people much more effectively.

Looking at events critically, Ojukwu was not prepared for peace or war, though he had ample time to be adequately prepared for both. But his personal hidden agenda and the corruption and incompetence of his cronies probably dissipated funds in the treacherous international illegal arms market. Besides, the allegation that civilians were sent to purchase arms[264]. This is the reason that despite efforts to acquire arms in early August 1966, Ojukwu's army did not have sufficient arms to "...fight an intensive battle for more than five minutes..."[265]

During the Aburi meeting, Ojukwu immediately got his colleagues to forsake the use of force as a means of resolving the problems that arise from the extant conflicts. But Ojukwu did not consider that secession was an act of force. For one, if any section secedes, the secessionist will now arrogate to itself the right to enforce its territorial boundaries as separate from Nigeria. If need be, by force of arms. Secondly, Ojukwu proposed that all sides should cease the recruitment of soldiers and either that no further arms should be purchased or that any arms purchased by the federal government or that became available should be distributed across the regions. Yea! Right! Do you want to believe that a potential adversary will share arms with you? Tell me about that!!! Ojukwu's proposition was diplomatically as well as militarily strategic since he had not been able to successfully arm himself. Somehow Ojukwu felt that his colleagues were naïve or plain fools. At the minimum, the secretaries who witnessed the discussions and the ones who read and discussed it would immediately conclude that this man probably did not have arms to fight if the matter came to a military confrontation. At that point, one would imagine that Nigerian actions would be inclined to set Ojukwu up in a checkmate.

---

[263] Njoku, Tragedy Without Heroes, Page 118

[264] *Akpan, Struggle for Secession, Page 63, Madiebo, The Nigerian revolution and the Biafra War, Pp. 377 – 91, and Anwunah, The Nigeria Biafra War: My Memoirs. Pp. 151 – 53.*

[265] *Njoku, Page 119*

And this Means War - Sic, Ita Vellent, et Sic Factum Est

Besides withholding the three-month salaries of displaced federal civil servants, at the end of March 1967, the federal government withheld Eastern Nigeria's share of statutory revenue allocations. In response to these provocations, Ojukwu passed the Revenue Edict to ensure funds for the region. On his part, Yakubu Gowon swiftly blockaded the Eastern Regions and deployed the Nigerian Navy to all sea approaches into Eastern ports: Calabar and Port Harcourt. In effect, the provocations of the Nigerian government played into Ojukwu's hands to justify secession and to set him up as a rebel who must be suppressed. After all, why would a potential adversary provide arms and money to the other side? There was nothing that justified withholding the salaries of displaced civil servants. On another side of the coin, if Ojukwu had accepted the modified or distorted Aburi agreement, it would have only been a matter of time for the federal government to find an excuse to declare a state of emergency in Eastern Nigeria. It would not have taken a long time to foment insurrection among the "minority" ethnic groups in Eastern Nigeria, who would be agitating for statehood. The attendant unrest and Ojukwu's high-handed attempt to suppress such unrest would immediately be grounds for a state of emergency. After all, the federal government was not oblivious to the efforts of the Ojukwu government's attempt to acquire arms in the black market. A plane smuggling arms into Eastern Nigeria had crash-landed in the Cameroons and was confiscated. Nigeria knew about this. About the end of January, a shipload of arms (without artillery guns or armored cars) arrived in Port Harcourt[266]. In his characteristic way, Ojukwu was so overjoyed that he practically broadcast it and personally supervised the offloading of the arms[267]. There is no gainsaying that Nigerian informants in the midst would make Nigeria aware of the haul, including its content and limitations[268].

Just like the systematic massacre of Igbo and Eastern Nigerian army officers even after there was an agreement on the cessation of hostilities in August 1966, the actions of the federal government in April 1967 were strategic. In April 1967, Gowon addressed diplomats during which he accused Ojukwu of violating the laws of the federal government by importing arms, appropriating the properties of the federal government, and frustrating peaceful resolutions. Gowon's speech was patently unfair and unjust. If Yakubu Gowon was sincerely honest, he needed to explain why the salaries of displaced civil servants had not been paid by the end of January and February 1967. There was an agreement about this and there was nothing that would have made the interpretation controversial. As supreme commander or commander-in-chief, he could have ordered it. The failure to implement even this simple gesture to the people caused a lot of alienation and was as much perceived as insensitivity and callousness as anything else that could have happened.

In September 1966, Gowon ordered federal workers who fled from Lagos amid the uncertainties to return by October 5, 1966 or lose their jobs. Shortly after Gowon's order and despite his condemnation of the atrocities against Igbos and other Eastern Nigerians, soldiers and civilians embarked on renewed massacres. I would raise the question to Gowon about what he would do if he had been in the position of these frightened Igbos. In as much as there were Igbos and other Eastern Nigerians who lived safely in Western Nigeria, there were still sporadic harassment activities against them. In this type of situation, not everyone has the same kind of luck, and for some people, the most prudent decision was to return home where safety was guaranteed—or at least one could be assured of no harassment or endangerment just for being Igbo or Eastern Nigerian.

Nigeria's strategic actions were motivated by the fact that the protagonists of a military solution saw that Nigeria was more militarily prepared than the Eastern Nigerian side— thanks to Ojukwu giving away his hands at the Aburi meeting and of course other intelligence-gathering activities. Comparatively, by the end of March 1967,[269] the Nigerian Army amassed troops in the Northern

---

[266] Akpan, *Struggle for Secession, Page, 52*

[267] *Ibid*

[268] *See Njoku, tragedy Without Heroes, Pp. 211 – 14 for Gowon's address to diplomats acknowledging his awareness that Ojukwu was purchasing arms illegally.*

[269] *Njoku, Tragedy Without Heroes, Pp. 126 – 27*

borders of Biafra that comprised two formidable brigades with artillery (76-mm Howitzers), armored cars, and British Ferret armored cars, earthmovers, among others. There was a navy with war vessels. Biafra had no artillery and no armored cars. A few helicopters were acquired, and an aged B-26 bomber from World War II vintage was in the arsenal. When Ojukwu was asked about weapons and informed by army officers that Biafra would not have sufficient weapons to fight a war, Ojukwu would dismiss them by saying that armaments were in the pipeline— though he provided no assuring evidence[270].

The protagonists of a pure military solution to the crisis had as their aim the ultimate subjugation of the Igbos by a coalition of extreme tribalists in Western Nigeria and the Northern ruling establishment. Their position was not necessarily borne out of a pure hatred of the Igbos but could be explained by a realistic political perspective. In other words, if we can do it, then so be it. Ojukwu himself was part of the ruling class. His error lay in the fact that he wanted to be the dominant player in the dominant class much like Napoleon Bonaparte or the Nazi Germans. Erroneously, Ojukwu sought to achieve his aims without making alliances and he made no compromises with constituent groups, such as the minority groups in Eastern Nigeria.

In effect, Ojukwu alienated and fought everyone, including his army officers, the declared enemy, the world at large, and even the Igbos that he purported to be speaking for or protecting. Ojukwu kept everyone in the dark and rejected all overtures for peace or consideration. He forsook reason like a man who was bewitched by the gods as a prelude for self-destruction and, like Don Quixote, rushed headlong and quite oblivious into the impending disaster. As will be argued later, for Ojukwu, it was all about his desire for self-aggrandizement both as a socially and politically powerful man and a wealthy man. Out of the pain and fears of his people he sought to profit, and he was not prepared to accommodate anyone in sharing the spoils.

After Decree No. 8, Ojukwu's survival edicts, and Yakubu Gowon's speech on April 8, 1967, it was clear that events were leading inevitably to war. The warmongers on both sides became intransigent and found excuses to reject any real and meaningful concessions that would bring about peace. What happened on both sides was akin to what the Roman delegation proposed to the Carthaginians to precipitate the Second Punic War, except that both sides were proposing simultaneously and both sides were responding simultaneously in accepting that war would be the ultimate resolution of the conflict.[271] For each side, it was all or nothing; sic, ita vellent, et sic factum est ("and so they wished and so it was").

Amid the tension between March and May 1967, efforts were made to find peace. Though Ojukwu failed to attend the meeting of the supreme military council in March 1967, he flew to Asaba to meet privately with Col. Adeyinka Adebayo (the military governor of Western Nigeria). Also, Lt. Col. David Ejoor (military governor of the Midwest Region) visited Ojukwu in Enugu to discuss the Aburi Accord[272]). No one knows the outcome or agenda of the discussion as no one has ever published the content of any propositions or offers made on either side. It might be safe to say that it was probably during Ejoor's visit that Ojukwu and Ejoor agreed on a nonaggression pact where Ojukwu may have promised not to attack the Midwest, the reason for which Ejoor made clear that he would not let the Midwest Region be turned into a war zone—that is until Biafra invaded the Midwest in August 1967.

Besides the meetings between Ojukwu and Ejoor and Adebayo, Yakubu Gowon wrote frantic missives to Ojukwu to find his way back into the Nigerian fold while avoiding offering the most

---

[270] Njoku, Ibid, Pp. 119 – 21, and Madiebo, The Nigerian Revolution and the Biafra War, Pp. 381 – 82

[271] *About 220 BC, while the Romans disputed the status of Sarguntum and Hannibal's investiture thereof, the Roman Senate sent a delegation to the Carthaginian Senate, demanding that Hannibal lift the siege of the disputed city. The leader of the delegation was Quintus Fabius Maximus. During the exchange, Quintus Fabius asked them what they would choose, war or peace? When the Carthaginians refused to answer, the leader of the embassy Fabius said: 'What is the delay? Here I bring you war and peace. Which do you choose?' In answer to their cry of "War!" he replied: "Thus you shall have war" (Titus Livius Patavinus, The History of Rome, Book 21. See also, Titus Livius Patavinus, The War with Hannibal)*

[272] Njoku, Tragedy Without Heroes, Pp. 118 – 20

basic non-controversial concessions that would protect Eastern NigeriansAmong other things, Gowon offered that

"The constitution can provide all safeguards necessary for state governments. Also, [the] program envisages the immediate appointment of a revenue allocation commission to find a new formula on basis of the principle of derivation and the need to provide adequate funds for essential government functions. The program will ensure justice and fair play for all the country.... Therefore, I earnestly appeal to you to cooperate to arrest further drift into disintegration. On the basis of the foregoing, representatives of all governments can meet without further delay to plan for smooth implementation of the political and administrative program adopted by your colleagues of the Supreme Military Council. Most immediate."[273]

More importantly, though, in early May 1967, Chief Awolowo led a delegation of a reconciliation committee that met Ojukwu in Enugu (May 6 and 7, 1967) to plead with Ojukwu not to take the East out of the Federation. The delegation included Chief Awolowo, Dr. Sam Aluko (a great friend of Ojukwu),[274] and Mr. Onyia, an Igbo man from the Midwest. During the meeting, Awolowo pleaded earnestly with Ojukwu and offered to transmit Ojukwu's demands to Yakubu Gowon. Among other things, Ojukwu demanded that all Northern Nigerian troops are withdrawn from Western Nigeria and the blockade of Eastern Nigeria must be lifted immediately.

In response to Awolowo's message, on or about May 17, 1967, the federal government sent a message that it was exploring the possibility of arranging British military protection for a meeting either in Benin or on a British Aircraft Carrier or Frigate off the shores of Lagos. Unfortunately, some information media immediately went public to say that arrangements were being made for the British to send troops to crush the East. Thus, this initiative died.[275] Nevertheless, on May 20, 1967, Yakubu Gowon accepted the recommendations of the National Reconciliation Committee, whereas Ojukwu declined to recognize the Committee and essentially insolently filibustered the meeting with Awolowo and Aluko. Ojukwu then dismissed the meeting as an ill-conceived child. Nevertheless, members of the Committee passed along his demands to the federal government.[276] After consultations, therefore, Gowon announced on May 25, that the supreme military council agreed to withdraw non-Yoruba troops from Abeokuta and Ibadan and establish a crash-training program to increase the Yoruba representation in the Army. This had always been one of Ojukwu's key demands, but it was also later echoed by Yoruba leaders. This move by Gowon was all a game. After all, the troops would be moved no further than Jebba Bridge and Ilorin and could be back in a minute. In any event, Ojukwu promptly rejected the proposition because the removal of Northern troops from Western Nigeria said nothing about Lagos. Based on intelligence information, it was clear to the policymakers in Lagos that Ojukwu had made up his mind to break away from Nigeria. During the meeting with Awolowo, Aluko, and Onyia, Ojukwu held a nocturnal meeting with Awolowo in which he made clear that the decision to secede was made and was irreversible.[277] Notwithstanding, one could criticize Ojukwu to the ends of the world, but even still, one needs to ask why it would take for Adebayo to come to Asaba in March 1967 to promise Ojukwu that the

---

[273] *Oluwatoyin Vincent Adepoju, Drums of Reconciliation, Drums of War: Efforts Between 1966 and 1967 to Persuade the South-Eastern Nigerian Leadership Not to Precipitate War,* https://www.scribd. com/ document/117715610/Drums-of-Reconciliation-Drums-of-War-Efforts-Against-the-Eruption-of-the-Nigerian-Civil-War-of-1967-1970

[274] *See Interview with Sam Aluko where Aluko claimed that he was a go between for Ojukwu and Gowon till the end of the war and even selected Ivory Coast – Cote D'Ivoire – as a place of exile for Ojukwu. https://www.nairaland.com/816532/what-ojukwu-told-me-before, Interview of Sam Aluko – Naira Land July 2020.*

[275] *Nowa Omoigui, Op. Cit*

[276] *Published by Online Editor, November 1, 2012, "Awo and the Nigerian Civil War: Memoranda of the Meetings Between His Excellency, Lt. Col. Odumegwu Ojukwu and A Delegation of the National Conciliation Committee Led by Chief Obafemi Awolowo.*

[277] *See Wole Soyinka, Op. CIt. See also https://www.nairaland.com/816532/what-ojukwu-told-me-before Interview of Sam Aluko – NairaLand July 2020*

Eastern Nigerian victims of the crisis would be paid their salaries as agreed at Aburi. Yakubu Gowon appeased the Yorubas but failed to extend the same gesture of support to the popular masses of Eastern Nigerians, especially the Igbos. The economic blockade that was imposed before secession did not help either.

On May 25, Ojukwu held a meeting with his consultative assembly to discuss secession. This consultative assembly that generally rubberstamped Ojukwu's propositions promptly mandated Ojukwu to declare the Republic of Biafra at the earliest possible opportunity. On the eve of the declaration of Biafran Independence, when the consultative assembly met, Ojukwu did not invite either Dr. Michael Okpara or Dr. Nnamdi Azikiwe to the meeting. At the behest of Dr. Michael Okpara, the former premier of Eastern Nigeria, Dr. Azikiwe, the past president, was invited to speak at the consultative assembly. According to Nwankwo,

"Dr. Azikiwe ... paid Ojukwu all the compliments due him as the reigning Governor of Eastern Nigeria. He even went ahead to acknowledge and agree with all the grievances adduced by Ojukwu... But Zik also rationalized that all that notwithstanding, the East must not allow itself to be stampeded or annoyed into a hasty and risky gambit or steps that are unsustainable. He pleaded with the audience to reflect deeply on what option to adopt over the critical questions that confronted the East at the time. He intimated, in fact pledged, that if he, Zik, was given the mandate, he would travel around the globe and persuade world leaders to compel the Gowon regime to pay adequate compensation for all the articles of trade and moveable properties abandoned or lost by Easterners in the North as well as pay reparation for the 30,000 Easterners butchered to death by blood-thirsty hordes in northern Nigeria, who had also previously massacred Ndigbo in Jos (1945) and Kano (1953) without any military coup as an excuse. But he pleaded that the East must not embark on secession – 'at least for now', because, he said, the action was fraught with danger and grave risk which the East was not equipped at the time to surmount. He was of course talking about the military situation on ground; the fact that virtually all the armaments of the Nigerian Military were stored in the North."[278]

The firm decision to secede must have been made about or before March 1967. Ojukwu had assembled his strategic committee, which included civilians and military personnel such as Lt. Col. Hillary Njoku, Lt. Col. Effiong, Lt. Col. Imo, Prof. Eni Njoku, Prof. Modebe, Prof. Nwakamma Okoro, and Mr. C. C. Mojekwu (Ojukwu's kinsman and right-hand man), among others. At their second meeting,[279] Col. Njoku presented a paper discouraging secession based on an analysis of the military and economic situation. Many others, including C. C. Mojekwu, Nwakamma Okoro, and Prof. Eni Njoku supported Njoku's proposition. Madiebo also reported extensively on the opposition to secession among the leaders. None of these people opposed secession entirely because they thought the east did not have legitimate grievances. Even Awolowo, the Western Nigerian leader (a Yoruba man) or Wole Soyinka (Yoruba man) acknowledged that much during their reconciliation ambassage of May 6 and May 7, 1967. For the most part, besides the genuine desire for the benefits of a united Nigeria, many, if not all, discouraged secession because it was not militarily feasible.

On May 27, 1967, Lt. Col. Yakubu Gowon announced the Decree that divided Nigeria into twelve states, three of which were in the Eastern Region. Ojukwu could not have been unaware of discussions to create states in Nigeria. Ojukwu acknowledged as much during a meeting of the consultative assembly in or about October 1966. He expressed a concern that states should not be created for the wrong reasons and acknowledged that constituencies should feel free to express their need for self-determination[280]. However, even before the federal government created new states, the discussions had been going on. What Ojukwu did, and I recollect this quite vividly, was to create twenty administrative provinces out of the original twelve provinces of Eastern Nigeria. Each province would have its own legislature and executive council. It was not clear, though, how

---

[278] *https://www.nairaland.com/1872985/zik-ojukwu-ndigbo-uchenna-nwankwo, Zik, Ojukwu and Ndigbo By Uchenna Nwankwo, August 25, 2014*

[279] *Njoku, Tragedy Without Heroes, Pp. 141 – 51*

[280] *Akpan, Struggle for Secession, Pp. 154 – 56.*

revenues or resources would be allocated or distributed to these provinces from the central pool—a question that the leaders of the minority areas had raised for which Ojukwu provided no clear answers.

Even in the proximity of the time for the promulgation of the Decree of May 27, 1967, the whispers for the creation of states were loud enough and many people from among the ethnic minorities were escaping and defecting to Lagos in anticipation. For the peoples of the ethnic minorities, the creation of states that gave them two states in the Calabar-Ogoja-Rivers area instead of the one that they had been lobbying for was a dream come true. For Gowon, the commander-in-chief on the Lagos side of the conflict, this was a masterstroke of diplomacy and a checkmate against Ojukwu. All along, both Gowon and the leaders in Lagos essentially gave Ojukwu a chance to see reason, at least their reason. I do not doubt, in my mind, that if Ojukwu had accepted Decree No. 8 from Aburi, it would have only been a matter of time for the Federal government to find an excuse to declare a state of emergency to either knock Ojukwu out or to neutralize him and still create states. However, if the leadership of Eastern Nigeria was militarily prepared, the Federal government will not be playing such a game. On the other hand, Ojukwu's hand would have been stronger in negotiating with the minorities for the creation of states in Eastern Nigeria and for Eastern Nigeria to have a united front. This conclusion goes to Njoku's point that God gave Eastern Nigerian leadership eleven months to prepare for peace or war and they prepared for neither.

During all the speculation, the rumors, and the maneuvers, a right-thinking strategist should have kept his options open and engaged the minorities in negotiations about the possibility of granting them their wishes. The first strategic move would have been to agree to the possibility and to negotiate boundaries. The next move would then be to get the minority elements in the army that fled from Lagos to allocate themselves to their roles as governors and other potentates in the state. Ojukwu would then work with them to align with the minorities in the north to create states in the north. Such a move would immediately earn him allies in the Middle Belt of Nigeria. Finally, Ojukwu could have worked on the state structure within the boundaries of Eastern Nigeria nested in a united Nigeria with the area commands in the military where Eastern Nigeria would be in a quasi-confederacy with Nigeria. Armed with these alliances, Ojukwu would have been able to present a united front, with himself as a heavy-weight player in the scheme of things where he could regularly shake concessions out of Nigeria and eventually achieve his aim of being a ruler or president of Nigeria. Upon negotiating with the minorities and being armed with the regional command, arrangements would have been made to recruit and arm soldiers in proportion to the ethnic composition of each region and deploy them strategically to protect the lives and property of his people and the Igbos, against strangulation. Indeed, the leaders of the ethnic minorities of the Eastern Region would have gladly worked with Ojukwu to procure arms to protect the entire periphery against federal domination.

One can only surmise that Ojukwu's adversaries could see that his demands at the meetings from April 1967 to May 1967 were faithless. Ojukwu was not negotiating the right things. He demanded to withdraw federal troops from all Western Nigeria, including Lagos, and to lift the blockade against Eastern Nigeria. Even the simplest analysis would lead to the conclusion that Ojukwu was demanding that Federal soldiers be withdrawn from the West with the hope that it would free the Yoruba ethnic group to rebel against the federal government, though such an expectation was naïve.

In response to the creation of states in Eastern Nigeria and Northern Nigeria, Ojukwu led the promulgation of secession of Eastern Nigeria and declared the independent and the sovereign Republic of Biafra. Yakubu Gowon immediately denounced the secession and urged Ojukwu to retrace his steps and return to Nigeria. Ojukwu would, of course, not heed such a call. In or about the first week of June 1967, the Supreme Military Council appointed governors for all twelve states. As a gesture of peace and goodwill, the Council appointed Ojukwu governor of the East Central State. Of course, he did not accept it. On July 1, 1967, Ojukwu was dismissed with ignominy from the Nigerian Army, but he did not care. On July 6, 1967, Yakubu Gowon and the supreme military council declared police action to forcibly return Biafra to Nigeria. In response to Gowon's declaration, Ojukwu made a broadcast declaring romantically that the Republic of Biafra would enter a total war with Nigeria—much like one sovereign state declaring war on another country.

Chapter XIII

QUEST FOR PEACE INTRA BELLUM

Illusions and Intransigence

There is a saying in ancient Rome, that goes: "Quaem Dei Perdere, Dementant Prius"[281] Whom the gods want to kill, they first make mad. On both sides of the conflict, there was a tendency to be oblivious to reason. The Nigerians manipulated the peace process because they believed that any war that comes out of the crisis would last no more than two weeks or four weeks. The Biafrans thought that if they frustrate Nigeria long enough that they would give up the enterprise. With these misguided attitudes, leaders on both sides led the populations into a traumatic experience. This attitude pervaded the entire peace process during the war. However, this madness was more apt for the Biafran leadership during the peace processes as the war wore on. There were opportunities for honorable peace that the Biafran leadership gave up because they appeared to be impervious to the evident degeneration of their situation.

Within one week of the war and before the third week of July, Nigerian forces captured the northern Biafran town of Nsukka and the home of the University of Nigeria. Nigeria also captured Ogoja, and the Third Marine Brigade (later called the Third Marine Commando Division) captured and or menaced the coastal port of Bonny, south of Biafra. The Nigerian Army offensive was not anything like a simple police action that Gowon had announced. The initial offensives were pure military action supported by artillery and armored cars. Maybe Yakubu Gowon thought it was minor military action. Notwithstanding, the swift military actions and successes of the Nigerian Army would not end the war as swiftly as Nigerians had anticipated. According to Maj Abubakar Atofarati,[282] "Delivery of arms and equipment for the Nigerian Army was hastened. Nigerian Army Headquarters (NAHQ) Operations plan envisaged a war that will be will be over within a month [*in four phases*]. The four phases were (1) Capture of Nsukka, (2) Capture of Ogoja, (3) Capture of Abakaliki, (4) Capture of Enugu [*and the war will end*]."[283] For example, some officials of the Nigerian Army had characterized the Biafran Army as an army of pen pushers, apparently referring to the fact that most Igbos and Eastern Nigerians in the army were in the clerical and service units and branches. They probably ignored the fact that the majority, or at least, a substantial proportion of the infantry commanders and artillery commanders, were also from Eastern Nigeria and Igbos. Many had combat training and could quickly train combat soldiers. Meanwhile, the strength of the Nigerian Army on the eve of the war was less than 12,000, of which 3,000 were in the East

---

[281] *He Who the Gods Wish to Destroy, they First Make Mad – This expression, taken from ancient Rome, is an adaptation from an earlier Greek saying that "Evil appears as good to whoever the gods want to destroy." In Latin, the actual expression is that "Who Jupiter wants to destroy, he first takes away the ability to reason," or "Quam Iupiter vult peredere, dementat prius." The English-speaking world adapted this to say, "...Whoever God wants to destroy, He first makes mad..."*

[282] *The Nigerian Civil War, Causes, Strategies, And Lessons Learnt, Abubakar A. Atofarati (Major)* <u>*https:// www.calitown.com/the-nigerian-civil-war-causes-strategies-and-lessons-learnt-by-major-abubakar-tofarati/*</u>

[283] *Words in Italics are mine*

despite the slaughter of many of its men. Moreover, of the remaining soldiers, there was a need for manpower in other parts of Nigeria. Therefore, given the determination of the Biafrans, the existing force of the Nigerian Army that attacked Biafra in July 1967 could not have achieved the stated objectives so swiftly. The units that attacked Ogoja were well equipped. Nevertheless, they could not easily overrun the territory and end the war as swiftly as they thought, especially considering the determination and apprehension of Biafrans regarding the intentions of the Nigerian Army and government. On the other hand, if the Nigerian Army had sufficient intelligence information about the limited armaments of the Biafran Army, they might have captured Enugu during the first two weeks of the war (see Njoku and Madiebo).[284] Or maybe not.

By the end of July and early August, the Nigerian Army had not come close to achieving its expectation of ending the war so swiftly. Biafra had recaptured Bonny. On August 9, 1967, Biafra invaded the Midwest and was moving to capture Lagos in a lightening military operation. This short-lived [hairbrained and myopic] military victory gave Biafrans the illusion that they were gaining the upper hand in the war. During Biafra's Midwest Offensive, the Organization of African Unity (OAU) was preparing for its meeting in Congo Kinshasa, slated for September 11 to 14, 1967. Biafra used the opportunity to make its case to the OAU, though the Nigerian government had received assurances that the Nigerian civil war, which it termed a strictly internal crisis, would not be on the agenda of the OAU meeting. The Biafran government protested and wrote, inter alia, "In this connection, the remorseless slaughter by Northerners of several thousand... unarmed Eastern Nigerians in May, July and September 1966, was merely the worst round of a continuing genocide unleashed in Jos in 1945 and followed up in Kano in 1953 against people of Eastern Nigerian origin."[285] This reference to genocide may have pressured members of the OAU to include the Nigerian conflict in its agenda for its September 1968 meeting. After its mid-September meeting, the OAU agreed to send a delegation of four heads of state to Lagos to attempt mediation of the conflict. As the delegation was about to meet in November 1967, Biafra's Midwest Offensive collapsed as the Nigerian Army rallied and recaptured the Midwest and began to menace Onitsha on the western boundaries of Biafra abutting the River Niger. When Nigerian troops captured Asaba, the last Igbo-speaking town in the Midwest of Nigeria, they engaged in a wanton, indiscriminate, and savage massacre and despoilation of the local population— men, women, and children.[286] On September 22, 1967, Ojukwu executed Victor Banjo, the commander of the Midwest offensive, along with three other experienced officers, calling them saboteurs and accusing them of attempting to overthrow him. Two of the six-member OAU delegation withdrew from the mission. Whether the delegation withdrew because Biafra's fortunes were waning or because of the heinous atrocities of Nigerian troops, it was all well and good by the Nigerian government, which did not want any meaningful mediation of the conflict.[287]

After repeated attempts by the Nigerian Army from October 1967 through January 1968 to take Onitsha and neutralize Biafra failed, the Nigerian government was under pressure to talk. After the fiasco that followed the failure to take Onitsha, some would say the military situation of the civil war stabilized into a stalemate, but that is not quite so. In October 1967, Nigeria captured Calabar, Biafra's eastern seaport, and connected Ogoja to the Northeast of Biafra in what could be called a brilliant strategic move that effectively sealed off the border with the Cameroons. Meanwhile, Biafra's propaganda machine, accompanied by images of malnourished children inundated global

---

[284] *See also Atofarati, Ibid.*

[285] *Roy Doron and Charles G Thomas, Introducing the New Lens of African Military History, In: Journal of African Military History, Dec 2019, Pp. 79 - 92*

[286] *See Emmanuel Okocha, Blood on the Niger: The First Black on Black Genocide, The Untold Story of the Asaba Massacre in the Nigerian Civil War Paperback – January 1, 2006 and Elizabeth Bird, Surviving Biafra: A Niger wife's Story, 2018 for detailed accounts.*

[287] *According to Naira land, retired Maj. Gen. Ibrahim Haruna is quoted as testifying during the Oputa Commission (1994), "whatever action he or his troops took during the war was motivated by a sense of duty to protect the unity of the Country ... As the Commanding Officer and leader of the troops that massacred in Asaba, Owerri and Ameke-Item, I acted as a soldier maintaining the peace and unity of Nigeria ... If General Yakubu Gowon apologized, he did it in his own capacity. As for me I have no apology, it was as barbaric as the 1966 coup; it was as barbaric as the pogrom."*

media outlets in the spring of 1968. The public outcry that ensued pressured Western governments, especially the British, to intervene to end the war and what the world saw as genocide. Furthermore, Biafra received diplomatic recognitions from Gabon, Ivory Coast, Zambia, and Tanzania, often citing the genocide that they saw as anathema to any genuine or legitimate justification to unite Nigeria. Even more so, in March 1968, the Biafran Army achieved an impressive military success against the Nigerian Army at the Battle of Abagana—where Biafra almost annihilated a 20,000-man division of the Nigerian Army that was on its way to connect Enugu to Onitsha. Though the Nigerian Army finally captured Onitsha, it was a hollow victory in which the Nigerian Army straggled into Onitsha much like Napoleon straggled into Moscow following the Battle of Borodino (1812). Though the Nigerian Army captured Onitsha, the link between Abagana and Enugu to Onitsha was never complete.

In response to world pressure, the British-led Commonwealth of Nations (composed of former British colonies in Asia, Africa, Australia, and the Americas) sponsored a peace conference in Kampala, Uganda, for May 1968. This peace conference finally gave Ojukwu and his government what they considered global attention. In a strange turn, the military and diplomatic successes that boosted Biafra's hope were beginning to be eroded by significant military losses and disasters. Nigeria captured the port city of Port Harcourt, further crippling Biafra's war effort as all sea lanes and connections to the outside world were now cut off. Thus, at the inception of the conference, Biafra's prospects for survival had waned considerably. However, in Ojukwu's miscalculation, he believed that the proximate diplomatic successes would force the Nigerians into a ceasefire or that international pressure would force the Nigerians to discuss peace on his terms.

In my view, neither side attended this conference in good faith. The Kampala conference ended in a confrontation and ended acrimoniously. On their way to the peace conference in Kampala, Ojukwu gave strict instructions to the delegates that Biafran sovereignty was nonnegotiable. According to Akpan[288] [289] and Odogwu[290], the instructions given to the delegates amounted to dictating terms of surrender to a vanquished enemy. Of significance in Ojukwu's instructions is the demand that Nigerian forces must withdraw from Biafran territory to the boundaries before the war started and then to pay reparations not only for the properties of Biafrans lost during the Northern crisis in 1966 but also for the destruction and anguish caused to Biafrans during the war. These kinds of demands indicate madness and self-delusion.[291] On the Nigerian side, their recent military successes, and observations of starving children among their adversaries, motivated them to become even more determined to achieve a military solution.

The Nigerian side came to the peace talks probably as a means to halt any other country's recognition of Biafra. For as long as the peace talks were going on, all action on recognition would cease, so the diplomatic world would not see a country as undermining the peace process. Specifically, the Gowon administration insisted that Biafra must renounce cessation before any peace talks could begin. On the one hand, Ojukwu insisted that there must be an unconditional cease-fire. But the Nigerian delegation saw such a demand as a ploy by Biafra to rearm if the peace talks failed. Subsequently, Biafra would be able to engage in a protracted military resistance. To his credit, Ojukwu had given signals to the Commonwealth Secretary, Arnold Smith, that he was prepared to negotiate a return to Nigeria.[292] But the Biafran delegation was not prepared to engage in a negotiation based on a united Nigeria unless they were certain what they were getting into. It

---

[288] *Akpan, The Struggle for Secession, Pp. 137 – 38, Stremlau, Pp. 160 - 80*

[289] *Stremlau, Pp. 160 – 82 for extra detailed rendition of the efforts by the Commonwealth Office to arrange peace.*

[290] *Benard Odogwu, No Where to hide, Pp. 133 – 34*

[291] *Why would an adversary withdraw from territory they have gained in a war? What should have been instructive to the Biafran leadership is that Israel, in spite of United Nations resolutions would not even heed the demand to withdraw from occupied Arab territory, which legitimately belonged to their adversaries—notwithstanding potential diplomatic consequences. Now, Biafran leaders are demanding that Nigeria should withdraw from territory they considered having been recovered from a rebellious section of the country.*

[292] *See Stremlau, Op, Cit., Page 142.*

is not clear whether Arnold Smith related his discussion with the Biafran Mission to Gowon and his administration.

For Biafra, its intransigence was a tactic to undermine the peace process with the hope that any countries that saw that the peace process collapsed would consider the ongoing genocide and weigh in on the side of recognition to undermine Nigeria's resolve. But the Biafran leadership under Ojukwu did not fully appreciate the realities of international diplomacy. At the time that the Kampala peace talks collapsed, the collapse of Biafra was all but a matter of time in the eyes of many in the diplomatic circles. Specifically, besides all the seaports falling into Nigerian hands, Aba and

Owerre, in the hinterland (the heartland of Igbo land) also fell to the federal forces and Umuahia was credibly threatened. Moreover, the Nigerian government engaged in a flurry of diplomacy while delaying and undermining the peace process. When Gabon recognized Biafra, the President of Togo Gnassingbe Eyadema and the leaders of other Francophone West African countries were immediately rattled and expressed concerns about pressures on them to recognize Biafra or at least express policies that were favorable to Biafra (Stremlau, Pp. 182 – 90). Notable among these countries were Dahomey, with a large Yoruba population, and the Niger Republic, with a substantial Hausa (with kindred in Nigeria) population. As the peace talks in Kampala tottered, Yakubu Gowon flew to Lome, the capital of Togo, to meet with Eyadema. Earlier in the year (1968), a plane carrying a load of Nigerian currencies—about £N7.1 or $21 million—had landed in Togo for refueling. Eyadema promptly seized the plane and returned all $21 million to the Nigerian government. The Nigerian government rewarded Eyadema with $200,000 at that time. During this later visit to discuss the Nigeria/Biafra crisis, Yakubu Gowon raised the reward to $2 million[293].[294] Besides, the hefty $2 million carrots, Gowon agreed to lift visa restrictions for Togolese traveling to Nigeria for fewer than ninety days. This relaxed visa restriction opened the way for a thriving smuggling business of Togolese merchants in Nigeria. In the same spirit that Gowon visited Eyadema in June 1968, he visited President Ahmadu Ahidjo of the Cameroons in July 1968. During the visit, Gowon sought assurances of neighborly help from the Cameroon president[295]. It was probably during this visit that Gowon conceded the oil-rich Bakassi Islands, off the coast of Calabar, Nigeria, to the Cameroonians. Besides, Ahmadu Ahidjo was a Fulani Muslim from the northern part of the Cameroons bordering on Nigeria. Therefore, he must have felt an affinity with the Nigerians and would naturally take sides with them. Finally, Ahidjo would not encourage secession given that Southern Cameroonians bordering on Eastern Nigeria were restive and could be encouraged to initiate a secession move if Biafra was supported by a Cameroonian president.

Following the failure of the Kampala peace talks, the OAU hosted another attempt in August 1968 to mediate the conflict in Addis Ababa under the auspices of Emperor Haile Selassie. This meeting began in July 1968 with a preliminary meeting in Niamey, the Niger Republic. Both Gowon and Ojukwu were invited but they never met. The delegations from Biafra and Nigeria agreed on the

---

[293] *Stremlau, International Politics of the Nigerian Civil War, P. 183*

[294] *Note should be made of Gowon's calculated move. It is instructive to note that Eyadema was the army chief who treacherously connived with the French to assassinate Togo's first post-independence president, Sylvanus Olympio, and later overthrew the next president Grunitzky for Eyadema to then become president for life from 1967 until he died in 2005. Eyadema was the perfect man to be bribed.*

[295] *Stremlau, The International Politics of the Nigerian Civil War, Pp. 186 – 87.*

Addis Ababa meeting for August 1968. Among the agenda items were conditions for the cessation of hostilities and the supply of relief materials for the civilian populations in Biafra. Once more, Biafra lived an illusion as they considered the peace talks to be a breakthrough given that they gave themselves the impression that Biafra was accorded diplomatic status through such an invitation. This meeting also ended in failure, and though Gowon was invited and Ojukwu expected to meet with him, Gowon declined to attend.

This meeting also ended with no agreement to end the war or the genocide. Once more, both intransigence and treacherous behavior on both sides caused this meeting to collapse[296].[297] During the Addis Ababa conference, Emperor Haile Selassie urged the Biafran delegation to consider a proposal that he had made that would have required Biafra to negotiate based on a united Nigeria. Although Aba and Owerre had fallen to Nigeria, the Nigerian troops at Owerre were surrounded and being strangulated. The Nigerian debacle at the Battle of Abagana was still fresh, and Nigeria's attempt to capture Umuahia and Oguta ended in miserable disasters. Nevertheless, the net result of several military moves was in Nigeria's favor. At the same time, Nigerian leadership under mounting world pressure was prepared to make concessions that guaranteed the security of the Igbos and to tolerate the presence of foreign peacekeeping soldiers[298]. Furthermore, they now realized that the war was going to be a costly affair, though their victory was all but assured. On the other hand, Yakubu Gowon initially demanded that the leadership of Igbos must be changed. Although he eventually did not insist, Gowon had no business proposing who should lead the Igbos.

On the other hand, while Biafra had achieved or demonstrated quite a bit of military credibility, the wise thing to do at the time of the Addis Ababa peace initiative was to accept, at least in principle, or negotiate based on One Nigeria, even if to buy time and diplomatic support. However, as Effiong and Odogwu report, Ojukwu gave the diplomatic delegation that included the likes of Nnamdi Azikiwe, Phillip Effiong (Ojukwu's second in command), Prof. Eni Njoku, and Prof. K. O. Dike no room for maneuver. Biafran insistence on the non negotiability of Biafran sovereignty gave the Nigerian side and the OAU mediators no cause for further tolerance. Sensing that victory would ultimately come, even if at a high cost, Nigeria decided to minimize further communication with the Biafran delegation. For example, while the Biafran and some Nigerian delegates remained in Addis Ababa, the leader of the Nigerians purportedly went home for consultations and never returned.

First, Ojukwu misconstrued or mismanaged the latitude given to him by the OAU. The leaders of the OAU—and especially the concerned Francophone countries—had gone to great lengths and bent over backwards to convince the recalcitrant Nigerian side to extend a direct invitation to Ojukwu. Out of sheer arrogance, the Nigerian government maintained this strange attitude that any OAU mediation should listen only to the Nigerian side of the conflict. Though at the November 1967 détentes, the OAU mediators wondered aloud how in the world there are two sides to a conflict and one side insists that there should be no contact with the other side, even if, as Nigeria put it, the matter was purely internal[299]. Secondly, Ojukwu conceded that the military situation weighed against Biafra and demanded that Biafrans would not agree to return to Nigeria until their many grievances were addressed. Secondly, Ojukwu proposed that he and Gowon meet privately as they did at Aburi

---

[296] *Ralp Uwechue (Pp. 139 – 41) describes post-Kampala explorations of alternative peace talks where Francis Nwokedi blew an opportunity for diplomatic help from the Tunisian government. Specifically, President Bourguiba of Tunisia proposed a possible discussion of a confederate arrangement and Francis interjected, with a choking mouth full of Caviar, "You mean we should surrender." It was this same Francis Nwokedi who single-handedly proposed and muscled through the infamous Decree 34 that riled the Northern Nigerians.*

[297] *Akpan, Struggle for Secession, Pp. 138 – 39, Effiong Nigeria and Biafra: My Story, Pp. 241 – 43, Uwechue, Reflections on the Nigerian Civil War, Pp. 140 – 41 and Odogwu, No Where to Hide, Pp. 137 – 42*

[298] Stremlau, Op. Cit, Pp. 202 – 03.

[299] *Stremlau, International politics of the Nigerian Civil War, Pp. 99 – 101.*

in January 1967. Gowon quickly rejected this proposition[300].[301] Ojukwu also insisted, and got his way, that the peace talks of August should not be done under the OAU Consultative Committee because he did not want to concede to the heavily biased position on the Committee that predicated the talks on the preservation of Nigerian unity. But this attitude is bewildering as Ojukwu had already hinted that Biafrans could return to Nigeria if their many grievances were addressed. Eventually, the talks proceeded to Addis Ababa, where the Nigerian delegation presented its conditions for settlement. Specifically, Nigeria presented the following key propositions, among others[302]:

1. *Renunciation of secession by a joint declaration which would proclaim the unity of Nigeria but would not require the other side to proclaim a unilateral pronouncement of renunciation.*
2. *"... the joint declaration ... could be followed by a cessation of hostilities and should be disarming of the rebel forces..."*
3. *After disarming the rebels, the normal policing of the rebel-held areas will be the responsibility of police ... drawn mostly from people of Igbo origin ..."*
4. *Until mutual confidence is restored, external forces should be stationed in Igboland from Ethiopia, India, and Canada ..."*
5. *The Military Governor and members of the executive should be Igbos ... Composition to be negotiated ...*
6. *"A general amnesty should be granted in most cases ... other claims could be examined ..."*

Other propositions are perfunctory and a matter of citizenship right and should not even be the subject of discussion. For example, the proposition (number 8) that Igbos will be reabsorbed into the civil service. What did Enahoro and the Nigerian delegation expect, if they seriously mean that Nigerians truly have equal rights?

The public Biafran counter proposition did not make sense and did not explicitly address the Nigerian propositions. However, privately and to Emperor Haile Selassie, Prof. Eni Njoku conceded that Biafra was prepared to make concessions and renounce secession[303]). Anthony Enahoro cabled this suggestion to Gowon[304]. Specifically, Biafra made the following propositions[305]:

1. *The maintenance of Law and Order in Biafra must be solely the responsibility of the Biafran government.*
2. *"We must maintain our own armed forces..."*
3. *"Biafra must be a member of international organizations..."*
4. *"Biafra must have the right to enter into international [economic] contracts ..."*

These Biafran propositions did not make sense vis-à-vis the Nigerian proposition, except on the matter of security within Biafran territory or just Igboland. Privately, Eni Njoku clarified that the use of Biafra in the propositions was more symbolic and did not substantively drive the position of the Biafran delegation. The implication is that secession could be renounced. Prof. Eni Njoku also indicated that Biafra was prepared to discuss and compromise on cease-fire lines and the composition of peacekeeping forces and territorial boundaries[306]. However, Njoku insisted that Biafra must maintain independent armed forces behind any ceasefire line and retain some degree of international standing, independent of Nigeria.

---

[300] *Stremlau, Ibid, Page 202*

[301] *Only God knows why Ojukwu would think that the matter between Biafrans and Nigerians would be settled just between him and Gowon. The conflict was not their private affair and should have had nothing to do with their private attitudes. Peoples were involved on both sides. What in the world was he going to discuss privately with Gowon that could not be put on the table by delegates from both sides?*

[302] *Stremlau, International Politics of the Nigerian Civil War, Page 202*

[303] Ibid, Page 204 footnote #81

[304] Ibid

[305] Ibid

[306] Stremlau, Op. Cit, Page 204, Footnote #82)

On balance, the propositions made on both sides were negotiable, though the Nigerian side made more meaningful propositions. Biafran propositions were not altogether outlandish, especially because Eni Njoku privately sent feelers to indicate that the use of Biafra was more symbolic than of substance and was prepared to discuss the composition of a peacekeeping force. While the Biafran proposition of an independent international standing and armed forces was simply untenable, these could easily have been negotiated away at the table with appropriate agreement on the strategic deployment of Nigerian forces, limited disarmament, and strategic deployment of Biafran or Igbo soldiers. For example, Biafran (Igbo) soldiers could be preponderantly disarmed, leaving only about 3,000 that were strategically deployed while Nigerian soldiers would also be strategically deployed away from the boundaries of Igboland. The Igbo soldiers could also be mixed in foreign observers as a way of monitoring their behavior and controlling their actions. The most objectionable proposition of the Nigerian side was the limited granting of amnesty. Nigeria had no moral locus standi to be talking about amnesty. If not for the senseless commencement of massacres of Igbos in late September 1966 and the continued harassment into December 1966, the strategic exodus of Igbos would not have occurred. If the Nigerian government had taken responsibility to truly rehabilitate the afflicted, the population of Igbos would not have felt so aggrieved to support the secession. The idea of limited amnesty, as objectionable as it was, would also have been negotiated away quite easily at the table.

In any event, Anthony Enahoro left for Lagos on August 8, 1968, and never returned. According to Stremlau[307] Gowon reviewed the propositions of the Biafran delegation, met with his military advisers and decided to discontinue the talks. Conceivably, Gowon and his military advisers and comrades could foresee victory and decided to terminate the talks. To the extent that Biafra frustrated the talks, their position was quite bizarre and was more the result of illusion. As of August 1968, Aba and Owerre had fallen into federal hands and Umuahia was credibly threatened. Meanwhile, there was limited realistic expectation of recognition by other African countries, much less from Europe or Asia, the latter of which had little or no interest in African matters. The peace talks continued in Algiers, Algeria, in September 1968.

The OAU conference in Algiers assembled around September 13, 1968. The outcome of the conference was all but predictable. By this time, the French government gave assurances to Nigeria that France would not recognize Biafra and would make no effort to persuade any other African country to recognize Biafra. The Biafran envoy in the Ivory Coast conveyed as much to Ojukwu, stating that Biafra had little hope of being addressed at the Algiers conference.[308] While Biafra's hope waned, Ojukwu had Biafra's African friends (Cote D'Ivoire, Tanzania, Gabon, and Zambia) distribute a 3,500-word appeal to the delegates at the conference. Several of the delegations, through their leadership, took a clearly anti-Biafra stand. The latter did not influence the conference. Specifically, Biafra's appeal to the OAU was that the only way to safeguard the life and liberty of Biafrans was to have two independent sovereign states of Biafra and Nigeria with an arrangement for cooperation along the lines of the East African Common Market. But the OAU paid no heed to the Biafran appeal. In the end, their final resolution was that Biafra should call off the secession and cooperate with Nigeria. However, the resolution also recommended that Nigeria should declare a general amnesty and cooperate with the OAU in ensuring the physical security of all Nigerians until mutual confidence was restored. Finally, the OAU called for cooperation in the delivery of humanitarian relief to the needy.

The peace talks of 1968 having failed, the OAU made other attempts, beginning in April 1969, to end the conflict by arranging other peace initiatives. All these failed, including initiatives in November 1969 as Biafra was about to collapse. Ojukwu rejected all of them, *quam dei perdere,* on some strange excuses. In April 1969, Biafra sent a representative to meet with Nigerian negotiators in Liberia (Monrovia) in conjunction with the OAU Consultative Committee on Nigeria. Before the meeting, Ojukwu impugned the integrity and sincerity of the Liberian president, but Gabon and

---

[307] Stremlau, Op. Cit, Page 205

[308] Stremlau, Op. Cit, Pp. 268 – 70

the Ivory Coast put pressure on him to become more flexible in his demands for preconditions[309]. Therefore, he relented and agreed to participate. At this meeting, Nigeria agreed to peacekeeping forces to ensure the security of the Igbos. But Biafra, once again, insisted on the cessation of hostilities as a precondition. The Nigerian delegation accepted wording that did not refer to the twelve-state structure, but the Nigerian Army needed to maintain control of the minority areas in Biafra. Nevertheless, the Biafran delegation scuttled the conference over semantics about a "United Nigeria."[310] In August 1969, the Pope once more was able to get delegates from both sides to meet in Kampala, Uganda.

These talks also went nowhere as Biafra would not agree to renounce cessation. About December 8, 1969, once more, the OAU attempted to broker peace. Ojukwu insisted that the peace talks were not arranged by the OAU but by Hailie Selassie in his personal capacity because Ojukwu had lost confidence in the OAU.[311] Ojukwu even rejected a meeting in Yaoundé, in the Cameroons, because he insisted that if Ahmadu Ahidjo had wanted him to attend, Mr. Ahidjo, the president of the Cameroons, should have invited him directly.[312]

According to Ben Gbulie[313]), on January 4, 1970, the secretary-general of the United Nations, U. Thant, had contacted Ojukwu and urged him to sue for peace under the auspices of the OAU. Though Ojukwu had rejected these recent overtures, it is doubtful that the Nigerian side would have been positively responsive to peace overtures by the end of November 1969. As of November 1969, the final offensive was commenced with newly acquired Soviet-supplied 122-mm rocket launchers If Ojukwu had agreed to all their terms by December 8, the peace offer under the auspices of the Pope in Kampala, Nigeria, may well have stalled and insisted on surrender terms that may have been only a notch less humiliating than the immediate rounding up and execution of our leaders. Specifically, according to Ben Gbulie,

"On Tuesday, January 6, 1970, I was summoned to an emergency ... meeting with the Head of State... I was at [this meeting] ... So was Brigadier Tim Onwuatuegwu ... appraising the situation ... which was that although the Nigerian forces had not crossed the Imo River ... considering the morale of our troops ... Biafra did not stand a dog's chance of surviving the latest offensive... and that unless there was a (doubtful) miracle, our leaders should do well to sue for peace... and it would be sheer suicide for Biafra to concede to the enemy the right to win the war militarily ... A good raconteur (storyteller), he (Onwuatuegwu) informed me that on Sunday, January 4, 1970, U Thant had appealed to Ojukwu to sue for peace through the OAU resolution on the war."[314]

It would have been too late to sue for such peace. If I were on the Nigeria side, I would not have listened to or entertained such an overture. In April 1969, shortly after the Biafran recapture of Owerre and the Biafran drive that nearly recaptured Port Harcourt, if Ojukwu had sued for peace and if Nigeria had rejected it, Biafra would have received massive support. The prospect of the latter would have compelled Nigeria to concede a no-questions-asked resolution based on twelve states but with greater control of self-destiny, without two armies as I suggested earlier. The Igbos and other groups within Biafra would have had a better deal today.

On January 10, 1970, less than six weeks from the OAU proposition of early December 1969 and less than ten days after the appeal from U. Thant (secretary-general of the United Nations), Ojukwu departed from Biafra, and on January 12, 1970, Biafra surrendered under the leadership of Maj. Gen. Phillip Effiong. Finally, we had a United Nigeria. But did we have peace? No! No peace was given

---

[309] *Stremlau, International Politics of the Nigerian Civil War. P. 312*

[310] Ibid, Page 318

[311] *Stremlau Ibid Pp. 363 - 66*

[312] *This is the point where I truly concluded that, all along, Ojukwu had actually lost his mind. All his defiance in the face of disaster was from a man that was not in control of his animated state.*

[313] *Ben Gbulie, The Fall of Biafra, Pp. 192 – 94*

[314] *At the meeting, Ben Gbulie, Op. Cit., Pp. 194 – 96, Ojukwu browbeat those attending the high-powered meeting, but none of them had the courage to come out clearly to tell Ojukwu to call off the war. Ojukwu actually gave the impression that there was no question of gift wrapping an olive branch to the Nigerian side (Page 97). Four days later, Ojukwu departed Biafra.*

to the Igbos. Now the real fear and suspense would begin. Ironically, when Gowon announced the end of the war, he declared "No victor, no vanquished." Really? I do not think so.

VAE VICTIS – Woe unto the Vanquished

The sad irony was that everything that the Igbos had sought to defend against was visited on them through most of the war and at the end of it. It was as if the other Nigerians said, "You are still talking, now we will give you more of the same until you stop complaining." The stated justification for the secession was that the Igbo people needed protection from a perceived annihilation and wanton slaughter. The fear was that their fellow Nigerians were determined to wipe them off the face of the earth, and there was probably a good reason to think so. For example, the observation by Legume of the *London Observer* was that there was no remorse for the wanton slaughter in Kano Airport nor was there any hesitation in a man's response at Oturkpo that they were doing the world a favor by eliminating the Igbos.[315] The pogrom of 1966 was not the first time that Igbos were attacked and slaughtered in Northern Nigeria. In 1948 and 1953, there was a planned rally by Awolowo's Action Group party. Instead of attacking the members of the Action Group (which was Yoruban-based), who had made substantial inroads into Northern Nigeria, the residents unleashed mayhem and engaged in wanton slaughter of Igbo residents in Kano and other Northern Nigerian cities. This time there was no pretense of a one-sided coup. Though the riot was provoked by the heckling of Northern Nigerian leaders in Lagos because they hesitated to argue for early independence for Nigeria, that was no excuse for the murderous riots that took place. But the insolent heckling was perpetrated by members of the Action Group, most of whom were Yoruba, not Igbo.[316] Therefore, the riots reflected a hatred for the Igbos. It was not, therefore, farfetched to assume that Igbos and even the rest of Biafrans had a cogent reason to seek a separation to protect their life and property. The sad irony though is that Ojukwu and some of his hawkish advisors contemplated secession immediately after the July coup[317, 318]. Ojukwu was dissuaded by the fact that no one knew the whereabouts or fate of Aguiyi Ironsi, the abducted supreme commander. But even more than that, and in opposition to some of his senior advisers, there were still Igbos in Northern Nigeria who could easily become victims of a secession move. When the massacre of Eastern Nigerians blazed in Northern Nigeria, the Eastern Nigerian government claimed that two Million Igbos and other Eastern Nigerians fled and became refugees in the East and later Biafra. Ironically, between one and two million Eastern Nigerians perished because of starvation during the civil war that followed, though the war of secession was fought as a means of protecting those two million people.

During the pogrom in Northern Nigeria, the Eastern Nigerian government propaganda reported that women were wantonly raped and property destroyed in an orgy of savagery.[319] During the war, Gen. Ojukwu urged Biafrans to fight on, reminding them that savage Northern Nigerians would rape their women and close their schools. During the war, Nigerian soldiers routinely roamed the villages and kidnapped and arrested women, and raped them. At Ovim, my hometown that fell to federal forces in March 1969, Nigerian soldiers on patrol routinely arrested women and raped them by the wayside, and went about their business. At other times, they simply went in and took people's wives and returned them after sexually abusing them for as many days as it pleased them. On July 10,

---

[315] *Charles Keil, The Price of Nigerian Victory, Africa Today, Jan – Feb. 1970 Vol. 17 (1). Pp. 1-3.*

[316] *There is no attempt here to suggest that Yorubas should have been lynched. It would have been equally wrong to lynch them.*

[317] *Take note that the contemplation of secession for Ojukwu was as convenient as it was strategic. The Northern mutineers of July/August 1966, gave as their condition for ending the killings of Igbo and Eastern Army officers that the North be allowed to secede from Nigeria, which suited Ojukwu quite well. Even Graham Douglas did not disagree but suggested that Eastern minority ethnic groups must be consulted*

[318] *Akpan, The Struggle for Secession, Page 68 and K. Whiteman, "Enugu: The Psychology of Secession, 20 July 1966 to 30 May 1967, in Nigerian Politics and Military Rule, Prelude to Civil War", S.K. Patrick Brick, Ed., University of London Press, 1970, Pp. 110 - 112)*

[319] *Nigerian Pogrom, 1966 – Eastern Nigerian Government, Op. Cit. Pp. 6 – 7.*

1967, four days after the war started, all schools—primary, secondary, and higher education—were closed to release resources (manpower and financial) for the war. The rape of Igbo women folk was even celebrated in song, at least by Nigerian troops at Ovim.

A major part of Eastern Nigerian propaganda reflected that the genuine fear among Igbos was the desire to annihilate the Igbo race through genocide. The behavior of the Northern Nigerians and the opportunism demonstrated by other ethnic groups, even in Western Nigeria, did not give the Igbos cause to be comfortable. The behavior of Nigerian forces during the early stages of the war and at Asaba and in other Igbo-speaking areas of the Midwest was clearly indicative of genocidal intent.[320] As the Nigerian Army captured parts of Biafra during the early stages of the war, the invaders pillaged and slaughtered the population. People fled at the sound of artillery and gunfire. From the air, the Nigerian Airforce avoided the battlefields, though Biafra had no air defenses, and instead bombed dense urban populations and heavily crowded marketplaces, killing numerous people in air raids that were designed to demoralize the populace. Ironically, these air raids hardened the resolve of the people to fight because they saw the fight as their only guarantee to eventual safety. Sadly enough, the struggle was to no avail. The Nigerian Army steadily constricted Biafra and herded the Igbo population into smaller and smaller spaces over time, like animals in a siege cage. Hunger and starvation set in to exterminate those that were not killed by gunfire on the ground or battery from the air. There was nowhere to hide from the onslaught. If Nigeria had truly wanted to slaughter all Igbos, who in the end were herded into less than one-quarter of Igboland, they would have done so. The world might have condemned them for it over the next one hundred years or into eternity, but that would merely be academic discourse.

The events that followed the end of the civil war make clear that there was a victor and there was a vanquished. Nigerian Army officers were asked to report to Lagos. Some were herded into detention camps around the East and flown to Lagos in cargo planes like livestock and detained. Though Gowon declared that "...there would be no Nuremberg trials...", something like the Nuremberg trials did take place because a kangaroo military tribunal was set up and the January boys were all imprisoned for four years and then released. All were dismissed. All senior Biafran Army officers who had been in the Nigerian Army before the crisis were dismissed with no benefits[321]. After about thirty years, the dismissals were converted to retirement, and even Ojukwu received a pension at his Nigerian Army rank of lieutenant colonel. However you look at it, the dismissals and detention of the January 1966 boys were unjust. Army officers who were reabsorbed selectively into the Nigerian Army lost years in advancement and could not rise above the rank of colonel, after which they were forcibly retired. The Igbos were punished and relegated in other ways as a people.

The crowning act of victimization was the nullification of the Biafran currency. According to Effiong,[322] he approached Adm. Akinwale Wey, the head of the Nigerian Navy, who stated that the Biafran currency was a counterfeit. Effiong (Pp. 317) made a passionate appeal to Yakubu Gowon, who responded vaguely by referring the matter to the central bank and saying that the matter was being considered. In fairness to Yakubu Gowon, he made clear that the Biafran pound could not be exchanged pound for pound with Nigerian currency. The Nigerian government decreed that Biafran

---

[320] *Considering that the Nigerian government insisted on a starvation and their murderous behavior at places like Asaba and Onitsha is clear indication of intent. Though they had the opportunity after the war but did not engage on a systematic arrest and execution, is irrelevant. The way they were going, if it took more years and more mass starvations, they would not have hesitated to exterminate the Igbo race just to achieve their objective. Such a vision was clear to President Richard Nixon of USA when he stated, in sum and substance that "... the extermination of a people to win a war is never justified no matter how morale the war...". Clearly, there was no fundamentally moral justification for the Nigerian war against Biafra. This is not to suggest that unification of the country was not justification enough. On the other hand, there is nothing that justifies forcing one group of people to be joined to another group to become one country, especially when the secessionist group is not guaranteed security of life and property.*
[321] *Njoku, Tragedy Without Heroes, Pp. 177 – 78. Effiong, Nigeria and Biafra,: My Story, Pp. 325 – 28 & PP. 359 – 68, Peter Odu, A Future that Vanished, Pp. 217 – 22, Anwunah. The Nigeria Biafra War, Pp. 277 - 80 and Fola Oyewole, The Reluctant Rebel, Pp. 200 - 10).*
[322] *Phillip Effiong, Nigeria, and Biafra: My Story, Pp. 316 – 17.*

money held in the hands of the people would become worthless. Biafrans were asked to deposit all their money and would receive a maximum of £N20 for all deposits, regardless of how much money they had in their possession. This was rather wicked, but it was also the vindictiveness of a victor against the vanquished (*vae victis*). In the middle of 1969, the Biafran pound exchanged at about £B30 to £N1. Immediately after the war, the Biafran pound exchanged for about £B50 to £N1. If the Nigerian government wanted to be fair, they should have exchanged the Biafran pound at some rate, say, £B60 to £N1 with a limit, say, of £N200 or even £N125. In 1970, this would have made a big difference as a genuine and sincere rehabilitation gesture on the part of the Nigerian government. Therefore, Gowon's statement of pursuing "rehabilitation, reconstruction, and reconciliation" was a travesty.

There were many rebellions in Nigeria, such as the Northern Crisis. But if treason prosperes, who dare call it treason? The more powerful get away with their treason. The mass slaughter of fellow citizens with the cry of "Araba!" was not the solution to anyone's grievances. The army and the police, branches of the federal government, perpetrated in no small measure the atrocities of savagery against Igbos during September/October 1966. These events, which continued into November and December 1966, contributed immensely and indeed were crucial in creating the fatal schism that precipitated the civil war. It was treason, but the offenders were powerful and got away with it.

At the end of the day, was it all worth it? This war was avoidable. But the four principal actors made their calculations. The coalition of Nigerian groups had concluded that they had to gang up against Ojukwu and the Igbos, as Ojukwu and the Igbos were in the clutches of Ojukwu's clique. The others in the conflict are the Northern Nigerian (Hausa-Fulani or Islamic) ruling class, Ojukwu's coterie of advisers with their hidden agendas, and the Igbos as a people. For the Igbos, there was a perception of "do or die," which was, in every way, justified. The Igbos also falsely believed that they had the wherewithal to engage the opposition. Even if they had the wherewithal, was it the optimal option? The answer is no. The optimal decision was not to secede from Nigeria. Given that the Nigerians had handed the Eastern territory to the leaders of Eastern Nigeria, the best decision was to bring the most experienced politicians into the process and develop military capacity to restructure Nigeria along the lines that Awolowo and Njoku had suggested.

There was genuine fear coupled with anger and indignation. For the fear, one could justify that it is sometimes better to fight and possibly be conquered or successfully defend oneself than to surrender and certainly be annihilated. At the same time, the better part of valor is discretion. A good soldier fights and lives to fight another day. If Ojukwu and his coterie of advisers had in their hidden agenda to appropriate the benefits of the pain and suffering of the people, certainly they overshot their mark. They all had the opportunity to think more strategically and live to fight another day. I believe that these leaders were taken more by greed than anything else. For the Nigerian and the Islamic ruling establishments, it was certainly worth it, even if it did come at a much higher cost than anticipated. If they had calculated the costs more accurately, they may have prepared better and would have concluded their enterprise more speedily. Today, they are reaping the benefits. All said and done, what lessons were learned and what can be concluded?

Chapter XIV

THE FOLLY OF THE IGBO MAN

Njo diri Nwantâ Âbuo Ọ gâ Ê buru Otû Mmanya (A Child Confronted with Two Adversities is Well Advised to Appease One of Them)

Truth be told, the core of the Biafran resistance was the Igboman or the Igbos. This is not to suggest that the so-called minority ethnic groups that made up 40 percent of Biafra were disinterested. Indeed, though they had their apprehensions about the Igbos, they were mostly sympathetic, though with divided loyalties. Under the circumstances, the war was led by the Igbos. Therefore, what the Igbo leadership did and did not do will be the reference point for the reflections and discussion that follow below..

The folly of the Igbo man during the period leading up to the war, during the war, and even after the war falls into three categories. One of them is complacency in their misguided sense of superiority. The second was and is still their lack of cohesion, which led to the absence of effective collective leadership. The third is their failure, especially during the war, of diplomacy. During the war, much of Biafran diplomacy was amateurish. Biafran war diplomacy was utopian and guided by simplistic notions that someone might consider, at best, idealistic and, at worst, quixotic. Throughout human history, manifest and overt diplomacy have been constrained by realistic self-interest. Covert support is a different thing altogether. Seeking covert support, therefore, is an optimizing or satisficing approach or stop-gap measure that may eventually lead to overt diplomatic support when the latter becomes realistically convenient. The Biafran leadership failed to grasp this—Ojukwu was responsible for this failure based on his attitudes and dispositions. Ojukwu's inner clique of advisers was also part of the problem or even the crux of the problem. A good example is their lamentation, after Ojukwu returned from Aburi, that Ojukwu did not bring them independence and sovereignty. Seriously? Did Ojukwu's inner circle of advisers expect the other regional governors of Nigeria to go to Aburi, Ghana, and elsewhere to negotiate the sovereignty of Biafra from the rest of Nigeria—in effect, handing Biafra to them on a platter? Somehow, they were living an illusion.

Diplomacy with the So-Called Eastern Minority Groups

Biafra was majority Igbo. But the Igbo majority was marginal in that there were fourteen million Biafrans of which 64 percent (nine million) were Igbos and 36 percent (five million) were other ethnic groups. While these five million "minorities" were made up of a polyglot of minor ethnic and linguistic groups, they were generally, if not uniformly, apprehensive of the Igbos. At least the Ibibio and the Efiks, though, constituted a substantial bloc that could not be taken lightly. Certainly, at the time of the crisis in 1966, the characteristic Igbo diffusion into all corners of Nigeria had given these small ethnic groups a sufficient enough experience of the Igbo that they saw the Igbo as neighbors that were barely tolerated. The diffusion of the Igbo was such that versions of the Igbo language were spoken among some of the Eastern minorities. For example, the Opobo and the Kalabari had distinct versions of the Igbo language, though they had their language and clear cultural identity. If the war had not given them a chance to break clean, the Igbo language over a period of fifty years might have become a lingua franca in some of these places, or at least a second official vernacular.

Besides their leverage in numbers, these other ethnic groups were in control of access to the sea aside from the estuary of the Imo River, which Biafra could only control with effective military force. It would have only required 10 to 15 percent of them to be formidable against Biafra, and as a matter of principle and if they had cooperated with Nigeria, they could have effectively doomed the Biafran struggle. For these reasons, the Igbos needed to work with them in a manner that brought along those among them that were either indifferent or hostile. If Biafra had succeeded with their preponderant support, these minority groups would have stood to gain more from an independent Biafra than from being part of a larger Nigeria. For starters, they were in a better position to be an effective pressure group within Biafra than within Nigeria. They had more valent kinship relationships with Igbos than with the larger Nigeria. It is in this context that one can say that the Igboman and the core Biafran leadership did a poor job of incorporating and motivating the minority groups to join the struggle.

Besides documented or alleged mistreatment of Biafra's ethnic minorities during the war and their lamentation thereof before the war,[323] the Biafran leadership did not give the minorities a real chance to identify with and support Biafra.[324] As earlier argued, there was no inherent reason for Biafra to include the Efiks, Ibibios, Kalabaris, or any other ethnic minorities as part of their sovereign entity. In late July and early August 1966, during the rebellion of the July coup plotters, one of their demands was that the killings of Southern army personnel would end if the North was allowed to secede from Nigeria[325]. Ojukwu responded that the Eastern Region would then go its way and revert to its sovereignty. Truth be told, there was no sovereign Eastern Nigerian entity with boundaries that included the ethnic groups that inhabited Eastern Nigeria in 1966. Eastern Nigeria was as much a convenient British contraption and mere geographical expression as Nigeria was and has been referred to. Any argument that justifies the superficiality of Nigeria and its disintegration equally justifies the superficiality of Eastern Nigeria and its disintegration. Therefore, Ojukwu's assertion that implied a sovereign state of Eastern Nigeria by whatever name it would choose was a travesty. During the nineteenth century (1885 and 1893) when the British established the Oil Rivers Protectorate, and later the Niger Coast Protectorate, they signed separate treaties with the sovereign Kings of Bonny, Opugbo (Opobo), Calabar, and, maybe later, Onitsha and Aro Chukwu. The concept of Biafra was taken from the Bight of Biafra that had been given to some area of the Atlantic Ocean by the Portuguese in the fifteenth and sixteenth centuries.[326] On that account, I could not agree better with Graham-Douglas,[327] who was not averse to Biafra if it was the solution that all Nigerians agreed to as a means of avoiding bloodshed in a forced Nigerian entity. This is what Douglas (Pp. 3 – 4) said:

"On July 29 [1966], we were awakened to the news of another coup ... We were paralyzed by fear ... which soon gave way to hope of immediate independence and sovereignty for Eastern Nigeria ...

---

[323] *See Nabo Graham-Douglas Ojukwu's Rebellion and World Opinion, Nigerian National Press, 1968, Pp. 16 – 17. See also Odogwu, No Where to Hide, Pp. 101 – 103 and Kenneth Ryeland, The Up-Country Man, Pp. 261 – 64.*

[324] *See also Arua Oko Omaka, The Forgotten Victims: Ethnic Minorities in the Nigeria-Biafra War, 1967-1970, Journal of Retracing Africa, Spring 2014, Pp. 25 - 40*

[325] *Akpan, The Struggle for Secession, Pp. 33 – 43, Graham-Douglas, Ojukwu's Rebellion and World Opinion, Pp. 3 – 9*

[326] *It is not likely that Biafra was an entirely imaginary concept or word that the Portuguese made up from thin air. During their explorations of the Atlantic Coast around Eastern Nigeria, there may have existed a potentiality or a cultural or political, or cult influence that caused them to refer to the general area as Biafra. However, unlike the Kingdom of Benin or the Kongo, there is no record of this Biafran entity or a reference to some cultural or political domination that was known, even in vague legend, as Biafra. It is also possible that a potentiality existed that was obliterated either by the military shock of the slave trade or an ecological disaster brought on by a European epidemic disease, like the chicken pox in the Americas, before the Europeans could make formal contact with its potentates.*

[327] *Graham Douglas, Op. Cit.*

by news reaching us ... that negotiations were going on ... that the firm stand of Northerners was the disintegration of Nigeria into four or so independent nations [based on] existing regions ... If the secession of the North from the Federation (Page 4) and the consequent disintegration of the Federation was the solution to the pestilence of periodic coups ... I was all for it ... but in the present circumstances ... I had advised the Military Governor to secure the solidarity of all the peoples of the Region lest the same divisive factors responsible for the imminent collapse of the Federation ... tended to the fragmentation of the East itself." Graham-Douglas later stated, inter alia,

"According to Ojukwu, ... since the January coup, the constitution was suspended and only the Army was holding the country together ... and following the July Coup ... the Army turned on itself ... the Federation had disintegrated ... each component of the Federation was free to go its own way... Going on the same premises one could argue that the East has also disintegrated ... and we are all thrown back into the position in the 1800s when the British ... were entering into treaties with the chieftains of the Oil Rivers Protectorates ... Accordingly, we would not have an Independent Eastern Nigeria ... but an independent Bokiland, Kalabari, Onitsha, Owerri ... If the peoples of these various entities wished to come together to be an independent country, they would do so by means of a treaty."[328]

It is on this point that the ruling Biafran clique was sorely misguided in their actions. In the first place, if Ojukwu argued that the Army turned on itself after the July 1966 coup, he was being dishonest. If one could make the argument that the Army turned on itself, that occurred on January 15, 1966. What happened on January 15, 1966, was that a group of army officers not only murdered the elected officials but also treacherously murdered senior army officers in an ethnically one-sided manner. The officers from the affected ethnic groups felt betrayed either genuinely or for convenience. Secondly, there was this presumption that Eastern Nigeria, a creation of the colonial British, automatically included the extant constituent ethnic groups. Indeed, the ruling group in Biafra purposely ignored and even suppressed the wishes and demands of the other ethnic groups. It is well known that minority ethnic groups in the original three regions of Nigeria had been agitating for the further division of Nigeria into states. Even as the Eastern Nigerian Constituent Assembly, created by Ojukwu, was preparing to meet in the later part of 1966, there were propositions for the creation of states—

The Midwest Region was created out of the Western Region in 1963. The Middle Belt region constituencies had been demanding the Middle Belt State out of the Northern Region, and there had been pressures for the Calabar-Ogoja-Rivers State from Eastern Nigeria. The Biafran ruling clique was fully aware of this. Furthermore, during the period of turbulence from July 1966 through January 1967, the constituencies in Eastern Nigeria made their wishes for separate states known and demanded as much. Ojukwu and his advisers argued at some point that the proposition to create states in Eastern Nigeria was an attempt to emasculate the East because the North would be one solid entity. But their attitude appeared to be a pretense of sorts since the winds of change were also blowing to create states in the Northern Region of Nigeria. As the crisis of 1966 wore on, Ojukwu, as governor, set up a constitutional committee to make recommendations on an appropriate constitution for Eastern Nigeria. Ojukwu himself acknowledged the work of the committee in a meeting of the

---

[328] *Ibid, Page 8.*

Consultative Assembly on October 4, 1966.[329] The recommendations of the committee, headed by Graham-Douglas, recommended, inter alia:

"Endorses both the principle of the creation of more states and the statement that the creation of more states is not what is needed... Since the desire on the part of minority groups ... [the desire] for self-determination is the drive behind the demand for the creation of states ... accordingly recommends that creation of any new states should be along linguistic and tribal boundaries."[330]

Even more directly, Ojukwu acknowledges that *"The representatives of the minority areas spoke frankly pointing out what they consider ... acts of neglect and injustice ... representative of the old Calabar Province ... submitted a memorandum that they wished to be grouped into one state ... and the representative of the old Rivers province... At these meetings, the people spoke boldly ... and fearlessly ... They, therefore, felt that a separate state ... would cure all these ills."*[331]

Ojukwu responded to the apprehensions of a major constituency and went on to offer lame and self-serving arguments that begged the real questions of the minority groups, specifically,

"I was encouraged by the fact that those before me were ... responsible people who were prepared to admit that the mere creation of states was not a panacea for the fears and rights of minorities ... Ladies and gentlemen, nobody in this region is opposed to the creation of states for healthy objectives ... All right-thinking persons who believe in Nigeria run on sound democratic principles have advocated this ... I would loathe being a party to any discussion about the creation of states on the poisoned principle of HATE, FEAR, and SPITE."[332]

First, no one ever suggested or believed that the mere creation of states was a panacea for political problems. However, given the proximate history of the peoples that made up Nigeria and the regions in 1966, the ethnic groupings and alliances of proximate groups was the best basis to use for the creation of states. Furthermore, most delegates attending the national Constituent Assembly supported this criterion for the creation of new states. Secondly, to the extent that Ojukwu had an alternative idea, he did not offer what he considered to be healthy reasons. Besides, Ojukwu should consider himself one voice among many. He had no authority—divine, natural, moral, or constitutional—to override the wishes of masses of a people.

This is where the challenge comes. Under the circumstances, the east was faced with the potential of being attacked by the north or an alliance of the other three regions. At the minimum, a Northern-dominated Nigeria where the other two regions were effectively silenced would have been a formidable foe against the east. The north had already agreed to concede to the creation of the Middle Belt state.[333] Since the minorities in the East were clear in their demand for a separate state and a monolithic north was perceived as a problem, a strategic thinker would have immediately agreed to concede the demands of the eastern minorities and then align with them to put more pressure on the other Nigerians to break up the north beyond the concession of a Middle Belt state. Furthermore, the Middle Belt, which had been writhing under the domination of the large Moslem North, would immediately work with Ojukwu and the Eastern Nigerian ruling elite to pressure the North to break up some more. All that Ojukwu needed was to negotiate boundaries if he had had an eye on the control of resources from the oil-producing areas. A far-thinking strategist would have negotiated boundaries and presented or created a united front and voice for Eastern Nigerians. As I pointed out earlier, the Eastern minorities stood to gain more from a united Eastern Nigeria than from a larger Nigerian entity. Even if the secession were to have become the outcome of the drift and

---

[329] *Ministry of Information Eastern Nigeria, Nigerian Crisis 1966, Eastern Nigerian Viewpoint, October 1966, Pp. 55 – 62.*

[330] *A. H. M Kirk-Greene, Crisis and Conflict in Nigeria, London, Oxford University Press, 1971, Pp. 255 – 58.*

[331] *Ministry of Information Eastern Nigeria, Nigerian Crisis 1966, Eastern Nigerian Viewpoint, October 1966, Pp. 56 – 59.*

[332] Ibid, Page 59

[333] Eastern Nigeria Government, Nigerian Crisis 1966, Eastern Nigerian Viewpoint, Oct. 1966Page 61

crisis leading from October 1966 to May 1967, the minorities may have seen states within Biafra as a satisfactory arrangement. Even if there had been no secession, the Eastern group of states would still present a united front with common services. Finally, by keeping his options open and keeping negotiations simmering at the bottom of things, Ojukwu would have played a trump card after the meeting of Northern Leaders of Thought on May 1, 1967. At this meeting, the Northern Leaders of Thought passed a resolution that additional states should be created in the Northern Region, even if states were not created in other regions. At that point, Ojukwu had time to offer state creation to the minorities and join in putting pressure on the other regions to make good on the resolution to create states in the Northern region. The minority groups in the east would have been glad to work with him and the majority Igbo ethnic group. At this point, he could have demanded that the governors of the eastern states be selected from among those who fled from the coup of July 1966 and that no Northern troops or those from any other region could be deployed in the east for at least five years. The officers from these eastern states and their political leaders would have been glad to cooperate with him because it would have given them a lot of bargaining control with the federal government. With the option of having their state under military control, the political leaders of the Eastern states would have gladly worked with him to smuggle arms into the east to ensure the enforcement of the agreement. But Ojukwu was selfish. The logic of my argument is borne out by the outcomes of post-military government civilian elections in 1999, 2003, 2007, 2011, 2015, and 2019. The eastern states voted to support the same party, though the candidates did not always have a person of Rivers State or Southeast origin. This time around, more than thirty years after independence, the Igbos and their ethnic neighbors voted along the same lines. They could not claim that they were coerced or dominated by the Igbos. There is a clear indication that the ethnic neighbors of the Igbos are willing to cooperate with the Igbos when they feel free to do so of their own volition. Therefore, one can only surmise that Ojukwu's resistance to state creation in the Eastern Region and working cooperatively with the ethnic neighbors of the Igbos were based on some unspoken agenda. Regardless, he failed.

Diplomacy with the Midwest and Western Nigeria

Relationships with the Midwest of Nigeria and Yorubaland are another example of a colossal failure of strategic diplomatic thinking. War is fought and won as much with lethal armaments as with diplomacy. There is no gainsaying that there were Western Nigerians as well as Midwestern Nigerians who were sympathetic with the Igbos and Biafrans and who made clear that they were not prepared to shed more Igbo blood to keep Nigeria united. These elements among the Yorubas and Midwesterners were not necessarily in support of Biafran secession, but they were indifferent as to whether Nigeria won or lost the war with Biafra. At the very least, they were not prepared to take up arms to compel the Igbos to return to Nigeria. Just before the war began, Yakubu Gowon vowed to crush the rebellion:

"When Gowon vouched to crush the rebellion, progressive Yoruba intellectuals deplored the language ... [For example] Professor Hezekiah Oluwasanmi, Vice-Chancellor of the University of Ife, described the use of the word as unfortunate. Justice Kayode Eso of the Western Court of Appeal said: "Crushing the East was not the way to make Nigeria one."[334]

Awolowo's statements cited earlier and as will be analyzed, later also indicate a lack of enthusiasm for military action against the Biafrans. The military governor of the Midwest, David Ejoor, maintained a policy of noninvolvement and warned Ojukwu not to invade the Midwest. For example, Njoku reports that he received a call from Brig. Imo when Nigeria attacked Biafra from the northern approaches and that Ojukwu wanted to see him. According to Njoku,

---

[334] *America's Secret Files: The Untold Biafran Story* National Custodian Newspaper, *https://www. facebook.com/1362516680591228/posts/americas-secret-files-the-untold-biafran-storysecret-american-diplomatic-dispatc/1408275649348664/* September 2019.

"When I got to Ojukwu in the State House, he had tears in his eyes and a glass of brandy in his hands ... He took some time to brief me on the latest situation...I wanted to know naturally if he had been hiding weapons away from the people in view of the Aburi Accord ... He [Ojukwu] said no... On whether the Western Region was going to fight with Nigeria against Biafra or whether there was an understanding that they too were seceding ... He said no, but that Banjo was in touch ... On whether the Midwest Governor, Lt Col. David Ejoor would fight on the Nigerian side or stay neutral ... he said that the Midwest was afraid of being turned into a battleground... He did not know how long that would last."[335]

The Yorubas of Western Nigeria were not all gung-ho to crush the Igbos or to defeat Biafra. Ojukwu was also aware that the federal military government of Nigeria desired to respect the neutrality of the Midwest and the governor's request to deploy mostly Nigerian troops of Midwestern origin along the Midwest border with Biafra. Indeed, all the top commanders of the Nigerian Army along the Biafran border were Igbos of Midwestern origin. For this reason, the Biafran government was confident that there would no invasion from the Midwest. Even if the federal government decided to attack Biafra, Biafra had friendly commanders in their midst who would inform the Biafran Army. Furthermore, if the Nigerian top command decided to override the governor of the Midwest, the Niger Bridge and the surrounding areas could have been mined using explosives, allowing the Biafran Army to stop such an invasion, as subsequent events proved in September 1967. This and previously discussed military inadequacy explain why Ojukwu and his advisers should not have invaded the Midwest in August 1967. Besides that, the Midwest could have been a corridor for breaching the economic blockade throughout the war. To the extent that the Igbo commanders and others in the Nigerian Army stationed in the Midwest cooperated in scheming the Biafran invasion of the Midwest, they were foolish. The economic argument in favor of not invading the Midwest is explained next.

Economic Strategic Logic for not Invading the Midwest.,

In any war, there are material shortages for food and basic civilian amenities such as clothing, transportation, and housing because priority is given to the production of war materiel. The Nigerian side of the conflict had full access to the sea and borders with friendly countries north (the vast Arab world), east (Cameroons), and west (all of West Africa). The Nigerian side also had a navy that they used to immediately monitor and later blockade Eastern Nigeria, and later Biafra, even before the secession was announced as early as November 1966 or a little later. The blockade was not limited to the sea, which blocked access to the outside world, but it was also a land blockade that constricted and practically forbade trade between Eastern Nigerians and other Nigerians, including their kindred in the Midwest of Nigeria.[336]

The Biafran side faced formidable disadvantageous obstacles from the beginning. Besides limited access to the sea (which was controlled by not-so-loyal constituents), Biafra was flanked by hostile neighbors to the east—the Cameroons. It was simply not possible to seek an alliance with the Cameroon government because their president at that time was a Moslem, probably Fulani, Northern Cameroonian (Ahmadu Ahidjo). Ahidjo was very hostile to Biafra and even admonished Igbos not to agitate openly. Besides, the major food-producing areas of Igboland were in the northeast of Biafra and close to the Nigerian border, which is easily vulnerable to attack and invasion. Finally, Biafra did not have a navy that could effectively mitigate the Nigerian sea blockade or at least minimize its adverse effects on Biafran shipping. Before the war began, critical food items such as beef, dried fish (Mangala), onions, and beans were brought into the east from Northern Nigeria. It would, therefore, have been clear to Biafran leadership that it would be imperative to keep open a corridor for food importation and that the Midwest provided such an opportunity.

---

[335] Njoku, A Tragedy Without Heroes, Pp. 125 – 26
[336] *See Egodi Uchendu, Women and Conflict in the Nigerian Civil War, Pp. 139 – 42*

Under the circumstances, Biafra was faced with three strategic alternatives. The first was the vigorous defense of the coastal waters to the south. This would require a good navy and forging of strong alliances, making peace with the coastal communities of the Ijaw, Ibibio, and Efik ethnic groups of Biafra. The second was a vigorous defense of the Biafran boundaries with the Cameroons because there was always a thriving and strong Igbo community in what was called the Southern Cameroons. The indigenous communities of this part of the Cameroons did not have any special allegiance to the larger Cameroons and would have cooperated in the continued smuggling of goods into Biafra. Many would have done it because they may have been secretly sympathetic and others for the profit they would make. Even military and border security personnel would do brisk business and look forward to the bribes and graft from the smuggling. As I narrated earlier, up and until the Cameroonian border was closed by Nigerian strategic invasion in November 1967, my great uncle and many others were still smuggling goods into Biafra through the Cameroons. Therefore, even if Nigeria captured Calabar and effectively blockaded the sea corridor into Calabar, Biafra would still have been able to do business through the Cameroons. The third strategic objective was to keep open the borders with the Midwest. This latter objective is explained next.

Considering Biafra's military weakness and lack of armaments or even if Biafra had been militarily strong and prepared, there is always the possibility that Biafra might lose access to the border with the Cameroons. In any strategic analysis, there is the basic requirement to consider Strengths, Weaknesses, Opportunities, and Threats—the well-known SWOT analysis. The major strength that Biafra had was the determination of the people to defend Biafra. In addition, the Midwest Region of Nigeria on the western border of Biafra had a substantial Igbo population that was fiercely loyal to Biafra. They had an equally good excuse to demand that Nigerian forces should not compel them to go to battle against their fellow Igbos to the East nor should they be expected to offer friendly assistance to the federal army. Moreover,

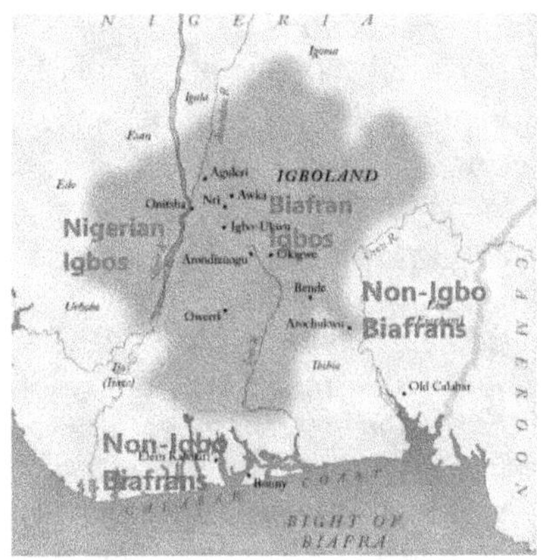

the policies and attitudes of the Midwest Governor David Ejoor buttressed the attitude of the predominant Igbo officers of the Midwest Command of the Nigerian Army. Specifically,

"during the Commander-in-Chief's (Gowon) conference on June 7 [1966] in Lagos, Lt. Col. David Ejoor (Military Governor) was told that 'Midwestern State will be kept free from active operations unless where necessary, but the border between the Eastern States and the Midwest will be completely sealed off.'"[337] Following this event, "on June 18 [1966], at a speech in Asaba, Ejoor reiterated a public commitment that the Midwest would not be turned into a battlefield... The prevailing wisdom at the time was that the war was a confrontation between the 'Northern' and 'Eastern' regions in the larger context of Nigerian unity.... On July 11, a week after 'police action' had commenced, Ejoor declared that the state would promptly and resolutely resist any incursion of its territory."[338] Accordingly, "three keys to the armory [in the Midwest contingent of the Nigerian Army] were made.... Midwest Ibo officers (Lt. Cols. Conrad Nwawo and Sylvanus Nwajei) held two keys, while Major Sam Ogbemudia (Bini-Edo) ostensibly held the third."[339] "To ensure the credibility of the promise not to involve the Midwest in the war, at the time of the Biafran Invasion, there had been no 'northern' troops in the Midwest. The Nigerian Army 4th Area Command had two battalions organized in nine (9) companies ... under the command of Lt. Col. Conrad Nwawo [Igbo

---

[337] *Nowamagbe A. Omoigui, The Midwest Invasion of 1967: Lessons for Today's Geopolitics,* Text of a keynote speech delivered at the Nigerian Independence Day Celebration sponsored by the Nigerian Women Association in Columbia, South Carolina on October 3, 1998 https://www. dawodu.com/midwest.htm

[338] Ibid. This later statement made on July 11, 1967, must be referring to Governor Ejoor's warning to Ojukwu or a reaffirmation of his earlier warning to Ojukwu not to invade the Mid-West (See A.H.M. Kirk-Greene, Crisis and Conflict in Nigeria, Volume II, Oxford University Press, 1971, Page 5).

[339] Ibid

and Igbo speaking] ... all but three officers on the ground ... of the rank of Major and above were Midwestern Ibos.... Indeed, in addition to possessing a sizable chunk of the rank and file, 13 out of 15 strategic command positions were held by Igbo or Igbo speaking officers. Specific selected examples are, Commander of the 4th Area Command (Lt. Col. Nwawo - Igbo) General Staff Officer for Operations, (Lt. Col. Nwanjei - Igbo), ...Commander, Benin Garrison, including two companies (Lt. Col. Ruddy Trimnell – Igbo speaking, though not Igbo, Battalion Commander (Lt. Col. Igboba – Igbo), ... Battalion Commander (Lt. Col. Ochei – Igbo),"[340] among others.

A further indication of the control that Igbo army officers had in the Midwest contingent of the Nigerian Army is illustrated by an event that took place in August 1967. "On August 5 [1967], a company of soldiers led by Lt. Igbinosa (Midwest – non-Igbo) arrived in Benin from Lagos with orders to escort a consignment of boats, procured by Ejoor from the Delta, to the Bonny sector in the East, where Lt. Col. Adekunle was operating. Igbinosa was promptly turned back by Lt. Col. Nwawo and other Midwest Ibo officers at the Area Command HQ...Ojukwu issued a public warning that day, to Ejoor, reminding him of his pledges to keep the region neutral."[341] Furthermore, the federal blockade was not enforced by troops of the fourth area command, none of whom were under the operational control of Ejoor. Trade with the Onitsha market continued unabated and flourished. The narrative of Egodi Uchendu[342] is instructive at this point. Specifically, According to Uchendu,

"The Federal Government's blockade on the Eastern region necessitated a boycott of the trading links with Eastern Nigeria... The Eastern Region utilized the months before the outbreak of hostilities to stock up on supplies .... Food items were moved in incredible quantities ... The sealing of the Niger Bridge did little to check the trade relations between the two Igbo groups as boats and canoes were employed to cross the River Niger ... Equally ineffective were directives prohibiting travelers going to Asaba from the Eastern Region to carry no more than five pounds (£5). The same injunctions banned foodstuffs from the Aniocha, Ika, and Ukwuani areas from finding their way to Eastern Nigeria and directed the seizure of lorries loaded with foodstuffs bound for Onitsha from Anioma ... Despite all these, Asaba had a site where canoes plied a thriving trade with the Eastern Region ... The trade association continued until the war broke out ... Until August 1967, the trade route was from Asaba to Onitsha ... After September 1967, the route changed ... Three months later when the Federal forces were alerted of the magnitude of trade with Biafra ... traders were forced to make some modifications."[343]

After the Biafran invasion of the Midwest, the Nigerian Army counterattacked and recovered the Midwest from Biafra. The Igbo army officers in the Midwest contingentof the Nigerian Army were no longer in charge and the Nigerian Army was now free to operate from the Midwest. Even with that, as previously narrated, the Nigerian Army's attempt to cross into Biafra failed miserably. You could imagine how much more woeful their failure would have been had they tried to defy the wall of Igbo sympathizers and an indifferent population that had made clear that the Midwest would not be turned into a war zone. Furthermore, with the war in a true stalemate, the Midwest Igbos would have continued to trade with the east (Biafra) and might have even been more blatant and defiant about it, ensuring the supply of basic items to Biafra or even openly supplying Biafra with food and other necessities.

In effect, Ojukwu and his advisers should have considered these factors and their strategic significance and opportunities for Biafra. They should have left the Midwest alone. Indeed, even at the height of the war, the Midwest Igbos continued to trade with Biafra. I would not even be

---

[340] Ibid (Italics are mine)

[341] *Nowamagbe A. Omoigui, The Midwest Invasion of 1967: Lessons for Today's Geopolitics, Text* of a keynote speech delivered at the Nigerian Independence Day Celebration sponsored by the Nigerian Women Association in Columbia, South Carolina on October 3, 1998. https://www. dawodu.com/midwest.htm. *On this event, Omoigui quotes Lt. Col. Ejoor and Major Ogbemudia.*

[342] *Egodi Uchendi, Women and Conflict in the Nigerian Civil War, Pp. 138 – 142. See also Fola Oyewole, Reluctant Rebel, Pp. 76 – 78.*

[343] *Ibid*

surprised at the possibility of importing limited quantities of arms through the Midwest had the invasion not occurred, as long as the Igbos in the Nigerian Army ensured that Nigerian forces did not use the Midwest as a staging post to invade Biafra. I would argue that they unwisely joined in the conspiracy to allow Biafra to invade the Midwest. If I had anything to say about it, they should have stayed away and used their contacts to provide the Biafran Army with intelligence, kept up the barrier, and even smuggled food and at least nonlethal supplies to Biafra. Biafra should have used the opportunity to build up a formidable defense on the Midwest border if Nigeria attempted to invade.

The Biafran invasion of the Midwest was also a diplomatic disaster for Biafra. Before the Biafran invasion of the Midwest, the Western Nigerians and the Yoruba ethnic group were sitting on the fence. This notwithstanding that Awolowo was deputy chairperson of the Federal Executive Council and had been released from prison by Yakubu Gowon. However, on August 12 or 13, 1967, Chief Obafemi Awolowo publicly appealed to Yorubas and expressed the feeling that it was necessary to counter appeals from the Eastern regime for Yorubas to desert the federal government. Awolowo then urged the Yorubas to "support the Federal Government in resisting the present rebellion."[344] With this call, many Yorubas of Western Nigeria and non-Igbos of Midwestern Nigeria enlisted in large numbers to join the fight against the Biafran regime. Information about Ojukwu's demand to appoint a military governor for Western Nigeria, Lagos, and the Midwest did not help matters.[345] This leads to the next diplomatic failure of the Igbos and the Biafran regime—the expectation that the Yoruba ethnic group would join Biafra against Nigeria.

Awolowo Sacramentum Fecit[346] – Did Awolowo Make a Promise and Why Rely on It?

During the war and since the end of the war more than fifty years ago, the Igbos have castigated or blamed the Yorubas for not supporting Biafra. The Yoruba ethnic group has been variously called treacherous and cowardly. For example, Okey Anueyiagu[347] asserts that "Yoruba neutrality was a lie." The attitude of the Igbos was that the Yorubas had a moral obligation to support the Igbos considering why the Igbos were making a bid for secession. What is more, the Igbos assert that Chief Awolowo, the leader of the Yorubas, had promised that if the Eastern Nigerians are allowed to opt-out of the Nigeria Federation, then the West and Lagos would also leave the Federation. The conclusions made based on Awolowo's statement, or even on moral grounds, are at least simplistic or, in the extreme, baseless and would not stand the test of rigorous logical scrutiny. Politics does not work the way the Igbos thought at that time and even now. While there was no shortage of moral sympathy for Biafra's cause around the world—and even among the Yorubas—diplomatic support or any support that might have military implications would have been highly ponderous undertakings. They must be convenient and, in the extreme, profitable. Under the circumstances, it was not convenient to support the Biafran cause in part because the Biafran decision-makers did not make it convenient. If Eastern Nigerians had forced a more equitable Nigeria, along the lines that Awolowo and the Yoruba leadership had proposed, it would have been profitable both for the

---

[344] *Nowamagbe A. Omoigui, The Midwest Invasion of 1967: Lessons for Today's Geopolitics. See also Luke Nnaemeka Aneke, The Untold Story of the Nigerian-Biafra War, New York, Triumph Publishing, 2007, Pp. 147 – 149. Aneke is quoting United Press International (UPI) and New York Times.*

[345] *See Adewale Ademoyega, Pp.202 – 15 and Njoku, previously cited. Ojukwu did not hide his intentions.*

[346] *Awolowo Sacramentum Fecit is borrowed from an inscription in the Bayou Tapestry of King Harold Godwinson and Duke Williams of Normandy fame that justified the Duke's invasion of England and the Battle of Hastings 1066. Specifically, Duke William of Normandy claimed that both King Edward (the Confessor) and Earl Harold of Essex had promised him the throne of England whenever the Confessor died. It was after a shipwreck in 1064 that Harold, held in the Duke's court, supposedly swore an Oath to help Duke William become King of England and this was said to have been recorded in the Bayou Tapestry. While the Earl may have been under duress, Awolowo was not.*

[347] *Okey Anueyiagu, Biafra, the Horrors of War: The Story of a Child Soldier, Atlanta, Brown Brommel Publishers, 2020.*

Yoruba ethnic group and other ethnic groups in Nigeria. If Biafra was defeated and the Igbos are out of the Federation, for now, it was strategically profitable for the Yorubas to occupy and take over the political and civil service positions Igbos had vacated. This, in turn, made it more profitable to join with the Nigerians against Biafra. Finally, the behavior of Biafran soldiers and Ojukwu's communications during the Midwest invasion effectively destroyed any incentives for the Yoruba nation and Awolowo to be neutral.

In the first place, Chief Awolowo did not have a grip on Western Nigerians and the Yoruba ethnic group as Ojukwu had on Eastern Nigeria. Although Awolowo had been avowed and declared a leader by the Yoruba ethnic group, he was not the governor of Western Nigeria. Secondly, it must be understood clearly that the Yoruba were not universally in support of the Igbos. At the minimum, about one-third of Yorubas despise Igbos as much as any other ethnic group. Furthermore, a significant percentage of the Yoruba population is Islamic. As such, they could easily be swayed to support the Islamic North. After all, this was what made it possible for the Northern People's Congress, a Northern-based party, to drive a bloody wedge between the Yorubas, leading to the violence and bloodletting that undergirded the Western election crisis immediately following independence between 1960 and 1964. This, in turn, laid the foundation for the military coup of January 1966. Besides all of this, the Western Nigerians did not have the military capability to sustain a secession if the Nigerian Army tried to force them back into Nigeria.

Finally, then, did Awolowo make a promise to lead the West and the Yoruba ethnic group out of Nigeria in support of Biafra? I do not think so. I do not agree that Awolowo's statement amounted to a promise. I equally disagree that the Yorubas were not truly neutral. See Ademoyega and a fuller excerpt of Awolowo's statements below. According to Eric Teniola,

"Chief Awolowo admitted on May 1, 1967, speech, that 'We have neither the military might, not the overwhelming advantage of numbers here in Western Nigeria and Lagos... If the West tried to secede before or in tandem with Biafra, at that time of Biafran secession, Western Region and Lagos would have been the battleground. The West did have the troops and was not prepared for a major war. At the time that Awolowo made those declarations, officers of the Western Region in the Nigerian Army were less than 7 percent. At that time Lagos, Ibadan, and Abeokuta garrisons were occupied by 'northern troops.' Even the then Governor of Western Region, Major General Adeyinka Adebayo was not prepared for war."[348]

Even if Awolowo made a promise, he certainly did not promise to be reckless or to subject his people to undue suffering. Nevertheless, one ought to read Awolowo's statements and analyze his position regarding war to understand what transpired.

Excerpts of Awolowo's Speech on May 1, 1967, to the Western Nigerian Leaders of Thought

"Only a peaceful solution must be found … The Eastern Region must be encouraged to remain part of the Federation. If the Eastern Region is *allowed* by acts of omission or commission to secede from or opt-out of Nigeria, then the West and Lagos must also stay out …" The operating word in Awolowo's statement is "allowed[349]." One could interpret Awolowo's statement cynically and see it as a hint to Nigeria that if the east seceded, then they should be forced back. That is to say, do not allow the east to secede. It could also mean that even if the east succeeds by military force to split from Nigeria, then the west must go. There is nothing in that statement that promises that if the east secedes then the west would secede or join them, even if with bare hands, to rise and to join in an uprising. The Western Nigerians, Awolowo being one of them, were fully aware of the suffocating

---

[348] Why Awo did not make West to Secede, The Guardian, 25 September 2017, https://guardian. ng/opinion/why-awo-did-not-make-west-to-secede/
[349] *Kirk-Greene, Crisis and Conflict in Nigeria, Vol. I, Pp. 414 – 18*

stranglehold that the Northern ruling establishment had on Nigerian affairs, and they lamented it like any other group. However, they were not prepared to commit mass suicide to resolve their issues.

Awolowo proceeds forcefully to condemn any act of war against the east, even if they were to secede. Very clearly, Awolowo states that the west would not join in such a war. Therefore, the prevailing attitude in the west and the Midwest was that the war that ensued in July, after the May 1 meeting, was a war between the north and the east. Therefore, when the war started in July 1967, the Nigerian Army attacked from the north, with essentially all Northern troops and commanders. Awolowo's statement, below, bears out his position, viz:

*"Those who advocate the use of force should stop a little and reflect. I can see no vital and abiding principle involved in any war between the North and the East. If the East attacked the North, it will be for revenge, pure and simple...If it is claimed that such a war is ... waged ... for recovering the real and personal properties left behind in the North ... personal effects left behind have been thoroughly looted or destroyed ... Since the real properties are immovable ... recovery of them can only be by means of forcible military occupation ... If the North attacks [**Eastern Nigeria**], it could only be for the purposes of further ... entrenching its position of dominance in the country ... If ... the attack on the East is going to be launched by the Federal Government ... designed for the Unity of the Federation ... it must be agreed to unanimously by the remaining units of the Federation ... In this connection, the West, Midwest, and Lagos have declared their implacable opposition to the use of force ..."*

Awolowo goes further, stating,

"Some... have likened an attack on the East to Lincoln's war against the Southern States in America. Two vital factors distinguish Lincoln's campaign from the one now ... the American civil war was aimed at abolishing slavery...If the Calabar-Ogoja-Rivers State is created after Eastern Nigeria would have made its severance from Nigeria Effective ... we will then be waging an unjust war against a foreign state ... because the purpose of it would be to remove ten minorities in the East from the domination of the Ibos ... only to subordinate them to the domination of the Efik/ Ibibio/Annang national group ...It is my considered view that while some of the demands of the East are excessive ... most of such demands are not only well-founded but are designed for smooth and steady association amongst various national units of Nigeria..."

It is evident from the two paragraphs above that Awolowo was firmly in support of the east, though not in secession. Accordingly, even if the east did decide to secede, knowing very well that it may well lead to war, it was up to the Biafran leadership to make support for its move convenient and attractive to the Midwest and the West. As events would show, that did not happen.

As described earlier, Ojukwu told Njoku that Banjo was in touch with the Yoruba leadership. It is well known that Banjo held Lt. Col. Ejoor hostage and negotiated between him and Ojukwu, with the British consulate acting as a go-between. Who is to say that the British consulate was not disclosing Banjo's propositions to the Yoruba leadership and Nigeria? Meanwhile, besides Ojukwu's clear directive that Biafran forces would occupy the west and appoint a military governor for the west, without consulting the Yorubas, Biafran forces brutalized the Midwestern Nigerian population.

Therefore, according to Waidi Adebayo,[350]

"In Lagos, the atmosphere of deep mistrust of Igbos left behind and those who recently made their way back from Biafra thickened. There was fear. There was panic. It had come to light that some of the Igbo minorities of the Midwest were used to sweep away Ejoor and put an Okonkwo in power. It will happen too in Lagos they reckoned. Banjo's troops were reported to be in Ore heading for Lagos. Was it going to be Chiedu? Or Emeka? Or Silvanus? Or would it be Calixtus? The atmosphere of suspicions thickened. Rubbles of the damaged Inland Revenue office, the British Library, the telephone exchange, and cinema house near Rowe Park in Yaba from the explosions

---

[350] Wadi Adebayo, *BIAFRA: The Untold Story of Nigeria's Civil War, BIAFRA: The Untold Story of Nigeria's civil war – Nigerian History (wordpress.com),* March 2013

of bombs conveyed in a petrol tanker on 19 July 1967 were there. Four people died and 56 were injured. On the night of 9th August, another Biafran plane flew in from the East and dropped bombs on a non-military area. 'Warning bombs,' Ojukwu called then in a lengthy midnight address on radio Biafra on 10 August 1967. The plane also dropped leaflets in Ikeja and Palmgrove areas "calling on people to overthrow Gowon's government and the Hausa imperialists." The American ambassador noted that the leaflets were similar to the ones being distributed by Biafran soldiers to gain their support in the Midwest. Around quarter past 4 on 16th August 1967, another Biafran plane flew in and dropped two bombs on Apapa. The more these bombs exploded, the more Lagos Igbos were put in trouble."

This bears restatement from Appendix 18 of Njoku's book (Pp. 224 – 25)[351]. After Banjo arrived in the Midwest, Ojukwu blasted a letter to Banjo, stating, inter alia,

"I have decided to place at your disposal Biafran forces for the liberation of Yorubaland on the following clear conditions: ... You will have nothing to do with the administration of the Midwest territory ... prior to your move to the West ... Biafran troops will, after the liberation of Yorubaland, remain in that territory ... for as long as we in Biafra consider it necessary... On the liberation of Yorubaland, you will be appointed Military Governor of that territory ... During the period of Biafra's presence in your territory, all political measures, statements, or decrees shall be subject to approval by myself ... Should our troops arrive and liberate Lagos, the Government of the Republic of Biafra reserves the right to appoint a military governor for that territory."[352]

Against this background, any support that Biafra had among Yorubas and with Awolowo dissipated and turned into open hostility. Western Yorubas and the ethnic groups of the Midwest began to enlist in the Nigerian Army in large numbers, especially heeding Awolowo's call to unite and crush the "present rebellion." The Yorubas and Awolowo would not stand to have an Igbo man appoint a governor for them and replace one army of occupation with another.

---

[351] Njoku, A Tragedy Without Heroes, Pp. 224 – 25.

[352] *Hilary Njoku, A Tragedy Without Heroes, Pp. 224 – 25. See also Adewale Ademoyega, Why we Struck, Pp. 207 – 208. Ademoyega, who became a commander in the Midwest operation after he was released by the Biafran Army, also reported that he had been initially appointed by Ojukwu to the post of military governor of Western Nigeria. It was on the basis of Ojukwu's conditions that Victor Banjo returned from his detention in Enugu to continue the operation to liberate the Midwest and Western Nigeria.*

CHAPTER XV

THE FOLLY OF THE IGBOMAN COUNTING THE CHICKENS? WHERE ARE THE EGGS?

Complacency in Crisis Management after January Coup

In the aftermath of the coup of January 1966, some described it as a coup inspired by the Igbo community to dominate and rule Nigeria. Though the coup was not successful, evidently nothing would have appeased or pacified the aggrieved. Anyone who wanted to avert the cataclysm that followed should have taken appropriate precautions. Neither Aguiyi Ironsi nor the Igbo ethnic group took appropriate precautions. The antagonists that emerged from the fracas were not sincere in their quest for peace. The conditions that set into motion the tragic events that followed could have been minimized, though probably would not have been averted altogether. The outcomes would not have been as cataclysmic and as tragic as they eventually turned out to be: the counter-coup of July 1966, the mass slaughter of Igbos in Northern Nigeria, and the subsequent civil war. It's possible that the latter may never have occurred, or if it did, it would not have ended in the untidy way that it did—as Ken Saro Wiwa[353] would put it. Madiebo even acknowledges this. For example, Madiebo states,

"In the first instance, we could have prevented the war by effectively challenging the counter-coup of July 1966 ... rather than allowing it to gain momentum ... we would not have a war to lose ... Gowon's counterrevolution having gained momentum, I believe it was still not impossible to have delayed the war ... if we had a more capable leader and better yet, collective leadership...[354]"

As soon as Ironsi established his government, he proscribed all political activities, especially "tribal" or ethnic-based organizations and political parties. However, as the other major ethnic groups—Yorubas and the Northern Hausa-Fulani establishment—began to organize themselves for a response, the Igbos did not engage themselves to scheme and organize if the situation degenerated into more serious unrest. Northern army officers not only began to complain, first procedurally and then in what amounts to defiant and threatening postures, but also began to hold meetings and engage in conspiracies. They also began to plot the logistics for action (see "The Crucible of Wahala"). Besides, the Northern Nigerian officers who wrote an angry letter to Lt. Col. Gowon, Northern civilian leaders began to hold meetings to rectify what they considered an injustice or at least to restore what they considered their position in the Nigerian political system. There was ample evidence and information to support plans for counteraction against the Igbos and possibly a military counter-coup that would be potentially deadly against Igbo and Eastern Nigerian army officers. According to Alexander Madiebo,[355]

---

[353] *Ken Saro Wiwa, A Month and a Day: A Detention Diary, London, Penguin, 1995*
[354] *Madiebo, The Nigerian Revolution and the Biafran War, Pp. 377 – 78*
[355] *Alexander Madiebo, The Nigerian Revolution and the Biafra War, P.34*

"As time went on [about April 1966], the clandestine campaign against Ironsi's government ... grew into an open and nationally organized exercise ... and appeared to have the blessing ...of Northern Nigerian government authorities ... By April [1966], top civil servants, ex-politicians and senior police officers were said to be holding frequent meetings which could no longer be said to be a secret ... Many politicians ... were ... buying up all the available short guns and cartridges in the local shops ... I called the [Governor's] attention to these developments."[356]

The Igbo army officers had all this information and what did they do? Madiebo acknowledges that when the coup started on the 29th of July 1966, Southern Army officers, lacking effective leadership ... ***because of Ironsi's political naïvete,*** went into confusion [and] hiding instead of challenging the move about which they had ample information[357]. Furthermore, Madiebo laments that

"General Ironsi's regime was a real tragedy for the people of Eastern Nigeria because it created the conditions which led to the killings [of Eastern Nigerians] and the ultimate civil war. In the first place he abolished the political parties and all ethnic organizations such as the Igbo State Union which provided ... protection for the people ... in the alien environments of some parts of Nigeria ... If the ... Igbo State Union had been in existence at the time of the May riots, ... it could have organized an effective defense or evacuation of the people ... as it did during the 1953 Kano riots ...that an Igbo man was at the helm gave the Igbos a false sense of security.[358]"

Madiebo's position to blame Ironsi is rather lame and indefensible. Madiebo and other Igbo leaders and army officers should be embarrassed. For example, Igbo leaders and even Madiebo himself were fully aware of potentially cataclysmic developments and yet failed to organize. Instead of getting organized, they were making reports to Ironsi. For example, Madiebo reports that a certain Alhaji Suya (a pseudonym) had disclosed to him a plot to kill Igbos in the northern part of the country. A certain Mr. Anueyiagu made a similar report, and both he and Madiebo[359] flew to Lagos to narrate the Alhaji Suya story to Aguiyi Ironsi. Madiebo was reprimanded by Ironsi and Anueyiagu was not able to render his report on the same matter.

What did Madiebo and the Igbo political and civilian leadership expect Gen. Ironsi to do? First of all, Ironsi is an Igboman being accused of a conspiracy to perpetuate Igbo domination of Nigeria based on a violent and murderous elimination of the leaders of other parts of the country. Therefore, Madiebo and other Igbo leaders should not have been making such reports openly to Ironsi. Since at least one of Ironsi's close aids, Lt. Nwankwo was an Igboman, such reports should have got to Ironsi through more clandestine channels to Nwankwo, or even through Ironsi's wife. Secondly, the fact that ethnic organizations and political parties were proscribed across the country did not prevent Northerners or even Western Nigerians to meet clandestinely and even, after a while, openly. Once the Northerners concluded that they felt aggrieved, they sprang to action and began to plot a strategy to strike back. If Madiebo chooses to describe Ironsi's behavior as political naivete, then it is fair to consider the Igbos, army officers, and all others to be equally naïve. Furthermore, on the same account that Northerners were organizing clandestinely, Eastern Nigerian civilian political and community-based organizations should also have been organizing. The military personnel, which included Madiebo, should have immediately sprung into action to organize. Indeed, they should not have involved Ironsi at all. When Ironsi chastised Madiebo and declined to listen to Mr. Anueyiagu in Igbo, this should have been seen as Ironsi's hint that the Igbo leadership, military and civilian, should bring no such reports to him. At least, not officially. Rather, they should take care of the situation without him. The moment that Madiebo witnessed Northern army officers and leading politicians buying up the short guns and cartridges in the community, two things should have immediately become obvious to both him and Mr. Anueyiagu, with whom he (Madiebo) and Col. Okoro met over Alhaji Suya's report. First, these people were buying guns in preparation for a

---

[356] *Ibid, Pp. 378 – 92*
[357] Ibid, Page, 379
[358] Ibid, Page 390
[359] Ibid, Pp. 46-47

violent confrontation. Secondly, they are probably making sure that there are no guns available for us to buy in the event of such a confrontation.

The first misstep of Igbo army officers was that they pulled off the January 15 coup in 1966. But that is a story for another day. Since there were rumors that Brig. Maimalari and pro–Northern People's Congress (NPC) army officers were planning the alleged Operation No Mercy, and being aware of their rank-and-file disadvantage in the army, the best approach for the Igbo officers would have been to stalk Brig. Maimalari and challenge them if and when they pulled off their alleged coup. On the counterrevolution, Eastern Nigerian army offices, if need be, should have immediately engaged in an intelligence-gathering operation to get an idea of when and how Operation Aure would be commenced. The Eastern Igbo officers could easily have begun disinformation gossip that all Southern officers would be targets. On that account, some Western and non-Igbo officers, for precautionary and, others, for self-defense would have obtained information that would enable the Igbo officers to achieve what Madiebo suggested: to challenge the counterrevolution and prevent it from gaining momentum. If need be, as close as April or even May 1966, they would have been able to clandestinely acquire military assault guns from within and outside the country. Once the coup commenced on July 29, 1966, the officers would not have been blindsided and would have sprung into action either defending themselves or hiding effectively until the situation came under control. One way to achieve neutralizing the coup would be to make it ineffective in Lagos and Western Nigeria. Ironsi and Fajuyi probably would not have died. They might have been overthrown, but they might have been able to escape from the statehouse in Ibadan. Besides, military preparations to consolidate the east could have been in place, regardless of Ojukwu's opinion or disposition.

Get Ye First the Earthly Kingdom

As an Igbo man, I can say without hesitation or fear of a jaundiced look that the Igboman is inclined to hunt for mice out of his burning house (_Ulô nâ â_ âgbâ _oku_, _Ndi_ Îgbô _â na â chu nta_ óké). There are many credible allegations that many Igbos diverted resources for prosecuting the war into their private pockets. For example, Madiebo reported that

"Whatever money Biafra ever had during the war was under the control of the Head of State while the actual spending was the responsibility of Mr. C.C. Mojekwu ... It goes without saying that better results may have been achieved if the above committee had been expanded to include a few other financial experts and credible accounts kept."[360] _The little money that Biafra had was wasted by civilians who purchased weapons for Biafra to the end of the war. "Rifles arrived either in unserviceable conditions ... or with the wrong caliber of ammunition ... Most of the artillery guns and mortars arrived ... without fuses."_[361] _"If qualified men were used to purchase these arms ...perhaps numerous aircraft which could not fly as soon as they were paid for would never have been bought ... How could complete honesty be expected when all Biafran funds that were raised and spent ... were under the names of individuals."_[362]

Effiong made similar allegations, claiming that funds were raised and ended up in the leaky pockets of some people. There were also allegations of individuals who were sent to Europe with several hundreds of thousands of Nigerian pounds to convert before they become worthless who returned from Europe with strange stories of how the money was confiscated when, in fact, they kept the conversion resources to themselves. Indeed, the cannibalistic fraud of Biafrans against the struggle was probably so bad that some ordinary Americans were aware of it. In 1983, I was among some African American friends, and I began to recount the story of suffering and starvation in Biafra. One of them screamed and said, "it's you people...we were out in the winter cold with cans going from house to house begging for donations, only to hear that your leaders pocketed all

---

[360] _Alexander Madiebo, Op. Cit. Pp. 382_
[361] _Ibid_
[362] Ibid, Page 386

the money and invested in real estate in New York." Behaviors such as these are what Madiebo was lamenting that Biafrans often left the straight path leading to our objectives in search of such frivolities as personal power and wealth and making one's name when such would have been automatic by-products of a successful establishment of the state of Biafra.[363]

Since the war ended in January 1970, there have been several coups that reveal the cracks in the cohesion of Biafra's former foes. In 1975, Yakubu Gowon was overthrown by Col. Murtala Mohamed. Somewhere in the subliminal recesses of Gowon's ethnic men, Murtala's coup was seen as the ultimate achievement of Murtala's original claim to leadership after the same Murtala Mohamed overthrew Ironsi, but Gowon "took" the spoils. In less than nine months, Lt. Col. Dimka shot Murtala in broad daylight in a failed coup attempt that some may interpret as a Middle Belt revenge. Several Middle Belt officers were rounded up and shot. In 1979, Nigeria returned to civilian rule under a Northern president by the name of Alhaji Shehu Shagari, but Gen. Mohamed Buhari (another Northerner) overthrew Shagari, only to be overthrown by another Northerner by the name of Gen. Ibrahim Babangida. While in office, a Middle Belt soldier, Maj. Gideon Orka attempted a coup after which several Middle Belt soldiers were rounded up and killed. Ibrahim Babangida then suspected another fellow Northerner, Gen. Mamman Vatsa, of plotting to overthrow him. Babangida arrested Vatsa and had executed him. The Igbo has not been involved in any of these. Biafra's former foes could engage in murderous conflicts among themselves and expose fissures in their alliances, but the Igboman does not dare say a word for one simple reason: They had been strong enough to engage in internal conflict, and if the Igboman tried to take advantage of it again, other groups could allocate minimal resources to suppress the Igboman again and return to settle their internal scores afterward. The moral of all this story is to remember to "Get Thou First the Earthly Kingdom" and everything else shall be added unto it. While we were at war, the Igboman had the heart to "eat money" that should have been used for the purchase of weapons for fighting. As Madiebo stated, though the civilians who were sent to purchase weapons wasted money by buying faulty equipment, they continued to purchase weapons for Biafra until the end. But it is not beyond the Igboman to pay more attention to hunting for mice while his house is burning. Not much has changed since the war ended fifty years ago.

Weak Historical Foundations

A weakness of the Igbos, the apparent common enemy of the other major and so-called minor groups, was the lack of a historical basis for an articulated or coordinated response to the political dynamics of the European era. There was no history of coordinated action or ideology that bound the traditional potentates together. The educated class that rose to prominence among colonial and post-colonial Igbos was not aligned one way or another to the ruling potentates. The emergent educated upper and middle class may have been in a struggle for domination with the traditional class of potentates. The Igbo Union that appeared to be potent was practically paralyzed following the aftershock of the coup of January 15, 1966, because Igbo Union was not part of a strategically coordinated scheme by a coordinated ruling establishment. If anything, the elite who were created through the Igbo Union and the elite who resulted from the Igbo effort toward education competed with the traditional establishment for influence and control. This struggle might well have been part of a dialectic process. However, the process had not achieved a dialectical synthesis that would have enabled it to operate in a coordinated manner under the circumstances. Therefore, individuals took advantage of the situation for personal gain. Ojukwu and the ruling clique in Biafra were not to be absolved in this self-defeating tactic. In this regard, Ojukwu was an opportunist that was in the right place at the right time.

---

[363] *Alexander Madiebo, Op. Cit., Pp. 382,384 and 389.*

As a people, the Igbos discovered themselves mostly during the European era, from about the early nineteenth century or even much later. According to Whiteman[364] "the name Ibo was originally derogatory, used apparently on the coast and the river to describe the people of the interior of Iboland and only became widespread during the colonial period ...especially as the colonial power was trying to standardize language and the Ibo was, above all, distinguishable as a language group."[365] While Igbos in their different localities were aware of each other and interacted, the Igbos of Onitsha on the Northwest boundaries were not aware of the Igbo-speaking people of Oboro Umuahia or the Igbos of Abam in the East. The Igbos in these latter areas knew more of Ibibios and Ogoja's than their fellow Igbo-speaking people in the northwest. Their potentates were not aware of each other and did not have diplomatic relations nor did they identify common interests, collaborations, and cooperation that would have led them to identify boundaries of conflicts and resolutions. They did not come to each other's common defenses.

It is remarkable though that, all along, the disarticulated Igbo communities referred to themselves as Igbo, for the name was not given to them only in recent history or by the Europeans. Even during the slave trade in the seventeenth and eighteenth centuries, Europeans referred to Igbos (Eboes), though that may have been about the derogated peoples that were transported from the interior where present-day Igbos occupy. Therefore, there was in existence a people who referred to themselves as Igbos, since there is ample evidence of a highly advanced bronzemaking Igbo civilization dating back to the ninth century—the Igbo Ukwu and Nri cultures.[366] However, even to this day, some people in Abakiliki, in the northeast fringes of Igboland, may refer to other Igbos as Igbo people, as if they are different. Even the Onitsha people and so-called Western Igbos in the western banks of the River Niger could refer to other Igbos as "..Nwa Onye Igbo" or the "progeny of Igbo." Once more, Whitehead reports that "Ukpabi Asika[367] records that ... wondering round the liberated parts of Iboland... without exception and in all cases, I have been told that we did not start this trouble, it is the Ibo who caused this trouble."[368] So, who are they, though they speak the language and understand other Igbos perfectly well? One could only speculate as to the origin of the Igbo ethnic group. It would appear that some core or kernel of some culture (Igbo-Ukwu) whose people called themselves Igbo may have developed in some central core and then began to spread out. For example, the Ikwere people near Port Harcourt refer to Igbos north of Port Harcourt as Isu[369] Ama (meaning "foreign invaders" or "barbarian invaders from outside (Ama)". The word "Isu" in Igbo refers to an outsider, invader, or barbarian much like its meaning from the ancient Greek concept (barbaroi) of unwelcome invaders from outside. The concept of Isu as an invader or foreigner could also be inferred from the reference to the legend of Igbuzo whose inhabitants were said to have migrated from Nri led by Eze Nwa Isu (King of the Isu[370]). Here, it is clear that the migrants were referred

---

[364] K. Whiteman, Enugu: The Psychology of Secession, 20 July 1966 to 30 May 1967, in Nigerian Politics and Military Pp. 115 – 16.

[365] K. Whiteman, Op. Cit. Page 115

[366] David Northrup, The Growth of Trade among the Igbo before 1800, The Journal of African History, 1972, Vol. 13(2) (1972), pp. 217-236. The Nri culture may also have referred to themselves as Igbo because the people of Igbouzo (migrant Igbos) are theorized to have migrated from Nri. If they were from Nri, why are they not called Nri Uzo (Migrant Nri)? But their neighbors who harbored them call them Igbouzo.

[367] Ukpabi Asika was the renegade who was appointed as Administrator of the East Central State in 1968 after Federal Nigerian forces felt sufficiently comfortable to appoint an Igboman to administer parts of captured Igbo territory.

[368] K.Whiteman, Op. Cit. Page 115

[369] The original barbaroi in ancient Greece referred to presumably less civilized people from the fringes of Greek civilization who did not speak proper Greek. But these barbaroi (Dorians) invasively migrated into the Greek city states in the wake of the ecological and social catastrophes that attended the end of the Bronze Age and may have established the concept of barbarian as uncivilized invaders.

[370] https://en.wikipedia.org/wiki/Igbuzo. Igbuzo, established about 1450... According to the oral history, Umejei Nwa Eze Isu (Prince Umejei of Isu) killed his opponent in a traditional wrestling bout, an act considered...Abomination...in the land and punishable by death. However, his death was commuted by his father who was also Eze Isu) the king of Isu..."

to as Isu, meaning outsiders, migrants, invaders, or even barbarians. The name Igbuzo, meaning migrant Igbos, also reinforces the notion that the Igbo language and culture may have originated from Nri and Igbo Ukwu (Greater Igbo). Considering that the Nri and Igbo Ukwu cultures and civilizations can be dated to the eighth and ninth centuries, the name Igbo did not originate as an adaptation of the derogatory reference by the riverine neighbors of the Igbos at the Atlantic coast. Because a lot of slaves were transported from the hinterland, north of the riverine communities at the Atlantic coast, the inhabitants of the riverine communities had attitude towards the source of these slaves, much like the word Negro became a synonym for slave in America and as the Slavs of eastern Europe gave their name to servitude, hence we have the word slave.

North of Ikwere land, the people of Owerre also refer to other Igbos north of Owerre as Isu Ama. North of Owerre, the people of Umuahia refer to the Igbos north of Umuahia as Îsu. Well, true to the reference north of Umuahia, are the people of Îsuikwuato (my native land, meaning "three kindred invaders or barbarians"), but also the people of Îsu Ochi and Îsu Njââbâ. The people of Îsuikwuato are kindred of the fearsome warlike people of Bende, Abiriba, Ohoofia, and other such neighbors who had been encroaching and making war with their neighbors before the era of the European. It may well be that violent migratory trends were putting pressure on people southward to the coast and eastward who, in feeling the pressure, referred to their new neighbors as barbarian invaders (Îsu). In the process, the invaders established their language as the prevailing language in their new environment.

One way or another, during the remote past, through this core or kernel, the Igbo language and culture spread. Igbo language and culture most likely originated from the Nri or Igbo Ukwu civilizations and cultures from about the ninth or tenth centuries and then spread through trade, religion, and proselytization. There are no legends of treaties, dominations, alliances, wars of conquest, cooperation, or even trade that created a united government of the entirety of present-day Igboland. There may have been a deliberate spread of the culture that created a domination, a hegemony, or even a coordinated potentiality. That unified corporate existence may have disintegrated because of some historical, ecological, or political shock. This disintegration may have occurred before the seventeenth or eighteenth century. Notwithstanding the disintegration, the cultural expansion may have continued, the language continuing to spread and to dominate their neighbors at the fringes without any reference to a central potentate or common cultural center. When the Europeans introduced the Trans-Atlantic slave trade in the seventeenth century, the Aros, who spoke Igbo, moved immediately to dominate it, and spread their colonies across Igboland and neighboring ethnicities. Although the colonies of the Aros, like ancient Roman settlements, paid homage to their homeland, the Aros did not establish independent potentialities, except maybe at Aro Ndi Izuogu.do so by means of a tr[371] In any event, the Aro potentiality did not engage the Onitshas in any coordinated diplomatic relationships that would have created common interests. There was no dominant group among the Igbos. With the arrival of the Europeans, and especially from the beginning of the twentieth century, the Igbos discovered that they had distant kith and kin beyond their immediate boundaries. Because this sudden discovery of distant kin was under colonial domination, it did not give rise to the establishment of protocols for collective action to resolve disputes among themselves or to address problems that arise from external challenges.

Contrary to the Igbo experience, the Yoruba peoples had interacted with each other and collectively with external foes for more than two hundred years before they encountered Europeans in the seventeenth and eighteenth centuries. For more than three hundred years at least, the Ife Kingdom was the dominant Yoruba potentiality until the eve of the seventeenth century, when the Oyo kingdom overthrew the Ile-Ife hegemony. From the twelfth or thirteenth centuries, when the Ile-Ife empire dominated Yoruba land, there may have been the usual internecine and endless wars of rivalry and mutual conquests. But as a group, the Yoruba were aware of each other and established a system of collective action that they could use if the need arose. Therefore, during the civil war,

---

[371] Ancient Greek civilization spread by establishing Greek colonies across the Mediterranean before the end of the Bronze Age (1,200 BC) but they had City States and established colonies that acknowledged their Greek identity but also established independent kingdoms and potentialities.

the Yorubas had a greater collective cohesion than the Igbos. Each constituency, the chiefs, and obas, the modern government apparatchik knew their place in the larger strategic context and acted collectively. The intelligentsia deferred collectively to the traditional ruling establishment and the latter group did not compete for the sphere of influence and direction of the other.

Although the Yorubas had a collective articulated past that enabled them to act collectively, they had schisms and rifts within them that made it possible for the NPC to drive a wedge between Awolowo and Akintola. Besides the traditional rivalries, I could only surmise that the internal class conflicts that manifested in the mutual selfishness between the two personalities provided an opportunity for the NPC to rend asunder the alliance between the National Council of Nigerian Citizens (NCNC) and the NPC and then to complete the project of consolidating the hegemony of the Hausa-Fulani based on a northern and western alliance. This was feasible because there are Moslems among the Yoruba with whom the NPC superstructure could find common ground. When the chips fell, the events that evolved and led to this fatal schism in the ranks of the Yoruba is a stark example that exposes the personalities involved in the Nigerian crisis as accomplices in the tragedy of the civil war for which we, the ordinary people, suffered an immeasurable calamity, with ignominy and nothing to show for it to this day.

The Hausa-Fulani superstructure, like the Yorubas, had a much longer coordinated history through their city-states dating back to at least the eleventh century and probably as early as the eighth century. The inhabitants and entities or potentialities knew each other, located each other economically, culturally, and diplomatically, if not in totality, then at least formally. The association may have been loose amid rivalries, but at least some formality established common interests. For example, in the ancient world, the city-states of Greece remained independent of each other and had their internal rivalries, and even fought wars against each other. Nevertheless, they came together to fight common enemies (the Trojan War of legend – circa 1200BCE and the Battle of Thermopylae 480 BCE of King Leonidas fame, the Battle of Marathon 490BCE and the Battle of Salamis 480 BCE, among others) and established protocols to resolve common disputes. However, each of the city-states had a different king. In the same way, the Hausa city-states had different independent rulers until the wars of Usman Dan Fodio unified them under the Sokoto Islamic Sultanate in the nineteenth century. Concerning the larger community of Northern Nigerians, Islam, an instrument and a platform for political and social organization and control, had existed for centuries and also provided the superstructure for a system of communications and coordination.

For several centuries, the Borno Empire had established communications and learned how to collectively address international diplomacy. As Islamic peoples, while they may not have been subdued by Usman dan Fodio, they probably had diplomatic communication and had common cause with them, at least in religion. For example, the Borno king, Mai Idris Alooma had iron-helmeted musketeers trained by Ottoman (present-day Turkey) military advisers. Idris Alooma had diplomatic relations and connections with Tripoli, Egypt, and the Ottoman Empire that sent ambassadors across the desert to Alooma's court at Ngazargamu. The Igbos, as a collective, lacked this stock of experience going into the war and also lacked the network, overt or subliminal, that such experiences could have provided or triggered.

The Absence of Collective Leadership

What the Igbos must learn is that they should never again allow themselves to be under the constricting grip of any one person. I could not agree better with Madiebo that what Biafra lacked was collective leadership[372]. Throughout the crisis, the leaders of the other major constituencies— the Hausa/Fulani in the north, and the Yorubas in the west— operated within a context of shared responsibilities within a superstructure of shared governance. For Biafra and the Igbos, in the grips of one dictator, there appeared to be a disconnection between the fundamental strategic objective of the group and what can only be considered the hidden strategic objective of the person at the

---

[372] Alexander Madiebo, The Nigerian Revolution and the Biafran War, Pp. 379 – 89

helm. Furthermore, the dictator received misleading information from ambitious cronies who had their hidden agendas. For this reason, Brig. Hillary Njoku lamented and proposed that henceforth when Igbos are called upon to respond to the call, "Igbo Kwenu!" or "Hark ye!, Harke ye! all Igbo," instead of responding "Nya" or "Hear, hear!" the Igbo should respond with a qualification, "Nke wu le'ezi," or "if there be truth in it."

This was the basic difference between Ojukwu and Gowon and Hassan Katsina and Adebayo. I will go beyond stating that Ojukwu did not understand his role in the broader strategic struggle. Ojukwu supplanted the strategic goals of the people and displaced them with his agenda. Gowon, however, worked with the politicians, as did Hassan Katsina and Adebayo. Hassan Katsina played his role as an administrator and soldier and performed his job by contributing his opinion on political issues and the decision-making about how the war was to be prosecuted and for what reasons. For example, during a meeting of the Northern Leaders of Thought on May 1, 1967, all that Hassan Katsina did was make a presentation and offer his opinion. He was not at the "head of the table" seeking a mandate from the Leaders of Thought as if he was the final decision-maker. It was at this meeting the Northern Nigerian leaders passed a resolution stating that States will be created in Northern Nigeria even if states are not created in other regions of the Federation. Awolowo was not governor, but he was proclaimed leader of Yorubas and represented them as a leader in peace talks and essentially was seen as the voice of the Yorubas. Col. Adebayo was governor and administrator who was the voice of Western Nigeria in the Supreme Military Council. If the Yorubas had an opinion, he presented it at the Supreme Military Council. In the east, Ojukwu had a Consultative Assembly that was a charade. He was the one making all the decisions, and any consultation that was held was simply a discussion of ideas and methods of how to implement his agenda. This is where, once more, I go back to Steven Harding and partially restate that:

"... overall control of a military force by a single all-powerful person, whose decisions are final and irrevocable...and who believes him or herself to be imbued with godlike powers or infallible judgment...With no requirement to heed the advice of inferiors, ... often make decisions that lead to widespread destruction and death, often followed by their own untimely demise and the end of their dynasties..."[373]

What then was the strategic objective that should have driven the executive actions of the administrator in the East and Biafra? What were the opportunities? The broader strategic objectives that faced the East were the security of the Igbos and the security of other Eastern Nigerians and the maintenance of prominence and cruciality in Nigerian political affairs. But also easing the yoke or even removing the yoke of domination from Eastern Nigerian ethnic minorities and other ethnic minorities in the remainder of Nigeria—the Tiv, Idomas, Igalas, and others. Events, as they developed, provided Ojukwu the opportunity very handily, but he lost it through greed or, at best, shortsightedness. When, two months after ceasing the government in July 1966, Northern Nigerian Army officers joined with civilians to brutalize and murder Eastern Nigerian civilians across the North, so Eastern Nigerians fled and evacuated the North. In addition, these same Northern soldiers began to harass Igbos in Western Nigeria wherefore Ojukwu understandably expelled all non-indigenes of Eastern Nigerian from the east because he could no longer guarantee their safety. Even Gowon agreed with Ojukwu on the expulsion. The way and arena were cleared for Ojukwu to have clear control of the territory. Other events, such as the Aburi Accord where concessions were made to him, gave Ojukwu ample opportunity to recruit and arm militarily without seceding. Even Awolowo agreed that Ojukwu's ideas were good for Nigeria, though some of his demands were excessive. Therefore, Ojukwu had ample room for bargaining forcefully through alliances and gaining advantages that may never have been otherwise achieved. Ojukwu had choices, but he was just not prepared militarily to accept peace or to make war. He needed to be a good strategist. Under the circumstances, he had the preponderance of all that he wanted including adulation and world sympathy. He had the opportunity to shake the tree as much as possible and could have achieved his

---

[373] Stephen Harding, The Perils of Hierarchy, *Letter From Military History – May 2016); https:// www. historynet.com/letter-from-military-history-may-2016.htm*

ambition except he might have waited a little longer. Finally, Igbos should disabuse their minds of the narcissistic attitude that they are better than others. There is no doubt that Igbos are ingenious, but there is ingenuity in every group. War is like a soccer match: it does not take a large population to assemble eleven players that can win the championship. For this reason, you cannot take any group for granted. Igbos thought that having a highly educated population was an advantage that Nigerians could not easily overcome. What the Igbos did not take into consideration was that the Yorubas and Midwesterners had as high a density of educated manpower as the Igbos. Make no mistake about it, Nigerians and the world were stunned by the ingenuity that the Igbos brought to the war. This is the reason why many Nigerians and the world marveled at the fact that the war lasted so long, contrary to the illusion that Nigerians would achieve victory in less than three months.

One thought that ran through the mind of the Igbo man was that the "Awusa" man could not defeat the Igbo man because the "Awusa" lacked the educated manpower to prosecute a war against the Igboman. Up to today, the Igbo credits the loss of the war to the support that Nigeria and the "Awusa" man received from the British and the Russians. If truth be told, the Igbo man's high education could not match that of the British and the Russians. If the Igbo was so highly educated, then they should not have engaged in hostile propaganda against the British. At least the British were neutral for a considerable amount of time during the early days of the conflict. Akpan, the secretary to the Biafran government, warned the Eastern Nigerians and Biafrans against attacking a superpower so openly. The best approach would have been to deal with the British through quiet diplomacy by engaging the services of political leaders and politicians who had longer and deeper connections with the British. The debacle with the Shell-BP company should have been avoided like a plague. With the British on the side of "Awusa" man, it does not take ingenuity to receive and make use of advice. Meanwhile, when it comes to education, it would be instructive to understand that the "Awusa" had experience with formal education for centuries before the Igboman encountered the Western world and began to acquire the kind of formal education that rules the modern world. For centuries, the Northern Nigerian, through Islam, could read and write. The fact that the education of reading and writing was concentrated within the aristocracy of the Hausa and later the Hausa-Fulani is irrelevant. Through the centuries and until the last two hundred years, education through reading and writing and international diplomacy was initiated, controlled, and monopolized by the aristocracy. In Northern Nigeria, which you may ridicule and mock for their feudalistic system, much of the benefits of education are carefully orchestrated for the benefit of the aristocracy. They are still mostly like that today, and their population lived by it for centuries and continue to live largely along those lines. Nevertheless, from the amalgamation of Nigeria more than one hundred years ago, the Northern ruling "feudalistic" aristocracy has controlled Nigeria and Nigerian politics with their structure for the benefit of their aristocracy.

Chapter XVI

THE FOLLY OF THE IGBO MAN
INTERNATIONAL DIPLOMACY

Rather Bear with Thee than Bear Thee.

Diplomatic support is not predictable. Preponderantly, personal, and national interest and often the instruments of blackmail could deter support for a friend or a cause for which nations or polities could have sympathy. For example, during the war, Awolowo and Enahoro reminded African leaders about their secessionist threats or other political upheavals, though they were not based on the same circumstances. Mobutu was also quick to remind Nigeria that Biafra and Katanga are not similar or even the same. Gowon promptly bribed him as Mobutu was susceptible to bribery.

Manifest and overt diplomatic support for a constituency at war has generally been constrained by realistic self-interest. No community will enter a war to support another unless there is something to gain or to prevent a loss that may come if the favored warring party loses. This applies to international diplomacy. The obliviousness of the Biafran leadership to this practicality of diplomacy explains the failure of Biafra's international diplomatic failures. In their conduct of international diplomacy, Biafran leaders made faulty assumptions and engaged in counterproductive behavior, all because one man (Ojukwu) was in charge and side-lined more experienced diplomats like Mathew Mbu. He also sidelined more experienced politicians like Azikiwe and Wenike Briggs[374]. In 1966, Wenike Briggs defected to Nigeria early enough, and Azikiwe did the same in August 1969. I will describe Biafra's experiences with Britain to illustrate the example of self-interest as well as counterproductive behavior. Israel, a sympathetic country will used to illustrate an example of self-interest and counterproductive behavior.

European, especially British, support was doubtful. Russians wanted an inroad into Nigeria and cash. The British wanted to protect investments and the balance of payments. Compared to Biafra, Nigeria had the vast Arab and Muslim world in support. Most Arab countries in North Africa were only restrained because of their connection with France. Biafra's appeal to European Christianity during the hostage crisis, to be described later, was naïve and amateurish, to say the least. Christianity may be European heritage, but it is never crucial in foreign policy decisions and positions regarding Africans. For Homo Sapiens, Sapiens, gens Europeanus, Christianity, which originated among the hated Jews, is only a convenient crutch. The European ruling classes did not embrace Christianity until it became politically expedient. Specifically, three hundred years after Christianity began to take root in Europe, Christians were still being persecuted brutally in the Roman Empire. The Christian religion was still in competition with Sun Worship. However, the masses of the European population were also gravitating toward the Christian religion because it promised salvation, equality, and eternal life for all irrespective of class, gender, or race. Subsequently, it was after the Battle of Milvan Bridge in October AD 325, when Constantine invoked the Christian cross to win a battle in the struggle for the Roman Imperial crown, that Christianity finally took off. For

---

[374] *See Njoku, A Tragedy Without Heroes, Madiebo, The Nigerian Revolution and the Biafran War, Effiong, Nigeria and Biafra: My Story and Akpan, The Struggle for Secession).*

the Europeans, money overrides doctrine. For example, during the Trans-Atlantic Slave Trade, the Catholic Church vehemently condemned the slave trade (see Hugh Thomas, Pp. 216 – 220) and questioned whether God sanctions such a trade. After a lot of pressure and defiance by slave dealers and their sponsoring devout Catholic Kings of Portugal, Spain, and England, the Catholic Church caved in and recommended that the slaves be baptized before they were transported in slave ships across to the Americas (Thomas, Pp. 397 – 99).[375] But for the Pope and the kings of Portugal, Spain, and England to find a way around the Christian Bible is a contradiction of faith, an aberration, and an abomination. The Christian Bible makes clear in Galatians 3:25–29, viz[376]:

[25]But after that faith comes, we are no longer under a schoolmaster; [26]*For ye are all the children of God by faith in Christ Jesus;* [27]*For as many of you as having been baptized into Christ have put on Christ;* [28]*There is neither Jew nor Greek, there is neither slave nor free, there is neither male nor female: for ye are all one in Christ Jesus;* [29]*And if ye be Christ's, then are ye Abraham's seed, and heirs according to the promise.*

Therefore, for the Pope and the slaving kings to even sanction the continuation of the slave trade after invoking the baptism of Christ is a sacrilege and blasphemy that took the name of God in vain. Yet, they all engaged in it because it was convenient. It was, therefore, futile for Biafra to count on the support of European ruling establishments by invoking the Christian faith against the Moslems of Northern Nigeria. There is a huge difference between the ordinary European man or woman and the ruling establishments.

Make no mistake about it, without European and Jewish public opinion and support, the cause of Biafra might have been smothered in silence. The point that I am getting at here is that Arab and Islamic ruling establishments will never have supported a Christian Nigeria against an Islamic Biafra. However, by appealing to Christian conscience during the war, Biafra succeeded marvelously in attracting humanitarian aid. The Nigerian government was quick to respond by appealing to the Pope and others that the war was not a religious war. The Nigerian government's counterpropaganda was fairly effective in neutralizing the sting of the religious appeal that sought to make it appear that it was about Christian Biafra against Islamic Northern Nigeria.[377]

Britain, Biafra, and Economic Self-Interests: You Have No Money in Your Purse

When Biafra declared secession in May 1967, many countries took a wait-and-see attitude, especially Britain, the United States, France, and China. The United States made a statement that they had not decided whether to recognize or not recognize Biafra, which was certainly not a statement of opposition. While Britain expressed support for a united Nigeria, they withheld the sale of arms to Nigeria.[378] Immediately after the secession was announced, "...On 30 May, the Commonwealth Office informed the British High Commission in Lagos that no decision had yet been made on recognition, while James Parker, the District High Commissioner in the Eastern capital of Enugu, was instructed to stay on good terms with the Biafrans..." US State Department informed the Foreign Office that it had '...no intention of taking the lead...' on recognition, and would cede to a Commonwealth initiative."[379] From all available information, Britain's ultimate decision to throw its weight on the Nigerian side was influenced largely by her investment interests, which changed with developments at the war front and Ojukwu's counterproductive diplomatic

---

[375] *Hugh Thomas, The Slave Trade: The Story of the Atlantic Slave Trade: 1440 – 1870.*
[376] *King James of the Christian Holy Bible, Galatians, Chapter 3 (25 – 29).*
[377] *Nicholas Ibeawuchi Omenka, Blaming The Gods: Christian Religious Propaganda in The Nigeria— Biafra War, The Journal of African History , 2010, Vol. 51, No. 3 (2010), pp. 367-389*
[378] George Thayer, The War Business: The International Trade in Armaments, New York, Simon, and Shuster, 1969, Pp. 163 – 72.
[379] *Gary Blank, Britain, Biafra and the Balance of Payments: The Formation of London's 'One Nigeria' Policy,* Revue Française De Civilisation Britannique – Vol. 18 N° 2.

behavior. The French initially took the attitude that *"La guerre est une chose aleatoire."* The outcome of a war is unpredictable.

While the British prevaricated on how to deal with Nigeria vis-à-vis Biafra, the British economic interest was paramount in diplomatic decision-making, as can be seen from what happened after the Biafran Army invaded the Midwest in August 1967. Specifically, quoting Gary Blank and archival communications of British Foreign Affairs,

"The sole immediate British interest in Nigeria is that the Nigerian economy should be brought back to a condition in which our substantial trade and investment in the country can be further developed, and particularly so that we can gain access to important oil installations. Our only direct interest in the maintenance of the Federation is that Nigeria has been developed as an economic unit, and any disruption of... this would have adverse effects on trade and development. Provided economic unity can be preserved, we have no direct interest in how this is done. The break-up of Nigeria into several independent States would not necessarily be averse to our interests provided that full economic cooperation was maintained between them. Indeed, to the extent that a break-up produced a more stable political arrangement, it might in the long term even be to our advantage."[380]

According to Aneke, quoting the *New York Times* on August 7, 1967, two days before the Biafran invasions of the Midwest, the Shell-BP Managing Director Mr. Stanley Grey told the Nigerian Government that his company would not make any oil royalty payments until the war ends. He made this known in a conference with Nigerian officials on his return from 10 days detention in Biafra.

"Mr. Grey who returned to Lagos after 10 days in detention in Enugu ... said his company was resting on the terms of the strictest legality in deciding that it did not have to pay on oil produced in 1967 until within two months of the end of the calendar in which the production occurred...He added that he had informed Lt. Col. Odumegwu Ojukwu ... of Shell-BP's refusal to pay royalties, ... he was ordered to leave the Region within 24 hours. Mr. Grey, who said that he had been treated with courtesy ... said that Ojukwu responded to the decision with an order to seize the assets [of Shell-BP] in the Region."[381]

Initially, the British essentially looked the other way when a private arms dealer called Parker-Haile sold 930 FN rifles to the Biafrans immediately after the secession.[382] One could argue that, at some point, the British did not care, except for their economic interests. Nothing is surprising about this attitude. If treason prospers, who dare call it treason? According to Thayer[383] "Because both the Federals and Biafrans wanted arms and could not get them from either the USA or Great Britain ... a vacuum was created which was promptly filled by all manner of suppliers ... private dealers gunrunners and governments...Inter-Arms UK which had been approached by both sides ... was at first denied an export license ... Later in the year (1967), the British authorities relaxed their restrictions on Inter-Arms activities ... Two B-26 bombers were delivered to the Biafrans ... obtained through a French dealer ... In October 1967 ...a transport under French registry traveling from Ireland also brought a load of Czech arms [to Biafra]."

Before war broke out and, as part of his Revenue Edict, and following it up when war broke out in July 1967, Ojukwu ordered that all royalties from the oil companies should be paid to Biafra. In response, the British High Commission wrote to the Commonwealth Office, stating, "In the new circumstances it must be a principal objective of British policy to avoid doing anything which could seriously antagonize the State of Biafra in case it is successful in vindicating its independence. Our

---

[380] *Ibid, Page 81 referencing communication with Secretary Thomas to the Prime Minister on August 18, 1967, when Biafran forces were still strongly entrenched in the Midwest and advancing towards Lagos, the Capital of Nigeria.*

[381] *Aneke, Luke, Untold Story of the Nigeria Biafra War, Shell BP Refuses to Pay Royalties to Nigeria August 7, 1967, Page 140 (New York Times, August 1967)*

[382] *Thayer, Op. Cit., Page 166. These may have been old 1950 versions – bolt action rifles that ported 7.92mm calibers.*

[383] *Thayer, Op. Cit, Pp. 165 – 67.*

interests, particularly in oil, are so great that they must override any lingering regret that we may feel for the disintegration of British-made Nigeria."[384] Regarding the blockade, Britain Minister of State for Commonwealth Affairs George Thomas was to meet Gowon in Lagos. " At the meeting, held on 8 July 1967, two days after the commencement of hostilities, Thomas maintained that the oil blockade was illegal under international law and that oil companies could not be blamed if they decided to pay royalties to Biafra, for it was the government in effective control of a disputed territory."[385] The Gowon administration did not flinch and suggested that Shell-BP be punished for the token payment of royalty to Biafra. About one or two months later, the British government eventually blocked the proposed token payment of £N250,000 to Biafra. The eventual cancellation of the proposed token royalty to Biafra was in part due to Ojukwu's counterproductive behavior, which will be described later.

There were other opposing views on the same theme. During a debate in the British House of Commons during the early stages of the secession, it was also argued that "Nevertheless, the facts are that Shell-BP ... invested £250 Million in Nigeria on which we now expect a large and increasing return of great importance to the British Balance of Payments. Other investments are worth up to £175 Million. Our annual export trade [to Nigeria] is about £90 Million ... All this would be at risk if we abandoned our policy of support for the Federal Government and others would quickly take our place."[386] In taking this latter position, the author also wanted to hedge against the possible cutoff of oil from the Middle East and also considered Nigeria a more cost-effective source of crude oils compared with the Middle East. It was all about economics and economic interests.

Israel, Biafra, and National Security Concerns

One of the grand illusions of the Biafran population, which, to my disappointment, also infected the apparently educated Biafran leadership, is that the international community's outpouring of sympathy and even indignation would be translated into strong diplomatic support. In this regard, it will be apt to honor Madiebo and his succinct summary of the illusion that he correctly credits for our people's endurance throughout the forty-two months of ordeal, horror, and torture—from the massacres of May 1966, September through December 1966, and the thirty months of civil war. According to Madiebo[387]. "...We felt that having been so unjustly treated and massacred, God and the international community would not stand idly by and allow us to be exterminated in our homeland ... Unfortunately, for our innocently naïve people political and military logic do not follow sentimental lines."[388] It is on this belief that the Biafran government and the Biafran population counted on the government of the State of Israel to support Biafra openly and to supply Biafra with arms sufficient to prosecute the war. It is equally for this reason that Igbos hold it against Awolowo when he said that starvation is a legitimate instrument of war.

In his Christmas speech, December 1967, Ojukwu appealed to the sentiments of the Jewish State of Israel. Specifically, Ojukwu exhorted,

"Like the Jews of old, we saw in the birth of our young republic the gateway to the freedom and survival of our people... But like Herod, ... Nigeria embarked on upon an adventure of indiscriminate slaughter and destruction ... Yet, I shudder to think that the leaders of the Christian worlds should watch in silence Nigeria's unprovoked war in a devilish bid to complete the genocide which she began last year ... I also shudder to think that the leaders of the Christian church in America and Europe should stand dumb and silent ... while the war machines of Britain and the

---

[384] Gary Blank, supra, quoting TNA, FCO 25/232, Lagos to Commonwealth Office [reproduced in Commonwealth Office Print of 7 July 1967]. This was a day after Nigeria attacked Biafra.
[385] *Ibid*
[386] *Chibuike Uche, Oil, British Interests and the Nigerian Civil War, Journal of African History, 2008 Vol 49 (1) Pp. 111 – 35*
[387] *Madiebo, The Nigerian Revolution, Pp. 377 – 78*
[388] *Madiebo, Ibid.*

godless Soviet Union are allowed to ... slaughter innocent men, women and children ... in hospitals and ... places of worship."[389]

This speech was designed to appeal to the Christian world and to a Jewish state that had several experiences similar to the ethnic cleansing pogrom of the Igbos.

There was no shortage of sympathy for the Igbos and even indignation toward Nigeria from the beginning of the six months of ethnic cleansing in 1966 through the genocidal orgy that raged. The genocidal actions of the Nigerian government were evident everywhere, including the mass starvation that was occurring and the indiscriminate bombing of civilians.

As explained earlier, moral and other forms of sympathy do not easily translate into diplomatic and political support. Individuals will provide support, but ruling establishments are compelled to deal with political realities and worry about their security, post factum when they give political support to a constituency on moral grounds. In the case of Israel, there is no doubt that they had sympathy for Biafra. After working to provide humanitarian support covertly and openly for Biafra from as far back as 1966, in July 1969, Abba Eban made known to the Nigerian government their indignation toward the Nigerian government about the plight of Biafran civilians.[390] Available evidence will show that the State of Israel provided tremendous bold and brave support for Biafra. Nevertheless, they could not come out openly to provide military support, nor were they even capable of being a major arms supplier to Biafra. The Jewish state had to worry about its security problems with its Arab neighbors, the possibility that Biafra could lose the war and thus cause the loss of its diplomatic relationship with Nigeria, and how that could affect Nigeria's vote at the Organization of Africa Unity (OAU) and the United Nations. Coupled with the natural caution of political diplomacy, the Biafran leadership, once more, approached the State of Israel in its typical amateurish way and exposed the Jewish state to pressure. Specifically:

"Nirgad, complained to officials in the Israeli government ... as for those whose approach is driven by emotions, I say that my heart ... is not with the Federal government in its barbaric war. As a Jew who lived under Nazi rule... yet as a state, we are bound by the political calculus and hypocrisy upon which modern statecraft is built ... We are too vulnerable, and the chances of an independent Biafra are exceedingly slim ... and ... any act of disloyalty to the Federal Government jeopardizes our position there and in other African countries."[391]

Indeed, under pressure from Aminu Kano, who maintained diplomatic contact with the Jewish state against the wishes of Ahmadu Bello, Israel supplied arms to Nigeria in mid-1968[392].

[389] *General C. Odumegwu Ojukwu, Biafra: Random Speeches with Journals of Events, London, Harper and Row, Vol. I, 1969*

[390] *JTA Daily news bulletin, Jewish Telegraphic Agency, July 10 (JTA) – "... Foreign Minister Abba Eban disclosed today that Israel has asked both Nigeria and its break-away eastern province of Biafra to make stronger efforts to end their civil war but the appeals have been in vain. Mr. Eban spoke in reply to questions in the Knesset. His disclosure was the first that Israel has made direct diplomatic representations in the Biafran situation. The Foreign Minister said that Israel would continue to provide humanitarian help to Biafra and will continue to let the Nigerian authorities in Lagos know of Israel's shock and indignation over the plight of Biafran civilians..."*

[391] *Zach Levey, Israel, Nigeria, and the Biafra Civil War, 1967 – 1970, in Dirk Moses and Lasse Heerten, Eds. Post-Colonial Conflict and the Question of Genocide, Routledge, 2019, Page 184.*

[392] *Ibid, Page 184*

As early as mid-August 1966, Ojukwu sent emissaries on a "clandestine" mission to purchase arms from the State of Israel.[393] Although the Israelis were supportive, the Eastern Nigerian emissaries left Israel empty-handed. Specifically, the Israeli government first assured the empty-handed Francis Nwokedi that "if there really does arise an independent Eastern Nigeria, Israel … would offer some support."[394] In October 1966, an official in the Israeli government, while expressing support and understanding of the sorrow of the Eastern Nigerians, also cautioned against getting into a misunderstanding with Lagos, because Lagos will interpret even a shipment of blankets to the East as succor for the rebels.[395] It must be noted that during this period, the State of Israel strained itself to assure the Nigerian government that it was not supplying arms to the Eastern Nigerian government. Moreover, the Israeli minister assured the Lagos government that Ojukwu had not made any contact with the Jewish state, though Nwokedi's visit was well known to people around and the visit was to a government official who would have all manner of eavesdroppers around.

In the first place, approaching Israel should never have been made through a government official and openly. This is where the naïveté of the Biafran leadership was exposed. Although the Jews may sympathize with the plight of the Igbos, they also had to hedge their bets and worry about their comfort around their neighborhood. Notwithstanding the assurances of the Jewish state to the Nigerian government, in November 1966, shortly after the visit by Eastern Nigerian emissaries, the Israelis put the Eastern Nigerians in touch with reliable arms dealers in Europe through Mossad (Israel's national intelligence agency), who could fly arms to Eastern Nigeria. This was an attempt to mitigate crooked arms dealers that had duped Ojukwu's arms supply agents. Indeed, Biafra's cheapest arms were procured through the State of Israel in the form of weapons captured from the Egyptians during the Six-Day War in 1967.[396] However, over the course of the war, Israel provided tremendous assistance through the Ivory Coast and other emissaries in the form of arms, money, and humanitarian aid.[397] Of particular importance is a series of secret missions called "Operation Relief Action Nigeria," where the Israeli government, working all but openly with the International Committee of the Red Cross (ICRC), hired Boeing C-97 cargo planes to ferry relief into Biafra. The Israeli government went far to assist Biafra, though making sure that they did not annoy Nigeria.[398]

The Biafran government continued its pressure on Israel and expressed disappointment that the Jewish state was not rendering sufficient assistance to Biafra.[399] While Israel played to the gallery of international diplomatic protocols, the Jewish state made its feelings well known to the government of Nigeria. As early as December 1967, in response to public opinion pressures, the Israeli government sent Nigerian officials a twenty-two-page essay titled, "Biafra: Struggle for National Survival." The Israeli government also made clear its empathy for Biafra as well as its concern for a Hausa-Muslim–dominated Nigeria. The Israelis also viewed the plight of Biafrans similar to what Israelis faced before the Six-Day War in June 1967 with the Egyptians and with the Holocaust.[400] Indeed, in July 1968, Abba Eban pointed out publicly that the intensity of the suffering in Biafra removed the situation in Nigeria-Biafra from the sphere of internal problem to an onus upon the conscience of all civilization.[401] It got to the point where the Israeli government openly sent an Israeli Air Force jet to a point near Biafra to deliver food into Biafra. Finally, in August 1968, through connections in the Ivory Coast, the Israeli government also supplied arms to the government

---

[393] *Jonh De St. Jorre, The Nigerian Civil War (A Brothers' War), London, Holder and Stoughton, 1972, Pp. 220 – 22.*

[394] *Zach Levey, Israel, Nigeria, and the Biafra Civil War, 1967 – 1970, in Dirk Moses and Lasse Heerten, Eds. Post-Colonial Conflict and the Question of Genocide, Routledge, 2019, Pp. 177 – 195.*

[395] *Ibid, Pp. 181 - 185*

[396] *Ibid, Page 182. See also Stremlau, The International Politics of the Nigerian Civil War, Princeton, NJ, Princeton University Press, 1977, Pp. 235 – 37.*

[397] *Zach Levey, Op. Cit.*

[398] *Eitan Press Biafran Airlift: Israel's Secret Mission to Save Lives, October 2013, https://unitedwithisrael. org/biafran-airlift-israels-secret-mission-to-save-lives/*

[399] *Zack Levey, Op. Cit., Page 185*

[400] *Ibid.*

[401] *Ibid, Page 186*

of Biafra. The only condition for the extensive shipment of arms to Biafra was that none of the arms should bear the markings of the Israeli Army.[402] Besides the substantial delivery of arms, Israel also made available to Biafra $US200,000 in cash in two separate $US100,000 transfers. The Israelis also sent medical doctors into Biafra. In effect, Israel provided substantial help to Biafra, but much of it, though not all, were undercover.

Counterproductive Behaviors – Fake News and Grabbing at Straws for Diplomatic Recognition

One of Biafra's greatest problems was transforming the tremendous amount of humanitarian sympathy into diplomatic support. As soon as Yakubu Gowon declared war on Biafra, he warned the international community that the crisis in Nigeria was a domestic problem and that other countries should not interfere. For this reason, diplomatic recognition would be considered interference and an unfriendly act. On its side, the Biafrans worked vigorously to achieve diplomatic recognition by other countries.

Shortly after the declaration of secession, Radio Biafra announced that several countries, including Israel, had already recognized Biafra.[403] I can recollect this moment myself—several other countries were named.[404] The truth was that no country, including Israel, recognized Biafra immediately after the declaration of secession. This is the first example of counterproductive diplomatic behavior. Propaganda, very often, is based on falsehood and half-truths. However, certain kinds of distortions should be made for internal consumption, but not where external constituencies can be affected adversely. According to Akpan, he inquired and found out that Ojukwu was aware of it, but no one was ever disciplined for the embarrassment. It would be an understatement to call this behavior childish. What is more important is that it demonstrates not only the desperation of the inner leadership clique of Biafra but also their incompetence in understanding how diplomacy works. The damage that was done to the Biafran diplomatic efforts would have been immense. The countries that were mentioned were embarrassed by the announcement because they accorded no such recognition to Biafra. The countries mentioned may have been countries that privately expressed sympathy for the Biafran cause and might have engaged Biafra with valuable and potent clandestine support. What is even worse about this misstep is that the Nigerian government was then alerted and would now bring behind-the-scenes pressure on these countries and put them on the defensive. The Nigerian government would now spy on the named countries and bring evidence to pressure them not to do anything to assist Biafra. It would have been better to spread this kind of morale-boosting propaganda as a rumor to be discarded later. Even at that, the initial morale-boosting effect could have created a more deleterious demoralization of the population when it would be found out that there was no such recognition. Therefore, such a story should not be allowed to spread even as a rumor.

Eventually, at some point, a few countries did recognize Biafra, specifically Tanzania (April 1968), Gabon, Ivory Coast, Zambia, and Haiti. However, the countries that recognized Biafra did so for two reasons: In their speeches to recognize Biafra, Julius Nyerere of Tanzania and Kenneth Kaunda of Zambia cited the brutality of the Nigerian slaughter of Biafrans and the conditions that led to the cessation move. Both of these countries had had their internal instabilities and had made statements in support of unity within colonial boundaries. But they were equally appalled and horrified by the brutality of the Nigerian government and that they could no longer hide behind the claim that the war in Nigeria was a domestic problem of Nigeria.[405] Another reason for recognizing Biafra was more as a means of forcing Nigeria to the negotiating table than to support

---

[402] Ibid, Page 187

[403] Zach Levey, Israel, Nigeria, and the Biafra Civil War, 1967 – 1970, in Dirk Moses and Lasse Heerten, Eds. Post-Colonial Conflict and the Question of Genocide, Routledge, 2019, Page 183.

[404] *Akpan, The Struggle for Secession,* Pp. 85 – 86

[405] *John de St.Jorre, The Brother's War: Biafra and Nigeria, Op. Cit., Pp. 192 – 210*

secession. If Nigeria agreed with the secession, so be it. If not, at least the recognition of Biafra and the possibility that other countries may follow could motivate Nigeria to make the concession that would bring about peace. If Ojukwu had understood so and used it more skillfully, he might have succeeded in negotiating a better deal for Biafra. Even Dr. Nnamdi Azikiwe, the first president of an independent Nigeria who had influenced the recognitions, made statements to confirm this conclusion. According to Dr. Azikiwe,

"The long and short of it all was that I and these great African statesmen agreed that if Gowon persisted with pre-conditions, then they would accord recognition [if the war did not end by March 31, 1968, as predicted by Yakubu Gowon] to force the hands of Gowon to go to the conference table and bring about peace."[406]

Besides the fact that the Biafrans were sorely disappointed by the absence of recognition, they also exaggerated to themselves the value of diplomatic recognition. Diplomatic recognition does not translate to bullets. Once countries began to recognize Biafra, the Nigerian government was even more determined to make nonsense of it through renewed and more brutal military action. Even the countries that recognized Biafra did not provide much military support for Biafra. Only the Ivory Coast worked vigorously to be a conduit for negotiating the purchase of military hardware for Biafra. Gabon also acted as a conduit to purchase arms for Biafra, and Zambia provided two DC-3 aircraft to support the humanitarian airlift into Biafra.[407]

Shell-BP and Oil Royalties

While Shell-BP prevaricated about payment of royalties to the Nigerian or Biafran government, Ojukwu demanded that Shell-BP pay all royalties to Biafra. In an attempt to hammer out a compromise, a meeting took place near the end of June 1967 in New York. Biafra put forth a proposal that 57.5 percent of the revenues deriving from the East should be paid to Biafra and the balance by July 1, and the remainder paid into a suspense account until a political settlement was reached.[408] Nigeria rejected the proposal. Within hours of Ojukwu's deadline of July 1, 1967, Shell promised to pay £UK250,000. But Biafra was determined to get a £7 Million, though the maximum they could justify since the beginning of the war was £1 Million. Biafra rejected the payment of the money to their ACB bank account and demanded payment to a Swiss Numbered account.[409] This was blocked by Britain.

Shell-BP at some point proposed to pay the royalties to a suspense account until the end of hostilities. As described earlier, the managing director of Shell-BP, Mr. Grey, had also declined to pay royalties to Biafra or Nigeria. However, when Biafra invaded the Midwest and it appeared that Biafra had military credibility, Ojukwu demanded immediate payment of £2 million. Thereupon, Ojukwu invited Mr. Grey to Enugu for discussion. Mr. Grey may have promised to pay more than that. According to Akpan[410] by the time Mr. Grey was invited to Enugu, he had promised to pay to Biafrans what would have been the Eastern Nigerian government's share of royalties. Ojukwu rejected the idea and threatened that he would detain Mr. Grey upon his arrival in Enugu. Akpan advised Ojukwu that such action would be unfortunate. Contrary to the advice of Akpan and Sir. Louis Mbanefo, Ojukwu had Mr. Grey placed under house arrest following a meeting in which Grey would not accede to Ojukwu's demands. While in detention, Mr. Grey instructed all Shell-BP staff in Port Harcourt to depart. After Mr. Grey was released from detention, he left Biafra, and for

---

[406] Center for Nigerian Progress – July 2020, Zik's version of what transpired between him and Ojukwu during the Biafra war https://lawakhigbe.com/2020/07/11/ziks-version-of-what-transpired-between-him-and-ojukwu-during-the-biafra-war/

[407] *John de St. Jorre, A Brother's War, Pp. 138 - 145*

[408] *John de. St. Jorre Pp. 139 – 141*

[409] *Ibid*

[410] Akpan, The Struggle for Secession, Page 148.

him and the British government, it was very likely the last straw.[411] The British government turned against Biafra after Mr. Grey's detention.

In this encounter with Shell-BP, what Ojukwu did not consider was that Mr. Grey, as managing director, was a representative of shareholders and the commercial interest of a powerful, sovereign nation. Mr. Grey did not hold all the decision-making power and could not even have been able to transfer the funds, even if he agreed with Ojukwu. While he argued with Shell-BP, the funds sat in some account, and following Ojukwu's behavior, the British government blocked the transfer of the £250,000 with the lame excuse that it was about exchange control. The wiser behavior for Ojukwu would have been to accept the £250,000 with alacrity and maintain good offices with Shell and the British government, and then follow up with more experienced and better-connected politicians and diplomats like Azikiwe and Mathew Mbu. Azikiwe, especially, had much more influence and more powerful influential connections with the British. Azikiwe also had bosom friends in the USA who would have been able to help with diplomatic support and, in all likelihood, the smuggling of arms. These people should have been sent as clandestine emissaries to England or to contact people in England and the United States that would have made valuable contacts. One of my colleagues (of blessed memory) at the City University of New York who stood with Biafra until after the Battle of Abagana repeatedly asked why Zik did not go on a mission to the United States and England. She stated to me that all the contacts she had in the United States were asking what Zik was saying and if Zik was saying nothing, why was he silent?

Captured Oilmen – The Ransom of AGIP Men

On May 9, 1969, Biafran Army Commandos stormed the Midwest and attacked oil installations and production facilities belonging to the Italian AGIP oil company. During the attack, eleven oilmen were killed and eighteen were captured. The Biafran government kept the information away from the news until about the end of May. Indeed, while I was still behind the Nigerian lines up till May 20, I had heard nothing about it in the news. It was after I settled at the 71B Battalion at Umuobiala that I heard the news. On June 2, 1969, the Biafran government purportedly put the oilmen on trial and condemned them to death while claiming that they were armed and fighting on the Nigerian side in a genocidal war against Biafra. There was an uproar in Europe and around the world to release the oilmen. As a means of putting pressure on Biafra, Portugal and France suspended all assistance to Biafra. Biafra's image and propaganda were tarnished. Some Europeans compared the Biafran courts to Nazi courts, implying that the trials were kangaroo. Also, many Europeans who raised money for Biafra suspended their efforts. After negotiations with the Italian and German governments, Biafra allegedly received what some considered as a ransom of $3 million. Biafra claimed that the money was more in the form of legitimate royalties to Biafra.

Overall, the hostage crisis tarnished Biafra's image as a victimized nation. Ojukwu lamented that the uproar signified that "White" lives mattered more than Black lives. Ojukwu asked, "How many dead blacks make one missing white." He then called on mathematicians to please help him. How could eighteen White men cause so much uproar? Even a Nigerian newspaper, the *New Nigerian*, decried the uproar over eighteen White men while thousands of Blacks on both sides of the conflict were dying daily on the battlefield. I happen to disagree with the lamentation of Ojukwu and even the *New Nigerian* on the matter. In the first place, the oilmen were not combatants. Even Ojukwu and the Biafran leadership knew that. The propaganda stunt that the oilmen were combatants was rather a blow below the belt. Secondly, if thousands of Blacks were dying daily on both sides of a conflict, it was because they put themselves in that position. On both sides, there had been opportunities to resolve the matter peacefully, yet neither side had been honest about it or, at least, one side should give way, or they should have found some compromise. Finally, whether it was one person or a thousand persons, the oil company was morally obligated to secure their release. Even the Europeans that went into an uproar were also morally obligated to plead for their release.

---

[411] Ibid., Pp. 147 – 150.

It appears that the Biafran government tried the oilmen and condemned them to death to call attention to its cause and gain some legitimacy as a government. If that was the purpose, it failed woefully and did more diplomatic and financial damage than it was worth. It was a clear indication of diplomatic incompetence on the part of Biafra. In the first place, Europeans considered these people their kith and kin who were not engaged in any combat. They were in Nigeria to make a living in normal trading activities. It was not their business that the people were fighting a war and killing themselves. It was not their responsibility to ask questions as to why they were fighting. Their European kin also did not see that they were in combat. Suppose for a moment that they were mercenaries, wearing army uniforms, and fighting on the Nigerian side fully armed and engaged in a firefight. I can bet that there would not be such an uproar. The European kin of the oilmen had been raising money to assist Biafrans to alleviate the suffering of the civilian population. If their noncombatant kin were captured and threatened with death, they would have every right to use every pressure that they could bring to bear to force Biafra to release them. In conclusion, it would have been much better for Biafra to immediately release the captured oilmen and admonish oil companies that they are operating in a war zone and should expect danger. Biafra would then simply explain that the ones that died were simply caught in a crossfire and there was no intention of killing them. Biafra would have been seen as a more civilized nation and their image would have been enhanced.[412]

The Gods Favor the Big Guns – The End Justifies the Means

Biafra lost the diplomatic war and ultimately the shooting war in part because, as Brig. Godwin Alabi[413] put it, "…they had a boss instead of a leader…," and as such did not have a collective leadership, as Madiebo[414] also stated. Their loss was also caused by the social superstructure of their struggle; borne out of a nebulous history that had neither foundations nor continuity from the remote past. Furthermore, the Igbos needed to disabuse their minds of the thought that they were more capable than other Nigerians and snap out of their false sense of superiority. It did not help that Igbos were living on the faulty assumption that their cause was so just that the world

would immediately come to their aid and not stand by and see them slaughtered in their homeland. Finally, Igbos need to learn to think more for the collective good in the long haul rather than on the individual gain in the short run based on internal treachery and mutual cannibalistic exploitation. I do not doubt that many Igbos will challenge what I have said because they are facts that are hard to swallow. However, all people need to look inward and engage in a soul-searching exercise. I will address each of these—some profoundly and others a little more loosely.

In War, Do Not Play Cry Baby – It Will Not Do You Any Good

Because the Igbos were not adequately prepared for war and relied on false assumptions, including oblique promises that were subject to interpretation, they relied so much on propaganda and repeatedly pointed the world to the justness of their cause. Without a doubt, and as has been said time and

---

[412] *For a fuller account of the hostage incident, see Roy Doron, Biafra and the Agip Oil Workers: Ransoming and the Modern Nation State in Perspective, African Economic History, 2014, Vol. 42 (2014), pp. 137-156*
[413] Brigadier Godwin Alabi, The Tragedy of Victory,
[414] Alexander Madiebo, The Nigerian Revolution and the Biafran War, Pp. 377 – 79.

again, there was no shortage of sympathy for the cause of Biafra, even among other Nigerians who, at least initially, did not throw their weight on the federal side of the confrontation. Because they believed in the justness of their cause, Biafrans misinterpreted Awolowo's statement about how the West would opt out of Nigeria if the East was "allowed" to opt-out. Furthermore, the Igbos expressed disappointment and still hold it against Awolowo that he said that starvation is a legitimate instrument of war. Two points need to be addressed here. The first is that all is fair in war. Therefore, starvation is a legitimate instrument of war. Secondly, so-called laws of war appear to me to be silly and meaningless. Once there is the issue of life and death, these rules are thrown out of the window because they are subject to interpretation and have nebulous meanings and boundaries. There are laws about the use of starvation as an instrument of war, but the details and definitions make such rules senseless because one could easily interpret them to suit the actions that are desired.[415] From about April 1968 to the end of the war, images of the mass starvation of children and the brutal ethnic cleansing pogrom of 1966 were used to influence the world. Biafra pointed to the genocidal behavior of the Nigerian Army and cried foul to a world where individuals responded but ruling establishments and the Nigerian public scoffed at the images either as false or as a just reward for the one-sided coup of January 1966. Unfortunately, the world of ruling establishments that have controlled the destiny of mankind for the greater part of human history does not care how many people are killed in a war. Throughout the history of warfare, it is well known that sieges intend to compel the enemy side into submission through starvation. And Biafra was under siege (see the Changing map of Biafra on this page). Usually, it is the civilian population that is the target since, sooner or later and even in between, the same civilian population supports the military combatants. Even the children, if the war lasts long enough, will grow into military combatants. Therefore, they might as well die now. Aptly, Brig. Benjamin Adekunle, commander of the Third Marine Commandos, stated that he wanted to see no Red Cross, Caritas, or Church Aid and wanted to see that no Igbo have a bite to eat until they capitulate. "If the children must die first, so be it." This statement came from a man who, if he did not yet have children, at least had relatives who had children. One would ask, what was this great sin of the Igbos that they should perish and where was it written that they must be Nigerians? Nevertheless, starvation is a perfectly legitimate instrument of war if the ultimate objective is to win. If you complain against Awolowo for his statement, you might as well complain about or condemn the Nigerian Army for prosecuting the war with guns and bullets.

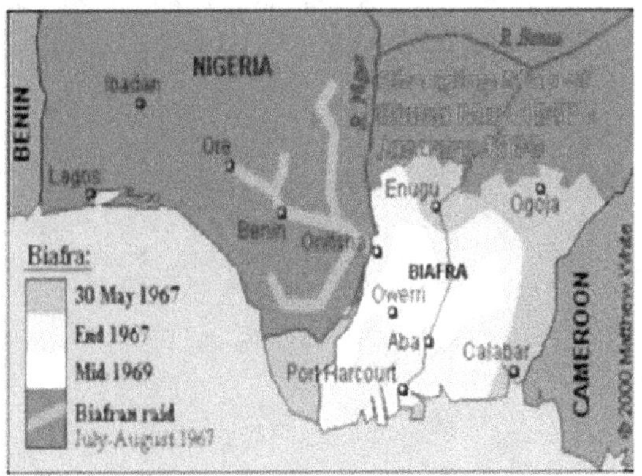

While Biafrans hoped in vain that the conscience of the world would come to their rescue, there are two things that the Igbo man should have borne in mind. The first is that other communities have their pressing challenges, one of which is feeding and supporting themselves.

The other is that the entire population of fourteen million Biafrans could have perished, and the world would not have blinked. The world did not become underpopulated because forty-eight million people died during the Second World War (1939–1945). It would have suited the Nigerians if all nine million Igbos of Biafra

---

[415] *For extensive review of the literature and the nebulous rules and laws, see Esbjörn Rosenblad, Starvation as a Method of Warfare — Conditions for Regulation by Convention, The International Lawyer, April 1973, Vol. 7, No. 2 (April 1973), pp. 252-270. Also George Alfred Mudge, Starvation As A Means Of Warfare, The International Lawyer, January, 1970, Vol. 4, No. 2, pp. 228-268 and Beth Van Schaack, Siege Warfare and the Starvation of Civilians as a Weapon of War and War Crime, February 4, 2016, https:// www.justsecurity.org/29157/siege-warfare-starvation-civilians-war-crime/ Intentional starvation of civilians should be considered a war crime worldwide: Federal Council supports International Criminal Court and Press release, Switzerland, Federal Department of Foreign Affairs (FDFA), May 2021*

perished. Then the lands and whatever resources were available in Igboland would belong to them. Over time, the annihilation of the Igbo race would be no more than a topic of academic interest.

When Igbos looked hopelessly upon the governments and ruling establishments of Christian Europe to pity the plight of starving children and to come to their rescue, the Igbos should first have looked at the statistics of death casualties of World War II (WWII). When we call World War II world war, we should know that this was a European war to resolve their internal power tussles and cleavages. Though Europeans have been fighting wars through the ages, WWII, in my opinion, was the grand finale of the Franco-German War that ended in 1871 and World War I that ended in 1918. In World War I, twenty-five million Europeans died. Except for 5,000 Ethiopians and 1,000 South Africans that may have included some Europeans (Whites), or twelve million Chinese and Japanese, all other casualties of WWII were European (White). That still leaves thirty-six million Europeans who died in World War II. England lost 388,000 people.

Against this backdrop, why did anyone think that the British would care if nine million Igbos perished so that the British could protect

Casualties of World War II 1939–1945			
Axis	**Military**	**Civilian**	**Total**
Germany	3,500,000	700,000	4,200,000
Japan	2,000,000	350,000	2,350,000
Other Axis	1,082,000	636,000	1,718,000
Axis Total	6,582,000	1,686,000	8,268,000
Allied	**Military**	**Civilian**	**Total**
Soviet Union	10,000,000	10,000,000	20,000,000
China	2,500,000	7,500,000	10,000,000
Poland	100,000	5,700,000	5,800,000
Other Allied	1,676,800	2,486,900	4,163,700
Allied Total	14,276,800	25,686,900	39,963,700
Total Casualties	20,858,800	27,372,900	48,231,700
Source: http://warchronicle.com/numbers/WWII/deaths.htm			

their investments? It was pointless appealing to the godless non-Christian communist Soviets, who do not believe in God and lost twenty million people in WWII. If that many of them were killed in a war, what makes anyone think that they would blink at nine million Igbos being killed in a war?

The first lesson that Igbos must learn is that nature does not owe anyone survival. It is true, as previously said, that it is better to fight and be conquered than to surrender to certain slaughter. It is equally true that discretion is the better part of valor. Those who rush into conflict are the ones who are not aware that conflict can be deadly.[416] To go into war, it is better to be strong. Even if it comes to the point where the lion and the lamb will lie together, try to be the lion. The logic of war has no respect for the unprepared. It does not matter whether you are right or wrong.

---

[416] *D. K. Achara, Ala Bingo (Igbo Literature Book) – Ndi ji oso â gbakwuru ôgû bû ndi â maghi nâ ôgû bu onwu*

Chapter XVII

EPILOGUE: LESSONS LEARNED OR NOT LEARNED POSTBELLUM

The Nigeria-Biafra civil war should teach us a lesson that should help us build a better nation. Nigeria gained independence in 1960 amid great expectations. Within six years of its existence, the country suffered a cataclysmic crisis that threatened to break up the country. The experience was traumatic in as much as it was bloody. There was tremendous pain and suffering that was one-sided, more so for some than for others. One thing that we should not do is continue to recriminate against each other and assign blame as to who was right or wrong. What I stand by is that the war was avoidable, except for the greed and petulance of the elite ruling classes on both sides for whom politics is a means of personal aggrandizement. For the ordinary Nigerian, we should not align ourselves with the factions of the elite because we are the cannon fodder who are sacrificed to protect the leisure of the elites, a statement that Lucius Mesterius Plutarchus is said to have attributed to Tiberius Gracchus. Rather, as a people, we should see the war as a "..foundation of blood, sweat, and tears ... upon which we built our nation ... If any side was wrong, then we were all wrong and if one side was right then we were all right..."[417] The extant arguments make it appear as if the war was caused singlehandedly by Ojukwu right out of the blue or at least in a cynical ploy to become a head of state. This is not true. Though I do not consider Ojukwu a hero of the Igbos, he should equally not be vilified, especially not by the Nigerian side. He was not a villain in any shape or form. He played his part as a member of the elite ruling class.

As I said earlier, we cannot continue to argue that the nation we have was an artificial creation of a colonial master. I will reiterate and maintain that the "White man" did us a favor by bringing us together in a common market that facilitates trade and economic prosperity, something we should exploit more wisely. What should have been instructive about the war is that the trauma occurred early enough—six years after independence. The gravity of the trauma and the pain and suffering should have shocked us enough to be cautious. The sad tragedy of our experience is that fifty years after the war, we do not seem to have learned critical lessons—or even any lessons at all.

Mockery, Honour, Reconciliation, Remembrance, and the Ghost of Nuremberg

Our insensitivity to the trauma that we suffered, as Nigerians and as Biafrans, began almost as soon as the war ended or just on the heels of the war. The victors, on the heels of the war and in subsequent years, continued the war in other ways and have continued to this day. The punishment of the vanquished was relentless as if to ignore the understandable reasons for the crisis of confidence and mutual trust that precipitated the war. The attitude of the Nigerian government was that the Igbos were unruly rebels who had no legitimate or understandable reason to rebel or to defend themselves.

---

[417] *Major General Joseph Nanven Garba, Fractured History, Pp. 149 – 50.*

243

Immediately after the war ended flowing Effiong's broadcast of January 12, 1970, the international relief agencies requested that Uli Airport, which had been used to ferry relief to the suffering peoples of Igboland, whom the Nigerian government claimed not to hate be immediately put to use to rush relief aid to the surviving Biafrans. Gen. Yakubu Gowon rejected their request. If the government of Nigeria was sincere all along, now that the so-called "rebel Ojukwu" had left the enclave, the Uli Airport could no longer be used to import arms. First and foremost, then Col. Olusegun Obasanjo, the commander of the Third Marine Commando Division that effectively conquered Biafra, ordered that Uli Airport be immediately destroyed and "converted back to what it was, … a road." In my opinion, Uli Airport should have been preserved as a monument to the monumental effort and sacrifice of the people on both sides of the struggle—the children that starved and died and the soldiers that shed their blood. These are ways to achieve true reconciliation: to acknowledge the legitimate and understandable complaints of all involved—the Biafrans as well as the Nigerians—for it was a brothers' war. But our leaders are extremely shallow in their thinking. But besides that, let's look at immediate considerations.

The Nigerian government could have taken advantage of Uli Airport's proximity to the ravaged region to provide immediate assistance to the tens of thousands of children and adults who were suffering. In his statement on January 12, 1970, to end the war, Effiong appealed "to all governments to give urgent thought to relief and to prevail on the Federal Military Government to order their troops to stop all military operations." But, in a move that still puzzles psychologists, Gowon refused relief materials from the so-called friends of Biafra as a punitive measure. Gowon said, "Let them keep their blood money. Let them keep their bloody relief supplies. We don't want it."[418] The question is, who were the "we" that did not want the relief? Was it the well-fed Gowon with members of his Supreme Military Council or the Easterners who were dying in their thousands after three years of starvation? Who were the "we"?[419]

"The relief agencies begged Gowon, since the war was already over, to allow them, at least temporarily, to flood Biafra with relief through Uli airport. But Gowon, … gave a bewildering "NO" and insisted that relief be trucked from Lagos, four hundred miles away, and then from North…of all places."[420]

You cannot say more for the insincerity of Gowon and the Nigerian government. But it is also easy to understand—*vae victis* "Woe unto the vanquished." The first genuine demonstration of reconciliation would have been to permit immediate relief to the suffering masses and the starving children who managed to survive the war, especially because the world had appealed to Gowon and his government. Therefore, the pronounced gesture of reconciliation and rehabilitation was, in many cases, a mockery, a farce, a façade, and political propaganda of the type that characterized some of the moves for reconciliation that attended the crisis of 1966 and eventually led to an avoidable war. The mockeries of reconciliation and reconstruction did not end there. There was also the change of currency, the administration of the East Central State after the war, the trials, detentions, and dismissals of Biafran Army officers, and the non-rehabilitation of the infrastructure of Igboland, among others. The conversion of the Biafran currency has already been described and discussed. The administrator of the East Central State should have been replaced within thirty days of the end of hostilities and replaced with a military governor. Mr. Ukpabi Asika, a renegade Igboman, was appointed during the war in 1968 to be the administrator of the East Central State. If the Nigerian government was sincere, it was not difficult to find an Igboman who was in the Nigerian military during the war or immediately reabsorbed from the so-called rebel army to become governor of the East Central State. Officers such as Lt. Col. Ogunewe who helped to avert bloodshed in Enugu during the July 1966 counter-coup should have been appointed governor. Even Lt. Col. (later Brig.) Njoku who was incarcerated for most of the war or Lt. Col. Ivenso or Lt. Col. Imo could have been

---

[418] *Nnaemeka Luke Aneke, Obong (General) Philip Efiong: A Tribute to An Uncommon Nigerian, January 19, 2004, https://nigeriaworld.com/articles/2004/jan/191.html*

[419] *Nnaemeka Aneke cites, Anthony Lewis, New York Times columnist, January 23, page 2, column 3*

[420] *Italics are my embellishments*

appointed. On the contrary, Ukpabi Asika remained administrator until Gowon's administration was overthrown in a military coup five years later in 1975.

Even when a military governor was appointed for East Central State, he was not an Igbo man. At the end of the war, besides destroying Uli Airport, the Nigerian government immediately set out to neutralize Biafran scientists and any reminder of the ingenuity that the Biafran people had developed in response to the war. After the war, it took the Nigerian government less than fifteen years to build oil pipelines from Port Harcourt to Kaduna and a refinery in Kaduna, more than five hundred miles away in northern Nigeria. Fifty years after the war, besides the refineries in Warri and Port Harcourt that were in existence before the war, successive Nigerian governments have forcefully resisted the construction of refineries in Igboland or even additional refineries in the oil-producing regions of the country, especially the East. A thoughtful and sincere government would immediately have tapped on the scientists from Biafra and would have commissioned them to construct a wholly Nigerian refinery within ten to fifteen years. But the Ghost of Biafra was and is still so strong in the minds of Nigerian leaders and civilians that it appears that the war is still being fought against the Igbos and the word Biafra has become a taboo or dirty word. But Biafra should not be a dirty word because we all contributed to making Biafra happen. On January 29, 1970, fourteen days after the formal termination of the war, Gen.

Gowon granted an interview and met with the diplomatic corps in Lagos. During this meeting, Gowon promised that his government would conduct nothing like Nuremberg trials of the leaders of the Biafran secession, and he also stated that there is general amnesty for those who were misled."[421] This is another farce and propaganda of deceit. One must applaud Gowon for all the restraint that he brought to bear on the crisis to mitigate wholesale vengeance against the vanquished and even in the crises that preceded the war. Nevertheless, his statement only said that there would be "nothing like" a Nuremberg trial[422] for the rebel officers. Gowon's statement did not say that no trials would be conducted. By the way, who are these so-called rebel officers?

Indeed, why should there be trials? German war leaders were tried for crimes against peace and other war atrocities including the mass murder of Jews, the crippled, and gypsies. The German Nazi government attacked Europe and made war on other countries for purposes of achieving domination. They expressed a philosophy of superiority and claimed territories as a justification for attacking their neighbors. On the contrary, Biafra did not attack Nigeria. It was Nigeria that attacked Biafra on the heels of the unprovoked attack against Eastern Nigerians by Nigerian Army personnel in Kano Airport and all across Northern Nigeria and even in Western Nigeria. These soldiers, along with the police officers, who committed these atrocities were detained (see Aburi proceedings) but were never charged with any offenses. The truth of the matter is that the actions of these soldiers and police and the Nigerian government's insensitivity to the displaced citizens of Eastern Nigeria, contributed, in no small measure, to the mass exodus of Eastern Nigerians and the bitterness and anger that eventually led to war. And, yes there were trials, detentions, and other punishments against Biafran Army officers, including prohibitions to seek elections and to seek employment.[423] At the end of the war, the federal military government set up a tribunal, a kangaroo tribunal, to try Biafran Army officers. Several of them were dismissed and others were detained. If any war crimes were committed, the division commander at Asaba in October 1967 should have been convicted of

---

[421] *William Borders, No 'Nuremberg Trials' for Rebels, Gowon Says, The New York Times, Jan. 30, 1970, https://www.nytimes.com/1970/01/30/archives/no-nuremberg-trials-for-rebels-gowon-says.html*

[422] After World War II, leaders of the Nazi Party in Germany were tried for war crimes in Nuremberg Germany in what is known as the Nuremberg Trials. The trials were conducted by an international tribunal made up of representatives from the United States, the Soviet Union, France, and Great Britain. The defendants faced charges ranging from crimes against peace, to crimes of war, to crimes against humanity. Several were executed. Others were jailed and some were acquitted.

[423] *P.J. Odu, The Future that Vanished, Pp.218 – 22. See also Ben Gbulie (Fall of Biafra) for details on the trials of Biafra officers. See also Hilary Njoku (A Tragedy without Heroes)*

war crimes.[424] The just thing to do after the war would have been for Gowon to order everyone to return to their jobs. No trials and no dismissals. If the intention was to dismiss any Biafran officers, such an action should have been taken during the war, especially for those who played an active part in commanding Biafran forces. On this point, it is important to note that on January 15, 1970, when Gowon gave his formal speech to end the war while acknowledging the Biafran delegation, he addressed the Biafran officers by their Nigerian ranks—Lt. Col. Philip Effiong, Lt. Col. Anwunah, etc. It took almost two years (November 1971) to decide to dismiss them. During those 23 months, these Biafran officers, now back in the Nigerian Army, retained their ranks in the Nigerian Army and were technically still in the Nigerian Army. Yakubu Gowon did his job, and very well too, by taking action to reunite the country. He knew well what forces were at play that led to the war. What would Yakubu Gowon have done if he was Igbo and if just being an Igbo was the reason for him to be in danger? What would Yakubu Gowon have done if he was one of the army officers who had to flee the North and the West because of the out-of-control Northern Nigerian army officers and soldiers? The Northern Nigerian army officers having taken the vengeful toll of so many Eastern Nigerian officers, should have been considered enough retribution. Instead, they initiated, orchestrated and perpetrated a wanton and despicable orgy of murder, pillaging, and ethnic cleansing to achieve the secession of the North. General Gowon should have recognized that this latter set of events contributed immensely to the secession and the war that followed. What followed the war was a continuation of mistrust and mutual anger. The dismissals of the Biafran Army officers continued to make clear that who puts who on trial after a war or even in most human conflicts has nothing to do with who was right or who was wrong—it is all about who has the military capability to prevail.

Ten years after the war, in 1979, Nigeria was returned briefly to civilian rule through an election process. Much like a stubborn nightmare, it appeared that we learned no lessons from the events of the previous twenty years—the crisis of 1966 that took four years to bring to an apparent closure and almost ten years of military rule that did not appear to have solved the problems that the coup planners of 1966 claimed they came to resolve. The political parties that emerged, to my chagrin, were exactly along the same lines of the years before the coup. There was the Nigerian People's Party (NPN)—another name for Northern People's Congress (NPC). The NPN was led by a previous minister from the NPC, Alhaji Shehu Shagari. Then there was the Unity Party of Nigeria (UPN), led by Chief Awolowo, that had its roots in the Western Yoruba region and the Midwest—another name for the Action Group of Chief Awolowo. The other parties were the People's Redemption Party (PRP), led by Aminu Kano, an obvious rebirth of the Northern Elements Progressive Union; the Nigerian People's Party (NPP), led by Nnamdi Azikiwe; and the Great Nigerian People's Party (GNPP), led by Waziri Ibrahim from Borno State. The GNPP, a pseudonym for the Borno Youth Movement (BYM), was a breakaway party from the NPP when the leaders could not agree on powersharing. What is instructive from the outcome of the elections in 1979 is that the voting lines ran exactly along ethnic lines as was before the crisis of 1964 to 1965 that made governance difficult (see election results map).

The only party that won the election along the slightest pretense of a national cross-section was the NPN because it took some of the eastern states that belonged to the Igbo-led NCNC and a part of the Middle Belt region. Finally, all the party leaders and presidential candidates were from the 1964 elections. The NPN won the election of 1979, was re-elected in 1983 and was overthrown in a military coup in December 1983, shortly after it was elected. What was the problem this time? The allegations included corruption, among others. Nonsense! The military men just wanted to remain in power. The true political (civilian) leaders of the country that could have worked things out had we left them alone began to build true reconciliation. Alex Ekwueme, an Igboman, was the vice president and may have been elected president in his own right in 1987. But, in my opinion, the Northern military brass and the underground tribalists, who were still fighting the war, could not see an Igboman become president so shortly after the war. Therefore, Gen. Muhammad Buhari

---

[424] *See Emma Okocha, Blood on the Niger: The First Black on Black Genocide, New York, Triatlantic Books, 2004 and also Elizabeth Bird and Rosaline Umelo, Surviving in Biafra: A Niger Wife's Story, London C. Hurst and Co., 2018*

overthrew the government only to be overthrown by another Northern Nigerian, Gen. Ibrahim Babangida. Ibrahim Babangida became very repressive, survived an active coup attempt, and lasted eight years in office. An election was conducted in 1993 that was won by a Yoruba man, Moshood Abiola. The election was annulled by Babangida. This annulment threw the country into a turmoil of the kind that almost precipitated another civil war, which caused Babangida to step aside amidst allegations of massive corruption and looting of the treasury. In an apparent hurry under pressure, Babangida handed the government to another Yoruba man, Earnest Shonekan, who was later overthrown by Gen. Sani Abacha, another Northern Moslem. It has been alleged that Abacha's regime was extremely corrupt and repressive. It was under Abacha's regime that Ken Saro Wiwa, a man from the Ogoni area of the River State of Nigeria where Nigeria's oil is produced, was executed after what many consider a kangaroo court. Saro Wiwa's offense was treason for agitating for a fair share of the revenues from the oil for his region of origin. After six years, Abacha died in office and Nigeria finally conducted an election in 1999, following thirty years of military involvement in national politics.

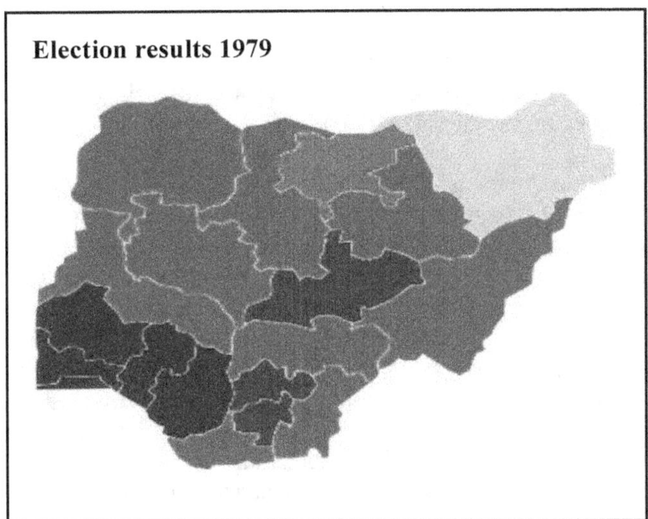

During those thirty years, corruption became even worse than it was, as successive military presidents were accused of extensive looting of the treasury. Why then did the military claim that corruption was one of their problems that justified overthrowing the government in 1966? It is evident today that the military failed to develop or establish structures for lasting political stability. At best, they took their turn under the sun to loot the treasury. Besides, after tottering attempts to return to civilian rule, having overthrown the elected government of 1979, the military underhandedly returned to power disguised as civilians.

In 1993, the military administration of Gen. Ibrahim Babangida annulled the general election won by Chief Abiola that was designed to return the country to civilian rule. Of course, for no other reason, though unspoken, than that Gen. Sani Abacha had not had his turn to rule. When Gen. Abacha died six years later, the military underhandedly returned the government to Gen. Olusegun Obasanjo, who had only had a three-year stint after Gen. Murtala Mohammed was assassinated in 1976. For in as much as Obasanjo had the appearance of Ijoba Alagbada, he was Ijoba Ologun disguised as Alagbada. Of course, he did not appoint military governors, but I get the impression that such were operating in the shadows. Similarly, Buhari, who served for two brief years (1983– 1985) as military president, was still itching to return to his presidency. Accordingly, he contested elections to become president over and over in 2003, 2007, 2011, and finally won in 2015 and satisfied his yearning to be president. Once more, we had Ijoba Ologun disguised as Alagbada.

But as a people, what have we done for ourselves, and have we demonstrated that we learned any valuable lessons? Since we returned to civilian rule in 1999, successive governments have not done a better job of stabilizing the country. Whereas Nigeria has generated more resources, even on a per capita basis, the plight of the common man has become even more desperate by basic standards of development and well-being. Unemployment and other forms of desperation are pervasive. Civil servants and many workers in the private sector are not paid their salaries, their wages, or pensions for months or even years, and our leaders are callous enough to go about their business. Our leaders despoil the country through looting and educational institutions are deteriorating while those that loot the treasury are sending their children overseas to be educated. Medical facilities are breaking down while our leaders run overseas for medical treatment. Therefore, they have no incentive to maintain the medical facilities in the country.

We have managed to conduct elections where the government is handed over peacefully. This might be the only lesson we have learned, albeit there are massive and almost evident fraud and rigging of elections. There is banditry at unprecedented levels with no signs of abatement. In today's Nigeria, we are witnessing lawlessness such as kidnapping for ransom, armed robbery in broad daylight, and armed extortion by police and soldiers. We also have unconcealed demand for bribes at public service locations and wholesale debauchery of the public treasury by public and elected officials. These are symptoms of a system's putrefaction—a decay that is threatening to cause the disintegration of our country.

There are complaints about marginalization by segments of the society and new agitations for separation. Fifty years after the war, there are new agitations for break up or sectional violence in different parts of the country—renewed calls for Biafra, Boko Haram, and their religious demands that are not clear to me, though it is a clear symptom of malaise. There are also dark calls for the Oduduwa Republic and the Niger Delta Avengers who were or are still demanding that the conquerors should desist from despoiling the oil-producing regions of the country. These complaints about marginalization, though not new or unique to the present regime, are not wholly unfounded. However, this is not to suggest that they should be entertained. In any event, addressing them by use of military force and violence fails to recognize the underlying causes: economic hardship, hopelessness, and desperation.

Those who call for Biafra should realize that the events that justified the Biafran secession are no longer taking place. The events that led to the Northern pogrom and genocide have not been repeated and will not be repeated. Nevertheless, the renewed calls for Biafra should not be met with the lethal force that the Nigerian government once brought to bear on the agitators. Even the arrest and detention of Nnamdi Kanu are uncalled for. Therefore, Nnamdi Kanu should be released without any further rancor or delay. The tragedy of the Nigerian government's attitude about Biafra is twofold: The first is the double standard compared with Boko Haram. If all that Boko Haram did was fly their flags and agitate for whatever their cause may be, the Nigerian government would not shoot their agitators to death. The second problem is that the Nigerian government and many civilian Nigerians make Biafra a dirty word when we were all equally responsible for what ultimately brought about Biafra. For this reason, I would urge our good dear President Mohammed Buhari to refrain from threatening to speak to the Biafran agitators in "the language that they understand." In making such a statement, Mohammed Buhari is referring to the brutal military suppression of the Biafran secession to which he (Buhari) mockingly reminds us that "we killed two million people" to keep Nigeria united. Unfortunately, a statesman should not be making a statement that only serves to reopen old wounds. I must equally ask Mohammed Buhari why he reminds us only of the two million people that were starved to death during the war. How about the 10,000 to 30,000 people that were murdered in Northern Nigeria with the help of the soldiers of the Fourth Battalion or Fifth Battalion of the Nigerian Army, of which Buhari was an officer. In what way did the murder of these innocent civilians help keep Nigeria united? Those innocent Igbo civilians at the Kano Airport who remained behind and held out hope that the crisis would end but were slaughtered on October 4 to October 5, 1966, and beyond through November and December 1966—in what way did they deserve the language that Buhari's battalion spoke to them? They were peaceful Nigerians who were hopeful and braved the dangers of the situation only to be forcefully driven out and then called rebels for protecting themselves from further carnage and defilement.

Honor to Whom Honor and the Tragedy of Defeat

"Render therefore to all their dues: a tribute to whom tribute is due; custom to whom custom; fear to whom fear; honor to whom honor."[425] In conclusion, we need to take stock of this trauma called

---

[425] *Romans 13:7 (Christian Holy Bible KJV)*

the civil war. As a teenager, largely influenced by my elders, I was an avid supporter of the war. I had no idea of what war is. The day after the war, as I was limping home, I forswore war. I could only hope that we, as Nigerians had learned lessons enough to avoid another war. Even Odumegwu Ojukwu who led the war on the Biafran side made clear, in an interview many years later, that we should avoid such an experience and that the war was a colossal waste of resources on both sides.

Six years after independence, a group of army officers overthrew the government because they felt that the post-independence leaders were corrupt, tribalistic, and incompetent. We cheered the military boys of January 1966 as heroes that came to save us. In hindsight, those post-independence leaders did a far better job than the subsequent military governments that we had. With far fewer resources per capita, the post-independence leaders (Azikiwe, Awolowo, Abubakar, Ahmadu Bello, Michael Okpara, and their colleagues) produced more food per capita at cheaper prices than the military governments. There was free education in Western Nigeria and the promotion of education and food in Eastern Nigeria. We owe them honors because I think they did a better job. The military boys did not demonstrate that they could solve the problem of tribalism better than the post-independence leaders, neither did they demonstrate themselves to be better politicians. They could not trade horses competently enough to avoid the cataclysm of war that ensued after they took over. We were more likely to speak each other's language before the war. I may be wrong on this one, but I happen to have the opinion that the army boys laid the foundation for the stupefying[426] level of corruption that we have today. Each of the past military presidents has been accused of amassing loot from the treasury that dwarfs the apparent ostentation of Okotie-Eboh.

In the end, the coup of January 1966 did not do us any good. The plotters of the coup were a polyglot of individuals who were not guided by a common political ideology. Ademoyega was a pure Marxist-Leninist. But it is not clear that the other ring leaders had his ideological perspective or would have been willing to adopt Ademoyega's ideological perspectives. For example, no one has claimed that Chukwuma Nzeogwu, the icon and apparent leader of the coup, had ideological motives except to end corruption and tribalism. Nzeogwu condemned the corruption and decadence of the government, but this does not make him an anti-capitalist ideologist. None of the others, such as Onwuatuegwu, Ifeajuna, or Ben Gbulie, had been known to profess even a modicum of socialist ideology let alone the stringent communist Marxist ideology that Ademoyega described as the aim of the coup plotters.

The common motive that held the plotters together was to unseat the extant government. If that was their aim, they might have succeeded in giving Nigerians an opportunity to start over on a truly popular democratic path with free elections. They may have released Awolowo and other political prisoners, as Ademoyega claims in his book. On the other hand, if they had taken over the government and politics of the country, they may have plunged the country into a civil war of a different kind, or maybe Ademoyega would easily have been swept away very early in the postcoup struggle, and the others would move on.

Ademoyega professed a pure Marxist-Leninist communist ideology. It appears from his renditions that Ademoyega also understood Marxist-Leninist processes and organizational tenets, precepts, and doctrines. Ademoyega also had plans for the future because he was working with and acknowledges the convictions and had confidence in a person like Phillip Alale who was executed with Banjo and Sam Agbam. Phillip Alale and Sam Agbam were well trained, competent, and avowed Communist Marxist organizers, agitators, and indoctrinators. The depth of Ademoyega's communist leaning is made clear from his dismissive attitude toward Awolowo's welfarism of free education and medical care. According to Ademoyega:

"We certainly would have created a mass political movement which would have led the... nation along the path of pure democratic socialism ... If farms were enlarged and owned collectively, everyone would have a sense of belonging ... Under the planned revolutionary system, workshops were to be collectively built ... construction work would be done communally ... civil engineers

---

[426] *Uduma Ukaegbu, Igbos and Folly of Biafra May 2020, https://www.westafricanpilotnews. com/2020/05/02/ igbos-and-folly-of-biafra-part-i/ PilotnewsPilotAfrican*

will work collectively ...Doctors would work collectively to cater to the health of the community... the Armed Forces were ...only separated under the capitalist system ...Welfarism [Free education and health care] will only dent the face of evil and never kill it ... as has been done in ... Russia and China...Extremely powerful capitalists ... force us to believe that those two countries are not successful.[427]

What Ademoyega describes here looks like Russia's Leninist-Bolshevik experiments of 1920 to 1960 and maybe a little beyond. Besides the ideological incompatibility of the plotters, there is no way that they would have been able to get the different Nigerian communities or ethnic groups to agree to organize themselves along the lines that Ademoyega described. The system that Ademoyega described would have been alien to them. The problem would have been made worse by the fact that the different ethnic groups would have seen Ademoyega's collectivist processes differently and would have been very hostile to it for the simple reason that such would have involved a herculean reeducation effort and program. The Northern Fulani/Hausa communities have been described as feudalistic, but the populations appear to be responsive to their leadership. The ruling establishment would have been fiercely opposed to any Marxist ideological reorganization of their systems of production and distribution. The Igbos and their neighbors in the east are individualistic and would not find a Marxist-Leninist organizational system of production along the lines practiced by Bolsheviks or Stalin and Lenin acceptable. You would also have to totally disrupt the superstructure of the Yoruba societies and their relationship with the peasantry of Yoruba land in the West and then get their intelligentsia to buy into the new ideological dispensation. What would anyone do with the obas, alafins, and alakes of Yoruba land? Or the obis and eze, obongs, and amanyangbos of the East? Or the emirs, the Shehu, and numerous other traditional rulers in the Northern part of Nigeria?

On the war, I have already argued in different ways and at different points that Ojukwu should not be made a villain of the war. I have also argued that he had better alternatives than to lead his people into war without adequate preparation. I could not agree better with Uduma Ukaegbu by paraphrasing that one cannot deny that Ojukwu was as near a genius of organizing as one could get. As Ukaegbu puts it,

"But make no mistake, Ojukwu was an extraordinary man. Only a few people can have the courage and audacity to embark upon and lead an endeavor of such magnitude, of starting a new country from scratch and facing mountainous odds. He was also not unmindful of the challenges that lay ahead. He was also an extraordinary organizer but equally foolish in his strategic analysis."

I will argue that the Biafran population stretched that war and put up a heroic resistance that stunned the world, not because of Ojukwu's ingenuity but, in spite, of Ojukwu. Nevertheless, Ojukwu's charisma and effective exhortation of the masses also brought out the genius of the people. Many other people could have been blessed with the same level of determination that the Igbos had and would not have galvanized the people as effectively as Ojukwu did. Operationally, Ojukwu demonstrated tremendous talent in his ability to make quick tactical adjustments that prepared the Biafrans to construct airports quickly, source out arms in all nooks and crannies of the world, and develop improvised technologies. He galvanized the people's talents as only a puny few ever did even in the history of the human race. But the successful undertaking of the war required much more than that.

I will not go as far as saying that Ojukwu was foolish in his strategic analysis. I believe that Ojukwu was carried away by a lethal combination of his understandable indignation at what happened to his people and his personal ambition to be their hero as well as his paranoia of securing his place in history. At some point, I wondered if he still had his full senses with him. He may have been so paranoid that he failed to understand the need to make alliances in a war, with a clear understanding that making such alliances also meant that one has to share the spoils. In this regard, he needed to bring in people more experienced than he was in the political and international

---

[427] *Adewale Ademoyega, Why We Struck: The Story of the First Nigerian Coup, Ibadan, Nigeria, Evans Brothers, 1981, Pp. 47 – 55*

diplomatic "jungle" and in the treacherous international black market for arms and weapons. These people were also more influential among the ruling establishments of Europe and the Americas—people like Azikiwe, Mathew Mbu, and Michael Okpara, whose friendship with Awolowo would have wrought magic in achieving the ultimate strategic objective of strengthening his hands and the hands of the minority ethnic groups. Ojukwu should have been strategic enough in his thinking to realize early enough that Biafra was not militarily prepared and should postpone or modify his ambition if that was at the foundation of his actions. Finally, I return to the folly of the Igbos. To the extent that the Igbo fought heroically, they must learn that they would not have lasted as long without the support of their neighbors, both as individuals and as communities. Focusing on the individuals, the Igbos must honor people like Maj. Gen. Phillip Effiong and Okokon Ndem. But even within Igboland, people like Njoku need to be rehabilitated and their honors restored. Brig. Njoku may have had his differences with Ojukwu, but his views were genuine. However, Njoku was unjustly incarcerated and vilified during most of the war based on the defamatory propaganda of Ojukwu's political machine. Such behaviors are not conducive to mass struggles.

The Igbos must be indicted for their neglect of Maj. Gen. Phillip Effiong and Mr. Okokon Ndem. The ignominy of these two individuals is deafening and despicable. Effiong struggled with the people to the very end and brought an orderly end to the war. Even after the war, he fought to integrate the Igbos and Biafrans properly with minimal pain into Nigeria. For details, see Effiong's *Nigeria and Biafra: My Story* or *The Caged Bird Sang No More*. Effiong was instrumental in ensuring that Ojukwu returned from exile. As for Okokon Ndem, even Ojukwu acknowledged that "Okokon Ndem made a worthy impression on Nigerians, especially on Ndigbo, that he will never be forgotten." Ojukwu is also quoted as saying that he was so proud to be with the family of Okokon Ndem at Ndem's funeral and proclaimed that Ndem was a genius.[428] Yes, there is no doubt about it: Okokon Ndem was a genius of a broadcast journalist. Yet, to the very end of their lives, the Igbos never conferred any honors on these two men. However, for Igbos who fought the war, the name, and News Talks of Okonon Ndem still ring like yesterday. Gen. Effiong was to lament this omission of not awarding him any honors openly. Nnaemeka Aneke put it succinctly in a tribute to Effiong:

"This last news conference by Gen. Effiong is not good news for the Igbos. He made it clear in his words that as much as some Igbos were friendly and some were not, the Ohaneze, itself fell short of his expectation in terms of reaching out. But why should the Igboman care or be concerned about the welfare or wellbeing of Gen Effiong? The simple answer is that, like it or not, Igbos are IOU to Gen Effiong. But equally important, if not more, is that Igbos, like many ethnic groups in Nigeria, need political alliances, coalitions, and amalgamations to make any impact at the center. And anybody or group contemplating such political cooperation with the Igbos will necessarily consider previous alliances of individuals and groups with the Igbos and how those people fared in success and failure. Surely, the story of Gen. Effiong is not an encouragement to such future alliances.... Even if Igbos can prevail in the argument that their own neglect and subjugation by the Federal Government left them with no ability to show gratitude and benevolence to Gen Effiong, they will be hard-pressed to explain to the neutral observer why his name should not be immortalized in Igboland."[429]

Both of these men, Effiong and Ndem, deserve monuments among the Igbos. Finally, the Igbos have not treated themselves to some true remembrance. For example, the Civil War Museum at Umuahia was built by the Nigerian government. However, pictures of it that I see online tell me that the Igbos are not maintaining it. The museum and Ojukwu's bunker at Umuahia are in total disrepair. Igbos should work with the Nigerian government to maintain such monuments and to be allowed to bury their dead with dignity. There should be a monument to the mass of malnourished children who were sacrificed by both sides to sustain the struggle and to compel capitulation. If the Nigerian government and peoples are sincere about reconciliation, Igbos should be allowed to

---

[428] *Nnaemeka Luke Aneke, A Tribute to an Uncommon Nigerian https://nigeriaworld.com/articles/2004/jan/191.html, January 19, 2004*
[429] *Aneke, A Tribute to an Uncommon Nigerian*

reconstruct Uli Airport as a monument to the suffering of a people who sought to defend themselves from possible extermination.

Global Issues Raised by the Biafra War – Genocide and the Limits of Self-Determination

Another sad irony of the human experience is comparative pain analysis and selective memories. In analyzing the war and its antecedents, even Biafrans are guilty of discounting and ignoring cogent arguments from the other side of the conflict. The Biafran War, among others, raised two questions that have captured the attention of analysts and the human conscience. One is the question of genocide. The other is the limit of self-determination. In the former, observers have been challenged to define what qualifies as genocide. During the Biafra War and for years after the war, the Nigerian government argued that genocide was not occurring. Two examples will be used to illustrate these arguments.

In his book, Brig. Alabi argues that there was no genocide. I do not know what he would make of events such as the cowardly and criminal massacre of innocent people in Asaba (October 1967) by the Second Division of the Nigerian Army. Similar massacres took place at Item and Onitsha. In his analysis of events during the war, Edokwe[430] focuses on the starvation that was occurring in Biafra and argues that what was going on was a civil war and not genocide because starvation was never explicitly prohibited, even by the Geneva Convention, as an instrument of war. There is a whole literature with convoluted arguments about whether genocide was taking place. For an extensive discourse on the question of genocide or no genocide in Biafra, (see Lasse Heerten and A. Dirk Moses.[431] This is not surprising to me. As is often said, the first casualty of war is the truth—as much as it is in many human conflicts. Evident truth is sometimes denied by extremists. Apologists distort the truth and make it difficult to interpret events for what they are. At other times, the truth is smothered by victimizing anyone who talks about it. Today, for example, many brazenly deny the Jewish Holocaust at the hands of the German Nazi Party or, at best, distort the extent of the event or its ideological foundations. Another example is the Ukrainian Holodomor ("Death by Starvation"). Specifically, during the 1930s, the Soviet regime under Joseph Stalin confiscated agricultural produce from the people of Ukraine, who had been forced to become part of the Russian-dominated state in about 1920. This Russian food confiscation was an attempt to collectivize Soviet agriculture by replacing Ukraine's small farms with state-run collectives. Aside from that, the policies of the Soviet government were designed to punish independence-minded Ukrainians who posed a threat to Soviet totalitarian authority. The consequence of this forced collectivization was to subject the Ukrainians to starvation that claimed the lives of four million to upwards of seven

---

[430] <u>Bridget Edokwe,</u> Revisiting Biafra: Starvation as A Strategy of Warfare: Was there really a Genocide? <u>https://barristerng.com/</u>, June 6, 2021

[431] *Lasse Heerten & A. Dirk Moses, The Nigeria–Biafra war: postcolonial conflict and the question of genocide, 2014, Journal of Genocide research, Pp. 169 – 203. See also, Lasse Heerten & A. Dirk Moses, Eds., Post-Colonial Conflict and the Question of Genocide, The Nigeria Biafra War (1967-70), Routledge Global Series, 2018 (This is a book that includes several articles on Starvation and discussion of Genocide during the War. The articles hardly defines genocide nor did they reach any tangible conclusion as to whether genocide occurred or whether the starvation of Biafrans should be condemned. But authors such as Douglas Anthony (Chapter 2, Pp. 47 – 71) – Irreconcilable Narratives: Biafra, Nigeria and Arguments about Genocide would argue that genocide was not taking place. On the other side Brian McNeil (Pp. 278 – 300 – Chapter 3), And Starvation is the Grim Reaper: The American Foundation to Keep Biafra Alive and the Question of Genocide During the Nigerian Civil War argue that genocide was taking place. James Farquharson (Pp. 301 – 326 – Black America Cares: The Response of African Americans to the Civil War and Genocide in Nigeria) also argues that genocide was taking place. Also Herbert Ekekwe, The Igbo genocide and its aftermath, https://www.pambazuka.org/human-security/igbo-genocide-and-its-aftermath, Feb 21, 2012 and* S. Elizabeth Bird & Fraser Ottanelli, The Asaba massacre and the Nigerian civil war: reclaiming hidden history, Journal of Genocide Research, Aug 2014, Pp. 379 – 99

million Ukrainians, about 13 percent of the population.[432] Unlike other famines in history caused by blight or drought, this famine was man-made. While the famine was going on and people were dying, the Soviet government increased the quotas for confiscation of food, making the food shortages and famine worse. Thousands of people were arrested, and orphaned children were shot if they became too numerous to feed. When people in distress tried to migrate out of the farms and areas where the famine was severe, they were blockaded and suppressed even more. For many years, even the European Union (EU) denied that genocide was what happened in Ukraine. In 2008, however, the EU finally declared that the Holodomor of Ukraine was genocide.

It has been argued that it is easy to prove that the Jewish Holocaust was genocide, but not so for the Holodomor of Ukraine. According to the United Nations Convention on Genocide (Article 2), genocide is defined as[433]:

"... acts committed with intent to destroy, in whole or in part, a national, ethnical, racial or religious group..." Which may include (1) Killing members of the group (2) Causing serious bodily or mental harm to members of the group (3) Deliberately inflicting on the group conditions of life calculated to bring about its physical destruction in whole or in part..."

Therefore, in every sense of the word, the Ukrainian man-made famine and the Biafran mass starvation can only be called genocide. Distortions of the argument about genocide have resorted to insisting on the intent declared by the perpetrators. Therefore, it has been argued both for the Ukrainian and the Biafran case that there was no genocide taking place.[434] However, Anthony Douglas, Karen E. Smith, and Roy Doron present inconclusive arguments while recognizing that mass destruction of a people was taking place.[435] On the contrary, Ekwekwe, Leitenberg, Chuku, and Njoku, among others, have reached clear conclusions that genocide was taking place inside Biafra.[436] In the case of the Holocaust and Holodomor, there were policy and political

Victims of Nigeria Air Raid - Time Life Magazine July 1968 Page 22 (R. Cagnozi)

---

[432] Ilie, Alexandra. (2011). Holodomor, the Ukrainian Holocaust? Studia Politica: Romanian Political Science Review, 11(1), 137-154. https://nbn-resolving.org/urn:nbn:de:0168-ssoar-445894. See also Hiroaki Kuromiya, Ukraine and Russia in the 1930s, Harvard Ukrainian Studies, December 1994, Vol. 18, No. 3/4 (December 1994), pp. 327-341 and *Klid, Bohdan, "Holodomor: Holodomor and UN Genocide Convention Criteria." Modern Genocide: Understanding Causes and Consequences. ABC-CLIO, 2013. Web. 21 Nov. 2013. Reprinted courtesy of ABC-CLIO. https://holodomor.ca/resource/ was-the-holodomor-a-genocide/*

[433] United Nations Convention on the Prevention of Genocide, https://www.un.org/en/ genocideprevention/ documents/atrocity-crimes/Doc.1 Convention%20on%20the%20 Prevention%20and%20Punishment%20 of%20the%20Crime%20of%20Genocide.pdf

[434] *Bridget Edokwe, Op. Cit.*

[435] *Anthony Douglas, Irreconcilable Narratives: Biafra, Nigeria and Arguments about Genocide, in Heearton and Moses, Eds, Post-Colonial Conflict and the Question of Genocide, The Nigeria Biafra War (1967-70), Routledge Global Series, 2018, (Chapter 2, Pp. 47 – 71) and Roy Doron, Marketing Genocide: Biafran Propaganda Strategies During the Nigerian Civil War, 1967 – 1970, , in Heearton and Moses, Eds, Post-Colonial Conflict and the Question of Genocide, The Nigeria Biafra War (1967-70), Routledge Global Series, 2018 (Chapter 3, Pp. 72 – 95) and Karen E. Smith The UK and "Genocide in Biafra", in Heearton and Moses, Eds, Post-Colonial Conflict and the Question of Genocide, The Nigeria Biafra War (1967-70), Routledge Global Series, 2018 (Chapter 6) and* Heerten, Lasse, and A. Dirk Moses. 2014. "The Nigeria–Biafra War: Postcolonial Conflict and the Question of Genocide." *Journal of Genocide Research* 16: 2–3, 169–203.

[436] *Goria Chuku, Women and the Nigeria-Biafra War, in Heearton and Moses, Eds, Post-Colonial Conflict and the Question of Genocide, The Nigeria Biafra War (1967-70), Routledge Global Series, 2018 (Chapter 6). See also, Leitenberg, Milton. 2006. "Deaths in Wars and Conflicts in the 20th Century." Cornell University, Peace Studies Program. Nd Njoku, Carol Ijeoma. 2013. "A Paradox of International Criminal Justice: The Biafra Genocide." Journal of Asian and African Studies 48:6, 710–26.*

reasons underlying the intention to kill. During the Holocaust, the Germans declared an ideology of anti-Semitism. In the Soviet Union, there was a political ideology that sought to eliminate a class of large farmers from a people of defined nationality and to bring the Ukrainians to capitulate and to strengthen and impose the rule and domination of the Soviet state over them. On this account, I could not agree better with Chima Korieh, when he argues that "…While it is plausible to argue that there was no complete annihilation of the Igbo when they lost the war, the actions and behavior of the federal Nigerian government during the war did not exclude such genocidal intent…"[437]. Examples include the mass slaughter of innocent defenseless civilians including children that were assembled to welcome Federal troops at Asaba. The mass slaughter of worshipers at Onitsha and Ozuitem. Added to these are air raids by the Nigerian Airforce that target churches, hospitals, marketplaces, refugee camps, and other civilian targets in villages and towns that could not be explained by mistaken bombs and avoiding military targets or battlefields. According to Gloria Chuku,[438]

"… I have seen things in Biafra that no man should have to see … Within six days that Alan Grossman of Time Magazine spent in Biafra, … civilian bombings took 300 lives … In a feeding center of 8,000 people at Owerrinta, a MiG fighter dropped bombs and killed 22 people and a raid at a hospital facility at Ihiala with 258 patients was reduced to only 8 patients. Also, 100 innocent civilians were killed along with four Red Cross staff at Okigwe…"[439]

Even the Nigerian government's own hired guns (so-called observers) acknowledged that the killings at Okigwe were unprovoked and inexcusable. Such killings were pervasive throughout the war.

Speeches by Northern leaders called for ethnic cleansing of the Igbo people from the North. Pogroms and mass killings of the Igbo population from a decade earlier leave no doubt that the war offered an opportunity to implement a "final solution" to what was perceived as an "Igbo problem."[440] While the Nigerian government did not declare a genocidal intent, its actions and the actions of the Nigerian Army speak to nothing but genocide. In effect, with the mass killings and indiscriminate air raids during the war and the starvation whose evidence was all over the world, the Nigerian government intended that if it takes the annihilation of the Igbo race to compel them to return the coveted territory to Nigeria, so be it.

Recognition and the Peace of Westphalia

Besides being outgunned and outmanned, Biafra struggled to gain diplomatic recognition during the war. For this reason, its legitimacy was constantly in question. As soon as the federal government declared war on Biafra, Yakubu Gowon admonished all countries that the government was engaged in what it called a police action and that the crisis was strictly an internal matter. Therefore, the federal government of Nigeria would consider any interference by any country an unfriendly act. Yakubu Gowon's reference to noninterference in what was considered an internal affair was invoking the United Nations charter of 1948, which was adopted by the Organization for African

---

[437] *Chima J Korieh Biafra and the discourse on the Igbo Genocide, Journal of Asian and African Studies, October 2013*

[438] *Gloria Chuku, in Heerten and Moses, Op. Cit, Pp. 334 - 337*

[439] *Ibid, Page 335*

[440] *Chima J Korieh Op. Cit*

Unity (OAU). These charters drew on the Westphalian model based on the treaty of Westphalia (1648).[441]

There was no shortage of sympathy for the plight of Biafrans—from to the pogroms of 1966 and even more so when pictures of the brutal starvation of innocent children hit the news media. However, as already explained, the logic of international diplomacy is heartless. Therefore, humanitarian sympathy only led to a massive airlift of food and medical care but not diplomatic support. The Nigerian government opposed strongly even the food relief, arguing that starvation was a legitimate instrument of war. Accordingly, several countries hesitated to recognize Biafra because they referred to the United Nations and OAU charters. However, I believe they were more concerned about possibly encouraging secession as they had their own internal potential separatist challenges. Secondly, as in the case of Israel, they had to worry about potential diplomatic fallout, since they expressed sympathy for Biafra and all but braved and defied the dangers to support Biafra, albeit covertly. For example, when Azikiwe approached several African countries, they expressed sympathy but cited potential internal insurrection that might be justified by their recognition of Biafra, for whatever reason. According to Nnamdi Azikiwe:

"President Senghor said he couldn't because the majority of his supporters were Muslims and rightly or wrongly, they felt it was a religious war. And he said well, if he granted recognition, then his government would fall. But he supported the idea of forcing the hands of Nigeria to the conference table. Houphouet Boigny was prepared, provided his people backed him. Ditto for the others except for Milton Obote who told us that Prince Mutesa and the Bagandans wanted to secede, and he couldn't support secession when his own state was confronted with similar problems. It left four of them...[442]"

Westphalia, United Nations charter and OAU charter—these nuances do not matter. In international diplomacy, it comes down to Biafra being able to assert its legitimacy. If treason succeeds, who dares call it treason? The Westphalian Peace principle on which the United Nations charter and OAU charter are based essentially recognized the supremacy of force. Specifically, after fighting each other for thirty years, Europeans got together and recognized that it was futile to continue fighting and destroying each other, devasting their populations and causing famines and pestilences in their countryside. When the treaty of Westphalia was signed, it provided, among other things assurances that (1) all states are equal, and one state cannot interfere in the internal affairs of another and (2) all disputes are to be settled peacefully and where possible through the use of economic sanctions or other means of collective security. Accordingly, when the United Nations Charter was drafted, it included a prohibition from interfering in the internal affairs of member states, viz:

"Nothing contained in the present Charter shall authorize the United Nations to intervene in matters that are essentially within the jurisdiction of any State or shall require the Members to submit such matters to settlement under the present Charter, but this principle shall not prejudice the application of enforcement measures ... where international peace and security are threatened."

But Westphalia did not make provisions for whether an individual state can brutalize its citizens and violate their basic human rights short of forcibly requiring them to follow the states' religion—things like engaging in genocidal mass slaughter as was claimed by Biafra and Nigeria. But the experiences of history would tell us that it all boils down to whether claimants to self-determination can sustain their claim by military force. For example, when Bangladesh sought to break away

---

[441] *Patton, Steven, "The Peace of Westphalia and it Affects on International Relations, Diplomacy and Foreign Policy," The Histories: Vol. 10 (5) https://digitalcommons.lasalle.edu/the_histories/vol10/iss1/5. See also Andreas Osiander, Sovereignty, International Relations, and the Westphalian Myth, International Organization 55, 2, Spring 2001, pp. 251–287 and Zreik, M, The Westphalia Peace and Its Impact On The Modern European State, Quantum Journal of Social Sciences And Humanities 2(1): 1-16. And Daud Hassan, The Rise of the Territorial State and The Treaty Of Westphalia, Yearbook of New Zealand Jurisprudence, Vol. 9, 2006*

[442] *Center for Nigerian Progress – July 2020, Op. Cit*

from Pakistan, it was a clear example of an internal affair. However, the army of India interfered and sent troops that forced the contingents of the Pakistani Army in Bangladesh to surrender, and Bangladesh was able to break away from Pakistan. After the elections in Vietnam in 1953, the United States and France intervened, and the United States intervened to keep the communist North Vietnamese from controlling the country in a matter that was an internal matter. In the end, the North Vietnamese communists prevailed, and Vietnam is united because the North Vietnamese had the military power to unite their country. Similarly, the United States intervened in Korea, but because the North Koreans were backed by communist China, they were able to break away from South Korea. However, the North Koreans were not able to invade and control South Korea.

When Katanga, a province of the Republic of the Congo sought to break away, the United Nations sent forces to resolve the crisis. The breakaway Katanga did not invite the United Nations to intervene. South Sudan broke away from the greater nation of Sudan as did Eritrea from Ethiopia. These two countries are now free, and they were contemporaries of Biafra. The question that arises is how Katanga represented a threat to international peace. Although the United Nations established a Human Rights Commission and reluctantly condemned genocide, Biafra had tremendous difficulty convincing the world and the United Nations to see the genocide that was going on in Biafra or that the pogrom of 1966 was a clear violation of the human rights of the citizens from a particular part of the country and of a specific ethnic group, especially given that military and police personnel were actively involved in such violation. In the final analysis, a hard and bitter lesson for Biafrans is that their post-independence claim of self-determination depends on whether you have the military force to sustain it and also on the strategic interests of the major powers. In the case of Biafra, British oil and investment interests were a determining factor. The Russians also supported Nigeria with fighter jets to bombard the Biafran population because they had a strong desire to establish a foothold in Nigeria.

The last several chapters of the book would make it appear as if I wrote this book to analyze the Nigeria Biafra War. This book is about me and my family (mother, father, brothers, sisters, and cousins) and how we made it through the trauma and other challenges that the war brought about. My purpose was to tie these experiences to the dynamics of societies, political entities, and the ruling establishments or classes, as some would want to put it. My lamentation applies to me and my family as well as to the community into which I was born and to the ordinary masses of the Nigerian and other societies.

For me, the challenges of the period from July 1967 were like a nightmare come true. Somewhere, I read that life imitates art or the other way. My family had close several calls to be annihilated. Yes, when the war wore on and I found myself out of school and the deprivations began to cause more pain, I began to wonder which of my extant experiences was in a dream. My belief that I was a high school student with privileges that 75% of society did not have made me wonder if I had been dreaming all along. Or was I dreaming that I was no longer in school and hoping that I would wake up and thank God that it was all a nightmare. I found myself in a situation where I was now going to the farmland and cultivating my food like other people my age and finding out that life in that manner was extremely difficult and fraught with uncertainties to boot. That was a real nightmare. How long would that last?

When I found myself in a forest hideout in a very uncomfortable grass house, or being pounded by heavy rain in the middle of a tropical rainforest in the dead of night and meandering hopelessly with no estimate of the remaining distance of my journey or even what the destination would look like, I was in a veritable nightmare. This was equally true of sitting in a dugout hole in the ground wondering what my destiny would be – whether I will be shot to death because I was accused of being an enemy spy. Yes, it was all a nightmare because two score years and ten later, and during all the years that passed two score and ten times, I have found myself in nightmares dodging Nigerian Army assaults and was either captured awaiting execution or crouching fearfully in a trench and enduring shellfire to confront an attack by the invading army. Each time, I would wake up and thank God that it was all a bad dream.

It was these nightmares that caused me to soliloquize that anyone who causes war in my lifetime would have to send their children and other kith and kin to fight such a war. My children will not join because the people that cause war do not fight them and do not send their children to fight and dodge bullets. If only the ordinary folks that make up the masses in society would harken unto my lamentation, there will be no more wars. The scions of the establishment will find more peaceful solutions to their differences or war will not be fought with machetes and guns and bullets. This is my story, and I would hope that I have made some valuable points. I would also hope that I have achieved my objective of being neutral in pointing out the foibles on both sides of the fratricide that occurred.

CHINYERE EMMANUEL EGBE, BSBA, MBA, MA, PH.D

Dr. Emmanuel Egbe was educated at the University of Nigeria, Nsukka, and later at Tulsa in Oklahoma.

He graduated BS in Business in 1977 and MBA in 1979, specializing in quantitative business methods. Later Dr. Egbe attended Washington State University in Pullman, Washington, and graduated with a MA (1983) and a Ph.D. in Economics, specializing in econometrics (1984).

Dr. Chinyere Emmanuel Egbe is an economist and currently a tenured full professor of Business at Medgar Evers College (CUNY), where he has taught business statistics and finance since 1989. During his tenure at the College, Dr. Egbe held various positions, including Deputy Chairperson, Interim Chairperson, and Dean of the School of Business. While he was dean, he led the School to complete a self-study that eventually enabled the School of Business to gain national accreditation through the Accreditation Council for Schools of Business and Programs (ACBSP) in 2003 and continued to provide leadership to reaffirm the accreditation of the School's business programs in 2013. Dr. Egbe also wrote proposals that established two new degree programs. Dr. Egbe led the faculty to establish a new degree in Financial Economics and a Financial Markets Simulation lab that brings Wall Street to Medgar Evers College. This new degree program has also been accredited by the ACBSP, graduated its first class after only three years, and established the first 100% online degree program among the comprehensive campuses of CUNY.

In addition to his administrative contributions, Dr. Egbe has been actively involved in local economic development. In October 2000, Dr. Egbe established the Community Outreach Partnership Center, funded by the US Department of Housing and Urban Development (HUD), and worked with small businesses in the Central Brooklyn Community. From May 2002 to June 2004, Dr. Egbe completed a major research study on Transportation Impediments to Job Access for Low-Income Residents in Brooklyn and Queens and completed several statistical surveys on the economic development of the Crown Heights neighborhood around the College. Dr. Egbe also established the Brooklyn International Trade and Development Center from 2006 – 2011 and served as its Deputy Director; helped to establish the project "Empowering Youth to Excel and to Succeed" (EYES) from 2010 – 2013. In 2018, Dr. Egbe participated with a team of researchers of the DuBois Bunch Center to complete a study on A Community Development & Wellness Initiative for Central Brooklyn: Baseline Measures commissioned by the New York State Department of Health, Office of Minority Health and Health Disparities Prevention. Dr. Egbe has also conducted research from which he published papers in various journals and presented research findings at many conferences.

Community leaders have also recognized Dr. Egbe for his contributions to community Development by the Caribbean American Chamber of Commerce and Industry (2018) and Certificate of Special Congressional Recognition – Educational leadership October 2018. In October 2018 (the Caribbean American Chamber of Commerce and Industry – CACCI) cited Dr. Egbe for Exemplary Service in Support of Small Business in the Brooklyn October 2001 Certificate of Special Congressional Recognition – Educational leadership and October 2001 – (Unity Democratic Club of Brooklyn) Recognitional for Community Educational Leadership.

Dr. Egbe's other professional activities include active involvement in accreditation and educational improvement. Since September 2005, Dr. Egbe has been actively involved in the activities of the Accreditation Council for Schools of Business and Programs (ACBSP). The ACBSP is an internationally acclaimed educational organization that provides accreditation in business education to higher education institutions around the world. Dr. Egbe served as Regional President (Region 1) of the ACBSP and served in the Council of Regional Presidents from 2010 – 2012. Dr. Egbe is also an avid student of military history and the history of human conflicts.

MR. PLINY ABEL IGWE
(P.A.I) EGBE (1918 – 1985)

Young Mazi Igwe Egbe as
a Student in London

A Short Profile

Mr. Pliny Abel Igwe Egbe (Igwe Abel Egbe) of Amaeke Elu, was a pioneer educator in Ovum and played significant roles in the development and advancement of the
name of Ovum throughout his life. Mr. Egbe's influence in the development of Ovum began very early but could not be attributed entirely to his efforts. However, historical circumstances provided him opportunities that he brought to bear on his contribution, in large part because he was a person whose perspective in life motivated him to give back. In the 1920s and 1930s, Ovum was a center of education and modern social developments. For example, people from our neighboring communities, from Ama'Aba, Ahaba, and probably beyond, attended the Methodist Central School in Ovum. The Spence Girls School, the Mission Hill of the Methodist missionaries that became the Methodist Girls School were also institutions that made Ovum to become well known. In this milieu, only a few privileged and foresighted people were able to attend school; Those who had the opportunity were also placed in a position to contribute. Only the conscientious and truly dedicated sons and daughters of the land leveraged their privileges to propagate the progress of their communities. Mr. Igwe Abel Egbe was one of those.

As a result of these pioneering institutions during the early days of colonialism, several people in Ovum went to school and became teachers. Early educators from Ovum included Mr. Azunna of Agbo Obayi and Mr. Obineche, also from Agbo Obayi and Jonah Achara of Amune. These were the early leaders, who no doubt, Mr. Igwe Abel Egbe emulated, along with his contemporaries such as Dr. E.A. Ukpabi of Ugwunta and, again, Mr. Jonah Achara.

It is not unusual for people who are privileged or lucky to take advantage of profitable trends to forget where they came from. The contribution of people like Mr. Igwe Abel Egbe lies in the fact that their presence in the educational sphere in the places that they worked in and around Igbo land and Nigeria brought attention to their origins. In addition, though, they all brought back home their various talents and insights into modern education and modern social and economic development to inspire others and propagate the foundations of social, educational, and economic development into Ovim. Mr. P.A.I Egbe, originally named Igwe Egbe, was born about 1918 to Chief Egbe Okêzie and Ækuagwu Ûgê at Amaeke-Elu Ovum. Ækuagwu Ûgê was a native of Umuagu Ôzârâ, a kindred town of Ovum. Ûgê, the mother of Ækuagwu was a native of Ndi Mmenme in Åhchâ Isu-Ikwuato.

Chief Egbe Okezie, the father of Igwe Abel Egbe, died when Mr. Igwe Egbe was still young; within thirty years after the first European colonists arrived in our area around Ovim. However, the young Igwe Egbe was a strong child. He probably identified quickly with the educational system that the Europeans had just introduced. Legend has it that many people despised European-type schools that were introduced into Ovim and neighboring communities. On the contrary, Igwe Egbe not only showed enthusiasm but at some point, suffered by working his way through school. Many people who went to school up to the 1960s will recollect that education was free only through what would be called Elementary One today. It was then that people had to pay for their education from Standard One and beyond.

The young Igwe Abel Egbe was also lucky in that he was quickly adopted and guided by a prominent and respected traveling teacher and supervisor by the name of Mr. Irogbenachi; a man from Arochukwu, sometimes known in Ovim as Uvara or Achinivu. Mr. Achinivu's children by his wife from Obichie had and still have a close relationship with Mr. Egbe's children. Mazi Igwe Egbe lived at Ikot Ekpene with Mr. Achînivu and went to School at Ikot Ekpene, hence Mazi. Igwe Egbe was able to speak the Ibibio language very fluently to the very end of his life.

After his elementary education, Igwe Egbe attended Methodist College Ozuækôlî and obtained the Grade Two Teachers' Certificate at a very young age in 1935. He then became a headmaster at Isuôchî. Mr. Egbe often said that some older women at the time that he was a headmaster at Isuôchî called him a headmaster that could still sit on his mother's lap. He must have been very popular at Isuôchî, because in 1973, a little over 40 years after he left Isuôchî, a man approached him very carefully at the Enugu Teaching hospital and asked him if he was Hey-matter (Headmaster). Mr. Egbe promptly affirmed and asked if the man was from Isuôchî.

From 1941 to 1943, Mr. Igwe Egbe attended the Rural Education Center at Umuahia in Eastern Nigeria. After his education at the Rural Education Center, Igwe Egbe worked at different places in Northern Nigeria including Okene and Zaria. While he worked at Okene and Zaria, Igwe Egbe completed his Advanced level GCE and London Matriculation Examinations and departed to England in 1948 to study at the University of London. Mr. Egbe returned in 1950 and worked at Idah in the Middle Belt of Nigeria; at Bauchi in Northern Nigeria and then returned to Eastern Nigeria in 1956 to become a senior staff teacher at the Rural Education Center (REC) in Umudike, Umuahia.

The Rural Education Center (REC) was an agricultural science school for elementary school headmasters. When the institution existed from the late 1930s through 1970 or 1971, it admitted only assistant headmasters or headmasters who were Grade Two teachers with at least five years' experience. The program was a two-year program, at the end of which graduates automatically received Grade One Teacher's Certificate. While at the institution, provisions were made to house the teachers and their families, while they received their full salaries.

Mr. P.A.I Egbe served as a senior staff teacher and Inspector of Education at the Rural Education Center from 1956-1959. On the eve of Nigerian independence, Mr. Egbe became the Vice Principal of the Rural Education Center. In 1962, he was promoted to Principal. Mr. Egbe served as Principal of the Rural Education Center (REC) from 1962 to 1965. During the period that Mr. Egbe served as Principal of the REC, the institution expanded its facilities tremendously and doubled its intake from 30 to 60 students a year. A new library, new science laboratories, student living quarters, and classrooms were constructed.

In 1965, Mr. Egbe was promoted to Senior Inspector of Education and posted to Owerre, where he continued to play a significant role in agricultural science education for teachers. In his role as Senior Inspector of Education, Mr. Egbe was responsible for a large portion of Eastern Nigeria.

When the Nigerian civil war disrupted life in Biafra, Mr. Egbe returned to Ovim in August 1968. In March 1969, the Nigerian army overran Ovim. After hiding out, with the rest of Ovim residents, in the forests and interior villages, in the northern parts of Ovim, and following a brief honor guard by Biafran soldiers, Mr. Egbe escaped to Biafra in the company of the 64th Brigade of the Biafran Army, under Lt. Col Ginger and Capt. C. C. Njeze of the 71B Battalion of the Biafran Army, on April 28, 1969. Three days after his escape, his house was raided, his family arrested, and nearly executed. The family was spared after the commander that ordered the arrest of the family identified him and his wife as his elementary or middle school teacher in a picture that Mr. Egbe, the commander, and Late Brig. Adekunle took as boy scouts. Mr. Igwe Egbe was the Scoutmaster. Later in July 1969, Mr. Egbe became a Liaison Officer of the Biafran Organization of Freedom Fighters (BOFF) stationed at Amo Ôgwûgwû near Umuahia

After the civil war, Igwe Abel Egbe returned as a civil servant and educator in the new East Central State, headed by the Administrator of the East Central State, Mr. Ukpabi Asika. At this time, Mr. Igwe Egbe continued his work as an educator and was posted to Enugu, the headquarters of the East Central State as a Senior Inspector of Education. Mr. Igwe Abel Egbe retired from civil service in January 1974 and went to reside at his family compound in Ovim. In September 1974, he was appointed to the State Schools Board of East Central State by the Asika Government. When the Imo State was created, Mr. Egbe transferred to the Schools Board in 1976 and retired finally in 1978.

During his working years, Igwe Abel Egbe was very actively involved in the affairs and development of Ovim. Besides helping to elevate the image of Ovum, like his predecessors and his contemporaries that I mentioned earlier, Igwe Abel Egbe was actively involved in taking initiatives that changed the landscape of Ovum, socially, culturally, and economically.

As many will attest, the Ovim Community League (OCL), which is alive till today was the brainchild of Mr. Egbe and several of his foresighted, activist, and visionary contemporaries such as the late Mr. I.E. Duroha of Umuanya and Jonah Achara of Amune. Mr. Igwe Abel Egbe was its founding President and received a certificate to that effect. From its inception till today, the OCL has been a great source of cohesion in Ovum. More importantly, the OCL became an organization that conceptualized many development and modernization ideas in Ovum. For example, the OCL spearheaded the modernization of the Oriendu Market in Ovim during the 1960s. Igwe Abel Egbe was instrumental in organizing, leading, and planning the modernization efforts. These modernizing effects have had a lasting effect on the organization of marketing in Oriendu. Following the modernization efforts, the Oriendu market had modern stores, a chemist, and modernized traditional stalls.

In other areas, Igwe Abel Egbe worked tirelessly alongside Dr. Ukpabi to establish the Secondary Technical School Ovim. He worked with Dr. Ukpabi to raise a request to Imo School Board. At many times they had long meetings and had to endure normal bureaucratic delays from the Ministry of Education.

In another sphere, Igwe Abel Egbe was part of the early formation of the Abia State Movement. In this endeavor, he was involved in this with Dr. J O J Okezie of Umuahia, Chief J J Ogbulafo of Umuahia and, Eze Ugo of Afikpo. They distributed pamphlets and attended meetings regularly also with Mr. Golden Okereke of Arochukwu, a longtime friend of his from the 1960s.

MRS. ANNA NNENNA EGBE
OUR BELOVED MOTHER

1928 – 2012: A Brief Profile

Mrs. Anna Nnenna Egbe was born in 1928 at Usaja, Ama'ukwu Amaeke Ovim. At a very early age, she was orphaned and was raised by her uncle, the late Mazi Okezie Ihedioha. As was the practice during her time, she was married off at an early age, probably 12 years of age to the Late Mazi Pliny Igwe Abel Egbe, who was a schoolteacher. As soon as she became of age, she wedded and began a life of dedication to her husband and her children. Our mother lived and supported our father (Mr. P.A.I Egbe, an educator and agricultural scientist) and her husband in all his endeavors. Our father, Mazi. Igwe Egbe lived and worked in various parts of Nigeria including Isu Ochi Okene, Zaria, Idah, Bauchi, and for a long time Umudike in Umuahia and Owerre and Enugu.

She was an exemplary wife and mother. One of her greatest legacies is her profound ability to be tolerant, forgiving, enduring, and generous. For us her children, it was not difficult to see that Mama would sacrifice all for her children just to make things possible for us. Another one of her enduring legacies in us as her children was that she always taught us to do the right thing and had faith that we would be rewarded by God and the community around us for our good behavior. During the civil war 1967 – 1970, she lived at Ovim with us. When our father escaped and I followed suit after three weeks, she managed to keep the family together. It was her quick wit and God-given charm that saved the family from being executed by the Nigerian soldiers that arrested her and all her children.

During the years that we all began to have children, Mama took time off to go and take care of the grandchildren that God was blessing her with. Indeed, in 1990, she even visited the United States and spent one year, taking care of one of her Grandsons (Amechi Egbe – a graduate of the University of Southern California). Within the extended family in the compound, Mama was a unifying force among the wives of her husband's brothers and cousins. They looked up to her for support in times of distress. In the Village (Our village Umueye, Amaeke-Elu), she was fondly known as Nnenna Abel, after our father, whose middle name is Abel.

Besides Mama's dedication to her husband and children, Mama was a woman of God. She was dedicated to God. Mama always relied on prayer to resolve all matters that confronted her. She similarly taught us all to rely on prayer. During the years that we lived in Umuahia, Mama was very active in the church. Mama continued to be active in her Christian Church affiliations wherever she lived. Accordingly, in March 2009, she was honored and awarded a plaque by the Christ Methodist Church of the World Bank Housing Estate (WBHE) as Mother of Faith, because of her dedication and exemplary Christian conduct.

Family Picture: 1973 on the occasion of our Big Sister Nneoma traveling to England From Left to Right, Standing Back Row: Leechi – Sister-in-Law, Uloaku Egbe, Sister-in-law and baby, our Mother, Our big Sister (Nneoma), our Father (Mazi Igwe Egbe), Ola, Myself (Chinyere). From Left to Right (Front Row): Agu, Okezie, and Iroegbu.

REFERENCES

Abamu, Elizabeth Ukeni	War From A Child's Point of View, Word Press
Achara, D. N.	*Ala Bingo (Igbo Literature Book)*
Achebe, Christie	Isbo Women in the Nigerian-Biafran War 1967-1970: An Interplay of Control, Journal of Black Studies, May 2010, Vol. 40, No. 5 Pp. 785-811
Adebayo, Wadi	BIAFRA: The Untold Story of Nigeria's Civil War, BIAFRA: The Untold Story of Nigeria's civil war – Nigerian History (wordpress.com), March 2013
Adeeko, Julius	Vanguard Online Community, February 2015 - http://community.vanguardngr.com/profile/ OtunbaJuliusOlusegunAdeeko
Ademoyega, Adewale	*Why we Struck: The Story of the First Nigerian Coup, Ibadan, Okley Printer, 1981*
Adepoju, Oluwatoyin Vincent	Drums of Reconciliation, Drums of War: Efforts Between 1966 and 1967 to Persuade the South-Eastern Nigerian Leadership Not to Precipitate War, https://www.scribd. com/ document/117715610/Drums-of-Reconciliation-Drums-of-War-Efforts-Against-the-Eruption-of-the-Nigerian-Civil-War-of-1967-1970
Adu, Fumilayo Mopdukpe. Oluwaseun Samulel Osadola & John UzomaNwachukwu	Clandestine Role of Religious Bodies in the Nigerian Civil War 1967-1970, American Journal of Humanities and Social Sciences January 2019, Pp. 73 - 85.
Afolalu, Julius	Secession of Biafra: Did Awolowo and Yoruba Betray Igbos Into War?, Middletwon, Delaware, USA 2020
Agbakoba, Nnamdi	Terrors of War: An Action Packed Story of the Experience of an Eight-Year Old Boy During the Nigeria-Biafra War, Astoria, NY Seaburn Press, 2008
Akinbode, Ayomide	A Carnage Before Dawn: Based on Nigeria's First Coup D'Etat, Lagos, Nigeria, Danieliherald Communications, 2020
Akinkunmi, Akintunde, A	Hubris: A Brief Political History of the Nigerian Army
Akinyemi, A. B,	The British Press and the Nigerian Civil War, AfricanAffairs , Oct., 1972, Vol. 71, No. 285 (Oct., 1972), pp. 408-426
Akpan, Ntieyong .U.	The Struggle for Secession, 1966 – 1970: A personal Account of the Nigerian Civil War, London, Frank Cass, 1976

Akuchu, Gemuh E.	Peaceful Settlement of Disputes: Unsolved Problem for the OAU (A Case Study of the Nigeria-Biafra Conflict) in Africa Today, Oct. - Dec., 1977, Vol. 24, No. 4, Nigeria: Impact of the Oil Economy (Oct. - Dec., 1977), pp. 39-58
Alabi, Godwin (Brig. General)	*The Tragedy of Victory: On the Spot Account of the Nigeria Biafra War in the Atlantic Theater, Ibadan, Nigeria, Spectrum Books, 2013*
Allen, Charles A.	Civilian Starvation and Relief During Armed Conflict: The Modern Humanitarian Law, Georgia Journal of International And Comparative Law 1989, PP 1 – 86 Vol 19 (5)
Amadi,Sam	Colonial Legacy, Elite Dissension and the Making of Genocide: The Story of Biafra, https://items.ssrc.org/ how-genocides-end/ colonial-legacy-elite-dissension- and-the-making-of-genocide-the-story-of-biafra/
Aneke, Luke Nnaemeka	*The Untold Story of the Nigerian-Biafra War, New York, Triumph Publishing, 2007*
Aneke, Nnaemeka Luke	Obong (General) Philip Efiong: ATribute to An Uncommon Nigerian, January 19, 2004, https://nigeriaworld.com/ articles/2004/jan/191.html
Anthony, Douglas	*Irreconcilable Narratives: Biafra, Nigeria and Arguments about Genocide, in Heearton and Moses, Eds, Post-Colonial Conflict and the Question of Genocide, The Nigeria Biafra War (1967-70), Routledge Global Series, 2018, (Chapter 2, Pp. 47 – 71)*
Anueyiagu, Okey	Biafra: The Horrors of War – The Story of a Child Soldier, Atlanta, Georgia USA, Brown Brommel Publishers, 2020
Anwunah, Patrick, A (Colonel)	*The Nigerian Biafra War (1967-70): My Memoirs, Ibadan, Nigeria, Spectrum Books, 2007*
Aremu, Johnson Olaosebikan and Lateef Oluwafemi Buhari	Sense and Senselessness of War: Aggregating the Causes, Gains and Losses of the Nigerian Civil War, 1967–1970, Journal of Arts and Humanities 2017 PP. 61 -78
Aremu, Johnson Olaosebikan	*Ghana's Role in the Nigerian War: Mediator or Collaborator? International Journal of Humanities and Cultural Studies December 2014 1 – 11*
Aremu, Johnson Olaosebikan	Midwifing Nigeria's Fragile Unity: The Role Of Obafemi Awolowo In The Nigerian Civil War, European Journal of Social Sciences Studies, Vol 2 (9) 165 – 183
Aremu, Johnson Olaosebikan	Ghana's Role in the Nigerian War: Mediator or Collaborator, International Journal of Humanities and Cultural Studies, Vol 1 (3), December 2014
Aremu, Johnson Olaosebikan and Oluwaseun Samuel Osadola	The Organisation of African Unity And Its Mediatory Role In The Nigerian Civil War: A Historical Assessment International Journal of Research,, May 2008 vol 5 (15) https:// edupediapublications.org/journals
Atofarati, Major Abubakar A.	*The Nigerian Civil War, Causes, Strategies, And Lessons Learnt,https://www.calitown.com/the-nigerian-civil- war-causes-strategies-and-lessons-learnt-by-major-abubakar- a-atofarati/*

Balogun, M.A. and G. P. Oyeyiola	Changes in the Nutrient Composition of Okpehe During Fermentation, Pakistan Journal of Nutrition 2012 Vol. 11(3) Pp. 270-275
Bamisaiye, Adepitan	The Nigerian Civil War in the International Press, Transition, 1974, No. 44 (1974), pp. 30-32 & 34-35
Baxter, Peter	Biafra: The Nigerian Civil War, 1967 – 1970, Helion and Co, Publishers Africa @War Series, Vol 16, P. 29
Bird, Elizabeth and Rosaline Umelo	Surviving in Biafra: A Niger Wife's Story, London C. Hurst and Co., 2018
Bird, S. Elizabeth and Fraser Ottanelli	The Asaba massacre and the Nigerian civil war: reclaiming hidden history, Journal of Genocide Research, Aug 2014, Pp. 379 – 99
Bird, S. Elizabeth and Fraser Ottanelli	The History and Legacy of the Asaba, Nigeria, Massacres, African Studies Review · December 2011
Blank, Gary	*Britain, Biafra and the Balance of Payments: The Formation of London's 'One Nigeria' Policy,* Revue Française De Civilisation Britannique – Vol. 18 N° 2.
Borders, William	*No 'Nuremberg Trials' for Rebels, Gowon Says, The New York Times, Jan. 30, 1970, https://www.nytimes. com/1970/01/30/ archives/no-nuremberg-trials-for-rebels-gowon-says.html*
Byrne, Tony	Airlift to Biafra: Breaching the Blockade, Blackrock, Dublin Ireland, the Columba Press, 1976
Center for Nigerian Progress	July 2020, Zik's version of what transpired between him and Ojukwu during the Biafra war, https://lawakhigbe. com/2020/07/11/ziks-version-of-what-transpired-between-him-and-ojukwu-during-the-biafra-war/
Chimee, Ihediwa Nkemjika	The Nigeria-Biafran War, Armed Conflicts and the Rules of Engagement, in Falola, et al, Eds, Warfare, Ethnicity and National Identity in Nigeria, trenton, NJ, Africa World Press, 2013
Chuku, Gloria Ifeoma	*From Petty Traders to International Merchants: A Historical Account of Three IGBO Women of Nigeria in Trade and Commerce, 1886 to 1970, African Economic History, 1999, No. 27 (1999), pp. 1-22*
Chukwurah, Diliorah	The Last Train to Biafra, Ibadan, Nigeria, Constelation Publishers, 2015
Collis, Robert	Nigeria in Conflict, Lagos, Nigeria, John West Publications, 1970
Conley, Bridget and Alex de Waal	The Purposes of Starvation Historical and Contemporary Uses Journal of International Criminal Justice 17 (2019), 699-722
Cronje, Suzanne	The World and Nigeria: The Diplomatic History of the Biafran War (1967 - 1970), London, Sidwick and Jackson, 1972
Daly, Samuel Fury Childs	A History of the Republic of Biafra Law, Crime, and the Nigerian Civil War, Cambridge University Press, 2020
De St. Jorre, Jonh	The Nigerian Civil War (A Brothers' War), London, Holder and Stoughton, 1972

Doron, Roy	We Are Doing Everything we Can, Which is Very Little - The Johnson Administration and the Nigerian Civil War, in Falola, et al, Eds, Warfare, Ethnicity and National Identity in Nigeria, trenton, NJ, Africa World Press, 2013
Doron, Roy	*Biafra and the Agip Oil Workers: Ransoming and the Modern Nation State in Perspective, African Economic History, 2014, Vol. 42 (2014), pp. 137-156*
Doron, Roy and Charles G Thomas,	Introducing the New Lens of African Military History, In: Journal of African Military History, Dec 2019, Pp. 79 - 92
Eastern Nigeria, Government	Nigerian Pogrom, Crisis 1966, Vol. 3, Publicity Division of the Ministry of Information, Eastern Nigeria, December 1966, Pp. 4 – 20.
Eastern Nigeria, Government	*Nigerian Crisis 1966, Eastern Nigerian Viewpoint, Ministry of Information, October 1966,*
Eastern Nigerian Government	The North and Constitutional Developments in Nigeria, Nigerian Crisis 1966, Vol. 5, Enugu, Government Printer, 1966
Eban, Abba (Foreign Minister)	JTA Daily news bulletin, Jewish Telegraphic Agency, July 10 (JTA), 1969
Ebbe, Obi N. Ignatius	Broken Back Axle: Unspeakable Events in Biafra, X-Libris Corporation, 2010.
Edokwe, Bridget	Revisiting Biafra: Starvation as A Strategy of Warfare: Was there really a Genocide? https://barristerng.com/, June 6, 2021
Effiong, Phillip (Major General)	Nigeria, and Biafra: My Story, Long Island, NY, African Tree Press, 2007
Effiong, Phillip (Major General)	The Caged Bird Sang No More: My Biafran Odyssey, 1966 - 1970, Pinetown, South Africa, 30* South Publishers, 2016
Ekekwe, Herbert	The Igbo genocide and its aftermath, https://www. pambazuka. org/human-security/igbo-genocide-and-its-aftermath, Feb 21, 2012
Emeagwali, Phillip	https://emeagwali.com/biafra/nigeria-biafra-civil-war-major-chukwuma-kaduna-nzeogwu.html
Enongchong, Charles Abi	Who Killed Major Nzeogwu: An Investigation Into the Greatest Cover-up of the Nigeria-Biafra War, Middletown, Delaware, USA, Century Books, 2019
Ezeogueri-Oyewole, Anne Nnenna	The Role of Olokoro Women in The Nigerian Civil War, 1967-1970, Asian Journal of Social Sciences, Vol. 4 (2), 2016.
Ezeonwuka, Innocent-Franklyn and Uchenna S. Ani	Biafra: Beyond the Realm, Sabotage and the Dearth of Intelligencein the Nigeria, Biafra Debacle, 1967 - 1970, Igwebuilke: An African Journal of Arts and Humanities, Vol. 4 (4), Pp. 25 - 41.
Falola, Toyin, Roy Doron and Okpeh O. Okpeh	Warfare, Ethnicity and National Identity in Nigeria, trenton, NJ, Africa World Press, 2013
Famoroti, Francis	Western Region crisis: HowAwolowo,Akintola Parted ways, October 2012, https://kwekudee-tripdownmemorylane. blogspot.com/2013/11/chief-samuel-ladoke-akintola-celebrated. html

Farquharson, James	*Black America Cares: The Response of African Americans to the Civil War and Genocide in Nigeria) in Heearton and Moses, Eds, Post-Colonial Conflict and the Question of Genocide, The Nigeria Biafra War (1967-70), Routledge Global Series, 2018, Pp. 301 – 326 –*
First, Ruth	*Barrel of a Gun: Political Power inAfrica and the Coup D'Etat, Penguin African Library, 1970*
Forsyth, Frederick	*The Biafra Story: The Making of an African Legend, Barnsley, England, Pen and Sword Military Books, 1972*
Fournie, Daniel A.	Second, Punic War: Hannibal's War in Italy, Military History magazine, March/April 2005.
Fowoyo, Patience Temitope	Microbiological and Proximate Analysis of Okpehe, a Locally Fermented Condiment, Food and Nutrition Journal, October 2017, Pp. 1 – 11 https://www. researchgate.net/ publication/331901184
Fronda, Michael P.	*Hegemony and Rivalry: The Revolt of Capua Revisited, Phoenix, Spring - Summer, 2007, Vol. 61, No. 1/2 (Spring - Summer, 2007), pp. 83-108*
Gabriel, Richard	Why Hannibal Lost, Military History Magazine, May 2016, Pp. 58 – 63.
Gabriel, Richard A	Scipio Africanus: Rome's Greatest General, Dulles, Virgina, Potomac Books, 2008
Garba, Joseph Nanven (Major General)	*Fractured History: Elite Shifts and Policy Changes in Nigeria, PrincetoN, NJ, Songhai Books, 1995*
Gbulie, Ben (Colonel)	*Fall of Biafra, Enugu, Nigeria, Benlie Publishers, 1989*
Gbulie, Ben (Colonel)	Nigeria's Five Majors: Coup d'etat of 15th January 1966, first inside account Kindle Edition, African Educational Publishers, (Revised Edition), 2016
Glover, Richard	*The Elephant in Ancient War, The Classical Journal, Feb., 1944, Vol. 39, No. 5 (Feb., 1944)*
Gould, Michael	The Biafran War: The Struggle for Modern Nigeria, London, I.B. Tauris, 2012
Government of Federal Republic of Nigeria	Meeting of the Nigerian Military Leaders held at Peduase Lodge, Aburi Ghana, January 4 – January 5, 1967, Federal Republic of Nigeria
Graham-Douglas, Nabo	*Ojukwu's Rebellion and World Opinion, Nigerian National Press, 1968, Pp. 16 – 17.*
Guttman, John	Hardware: Carthaginian War Elephant, Military History Magazine, May 2016, Pp. 20 - 21
Hanbury, H. G.	Biafra: A Challenge to the Conscience of Britain, London, Britain-Biafra Association, 1968
Harding, Stephen	The Origins of War, Military History Magazine – July 2016, Page 21 http://dev.historynet.com/letter-military-history-july-2016.htm
Harding, Stephen	The Perils of Hierarchy, Letter From Military History – May 2016, Page 23; https://www.historynet.com/letter-from-military-history-may-2016.htm

Harneit-Sievers, Axel, Jones O. Ahuziem and Sydney Emezue	A Social History of the Nigerian Civil War: Perspectives from Below, Enugu, Nigeria, Jemezie Associates, 1997
Hassan, Daud	*The Rise of the Territorial State and The Treaty Of Westphalia, Yearbook of New Zealand Jurisprudence, Vol. 9, 2006*
Heerten, Lasse and A. Dirk Moses	*The Nigeria–Biafra war: postcolonial conflict and the question of genocide, 2014, Journal of Genocide research, Pp. 169 – 203.*
Heerten, Lasse and A. Dirk Moses, Eds.	Post-Colonial Conflict and the Question of Genocide, The Nigeria Biafra War (1967-70), Routledge Global Series, 2018
Higham, Charles	Trading with the Enemy: The Nazi-American Money Plot 1933 - 49, New York, Barnes and Nobles Books, 1983
Hildinger, Erik	Swords Against the Senate: The Rise of the Roman Army and the Fall of the Republic, DaCapo Press, 2002,
Hoyos, B.D	Hannibal, What Kind of Genius, in Greece and Rome, Vol. XXX # 2, 1983
Hunt, David	On the Spot: An Ambassador Speaks, London, Peter Davis, 1975
Hunt, Patrick	*Hannibal, New York, Simon and Schuster, 2017*
Ilie, Alexandra	Holodomor, the Ukrainian Holocaust? Studia Politica: Romanian Political Science Review, 2011, 11(1), 137-154. https://nbn-resolving.org/urn:nbn:de:0168-ssoar-445894
Keil, Charles	The Price of Nigerian Victory, Africa Today, Jan – Feb. 1970 Vol. 17 (1). Pp. 1-3.
Kirk-Greene, A.H.M.	*Crisis and Conflict in Nigeria, Volume II, Oxford University Press, 1971*
Kirk-Greene, A. H. M	*Crisis and Conflict in Nigeria, Volume I, Oxford University Press, 1971,*
Klid, Bohdan,	"Holodomor: Holodomor and UN Genocide Convention Criteria." Modern Genocide: Understanding Causes and Consequences. ABC-CLIO, 2013. Web. 21 Nov. 2013. Reprinted courtesy of ABC-CLIO. https://holodomor.ca/resource/was-the-holodomor-a-genocide/
Koren, David	Far Away in the Sky: A Memoir of the Biafran Airlift, New York, Peace Corp Writers, 2016
Korieh, Chima J	Biafra and the discourse on the Igbo Genocide, Journal of Asian and African Studies, October 2013
Korieh, Chima J	The Nigeria-Biafra War, Oil and the Political Economy of State Induced Development Strategy in Eastern Nigeria, 1967–1995 Social Evolution & History, Vol. 17 No. 1, March 2018 76–107
Korieh, Chima J.	Biafra and the Discourse on the Igbo Genocide (2013). History Faculty Research and Publications. 145. https:// epublications.marquette.edu/hist_fac/145
Kotun, Ajiroba Yemi	A Stab in the Back, The Nigerian Voice, June 2013 https://www.thenigerianvoice.com/news/117069/a-stab-in-the-back.html

Kuromiya, Hiroaki	Ukraine and Russia in the 1930s, Harvard Ukrainian Studies, December 1994, Vol. 18, No. 3/4 (December 1994), pp. 327-341
Lacey,James	Ghosts of Cannae, by Robert L. O'Connell, Book Review: Ghosts of Cannae, by Robert L. O'Connell (historynet.com).
Leitenberg, Milton	"Deaths in Wars and Conflicts in the 20th Century." Cornell University, Peace Studies Program.
Levey, Zach	Israel, Nigeria, and the Biafra Civil War, 1967 – 1970, in Dirk Moses and Lasse Heerten, Eds. Post-Colonial Conflict and the Question of Genocide, Routledge, 2019
Luckham, Robin	*The Nigerian Military: A Sociological Analysis of Authority and Revolt 1960 – 67, Cambridge, University Press 1971*
Madiebo, Alexander (Major General)	*The Nigerian Revolution and the Biafra War, Enugu Nigeria, Fourth Dimensions Publishers, 1980*
Maduabum, Regina	A soldier's Spouse, Bloomfield, NJ, Redbuck Books, 2008
Maier, Karl	This House Has Fallen: Nigeria in Crisis, Cambridge, Massachusettes, Westview Press, 2000
Mark, Joshua J.	Hasdrubal Barca, https://www.worldhistory.org/ Hasdrubal_Barca/ 05 April 2018
Mbu, Mathew T	Dignity in Service, Ibadan, Nigeria, Safari Books, 2018
McNeil, Brian	*And Starvation is the Grim Reaper: The American Foundation to Keep Biafra Alive and the Question of Genocide During the Nigerian Civil War in Heearton and Moses, Eds, Post-Colonial Conflict and the Question of Genocide, The Nigeria Biafra War (1967-70), Routledge Global Series, 2018 (Chapter 3, Pp. 278 – 300*
Mezu, S. Okechukwu	*Behind the Rising Sun*, Heinemann, London, (1971)
Miles, Richard	*Carthage Must be Destroyed: The Rise and Fall of an Ancient Civilization, London, Penguin Books, 2010*
Milton, Keith	How Hannibal Hammered the Roman Army; https:// warfarehistorynetwork.com/2015/11/15/how-carthaginian-hannibal-hammered-the-roman-army/ November 15, 2015
Morey, William C.	*Second Punic War (218-201 B.C.) in "Outlines of Roman History". New York, American Book Company (1901), published in https://factsanddetails.com/world/cat56/ sub407/ entry-6249.html#chapter-9*
Mshelia, Ayuba	Araba, Let's Separate: The Story of the Nigerian Civil War, Bloomington, Indiana, Author House, 2021
Mudge, George Alfred	*Starvation As A Means Of Warfare, The International Lawyer, January, 1970, Vol. 4, No. 2, pp. 228-268*
Mulder, Nicholas & Boyd van Dijk	Why Did Starvation Not Become the Paradigmatic War Crime in International Law?, Oxford Scholarship Online, https:// oxford.universitypressscholarship.com/ view/10.1093/oso/9780192898036.001.0001/ oso-9780192898036-chapter-22
Muusers, Christianne	Roman Fish Sauce: Liquamen or Garum, https:// coquinaria.nl/ en/roman-fish-sauce/

Nafziger, E. Wayne	The Economic Impact of the Nigerian Civil War, The Journal of Modern African Studies, Jul., 1972, Vol. 10, No. 2 (Jul., 1972), pp. 223-245
National Custodian Newspaper	AMERICA'S SECRET FILES: THE UNTOLD BIAFRAN STORY, https://www. facebook. com/1362516680591228/posts/americas-secret-files-the-untold-biafran-storysecret-american-diplomatic-dispatc/1408275649348664/
Nixon, Charles R.	Self-Determination: The Nigeria/Biafra Case, World Politics, Jul., 1972, Vol. 24, No. 4 (Jul., 1972), pp. 473-497
Njoku, Carol Ijeoma	"A Paradox of International Criminal Justice: The Biafra Genocide." *Journal of Asian and African Studies* 48:6, 2013, Pp. 710–26.
Njoku, Hilary (Brigadier)	*A Tragedy Without Heroes, Enugu, Nigeria, Fourth Dimensions Publishers, 1987*
Nkwocha, Onyema, G	The Republic of Biafra: Once Upon a Time in Nigeria, Bloomington, Indiana, AuthorHouse, 2010
Northrup, David	The Growth of Trade among the Igbo before 1800, The Journal of African History, 1972, Vol. 13(2) (1972), pp. 217-236
Nwadike, Jerome Agu	A Biafran Soldier's Survival from the Jaws of Death, Xlibris 2010
Nwankwo, Uchenna	https://www.nairaland.com/1872985/zik-ojukwu-ndigbo-uchenna-nwankwo, Zik, Ojukwu And Ndigbo, August 25, 2014
O'Connell, Robert L.	*Ghosts of Cannae: Hannibal and the Darkest Hour of the Roman Republic,* by, Random House, 2010.
Obasanjo, Olusegun (General)	My Command: An Account of the Nigerian Civil War (1967 - 1970), Ibadan, Nigeria, Heinemann Books, 1980
Obasanjo, Olusegun (General)	Nzeogwu: An Intimate Portrait of Major Chukwuma Kaduna Nzeogwu, Ibadan, Nigeria, Spectrum Books, 1987
Ober, Josiah	Hannibal's Dilemma, Military History Quarterly, Summer 1990, Pp. 50 – 60.
Odogwu, Benard	No Where to Hide: Crisis and Conflict Inside Biafra, Enugu, Nigeria, Fourth Dimensions Publishers, 1987
Odu, Peter	The Future that Vanished, Thorough Fare, NJ, Xlibris Publishing, 2009
Ogali, Ogali A	Veronica my Daughter, in Veronica my Daughter and Other Onitsha Market Plays and Stories, Reinhard Sander and Peter K. Ayers, Eds., Washington, DC, Three Continents Press, 1980, Pp. 137 - 171
Ogbechie, Mike Uriel	Eclipse at Noonday: Biafran Diaries of Unwritten Stories, X-Libris, 2012
Ogbonna, Ngozi	The Nigerian Civil War: Personal Experiences of a Student Nurse, Enugu, Nigeria, Chizo Press, 2012

Ogbonnaya, HRH, Uwadiegwu	https://www.nationallightngr.com/byline/by-uwadiegwu-c-ogbonnaya/, May 16, 2019; Also Google: "Famous Educationist from Ovim"
Ojukwu, Odumegwu C. (General)	Biafra: Random Speeches with Journals of Events, London, Harper and Row, Vol. I, 1969
Okocha, Emmanuel	Blood on the Niger: The First Black on Black Genocide, The Untold Story of the Asaba Massacre in the Nigerian Civil War Paperback – January 1, 2006
Okocha, Emmanuel	*Blood on the Niger: The First Black on Black Genocide, New York, Triatlantic Books, 2004*
Okonta, Ike and Oronto Douglas	*Where the Vultures Feast: Shell, Human Rights and Oil in the Niger Delta, San Francisco, Sierra Club Books, 2001*
Okoro, Daniel	I Cry, Xlibris, 2020
Oladipo Ojo, Emmanuel	The Awolowo – Akintola Leadership Tussle: A Reinterpretation, the Journal of Arts and Humanities, Vol 1 (5) 2016 (https://theartsjournal.org/index.php/site/ article/ view/896)
Oleka, Ogbonna and Ndubuisi Ofondu	Power with Civility. A Biography of Rear Admiral Godwin Ndubuisi Kanu. Nekson Publishers, 1998
Omaka, Arua Oko	The Forgotten Victims: Ethnic Minorities in the Nigeria-Biafra War, 1967-1970, Journal of Retracing Africa, Spring 2014, Pp. 25 - 40
Omenka, Nicholas Ibeawuchi	Blaming The Gods: Christian Religious Propaganda in The Nigeria—Biafra War, The Journal of African History , 2010, Vol. 51, No. 3 (2010), pp. 367-389
Omigbodun, Olayinka	The Nation, Sunday Interview Archives - Latest Nigeria News, Nigerian Newspapers, Politics (thenationonlineng. net)
Omoigui, Nowa	January 15, 1966: The role of Major Hassan Usman Katsina, https://dawodu.com/katsina1.htm
Omoigui, Nowamagbe A.	OPERATION 'AURE': Northern Nigerian Military Counter-Rebellion, July, 1966, Uhrhobo Historical Society, 17 Aug 2002
Omoigui, Nowamagbe A.	The Midwest Invasion of 1967: Lessons for Today's Geopolitics, https://www.dawodu.com/midwest.htm
Onyejekwe, Ignatius Chukwuka	*Nigeria Civil War: The Country Biafra and the Fall of an Iroko Tree, Frederick Maryland, USA, America Star Books, 2014*
Onyema, Henry Chukwuemeka	July 29 1966 on my Mind: Did General Aguyi-Ironsi Deserve to Die? Part Two: Ironsi's Role in The January 15 1966 Coup, https://www.author-me.com/nonfiction/ julyonmymind2.htm
Osaghae, Eghosa, E	Crippled Giant: Nigeria Since Independence, Bloomington, Indiana, Indiana University Press 1998
Osiander, Andreas	*Sovereignty, International Relations, and the Westphalian Myth, International Organization 55, 2, Spring 2001, pp. 251–287*
Osuchukwu, Emmanuel Chigozie	1966 and the Evolution of Nigerian Politics, London and Aba, Nigeria, Creative People

Ottah, Neslon	Drum Magazine (of Nigeria, June 1970).
Oyewole, Fola	The Reluctant Rebel, London, Rex Collins Books, 1975
Panther-Brick, S.K (Editor)	Nigerian Politics and Military Rule: Prelude to the Civil War, London, the Athalon Press, 1970
Patavinus, Titus Livius (Livy)	*The History of Rome, Book 21*
Patavinus, Titus Livius (Livy)	The War with Hannibal, London Penguin Classics, 1965
Press, Eitan	Biafran Airlift: Israel's Secret Mission to Save Lives, October 2013, https://unitedwithisrael.org/ biafran-airlift-israels-secret-mission-to-save-lives/
Prevas, John	*Hannibal's Oath: The Life and Wars of Rome's Greatest Enemy, Boston, DeCapo Press, 2017*
Rosenblad, Esbjörn	*Starvation as a Method of Warfare — Conditions for Regulation by Convention, The International Lawyer, April 1973, Vol. 7, No. 2 (April 1973), pp. 252-270*
Ryeland, Kenneth C	The Up-Country Man: A personal Account of the First 100 Days in Secessionist Biafra, Lagos, Ogun's Fire Books, 2012
Schaack, Beth Van	*Siege Warfare and the Starvation of Civilians as a Weapon of War and War Crime, February 4, 2016, https:// www.justsecurity.org/29157/ siege-warfare-starvation-civilians-war-crime/*
Schwarz, Walter	Nigeria, New York, Frederick Preager Publishers, 1983
Seibert, Gerhard	São Tomé and the Biafran War (1967–1970), International Journal of African Historical Studies Vol. 51, No. 2 (2018) 263 - 92
Sherman, John	War Stories: A Memoire of Nigeria and Biafra, Indianapolis, USA, Mesa Verde Press, 2003
Siollun, Max	Oil, Politics and Violence: Nigeria's Military Coup Culture (1966 - 1976), New York, USA, Algora Publishing, 2009
Siollun, Max	The Inside Story of Nigeria's First Military Coup - Part http:// www.gamji.com/article6000/news6574.htm,
Smith, Karen E.	The UK and 'genocide' in Biafra. Journal of Genocide Research, 16 (2-3) (2014) . pp. 247-262
Smith, Karen E.	*The UK and "Genocide in Biafra",, in Heearton and Moses, Eds, Post-Colonial Conflict and the Question of Genocide, The Nigeria Biafra War (1967-70), Routledge Global Series, 2018 (Chapter 6)*
Soyinka, Wole	The Man Died: Prison Notes of Wole Soyinka, London, Rex Collins 1972
Soyinka, Wole	You Must Set Forth at Dawn, New York, Random House, 2006
Steven, Patton	"The Peace of Westphalia and it Affects on International Relations, Diplomacy and Foreign Policy," The Histories: Vol. 10 (5) https://digitalcommons.lasalle.edu/ the_histories/vol10/ iss1/5
Stremlau, John J	The International Politics of the Nigerian Civil War 1967 - 70, Princeton, NJ, 1977

Symes, Peter	The Bank Notes of Biafra, *International Bank Note Society Journal Volume 36, No.4, 1997*
Talbot, Amauri, P	Tribes of the Niger Delta: The Religious Customs, New York, Barnes and Nobles Books, 1932 and 1967
Tannahill, Reay	Food in History, New York, Three Rivers Press, 1973 & 1985
Teniola, Erick	Why Awo did not make West to Secede, The Guardian, 25 September 2017, https://guardian.ng/opinion/why-awo-did-not-make-west-to-secede/
Thayer, George	The War Business: The International Trade in Armaments, New York, Simon, and Shuster, 1969
Thomas, Hugh	*The Slave Trade: The Story of the Atlantic Slave Trade: 1440 – 1870*
Uche, Chibuike	Money matters in a war economy: The Biafran experience, Nationalism and Ethnic Politics, 2002, Vol 8 (1) Pp. 29-54,
Uche, Chibuike	Oil, British Interests and the Nigerian Civil War, The Journal of African History, 2008, Vol. 49, No. 1 (2008), pp. 111-135
Uchendu, Egodi	Recollections of Childhood Experiences During The Nigerian Civil War, Africa 77 (3), 2007, Pp. 393 - 418
Uchendu, Egodi	*Women and Conflict in the Nigerian Civil War, Trenton, New Jersey, Africa World Press, 2007*
Ukaegbu, Uduma	*Igbos and Folly of Biafra May 2020, https://www. westafricanpilotnews.com/2020/05/02/igbos-and-folly-of-biafra-part-i/ PilotnewsPilotAfrican*
Ukaogo, Victor	Ahia Attaakie' and 'Yakambaya' : Interrogating the Moral Dilemma and the Role of Ozuitem-Bende Women in the War Economy of Biafra, 1967-1970, UZU: Journal of History and International Affairs...January 2012
Umoh, Ubong Essien	The Making of Arms in Civil War Biafra, 1967-1970, Vol. 5, Nos. 1 & 2, December 2011, pp. 339-359
Umweni, Samuel	888 Days in Biafra, London, iUniverse, Inc, 2007
Uwechue, Raplh	*Reflections on the Nigerian Civil War: Facing the Future, Victoria, BC Canada, Trafford Publishers, 1969 and 2004*
Uzokwe, Alfred	Surviving in Biafra, Lincoln, Nebraska, iUniverse, 2003
Van Schaack, Beth	*Siege Warfare and the Starvation of Civilians as a Weapon of War and War Crime, February 4, 2016, https://www. justsecurity.org/29157/siege-warfare-starvation-civilians-war-crime/*
Venter, Al J	Biafra Genocide: Nigeria Bloodletting and Mass Starvation (1966 - 1970), Barnsley, England, Pen and Sword Military Books, 2018
Venter, Al J	Biafra's War (1967 - 1970): A Tribal Conflict in Nigeria that Left a Million Dead, West Midlands, Helion and Company, 2015
Warchronicle.com	How Many People Died in World War 2, http:// warchronicle.com/numbers/WWII/deaths.htm

Weapons and Warfare	Heraclea (280 BC), History and Hardware of Warfare https://weaponsandwarfare.com/2018/03/19/heraclea-280-bc/, March 19, 2018
Whiteman, K.	Enugu: The Psychology of Secession, 20 July 1966 to 30 May 1967, in Nigerian Politics and Military Rule, Preude to Civil War", S.K. Patrick Brick, Ed., University of London Press, 1970, Pp. 110 - 127)
Wiwa, Ken Saro	*A Month and a Day: A Detention Diary, London, Penguin, 1995*
Yesufu, Deji	I am Not Dead Yet: The Sad Story of Banjo's Death | Al Jazirah News, June 2017
Yocherer, Greg	Second Punic War: Battle of Cannae, Military History Magazine, February 2000
Zreik, M,	*The Westphalia Peace and Its Impact On The Modern European State, Quantum Journal of Social Sciences And Humanities 2(1): 1-16.*

TABLE OF PHOTO CREDITS

Photo Credits for Cover Design:
Woman and Child: Alamy Stock Photos by license Severed Head: Government of Eastern Nigeria, (1966)

Table of Photo Credits			
Location	**Picture**	**Description**	**Photo Credit**
Preface		Map of Italy During Second Punic War and Hannibal's Routes 220 BCE to 203 BCE	Internet
Preface		Map of Spain at Showing River Ebro that marked the Boundary for Peace Between Rome and Carthgae Before the Beginning of the Second Punic War (219 BCE)	Internet
Preface		Picture of Mangled and Wounded Child – Victim of the Northern Nigerian Pogroms 1966	Government of Eastern Nigeria Ministry of Information 1966

Table of Photo Credits			
Location	**Picture**	**Description**	**Photo Credit**
Preface		Picture of Mangled and Wounded Man – Victim of the Northern Nigerian Pogroms 1966	Government of Eastern Nigeria Ministry of Information 1966
Introduction		Ethnic Map of Nigeria Showing Regions	Internet
Introduction		Praying Soldier	Alamy Stock Photo by License
Chapter 1		Our Daddy came back from the War with a Gun that looked like this Glock.	Internet
Chapter 1		Picture of Dead Skulls	Internet

Table of Photo Credits			
Location	**Picture**	**Description**	**Photo Credit**
Chapter 1		Picture of Dead Skulls	Internet
Chapter 3		Severed Head – Victim of Northern Nigerian Pogrom 1966	Government of Eastern Nigeria, Ministry of Information 1966
Chapter 3		Wounded Victim of Northern Nigeria Pogrom 1966	Government of Eastern Nigeria, Ministry of Information 1966
Chapter 4		Relic of the Drug Store (Chemist) that I managed during the War, September 1967 - March 1969	Family Archive
Chapter 4		Certificate of Achievement – First Prize in Photography Won by our Big Brother, Chukwumaeze Egbe at the Eastern Nigerian Festival of the Arts 1965	Family Archive

Table of Photo Credits			
Location	**Picture**	**Description**	**Photo Credit**
Chapter 4		Surviving Photograph of Chukwumaeze 1966, One Year Before He joined Biafran Army	Family Archive
Chapter 7		Picture of Our Mother	Family Archive
Chapter 9		Picture of Okoso, the Conical Object Used for Playing a Rough Spinning Game by Rascally Boys. Failure to Overturn the Cone on Its Top Earns the Loser a Painful Spin on the Back of the Palm	Internet

<table>
<tr><th colspan="4">Table of Photo Credits</th></tr>
<tr><th>Location</th><th>Picture</th><th>Description</th><th>Photo Credit</th></tr>
<tr><td>Chapter 11</td><td></td><td>Biafran Stamp – With Symbol of Savage Pogrom – Severed Head of a Man Placed in Train for Transportation to Ojukwu as Gift</td><td>Purchased Internet</td></tr>
<tr><td>Chapter 11</td><td></td><td>Biafran refugee Camp</td><td>Alamy Stock Photos By License</td></tr>
<tr><td>Chapter 11</td><td></td><td>Changing Political Map of Nigeria – 1967 to 1976 (12 State Structure)</td><td>Internet</td></tr>
<tr><td>Chapter 11</td><td></td><td>Fleeing Biafran Refugees (1967 – 1968)</td><td>Alamy Stock Photos by License</td></tr>
<tr><td>Chapter 14</td><td></td><td>Map of Igboland in Nigerian and Biafra</td><td>Internet</td></tr>
</table>

Table of Photo Credits			
Location	**Picture**	**Description**	**Photo Credit**
Chapter 14		Starving Children of Biafra	Alamy Stock Photos by License
Chapter 16		Shrinking Map of Biafra	Internet
Chapter 16		Wounded Victim of Northern Pogrom 1966	Government of Eastern Nigeria, Ministry of Information 1966
Chapter 16		Starving Biafran Children at Refugee Camp 1969	International Committee of the Red Cross (ICRC) Free Access.

Table of Photo Credits			
Location	**Picture**	**Description**	**Photo Credit**
Chapter 17	Victims of Nigeria Air Raid - Time Life Magazine July 1968 Page 22 (R. Cagnozi)	Victims of Nigerian Airforce Raid at Aba 1968	Time Life Magazine July 1968
Chapter 17		Post War (1979) Election Map of Nigeria	Internet

W

The West 218
Western Nigeria 23, 24, 26, 28, 51, 53, 54, 55,
56, 59, 63, 65, 66, 72, 76, 78, 80, 81, 101,
103, 109, 110, 178, 182, 184, 185, 187,
192, 193, 194, 196, 206, 213, 214, 217,
218, 220, 223, 228, 245, 249

Y

Yoruba 23, 26, 28, 29, 33, 47, 51, 52, 56, 58,
59, 60, 61, 62, 63, 71, 73, 75, 76, 80, 81,
83, 98, 101, 102, 103, 104, 105, 111, 112,
147, 161, 169, 173, 178, 185, 194, 195,
196, 200, 205, 213, 217, 218, 219, 226,
227, 246, 247, 250, 267

Z

Zambia 116, 199, 203, 237, 238